Library of America, a nonprofit organization,
champions our nation's cultural heritage
by publishing America's greatest writing in
authoritative new editions and providing resources
for readers to explore this rich, living legacy.

CRIME NOVELS OF THE 1960s
VOLUME 2

Crime Novels

FOUR CLASSIC THRILLERS 1964–1969

Volume 2

The Fiend • Margaret Millar

Doll • Ed McBain

Run Man Run • Chester Himes

The Tremor of Forgery • Patricia Highsmith

Geoffrey O'Brien, *editor*

THE LIBRARY OF AMERICA

CRIME NOVELS: FOUR CLASSIC THRILLERS 1964–1969

Published in the United States by Library of America.
Visit our website at www.loa.org.

This paper exceeds the requirements of
ANSI/NISO Z39.48–1992 (Permanence of Paper).

Distributed to the trade in the United States
by Penguin Random House Inc.
and in Canada by Penguin Random House Canada Ltd.

Library of Congress Control Number: 2022947205
ISBN 978-1-59853-738-3

First Printing
The Library of America—371

Manufactured in the United States of America

Contents

Introduction

BY GEOFFREY O'BRIEN

American crime fiction has always tended to reflect the culture's rougher edges and more unstable elements. In the twentieth century, genteel puzzle mysteries in the Agatha Christie mode had their devotees and imitators, but the native product was more typically characterized by an acute awareness of social fissures and mental borderlines. The pressures and dangers of the Prohibition era, the Depression, World War II and its anxious aftermath are never far away. Likewise, the crime novels of the 1960s are suffused with the outward ills and troubled undercurrents of their time—urban chaos, racist hatreds, proliferating drug use, the suspicions and jangled nerves of suburban enclaves, the nihilistic rejection of established moral codes, the dissolution of personality itself—as perceived by very different writers from multiple angles.

As a genre, crime fiction has always also had a symbiotic relation with emerging media and with evolutionary changes in publishing formats. The pulp magazines of the 1920s and '30s fostered the rise of the hard-boiled style exemplified by Dashiell Hammett and Raymond Chandler. In the 1940s—a decade during which crime stories of all sorts maintained a dominant position in the world of entertainment—the same tropes, and often the same writers, could be found in novels, popular magazines, movies, and radio. It was typical for a successful mystery novel to be serialized in a magazine, adapted for radio and the movies, and eventually reissued as an inexpensive paperback. At this moment of peak popularity, the genre embraced a wide range of approaches, from the tough guy school to the psychological realism of women writers such as Helen Eustis and Elisabeth Sanxay Holding. In the 1950s, the success of paperback reissues ushered in the era of paperback originals, driving the remaining pulps toward extinction, just as the conventions of the half-hour radio play migrated to television. Increasingly in evidence was a grittier, more male-oriented vein exemplified by the novels of Mickey Spillane, movies offering violent ripped-from-the-headlines exposés of gangsterism, or televised celebrations of law enforcement such as *M Squad* or *Highway Patrol.*

By the 1960s, crime fiction, although still a reliably popular genre, no longer occupied such a commanding cultural position. Even Ross Macdonald, the preeminent literary heir of Hammett and Chandler, did not become a best-selling author until late in the decade. (Macdonald's work, central to any consideration of crime fiction in the 1960s, is available in three Library of America volumes.) Conventions that had flourished for decades seemed to have reached a point of diminishing returns. The era of the private eye and the romantic noir melodrama along the lines of *Double Indemnity* or *Laura* tended to inspire parody or evoke nostalgia. Other genres emerged as strong competitors to traditional crime fiction: science fiction and fantasy as developed by Robert Heinlein, Frank Herbert, and others (including the belatedly popularized J.R.R. Tolkien), and extended by *The Twilight Zone* and *The Outer Limits*; the fusion of crime story with horror as in Alfred Hitchcock's *Psycho*, from a novel by Robert Bloch; the political thriller making drama out of global crisis, exemplified by best-selling novels like *Seven Days in May* and *Fail-Safe*; the harsh realism and psychological probing of true crime breaking through to a wider public with Truman Capote's *In Cold Blood*; and above all the phalanx of secret agents led by James Bond and given more substantial credibility by the clandestine bureaucrats of John le Carré.

Facing this stiff competition, writers working in a more traditional vein felt the pressure to go beyond the predictable limits of the standard whodunit or police procedural. By widening the breadth of their subject matter, addressing themes that might once have seemed risky, perhaps availing themselves of the audacity allowed by a new permissiveness in publishing, or experimenting with formal approaches befitting a flashier and speeded-up era, the best crime writers reinvented the genre in strikingly distinctive ways.

In such novels as *Beast in View* (1955), *An Air That Kills* (1957), *The Listening Walls* (1959), and *A Stranger in My Grave* (1960), Margaret Millar pushed the mystery form—her mastery of which she had demonstrated in her novels of the 1940s and early '50s—toward an ambiguous exploration of borderline mental states and free-floating anxieties. *The Fiend* (1964) sketches the collective portrait of a city—Santa Barbara masquerading as San Felice—as a whirlpool of suspicions, animosities, delusions, and irrepressible compulsions, with two very different nine-year-olds finding themselves involuntarily at the center of the vortex. Exactly who "the fiend" is, and what actual crimes and transgressions have taken place, unfolds with slow and painful precision, as Millar deftly slides in and out of different viewpoints, in a dark journey to the end of the suburban night.

Like Donald E. Westlake in the novels he wrote as Richard Stark, Evan Hunter (author of mainstream best sellers such as *The Blackboard Jungle*, *Strangers When We Meet*, and *Last Summer*) assumed an entirely different literary persona under the name of Ed McBain. As McBain, he wrote like a pulp modernist, racing at breakneck speed while he juxtaposed extreme violence with the deadpan humor of harried cops, lyrical intermezzos, a kaleidoscope of urban snapshots, and a cacophony of street voices. The speed with which he produced his 87th Precinct police procedurals—fifty-four in all by the time he was done—belied the structural virtuosity he regularly displayed. *Doll*, the nineteenth in the series, weaves together murder, drugs, psychotherapy, the modeling business, and an array of vividly drawn characters.

After he moved to France, Chester Himes initiated a new phase of his work in his late forties with a series of crime novels—eight in all—featuring the Harlem police detectives Coffin Ed Johnson and Grave Digger Jones, beginning with *For Love of Imabelle* (1957, also known as *A Rage in Harlem*). *Run Man Run*, which does not feature the detective duo, is a different kind of crime novel. Like most of the others it was originally published in French as part of Gallimard's famous Série Noire; although the French edition appeared in 1959, the first English-language version, clearly deriving from a significantly different manuscript, was not published until 1966. The book was prompted by an incident in which Himes, working temporarily in New York in 1955 as a porter at a Horn & Hardart Automat, had a potentially deadly encounter with an inebriated cop. Extrapolating from this incident, Himes envisions an outcome in which the racial paranoia of a drunken police detective leads to a double killing and the relentless pursuit of a young Black college student who witnessed the event. The novel has a careening nightmarish energy as it underscores the hero's belated realization: "White cops were always shooting some Negro in Harlem. This was a violent city, these were violent people. Read any newspaper any day. What protection did he have?"

The Tremor of Forgery by Patricia Highsmith is a book about a man whose personality is crumbling while he writes a book—entitled *The Tremor of Forgery*—about a man whose personality is crumbling, "like a mountain collapsing from within." Stranded unexpectedly in Tunisia when a film project falls apart, Howard Ingham finds himself strangely paralyzed, drifting away from his own identity and values. Seeing the world through his eyes—as he views the Arabs around him with contempt and suspicion and slides away from any firm emotional commitment to anything—we may begin to wonder what that identity and those values consisted of in the first place. Like so much of Highsmith's work, it is a book about an internal splintering observed with such objectivity that it seems like a merciless self-portrait at one remove. Employing the techniques of the suspense novel, Highsmith pushes the genre toward the edge of abstraction, as Ingham ponders whether a crime has really taken place, while carefully repairing the damaged typewriter that may be the only remaining trace of a killing.

Each of these works establishes a very personal connection with a transitional and often chaotic cultural era, while continuing to draw on the strengths of a mature tradition. The novels collected in this volume, along with its companion volume, *Crime Novels: Five Classic Thrillers 1961–1964*, reveal not so much a period style as a varied and inventive range of approaches. In going beyond earlier templates for crime fiction, these writers continued to redefine its nature and widen its possibilities.

THE FIEND

Margaret Millar

For Jewell and Russ Kriger,
with deep affection, as always

The fiend with all his comrades
Fell then from heaven above,
Through as long as three nights and days . . .

Caedmon

I

IT WAS the end of August and the children were getting bored with their summer freedom. They had spent too many hours at the mercy of their own desires. Their legs and arms were scratched, bruised, blistered with poison oak; sea water had turned their hair to straw, and the sun had left cruel red scars across their cheekbones and noses. All the trees had been climbed, the paths explored, the cliffs scaled, the waves conquered. Now, as if in need and anticipation of the return of rules, they began to hang around the school playground.

So did the man in the old green coupé. Every day at noon Charlie Gowen brought his sandwiches and a carton of milk and parked across the road from the playground, separated from the swings and the jungle gym by a steel fence and some scraggly geraniums. Here he sat and ate and drank and watched.

He knew he shouldn't be there. It was dangerous to be seen near such a place.

"—where children congregate. You understand that, Gowen?"

"I think so, sir."

"Do you know what *congregate* means?"

"Well, not exactly."

"Don't give me that dumb act, Gowen. You spent two years at college."

"I was sick then. You don't retain things when you're sick."

"Then I'll spell it out for you. You are to stay away from any place frequented by children—parks, certain beach areas, Saturday afternoon movies, school playgrounds—"

The conditions were impossible, of course. He couldn't turn and run in the opposite direction every time he saw a child. They were all over, everywhere, at any hour. Once even at midnight when he was walking by himself he'd come across a boy and a girl, barely twelve. He told them gruffly to go home or he'd call the police. They disappeared into the darkness; he never saw them again even though he took the same route at the same time every night after that for a week. His conscience gnawed at him. He loved children, he shouldn't have threatened the boy and girl, he should have found out why they were on the streets at such an hour and then escorted them home and lectured their parents very sternly about looking after their kids.

He started on his second sandwich. The first hadn't filled the void in his stomach and neither would the second. He might as well have been eating clouds or pieces of twilight, though he couldn't express it that way to his brother, Benjamin, who made the lunches for both of them. He had to be very careful what he said to Benjamin. The least little fanciful thought or offbeat phrase and Ben would get the strained, set look on his face that reminded Charlie of their dead mother. Then the questions would start: Eating clouds, Charlie? Pieces of twilight? Where do you get screwy ideas like that? You're feeling all right, aren't you? Have you phoned Louise lately? Don't you think she might want to hear from you? Look, Charlie, is something bothering you? You're sure not? . . .

He knew better, by this time, than to mention anything about clouds or twilight. He had said simply that morning, "I need more food, Ben."

"Why?"

"Why? Well, because I'm hungry. I work hard. I was wondering, maybe some doughnuts and a couple of pieces of pie—"

"For yourself?"

"Sure, for myself. Who else? Oh, now I see what you're thinking about. That was over two years ago, Ben, and the Mexican kid was half starved. Everything would have been fine if that busybody woman hadn't interfered. The kid ate the sandwich, it filled him up, he felt good for a change. My God, Ben, is it a crime to feed starving children?"

Ben didn't answer. He merely closed the lid of the lunchbox on the usual two sandwiches and carton of milk, and changed the subject. "Louise called last night when you were out. She's coming over after supper. I'll slip out to a movie and leave you two alone for a while."

"Is it? Is it a crime, Ben?"

"Louise is a fine young woman. She could be the making of a man."

"If I were a starving child and someone gave me food—"

"Shut up, Charlie. You're not starving, you're overweight. And you're far from being a child. You're thirty-two years old."

It was not the command that shut Charlie up, it was the sudden cruel reference to his age. He seldom thought about it on his own because he felt so young, barely older than the little girl hanging upside down from the top bar of the jungle gym.

She was about nine. Having watched them all impartially now for two weeks, Charlie had come to like her the best.

She wasn't the prettiest, and she was so thin Charlie could have spanned her waist with his two hands, but there was a certain cockiness about her that both fascinated and worried him. When she tried some daring new trick on the jungle gym she seemed to be challenging gravity and the bars to try and stop her. If she fell—and she often did—she bounced up off the ground as naturally as a ball. Within five seconds she'd be back on the top bar of the jungle gym, pretending nothing had happened, and Charlie's heart, which had stopped, would start to beat again in double time, its rhythm disturbed by relief and anger.

The other children called her Jessie, and so, inside the car with the windows closed, did Charlie.

"Careful, Jessie, careful. Self-confidence is all very well, but bones can be broken, child, even nine-year-old bones. I ought to warn your parents. Where do you live, Jessie?"

The playground counselor, a physical education major at the local college, was refereeing a sixth-grade basketball game. The sun scorched through his crew cut, he was thirsty, and his eyes stung from the dust raised by scuffling feet, but he was as intent on the game as though it were being played in the Los Angeles Coliseum. His name was Scott Roberts, he was twenty, and the children respected him greatly because he could chin himself with one hand and drove a sports car.

He saw the two little girls crossing the field and ignored them as long as possible, which wasn't long, since one of them was crying.

He blew the whistle and stopped the game. "O.K., fellas, take five." And, to the girl who was crying, "What's the matter, Mary Martha?"

"Jessie fell."

"It figures, it figures." Scott wiped the sweat off his forehead with the back of his hand. "If Jessie was the one who fell, why isn't she doing the crying?"

"I couldn't be bothered," Jessie said loftily. She ached in a number of places but nothing short of an amputation could have forced her to tears in front of the sixth-grade boys. She had a crush on three of them; one had even spoken to her. "Mary Martha always cries at things, like sad events on television and people falling."

"How are your hands? Any improvement over last week?"

"They're O.K."

"Let me see, Jessie."

"Here, in front of everybody?"

"Right here, in front of everybody who's nosy enough to look."

He didn't even have to glance at the sixth-graders to get his message across. Immediately they all turned away and became absorbed in other things, dribbling the ball, adjusting shoelaces, hitching up shorts, slicking back hair.

Jessie presented her hands and Scott examined them, frowning. The palms were a mass of blisters in every stage of development, some newly formed and still full of liquid, some open and oozing, others covered with layers of scar tissue.

Scott shook his head and frowned. "I told you last week to get your mother to put alcohol on your hands every morning and night to toughen the skin. You didn't do it."

"No."

"Don't you have a mother?"

"Of course. Also a father, and a brother in high school, and an aunt and uncle next door—they're not really blood relations but I call them that because they give me lots of things, etcetera—and heaps of cousins in Canada and New Jersey."

"The cousins are too far away to help," Scott said. "But surely one of the others could put alcohol on your hands for you."

"I could do it myself if I wanted to."

"But you don't want to."

"It stings."

"Wouldn't you prefer a little sting to a big case of blood poisoning?"

Jessie didn't know what blood poisoning was, but for the benefit of the sixth-grade boys she said she wasn't the least bit scared of it. This remark stimulated Mary Martha to relate the entire plot of a medical program she'd seen, in which the doctor himself had blood poisoning and didn't realize it until he went into convulsions.

"By then it was too late?" Jessie said, trying not to sound much interested. "He died?"

"No, he couldn't. He's the hero every week. But he suffered terribly. You should have seen the faces he made, worse than my mother when she's plucking her eyebrows."

Scott interrupted brusquely. "All right, you two, knock it off. The issue is not Mother's eyebrows or Dr. Whoozit's convulsions. It's Jessie's hands. They're a mess and something has to be done."

Flushing, Jessie hid her hands in the pockets of her shorts. While she was playing on the jungle gym she'd hardly noticed the pain, but now, with everyone's attention focused on her, it had become almost unbearable.

Scott was aware of this. He touched her shoulder lightly and the two of them began walking toward the back-exit gate, followed by an excited and perspiring Mary Martha. None of them noticed the green coupé.

"You'd better go home," Scott said, "Take a warm bath, put alcohol on your hands with a piece of cotton, and stay off the jungle gym until you grow some new skin. You'd better tell your mother, too, Jessie."

"I won't have to. If I go home at noon and take a bath she'll think I'm dying."

"Maybe you are," Mary Martha said in a practical voice. "Imagine me with a dying best friend."

"Oh, shut up."

"I'm only trying to help."

"That's the kind of help you ought to save for your best enemy," Scott said and turned to go back to the basketball game.

Out of the corner of his eye he noticed the old green coupé pulling away from the curb. What caught his attention was the fact that, although it was a very hot day, the windows were closed. They were also dirty, so that the driver was invisible and the car seemed to be operating itself. A minute later it turned onto a side street and was out of sight.

So were the two girls.

"We could stop in at my house," Mary Martha said, "for some cinnamon toast to build your strength up."

"My strength is O.K., but I wouldn't mind some cinnamon toast. Maybe we could even make it ourselves?"

"No. My mother will be home. She always is."

"Why?"

"To guard the house."

Jessie had asked the same question and been given the same answer quite a few times. She was always left with an incongruous mental picture of Mary Martha's mother sitting large and formidable on the porch with a shotgun across her lap. The real Mrs. Oakley was small and frail and suffered from a number of obscure allergies.

"Why does she have to stay home to guard the house?" Jessie said. "She could just lock the doors."

"Locks don't keep him out."

"You mean your father?"

"I mean my *ex*-father."

"But you can't have an *ex*-father. I asked my Aunt Virginia and she said a wife can divorce her husband and then he's an *ex*-husband. But you can't divorce a father."

"Yes, you can. We already did, my mother and I."

"Did he want you to?"

"He didn't care."

"It would wring my father's heart," Jessie said, "if I divorced him."

"How do you know? Did he ever tell you?"

"No, but I never asked."

"Then you don't know for sure."

The jacaranda trees, for which the street was named, were in full bloom and their falling petals covered lawns and sidewalks, even the road itself, with purple confetti. Some clung to Jessie's short dark hair and to Mary Martha's blond ponytail.

"I bet we look like brides," Jessie said. "We could pretend—"

"No." Mary Martha began brushing the jacaranda petals out of her hair as if they were lice. "I don't want to."

"You always like pretending things."

"*Sensible* things."

Jessie knew this wasn't true, since Mary Martha's favorite role was that of child spy for the FBI. But she preferred not to argue. The lunch she'd taken to the playground had all been eaten by ten o'clock and she was more than ready for some of Mrs. Oakley's cinnamon toast. The Oakleys lived at 319 Jacaranda Road in a huge redwood house surrounded by live oak and eucalyptus trees. The trees had been planted, and the house built, by Mr. Oakley's parents. When Jessie had first seen the place she'd assumed that Mary Martha's family was terribly rich, but she discovered on later visits that the attic was just full of junk, the four-car garage contained only Mrs. Oakley's little Volkswagen and Mary Martha's bicycle, and some of the upstairs rooms were empty, with not even a chair in them.

Kate Oakley hated the place and was afraid to live in it, but she was even more afraid that, if she sold it, Mr. Oakley would be able by some legal maneuver to get his hands on half of the money. So she had stayed on. By day she stared out at the live oak trees wishing they would die and let a little light into the house, and by night she lay awake listening to the squawking and creaking of eucalyptus boughs, and hoping the next wind would blow them down.

Mary Martha knew how her mother felt about the house and she couldn't understand it. She herself had never lived any other place and never wanted to. When Jessie came over to play, the two girls tried on old clothes in the attic, put on shows in the big garage, rummaged through the cellar for hidden treasure, and, when Mrs. Oakley wasn't looking, climbed the trees or hunted frogs in the creek, pretending the frogs were handsome princes in disguise. None of the princes ever had a chance to become undisguised since Mrs. Oakley always made the girls return the frogs to the creek: "*The poor little creatures. . . . I'm ashamed of you, Mary Martha, wrenching them away from their homes and families. How would you like it if some enormous giant picked you up and carried you away?*"

The front door of the Oakley house was open but the screen was latched and Mary Martha had to press the door chime. The sound was very faint. Mrs. Oakley had had it muted shortly after Mr. Oakley moved out because sometimes he used to come and stand at the door and keep pressing the chime, demanding admittance.

"If she's not home," Jessie said hopefully, "we could climb the sycamore tree at the back and get over on the balcony of her bedroom and just walk in. . . . What's the matter with your doorbell?"

"Nothing."

"Ours is real loud."

"My mother and I don't like loud noises."

Mrs. Oakley appeared, blinking her eyes in the light as if she'd been taking a nap or watching television in a darkened room.

She was small and pretty and very neat in a blue cotton dress she had made herself. Her fair hair was softly waved and hung down to her shoulders and she wore high-heeled shoes without any backs to them. Sometimes, when Jessie was angry at her mother, she compared her unfavorably with Mrs. Oakley: her mother liked to wear sneakers and jeans or shorts, and she often forgot to comb her hair, which was as dark and straight as Jessie's own.

Mrs. Oakley kissed Mary Martha on the forehead. "Hello, lamb." Then she patted Jessie on the shoulder. "Hello, Jessie. My goodness, you're getting big. Each time I see you, I truly swear you've grown another inch."

Whenever Mrs. Oakley said this to her, which was at least once a week, Jessie felt highly complimented. Her own mother said, "Good Lord, do I have to buy you another pair of shoes *already*?" And her brother called her beanpole or toothpick or canary legs.

"I eat a lot," Jessie said modestly. "So does my brother, Mike. My father says he should get double tax exemptions for us."

As soon as she'd made the remark Jessie realized it was a mistake. Mary Martha nudged her in the side with her elbow, and Mrs. Oakley turned and walked away, her sharp heels leaving little dents in the waxed linoleum.

"You shouldn't talk about fathers or taxes," Mary Martha whispered. "But it's O.K., because now we won't have to tell her about your hands. She hates the sight of blood."

"I'm not bleeding."

"You might start."

Charlie wrote the name and address on the inside cover of a book of matches: Jessie, 319 Jacaranda Road. He wasn't sure yet what he intended to do with the information; it just seemed an important thing to have, like money in the bank. Perhaps he would find out Jessie's last name and write a letter to her parents, warning them. Dear Mr. and Mrs. X: I have never written an anonymous letter before, but I cannot stand by and watch your daughter take such risks with her delicate bones. Children must be cherished, guarded against the terrible hazards of life, fed good nourishing meals so their bones will be padded and will not break coming into contact with the hard cruel earth. In the name of God, I beg you to protect your little girl. . . .

2

FOR MANY years the Oakley house had stood by itself, a few miles west of the small city of San Felice, surrounded by lemon and walnut groves. Most of the groves were gone now, their places taken by subdivisions with fanciful names and low down payments. Into one of these tract houses, a few blocks away from the Oakleys, Jessie had moved a year ago with her family. The Brants had been living in an apartment in San Francisco and they were all delighted by the freedom of having their own private house and plot of land. Like most freedoms, it had its price. David Brant had been forced to renew his acquaintance with pliers and wrenches and fuse boxes, the children were expected to help with the housework, and Ellen Brant had taken over the garden. She bought a book on landscaping and another on Southern California flowers and shrubs, and set out to show the neighbors a thing or two.

Ellen Brant was inexperienced but obstinate. Some of the shrubs had been moved six or seven times and were half dead from too much attention and overfeeding. The creeping fig vine, intended to cover the chimney of the fireplace, refused to creep. The leaves of the jasmine yellowed and dropped from excess dampness, and Ellen, assuming their wilting was due to lack of water, turned on the sprinkling system. Bills from the nursery and the water department ran high but when Dave Brant complained about them Ellen pointed out that she was actually increasing the value of the property. In fact, she didn't know or care much about property values; she simply enjoyed being out-of-doors with the sun warm on her face and the wind smelling mysteriously of the sea.

She was busy snipping dead blossoms off the rosebushes when Jessie arrived home at one o'clock.

Ellen stood up, squinting against the sun and brushing dirt off her denim shorts and bare knees. She was slim and very tanned, like Jessie, and her eyes were the same unusual shade of grayish green.

"What are you doing home so early?" she said, pushing a strand of moist hair off her forehead with the pruning shears.

"By the way, you didn't straighten up your room before you left. You know the rules, you helped us write them."

It seemed to Jessie a good time to change the subject as dramatically as possible. "Mary Martha says I may be dying."

"Really? Well, you wouldn't want to be caught dead in a messy room, so up you go. Start moving, kiddo."

"You don't even believe me."

"No."

"I bet if Mary Martha went home and told *her* mother she was dying, there'd be a terrible fuss. I bet there'd be ambulances and doctors and nurses and people screaming—"

"If it will make you feel any better I'll begin screaming right now."

"No! I mean, somebody might hear you."

"That's the general purpose of screaming, isn't it?" Ellen said with a smile. "Come on, let's have it, old girl—what's the matter?"

Jessie exhibited her hands. A dusting of cinnamon hadn't improved their appearance but Ellen Brant showed neither surprise nor dismay. She'd been through the same thing with Jessie's older brother, Mike, a dozen times or more.

She said, "I have the world's climbingest children. Where'd you do this?"

"The jungle gym."

"Well, you go in and fill the washbasin with warm water and start soaking your hands. I'll be with you in a minute. I want to check my record book and see when you had your last tetanus booster shot."

"It was the Fourth of July when I stepped on the stingray at East Beach."

"I hope to heaven you're not going to turn out to be accident-prone."

"What's that?"

"There were at least a thousand people on the beach that afternoon. Only you stepped on a stingray."

Although Jessie knew this was not intended as a compliment, she couldn't help taking it as such. Being the only one of a thousand people to step on a stingray seemed to her quite distinctive, the sort of thing that could never happen to someone like Mary Martha.

Half an hour later she was ensconced on the davenport in the living room, watching a television program and drinking chocolate milk. On her hands she wore a pair of her mother's white gloves, which made her feel very sophisticated if she didn't look too closely at the way they fitted.

The sliding glass door was partly open and she could see her mother out on the lawn talking to Virginia Arlington, who lived next door. Jessie was quite fond of Mrs. Arlington and called her Aunt Virginia, but she hoped both women would stay outside and not interrupt the television movie.

Virginia Arlington's round pink face and plump white arms were moist with perspiration. As she talked she fanned herself with an advertisement she'd just picked up from the mailbox.

Even her voice sounded warm. "I saw Jessie coming home early and I was worried. Is anything the matter?"

"Not really. Her hands are sore from playing too long on the jungle gym."

"Poor baby. She has so much energy she never knows when to stop. She's like you, Ellen. You drive yourself too hard sometimes."

"I manage to survive." She dropped on her knees beside the rosebush again, hoping Virginia would take the hint and leave. She liked Virginia Arlington and appreciated her kindness and generosity, but there were times when Ellen preferred to work undisturbed and without someone reminding her she was driving herself too hard. Virginia had no children, and her husband, Howard, was away on business a great deal; she had a part-time gardener and a cleaning woman twice a week, and to open a can or the garage doors or the car windows, all she had to do was press a button. Ellen didn't envy her neighbors. She knew that if their positions were reversed, she would be doing just as much as she did now and Virginia would be doing as little.

Virginia lingered on, in spite of the sun which she hated and usually managed to avoid. Even five minutes of it made her nose turn pink and her neck break out in a rash. "I have an idea. Why don't I slip downtown and buy Jessie a couple of games?—you know, something absorbing that will keep her quiet."

"I thought Howard was home today."

"He is, but he's still asleep. I could be back by the time he wakes up."

"I appreciate your offer, naturally," Ellen said, "but you've already bought Jessie so many toys and books and games—"

"That won't spoil her. I was reading in a magazine just this morning that buying things for children doesn't spoil them unless those things are a substitute for something else."

Ellen had read the same magazine. "Love."

"Yes."

"Jessie gets plenty of love."

"I know. That's my whole point. If she's already loved, the little items I buy her can't harm her."

Ellen hesitated. Some of the items hadn't been so little—a ten-gear Italian bicycle, a cashmere sweater, a wrist watch—but she didn't want to seem ungrateful. "All right, go ahead if you like. But please don't spend too much money. Jessie might get the idea that she deserves an expensive gift every time something happens to her. Life doesn't work out that way."

There was a minute of strained silence between the two women, like the kind that comes after a quarrel over an important issue. It bothered Ellen. There had been no quarrel, not even a real disagreement, and the issue was hardly important, a two-dollar game for Jessie.

Virginia said softly, "I haven't offended you, have I, El? I mean, maybe you think I was implying that Jessie didn't have enough toys and things." Virginia's pale blue eyes were anxious and the tip of her nose was already starting to turn red. "I'd feel terrible if you thought that."

"Well, I don't."

"You're absolutely sure?"

"Don't go *on* about it, Virginia. You want to buy Jess a game, so buy it."

"We could pretend it was from you and Dave."

"I don't believe in pretending to my children. They're subjected to enough phoniness in the ordinary course of events."

From one of the back windows of the Arlington house a man's voice shouted, "Virgie! Virgie!"

"Howard's awake," Virginia said hastily. "I'll go and make

his breakfast and maybe slip downtown while he's eating. Tell Jessie I'll be over later on."

"All right."

Virginia walked across the lawn and down her own driveway. It was bordered on each side with a low privet hedge and small round clumps of French marigolds. Everything in the yard, as in the house, was so neat and orderly that Virginia felt none of it belonged to her. The house was Howard's and the cleaning woman's, and the yard was the gardener's. Virginia was a guest and she had to act like a guest, polite and uncritical.

Only the dog, a large golden retriever named Chap, was Virginia's. She had wanted a small dog, one she could cuddle and hold on her lap, and when Howard brought Chap home from one of his trips she had felt cheated. Chap was already full-grown then and weighed ninety pounds, and the first time she was left alone with him she was frightened. His bark was loud and ferocious; when she fed him he nearly gobbled her hand; when she took him out on a leash he'd dragged her around the block like a horse pulling a wheelless carriage. She had gradually come to realize that his bark was a bluff, and that he had been underfed by his previous owners and never taught to obey any orders.

From the beginning the dog had attached himself to Virginia, as if he knew she needed his company and protection. He was indifferent to Howard, despised the cleaning woman, and held the gardener in line with an occasional growl. He slept inside at night and kept prowlers away not only from Virginia but from the immediate neighbors as well.

Howard had gotten up and let the dog out. Chap came bounding down the driveway, his plumed tail waving in circles.

Virginia leaned down and pressed her cheek against the top of his huge golden head. "You silly boy, why the big greeting? I've only been away for ten minutes."

Through the open kitchen window Howard overheard her and said, "A likely story. You've probably been over at the Brants' gabbing with Ellen all morning."

She knew he intended it mainly, though not entirely, as a joke. Without replying, she went in the back door, through the service porch to the kitchen. The dog followed her, still making a fuss, as if she were the one, not Howard, who'd been gone for two weeks.

Howard had made coffee and was frying some bacon on the grill in the middle of the stove. When he was home he liked to mess around the kitchen because it was a pleasant contrast to sitting in restaurants, being served food he didn't enjoy. He was a fussy eater for such a large man.

A head taller than Virginia, he had to lean way down to kiss her on the mouth. "You're a sight for sore eyes, Virgie."

"Am I?" Virginia said. "The bacon's burning."

"Let it. Did you miss me?"

"Yes."

"Is that all, yes?"

"I missed you very much, Howard."

He flipped the bacon expertly with a spatula, all four slices at once. "Still want me to quit my job, Virgie?"

"I haven't brought that subject up for over a year."

"I know. It makes me wonder how you've been spending your time while I'm away."

"If you want to know, ask me."

"I'm asking you."

"All right." Virginia sat down at the kitchen table, her pale pretty hands folded in her lap. "I start off each day with a champagne breakfast. After that, it's luncheon with the girls, with plenty of drinks, of course. We play bridge for high stakes all afternoon and end up at a cocktail party. Then I have dinner at a nightclub and carouse until dawn with a group of merry companions."

"Sounds rigorous," Howard said, smiling. "How do you manage to stay so beautiful?"

"Howard—"

"Put a couple of slices of bread in the toaster, will you?"

"Howard, were you serious when you asked me how I spent my time?"

"No."

"I think you were. Perhaps you'd like me to keep a diary. It would make fascinating reading. Juicy items like how I took some clothes to the cleaners, borrowed a book from the library, bought groceries—"

"Cut it out, will you, Virgie? Something popped into my head and I said it and I shouldn't have. I'm sorry. Let's forget it."

"I'll try."

He brought his plate of bacon to the table and sat down opposite her. "I hope I didn't wake you when I came in this morning. Chap made a hell of a fuss, he almost convinced me I had the wrong house. You'd think he'd know me by this time."

"He's a good watchdog," she said, adding silently: *You'd think I, too, would know you by this time, Howard, but I don't.* "How was the trip?"

"Hot—103 degrees in Bakersfield, 95 in L.A."

"It's been hot here, too."

"I have an idea. Why don't we head for the beach this afternoon? We'll loll around on the sand, have a walk and a swim—"

"It sounds nice, Howard, but I'm afraid I can't. You know how badly I sunburn."

"You could wear a wide straw hat and we'll take along the umbrella from the patio table."

"No."

He stared at her across the table, his eyes puzzled. "That was a pretty definite no, Virginia. Are you still sore at me?"

"Of course not. It's just that—well, the umbrella's no good any more. It was torn. I threw it away."

"It was practically brand-new. How did it get torn?"

"The wind. I intended to tell you. We had a big wind here Tuesday afternoon, a Santa Ana from the desert. I was downtown when it started and by the time I got home the umbrella was already damaged."

"Why didn't you take it to one of those canvas shops to have it repaired?"

"The spokes were bent, too. You should have seen it, Howard. It looked as if it had been in a hurricane."

"The bougainvillea beside the garage usually blows over in a Santa Ana. I didn't notice anything wrong with it."

"Salvador may have tied it up."

She knew this was safe enough. Salvador, who spoke or pretended to speak only Spanish, wasn't likely to deny or confirm anything. He would merely smile his stupid silver-toothed smile and crinkle up his wise old eyes and go right on working. *You speak, señor, but if I do not hear you, you do not exist.*

There had been no Santa Ana on Tuesday afternoon, just a fresh cool breeze blowing in from the ocean. Virginia had not been downtown, she'd been sitting on the front porch watching Jessie and Mary Martha roller-skate up and down the sidewalk. It was Jessie's idea to borrow the umbrella to use as a sail, and it had worked all too well. The two girls and the umbrella ended up against the telephone pole at the corner. Over cookies and chocolate malted milks Virginia told the girls, "There's no need to go blabbing to your parents about this. You know your mother, Jessie. She'd insist on paying for the umbrella and she can't really afford to. So let's keep this our secret, shall we?"

Virginia got up and poured Howard some coffee. Her hands were shaking and she felt sick with fear that Howard suspected her of lying. "I'm terribly sorry about the whole thing, Howard."

"Come on now. I hardly expect you to apologize for a Santa Ana. As for the umbrella, it was just an object. Objects can be replaced."

"I could go downtown right now and buy one, while you're reading the newspaper."

"Nonsense. We'll have one sent out."

"I'm going down anyway."

"Do you have to? We've hardly had a chance to talk."

We've had a chance, Howard, she thought, *we just haven't used it to very good advantage.* She said, "You'll be reading the paper anyway. It seems silly for me merely to sit and watch you when I could be accomplishing something."

"Since you put it like that," Howard said, taking her hand, "go ahead. Do you need money? What do you want to accomplish?"

"An errand."

"Ah, we're playing the woman of mystery today, are we?"

"There's no mystery about it," she said bluntly. "Jessie's sick. I want to buy her a little game or two to keep her quiet."

"I see."

She could tell from his tone that what he saw gave him little pleasure.

"I'm sorry the kid's sick," he added. "What's the matter with her?"

"According to Ellen, Jessie's hands are sore from playing on the jungle gym."

"It hardly sounds catastrophic."

"I know, but Ellen tends to minimize things like that. Sometimes I think she's not sympathetic enough with the child."

"Sympathy can be overdone and children can take advantage of it."

"Not Jessie. She's really a wonderful girl. You know, when she and I are alone together, I never have the least trouble with her. The problem of discipline doesn't even come up."

"Why should it?" Howard said dryly. "She calls the shots."

Virginia looked shocked. "That's not true."

"All right, it's not true. I'm just imagining that she comes barging in here without knocking, helps herself to whatever is in the refrigerator, bangs on the piano, feeds the dog until he's too stuffed to move—"

"It so happens that she has my permission to feed both the dog and herself and to come in here when she feels like it. She has no piano of her own so I'm giving her lessons on ours because I think she has talent."

"Listen, Virginia, I've wanted to say this before but I hated to cause trouble. Now that trouble's here anyway, I might as well speak my piece. You're getting too bound up with Jessie."

"I won't listen to you."

She put her hands over her ears and shook her head back and forth. After a moment's hesitation, Howard grabbed her by the wrists and forced her hands to her sides.

"You'll listen, Virginia."

"Let go of me."

"Later. It's natural enough for you to be fond of the kid since we don't have any of our own. What isn't natural is that she's taken everybody's place in your life. You don't see your friends any more, you don't even seem to want to spend much time with me when I'm home."

"Why should I, when all you do is pick on me?"

"I'm not picking on you. I'm warning you for your own good not to make yourself vulnerable to a heartbreak. Jessie doesn't belong to you, you have no control over her. What if something happens to her?"

"Happens? What?"

"For one thing, Dave Brant could lose his job or be laid off and forced to move away from here."

Virginia was staring at him bleakly, her face white. "That would suit you fine, wouldn't it?"

"No. I happen to like the Brants and enjoy their company. They're not, however, my sole interest in life. I'm prepared to survive without them. Are you?"

"I think you're jealous," Virginia said slowly. "I think you're jealous of a nine-year-old girl."

He let go of her wrists as if the accusation had suddenly paralyzed him. Then, with a sound of despair, he walked away into the living room. She stood motionless in the middle of the kitchen, listening to the rustle of Howard's newspaper, the sighing of his leather chair as he sat down, and the rebellious beat of her own heart.

3

AT 12:50 Charlie Gowen went back to the wholesale paper supply company where he was employed. He was always punctual, partly by nature, partly because his brother, Benjamin, had been drumming it into him for years. "So you have your faults, Charlie, and maybe you can't help them. But you can be careful about the little things, like being on time and neat and keeping your hair combed and not smoking or drinking, and working hard— A bunch of little things like that, they all add up, they look good on a man's record. Employment record, I mean."

Charlie knew that he didn't mean employment record but he let it go and he listened to Ben's advice because it sounded sensible and because, since the death of his mother, there was no one else to listen to. He felt, too, that he had to be loyal to Ben; Ben's wife had divorced him on account of Charlie. She'd walked out leaving a note in the middle of the bed: "I'm not coming back and don't try to find me. I'm sick of being disgraced."

Charlie worked at the paper supply company as a stock boy. He liked his job. He felt at home walking up and down the narrow aisles with shelves, from floor to ceiling, filled with such a variety of things that even Mr. Warner, the owner, couldn't keep track of them: notebooks, pens, pencils, party decorations and favors, brooms and brushes and mops, typewriter ribbons and staplers and stationery, signs saying No Trespassing, For Rent, Private, Walk In, erasers and bridge tallies and confetti and plastic lovers for the tops of wedding cakes, huge rolls of colored tickets to functions that hadn't even been planned yet, maps, charts, chalk, ink, and thousands of reams of paper.

The contents of the building were highly inflammable, which was one of the main reasons why Charlie had been hired. Though he carried matches for the convenience of other people, he hadn't smoked since the age of fourteen when Ben had caught him trying it and beaten the tar out of him. Mr.

Warner, the owner, had been so delighted to find a genuine nonsmoker, not just someone who'd quit a few weeks or months ago, that he'd given Charlie the job without inquiring too closely into his background. He knew in a general way that Charlie had had "trouble," but there was never any sign of it at work. Charlie arrived early and stayed late, he was pleasant and earnest, always ready to do a favor and never asking any in return.

In the alley behind the building Charlie found one of his coworkers, a young man named Ed Hines, leaning against the wall with an unlit cigarette in his hand.

"Hey, Charlie, got a match?"

"Sure." Charlie tossed him a packet of book matches. "I'd appreciate having them back, if you don't mind. There's an address written on the cover."

Ed grinned. "And a phone number?"

"No. Not yet."

"You gay old dog, you!"

"No. No, it's not like that actually—" Charlie stopped, realizing suddenly that Ed wouldn't understand the truth, that there was a family at 319 Jacaranda Road who were neglecting their pretty little girl, Jessie.

Ed returned the matches. "Thanks, Charlie. And say, the old man's in a stew about something. You better check in at the front office."

Warner was behind his desk, a small man almost lost in the welter of papers that surrounded him: order forms, invoices, sales slips, bills, correspondence. Some of this stuff would be filed, some would simply disappear. Warner had started the business forty years ago. It had grown and prospered since then, but Warner still tried to manage the place as if he personally knew, as he once had, every customer by name, every order from memory. Many mistakes were made, and with each one, Warner got a little older and a little more stubborn. The business continued to make money, however, because it was the only one of its kind in San Felice.

Charlie stood in the doorway, trying to hold his head high, the way Ben kept telling him to. But it was difficult, and Mr. Warner wasn't watching anyway. He had the telephone perched on his left shoulder like a crow. The crow was talking, loud and fast, in a woman's voice.

Mr. Warner put his hand over the mouthpiece and looked at Charlie. "You know anything about some skeletons?"

"Skeletons?" The word emerged from Charlie's throat as if it had been squeezed out of shape by some internal pressure. Then he went dumb entirely. He couldn't even tell Mr. Warner that he was innocent, he had done nothing, he knew nothing about any skeletons. He could only shake his head back and forth again and again.

"What's the matter with you?" Warner said irritably. "I mean those life-size cardboard skeletons we have in stock around Halloween. Some woman claims she ordered a dozen for a pathologists' convention dance that's being held tomorrow night." Then into the telephone, "I can't find any record of your order, Miss Johnston, but I'll check again. I promise you you'll get your skeletons even if I, ha ha, have to shoot a couple of my employees. Yes, I'll call you back." He hung up, turning his attention to Charlie. "And believe me, I meant everything but the ha ha. Now let's start searching."

Charlie was so dizzy with relief that he had to hold on to the doorjamb to steady himself. "Yes, sir. Right away. If I knew exactly what to search for—"

"A package from Whipple Novelty in Chicago."

"That came in this morning, Mr. Warner."

"It did? Well, I'll be damned." Warner looked pleasantly surprised, like a man who doesn't expect or deserve good news. "Well, I hand it to you, Charlie. You're getting to know the business. I ask for skeletons, you produce skeletons."

"No. No, I—"

"I saw you at the drive-in the other night, by the way. You were with a nice-looking young woman. Funny thing, I could have sworn I've seen her before. Maybe she's one of our customers, eh?"

"No, sir. She works at the library, in the reference department."

"That explains it, then," Warner said. "So she's a librarian, eh? She must be pretty smart."

"Yes, sir."

"It pays to have a smart wife."

"No, no. She's not—I mean, we're not—"

"Don't fight it, Charlie. We all get hooked sooner or later."

Charlie would have liked to stay and explain to Mr. Warner about his relationship with Louise, but Mr. Warner had picked up the phone and was dialing, and Charlie wasn't sure he could explain it anyway.

He felt sometimes that he had known Louise all his life and at other times that he didn't know her at all. In fact, he had met her about a year ago at the library. Charlie was there at Ben's insistence: "You don't want to be a stock boy forever, Charlie. I bet there are careers you never even heard about. One of them might be just down your alley but you've got to investigate, look around, find out what's available."

And so, night after night, Charlie went to the library and read books and magazines and trade journals about electronics, photography, turkey farming, real estate, personnel management, mining engineering, cartooning, forestry, interior design, cabinet-making, raising chinchillas, mathematics. He barely noticed the woman who helped him locate some of this material until one night she said, "My goodness, you certainly have a wide range of interests, Mr. Gowen."

Charlie merely stared at her, shocked by the sudden attention and the fact that she even knew his name. He thought of a library as a warm, safe, quiet place where people hadn't any names or faces or problems. The woman had no right to spoil it, no right—

But the next time he went, he wore a new shirt and tie, and a very serious expression which befitted a man with a wide range of interests. He took out an imposing book on architecture and sat with it open on the table in front of him and watched Louise out of the corner of his eye as if he had never seen a woman before and wasn't sure what to expect from the strange creature.

He guessed, from the way her colleagues deferred to her, that she was head of the department and so must be at least in her late twenties. But she had a tiny figure like a girl's with the merest suggestion of hips and breasts, and her movements were quick and light as if she weighed scarcely anything at all. Every time Charlie caught her glancing at him, something expanded inside of him. He felt larger and stronger.

He was only vaguely aware that it was getting late and people were leaving the library.

Louise came from behind the desk and approached the table where he was sitting. "I hate to disturb you, Mr. Gowen, but we're getting ready to lock up."

Charlie rose awkwardly to his feet. "I'm terribly sorry, I didn't notice. I—I was absorbed."

"You must have great powers of concentration to study in a noisy place like this."

"No. No, I really haven't."

"I wish I could let you take this book home but it's from the reference shelves and isn't allowed out. Unless, of course, there are special circumstances—"

"No. No, there aren't." Charlie hung his head and stared down at the floor. He could almost feel Ben behind him, telling him to square his shoulders and keep his head up and look proud. "I mean, I'm not an architect or anything. I don't know anything about architecture."

He hadn't planned on telling her this, or, in fact, talking to her at all. He'd intended to let her think he was a man of some background and education, a man to be respected. Now he could hear his own voice ruining everything, and he was powerless to stop it.

"Not a thing," he added.

"Neither do I," Louise said cheerfully. "Except about this building, and here I qualify as an expert. I can predict just where the roof will be leaking, come next January."

"You can? Where?"

"The art and music department. You see, last year it was the children's wing, they patched that up. And the year before, it was here, practically above my desk. So next time it's art and music's turn."

"I'll have to come back in January and find out if you were right."

There was a brief silence; then Louise said quietly, "That sounds as if you're going away some place. Will you be gone long, Mr. Gowen?"

"No."

"We'll miss you."

"No. I mean, I must have given you the wrong impression. I'm not going anywhere."

"You didn't give me the wrong impression, Mr. Gowen. I simply jumped to a wrong conclusion. My dad says I'm always doing it. I'm sorry."

"Even if I wanted to, I couldn't go anywhere."

Charlie could feel Ben behind him again: *Stop downgrading yourself, Charlie. Give people a chance to see your good side before you start blabbing. You've got to put up a front, develop a sense of self-preservation.*

"In fact," Charlie said, "I can't even leave the county without special permission."

Louise smiled, thinking it was a joke. "From whom?"

"From my parole officer."

He didn't wait to see her reaction. He just turned and walked away, stumbling a little over his own feet like an adolescent not accustomed to his new growth.

For the next three nights he stayed home, reading, watching television, playing cards with Ben. He knew Ben was suspicious and Charlie tried to allay the suspicion by talking a lot, reminiscing about their childhood, repeating jokes and stories he heard at work.

Ben wasn't fooled. "How come you don't go to the library any more, Charlie?"

"I've been a little tired this week."

"You don't act tired."

"A man needs a change now and then. I've been getting into a rut spending every night at the library."

"You call this a nonrut?" Ben gestured around the room. Since their mother's death nothing in the house had been moved. It was as if the chairs and tables and lamps were permanently riveted in place. "Listen, Charlie, if anything happened, I have a right to know what it was."

"Why?"

"Because I'm your older brother and I'm responsible for you."

"No. No, you're not," Charlie said, shaking his head. "I'm responsible for myself. You keep telling me to grow up. How can I, with you breathing down my neck? You won't allow me to do anything on my own."

"I won't allow you to make a fool of yourself if I can help it."

"Well, you can't help it. It's over. It's done." Charlie began pacing up and down the room, his arms crossed on his chest in a despairing embrace. "I made a fool of myself and I don't care, I don't give a damn."

"Tell me about it, Charlie."

"No."

"You'd better. If it's not too serious I may be able to cover up for you."

"I keep uncovering and you keep covering up. Back and forth, seesaw, where will it end?"

"That's up to you."

Charlie paused at the window. It was dark outside, he could see nothing on the street, only himself filling the narrow window frame like a painting that had gotten beyond control of the artist and outgrown its canvas. A layer of greasy film on the glass softened his image. He looked like a very young man, broad-shouldered, slim-waisted, with a lock of light brown curly hair falling over his forehead and twin tears rolling down his cheeks.

Ben saw the tears, too. "My God, what have you done this time?"

"I—I ruined something."

"You sound surprised," Ben said bitterly, "as if you didn't know that ruining things was your specialty in life."

"Don't. Don't nag. Don't preach."

"Tell me what happened."

Charlie told him, while Ben sat in the cherrywood rocking chair that had belonged to his mother, rocking slowly back and forth the way she used to when she was worried over Charlie.

"I don't know why I said it, Ben, I just don't *know*. It popped out, like a burp. I had no control over it, don't you understand?"

"Sure, I understand," Ben said wearily. "I understand you've got to put yourself in a bad light. Whenever things are going all right you've got to open your big mouth and wreck them. Who knows? This woman might have become interested in you, a nice relationship might have developed. God help you,

you could use a friend. But no, no, you couldn't keep your trap shut long enough even to find out her name. . . . Don't you *want* a friend, Charlie?"

"Yes."

"Then why in hell do you do these things?"

"I don't know."

"Well, it's over with, it's finished. There's not much use discussing it." Ben rose, heavily, from the rocking chair. "I suppose this means you won't be going to the library any more?"

"I can't."

"You could if you wanted to. If it were me, I'd just sail in there one of these nights with a smile on my face and pretend the whole thing was a joke."

"She knew it wasn't a joke."

"How can you be sure? You said you turned and walked out. If you didn't stick around to watch her reaction, you can't tell what it was. She might have gotten a big laugh out of it, for all you know."

"Stop it, Ben. It's no use."

"It's no use always looking on the black side, either. You're a good-looking man, Charlie. A woman could easily flip over you if you gave her a chance. If you held your head up, squared your shoulders, if you thought white instead of black for a change, if you put on a front—"

Charlie knew all the if's, including the one that was never spoken: If you got married, Charlie, some of your weight would be lifted off my back.

The following afternoon, when Charlie got home from work, there was a letter waiting for him, propped up against the sugar bowl on the kitchen table. Charlie received few letters and he would have liked to sit with it in his hands for a few minutes, wondering, examining the small neat handwriting. But Ben came out of the bedroom where he had changed from his good gabardine suit into jeans and T-shirt.

"There's a letter for you."

"Yes."

"Aren't you going to open it?"

"If you want me to."

"If *I* want you to?" Ben said irritably. "For Pete's sake, what have *I* got to do with it? It's your letter."

Charlie didn't argue, though he knew the letter wasn't really his. He had nothing that was privately, exclusively his own, any more than a five-year-old child has. The letter might as well have been addressed to Ben, because Ben would read it anyway, just as if Charlie, in his times of trouble, had lost the ability to read.

Charlie slit the envelope open with a table knife and unfolded the small sheet of stationery:

> Dear Mr. Gowen:
>
> I wanted to tell you this in person, but since you haven't appeared at the library, I must do it by letter. I was deeply moved by your courage and forthrightness on Monday evening. Very few people are capable of such honesty. Perhaps I'm being too presumptuous but I can't help hoping that what you did was an act of trust in me personally. If it was, I will try to deserve this trust, always.
>
> Very sincerely yours,
> Louise Lang
>
> P.S. About that reference book on architecture, I have arranged for you to borrow it for a month, if you'd like to.

"Well," Ben said, "who's it from?"

"Her."

"Her?"

Charlie's left hand was clenched into a fist and he kept rubbing it up and down his jaw as if he were testing it for a vulnerable place to strike a blow. "She—she misunderstood. It wasn't like that. I'm not like that. I'm not any of those things she said."

"What in hell are you talking about?"

"I'm not, I'm not brave and forthright and honest."

Ben picked up the letter and read it, his eyebrows raised, one corner of his mouth tucked in.

Charlie was watching him anxiously. "What's it mean, Ben?"

"It means," Ben said, "that she wants to see you again."

"But why?"

"Because she likes you. Don't try to figure it out. Just enjoy it. She likes you, she wants to see you again. You want to see her too, don't you?"

"Yes."

"All right, then. Go and do it. Right after supper."

"I will," Charlie said. "I have to set her straight. I can't let her go on thinking all those good things about me when they aren't true."

Ben took it very quietly, without arguing or making a fuss or giving a lecture. But after supper, when the dishes were done, he changed back into the brown gabardine suit he wore to the cafeteria he managed. Then he told Charlie, "It's such a nice night I think I'll take a little walk to the library."

"It's foggy out, Ben."

"I like fog."

"It's bad for your bronchial tubes."

"I'm going with you," Ben said heavily, "because I know that if I don't, you'll louse things up for yourself. You may, anyway; in fact, you probably will. But the least I can do is try and stop you."

The rest of that night was never quite clear in Charlie's mind. He remembered the fog and Ben walking grayly beside him, in absolute silence. He remembered how, at the library, he'd stood beside the newspaper rack while Ben and Louise talked at Louise's desk. Every now and then they would glance, sympathetically and kindly, over at Charlie, and Charlie knew that between the two of them they were creating a fictional character, a person who didn't exist, called Charlie Gowen; a brave, forthright, honest man, too modest to admit his good qualities; every maiden's dream, every brother's joy.

The scene in the library had taken place a year ago. Since then Louise had become almost part of the family, but Charlie often felt that there had been no real change during the year. He was still standing apart, across a room, unrecognized, unidentified, while Ben and Louise talked, adding more touches to their creation, the Charlie doll. They were so proud of their doll that Charlie did his best to copy it.

Charlie located the package of cardboard skeletons and took them up to the front of the building. Mr. Warner's secretary hadn't returned from her lunch hour and Warner had just left for his, so the office was empty. This was the first time Charlie had been in the office when it was empty and it gave him an odd but not unpleasant feeling that he was doing something wrong. It was like entering a private bedroom while the owner slept, exposed, defenseless, and searching through the contents of pockets and purses and bureau drawers and suitcases.

To make room for the package on Mr. Warner's desk, Charlie had to move the telephone. As he touched it, an impulse seized him to call Louise. He dialed the number of the library and asked for the reference department.

"Louise? It's me, Charlie."

"Hello, Charlie." She seemed, as she always did, very happy to hear his voice. "Your timing is good. I just this minute arrived at work."

"Louise, would you do me a small favor?"

"Consider it done."

"Would you look up an address in the city directory and tell me who lives there? It's 319 Jacaranda Road. You don't have to do it immediately. Just make a note of the name and give it to me tonight when you come over."

"What's the mystery?"

"Nothing. I mean, it's not a mystery, I'll tell you about it tonight."

"Are you feeling all right, Charlie?"

"Sure I am. Why?"

"You sound kind of excited."

"No. No, I don't," Charlie said, and hung up.

She must be crazy, he thought. *Why should I be excited? What have I got to be excited about?*

4

MARY MARTHA OAKLEY was on the window seat in the front room, playing with her cat, Pudding. Her feelings toward the cat were ambivalent. Sometimes she loved him as only a solitary child can love an animal. At other times she didn't want to see him because he symbolized all the changes that had taken place in her life during the last two years. Her mother had brought the cat home from the pet shop on the same day her father had moved out of the house.

"*See, lamb? It's a real live kitten, just what you've always wanted.*"

Where had her father gone?

"*Look at his adorable eyes and his silly little nose. Isn't he adorable?*"

Was he coming back?

"*Let's think of a real yummy name for him. How about Pudding?*"

After the cat there were other changes: new locks on the doors and the downstairs windows and the garage, a private phone with an unlisted number that Mary Martha wasn't allowed to tell anyone, even her teachers at school or her best friend, Jessie. Furniture began to disappear from the upstairs rooms, silver and china from the dining room, pictures from the walls, and all the pretty bottles from the wine cellar. The cook and the gardener stopped coming, then the cleaning woman, the grocery boy, the once-a-month seamstress, the milkman. Kate managed everything herself, and did her own shopping at a cash-and-carry supermarket.

Pudding was the only one of these changes that Mary Martha liked. Into his furry and uncritical ear she whispered her confidences and her troubled questions, and if Pudding couldn't give her any answers or reassurance, he at least listened, blinking his eyes and now and then twitching his tail.

"Mary Martha, I've been calling you."

The child raised her head and saw her mother standing in the doorway looking hot and fretful as she always did when she worked in the kitchen. "I didn't hear you."

"It's all right, it's not important. I just—" *I just wanted to talk to somebody.* "I just wanted to tell you that dinner will be a little late. It's taking the hamburgers longer to thaw than I reckoned it would. . . . Stop letting the cat bite your ponytail. It's not sanitary."

"He's as clean as I am."

"No, he isn't. Besides, he should go outside now. He doesn't get enough fresh air and sunshine."

Mrs. Oakley leaned over to pick up the cat and it was then that she saw the old green coupé parked at the curb across the street. At noon when she'd unlatched the front screen door to let the girls in, she'd seen it too, but this time she knew it couldn't be a coincidence. She knew who was behind the wheel, who was staring out through the closed, dirty window and what was going on in his closed, dirty mind.

Her hands tightened around the cat's body so hard that he let out a meow of pain, but she kept her voice very casual. "Mary Martha, I've been concerned about those book reports that were assigned to you for summer work. How many do you have to write?"

"Ten. But I've got a whole month left."

"A month isn't as long as you think, lamb. I suggest you go up to your room right now and start working on one. After all, you want to make a good first impression on your new teacher."

"She already knows me. It's just Mrs. Valdez."

"Are you going to argue with me, lamb?"

"I guess not."

"That's my angel. You may take Pudding up with you if you like."

Mary Martha went toward the hallway with the cat at her heels. Though she couldn't have put her awareness into words, she realized that the more pet names her mother called her, the more remote from her she actually was. Behind every lamb and angel lurked a black sheep and a devil.

"Mother—"

"Yes, sweetikins?"

"Nothing," Mary Martha said. "Nothing."

As soon as Kate Oakley heard Mary Martha's bedroom door slam shut, she rushed out to the telephone in the front hall. With the child out of the way she no longer had to exercise such rigid control over her body. It was almost a relief to let her hands tremble and her shoulders sag as they wanted to.

She dialed a number. It rang ten, twelve, fifteen times and no one answered. She was sure, then, that her suspicions were correct.

She dialed another number, her mouth moving in a silent prayer that Mac would still be in his office, detained by a client or finishing a brief. She thought of how many times she had been the one who detained him, and how many tears she had shed sitting across the desk from him. If they had been allowed to collect, Mac's office would be knee-deep in brine, yet they had all been in vain. She had been weeping for yesterday as though it were a person and would be moved to pity by her tears and would promise to return . . . *Don't cry, Kate. You will be loved and cherished forever, and forever young. Nothing will change for you.*

Mac's secretary answered, sounding as she always did, cool on the hottest day, dry on the wettest. "Rhodes and MacPherson. Miss Edgeworth speaking."

"This is Mrs. Oakley. Is Mr. MacPherson in?"

"He's just going out the door now, Mrs. Oakley."

"Call him back, will you? Please."

"I'll try. Hold on."

A minute later Mac came on the line, speaking in the brisk, confident voice that had been familiar to her since she was Mary Martha's age and her father had died. "Hello, Kate. Anything the matter?"

"Sheridan's here."

"In the house? That's a violation of the injunction."

"Not in the house. He's parked across the street, in an old green car he probably borrowed from one of his so-called pals. He won't use his own, naturally."

"How do you know it's Sheridan? Did you see him?"

"No, he's got the windows closed. But it couldn't be anyone else. There's nothing across the street except a vacant lot. Also, I called his apartment and he wasn't home. When you add two and two, you get four."

"Let's just add one and one first," Mac said. "Do you see anybody in the car?"

"No. I told you, the windows are closed—"

"So you're not sure that there's even anyone in it?"

"I *am* sure. I *know*—"

"It's possible the car stalled or ran out of gas and was simply abandoned there."

"No. I saw it at noon, too." Her voice broke, and when she spoke again, it sounded as if it had been pasted together by an amateur and the pieces didn't fit. "He's spying on me again, trying to get something on me. What does he hope to gain by all this?"

"You know as well as I do," Mac said. "Mary Martha."

"He can't possibly prove I'm an unfit mother."

"I'm aware of that, but apparently he's not. Divorces can get pretty dirty, Kate, especially if there's a child involved. When money enters the picture too, even nice civilized people often forget every rule of decency they ever knew."

Kate said coldly, "You're speaking, I hope, of Sheridan."

"I'm speaking of what happens when people refuse to admit their own mistakes and take cover behind self-righteousness."

"You've never talked to me like this before."

"It's been a long day and I'm tired. Perhaps fatigue works on me like wine. You and Sheridan have been separated for two years and you're still bickering over a financial settlement, you haven't come to an agreement about Mary Martha, there have been suits, countersuits—"

"Please, Mac. Don't be unkind to me. I'm distracted, I'm truly distracted."

"Yes, I guess you truly are," Mac said slowly. "What do you want me to do about it?"

"Tell Sheridan to get out of town and I'll settle for eight hundred dollars a month."

"What about Mary Martha? He insists on seeing her."

"He'll see her over my dead body and no sooner. I won't change my mind about that."

"Look, Kate, I can't tell a man that simply because his wife no longer loves him he has to quit his job, leave the city he was born and brought up in and give up all rights to his only child."

"He's always loathed this town and said so. As for that silly little job, he only took it to get out of the house. He has enough money from his mother's trust fund. He can well afford to pay me a thousand dollars—"

"His lawyer says he can't."

"Naturally. His lawyer's on his side." She added bitterly, "I only wish to God my lawyer were on mine."

"I can be on your side without believing everything you do is right."

"You don't know, you don't *know* what I've gone through with that man. He's tried everything—hounding me, holding back on support money so I've had to sell half the things in the house to keep from starving, following me around town, standing outside the door and ringing the bell until my nerves were shattered—"

"That's all over now. He's under a court order not to harass you."

"Then what's he doing parked outside right this minute? Waiting to see one of my dozens of lovers arrive?"

"Now don't work yourself up, Kate."

"Why can't he leave us alone? He's got what he wanted, that fat old gin-swilling whore who treats him like little Jesus. Does he actually expect me to allow Mary Martha to associate with *that*?"

Lying on her stomach on the floor of the upstairs hall, Mary Martha suddenly pressed her hands against her ears. She had eavesdropped on dozens of her mother's conversations with Mac and this was no different from the others. She knew from experience that it was going to last a long time and she didn't want to hear any more.

She thought of slipping down the back stairs and going over to Jessie's house, but the steps creaked very badly. She got to her feet and tiptoed down the hall to her mother's room.

To Mary Martha it was a beautiful room, all white and pink and frilly, with French doors opening onto a little balcony. Beside the balcony grew a sycamore tree where she had once found a hummingbird's tiny nest lined with down gathered from the underside of the leaves and filled with eggs smaller than jelly beans.

It was the cat, Pudding, who had alerted Mary Martha to the possibilities of the sycamore tree. Frightened by a stray dog, he had leaped to the first limb, climbed right up on the balcony and sat on the railing, looking smugly down on his enemy. Mary Martha wasn't as fearless and adept a climber as either Pudding or Jessie, but in emergencies she used the tree and so far her mother hadn't caught her at it.

She stepped out on the balcony and began the slow difficult descent, trying not to look at the ground. The gray mottled bark of the tree, which appeared so smooth from a distance, scratched her hands and arms like sandpaper. She passed the kitchen window. The hamburger was thawing on the sink and the sight of it made her aware of her hunger but she kept on going.

She dropped onto the grass in the backyard and crossed the dry creek bed, being careful to avoid the reddening runners of poison oak. A scrub jay squawked in protest at her intrusion. Mary Martha had learned from her father how to imitate the bird, and ordinarily she would have squawked back at him and there would have been a lively contest between the two of them. But this time she didn't even hear the jay. Her ears were still filled with her mother's voice: "*He's got what he wanted, that fat old gin-swilling whore who treats him like little Jesus.*" The sentence bewildered her. Little Jesus was a baby in a manger and her father was a grown-up man with a mustache. She didn't know what a whore was, but she assumed, since her father was interested in birds, that it was an owl. Owls said, "Whoo," and were fat and lived to be quite old.

Mr. and Mrs. Brant were in the little fenced-in patio at the back of their house, preparing a barbecue. Mr. Brant was trying to get the charcoal lit and Mrs. Brant was wrapping ears of corn in aluminum foil. They both wore shorts and cotton shirts and sandals.

"Why, it's Mary Martha," Ellen Brant said, sounding pleased and surprised, as though Mary Martha lived a hundred miles away and hadn't seen her for a year. "Come in, dear. Jessie will be out in a few minutes. She's taking a bath."

"I'm glad she didn't get blood poisoning and convulsions," Mary Martha said gravely.

"So am I. Very."

"Jessie is my best friend."

"I know that, and I think it's splendid. Don't you, Dave?"

"You bet I do," Dave said, turning to give Mary Martha a slow, shy smile. He was a big man with a low-pitched, quiet voice, and a slight stoop to his shoulders that seemed like an apology for his size.

It was his size and his quietness that Mary Martha especially admired. Her own father was short in stature and short of temper. His movements were quick and impatient and no matter what he was doing he always seemed anxious to get started on the next thing. It was restful and reassuring to stand beside Mr. Brant and watch him lighting the charcoal.

He said, "Careful, Mary Martha. Don't get burned."

"I won't. I often do the cooking at home. Also, I iron."

"Do you now. In ten years or so you'll be making some young man a fine wife, won't you?"

"No."

"Why not?"

"I'm not going to get married."

"You're pretty young to reach such a drastic decision."

Mary Martha was staring into the glowing coals as if reading her future. "I'm going to be an animal doctor and adopt ten children and support them all by myself so I don't have to sit around waiting for a check in the mail."

Over her head the Brants exchanged glances, then Ellen said in a firm, decisive voice, "No loafing on the job, you two. Put the corn on and I'll get the hot dogs. Would you like to stay and eat with us, Mary Martha?"

"No, thank you. I would like to but my mother will be alone." *And she will have a headache and a rash on her face and her eyes will be swollen, and she'll call me sweetie-pie and lambikins.*

"Perhaps your mother would like to join us," Ellen said. "Why don't you call her on the phone and ask her?"

"I can't. The line's busy."

"How do you know that? You haven't tried to—"

"She wouldn't come, anyway. She has a headache and things."

"Well," Ellen said, spreading her hands helplessly. "Well, I'd better get the hot dogs."

She went inside and Dave was left alone with Mary Martha. He felt uneasy in her presence, as if, in spite of her friendliness and politeness, she was secretly accusing him of being a man and a villain and he was secretly agreeing with her. He felt heavy with guilt and he wished someone would appear to help him carry it, Jessie or Ellen from the house, Michael from the football field, Virginia and Howard Arlington from next door.

But no one came. There was only Mary Martha, small and pale and mute as marble.

For a long time the only sound was an occasional drop of butter oozing from between the folds of the aluminum foil and sputtering on the coals. Then Mary Martha said, "Do you know anything about birds, Mr. Brant?"

"No, I'm afraid not. I used to keep a few homing pigeons when I was a boy but that's about all."

"You didn't keep any owls?"

"No. I don't suppose anyone does."

"My ex-father has one."

"Does he now," Dave said. "That's very interesting. What does he feed it?"

"Gin."

"Are you sure? Gin doesn't sound like a suitable diet for an owl or for anything else, for that matter. Don't owls usually eat small rodents and birds and things like that?"

"Yes, but not this one."

"Well," Dave said, with a shrug, "I don't know much either about owls or about your fath—your ex-father, so I'll just have to take your word for it. Gin it is."

Twin spots of color appeared on Mary Martha's cheeks, as if she'd been stung by bees or doubts. "I heard my mother telling Mac about it on the telephone. My ex-father has a fat old whore that drinks gin."

There was a brief silence. Then Dave said carefully, "I don't believe your mother was referring to an owl, Mary Martha. The word you used doesn't mean that."

"What does it mean?"

"It's an insulting term, and not one young ladies are supposed to repeat."

Mary Martha was aware that he had replied but hadn't answered. The word must mean something so terrible that she could never ask anyone about it. Why had her mother used it then, and what was her father doing with one? She felt a surge of anger against them all, her mother and father, the whore, David, and even Jessie who wasn't there but who had a real father.

Inside the kitchen the phone rang and through the open door and windows Ellen's voice came, clear and distinct:

"Hello. Why yes, Mrs. Oakley, she's here. . . . Of course I had no idea she didn't have your permission. . . . She's perfectly all right, there's no need to become upset over it. Mary Martha isn't the kind of girl who'd be likely to get in trouble. . . . I'll have Dave bring her right home. . . . Very well, I'll tell her to wait here until you arrive. Good-bye."

Ellen came outside, carrying a tray of buttered rolls and hot dogs stuffed with cheese and wrapped in bacon. "Your mother just called, Mary Martha."

Mary Martha merely nodded. Her mother's excitement had an almost soothing effect on her. There would be a scene, naturally, but it would be like a lot of others, nothing she couldn't handle, nothing that hadn't been said a hundred times. "*If you truly love me, Mary Martha, you'll promise never to do such a thing again.*" "*I truly love you, Mother. I never will.*"

"She's driving over to get you," Ellen added. "You're to be waiting on the front porch."

"All right."

"Jessie will wait with you. She's just putting her pajamas on."

"I can wait alone."

"Of course you can, you're a responsible girl. But you came over here to see Jessie, didn't you?"

"No, ma'am."

"Why did you come, then?"

Mary Martha blinked, as if the question hurt her eyes. Then she turned and walked into the house, closing the screen door carefully and quietly behind her.

Dave Brant watched his wife as she began arranging the hot dogs on the grill. "Maybe you shouldn't question her like that, Ellen."

"Why not?"

"She might think you're prying."

"She might be right."

"I hope not."

"Oh, come on, Dave. Admit it—you're just as curious as I am about what goes on in that household."

"Perhaps. But I think I'm better off not knowing." He thought of telling Ellen about the fat old whore but he couldn't predict her reaction. She might be either quite amused by the story or else shocked into doing something tactless like repeating it to Mrs. Oakley. Although he'd been married to Ellen for eighteen years, her insensitivity to certain situations still surprised him.

"Dave—"

"Yes?"

"We'll never let it happen to our children, will we?"

"What?"

"Divorce," Ellen said, with a gesture, "and all the mess that goes with it. It would kill Michael, he's so terribly sensitive, like me."

"He's going to have plenty of reason to be sensitive if he's not home by 6:30 as he promised."

"Now, Dave, you wouldn't actually punish him simply for losing track of the time."

"He has 20-20 vision and a wrist watch," Dave said. But he wasn't even interested in Michael at the moment. He merely wanted to change the subject because he couldn't bear to talk or even think about a divorce. The idea of Jessie being in Mary Martha's place appalled him. Michael was sixteen, almost a man, but Jessie was still a child, full of trust and innocence, and the only person in the world who sincerely believed in him. She wouldn't always. Inevitably, the time would come when she'd have to question his wisdom and courage, perhaps even his love for her. But right now she was nine, her world was small, no more than a tiny moon, and he was the king of it.

The two girls sat outside the front door on the single concrete step which they called a porch. Jessie was picking at the loose skin on the palm of one hand, and Mary Martha was watching her as if she wished she had something equally interesting to do.

Jessie said, "You'll probably catch it when your mother comes."

"I don't care."

"Do you suppose you'll cry?"

"I may have to," Mary Martha said thoughtfully. "It's lucky I'm such a good crier."

Jessie agreed. "Maybe you should start in right now and be crying when she arrives. It might wring her heart."

"I don't feel like it right now."

"I could make up a real sad story for you."

"No. I know lots of real sad stories. My ex-father used to tell them to me when he was you-know-what."

"Drunk?"

"Yes."

It had been two years now since she'd heard any of these stories but she remembered them because they were all about the same little boy. He lived in a big redwood house which had an attic to play in and trees around it to climb and a creek at the back of it to hunt frogs in. At the end of every story the little boy died, sometimes heroically, while rescuing an animal or a bird, sometimes by accident or disease. These endings left Mary Martha in a state of confusion: she recognized the house the little boy lived in and she knew he must be her father, yet her father was still alive. Why had the little boy died? "*He was better off that way, shweetheart, much better off.*"

"I wish you could stay at my house for a while," Jessie said. "We could look at the big new book my Aunt Virginia gave me. It's all about nature, mountains and rivers and glaciers and animals."

"We could look at it tomorrow, maybe."

"No. I have to give it back as soon as she gets home from the beach."

"Why?"

"It was too expensive, twenty dollars. My mother was so mad about it she made my father mad too, and then they both got mad at me."

Mary Martha nodded sympathetically. She knew all about such situations. "My father sends me presents at Christmas and on my birthday, but my mother won't even let me open the packages. She says he's trying to buy me. Is your Aunt Virginia trying to buy you?"

"That's silly. Nobody can buy children."

"If my mother says they can, they can." Mary Martha paused. "Haven't you even heard about nasty old men offering you money to go for a ride? Don't you even know about *them*?"

"Yes."

"Well, then."

She saw her mother's little Volkswagen rounding the corner. Running out to the curb to meet it she tried to make tears come to her eyes by thinking of the little boy who always died in her father's stories. But the tears wouldn't come. Perhaps her father was right and the little boy was better off dead.

Kate Oakley sat, pale and rigid, her hands gripping the steering wheel as if she were trying to rein in a wild horse with a will of its own. Cars passed on the road, people strolled along the sidewalk with children and dogs and packages of groceries, others watered lawns, weeded flower beds, washed off driveways and raked leaves. But to the woman and child in the car, all the moving creatures were unreal. Even the birds in the trees seemed made of plastic and suspended on strings and only pretending to fly free.

Mary Martha said in a whisper, "I'm sorry, Momma."

"Why did you do it?"

"I thought you'd be talking on the telephone for a long time and that I'd be back before you even missed me."

"You heard me talking on the telephone?"

"Yes."

"And you listened, deliberately?"

"Yes. But I couldn't help it. I wanted to know about my father, I just wanted to *know*, Momma."

Real tears came to her eyes then, she didn't have to think of the little dead boy.

"God forgive me," her mother said as if she didn't believe in God or forgiving. "I've tried, I'm still trying to protect you from all this ugliness. But how can I? It surrounds us like a lot of dirty water, we're in it right up to our necks. How can I pretend we're standing on dry land, safe and secure?"

"We could buy a boat," Mary Martha suggested, wiping her eyes.

There was a silence, then her mother said in a bright, brittle voice, "Why, lamb, that's a perfectly splendid idea. Why didn't I think of it? We'll buy a boat just big enough for the two of us, and we'll float right out of Sheridan's life. Won't that be lovely, sweetikins?"

"Yes, ma'am."

5

QUICKLY AND QUIETLY, Charlie let himself in the front door. He was late for supper by almost an hour and he knew Ben would be grumpy about it and full of questions. He had his answers ready, ones that Ben couldn't easily prove or disprove. He hated lying to Ben but the truth was so simple and innocent that Ben wouldn't believe it: he'd gone to 319 Jacaranda Road, where the child Jessie lived, to see if she was all right. She'd taken a bad fall at the playground, she could have injured herself quite seriously, her little bones were so delicate.

He knew from experience what Ben's reaction would be. Playground? What were you doing at a playground, Charlie? How did you learn the child's name? And where she lives? And that her little bones are delicate? How did she fall, Charlie? Were you chasing her and was she running away? Why do you want to chase little girls, Charlie?

Ben would misunderstand, misinterpret everything. It was better to feed him a lie he would swallow than a truth he would spit out.

Charlie took off the windbreaker he always wore no matter what the weather and hung it on the clothes rack beside the front door. Then he went down the dark narrow hall to the kitchen.

Ben was standing at the sink, rinsing a plate under the hot-water tap. He said, without turning, "You're late. I've already eaten."

"I'm sorry, Ben. I had some trouble with the car. I must have flooded it again. I had to wait half an hour before the engine would turn over."

"I've told you a dozen times, all you've got to do when the engine's flooded is press the accelerator down to the floorboard and let it up again very slowly."

"Oh, I did that, Ben. Sometimes it doesn't work."

"It does for me."

"Well, you've got a real way with cars. You command their respect."

Ben turned. He didn't look in the least flattered, as Charlie had hoped he would. "Louise called. She'll be over early. She's getting off at seven because she's taking another girl's place tomorrow night. You'd better hurry up and eat."

"Sure, Ben."

"There's a can of spaghetti in the cupboard and some fish cakes."

Charlie didn't particularly like fish cakes and spaghetti but he took the two cans out of the cupboard and opened them. Ben was in a peculiar mood, it would be better not to cross him even about so minor a thing as what to have for supper. He wanted to cross him, though; he wanted to tell him outright that he, Charlie, was a grown man of thirty-two and he didn't have to account for every minute of his time and be told what to eat and how to spend the evening. So Louise was coming. Well, suppose he wasn't there when she arrived. Suppose he walked out right now . . .

No, he couldn't do that, not tonight anyway. Tonight she was bringing him something very important, very urgent. He didn't understand why he considered it so important but it was as if she were going to hand him a key, a mysterious key which would unlock a door or a secret box.

He thought of the hidden delights behind the door, inside the box, and his hands began to tremble. When he put the fish cakes in the frying pan, the hot grease splattered his knuckles. He felt no pain, only a sense of wonder that this grease, which had no mind or will of its own, should be able to fight back and assert itself better than he could.

"For Pete's sake, watch it," Ben said. "You're getting the stove dirty."

"I didn't mean to."

"Put a lid on the frying pan. Use your head."

"My head wouldn't fit, Ben. It's too small."

Ben stared at him a moment, then he said sharply, "Stop doing that. Stop taking everything literally. You know damned well I didn't mean for you to decapitate yourself and use your head as a lid for the frying pan. Don't you know that?"

"Yes."

"Damn it all, why do you do it then?"

Charlie turned, frowning, from the stove. "But you said, put a lid on the frying pan, use your head. You *said* that, Ben."

"And you think I meant it like that?"

"I wasn't really thinking. My mind was occupied with other things. Maybe with Louise coming and all like that."

"Look, Charlie, I'm only trying to protect you. You pull something like this at work and they'll consider you a moron."

"No," Charlie said gravely. "They just laugh. They think I'm being funny. Actually, I don't have much of a sense of humor, do I?"

"No."

"Did I ever? I mean, when we were boys together, Ben, before—well, before anything had happened, did I have a sense of humor then?"

"I can't remember."

"I bet you can if you tried. You've always had a good memory, Ben."

"Now I've got a good forgetter," Ben said. "Maybe that's more essential in this life."

"No, Ben, that's wrong. It's important for you to remember how it was with us when we were kids. Mother and Dad are dead, and I can't remember, so if you don't, it's like it never happened and we were never kids together—"

"All right, all right, don't get excited. I'll remember."

"Everything?"

"I'll try."

"Did I have a sense of humor?"

"Yes. Yes, you did, Charlie. You were a funny boy, a very funny boy."

"Did we do a lot of laughing together, you and I and Mom and Dad?"

"Sure."

"Louise laughs a lot. She's very cheerful, don't you think?"

"Louise is a very cheerful girl, yes."

Slowly and thoughtfully, Charlie turned the fish cakes. They were burned but he didn't care. It would only be easier to pretend they were small round tender steaks. "Ben?"

"Yes."

"She wouldn't stay cheerful very long if she married me, would she?"

"Stop talking like—"

"I mean, you haven't leveled with her, Ben. She doesn't realize what a drag I am and how she'd have to worry about me the way you do. I would hurt her. I would be hurting her all the time without meaning to, maybe without even knowing it. Would she be cheerful then? Would she?"

Ben sat down at the table, heavily and stiffly, as if each of the past five minutes had been a crippling year.

"Well? Would she, Ben?"

"I don't know."

Charlie looked dismayed, like a child who's been used to hearing the same story with the same happy ending, and now the ending has been changed. It wasn't happy any more, it wasn't even an ending. Did the frog change into a prince? *I don't know*. Did he live happily ever after with his princess? *I don't know.*

Charlie said stubbornly, "I don't like that answer. I want the other one."

"There is no other one."

"You always used to say that marriage changed a man, that Louise could be the making of me and we could have a good life together if we tried. Tell it to me just like that all over again, Ben."

"I can't."

"All right then, give me hell. Tell me I'm downgrading myself, that I'd better look on the bright side of things, start putting on a front—that's all true, isn't it?"

"I don't know," Ben said. "Eat your supper."

"How can I eat, not knowing?"

"The rest of us eat, not knowing. And work and sleep, not knowing." He added in a gentler voice, "You're doing all right, Charlie. You're holding down a job, you've got a nice girl friend, you're keeping your nose clean—you're doing fine, just fine."

"And you're not mad at me any more for being late?"

"No."

"I flooded the engine, see. I had to wait and wait for the gas to drain out of it. I thought of calling you, but then I thought,

Ben won't be worrying, he knows I'm behaving myself, keeping my nose clean. . . ." *I watched from the road. The house is a long way back among the trees but I could see the child sitting at one of the front windows. Poor Jessie, poor sweetheart, resting her little bruised body. Why don't her parents protect her? If anything happens to the girl it will be their fault, and their fault alone.*

6

THE ARLINGTONS arrived home from the beach at seven o'clock and Virginia went directly to her room, without saying a word. Howard was in the kitchen unpacking the picnic basket when the dog, Chap, began barking and pawing at the back door.

Howard called out, "Who's there?"

"It's me, Uncle Howard. Jessie."

"Oh. Well, come on in."

Jessie went in, wearing a robe over her pajamas and carrying the book that weighed nearly half as much as she did. "Is Aunt Virginia here?"

"Oh, she's here all right, but she's incommunicado."

"Does that mean in the bathroom?"

Howard laughed. "No, it means she's sore at me."

"Why?"

"A dozen reasons. She's sunburned, she's got sand in her hair, she doesn't like the way she looks in a bathing suit, a bee stung her on the foot—all my fault, of course." Howard put the picnic basket, now empty, on the top shelf of the broom closet, and closed the door. "When you grow up, are you going to fuss about things like that?"

"I don't think so."

"Atta girl."

Jessie put the book on the table, then leaned over to pet the dog. Chap, smelling the butter that had dribbled down her chin from an ear of corn, began licking it off. Jessie was so flattered she stood the tickling without a giggle, though it was almost unbearable. "Do you think Chap likes me, Uncle Howard?"

"Obviously."

"Does he like everybody?"

"As a matter of fact, no," Howard said dryly. "He doesn't even like me."

"Why? Is he afraid of you?"

"Afraid of me? Why should he be? What gave you that idea?"

"I don't know."

"Well, I don't beat him, kid, if that's what you mean. He's just been spoiled rotten by women. All he has to do is roll his eyes and he gets a T-bone steak. A little more," he added, "is required of the human male though God knows what it is."

Jessie wasn't sure what he was talking about but she realized he was in a bad mood and she wished Aunt Virginia would come out of communicado.

Howard said, "Who's the book for?"

"Aunt Virginia. She gave it to me this afternoon, only when my mother saw it she told me I had to give it back."

"Why?"

"It cost twenty dollars."

"Oh?" Howard opened the book and looked at the price on the inside back jacket. "So it did. Twenty dollars."

He sounded very calm but his hands were shaking and both the child and the dog sensed trouble.

"Virginia!"

There was no response from the bedroom.

"You'd better come out here, Virginia. You have a visitor, one I'm sure you wouldn't want to miss."

Virginia's voice answered, soft and snuffly, "I'm in bed."

"Then get out of bed."

"I—I can't."

"You can and you will."

The dog, tail between his legs, crawled under the table, his eyes moving from Howard to the bedroom door and back to Howard.

The door opened and Virginia came out, clutching a long white silk robe around her. All of her skin that was visible was a fiery red and her eyes were bloodshot. "I'm not feeling very well, Howard. I have a fever."

"You also have a visitor," Howard said in the same calm voice. "Jessie has come to return the book you gave her this afternoon. It seems her mother considered it too expensive a gift for her to accept. How much did it cost, Virginia?"

"Please, Howard. Not in front of the child. It's—"

"How much?"

"Twenty dollars."

"And where did you get the twenty dollars, Virginia?"

"From my—purse."

Howard laughed.

"Where did you get the money in your purse? Perhaps you've taken a job and the twenty came out of your salary?"

"You know I haven't, it didn't. . . . Jessie, you'd better go home now. Right away, dear."

"Let her stay," Howard said.

"Please, Howard. She's only a little girl."

"Little girls can cause big troubles. And do. I want you to tell me, in front of Jessie, just where the twenty dollars came from."

"From you, Howard."

"That's right. From my pay check. So that makes me the Santa Claus of the neighborhood, not you, Virginia. Right?"

"Yes."

He picked the book up from the table and held it out toward Jessie. "Here you are, kid. Take the book, it's all yours, with love and kisses from Santa Claus."

Jessie stared at him, wide-eyed. "I can't. My mother won't let—"

"Take it. Get it out of here. I'm sick of the sight of it."

"I don't want it."

"You don't want it. I see. Maybe you'd rather have the money, eh? All right."

He reached for his wallet, pulled out two ten-dollar bills and thrust them into her hand. Behind his back she saw Virginia nod at her and smile a shaky little smile that asked her to humor Howard. Jessie looked down at the bills in her hand, then she put them in the pocket of her bathrobe, quickly, as though she didn't like the feel of them. She remembered the conversation she'd had with Mary Martha about grownups buying children and she wondered if she had been bought and what buying and selling really meant.

Sex had no particular interest or mystery for Jessie. Her mother and father had explained it to her quite carefully. But nobody had ever explained money and why people were affected by it. To Jessie it seemed like black magic, nice when it was on your side and bad when it wasn't, but you couldn't tell in advance which it would be. Money was what bought things to make people happy, like the new house, but it was also what parents quarreled about when they thought the children were sleeping; it caused Virginia to cringe in front of Howard, and lie about the patio umbrella; it made her mother irritable when the mail arrived and made her brother Michael threaten to quit school and get a job. It was as mysterious as God, who had to be thanked for blessings but couldn't be blamed for their lack.

The pocket of her bathrobe felt heavy with power and with guilt. She could buy things now, but she had also been bought.

"What are you standing around for, kid?" Howard said. "You have your money and your earful. That's about all you can expect from one visit."

Virginia walked quickly to the back door and opened it. Her face appeared very peculiar because she was trying, with one part of it, to give Howard a dirty look, and with the other part, to smile reassuringly at Jessie. "Good night, dear. Don't worry. I'll explain things to your mother in the morning."

"I bet you will," Howard said when Jessie had gone. "The explanation should be a doozy. I wish I could stick around to hear it but I can't. I'm leaving."

"Why? Haven't you done enough damage for one night?"

"I'm afraid I might do more if I stay."

He went into the bedroom. His suitcase was lying on the floor, open but still unpacked except for his toothbrush and shaving kit. He gave it a kick and the lid fell shut.

Virginia said from the doorway, "You don't have to be childish."

"It's better than kicking you or the dog, isn't it?"

"Why do you have to kick anything?"

"Because I'm a bully, I'm the kind of guy who forces sweet little wife to go out in the nasty sun and fresh air down to the nasty beach. That's your version of this afternoon, isn't it?"

"I can't help it if I sunburn easily."

"Well, here's my version. This is my first day at home in two weeks. I wanted to be with my wife and I also wanted to get some fresh air and exercise which I happen to need. That's all. Not exactly reaching for the moon, was I, Virginia?"

"No. But—"

"Let me finish. I realized my wife had a delicate skin so I bought her a large straw hat and a beach umbrella. She decided the hat wasn't becoming enough, and after a while she got bored sitting under the umbrella so she went for a walk. The sun was strong, there was a wind and there was also, unfortunately, a half-dead bee which she stepped on. To complicate matters, she became conscious of all the young girls on the beach with young figures and by the time we were ready to eat she'd decided to go on a diet. She didn't eat anything. I did, though, the way any man would when he hasn't had a meal at home in two weeks. My wife sat and watched me. She was sunburned, hungry, nursing a sore foot and silent as a tomb. It was an interesting afternoon. I thank you for it, Virginia. It makes going back to work a real pleasure."

"Is that where you're going now, back to work?"

"Why not?"

He picked his suitcase up off the floor and tossed it on the bed. A sock and a drip-dry shirt fell out and Virginia went over to pick them up. The shirt was clean but wrinkled, as if Howard had laundered it himself and hung it up on the shower rod of any of a dozen anonymous motor courts or hotels.

Virginia held the shirt against her breasts as if it, more than the man who wore it, could move her to pity. "Did you wash this yourself, Howard?"

"Yes."

"Where? I mean, what city, what hotel?"

He looked at her, puzzled. "Why do you want to know that?"

"I just do."

"It was the Hacienda Inn in Bakersfield. There was an all-night party going on next door. Instead of taking a sleeping pill I got up and did some laundry."

"Howard, your job isn't much fun, is it?"

"Sometimes it is, in some ways," he said brusquely. "I don't expect to go around laughing all the time."

After a moment's hesitation Virginia went over to the bed and started taking the things out of his suitcase and putting them away in the clothes closet and the bureau drawers. She worked quickly and nervously as if she wanted to get it done before he had a chance to protest. Neither of them spoke until the suitcase was empty and snapped shut and hidden under the bed. Then Virginia said, "I'm sorry I was such a poor sport this afternoon."

"I knew you were a poor sport when I married you," Howard said quietly. "I should have had more sense than to plan a beach picnic."

"But you wanted one, you deserved one. You work hard at a difficult job and—"

"Come on now, don't go to extremes. I do a job, like any other man. I also get mad and lose my temper. Yes, and I guess I get jealous, too. . . . I'm sorry I made an ass of myself in front of the kid. Giving her twenty dollars like that—God, what'll Dave and Ellen think when she tells them?"

"Nothing. She won't tell them."

"Why not?"

"Because they'd make her return the money and she doesn't want to."

Howard sat down on the edge of the bed, shaking his head ruefully. "I'm sorry. I'm very sorry."

"Stop thinking about it. We were both wrong and we're both sorry." Virginia sat down beside him and put her head on his shoulder. "I'm a poor sport and you're a jealous idiot. Maybe we deserve each other."

"Your sunburn—"

"It doesn't hurt so much any more."

After a time he said, "I'll be very gentle with you, Virginia."

"I know."

"I love you."

"I know that, too."

She lay soft in his arms, her eyes closed, thinking that it had been exactly seven months and one week since she'd told Howard that she loved him.

7

LOUISE DRESSED carefully in a blue linen sheath with a Peter Pan collar, matching flat-heeled shoes that emphasized the smallness of her feet, and white gloves so tiny that she had to buy them in the children's department. At the last minute she pinned a bow in her short brown hair because Charlie liked girls to wear bows in their hair.

She went to the living room to say good night to her parents. Mr. Lang was doing the crossword puzzle in the evening newspaper, and Mrs. Lang was embroidering the first of a dozen pillow slips she would send to her relatives at Christmas.

"Well, I'm off," Louise said from the doorway. "I won't be late, but don't wait up."

Mrs. Lang peered at her over the top of her spectacles. "You look just lovely, dear. Doesn't she, Joe, look lovely?"

Mr. Lang put down his paper and stood up, as if Louise were a stranger he had to be polite to. Sitting, he had appeared to be of normal size, but when he stood up he wasn't much taller than Louise, though he held himself very straight. "You look very lovely indeed, my dear. Is this a special occasion?"

"No."

"Where are you going?"

"To Ben and Charlie's."

"It sounds like the name of a bar and grill on lower State Street."

"What a way to talk," Mrs. Lang said quickly. "You stop that, Joe, you just stop it. You know perfectly well who Ben and Charlie are. They're nice, respectable—"

Her husband silenced her with a gesture, then he turned his attention back to Louise. "Other girls seem to find satisfaction in dating only one gentleman at a time. They are also, I believe, called for at home by the gentleman. Are you different, Louise?"

"The situation is different."

"Exactly what is the situation?"

"One that I'm old enough to handle by myself."

"Old enough yes—at thirty-two, you should be—but are you equipped?"

"Equipped?" Louise looked down at her body as if her father had called attention to something that was missing from it, a part that had failed to grow, or one she had carelessly lost somewhere between the house and the library. She said, keeping her voice steady, "Daddy, I'm going over to play cards with two friends who happen to be male. Either one of them would be glad to pick me up here, but I have my own car and I enjoy driving it."

"Louise, honey, I'm not questioning your motives. I'm simply reminding you that you've had very little experience in—well, in keeping men in line."

"Haven't I just."

"I also remind you that appearances still count, even in this licentious world. It doesn't look right for a girl of your class and position to go sneaking off surreptitiously at night to visit two men in their house."

"Home, if you don't mind."

"Call it what you will."

"I'll call it what it is," Louise said sharply. "A *home*, where Charlie and Ben have lived since they were children. As for my sneaking off surreptitiously, that's some trick when you drive a sports car that can be heard a mile away. I must be a magician. Or are you getting deaf?"

Mrs. Lang moved her heavy body awkwardly out of her chair, grunting with the effort. She stood between her husband and daughter like a giant referee between two midget boxers who weren't obeying the rules. "Now I've heard just about enough from you two. Louise, you ought to be ashamed, talking fresh to your father like that. And you, Joe, my goodness, you've got to realize you're living in the modern world. People don't put so much stock in things like a man calling for his date at home. It's not as if Charlie was a stranger you didn't know. You've met him and talked to him. He's a nice, agreeable man."

"Agreeable, yes." Mr. Lang nodded dryly. "I said it was hot and he agreed. I said it was too bad about the stock market and he agreed. I—"

Louise interrupted. "He's shy. You embarrassed him by asking him personal questions about his background and his job."

"I don't mind people asking me about my job and my background."

"You're not shy like Charlie."

"What makes Charlie shy?"

"Sensitivity, *feeling*—"

"Which I don't have?"

Mrs. Lang put her hands, not too gently, on Louise's shoulders and pushed her out of the door into the hall. "You go along now, dear, or you'll be late. Don't pay too much attention to Dad tonight, he's having some trouble with his supervisor. Do you have your latchkey?"

"Yes."

"Enjoy yourself, dear."

"Yes." Slowly, Louise reached up and touched the bow in her hair. She could scarcely feel it through the fabric of her glove but it was still there, for Charlie. "Do I—look all right?"

"Just lovely. I told you that before, at least I think I did."

"Yes. Good night, Mother."

Mrs. Lang made sure the door was locked behind Louise, then she went back into the living room, panting audibly, as if it took more energy to be a referee than to be a contestant. She wished Joe would go to bed and leave her to dream a little: *Louise will be married in the church, of course. With a long-sleeved, floor-length bridal gown to hide her skinny arms and legs, and the right make-up to enlarge her eyes, she'll look quite presentable. She has a nice smile. Louise has a very nice smile.*

Joe was standing where she'd left him, in the middle of the room. "Sensitivity, feeling, my foot. He seemed plain ordinary stupid to me. Hardly opened his mouth."

"Oftentimes you don't bring out the best in people, Joe."

"Why shouldn't I ask him questions about his job? What's he got to hide?"

"Nothing," his wife said mildly. "Now stop carrying on, it's bad for your health. Charlie Gowen is a fine-looking young man with good manners and gainful employment. He probably has a wide choice of female companions. You should consider it a lucky thing that he picked Louise."

"Should I?"

"As for his being shy, I, for one, find it refreshing. There are so many smart-alecky young men going around tooting their own horn these days. That kind doesn't appeal to Louise. She has a spiritual nature." She added, without any change of tone, "I'm warning you, Joe. Don't ruin her chances or you'll regret it."

"Her chances for what? Becoming the talk of the town? Acquiring a bad reputation that might even cost her her job?"

"Louise and Charlie will be getting married."

For a moment Joe was stunned into silence. Then, "I see. Louise told you?"

"No."

"Charlie told you?"

"No. Nobody told me. Nobody had to. I can feel it in the air." She settled herself in the chair again and picked up her embroidery. "You may laugh at my intuition, but wasn't I right last fall when I said I could feel it in my bones that we'd have a wet winter? And about Mrs. Cudahy when I said she couldn't last more than a week and she died the next day? Wasn't I right?"

He didn't answer. It had been a wet winter, Mrs. Cudahy had died, Louise was marrying Charlie.

Ben met her at the door. He was freshly shaved—she could smell his shaving cream when they shook hands—and he had on a business suit, not the jeans and T-shirt he usually wore around the house.

"Well, you're all dressed up," Louise said, smiling. "Are we going out some place?"

Ben looked uneasy. "No. I mean, I'm going out. You and Charlie can do what you like, of course."

"But I thought we were all three of us going to play cards as usual. What made you change your mind? Has anything happened?"

"No. I just figured you and Charlie might want to be alone together for a change."

She was seized by a panic so severe that for several seconds her heart stopped. She could feel it in the middle of her chest, as heavy and silent as a stone. "If Charlie wanted to be alone with me, he'd arrange it that way, wouldn't he?"

"Not necessarily. Charlie may want something but he often doesn't know he wants it until I tell him."

"Until you tell him," she repeated. "Well, did you?"

"What?"

"Tell him he wanted to be alone with me tonight?"

"No. I just said I was going out."

"And he didn't run away," she said, "so that means he wants to be alone with me? How very romantic."

"Don't be childish, Louise. You know Charlie as well as I do. He doesn't spell romance for anyone."

A slight noise at the end of the hall made them both turn simultaneously. Charlie was standing at the door of his bedroom, coatless and with one hand on his tie as if he hadn't quite finished dressing.

"Why, I can so," he said with a frown. "I can spell *romance*. R-o-m-a-n-c-e."

Louise hesitated a moment, then gave him a quick little nod of approval. "That's very good, Charlie."

"Not really. It's an easy word. I bet I could spell it when I was nine years old."

"I bet you could."

"Maybe not, though. I can't remember much about when I was nine. Ben does my remembering for me. You know what he remembered tonight, Louise?"

"No. What?"

"That I had a nice sense of humor when I was young."

"I'm not surprised."

"I am." He turned to Ben. "I thought you were going out tonight. Didn't you tell me that?"

"Yes."

"You'd better hurry. Louise and I have something to talk about."

Louise flushed and stared down at the stained and worn carpet. One of the first things she'd do would be to replace it. She had money in the bank, she would use it to fix the place up before she invited anyone, even her parents, to visit her in her own home.

"Well, I can take a hint," Ben said, sounding very pleased. "I know when I'm not wanted. Good night, you two. Have fun."

He went outside, closing the door softly behind him, as if the slightest sound might change Charlie's mood. The night air was cool but sweat was running down behind his ears and under his collar like cold, restless worms. Before he got into his car he turned to glance back at the house. The drapes in the front room hadn't been drawn and he could see Louise sitting on the davenport and Charlie standing facing her, bending over a little, ready to whisper into her ear.

Ben let out his breath suddenly and violently, as if he'd been holding it for years. He stood on the driveway for a long time, not watching the house any more, just breathing in and out, in and out, like any free man on a summer night.

Charlie said, "Are you comfortable, Louise?"

"Yes."

"If it's too cool for you in here, I could turn on the heater."

"I'm fine, I really am."

"You don't think I hurt Ben's feelings, practically ordering him to get out of the house like that?"

"I'm sure he's not hurt. Stop worrying and sit down."

He sat beside her and she leaned toward him a little so that their shoulders touched and she could feel the smoothness of his arm and the hardness of its muscle. She wanted to tell him how strong he was and how much she admired strength when it was combined with gentleness like his. But she was afraid he would become mute with embarrassment, or else claim, quite flatly, that he wasn't the way she imagined him at all, he was weak and brutal.

"I had to get rid of him," Charlie said, "so you and I could talk. Ben doesn't have to be in on everything, does he?"

"No."

"When he's around and I make a remark or ask a question, he always has to know why. Ben always has to know the why of things. Sometimes there *is* no why. You understand that, don't you?"

"Of course," Louise said softly. "It's that way with love."

"Love?"

"Nobody can explain what it is, what makes people fall in love with each other. Do you remember that first night when you were sitting in the library and I looked over and there you were with that book on architecture? I felt so strange, Charlie, as if the world had begun to move faster and I had to cling like mad to stay on it. It hasn't slowed down even for a minute, Charlie."

He stared down at the floor, frowning, as if he were trying to see it move in space. "I don't like that idea. It makes me dizzy."

"I'm dizzy, too. So we're two dizzy people. What's the matter with that?"

"It's not scientific. Nobody can feel the world move."

"I can."

He drew away from her as if she'd confessed having a disease he didn't want to catch. Then he got up entirely and walked over to the window. He could see the dark figure of a man standing in the driveway and he knew it must be Ben. It worried him. Ben didn't stand quietly in driveways, he was always busy, always moving like the world and making people dizzy, unsure of themselves, unable to figure out the why of anything even if there was one.

He said, "Did you tell Ben what we talked about on the telephone?"

"What we talked—?"

"The information I asked you to get for me. The house, who lives in the house on Jacaranda Road. You found out for me, didn't you?"

Louise was sitting so still he thought she'd suddenly gone to sleep with her eyes open, a dreamless sleep because her face held no expression whatever. In nice dreams you smiled, in bad ones you cried and woke up screaming and Ben came in and asked *why*?

He went over and put his hand on her shoulder to wake her up. "Louise? You didn't forget about it, did you? It's important to me. You see, these people—the people who live in the house—have a dog, a little brown dog. When I drove past there this morning on my way to work the dog chased my car and I nearly hit the poor creature. One inch closer and I would have killed it. I must tell those people they've got to take better care of their little dog unless they want it to be killed by a car or something. Isn't that the right thing for me to do?"

He knew she wasn't sleeping because she stirred and blinked her eyes, though she still didn't speak.

"Louise?"

"Is—this what you wanted to talk to me about, Charlie?"

"Why, yes. It may not seem important to you, but I love dogs. I couldn't bear to hurt one, see it all mangled and bloody."

She looked down at her blue dress. It was spotless, unwrinkled. It bore no sign that she had run out into the street after Charlie's car and been dragged under the wheels and lacerated; and Charlie, unaware that anything had happened, had driven on alone. He had seen nothing and felt little more. *Maybe I felt a slight bump but I thought it was a hole in the road, I certainly didn't know it was you, Louise. What were you doing out on the road chasing cars like a dog?*

"Oakley," she said in a high, thin voice. "Mrs. Cathryn Oakley."

"The little dog has no father?"

"I guess not."

"Do you spell her first name with a *C* or a *K*?"

"C-a-t-h-r-y-n."

"You must have looked it up in the city directory?"

"Yes. Mrs. Oakley is listed as head of the household, with one minor child."

Charlie's face was flushed, as if he'd come out of the cold into some warm place. "It's funny she'd want to live alone in that big house with just a little girl."

He knew, as soon as the words left his mouth, that he'd made a mistake. But Louise didn't seem to notice. She had stood up and was brushing off her dress with both hands. He could see the outline of her thighs, thin, delicate-boned, with hardly any solid flesh to protect them from being crushed under a man's weight. She wasn't wearing any garters and he would have liked to ask her how she kept her stockings up. It was a perfectly innocent question on his part, but he was afraid she would react the way Ben would, as if such thoughts didn't occur to normal men, only to him, Charlie. *"Why do you ask that, Charlie?" "Because I want to know." "But why do you want to know?" "Because it's interesting." "Why is it interesting?"*

"Because gravity is pulling her stockings down and she must be doing something to counteract it."

Louise had taken her gloves out of her handbag and was putting them on, holding her fingers stiff and smoothing the fabric down over each one very carefully. Charlie looked away as if she were doing something private that he had no right to watch.

She said, "I'd better be going now."

"But you just got here. I thought you and I were going to have a talk."

"We already have, haven't we?"

"Not real—"

"I think we've covered the important thing, anyway—Mrs. Oakley and her dog and her child. That was the main item on tonight's agenda, wasn't it? Perhaps the only one, eh, Charlie?"

She sounded friendly and she was smiling, but he was suddenly and terribly afraid of her. He backed away from her, until his buttocks and shoulders touched the wall. It was a cool wall with hot red roses climbing all over it.

"Don't," he whispered. "Don't hurt me, Louise."

Her face didn't alter except that one end of her smile began to twitch a little.

"Louise, if I've done anything wrong, I'm sorry. I try to do what you and Ben tell me to because my own thinking isn't too good sometimes. But tonight nobody told me."

"That's right. Nobody told you."

"Then how was I to know? I saw you and Ben looking at each other in the hall and I could sense, I could feel, you were expecting me to do something, but I didn't understand what it was. You and Ben, you're my only friends. I'd do anything for you if you'd just tell me what you want."

"I won't do that."

"Why not?"

"You must figure it out for yourself, apart from Ben and me."

"I can't. I *can't*. Help me, Louise. Hold out your hand to me."

She walked toward him, her arms outstretched stiffly like a robot obeying an order. He took both her hands and pressed them hard against his chest. She could feel the fast, fearful beating of his heart and she wished it would stop suddenly and forever, and hers would stop with it.

"Oh God, Louise, don't leave me here alone in this cold dark."

"I can't make it any lighter for you," she said quietly. "Warmer, yes, because there would be two of us. I've had foolish dreams about you, Charlie, but I've never kidded myself that I could turn on any lights for you when other people, even professionals, have failed. I can share your darkness, though, when you need me. I know what darkness is, I have some of my own."

"For me to share?"

"Yes."

"And I can help you, too?"

"You already have."

He held her body close against his own. "It's warmer already, isn't it, Louise? Don't you feel it?"

"Yes."

"Imagine me helping anybody, that's a switch. I could laugh. I could laugh out loud."

"Don't."

She put one hand gently over his mouth, staring into his eyes as she would twin pools of water. On the surface she saw her own reflection, but underneath there were live creatures of every shape and size, moving mysteriously in and out, toward and past each other; arriving, departing, colliding, unconcerned with time or joy or grief. At the bottom of the cold, dark water lay the stones of death, but small green creatures clung to them and survived, unafraid. There was enough light to live by, even down there, and they had each other for comfort.

Charlie said, "Why—are you looking at me like that?"

"Because I love you."

"That's not a reason."

"It's reason enough for anything."

"You talk sillier than I do," he said, touching her hair and the ribbon in it. "I like silly girls."

"I've never been called a silly girl before. I'm not sure I approve."

"You do, though. I can tell."

He laughed, softly and contentedly, then he swooped her up in his arms and carried her over to the davenport. She sat on his lap with her face pressed against the warm moist skin of his neck.

"Louise," he said in a whisper, "I want you and me to be married in a church and everything, like big shots."

"I want that too."

"You in a long fluffy dress, me in striped trousers and a morning coat. I can rent an outfit like that down at Cosgrave's. One of the fellows at work rented one for his sister's wedding and he said it made him feel like an ambassador. He hated to take it back because actually he's just a truck driver. I wouldn't mind feeling like an ambassador, for a few hours anyway."

"An ambassador to where?"

"Anywhere. I guess they all feel pretty much the same."

"I suppose I could stand being an ambassador's wife for a few hours," Louise said dreamily, "as long as I could have you back again exactly the way you are now."

"Exactly?"

"Yes."

"Now you're talking silly again. I mean, it's not sensible to want me just as I am, with all my—my difficulties."

"Shhh, Charlie. Don't think about the difficulties, think about us. We must start planning. First, we'll have to decide on a church and a date and make a reservation. Someone told me that autumn weddings are starting to outnumber June weddings."

"Autumn," he repeated. "It's August already."

"If that's too soon for you," she said quickly, "we'll postpone it. Is it too soon, Charlie?"

She knew the answer before she asked the question. The muscles of his arms had gone rigid and the pulse in his neck was beating fast and irregularly. It was as if he could picture her in a long fluffy dress and himself in a morning coat, looking like an ambassador, but he couldn't put the two of them together, at one time and in one place.

"Actually," she said, "when I consider it, it does seem like rushing things. There are so many plans to make, and as you said, it's August already."

"Yes."

"I've always thought Christmas would be a good time for a wedding. Things are so gay then, with all the pretty parcels and people singing carols. And the weather's usually good here at Christmas too. Sometimes it's the very best weather of the year. You wouldn't have to worry about rain getting your striped trousers wet. You couldn't very well feel like an ambassador with your trousers wet, could you?"

"I guess not."

"You like Christmas, don't you, Charlie? Opening packages and everything? Of course I don't want to rush you. If you'd rather wait until early spring or even June—"

"No," he said, touched by her desire to please him and wanting to please her in return. "I don't want to wait even until Christmas. I think we should be married right away. Maybe the first week of September, if you can be ready by then."

"I've been ready for a year."

"But we just met a year ago."

"I know."

"You mean you fell in love with me right away, just looking at me, not knowing a thing about me? That's funny."

"Not to me. Oh, Charlie, I'm so happy."

"Imagine me making anyone happy," Charlie said. "Ben will certainly be surprised."

Ben wouldn't be able to say *I don't know* any more. He'd have to admit that the frog turned into a prince and lived happily ever after with his princess.

"Louise, I just thought, what if your parents don't approve? Your father doesn't seem to like me very much."

"Yes, he *does*. He told me tonight as I was leaving that you were a fine young man."

"Did he really?"

"It wouldn't matter anyway, Charlie."

"Yes, it would. I want everything to be right, everyone to be—well, on our side."

"Everything will be right," she said. "Everyone is on our side."

She thought of the small green creatures clinging to the stones at the bottom of the cold dark water. They survived, with nothing on their side but each other.

8

IT WAS the following noon that Kate Oakley received the letter. She was alone in the house; Mary Martha had gone to the playground with Jessie and Jessie's brother, Mike, who was supposed to see to it that the girls stayed off the jungle gym and kept their clothes clean. Kate had promised to drive them to the Museum of Natural History right after lunch.

She liked to take the girls places and let people assume they were both her daughters, but she was dreading this particular excursion. The museum used to be—and perhaps still was—one of Sheridan's favorite hangouts. He hadn't seen Mary Martha for four months and Kate was afraid that if he ran into her now there would be a scene in front of everybody, quiet and sarcastic if he was sober, loud and weepy if he wasn't. Still, she had to risk it. There weren't many places she could take Mary Martha without having to pay, and money was very short.

She had received no check from Sheridan for temporary support for nearly two months. She knew it was Sheridan's way of punishing her for keeping him away from Mary Martha but she was determined not to give in. She was strong—stronger than he was—and in the end she would win, she would get the money she needed to bring Mary Martha up in the manner she deserved. Things would be as they were before. She would have a woman to do the cleaning and laundering, a seamstress to make Mary Martha's school clothes, a gardener to mow the vast lawn and cut the hedges and spray the poison oak. The groceries would be delivered and she would sign the bill without bothering to check it and tip the delivery boy with real money, not a smile, the way she had to tip everyone now.

These smile tips didn't cost her anything but they were expensive. They came out of her most private account, her personal capital. Nothing had been added to this capital for a long time; she had been neither loved nor loving, she offered no mercy and accepted none; hungry, she refused to eat; weary, she couldn't rest; alone, she reached out to no one. Sometimes at night, when Mary Martha was in bed asleep and the house seemed like a huge empty cave, Kate could feel her impending bankruptcy but she didn't realize that it had very little connection with lack of money.

She was vacuuming the main living room when she saw the postman coming up the flagstone walk. She went out into the hall but she didn't open the door to exchange greetings with him. She waited until he dropped the mail in the slot, then she scooped it up greedily from the floor. There was no check from Sheridan, only a couple of bills and a white envelope with her name and address printed on it. The contents of the envelope were squeezed into one corner like a coin wrapped in paper and her first thought was that Sheridan was playing another trick on her, sending her a dime or a quarter to imply she was worth no more than that. She ripped open the envelope with her thumbnail. There was no coin inside. A piece of notepaper had simply been folded and refolded many times, the way a child might fold a note to be secretly passed during class.

The note was neatly printed in black ink:

> Your daughter takes too dangerous risks with her delicate body. Children must be guarded against the cruel hazards of life and fed good, nourishing food so their bones will be padded. Also clothing. You should put plenty of clothing on her, keep arms and legs covered, etc. In the name of God please take better care of your little girl.

She stood for a minute, half paralyzed with shock. Then, when her blood began to flow again, she reread the note, more slowly and carefully. It didn't make sense. No one—not even Sheridan, who'd accused her of everything else—had ever accused her of neglecting Mary Martha. She was well fed, well clothed, well supervised. She was, moreover, rather a timid child, not given to taking dangerous risks or risks of any kind unless challenged by Jessie.

Kate refolded the note and put it back in the envelope. She thought, *it can't be a mistake because it's addressed to me and my name's spelled correctly. Perhaps there's some religious crank in the neighborhood who's prejudiced against divorced women, but it hardly seems possible now that divorce is so common.*

Only one thing was certain: the letter was an attack, and the person most likely to attack her was Sheridan.

She went out into the hall and telephoned Ralph MacPherson's office. "Mac, I hate to bother you again."

"That's all right, Kate. Are you feeling better today?"

"I was, until the mail came. I just received an anonymous letter and I think I know who—"

"Don't think about it at all, Kate. Tear it up and forget it."

"No, I want you to see it."

"I've seen quite a few of them in my day," Mac said. "They're all the same, sick and rotten."

"I want you to see it," she repeated, "because I'm pretty sure it's from Sheridan. If it is, he's further gone than I imagined. He may even be—well, committable."

"That's a big word in these parts, Kate. Or in any parts, for that matter."

"People are committed every day."

"Not on the word of a disgruntled spouse. . . . All right. Bring the letter down to my office. I'll be here until I leave for court at 1:30."

"Thank you, Mac. Thank you very much."

She dressed hurriedly but with care, as if she were going to be put on exhibition in front of a lot of people, one of whom had written her the letter.

Before leaving the house she made sure all the windows and doors on the ground floor were locked, and when she had backed her car out of the garage she locked the garage doors behind her. She had nothing left to steal, but the locking habit had become fixed in her. She no longer thought of doors as things to open; doors were to close, to keep people out.

She usually handled her small car without thinking much about it, but now she drove as she had dressed, with great care, as though a pair of unfriendly eyes was watching her, ready to condemn her as an unfit mother if she made the slightest mistake, a hand signal executed a little too slowly, a corner turned a little too fast.

She headed for the school playground, intending to tell the girls that she would be late picking them up. She had gone about three blocks when she stopped for a red light and saw, in the rear-view mirror, an old green coupé pull up behind her. Kate paid more attention to cars than most women, especially since she'd been living alone, and she recognized it instantly as the car she'd noticed parked outside her house the previous afternoon.

She tried to keep calm, the way Mac had told her to: *Don't jump to conclusions, Kate. If you thought Sheridan was driving that car, why didn't you go out and confront him, find out why he was there? If it happens again—*

Well, it was happening again.

She opened the door and had one foot on the road when the light changed. The left lane was clear and the green coupé turned into it and shot past her with a grinding of gears. Its grimy windows were closed and she could see only that a man was behind the wheel. It was enough. Sheridan was following her. He may even have been waiting outside the house while the postman delivered his letter, eager to watch its effect on her. She thought, *Well, here it is, Sheridan, here's the effect.*

She didn't hesitate even long enough to close the door. She pressed down on the accelerator and the door slammed shut with the sudden forward thrust of her car. For the next five minutes she was not in conscious control either of herself or of the car. It was as though a devil were driving them both and he was responsible to no one and for no one; he owned the roads, let others use them at their own risk.

Up and down streets, around corners, through a parking lot, down an alley, she pursued the green coupé. Twice she was almost close enough to force it over to the curb but each time it got away. She was not even aware of cars honking at her and people yelling at her until she ran a red light. Then she heard the shrieking of her own brakes as a truck appeared suddenly in front of her. Her head snapped forward until it pressed against the steering wheel. She sat in a kind of daze while the truck driver climbed out of the cab.

"For Chrissake, you drunk or something? That was a red light."

"I didn't—see it."

"Well, keep your eyes open next time. You damn near got yourself killed. You woulda spoiled my record, I got the best record in the company. How they expect a guy to keep his record with a lot of crazy women scooting around in kiddie cars?"

"Shut up," she said. "Please shut up."

"Well, well, now you're trying to get tough with me, eh? Listen, lady, you'll be damn lucky if I don't report you for reckless driving, maybe drunk driving. You been drinking?"

"No."

"They all say that. Where's your driver's license?"

"In my purse."

"Get it out."

"Please don't—"

"Lady, a near accident like this happens and I'm supposed to check on it, see? Maybe you've got some kind of restriction on your license, like you're to wear glasses when you're driving, or a hearing aid."

She fumbled around in her purse until she found her wallet with her driver's license in it. On the license there was a little picture of her, taken the day she'd passed her test. She was smiling confidently and happily into the camera.

She saw the truck driver staring at the picture in disbelief. "This is you, lady?"

She wanted to reach out and strike him between the eyes, but instead she said, "It was taken three years ago. I've been—things have happened to me. When you lose weight, it always shows in the face, it makes you appear—well, older. I was trying to think of a nicer word for it but there isn't one, is there? More aged? That's no improvement. More ancient, decrepit? Worn out? Obsolete?"

"Lady, I didn't mean it like that," he said, looking embarrassed. "I mean—oh hell, let's get out of here."

A crowd had begun to gather. The truck driver waved them away and climbed back into his cab. The green coupé had long since disappeared.

The two girls, on Mike's orders, were sitting on a bench in an area of the playground hidden from the street by an eight-foot oleander hedge. Mike was lying face down on the grass nearby, listening to a baseball game on a transistor radio. Every now and then he raised his head, consulted his wrist watch in an authoritative manner, and gave the girls what was intended to be a hypnotic glance.

They had both been absolutely silent and motionless for seven minutes except for the occasional blink of an eye or twitch of a nose. Mike was beginning to worry about whether he actually had hypnotized them and how he was going to snap them out of it, when Jessie suddenly jumped off the bench.

"Oh, I hate this game! It's not even a *game*, seeing who can stay stillest the longest."

"You're just sore because Mary Martha won," Mike said airily. "I was betting she would. You can't keep your trap shut for two seconds."

"I can if I want to."

"Yackety yak."

"Anyhow, I know why you're making us sit here."

"O clever one, do tell."

"So none of your buddies going past will see you baby-sitting. I heard you tell Daddy you'd never be able to hold up your head in public again if they saw you playing with two little girls. But Daddy said you had to play with us anyway. Or else."

"Well, I wish I'd taken the *or else*," Mike said in disgust. "Anything'd be better than looking after a pair of dimwitted kids who should be able to look after themselves. *I* didn't need a baby-sitter at your age."

Jessie blushed, but the only place it showed was across the bridge of her nose where repeated sunburns had peeled off layers of skin. "I don't need one either except I've got sore hands."

"You're breaking my heart with your itty bitty sore hands. Man, oh man, you get more mileage out of a couple of blisters than I could get from a broken neck."

"If I won the game," Mary Martha said wistfully, "may I move now? There's a bee on my arm and it tickles me."

"So tickle it back," Mike said and turned up the volume of the radio.

"My goodness, he's mean," Mary Martha whispered behind her hand. "Was he born that way?"

"I've only known him for nine years, but he probably was."

"Maybe some evil witch put a curse on him. Do you know any curses?"

"Just g-o-d-d-a-m, which I never say."

"No, I mean real curses." Mary Martha contorted her face until it looked reasonably witchlike. Then she spoke in a high eerie voice:

"Abracadabra,
Purple and green,
This little boy
Will grow up mean."

"Did you just make that up?" Jessie asked.

"Yes."

"It's very good."

"I think so, too," Mary Martha said modestly. "We could make up a whole bunch of them about all the people we hate. Who will we start with?"

"Uncle Howard."

"I didn't know you hated your Uncle Howard."

Jessie looked surprised, as if she hadn't known it herself until she heard her own voice say so. She stole a quick glance at Mike to see if he was listening, but he was engrossed in the ball game, his eyes closed. She said, "You won't ever tell anyone, will you?"

"Cross my heart and hope to die. Now let's start the curse. You go first."

"No, you go first."

Mary Martha assumed her witchlike face and voice:

"Abracadabra,
Yellow and brown,
Uncle Howard's the nastiest
Man in town."

"I don't like that one very much," Jessie said soberly.

"Why not?"

"Oh, I don't know. Let's play another game."

From the street a horn began to blow, repeating a pattern of three short, two long.

"That's my mother," Mary Martha said. "We'd better wake Mike up and tell him we're leaving."

"I'm awake, you numbskull," Mike said, opening his eyes and turning down the volume of the radio. Then he looked at his watch. "It's only a quarter after twelve. She's not supposed to be here until one." He rolled over on his back and got up. "Well, who am I to argue with good fortune? Come on, little darlings. Off to the launching pad."

"You don't have to come with us," Jessie said.

"No kidding? You mean you can actually walk out of here without breaking both your legs? I don't believe it. Show me."

"Oh, shut up."

"Yes, you shut up," Mary Martha added loyally.

The two girls went out through the stone arch, arm in arm, as if to show their solidarity against the enemy.

Mike waited a couple of minutes before following them. He saw Mrs. Oakley standing on the curb talking to them, then Mary Martha and her mother got into the car and Jessie turned and walked back to the playground, alone. She was holding her head high and her face was carefully and deliberately blank.

Mike said, "What's the matter?"

"We're not going to the Museum today."

"Why not?"

"Mrs. Oakley has some errands to do in town. Mary Martha didn't want to go along but she had to."

"Why?"

"Mrs. Oakley won't leave her at the playground alone any more."

"What does she mean, alone?" Mike said, scowling. "*I'm* here."

"I guess she meant without a grownup."

"For Pete's sake, what does she think I am? A two-year-old child? Man, oh man, women sure are hard to figure. . . . Well, come on, no use hanging around here any more. Let's go home."

"All right."

"Aren't you even going to argue?"

"No."

"You're sick, kid."

*

"I'm sorry," Kate Oakley repeated for the third or fourth time. "I hate to disappoint you and Jessie but I can't help it. Something unexpected came up and I must deal with it. You understand that, don't you?"

Mary Martha nodded. "But I could have stayed at the playground with Jessie while you were dealing."

"I want you with me."

"Why? To protect you?"

"No," Kate said with a sharp little laugh. "You've got it all wrong, sweetikins. *I'm* protecting *you*. What on earth gave you the silly idea that I need your protection?"

"I don't know."

"Sometimes your mind works in a way that truly baffles me. I mean, really, angel, it doesn't make sense that I need your protection, does it? I am a grownup and you're a little girl. Isn't that right?"

"Yes, ma'am," Mary Martha said politely. She would have liked to ask what her mother was protecting her from, but she was aware that Kate was already upset. The signs were all there: some subtle, like the faint rash that was spreading across her neck; some obvious, like the oversized sunglasses she was wearing. Mary Martha didn't understand why her mother put on these sunglasses when she was under pressure, she knew only that it was a fact. Even in the house on a dark day Kate sometimes wore them and Mary Martha had come to hate the sight of them. They were like a wall or a closed door behind which untold, untellable things were happening. If you threw questions at this wall they bounced back like ping-pong balls: *what on earth do you mean, lamb?*

They had reached the center of town by this time. Kate drove into the parking lot behind the white four-story building where Mac had his office. It was the first inkling Mary Martha had of where her mother was going and she dreaded the thought of waiting in Mac's outer office, listening to the rise and fall of voices, never hearing quite enough and never understanding quite enough of what she heard. If the voices became distinct enough, Miss Edgeworth, Mac's receptionist, started talking loudly and cheerfully about the weather and how Mary Martha was doing in school and what a pretty dress she was wearing.

When her mother got out of the car Mary Martha made no move to follow her.

"Well?" Kate said. "Aren't you coming?"

"I can wait here."

"No. I don't like the look of that parking-lot attendant. You can't trust these—"

"Or I could go to the library and maybe start on one of my book reports."

"I don't think a nine-year-old should be wandering around downtown by herself."

"The library's only a block away."

Kate hesitated. "Well, all right. But you've got to promise you'll go straight there, not loiter in the stores or anything. And once you're there, you're to stay. No matter how long I am, don't come looking for me, just wait right there."

"I promise."

"You're a good girl, Mary Martha."

Mary Martha got out of the car. She was glad that her mother called her a good girl but she couldn't understand why she said it in such a strange, sad voice, as if having a good child was somehow harder to bear than having a bad one. She wondered what would happen if she turned bad. Maybe Kate would give her to Sheridan and that would be the end of the fighting over the divorce terms. Or maybe Sheridan wouldn't want her either, and she'd have to go and live with a foster family like the Brants and be Jessie's almost-sister.

Once the idea occurred to her, the temptation to try being bad was irresistible. The problem was how to begin. She thought of loitering in the stores, but she wasn't sure what loitering was or if she could do it. Then she heard her mother say, "I don't know what I'd do without you, Mary Martha," and the temptation died as suddenly as it had been born. She felt rather relieved. Loitering in stores didn't sound like much fun and probably the Brants couldn't afford to feed another mouth anyway.

Kate went in the rear entrance of the building and up the service stairs to avoid meeting anyone. After the bright light of noon the stairway seemed very dark. She stumbled once or twice but she didn't remove her sunglasses, she didn't even think of it. By the time she reached Mac's office on the third floor she was breathing hard and fast and the rash on her neck had begun to itch.

Miss Edgeworth was out to lunch. Her typewriter was covered and her desk was bare of papers, as though she'd tidied everything up in case she decided never to come back.

The door of Mac's office was open and he was sitting at his desk with his chair swiveled around to face the window. He was eating a sandwich, very slowly, as if he didn't like it or else liked it so much he didn't want to reach the end of it. Kate had known him for over twenty years and it seemed to her that he hadn't changed at all since she first met him. He was still as thin as a rake, and his hair was still brown and curly and cut very short to deny the curl. He had the reddish tan and bleached eyes of a sailor.

"Mac?"

He turned in surprise. "I didn't hear the elevator."

"I used the back steps."

"Well, come in, Kate, if you don't mind watching me eat. There's extra coffee, would you like some?"

"Yes, please."

He poured some coffee into a plastic cup. "Sit down. You look a bit under the weather, Kate. You're not dieting, I hope."

"Not by choice," she said grimly. "The support check's late again. Naturally. He's trying to make me crawl. That I'm used to, that I can stand. It's these—these awful other things, Mac."

"Have you seen him today?"

"About half an hour ago, on my way here. He was driving that same old green car he drove yesterday when he was parked outside the house. When I saw it in the rear-view mirror, something terrible came over me, Mac. I—I just wanted to *kill* him."

"Now, now, don't talk like that."

"I mean it. All I could think of was chasing him, ramming his car, running him down, getting rid of him some way, any way."

"But you didn't."

"I tried."

"You tried," he repeated thoughtfully. "Tell me about it, Kate."

She told him. He listened, with his head cocked to one side like a dog hearing a distant sound of danger.

"You might have been killed or seriously injured," he said when she'd finished.

"I know that now. I may even have known it then, but it didn't matter. I wasn't thinking of myself, or even, God help me, of Mary Martha. Just of him, Sheridan. I wanted to—I *had* to get even with him. This time he went too far."

"This time?"

"The letter, the anonymous letter."

"Have you got it with you?"

"Yes."

"Show it to me."

She took the letter out of her handbag and put it on his desk.

He studied the envelope for a minute, then removed the wad of paper and began unfolding it. He read aloud: "Your daughter takes too dangerous risks with her delicate body. Children must be guarded against the cruel hazards of life and fed good, nourishing food so their bones will be padded. Also clothing. You should put plenty of clothing on her, keep arms and legs covered, etc. In the name of God please take better care of your little girl."

"Well?" Kate said.

He leaned back in his chair and looked up at the ceiling. "It's a curious document. The writer seems sincere and also very fond—if fond is the correct word—of children in general."

"Why in general? Why not Mary Martha in particular? Sheridan's never particularly liked children; he's crazy about Mary Martha because she's an extension of his ego, such as it is."

"This doesn't sound like Sheridan's style to me, Kate."

"Who else would accuse me of neglecting my daughter?"

"I don't read this as an accusation, exactly. It seems more like a plea or a warning, as if the writer believes he has advance knowledge that something will happen to Mary Martha unless you take preventative steps." Alarmed by her sudden pallor, he added quickly, "Notice I said he *believes* he has such knowledge. Beliefs often have little relationship to fact. My own feeling is that this is from some neighborhood nut. Have you or Mary Martha had any unpleasantness with any of your neighbors recently?"

"Of course not. We mind our own business and I expect other people to mind theirs."

"Perhaps you expect too much," Mac said with a shrug. "Well, I wouldn't worry about the letter if I were you. It's unlikely, though not impossible, that Sheridan wrote it. If he did, he's flipped faster and further than I care to contemplate."

"Will you find out the truth?"

"Naturally I'll try to contact him. If he's pulling these shenanigans he's got to be stopped, for his own sake as well as yours and Mary Martha's. Meanwhile I'll keep the letter, with your permission. I have a friend who's interested in such things. By the way, was it folded half a dozen times like this when it was delivered?"

"Yes."

"Kid stuff, I'd say. Just one more question, Kate. Did you manage to get the license number of the green car?"

"Yes. It's GVK 640."

"You're sure of that?"

"I should be," she said harshly. "I rammed his license plate."

"Kate. Kate, listen to me for a minute."

"No. I can't. I can't listen any more. I want to talk, I've got to *talk* to somebody. Don't you understand, Mac? I spend all my time with a child. She's a wonderful girl, very bright and sweet, but she's only nine years old. I can't discuss things with her, I can't burden her with my problems or ask her for help or support. I've got to put up a front, pretend that everything's all right, even when I can feel the very earth crumbling under my feet."

"You've isolated yourself, Kate," he said calmly. "You used to have friends you could talk to."

"Friends are a luxury I can't afford any more. Oh, people were very kind when Sheridan first moved out. They invited me over to cheer me up and hear all the gruesome details. One thing I learned, Mac, and learned well: the only people who really enjoy a divorce are your best friends. All that vicarious excitement and raw emotion, all the blood and guts spilled—why, it was almost as good as television."

"You're being unfair to them."

"Perhaps. Or perhaps I didn't have the right kind of friends. Anyway, I stopped accepting invitations and issuing them. I didn't want people coming over and feeling sorry for me because I was alone, and sorry for themselves because I couldn't afford to offer them drinks. You want to lose friends, Mac? Stop buying liquor. No money down, results guaranteed."

"What about Mary Martha?" Mac said.

"What about her?"

"She needs some kind of social environment."

"She has friends. One friend in particular, Jessie Brant. I don't especially care for the Brants—Ellen's one of these pushy modern types—but Jessie's an interesting child, free-wheeling and full of beans. I think she's a good influence on Mary Martha, who's inclined to be overcautious. . . . That's another thing about the letter, Mac. It was inaccurate. Mary Martha doesn't take dangerous risks, and I certainly wouldn't call her delicate. She's the same age and height as Jessie but she outweighs her by eight or ten pounds."

"Perhaps the 'risks' mentioned didn't refer to a physical activity like tree-climbing, but to something else that Mary Martha did. Say, for instance, that she was a little reckless while riding her bike and one of the neighbors had to swerve his car to avoid hitting her—"

"Mary Martha is very careful on her bicycle."

"Yes. Well, it was only a suggestion."

She was silent for a minute. Then she said in a low bitter voice, "You see? It's happened the way it always does. I was talking about myself, and now we're suddenly talking about Mary Martha again. There is no me any more. There's just the woman who lives in the big house who looks after the little girl. I've lost my personship. I might just as well have a number instead of a name."

"Calm down now, Kate, and get hold of yourself."

"I told you, myself doesn't exist any more. There is no me, there's nothing to get hold of."

In the outer office Miss Edgeworth had come back from lunch. As soon as she'd found out that Mrs. Oakley had made an appointment with Mac, she'd gone out and bought two chocolate bars to give to Mary Martha. When she saw that Mrs. Oakley hadn't brought Mary Martha along after all, Miss Edgeworth was so relieved she ate both of the chocolate bars herself.

9

AFTER THE noon lunchers departed and before the one o'clock lunchers arrived there was always a short lull in the cafeteria which Ben managed for the owner. Ben used this period to stand out in the alley behind the cafeteria and soak up a little sun and smoke his only cigarette of the day. Ben didn't enjoy smoking but he became sick of food odors and he believed that smoking would dull his sense of smell.

He watched a flock of seagulls circling overhead, waiting for a handout. He thought what a fine day it was for the beginning of his new life. Charlie was engaged. Charlie and Louise were going to be married. Ben had told the good news to his employees and some of his regular customers, and though most of them didn't even know Charlie, they were pleased because Ben was. The whole place seemed livelier. A wedding was in the air, it hardly mattered whose.

Ben leaned against the sunny wall, letting the smoke curl up through his nostrils like ether. He felt a little dizzy. He wasn't sure whether it was from the cigarette or from the surges of happiness that had been sweeping over him off and on all morning. *I'll let Louise and Charlie have the house, Mother always planned it that way. I'll get a little apartment down near the beach and buy a dog. I've always wanted a dog. I could have bought one years ago—Charlie would never have mistreated an animal, he's crazy about animals—but I never got around to it. I don't know the reason. Why, Charlie would cut off his right arm before he'd hurt a dog.*

"Ben."

At the sound of his name Ben turned, although he didn't recognize the voice. It was a little boy's voice, high and thin, not like Charlie's at all. Yet it was Charlie running toward him, down the alley from the street. His clothes were disheveled and he was clutching his stomach with both hands as though he were suffering an acute attack of cramps. Ben felt the happiness draining out of him. All the pores of his skin were like invisible wounds from which his life was spurting.

"What's—the matter, Charlie?"

"Oh God, Ben. Something terrible. She tried to kill me. A woman, a woman in a little blue car. I swear to God, Ben, she meant to kill me and I don't even know her, I never saw her before."

"Sshhh." Ben looked quickly up and down the alley. "Keep your voice down. Someone might hear you."

"But it's true! I didn't imagine it. I don't imagine things like that, ever. Other things, maybe, but not—"

"Calm down and tell me about it, quietly."

"Yes. Yes, I will, Ben. Anything you say."

"Take a deep breath."

"Yes."

"Now where did this happen?"

Charlie leaned against the wooden rubbish bin. His whole body was shaking and the more he tried to control it, the more violently it shook, as though the lines of communication between his brain and his muscles had been cut. "I d-don't remember the name of the street but it was over on the north side. I'd gone to Pinewood Park to eat my lunch."

"Why?"

"Why?" Charlie repeated. "Well, for the fresh air. Sun and fresh air, they're nice, they're good for you. Didn't you tell me that, Ben?"

"Yes. *Yes.* Now go on."

"I was driving back to work and this little blue car was in front of me, with a lady at the wheel. She was going real slow like maybe she was drunk and trying to be extra careful to avoid an accident. Well, I passed her. That's all I did, Ben, I just passed her."

"You didn't honk your horn?"

"No."

"Or look at her in a way that she might have—well, misinterpreted?"

"*No.* I swear to you, Ben, I just *passed* her. Then I heard this terrible sound of gears and I looked around and she was after me. I stepped on the gas to get away from her."

"Why?"

"What else could I have done? What would you have done?"

"Pulled over to the curb, or into a gas station, and asked the lady what the hell she thought she was doing."

"I never thought of that," Charlie said earnestly. "When someone chases me, I run."

"Yes, I guess you do." Ben wiped the sweat off his forehead with the back of his hand. Only a few minutes ago the sun had been like a warm, kindly friend. Now it was his enemy. It stabbed his eyes and temples and burned the top of his head where his hair was thinning, and the dry tender skin around his mouth. It imprisoned him in the alley with the smell of cooking food and the smell of Charlie's fear.

He lit another cigarette and blew the smoke out through his nostrils to deaden them. It was when he threw away the spent match that he noticed the little plant growing out of a crack in the concrete a yard or so from where Charlie was standing. It was about six inches high. It was covered with city dust and some of its leaves had been squashed by the wheel of a car, but it was still growing, still alive. He was filled with a sense of wonder. The little plant had nothing going for it at all: seeded by accident out of garbage, driven over, walked on, unwatered, with no rain since March, it was still alive.

He said, "Everything's going to be O.K., Charlie. Don't worry about it. Things work out one way or another."

"But what do I do now, Ben?"

"Get back on the job or you'll be late."

"I can't use my own car."

"What's the matter with it?"

"Nothing," Charlie said. "The engine's running fine, only—well, here's how I figure it, Ben. That woman, she couldn't have anything against me when I don't even know her. So it must be the car. She has a grudge against the former owner and she thought he was driving, not me. So it seems obvious what I've got to do now."

"To you, perhaps. Not to me."

"Don't you see, Ben? Everything will be solved if I buy a new car. Oh, not a brand-new one but a different one so that woman won't chase me again."

If there was a woman, Ben thought, *and if there was a chase. Maybe he invented the whole thing as an excuse to change cars again.* "You can't afford to buy a car now," he said bluntly, "with the wedding coming up so soon."

Charlie looked surprised as if he'd forgotten all about the wedding. "I have money in the bank."

"You'll be needing it to buy Louise's ring, pay for the honeymoon, buy yourself some new clothes—"

"I'm old enough to make my own decisions," Charlie said, kicking the side of the rubbish bin. "I'm an engaged man. An engaged man has to plan things for himself."

Ben looked down at the little tomato plant growing out of the crack in the concrete. "Yes. Yes, I suppose he does."

"Thank you, Ben. I really do thank you."

"What for?"

"For everything. Even just for being around."

"You're an engaged man now, Charlie. I'm not going to be around much longer. You and Louise will be making a life of your own."

One of the Mexican busboys came out into the alley and said something to Ben in Spanish. The boy spoke softly, smiled softly, moved softly. Ben gave him fifty cents and the boy went back inside.

Charlie had paid no attention to the interruption. His eyes were fixed on Ben's face and his thin silky brows were stitched together in a frown. "You talk as if everything's going to change between us. But it's not. You'll be living with Louise and me, we'll be eating our meals together and playing cards in the evening the way we used to. Why should we let things change?"

"Things change whether we let them or not. And that's good—it keeps us from getting bored with life and with each other."

"But I'm *not* bored."

"Listen to me, Charlie. I won't be living with you and Louise, first because I don't want to, and second, because Louise wouldn't want me to, and third be—"

"Louise wouldn't mind. She's crazy about you, Ben. Why, I bet when you come right down to it, she'd just as soon marry you as marry me."

Ben reached out and grabbed him by the shoulder. "Goddam it, don't you talk like that. It's not fair to Louise. Do you hear me?"

"Yes," Charlie said in a whisper. "But I was only—"

"Sure, you were *only*. You're always *only*. You know what happens when you're *only*? Things get so fouled up—"

"I'm sorry, Ben."

"Yeah. Sure. Well."

"I only meant it as a compliment, to show you how much Louise likes you and that she wouldn't mind at all if you lived with us."

Ben took a deep drag on his cigarette. "I have to go back inside."

"You're not really mad at me?"

"No."

"And it's O.K. if I buy another car, say right after work?"

"It's your money."

"Wouldn't you like to come along and give me advice on what make and model to get and things like that?"

"Not this time."

Charlie heard the finality in his voice and he knew Ben meant *not this time and not any time ever again.*

He watched Ben go back into the cafeteria kitchen and he felt like a child abandoned in the middle of a city, in a strange noisy alley filled with the clatter of dishes and the clanking of pots and pans, and voices shouting, in Spanish, words he couldn't understand.

I'm frightened. Help me, Ben!

Not this time. Not any time ever again.

The two Charlies walked, together but not quite in step, down the alley and into the street, the engaged man about to buy a new car, and the little boy looking for a little girl to play with.

10

Miss Albert first noticed the child because she was so neat and quiet. Most of the children who came to the library during summer vacation wore jeans or shorts with cotton T-shirts, as if they were using the place as a rest stop between beach and ball game, movie and music lesson. In groups or alone, they were always noisy and always chewing something—chocolate bars, bubble gum, peanut brittle, apples, ice cream cones, bananas, occasionally even cotton candy. Miss Albert had a recurrent nightmare in which she opened up one of the valuable art books and found all the pages glued together with cotton candy.

The little girl with the blond ponytail was not chewing anything. She wore a pink dress with large blue daisies embroidered on the patch pockets. Her shoes had the sick-white color that indicated too many applications of polish to cover too many cracks in the leather. The child's expression was blank, as if her hair was drawn back and fastened so tightly that her facial muscles couldn't function. *It must be just like having your hair pulled all the time*, Miss Albert thought. *I wouldn't like it one bit. She probably doesn't either, poor child.*

The girl picked a magazine from the rack and sat down. She opened it, turned a few pages, then closed it again and sat with it on her lap, her eyes moving from the main door to the clock on the mezzanine and back again. The obvious conclusion was that the girl was waiting for someone. But Miss Albert didn't care for the obvious; she preferred the elaborate, even the bizarre. The child's family had just arrived in town, possibly to get away from a scandal of some kind—what kind Miss Albert would decide on her lunch hour—and the girl, alone and friendless, had come to the library for the children's story hour at half past one. But Miss Albert was not satisfied with this explanation. The girl had no look of anticipation on her face, no look of anything, thanks to that silly hair-do. *She'd be cute as a bug with her hair cut just below her ears and a fluffy bang. Or maybe with an Alice-in-Wonderland style like Louise, except on Louise it looks ridiculous at her age. Imagine Louise getting married, I think it's just wonderful. It shows practically anything can happen if you wait long enough.*

Half an hour passed. Miss Albert's stomach was rumbling and her arms were tired from taking books from her metal cart and putting them back on their proper shelves. From the children's section adjoining the main reading room, she could hear a rising babble of voices and the scrape of chairs being rearranged. In ten minutes the story hour would begin and Mrs. Gambetti, with nothing to do at children's checkout, would come and relieve Miss Albert for lunch. And Miss Albert would take her sandwich and Thermos of coffee over to Encinas Park to watch the people with their sandwiches and their Thermoses of coffee.

But I really can't leave the child just sitting there, she thought. *Very likely she doesn't know where to go and she's probably too timid to ask, having been through all that scandal whatever it was but I'm sure it was quite nasty.*

Miss Albert pushed her empty cart vigorously down the aisle like a determined week-end shopper. At the sound of its squeaking wheels, Mary Martha turned her head and met Miss Albert's kindly and curious gaze.

Miss Albert said, "Hello."

Mary Martha had been instructed not to speak to strangers but she didn't think this would apply to strangers in a library, so she said, "Hello," back.

"What's your name?"

"Mary Martha Oakley."

"That's very pretty. You're new around here, aren't you, Mary?"

The child didn't answer, she just looked down at her shoes. Her toes had begun to wiggle nervously like captive fish. She didn't want the lady to notice so she attempted to hide her feet under the chair. During the maneuver, the magazine slid off her lap onto the floor.

Miss Albert picked it up, trying not to look surprised that a child so young would choose *Fortune* as reading material. "Did you move to town recently, Mary?"

"I'm not supposed to answer when people call me Mary because my name is Mary *Martha*. But I guess it's all right in a library. We didn't move to town, we've always lived here."

"Oh. I thought—well, it doesn't matter. The story hour is beginning in a minute or two. You just go through that door over there"—Miss Albert pointed—"and turn to the right and take a seat. Any seat you like."

"I already have a seat."

"But you can't hear the story from this distance."

"No, ma'am."

"You don't want to hear the story?"

"No, ma'am, I'm waiting for my mother."

Miss Albert concealed her disappointment behind a smile. "Well, perhaps you'd like something to read that would be a little more suitable for your age bracket."

Mary Martha hesitated, frowning. "Do you have books about everything?"

"Pretty nearly everything, from aardvarks to zulus. What kind of book are you interested in?"

"One about divorce."

"Divorce?" Miss Albert said with a nervous little laugh. "Goodness, I'm not sure I— Wouldn't you like a nice picture book to look at instead?"

"No, ma'am."

"Well, I'm afraid I don't—that is, perhaps we'd better ask Miss Lang in the reference department. She knows more about such situations than I do. Come on, I'll take you over and introduce you."

Behind the reference desk Louise was acting very busy but Miss Albert wasn't fooled. Checking the number of sheep in Australia or the name of the capital of Ghana hadn't put the color in her cheeks and the dreamy, slightly out-of-focus look in her eyes.

"I hope I'm not interrupting anything," Miss Albert said, knowing very well she was, but feeling that it was the kind of thing that should be interrupted, especially during working hours. "This is Mary Martha Oakley, Louise. Mary Martha, this is Miss Lang."

Louise stared at the girl and said, "Oh," in a cold way that puzzled Miss Albert because Louise was usually very good with children.

"Mary Martha," Miss Albert added, "wants a book on divorce."

"Does she, indeed," Louise said. "Am I to gather, Miss Albert, that you've encouraged the child in her request by bringing her over here?"

"Not exactly. My gosh, Louise, I thought you'd get a kick out of it, a laugh."

"You know the rules of the library as well as I do, or you should. You're excused now, Miss Albert."

"Good," Miss Albert said crisply. "It happens to be my lunch hour."

Over Mary Martha's head she gave Louise a dirty look, but Louise wasn't even watching. Her eyes were still fixed on Mary Martha, as if they were seeing much more than a little girl in a pink dress with daisies.

"Oakley," she said in a thin, dry voice. "You live at 319 Jacaranda Road?"

"Yes, ma'am."

"With your mother."

"Yes."

"And your little dog."

"I don't have a little dog," Mary Martha said uneasily. "Just a cat named Pudding."

"But there's a dog in your neighborhood, isn't there? A little brown mongrel that chases cars?"

"I never saw any."

"Never? Perhaps you don't particularly notice dogs."

"Oh yes, I do. I always notice dogs because they're my favorites even more than cats and birds."

"So if you had one, you'd certainly protect it, wouldn't you?"

"Yes, ma'am."

Louise leaned across the desk and spoke in a smiling, confidential whisper. "If I had a dog that chased cars, I wouldn't be anxious to admit it, either. So of course I can't really blame you for fibbing. Just between the two of us, though—"

But there was nothing between the two of them. The child, wary-eyed and flushed, began backing away, her hands jammed deep in her pockets as if they were seeking the roots of the embroidered daisies. Ten seconds later she had disappeared out the front door.

Louise watched the door, in the wild hope that the girl would decide to come back and change her story—yes, she had a little dog that chased cars; yes, one of the cars was an old green Ford coupé.

There was a dog, there had to be, because Charlie said so. It had chased his car and Charlie, afraid for the animal's safety, felt that he should warn the owner. That's why he wanted to find out who lived at 319 Jacaranda Road. What other reason could he possibly have had?

He's not a liar, she thought. *He's so devastatingly honest sometimes it breaks my heart.*

She rubbed her eyes. They were dry and gritty and in need of tears. It was as if dirt, blowing in from the busy street, had altered her vision and blurred the distinctions between fact and fantasy.

"Don't talk so fast, lamb," Kate Oakley said. "Now let me get this straight. She asked you if you had a little brown dog that chased cars?"

Mary Martha nodded.

"And she wouldn't believe you when you denied it?"

"No, ma'am."

"It's crazy, that's what it is. I declare, I think the whole world has gone stark staring mad except you and me." She spoke with a certain satisfaction, as if the world was getting no more than it deserved and she was glad she'd stepped out of it in time and taken Mary Martha with her. "You'd expect a librarian, of all people, to be sensible, with all those books around."

Immediately after Kate's departure, Ralph MacPherson made two telephone calls. The first was to the apartment where Sheridan Oakley claimed to be living. He let the phone ring a dozen times, but, as on the previous afternoon and evening, there was no answer.

The second call was to Lieutenant Gallantyne of the city police department. After an exchange of greetings, Mac came to the point:

"I'm in the market for a favor, Gallantyne."

"That's no switch," Gallantyne said. "What is it?"

"A client of mine claims that her husband, from whom she's separated, is harassing her and her child. She says he's driving around town in a green Ford coupé, six or seven years old, license GVK 640."

"And?"

"I want to know if he is."

"All I can do is check with Sacramento and find out who owns the car. That may take some time, unless you can come up with a more urgent reason than the one you've given me, say like murder, armed robbery—"

"Sorry, no armed robbery or murder. Just a divorce, with complications."

"I think your cases are often messier than mine are," Gallantyne said with a trace of envy.

"Could be. We'll have to get together on one sometime."

"Let's do that. Now, you want us to contact Sacramento about the green Ford?"

"Yes, but meanwhile pass the license number around to the traffic boys. If they spot the car anywhere I'd like to hear about it, any time of the day or night. I have an answering service."

"What's that license again?"

"GVK, God's Very Kind, 640."

II

HE BOUGHT the new car right after work, a three-year-old dark, inconspicuous sedan. As soon as he got behind the wheel he felt safe and secure as though he'd acquired a whole new body and nobody would recognize the old Charlie any more. He felt quite independent, too. He had chosen the car by himself, with no help from Ben, and he had paid for it with his own money. The used-car salesman had taken his check without hesitation as if he couldn't help but trust a man with such an honest face as Charlie's. And Charlie, inspired by this trust, was absolutely convinced that the car had been driven only 10,000 cautious miles by one owner and a Detroit-trained garage mechanic at that. A man so skillful, Charlie reasoned, would have practically no spare time and that would account for the extremely low mileage on the car.

It seemed to him that the salesman, who had paid little attention to him when he first started browsing around the lot, noticed the change in him, too. He started to call him sir.

"I hope you'll be very happy with your car, sir."

"Oh, I will. I already am."

"There's no better advertising than a satisfied customer," the salesman said. "The only trouble with selling a man a good car like this is that we don't see him around for a long time. Good luck and safe driving to you, sir."

"Thank you very much."

"It was a pleasure."

Charlie eased the car out into the street. It was getting quite late and he knew Ben would be starting to worry about him, but he didn't want to go home just yet. He wanted to drive around, to get the feel of his new car and test the strength of his new body before he exposed either to Ben or Louise. They would both be suspicious, Ben of the car and the salesman and the garage mechanic, Louise of the change in him. He realized, in a vague way, that Louise didn't really want him to change, that she was dependent on his weakness though he couldn't understand why.

When he started out, he had, at the conscious level, no destination in mind. At crossroads he made choices seemingly unconnected with what he was thinking. He turned left because the car in front of him did; he turned right to watch a flock of blackbirds feeding on a lawn; he went straight because the road crossed a creek and he liked bridges; he turned left again because the setting sun hurt his eyes. The journey took on an air of adventure, as if the streets, the bridge, the blackbirds, the setting sun were all strange to him and he was a stranger to them. He wasn't lost—nobody could get lost in San Felice where the mountains were to the east and the sea to the west, with one or the other, or both, always visible—he was deliberately misplaced, as if he were playing a game of hide-and-seek with Ben and Louise. An hour must have passed since the game started. *Ready or not, you must be caught, hiding around the goal or not.*

The sun had gone down. Wisps of fog were floating in from the sea and gathering in the treetops like spiders' webs. It was time to turn on the headlights but he wasn't sure which button to press, there were so many of them on the dashboard. He pulled over to the curb and stopped the car about fifty feet from an intersection. The intersection looked familiar to him although he didn't recognize it. It wasn't until he switched on the headlights and their beam caught the street sign and held it, that he knew where he was. Jacaranda Road, 300 block.

He felt a sudden and terrible pain in his head. He heard his own voice in his ears but he couldn't tell whether it was a whisper or a scream.

"Ben! Louise! Come and find me, I'm not hiding. It's not a game any more. Help me. Come and take me home, Louise, don't leave me in this bad place. You don't know, nobody knows, how bad—dirty—dirty bad—"

At 8:30 the phone rang and Ben, who'd been sitting beside it for a long time, answered on the first ring.

"Hello."

"Ben, this is Louise. Charlie was supposed to pick me up half an hour ago. He may have forgotten, so I thought I'd call and jog his memory a bit."

"He's not here."

"Well, he's probably on his way then. I'll just go wait on the steps for him. It's a nice night."

"It's cold."

"No, it's not," Louise said, laughing. "You know how it is when you're in love, Ben. All the weather is wonderful."

"You'd better stay in the house, Louise. I don't think he's on his way over."

"Why not? Is something the matter?"

"I'm not sure," Ben said in his slow careful voice. "He came to the cafeteria at noon with some crazy—a far-fetched story about a strange woman trying to kill him with her car. I didn't know how much of it, if any, to believe. He may have invented the whole thing as an excuse to buy a new car. You know Charlie, he can't just go ahead and do something; he has to have a dozen reasons why, no matter how nutty some of them are. Anyway, he told me he was going to buy a new car after work."

"He got off work three and a half hours ago. How long does it usually take him to buy a car?"

"Judging from past performance, I'd say five minutes. He sees one he likes the look of, kicks a couple of the tires, sounds the horn, and that's it. It can be the worst old clunker in town but he buys it."

"Then he should be home by now."

"Yes."

"Ben, I'm coming over."

"What good will that do? It will simply mean two of us sitting around worrying instead of one. No, you stay where you are, Louise. Get interested in something. Read a book, wash your hair, call a girlfriend, anything."

"I can't. I won't."

"Look, Louise, I don't want to be brutal about this, but waiting for Charlie is something you must learn to handle gracefully. You may be doing quite a bit of it. Ten chances to one, he's O.K., he's just gotten interested in something and—"

"I can't afford to bet on it, even at those odds," Louise said and hung up before he could argue any further.

She went down the hall toward her bedroom to pick up a coat. All the weather was wonderful, but sometimes it paid to carry a coat.

She walked quickly and quietly past the open door of the shoebox-sized dining room where her parents were still lingering over coffee and the evening paper, going line by line over the local news, the obituaries and divorces and marriages, the water connections and delinquent tax notices and building permits and real estate transfers. But she didn't move quietly enough. *No one could*, she thought bitterly. *Not even the stealthiest cat, not even if the carpet were velvet an inch thick.*

"Louise?" her father called out. "Are you still here, Louise?"

"Yes, Daddy."

"I thought you were going out tonight."

"I am. I'm just leaving now."

"Without saying good-bye to your parents? Has this great romance of yours made you forget your manners? Come in here a minute."

Louise went as far as the door. Her parents were seated side by side at the table with the newspaper spread out in front of them, like a pair of school children doing their homework together.

Mr. Lang rose to his feet and made a kind of half-bow in Louise's direction. For as long as Louise could remember he had been doing this whenever she entered a room. But his politeness was too elaborate, as if, by treating her like a princess, he was actually calling attention to her commonness.

Louise stared at him, wondering how she could ever have been impressed by his silly posturings or affected by his small, obvious cruelties. She said nothing, knowing that he hated silence because his weapon was his tongue.

"I understood," he said finally, "that this was the night your mother and I were to congratulate our prospective son-in-law. Am I to assume the happy occasion has been postponed?"

"Yes."

"What a pity. I had looked forward to some of his stimulating conversation: yes, Mr. Lang; no, Mr. Lang—"

"Good night."

"Wait a minute. I haven't finished."

"Yes, you have," Louise said and walked down the hall and out the front door. For once, she was grateful for her father's cruelty. It had saved her from trying to explain where Charlie was and why he hadn't kept their date.

Ben must have been watching for her from the front window because as soon as she pulled up to the curb in front of the house he came out on the porch and down the steps.

To the question in her eyes he shook his head. Then, "You might as well go home, Louise."

"No."

"All right. But it's silly to start driving around looking for him when I haven't the slightest idea where he is."

"I have," she said quietly. "It's just a feeling, a hunch. It may be miles off but it's worth trying. We've got to find him, Ben. He needs us."

"He needs us." Ben got in the car and slammed the door shut. "Where have I heard that before? Charlie needs this, Charlie needs that, Charlie needs, period. Some day before I die, *I'm* going to have a need. Just once somebody's going to say, *Ben* needs this or that. Just once— Oh, what the hell, forget it. I don't really need anything."

"I do."

"What?"

"I need Charlie."

"Then I'm sorry for you," Ben said, striking his thigh with his fist. "I'm so sorry for you I could burst into tears. You're a decent, intelligent young woman, you deserve a life. What you're getting is a job."

"Don't waste any pity on me. I'm happy."

"You're happy even now, with Charlie missing and maybe in the kind of trouble only Charlie can get into?"

"He's alive—you'd have been notified if he'd been killed in an accident or anything—and as long as Charlie's alive, I'm happy."

"I'm not," he said bluntly. "In fact, there have been times, dozens, maybe hundreds of times, when I've thought the only solution for Charlie would be for him to step in front of a fast-moving truck. Before this is all over, you might be thinking the same thing."

"That's a—a terrible thing to say to me."

"I'm sorry, I had to do it. I didn't want to hurt you, but—"

"Isn't it funny how many times people don't want to hurt you, *but*?"

"I suppose it's pretty funny, yes."

She was staring straight ahead of her into the darkness but her eyes were squinting as if they were exposed to too much light. "Stop worrying about Charlie and me. If you want us to get married, give us your blessing and hope we'll muddle through all right. If you don't want us to get married, say so now, tonight."

"You have my blessing and my hope. I'm not much of a hoper, or a blesser either, but—"

"Sssh, no buts. They ruin everything." She smiled and touched his arm. "You see, Ben, you've been very good to Charlie. I think, though, that I'll be better *for* him."

"I hope so."

"Thanks for talking to me, and letting me talk. I feel calmer and more sure of myself, and of Charlie, than I ever have before. Good night, Ben."

"Good night? I thought we were going out to look for Charlie."

"You're not, I am. Looking for Charlie is my job now."

"All right." He got out of the car and stood on the curb with the door open, trying to decide whether to get back in. Then he leaned down and shut the door very firmly, as if this was a door he'd had trouble with in the past and he knew it needed a good slam to stay closed. "Good night, Louise."

If she said good night to him again he didn't hear it above the roar of the engine. She was out of sight before he reached the top of the steps.

He felt no sharp, sudden pain, only a terrible sadness creeping over him like fog over the city. He thought, *she's driving blind, following a wild hunch*, and he wondered how many hunches she would have before she gave up. One in twenty might be correct and she'd bank on that one, believing that she finally understood Charlie, that she'd pressed the right button and come up with the right answer. It would take her a long time to realize that with Charlie the buttons changed position without reason, and yesterday's answer was gibberish and today's only a one-in-twenty hunch.

Ben remembered the document word by word, though it had been years since he'd seen it:

> We are recommending the release of Charles Edward Gowen into the custody and care of his brother. We feel that Gowen has gained insight and control and is no longer a menace to himself or to others. Further psychiatric treatment within the closed environment of a hospital seems futile at this time. Gainful employment, family affection and outside interests are now necessary if he is to become a useful and self-sufficient member of society.

12

THE FOG thickened as she drove. Trees lost their tops, whole sections of the city disappeared, and street lights were no more than dim and dirty halos. But inside her mind everything was becoming very clear, as if the lack of visibility around her had forced her to look inward.

What she had called a hunch to Ben was now a conclusion based on a solid set of facts. Charlie was frightened beyond the understanding of anyone like Ben or herself; he was running away from Ben, from her, from marriage, from the responsibility of growing up. He must be treated like a scared boy, shown the dark room and taught that it had no more terrors than when it was light; he must be trusted even when trust was very difficult. But first he must be found because he was trying to escape into a world that seemed safe to him, that seemed to present no challenge. Yet it was a dangerous place for Charlie, this world of children.

Her hands were gripping the steering wheel so tightly that the muscles of her forearms ached, but she felt compelled to go on thinking calmly and reasonably, like a mathematician faced with a very long and difficult equation. *If I am to deal with this thing, if I am to help Charlie deal with it, I must know what it is. I must know. . . .*

Charlie had never even mentioned children to her, he never looked at them passing on the street or watched them playing in the park. Yet somehow, somewhere, he had seen the girl, Mary Martha, and found out where she lived. Louise remembered his excitement the previous night when he was talking about 319 Jacaranda Street and the little dog that chased cars. Well, there was no little dog; there was a child, Mary Martha. Charlie had said so himself and though Louise had deafened her ears at the time, his words rang in them now like the echo of tolling bells: "*It's funny she'd want to live alone in the big house with just a little girl.*"

She wondered whether it had been a slip of the tongue or whether Charlie, in some corner of his mind, wanted her to know about it and was asking for her help.

"Oh God," she said aloud, "how do you help someone like Charlie?"

She found him at the corner of Toyon Drive and Jacaranda Road. He was leaning against the hood of a dark car she didn't recognize, his hands folded across his stomach, his head sunk low on his chest. A passing stranger might think he'd had engine trouble, had lifted the hood and discovered something seriously wrong and given up in despair.

Although he must have heard her car stop and her footsteps as she approached, he didn't move or open his eyes. Jacaranda petals clung thickly to his hair and his windbreaker. They looked very pale in the fog, like snowflakes that couldn't melt because they'd fallen on something as cold as they were.

She spoke his name very softly so she wouldn't startle him.

He opened his eyes and blinked a couple of times. "Is that —is that you, Louise?"

"Yes."

"I was calling you. Did you hear me?"

"No. Not in the way you mean. I heard, though, Charlie. I'll always hear you."

"How can you do that?"

"It's a secret."

He stood up straight and looked around him, frowning. "You shouldn't be here, Louise. It's a bad place for women and children. It's—well, it's just a bad place."

"The children are all safe in bed," she said with calm deliberation. "And, as a woman, I'm not afraid because I have you to look after me. It's awfully cold, though, and I'll admit I'd feel more comfortable at home. Will you take me home, Charlie?"

He didn't answer. He was staring down at the sidewalk, mute and troubled.

"You've bought a new car, Charlie."

"Yes."

"It's very sleek and pretty. I'd like a ride in it."

"No."

"You were calling me, Charlie. Why did you call me if you didn't want to see me?"

"I did, I do want to see you."

"But you won't drive me home?"

"No," he said, shaking his head. "It would be too complicated."

"Why?"

"Well, you see, there are two cars and two people, so each of the cars has to be driven by one person. That's just plain arithmetic, Louise."

"I suppose it is."

"If I take you home, your car will be left sitting here alone, and I told you what kind of place this is."

"It looks like a perfectly nice residential neighborhood to me, Charlie."

"That's on the surface. I see what's underneath. I see things so terrible, so—" He began to grind his fists into his eyes, as though he were trying to smash the images he saw into a meaningless pulp.

She caught his wrists and held them. "Stop it. Stop it, please."

"I can't."

"All right," she said steadily. "So you see terrible things. Perhaps they exist, in this neighborhood and in yourself. But you mustn't let them blind you to the good things and there are more of them, many more. When you take a walk in the country, you can't stop and turn over every stone. If you did, you'd miss the sky and the trees and the flowers and the birds. And to miss those would be a terrible thing in itself, wouldn't it?"

He was watching her, earnest and wide-eyed, like a child listening to a story. "Are there good things in me, Louise?"

"Too many for me to tell you."

"That's funny. I wonder if Ben knows."

"Ben knows."

"Is that why he never tells me about them? Because there are too many?"

"Yes."

"That's nice, that's very nice," he said, nodding. "I like that about the stones, Louise. Ben and I used to turn over a lot of stones when we went hiking in the mountains. We used to find some very interesting things under stones. No birds, naturally, but sow bugs and lizards and Jerusalem crickets. . . . I made a crazy mistake the first time I ever saw a young Jerusalem cricket. It lay there on its back in the ground, flesh-colored and wriggling its—well, they looked like arms and legs. And I thought it was a real human baby and that that was where they came from. When I asked Ben about it he told me the truth, but I didn't like it. It didn't seem nearly so pleasant or so natural as the idea of babies growing in the ground like flowers. If I could start all over again, I'd want to start like that, growing up out of the ground like a flower. . . . You're shivering, Louise. Are you cold?"

"Yes."

"I'll take you home."

"That's a good idea," she said soberly, as if it had not occurred to her before.

He opened the door for her and she got into the car. The seat covers felt cold and damp like something Charlie had found under a stone.

He walked around the front of the car. The headlights were still on and as he passed them he shielded his entire face with his hands like a man avoiding a pair of eyes too bright and knowing. But as soon as he got behind the wheel of the car and turned on the ignition, he began to relax and she thought, *the crisis is over. At least, one part of one crisis is over. That's all I dare ask right now.*

She said, "The engine sounds very smooth, Charlie."

"It does to me, too, but of course I'm not an expert like Ben. Ben will probably find a dozen things the matter with it."

"Then we won't listen to him."

"I don't have enough courage not to listen to Ben. In fact, I just don't have enough courage, period."

"That's not true," she said, thinking, *for people with problems, like Charlie, just to go on living from day to day requires more courage than is expected of any ordinary person.* "Does the fog bother you, Charlie?"

He gave a brief, bitter laugh. "Which fog, the one out there or the one in here?"

"Out there."

"I like it. I'd like to lose myself in it forever and that'd be the end of me, and good riddance."

"It would be the end of me too, Charlie. And I don't want to end yet. I feel I only began after I met you."

"Don't say that. It scares me. It makes me feel responsible for you, for your life. I'm not fit for that. Your life's too valuable and mine's not worth a—"

"All lives are valuable."

"Oh God, I can't *explain* to you. You won't *listen*."

"That's right, I won't listen."

"You're stubborn like Ben."

"No," she said, smiling. "I'm stubborn like myself."

For the next few blocks he didn't speak. Then, stopping for a red light, he blurted out, "I didn't mean it to be like this, Louise."

"Mean what to be like what?"

"Tonight, our date, the car. I was—I was going to come to your house and surprise you with the new car. But I decided I'd better drive around a bit first and get used to the motor so I wouldn't make any mistakes in front of you. I started out, not thinking of where or why, not thinking of anything. Then I stopped, I just stopped, I don't even remember if I had a reason. And there I was, in that place I hate. I hate it, Louise, I hate that place."

"Then you mustn't go there any more," she said calmly. "That makes sense, doesn't it, Charlie? To avoid what makes you feel miserable?"

"I didn't *go* there. I was led, I was driven. Don't you understand that, Louise?"

"I'm trying."

She watched the street lights step briskly out of the fog and back into it again like sentries guarding the greatness of the night. She wondered how much she could afford to understand Charlie and whether this was the time to try. Perhaps she might never have a better opportunity than now, with Charlie in a receptive mood, humble, wanting to change himself, and grateful to her for finding him.

She bided her time, saying nothing further until they arrived at her apartment house and Charlie parked the car at the curb. He reached for her hands and held them tightly in his own, against his chest. She almost lost her nerve then, he looked so tired and defenseless. She had to remind herself that it wasn't enough just to get by, to smooth things over for one day when there were thousands of days ahead of them. *I must do it*, she thought. *I can't hurt him any more than he's already hurting himself.*

"To me," she said finally, "Jacaranda Road is like any other. Why do you hate it, Charlie? Why do you call it a bad place?"

"Because it is."

"The whole street is?"

He let go of her hands as if they'd suddenly become too personal. "I don't want to dis—"

"Or just one block? Or perhaps one house?"

"Please stop. Please don't."

"I have to," she said. "The bad part, is it the house where the little Oakley girl lives with her mother?"

He kept shaking his head back and forth as though he could shake off the pain like a dog shaking off water. "I don't—don't know any Oakley girl."

"I think you do, Charlie. It would help you, it would help us both, if you'd tell me the truth."

"I don't know her," he repeated. "I've seen her, that's all."

"You've never approached her?"

"No."

"Or talked to her?"

"No."

"Then nothing whatever has happened," she said firmly. "You have no reason to feel so bad, so guilty. Nothing's *happened*, Charlie, that's the important thing. It doesn't make sense to feel guilty about something that hasn't even happened."

"Do you think it's that simple, Louise?"

"No. But I think it's where we have to start, dividing things into what's real and what isn't. You haven't harmed anyone. The Oakley girl is safe at home, and I believe that even if I hadn't found you when I did, she'd still be safe at home."

He was watching her like a man on trial watching a judge. "You honest to God believe that, Louise?"

"Yes, I do."

"Tell it to me again. Say it all over again."

She said it over again and he listened as if he'd been waiting all of his life to hear it. It wasn't like anything he would have heard from Ben: "*Can't you use your head for a change? You've got to avoid situations like that. God knows what might have happened.*"

"Nothing happened," he said. "Nothing happened at all, Louise."

"I know."

"Will you—that is, I suppose you'll be telling Ben about all this business tonight."

"Not if you don't want me to."

"He wouldn't understand. Not because he's dumb or anything, but because I've disappointed him so often, he can't help expecting the worst from me. . . . You won't tell him where you found me?"

"No."

"How did you find me, Louise? Of all the places in the city, what made you go there?"

"A lucky guess based on a lucky coincidence," she said, smiling. "The little Oakley girl was in the library this afternoon. She wanted a special book and Miss Albert brought her to my department and introduced her to me. Since I'd just looked up who lived at 319 Jacaranda Road for you, I asked her if that was her address and she said yes. It was that simple."

"No, it couldn't have been. You couldn't have even guessed anything from just that much."

"Well, we talked a little."

"Not about me. She's never even seen me."

"We talked," Louise said, "about her cat. She doesn't own a dog."

He turned away from her and looked out the window though there was nothing to see but different shades of grayness. "That wasn't a very good lie about the little dog that chased cars, I guess."

"No, it wasn't."

"It's a funny thing, her coming to the library like that. It's as if someone planned it, God or Ben or—"

"Nobody planned it. Kids go to libraries and I work in one, that's all. . . . You see lots of little girls, Charlie. What made you—well, take a fancy to that particular one?"

"I don't know."

"Was it because she reminded you of me, Charlie? She reminded me of me right away, with those solemn eyes and that long fine blond hair."

"Blond?"

"Don't sound so incredulous. I used to be a regular towhead when I was a kid."

He put his hands on the steering wheel and held on tight like a racing driver about to reach a dangerous curve. *Blond,* he thought. *That crazy mother has dyed Jessie's hair blond. No, it's impossible. Jessie's hair is short, it couldn't have grown long in a day. A wig, then. One of those new wigs the young girls are wearing now—*

"There must be trouble in the family," Louise said. "Mary Martha wanted a book on divorce."

"Who?"

"The Oakley girl, Mary Martha. . . . You look upset, Charlie. I shouldn't go on talking about her like this, and I won't. I promise not to say another word." She pressed her cheek against his shoulder. "I love you so much, Charlie. Do you love me, too?"

"Yes."

"You're tired, though, aren't you?"

"Yes."

"Do you want to go home?"

"Yes," he said. "*Yes.* I—it's late, it's cold."

"I know. You go home and get a good night's sleep and you'll feel much better in the morning."

"Will I?" He looked straight ahead of him, his eyes strained, as if he was trying to make out the outlines of the morning through the fog. But all he could see was Jessie coming out of the playground with Mary Martha. Their heads were together and they were whispering, they were planning to trick him. All the time he thought they hadn't noticed him and they'd been on to him right from the start. They'd looked at him and seen even through the dirty windows of the old green car, something different about him, something wrong. And Jessie—it must have been Jessie, she was always the leader—had said, "*Let's fool him. Let's pretend I live in your house.*"

Children were subtle, they could see things grownups couldn't. Their attention wasn't divided between past and present, it was focused on the present. But what was there about him that had made Jessie notice him? How had she found out he was different?"

Louise said, "Good night, Charlie."

Although he said, "Good night," in return, he was no longer even aware of Louise except as a person who'd come to bring him bad news and was now leaving. *Good riddance, stranger.*

The car door opened and closed again. He turned on the ignition and pulled out into the street. Somewhere in the city, in some house hidden now by night and fog, a little girl knew he was different—no, she was not a little girl, she was already a woman, devious, scheming, provocative. She was probably laughing about it right at this minute, remembering how she'd tricked him. He had to find her.

Reasons why he had to find her began to multiply in his mind like germs. *I'll reprimand her, without scaring her, of course, because I'd never scare a child no matter how bad. I'll ask her what there was about me she noticed, why I looked different to her. I'll tell her it's not nice, thinking such terrible thoughts. . . .*

13

JESSIE CALLED out from her bedroom, "I got up for a glass of water and now I'm ready to be tucked in again, somebody!"

She didn't especially need tucking in for the third time but she could hear her parents arguing and she wanted to stop the sound which was keeping her awake. She thought the argument was probably about money, but she couldn't distinguish any particular words. The sound was just a fretful murmur that crept in through the cracks of her bedroom door and made her ears itch. It wasn't a pleasant tickle like the kind she got when she hugged the Arlingtons' dog, Chap; it was like the itch of a flea bite, painful, demanding to be scratched but not alleviated by scratching.

She called again and a minute later her father appeared in the doorway. He had on his bathrobe and he looked sleepy and cross. "You're getting away with murder, young one. Do you realize it's after ten?"

"I can't help it if time passes. I couldn't stop it if I wanted to."

"No, but you might make its passing a little more peaceful for the rest of us. Mike's asleep, and I hope to be soon."

She knew from his tone that he wasn't really angry with her. He even sounded a little relieved that his conversation with Ellen had been interrupted.

"You could sit on the side of my bed for a minute."

"I think I will," he said, smiling slightly. "It's the best offer I've had today."

"Now we can talk."

"What about?"

"Oh, everything. People can always find something to talk about."

"They can if one of the people happens to be you. What's on your mind, Jess?"

She leaned against the headboard and gazed up at the ceiling. "Are Ellen and Virginia best friends?"

"If you're referring to your mother and your Aunt Virginia, yes, I suppose you'd call them best friends."

"Do they tell each other everything?"

"I don't know. I hope not."

"I mean, like Mary Martha and me, we exchange our most innermost secrets. Did you ever have a friend like that?"

"Not since I was old enough to have any secrets worth mentioning," he said dryly. "Is something worrying you, Jessie?"

She said, "No," but she couldn't prevent her eyes from wandering to the closed door of her closet. A whole night and day had passed since she'd taken back the book Virginia had given her and Howard had pressed the twenty dollars into her hand. The money was out of sight now, hidden in the toe of a shoe, but she might as well have been still carrying it around in her hand. She thought about it a good deal, and always with the same mixture of power and guilt; she had money, she could buy things now, but she had also been bought. She wondered what grownups did with children they bought. Did they keep them? Or did they sell them again, and to whom? Perhaps if she returned the twenty dollars to Howard and Virginia, they would give her back to her father and everything would be normal again. She hadn't wanted the money in the first place, Howard had forced it on her; and she had a strong feeling that he would refuse to take it back.

She said in a rather shaky voice, "Am I *your* little girl?"

"That's an odd question. Whose else would you be?"

"Howard and Virginia's."

He frowned slightly. "Where'd you pick up this idea of calling adults by their first names?"

"All the other kids do it."

"Well, you don't happen to be all the other kids. You're my special gal." He added casually, "Were you over at the Arlingtons' today?"

"No."

"You seem to be doing a lot of thinking about them."

"I was wondering why they don't have children of their own."

"I'm afraid you'll have to go on wondering," he said. "It's not the kind of question people like being asked."

"They could *buy* some of their own, couldn't they? They have lots of money. I heard Ellen say—"

"Your mother."

"—my mother say that if she had a fraction of Virginia's money, she'd join a health club and get rid of some of that fat Virginia carries around. Do you think Virginia's too fat? Howard doesn't. He likes to kiss her, he kisses her all the time when he's not mad at her. Boy, he was mad at her last night, he—"

"All right, that's enough," Dave said brusquely. "I don't want to hear any gossip about the Arlingtons from a nine-year-old."

"It's not gossip. It really happened. I wanted to tell you about the twenty dollars he—"

"I don't want to listen, is that clear? Their private life isn't my business or yours. Now you'd better settle down and go to sleep before your mother comes charging in here and shows you how mad someone can really get."

"I'm not afraid of her. She never *does* anything."

"Well, *I* might do something, kiddo, so watch it. No more drinks of water, no more tucking in, and no more gossip. Understand?"

"Yes."

"Lie down and I'll turn out your light."

"I haven't said my prayers."

"Oh, for heaven's sa— O.K. O.K., say your prayers."

She closed her eyes and folded her hands.

"Dear Jesus up in heaven,
Like a star so bright,
I thank you for the lovely day,
Please bless me for the night.

"Amen. I don't really think it's been such a lovely day," she added candidly. "But that's in the prayer so I have to say it. I hope God won't consider me a liar."

"I hope not," her father said. His hand moved toward the light switch but he didn't turn it off. Instead, "What was the matter with your day, Jessie?"

"Lots of things."

"Such as?"

"I was treated just like a child. Mike even went to the school with me and Mary Martha to make sure I didn't play on the jungle gym because of my hands. He acted real mean. I'm thinking of divorcing him."

"Then you'd better think again," Dave said. "You can't divorce a brother or any blood relative."

"Mary Martha did. She divorced Sheridan."

"That's silly."

"Well, she never ever sees him, so it's practically the same thing as divorce."

"Why doesn't she ever see him?"

Jessie looked carefully around the room as if she were checking for spies. "Can you keep a secret even from Ellen?"

Although he smiled, the question seemed to annoy him. "It may be difficult but I could try."

"Cross your heart."

"Consider it crossed."

"Sheridan went to live with another woman," Jessie whispered, "so he can't see Mary Martha ever again. Not ever in his whole life."

"That seems a little unreasonable to me."

"Oh no. She's a very bad woman, Mary Martha told me this morning. She looked up a certain word in the dictionary. It took her a long time because she didn't know how to spell it but she figured it out."

"She figured it out," Dave repeated. "Yes, that's Mary Martha all right."

"Naturally. She's the best speller in the school."

"And you, my little friend, are about to become the best gossip."

"Why is it gossip if I'm only telling the truth?"

"You don't know it's the truth, for one thing." He paused, rubbing the side of his neck as if the muscles there had stiffened and turned painful. "The woman involved might not be so bad. Certainly Mrs. Oakley's opinion of her is bound to be biased." He paused again. "How on earth I get dragged into discussions like this, I don't know. Now you settle down and close your eyes and start thinking about your own affairs for a change."

She lay back on the pillow but her eyes wouldn't close. They were fixed on Dave's face as if she were trying to memorize it. "If you and Ellen got divorced, would I ever see you again?"

"Of course you would," he said roughly and turned out the light. "I want no more nonsense out of you tonight, do you hear? And kindly refer to your mother as your mother. This first-name business is going to be nipped in the bud."

"I wish the morning would hurry up and come."

"Stop wishing and start sleeping and it will."

"I hate the night, I just hate it." She struck the side of the pillow with her fist. "Nothing to do but just lie here and sleep. When I'm sleeping I don't feel like me, myself."

"You're not supposed to feel like anything when you're sleeping."

"I mean, when I'm sleeping and wake up real suddenly, I don't feel like me. It's different with you. When you wake up and turn on the light, you see Ellen in the other bed and you think, that's Ellen over there so I must be Dave. You know right away you're Dave."

"Do I?" His voice was grave and he didn't rebuke her for using first names. "Suppose I woke up and Ellen wasn't in the other bed?"

"Then you'd know she was just in the kitchen getting a snack or making a cup of tea. Ellen's always around some place. I never worry about her."

"That sounds as if you worry about me, Jess. Do you?"

"I guess not."

"But you're not sure?"

She put one hand over her eyes to shade them from the hall light coming through the door. "Well, fathers are different. They can just move out, like Sheridan, and you never see them any more."

"That's nonsense," he said sharply. "The Oakley case is a very special one."

"Mary Martha says it always happens the same way."

"If it makes Mary Martha feel better to believe that, let her. But you don't have to." He leaned over and smoothed her hair back from her forehead. "I'll always be around, see? In fact, I'll be around for such a long time that you'll get mighty sick of me eventually."

"No, I won't."

"Wait until the young men start calling on you and you want the living room to entertain them in. You'll be wishing dear old Dad would take a one-way trip to the moon."

She let out a faint sound which he interpreted as a giggle.

"There now," he added. "You're feeling better, aren't you? No more worrying about me and no more thinking about the Oakleys. They're in a class by themselves."

"No, there are others."

"Now what do you mean by that, if anything? Or are you just trying to prolong the conversation by dreaming up—"

"*No*. I heard with my own ears."

"Heard what?"

"You might call it gossip if I tell you."

"I might. Try me."

She spoke in a whisper as if the Arlingtons might be listening at the window. "Howard is moving out, exactly the way Sheridan did. He told Virginia last night, right in front of me. 'I'm leaving,' he said, and then he stomped away."

"He didn't stomp very far," Dave said dryly. "I saw him outside helping the gardener this morning. Look, Jessie, married people often say things to each other that they don't mean. Your mother and I do it sometimes, although we shouldn't. So do you and Mike, for that matter. You get mad at each other or your feelings are hurt and you start making threats. You both know very well they won't be carried out."

"Howard *meant* it."

"Perhaps he did at the time. But he obviously changed his mind."

"He could change it back again, couldn't he?"

"It's possible." He stared down at her but he could tell nothing from her face. She had averted it from the shaft of light coming from the hall. "You sound almost as if you wanted Howard to leave, Jessie."

"I don't care."

"The Arlingtons have always been very nice to you, haven't they?"

"I guess so. Only it would be more fun if somebody else lived next door, a family with children of their own."

"What makes you think the Arlingtons are going to sell their house?"

"If Howard leaves, Virginia will have to because she'll be without money like Mrs. Oakley."

He stood up straight and crossed his arms on his chest in a gesture of suppressed anger. "I'm getting pretty damned tired of the Oakleys. Best friend or no best friend, I may have to insist that you see less of Mary Martha if you're going to let her situation dominate your thinking."

She sensed that his anger was directed not against the Oakleys, whom he didn't even know except for Mary Martha, but against the Arlingtons and perhaps even Ellen and himself. One night she had overheard him telling Ellen he wanted to move back to San Francisco and Ellen had appeared at breakfast the next morning with her eyes swollen. Nobody questioned her story about an eye allergy but nobody believed it either. For a whole week afterward Dave had acted very quiet and allowed Mike and Jessie to get away with being late for meals and fighting over television programs.

"Did you hear me, Jessie?"

"Yes. But I'm getting sleepy."

"Well, it's about time," Dave said and went out and shut the door very quickly as if he were afraid she might start getting unsleepy again.

Left alone, Jessie closed her eyes because there was nothing to see anyway. But her ears wouldn't close. She heard the Arlingtons arriving home in Howard's car—it was noisier than Virginia's—the barking of their dog Chap, the squawk of the garage door, the quick, impatient rhythm of Howard's step, the slow one of Virginia's that sounded as if she were being dragged some place she didn't want to go.

"The Brants' lights are still on," Virginia said, her voice slurred and softened by fog. "I think I'll drop over for a minute and say good night."

"No you won't," Howard said.

"Are you telling me I *can't*?"

"Try it and see."

"What would you do, Howard? Embarrass me in front of the Brants? That's old stuff, and I don't embarrass so easily any more. Or perhaps you'd try and bring Jessie into the act. It's funny you can't solve your problems without dragging in the neighbors. You're such a big, clever man. Can't you handle one wife all by yourself?"

"I could handle a wife. I can't handle an enemy."

Jessie tiptoed over to the window and looked out through the slats of the Venetian blind. The floodlight was turned on in the Arlingtons' yard and she could see Howard bending over unlocking the back door. Virginia stood behind him holding her purse high against her shoulder as if she intended to bring it down on the back of Howard's neck. For a moment everything seemed reversed to Jessie: Howard was the smaller, weaker of the two and Virginia was the powerful one, the boss. Then Howard stood up straight and things seemed normal again.

Howard opened the door and said, "Get inside," and Virginia walked in quickly, her head bowed.

The floodlight went off, leaving the yard to the fog and the darkness, and the only sound Jessie heard was the dripping of moisture among the loquat leaves.

14

THE FOLLOWING morning Ralph MacPherson rose, as usual, at 5:30. Since his wife had died he found it possible to fill his days, but the nights were unbearably lonely. He minimized them by getting up very early and going to bed when many lawyers were just finishing dinner. His matchmaking friends disapproved of this routine but Mac thrived on it. It was a healthy life.

Before breakfast he took his two dogs for a run, worked in the garden and put out food and water for the wild birds and mammals. After breakfast he read at the dining-room window, raising his head from time to time to watch the birds swooping down from the oaks and pines, the bush bunnies darting out of poison oak thickets at the bottom of the canyon and the chipmunks scampering up the lemon tree after the peanuts he'd placed in an empty coconut shell. Helping the wild creatures survive made him feel good, like a secret conspirator against the depredations and greed of man.

He reached his office at 8:30. Miss Edgeworth was already at her desk, looking fresh and crisp in a beige silk suit. Although he'd never accused her of it—Miss Edgeworth didn't encourage personal conversation—Mac sometimes had the notion that she was making a game out of beating him to the office, no matter how early he arrived, and that winning this game was important to her; it reinforced her low opinion of the practicality and efficiency of men.

There was always a note of triumph in her "Good morning, Mr. MacPherson."

"Good morning, Miss Edgeworth."

Her name was Alethea and she had worked for him long enough to be on a first-name basis. But it seemed to him that "Good morning, Alethea," was even more formal than "Good morning, Miss Edgeworth." He was afraid the day would come when he would accidentally call her what the girls in the office called her behind her back—Edgy.

He said, "Any calls for me?"

"Lieutenant Gallantyne wants you to contact him at police headquarters. It's about a car. Shall I get him for you?"

"No. I'll do it."

"Mrs. Oakley also—"

"That can wait."

He went into his office, closed the door and dialed police headquarters.

"Gallantyne? MacPherson here."

"Hope I didn't wake you up," Gallantyne said in a tone that hoped the opposite. "You lawyers nowadays keep bankers' hours."

"Do we. Any line on the green coupé?"

"One of the traffic boys spotted it an hour ago. It's standing in Jim Baker's used-car lot on lower Bojeta Street near the wharf."

"How long has it been there?"

"Garcia didn't ask any questions. He wasn't instructed to."

"I see. Well, thanks a lot, Gallantyne. I'll check it out myself."

He hung up, leaned back in the swivel chair and frowned at the ceiling. The fact that the green car had been sold made it more likely that Kate was right in claiming that the man behind the wheel had been Sheridan. Ordinarily Mac took her accusations against Sheridan with a grain of salt. A number of them were real, a number were fantasy, but most of them fell somewhere in the middle. If she walked across a room and stubbed her toe she would blame Sheridan even if he happened to be several hundred miles away. On the other hand, Sheridan had pulled some pretty wild stuff. It was quite possible that he'd tried to frighten her into coming to terms over the divorce and had ended up being frightened himself when she pursued him with her car.

Mac thought, as he had a hundred times in the past, that they were people caught like animals in a death grip. Neither was strong enough to win and neither would let go. The grip had continued for so long that it was now a way of life. It was not the sun that brightened Kate's mornings or the sea air that freshened Sheridan's. It was the anticipation, for each of them, of a victory over the other. They could no longer live without the excitement of battle. Mac remembered two lines from the children's poem about a gIngham dog and a calico cat who had disappeared simultaneously:

> "The truth about the cat and pup
> Is this: they ate each other up."

It hardly mattered now who took the first bite, Kate or Sheridan. The important thing was how to prevent the last bite, and so far Mac hadn't found any way of doing it. With the idea that perhaps someone else could, he had tried many times to persuade Kate to engage another lawyer. She always had the same answer: "*I couldn't possibly. No other lawyer would understand me.*" "*I don't understand you either, Kate.*" "*But you must, you've known me since I was a little girl.*"

Kate's attitude toward men was one of unrealistic expectation or unjustified contempt, with nothing in between. If they behaved perfectly and lived up to the standards she set, they were god figures. When they failed as gods, they were immediately demoted to devils. Mac had avoided demotion simply by refusing either to accept her standards or to take her expectations seriously.

Sheridan's demotion had been quick and thorough, and there was no possibility of a reversal. Sheridan was aware of this. One of the main reasons why he went on fighting her was his knowledge that no matter how generous a settlement he made or how many of her demands he satisfied, he could never regain his godship.

Mac was sorry for them both and sick of them both. He almost wished they would move away or finish the job of eating each other up. Mary Martha might be better off in a foster home.

He told Miss Edgeworth he'd be back in an hour, then he drove down to the lower end of Bojeta Street near the wharf. It was an area of the city that was doomed now that newcomers from land-locked areas were moving in and discovering the sea. Real estate speculators were greedily buying up ocean-front lots and razing the old buildings, the warehouses and fish-processing plants and shacks for Mexican agricultural workers. All of these had been built in what the natives considered the damp and undesirable part of town.

Jim Baker's used-car lot was jammed between a three-story motel under construction and a new restaurant and bar called the Sea Aira Club. A number of large signs announced bargains because Baker was about to lose his lease. Baker himself looked as if he'd already lost it. He was an elderly man with skin wrinkled like an old paper bag and a thick, husky voice that sounded as if he'd swallowed too many years of fog.

He came out of his oven-sized office, chewing something that might have been gum or what was left of his breakfast, or an undigested fiber of the past. "Can I do anything for you?"

"I'm interested in the green coupé at the rear of the lot."

"Interested in what way?" Baker said with a long, deliberate look at Mac's new Buick. "Something fishy about the deal?"

"Not that I'm aware of. My name is Ralph MacPherson, by the way. I'd like to know when the car was sold to you."

"Last night about six o'clock. I didn't handle the transaction—my son, Jamie, did—but I was in the office. I'd brought Jamie's dinner to him from home. We're open fourteen hours out of the twenty-four, and Jamie and I have to spell each other. He sold the young man a nice clean late-model Pontiac that had been pampered like a baby. I hated to see it go, frankly, but the young man seemed anxious and he had the cash. Sooo—" Baker shrugged and spread his hands.

"How young a man was he?"

"Oh, about Jamie's age, thirty-two, thirty-five, maybe."

Sheridan was thirty-four. "Do you remember his name?"

"I never knew it. It's in the book but I'm not sure I ought to look it up for you. I wouldn't want to cause him any trouble."

"I'm trying to prevent trouble, Mr. Baker. A client of mine—I'm a lawyer—is convinced that the husband she's divorcing has been using the green coupé to spy on her. I've been a family friend for many years and I'm simply trying to find out the truth one way or the other. Even a description of the man would be a big help."

Baker thought about it. "Well, he was nice, clean-cut,

athletic-looking. Tall, maybe six feet, with kind of sandy hair and a smile like he was apologizing for something. Would that be the husband?"

Sheridan was short and dark and wore glasses, but Mac said, "I'm not sure. Perhaps you'd better look up the name."

"I guess it'd be all right, being as it's just a divorce case and nothing criminal. I don't want to get caught up in anything criminal. It plays hell with business."

"To the best of my knowledge, nothing criminal is involved."

"O.K., wait here."

Baker went into the office and returned in a few minutes with a name and address written on an old envelope: Charles E. Gowen, 495 Miria Street.

"Is that the man?" Baker asked.

"I'm glad to say it's not." Mac returned the envelope. "This will be good news to my client."

"Women get funny ideas sometimes."

"Do they not."

If it was good news to Kate, she didn't show it. She met him at the front door, wearing a starched cotton dress and high-heeled shoes. Her face was carefully made up and her hair neat. It seemed to Mac that she was always dressed for company but company never came. He knew of no one besides himself who any longer got past the front door.

They went into the smaller of the two living rooms and she sat on the window seat while he told her what he'd found out. With her face in shadow and the sun at her back illuminating her long, fair hair, she looked scarcely older than Mary Martha. *She's only thirty*, Mac thought. *Her life has been broken and she's too brittle to bend down and pick up the pieces.*

"You can stop worrying about the green car," he told her. "Sheridan wasn't in it."

She didn't look as if she intended or wanted to stop worrying. "That hasn't been proved."

"The car was registered to Charles Gowen. He traded it in last night."

"Funny coincidence, don't you think?"

"Yes. But coincidences happen."

"A lot of them can be explained. I told you from the beginning that Sheridan was too crafty to use his own car. Obviously, he borrowed the green coupé from this man Gowen. The kind of people Sheridan runs around with nowadays exchange cars and wives and mistresses as freely as they exchange booze. Sheridan's moved away down in the world, farther than you think."

"I haven't time to go into that now, Kate. Let's stick to the point."

"Very well. He used Gowen's car to harass me. Then when I fought back, when I chased him, he got scared and told Gowen to sell it."

"Why? Why didn't he simply return it to Gowen and let the matter drop? Selling the car was what led me to Gowen."

"Sheridan's mind is usually, I might say always, befuddled by alcohol. He probably considered the gambit quite a cunning one."

"What about Gowen?"

"I don't know about Gowen," she said impatiently. "I've never heard of him before. But if he's typical of Sheridan's current friends, he'll do anything for a few dollars or a bottle of liquor. Don't forget, Sheridan has money to fling around. It makes him pretty popular, and I suppose powerful, in certain circles." She paused, running her hand along her left cheek. The cheek was bright red as though it had been slapped. "You asked, 'What about Gowen?' Well, why don't you find out?"

"I don't think there's enough to warrant an investigation."

She looked at him bitterly. "Not *enough*? I suppose you think I've imagined the whole thing?"

"No, Kate. But—"

"I didn't imagine that car parked outside my house, watching me. I didn't imagine an anonymous letter accusing me of neglecting my daughter. I didn't imagine that chase around town yesterday. Would an innocent man have fled like that?"

"Perhaps there are no innocent men," Mac said. "Or women."

"Oh, stop talking like a wise old philosopher. You're not old, and you're not very wise either."

"Granted."

"If you had been in that car, would you have run away like that? Answer me truthfully."

"You seem concerned only with the fact that he ran away. I'm more concerned with the fact that you chased him."

"I was upset. I'd just received that letter."

"Perhaps he had had a disturbing experience, too, and was reacting in an emotional rather than a logical manner."

She let out a sound of despair. "You won't *listen* to me. You won't take me seriously."

"I do. I am."

"No. You think I'm a fool. But I feel a terrible danger, Mac, I know it's all around me. Something awful is waiting to happen, it's just around the corner, waiting. It can't be seen or heard or touched, but it's as real as this house, that chair you're sitting on, the tree outside the window."

"And you think Sheridan is behind this danger?"

"He must be," she said simply. "I have no other enemies."

Mac thought what a sad epitaph it made for a marriage: *I have no other enemies.* "I'll try again to contact Sheridan. As you know, he hasn't been answering his telephone."

"Another sign of guilt."

"Or a sign that he's not there," Mac said dryly. "As for Charles Gowen, I can't go charging up to him with a lot of questions. I haven't the legal or moral right. All I can do is make a few discreet inquiries, find out where he lives and works, and what kind of person he is, whether he's likely to be one of Sheridan's cronies, and so on. I may as well tell you now, though: I don't expect anything to come of it. If Gowen had a guilty reason for not wanting the green coupé found, it seems to me he'd have taken a little more trouble in disposing of it. There are at least a hundred used-car dealers between here and Los Angeles, yet Gowen sold it right here, practically in the center of town."

"He may simply be stupid. Sheridan's friends nowadays are not exactly intellectual giants."

Mac's smile was more pained than amused. "One of the things a lawyer has to learn early in his career is not to assume that the other guy is stupid."

He rose. His whole body felt heavy, and stiff with tension. He always felt the same way when he was in Kate's house, that he couldn't move freely in any direction because he was under constant and judgmental surveillance. He could picture Sheridan trying, at first anyway, to conform and to please her, and making mistakes, more and more mistakes every day, until nothing was possible but mistakes.

He knew he was not being fair to her. To make amends for his thoughts, he crossed the room and leaned down and kissed her lightly on the top of her head. Her hair felt warm to his lips, and smelled faintly of soap.

She looked up at him, showing neither surprise nor displeasure, only a deep sorrow, as if the show of tenderness was too little and too late and she had forgotten how to respond. "Is that a courtesy you extend to all your clients?"

"No," he said, smiling. "Only the ones I like and have known since they were freckle-faced little brats."

"I never had freckles."

"Yes, you did. You were covered with them every summer. You probably still would be if you spent any time in the sun. Listen, Kate, I have an idea. Why don't you and Mary Martha come sailing with me one of these days?"

"No. No, thank you."

"Why not?"

"I wouldn't be very good company. I've forgotten how to enjoy myself."

"You could relearn if you wanted to. Perhaps you don't want to."

Her sorrow had crystallized into bitterness, making her eyes shine hard and bright like blue glass. "Oh, stop it, Mac. You're offering me a day of sailing the way you'd throw an old dog a bone. Well, I'm not that hungry. Besides, I can't afford to leave the house for a whole day."

"You can't afford not to."

"Sheridan might force his way in and steal something. He's done it before."

"Once."

"He might do it ag—"

"He was drunk," Mac said, "and all he took was a case of wine which belonged to him anyway."

"But he broke into the house."

"You refused to admit him. Isn't that correct?"

"Naturally I refused. He was abusive and profane, he threatened me, he—" She stopped and took a long, deep breath.

"You're always making excuses for him. Why? You're supposed to be on my side."

"I'm a man. I can't help seeing things from a man's point of view occasionally."

"Then perhaps," she said, rising, "I'd better hire a woman lawyer."

"That might be a good idea."

"You'd like to get rid of me, wouldn't you?"

"Let's put it this way: I'd like for us both to be rid of your problems. My going along with you and agreeing with everything you say and do is not a solution. It gets in the way of a solution. Your difficulties can't just be dumped in a box labeled Sheridan. You had them before Sheridan, and you're having them now, after Sheridan. I'd be doing you no favor by pretending otherwise."

"I was a happy, healthy, normal young woman when I married him."

"Is that how you remember yourself?"

"Yes."

"My memory of you is different," he said calmly. "You were moody, selfish, immature. You flunked out of college, you couldn't hold on to a job, and your relationship with your mother was strained. You tried to use marriage as a way out of all these difficulties. It put a very heavy burden on Sheridan, he wasn't strong enough to carry it. Can you see any truth in what I'm saying, Kate? Or are you just standing there thinking how unfair I'm being?"

They were face to face, but she wasn't looking at him. She was staring at a piece of the wall beyond his left shoulder, as if to deny his very presence. "I no longer expect fairness, from anyone."

"You're getting it from me, Kate."

"You call that fairness—that repulsive picture of me when I was nineteen?"

"It's not repulsive, or even particularly unusual. A great many girls in the same state go into marriage for the same reason."

"And what about Sheridan's reasons for getting married?" she said shrilly. "I suppose *they* were fine, *he* was mature, *he* got along great with *his* mother, *he* was a *big* success in the world—"

He took hold of her shoulders, lightly but firmly. "Keep your voice down."

"Why should I? Nobody will hear. Nobody can. The Oakleys were very exclusive, they liked privacy. They had to build the biggest house in town on the biggest lot because they didn't want to be bothered by neighbors. I could scream for help at the top of my lungs and not a soul would hear me. I've got enough privacy to be murdered in. Sheridan knows that. He's probably dreamed about it a hundred times: *wouldn't it be nice if someone came along and murdered Kate?* He may even have made or be making some plans of his own along that line, though I don't believe he'd have enough nerve to do it himself. He'd probably hire someone, the way he hired Gowen."

Her quick changes of mood and thought were beginning to exhaust Mac. Trying to keep track of them was like following a fast rat through a tortuous maze: Sheridan had borrowed the car from Gowen, who was one of his drunken friends—Sheridan had been at the wheel—Sheridan hadn't been at the wheel—Gowen wasn't his friend, he'd been hired—Gowen had driven the car himself. At this point Mac might have dismissed her whole story as fictional if she hadn't produced the real license number of a real car. The car existed, and so did Gowen. They were about the only facts Mac had to go on.

"Now you're suggesting," he said, "that Gowen was hired by Sheridan to intimidate you."

"Yes. He's probably some penniless bum that Sheridan met in a bar."

He didn't point out that penniless bums didn't pay cash for late-model sedans. "That should be easy enough to check."

"Would you, Mac? Will you?"

"I'll try my best."

"You're a dear, you really are."

She seemed to have forgotten her ill-feeling toward him. She looked excited and flushed as if she'd just come in from an hour of tennis in the sun and fresh air. But he knew the game wasn't tennis and the sun wasn't the same one that was shining in the window. What warmed her, brightened her, made her blood flow faster, was the thought of beating Sheridan.

15

CHARLIE HAD lain awake half the night making plans for the coming day, how he would spend his free hour at noon and where he'd go right after work. But before noon Louise phoned and invited him to meet her for lunch, and at five o'clock his boss Mr. Warner asked him to take a special delivery to the Forest Service ten miles up in the mountains. He couldn't refuse either of these requests without a good reason. His only reason would have seemed sinister to Louise and peculiar to Mr. Warner, but to Charlie himself it made sense: he had to find a little girl named Jessie to warn her not to play any more tricks on him because it was very naughty.

It was six o'clock before he arrived back at the city limits. He drove to the school grounds as fast as he could without taking any chances on being stopped by the police. The mere sight of a police car might have sent him running home to Ben, but he saw none.

At the rear of the school the parking lot, usually empty at this time, contained half a dozen cars. Charlie's first thought was that an accident had happened, Jessie had taken another fall and hurt herself very seriously and would be in the hospital for a long period; she would be safe in a hospital with all the doctors and nurses around; no stranger could reach her, a stranger would be stopped at the door and sent packing. Alternate waves of relief and despair passed over him like cold winds and hot winds coming from places he had never visited.

He drove around to the side of the school and saw that no accident had happened. A group of older boys were playing baseball and a few spectators were watching the game, including a man and woman who acted like parents. There were no young children in sight.

Charlie pulled over to the curb and turned off the ignition. He had no reason to stay there, with Jessie gone, but he had no reason to go home either. He had called Ben from work and told him that he was going on an errand for the boss and not to expect him home until seven or later. Though Ben had sounded suspicious at first, the words "special delivery" and

"Forest Service" seemed to convince him not only that Charlie was telling the truth but that Mr. Warner trusted him enough to send him on an important mission.

Charlie watched the game for a few minutes without interest or attention. Then one of the players he hadn't noticed before came up to bat. He was a boy about sixteen, tall and thin as a broom handle. Even from a distance his cockiness was evident in every movement he made. He tapped the dirt out of his cleats, took a called strike, swung wildly at the second pitch and connected with the third for a home run that cleared the fence. With a little bow to his teammates he began jogging nonchalantly around the bases. As he rounded second base Charlie recognized him as the boy he'd seen several times with Jessie. There was no doubt about his identity: he even looked like Jessie, dark, with thin features and bright, intense eyes.

Charlie sat motionless, hardly even breathing. This was Jessie's brother. The phrase kept running through his head like words on a cracked record: *Jessie's brother, Jessie's brother, Jessie's brother.* Jessie's brother would live in the same house as Jessie, so it was now simply a question of following him, cautiously so the boy wouldn't get suspicious, but keeping him in sight at all times until he stopped at a house and went inside. Charlie's throat felt so thick that he had to touch it with his fingers to make sure he was not swelling up like a balloon. *The house he goes into will be Jessie's house. If I'm lucky there'll be a name on the mailbox and I won't have to ask Louise to help me. I'll be on my own, I'll do it all by myself.*

The home run had broken up the game. There was a round of cheers and applause, with the man and woman deliberately abstaining. They walked onto the field and started talking to the pitcher, who turned his back on them. Players and spectators were dispersing, toward the parking lot and the side gate. Within five minutes the playground was empty of victors and vanquished alike, and a flock of blackbirds were walking around in the dust, nodding their heads as if they'd known right from the beginning how it would all end: someone would win, someone would lose. Charlie had done both.

The boys drifted off in twos and threes, wearing their uniforms but carrying their cleated shoes and bats and baseball mitts. Some of them passed Charlie's car, still discussing the game, but Jessie's brother and two of his teammates went out the gate on the other side of the school.

Charlie drove around the block, passed them, and parked in front of a white stucco house. As they went by the car Charlie pretended to be searching for something in the glove compartment in order to keep his face hidden from them. Their voices were so loud and clear that he had a moment's panic when he thought they were talking directly to him. They knew all about him, they were baiting him—

"—four o'clock in the morning, man, she'll have a fit," Jessie's brother said. "She's always grouching about me waking everybody up too early when I go fishing."

"We could all stay at my house overnight. My folks sleep like they're in a coma."

"Good thinking, man. I'll just check in at the house and check right out again."

"Maybe we should leave even earlier than four. We'll catch the fish before they've got their eyes open—"

The boys passed out of earshot. Cautiously, Charlie raised his head. The snatch of conversation he'd overheard worried him. He couldn't shake off the feeling that Jessie had told her brother about him and the brother had told his two friends and the three of them were taunting him: he was the fish who would be caught before he opened his eyes. They had found out from some secret source that he always woke up at four o'clock in the morning. Or was it five? Or six?

The ordinary facts of his existence were all crowding together in one part of his mind and trampling each other like frightened horses in the corner of a corral. Some died, some were mutilated beyond recognition, some emerged as strange, unidentifiable hybrids. Four and five and six were all squashed together; he didn't know what time it was now or what time he woke in the morning. The setting sun could have been a rising moon or the reflected glow of a fire or a lighted spaceship about to land. Jessie and her brother merged into a single figure, a half-grown boy-girl. Louise and Ben had faces but they wouldn't let him see; they kept their backs to him because he'd done something they didn't like. He couldn't remember what it was he'd done but it must have been terrible, their backs were rigid with disapproval and Louise had deliberately let her hair grow long and braided it around her head the way his mother used to. He hated it. He wanted to take a pair of scissors and cut it off. But the scissors wasn't in the kitchen drawer where it was always kept, and the drawer had lost its handle. It didn't even open like a drawer. It sprung out when he pushed a little silver button, like the glove compartment in a car.

Glove compartment. Car. He blinked his eyes painfully, as though he were emerging from a long and dreadful sleep. The sun was beginning to set. It was a quarter to seven by his watch. Three boys were walking up the street. He followed them.

Ralph MacPherson worked at the office until nearly seven o'clock. He felt too weary to contact Kate again but he could picture her waiting at the telephone for his call, getting herself more and more worked up, and he knew he couldn't postpone it any longer.

She answered before the second ring, in the guarded half-disguised voice she always used before he identified himself.

"Hello."

"Kate, this is Mac."

"Have you found anything out about Gowen?"

"Yes."

"Well? Was I right? He's some bum Sheridan picked up in a bar and hired to do his dirty work for him."

"I hardly think so," Mac said as patiently as he could. "I went over to Miria Street this afternoon and dropped in at a drugstore around the corner from Gowen's house. I pretended I'd lost the address. Not very subtle, perhaps, but it worked. The druggist knows the Gowen family, they've been his customers for years. It didn't take much to start him talking. Business was slow."

She made an impatient sound. "Well, what did he *say*?"

"Charles Gowen lives with his brother Ben. Ben manages a downtown cafeteria, Charles has a job with a paper company. They're both hard-working and clean-living. They don't smoke or drink, they pay their bills on time, they mind their own business. There's a neighborhood rumor that Charles is going to marry one of the local librarians, a very nice woman who is also hard-working and clean-living, etcetera, etcetera. In brief, Gowen's not our man."

"But he must be," she said incredulously. "He ran away from me. He acted guilty."

"It's possible that you scared the daylights out of him. He may not be used to strange women chasing him around town. Not many of us are. Make me a promise, will you, Kate?"

"What is it?"

"That you'll stop thinking about Sheridan's machinations just for tonight and get yourself a decent rest."

She didn't argue with him but she didn't promise either. She simply said she was sorry to have bothered him and hung up.

Parked half a block away, Charlie watched the three boys turn in the driveway of a house on Cielito Lane. Only a difference in planting and a ribbon of smoke rising from a backyard barbecue pit distinguished it from its neighbors, but to Charlie it was a very special house.

He drove past slowly. The mailbox had a name on it: David E. Brant.

16

IT WAS Howard Arlington's last night in the city for two weeks and he and Virginia had been invited to a farewell barbecue in the Brants' patio. They didn't want to go but neither of them indicated this in any way. Ever since their unpleasant scene the previous night, they'd been excessively polite to each other, to Dave and Ellen and Jessie, even to the gardener and the cleaning woman. It was as if they were trying to convince everyone, including themselves, that they were not the kind of people who staged domestic brawls—not they.

This new formal politeness affected not only their speech and actions but their style of dress. They both knew that Ellen and Dave would be in jeans and sneakers, but Howard had put on a dark business suit, white shirt and a tie, and Virginia wore a pink-flowered silk dress with a stole and matching high-heeled sandals. They looked as though they were going out to dinner and a symphony instead of to the neighbors' backyard for hamburgers and hi-fi, both of which would be overdone.

The hi-fi was already going and so was the fire. Smoke and violins drifted into the Arlingtons' kitchen window. Normally, Howard would have slammed the window shut and made some caustic remark about tract houses. Tonight he merely said, "Dave's sending out signals. What time does Ellen want us over there?"

Virginia wasn't sure Ellen wanted them over there at all but the invitation had been extended and accepted, there was nothing to be done about it. "Seven o'clock."

"It's nearly that now. Are you ready?"

"Yes."

"Perhaps we'd better leave Chap in the house."

"Yes, perhaps we'd better." Her voice gave no hint of the amused contempt she felt. The big retriever was already asleep on the davenport and it would have taken Howard a long time to wake him up, coax, bribe, push and pull him outside. Chap would not be mean about it, simply inert, immovable. Sometimes she wondered whether the dog had learned this passive resistance from her or whether she'd learned it from him. In any case the dog seemed just as aware as Virginia that the technique was successful. Inaction made opposing action futile; Howard was given no leverage to work with.

They went out the rear door, leaving a lamp in the living room turned on for Chap, and the kitchen light for themselves. At the bottom of the stairs, Howard suddenly stopped.

"I forgot a handkerchief. You go on without me, I'll join you in a minute."

"I'd rather wait, thank you. We were invited as a couple, let's go as a couple."

"A couple of what?" he said and went back in the house.

Virginia's face was flushed with anger, and the rush of blood made her sunburn, now in the peeling stage, begin to itch painfully. She no longer blamed the sun as the real culprit, she blamed Howard. It was a Howardburn and it itched just as painfully inside as it did outside. There was a difference, though: inside, it couldn't be scratched, no relief was possible.

When Howard returned, he was holding the handkerchief to his mouth as if to prove to her that he really needed it. His voice was muffled. "Virginia, listen."

"What is it?"

"You don't suppose the kid told her parents about that twenty dollars I gave her?"

"I talked to Ellen today, nothing was mentioned about it. By the way, Jessie has a name. I wish you'd stop referring to her as 'the kid.'"

"There's only one kid in our lives. It hardly seems necessary to name her."

"I thought we'd agreed to be civil to each other for the rest of your time at home. Why do you want to start something now? We've had a pleasant day, don't ruin it."

"You think it's been a pleasant day, do you?"

"As pleasant as possible," Virginia said.

"As pleasant as possible while I'm around, is that what you mean? In other words, you don't expect much in my company."

"Perhaps I can't afford to."

"Well, tomorrow I'll be back on the road. You and the kid can have a real ball."

"Let's stop this right now, Howard, before it goes too far. We're not saying anything new anyway. It's all been said."

"And done," Howard added. "It's all said and done. Amen." He looked down at her with a smile that was half-pained, half-mocking. "The problem is, what do people do and say after everything's said and done? Where do we go from here?"

"To the Brants' for a barbecue."

"And then?"

"I can't think any further than that now, Howard. I can't think."

She leaned against the side of the house, hugging her stole around her and staring out at the horizon. Where the sea and sky should have met, there was a gray impenetrable mass of fog between them. She dreaded the time when this mass would begin to move because nothing, no one, could stop it. The sea would disappear, then the beaches, the foothills, the mountains. Streets would be separated from streets, houses from houses, people from people. Everyone would be alone except the women with a baby growing inside them. She saw them nearly every day in stores, on corners, getting into cars. She hated and envied the soft, confident glow in their eyes as if they knew no fog could ever be thick enough to make them feel alone.

Howard was watching her. "Let me get you a sweater, Virginia."

"No, thank you."

"You look cold."

"It's just nerves."

They crossed the lawn and the concrete driveway and Ellen's experimental patch of dichondra with a Keep Off sign in the middle. From the beginning, neither the dichondra nor the sign had stood much of a chance. The sign had been bumped or kicked or blown to a 45° angle, and between the dichondra plants were the marks of bicycle tires and children's sneakers. The sneaker marks were about the size that Jessie would make, and Virginia had an impulse to lean down and push some dirt over them with her hand so that Jessie wouldn't be blamed. But she realized she couldn't do such a thing in front of Howard; it would only aggravate his jealousy of the child. So, instead, she stepped off the flagstone path into the dichondra patch, putting her feet deliberately over the imprints of Jessie's.

Howard opened his mouth to say something but he didn't have time. Mike was coming out of the gate of the patio fence, carrying some fishing tackle, a windbreaker, and three hamburgers still steaming from the grill.

Mike grinned at Howard and Virginia but there was impatience behind the grin, as though he suspected they would try to keep him there talking when he had other and more interesting things to do.

Howard said formally, "Good evening, Michael."

"Oh hi, Mr. Arlington, Mrs. Arlington. If you'll excuse me now, I've got some of the gang waiting for me. We're going fishing at two o'clock in the morning."

"That's pretty early even for fish, isn't it?"

"Maybe. I'm not sure whether fish sleep or not."

"I'm not, either. Well, good luck anyway."

"Thanks, Mr. Arlington. So long."

Virginia hadn't spoken. She was still standing in the dichondra patch looking vague and a little puzzled, as if she was wondering how she got there, and whether fish slept or not. Her high heels were sinking further and further into the ground like the roots of a tree seeking nourishment and moisture. For a moment she imagined that she was a tree, growing deeper, growing taller, putting out new leaves and blossoms, dropping fertile seeds into the earth.

Then Howard grasped her by the arm and it was an arm, not a branch, and it would never grow anything but old.

"For heaven's sake, what are you doing, Virginia?"

"Would you really like to know?"

"Yes."

She let out a brief, brittle laugh. "I'm pretending to be a tree."

"You're acting very peculiar tonight."

"I'm a very peculiar woman. Hadn't you noticed that before, Howard? Surely those sharp eyes of yours couldn't miss anything so obvious. I'm not like other women, I'm a freak. There's something missing in me."

"Take my hand and I'll help you out of there."

"I don't want to get out. I *like* being a tree."

"Stop playing games. Are you going to let me help you?"

"No."

"All right." Without further argument he picked her up and lifted her out of the dichondra patch. He had to exert all his strength to do it because she'd made herself limp—arms, legs, waist, neck. "O.K., tree, you've just been uprooted."

"Damn you. *Damn* you."

"That's better. Now suppose we go inside and you can start pretending you're a person." He opened the gate for her. "Coming?"

"I have no choice."

"You'd have even less choice if you were a tree."

They went into the patio and Howard closed the gate behind them with unnecessary force. The loud bang seemed to Virginia to be a warning, like a shot fired over her head.

"Come in, come in," Dave said. "Welcome to Brants' Beanery."

He was standing at the barbecue grill wearing an apron over his Bermuda shorts and T-shirt, and drinking a can of beer. Ellen sat barefoot at the redwood picnic table, slicing an onion. Neither of them looked as though they expected company or particularly wanted any.

Even though Virginia had known this was how it was going to be, she felt a stab of resentment, aggravated by a feeling, a hangover from her childhood, that she was the one who was wrong, and no matter how hard she tried, she always would be. She had spent an hour dressing and fixing her hair but Dave didn't even look at her. He had opened a can of beer for Howard and the two men were already deep in conversation, one on each side of the barbecue pit.

Virginia sat down beside Ellen. "Anything I can do to help?"

"It's all done, thanks. I wouldn't allow you to touch a thing in that dress, anyway. I'd feel so guilty if you spilled something on it. It's simply gorgeous."

Virginia had to take it as a compliment but she knew it wasn't. Ellen's voice was too objective, as though the dress had nothing to do with Virginia personally; a gorgeous dress was a gorgeous dress and it didn't matter who wore it or who owned it.

"It's not new," Virginia said. "I mean, it's just been lying around." For a whole week it had been lying around, waiting for an occasion. Now the occasion had arrived, hamburger and onions and baked beans in the next-door neighbors' backyard. She thought wildly and irrationally, *damn you, Howard. You didn't have to bring me here.*

"I thought perhaps it was the one you bought last week at Corwin's," Ellen said. "You told me about it."

"No, no, I took that back. I've had this dress since—well, since before you even moved here. That seems ages ago, doesn't it? I feel so close to you and Dave and Mike and, of course, Jessie." She glanced hastily in Howard's direction to make sure he hadn't overheard the name. He was still engrossed in his conversation with Dave. "Where is Jessie?"

"In the front room watching television."

"I'll go in and say hello. I have a little something for her."

"Virginia, you shouldn't, you'll—"

"It's nothing at all, really, just a piece of junk jewelry. I saw it in a store window this afternoon and I thought Jessie would like it."

"She's too young to wear jewelry."

"It's only a small ring with an imitation pearl. I had one exactly like it when I was six years old. I remember it so clearly. My hands grew too fast and it had to be filed off."

"It won't have to be filed off Jessie," Ellen said dryly. "She'll lose it within a week."

"Then you don't mind if I give it to her?"

"I suppose not."

Virginia rose and crossed the patio, moving with unaccustomed agility as though she wanted to get away before she could be called back.

Jessie was curled up in a corner of the davenport, her chin resting on her knees, her arms hugging her legs. Her eyes widened a little when she saw Virginia in the doorway but it was the only sign of recognition she gave.

"Hello, Jessie." Virginia went over to the television set. "May I turn this down a minute?"

"I—yes, I guess."

"I haven't seen you for two days."

"I've been busy," Jessie said, looking down at the floor as if she were talking to it and not Virginia. "My mother took me swimming this afternoon. To see if the salt water would hurt my hands."

"And did it?"

"Not much."

Virginia sat down on the davenport beside her. "You know what I did this afternoon? I went downtown shopping."

"Did you buy something?"

"Yes."

"Was Howard with you to pay for it?"

Virginia sucked in her breath as though the question had knocked it out of her. "No, no, he wasn't. I paid for it myself."

"But the other night he said—"

"The other night he said a lot of things he didn't mean. He was tired and out of sorts. We all get like that sometimes, don't we?"

"Yes, sometimes."

"When two people are married, they share whatever money comes into the house, whether it's the man's salary or the woman's or both. If I see something I want and can afford, I buy it. I don't need Howard's permission." *But it helps,* she added bitterly to herself. *He likes to play Big Daddy, spoiling his foolish and extravagant little girl, as long as the little girl is duly appreciative.*

Jessie was considering the subject, her mouth pursed, her green eyes narrowed. "I guess Howard gives you lots of money, doesn't he?"

"Yes."

"Every month my daddy gives money to the bank for this house. In nineteen more years we're going to own it. When is Howard going to own you?"

"Never," Virginia said sharply. Then, seeing Jessie's look of bewilderment, she added in a softer voice, "Look, dear, I'm not a house. Howard isn't making payments on me."

"Then why does he give you money?"

"He doesn't exactly give it to me. We share it. If Howard didn't have me to look after the house for him, he'd have to hire someone else to perform the same services for him."

"If he hires you, that makes him the boss."

"*No.* I mean—how on earth did we get off on this subject? You're too young to understand."

"Will I understand when I'm older?"

"Yes," Virginia said, thinking, *I hope you never grow up to understand what I do. I hope you die before your innocence is torn away from you.*

Jessie was frowning and biting the nail of her left thumb. "I certainly have tons of stuff to learn when I grow up. I wish I could start right now."

"No. No, don't wish that. Stay the way you are, Jessie. Just stay, stay like this, like tonight."

"I can't," Jessie said in a matter-of-fact voice. "Mary Martha would get way ahead of me. She's already taller and spells better. Mary Martha knows a lot."

"Some of them are things I couldn't bear having you know, Jessie."

"Why not? They're not bad, they don't hurt her."

"They hurt. I see her hurting."

Jessie shook her head. "No. If she was hurting, she'd cry. She's an awful sissy sometimes, she can't stand the sight of blood or anything oozing."

"Do you ever see me cry, Jessie?"

"No."

"Well, I hurt. I hurt terribly."

"Because of your sunburn?"

Virginia hesitated a moment, then she laughed, the harsh, brief laugh she heard herself utter so often lately. It was like the distress signal of an animal that couldn't communicate in words. "Yes, of course. Because of my sunburn. I must be as big a sissy as Mary Martha."

"She's not a sissy about everything."

"Perhaps I'm not either, about everything. I don't know. Not everything's been tried on me yet. Not quite."

Jessie would have liked to ask what had or had not been tried, but Virginia had averted her face and was changing the subject, not very subtly or completely, by opening her purse. It was a pink silk pouch that matched her dress. Inside the pouch was a tiny box wrapped in white paper and tied with a miniature golden rope.

Jessie saw the box and immediately and deliberately turned her head away. "Your shoes are dirty."

"I stepped off the path. Jessie, I have a little pres—"

"You're not supposed to step off the path."

Virginia's face was becoming white even where she was sunburned, on her cheekbones and the bridge of her nose, as though whiteness was not a draining away of blood but a true pigmentation that could conceal other colors. "Jessie, dear, you're not paying attention to what I'm telling you. I said, I have a little present for you. It's something I'm sure you'll love."

"No, I won't. I *won't* love it."

"But you don't even know what it is yet."

"I don't care."

"You don't want it, is that it?"

"No."

"You won't—won't even open it?"

"No."

"That's too bad," Virginia said slowly. "It's very pretty. I used to have one exactly like it when I was a little girl and I was so proud of it. It made me feel grown-up."

"I don't want to feel grown-up any more."

"Oh, you're quite right, of course. You're really very sensible. If I had it to do over again, I wouldn't choose to grow up either. To live the happy years and die young—"

"I'm going to watch television." Jessie's lower lip was quivering. She had to catch it with her teeth to hold it still so that Virginia wouldn't see how frightened she was. She wasn't sure what had caused the sudden, overwhelming fear but she realized that she had to fight it, with any weapon at all that she could find. "My—my mother doesn't like you."

Virginia didn't look surprised, her eyes were merely soft and full of sadness. "I'm sorry to hear that because I like her."

"You're not supposed to like someone who doesn't like you."

"Really? Well, I guess I do a lot of things I'm not supposed to. I step off paths and get my shoes dirty, I buy presents for little girls— Perhaps some day I'll learn better."

"I'm going to watch television," Jessie repeated stubbornly. "I want to see the ending of the program."

"Go ahead."

"You turned it off. When company turns it off my mother makes me keep it that way."

"Turn it on again. I'm not company."

Awkwardly, Jessie unfolded her arms and legs and went over to the television set. Her head felt heavy with what she didn't yet recognize as grief: something was lost, a time had passed, a loved one was gone. "You—you could watch the ending with me, Aunt Virginia."

"Perhaps I will. That's the nice part about television programs, they start with a beginning and end with an ending. Other things don't. You find yourself in the middle and you don't know how you got there or how to get out. It's like waking up in the middle of a water tank with steep, slippery sides. You just keep swimming around and around, there's no ladder to climb out, nobody flings you a rope, and you can't stop swimming because you have this animal urge to survive. . . . No television program is ever like that, is it, Jessie?"

"No, because it has to end to make room for another program. Nobody can be left just swimming around."

"How would it end on television, Jessie?"

Jessie hesitated only long enough to take a deep breath. "A dog would find you and start barking and attract a lot of people. They'd tie all their jackets and sweaters and things together to make a rope and they'd throw it to you and lift you out. Then you'd hug the dog and he'd lick your face."

"Thanks for nothing, dog," Virginia said and got up and went over to the doorway. "I'll see you later."

"Aren't you going to stay for the ending?"

"You've already told me the ending."

"That's not *this* program. *This* is about a horse and there's no water tank in it, just a creek like the one behind Mary Martha's house."

But Virginia had already gone. Jessie turned up the sound on the television set. Horses were thudding furiously across the desert as if they were trying to get away from the loud music that pursued them. Above the horses' hoofs and trumpets, Jessie could hear Virginia laughing out on the patio. She sounded very gay.

17

THE PAIN BEGAN, as it usually did, when Charlie was a couple of blocks away from his house. It started in his left shoulder and every heartbeat pushed it along, down his arm and up his neck into his head until he was on fire. Alone in his room with no one to bother him, he could endure the pain and even derive some satisfaction from not taking anything to relieve it. But tonight Ben was waiting for him. Questions would be asked—some trivial, some innocent, some loaded—and answers to them would be expected. It would be at least an hour before he was allowed to go into his room and be by himself to plan what he would say to Jessie.

He stopped for a red light and was reaching into the glove compartment for the bottle of aspirin he kept there when he remembered that he wasn't driving the green coupé any more. There was no bottle of aspirin in this one, only a map of Los Angeles, unfolded and torn, as if someone had crammed it into the glove compartment in a fit of impatience.

The light turned green. He drove past the house. Ben's car was parked in the driveway, looking, to Charlie, exactly like its owner, not new any more but sturdy and clean and well taken care of, with no secret trouble in the engine.

The drug store was around the corner, one block down. There was no one in the store but Mr. Forster, the owner, who was behind the prescription counter reading the evening newspaper.

"Well, it's you, Charlie." Mr. Forster took off his spectacles and tucked them in the pocket of his white jacket. "Long time no see. How are you?"

"Not so good, Mr. Forster."

"Yes, I see that. Yes, indeed." Mr. Forster was the chief diagnostician of the neighborhood, even for people who had their own doctors. Out of respect for his position his customers always addressed him as Mr. Forster and so did his wife. He took his responsibilities very seriously, subscribing to the A.M.A.

journal and *Lancet*, and reading with great care the advertising material that accompanied each new drug sample.

"A bit feverish, aren't you, Charlie?"

"I don't think so. I have a headache. I'd like some aspirin."

"Any nausea or vomiting?"

"No."

"What about your eyes? Are they all right?"

"Yes."

"Had your blood pressure checked recently?"

"No. I just want some—"

"It sounds like a vascular headache to me," Forster said, nodding wisely. "Maybe you should try one of the new reserpine compounds. By the way, did the man find your house?"

"What—what man?"

"Oh, he was in here a while ago, nice-looking gray-haired fellow around fifty. Said he'd lost your address."

"I haven't been home yet tonight."

"Well, he may be there right now, waiting for you."

"Not for me," Charlie said anxiously. "For Ben. People come to the house to see Ben, not me."

"Isn't your name Charles Gowen?"

"You know it is, Mr. Forster."

"Well, Charles Gowen is who he wanted to see." Forster took a bottle of aspirin off a shelf. "Shall I put this in a bag for you?"

"No. No, I'll take one right away." Charlie reached for the bottle. His hands were shaking, a fact that didn't escape Forster's attention.

"Yes, sir, if I were you, Charlie, I'd have my blood pressure checked. A niece of mine had a vascular headache and reserpine fixed her up just like magic. She's a different woman."

Charlie unscrewed the cap of the bottle, removed the cotton plug and put two aspirins in his mouth. The strong bitter taste spread from his tongue all the way to his ears and his forehead. His eyes began to water so that Mr. Forster's face looked distorted, like a face in a fun-house mirror.

"Let me get you a glass of milk," Forster said kindly. "You should always take a little milk with aspirin, it neutralizes the stomach acids."

"No, thank you."

"I insist."

Forster went into the back room and came out carrying a paper cup full of milk. He stood and watched Charlie drink it as though he were watching a stomach fighting a winning battle over its acids.

"I can understand your being nervous," Forster said, "at this stage of the game."

"What game?"

"The marriage game, of course. The word's gotten out how you're engaged to a nice little woman that works in the library. Marriage is a great thing for a man, believe me. You might have a few qualms about it now but in a few years you'll be glad you took the big step. A man stays single just so long, then people begin to talk." Forster took the empty paper cup from Charlie's hand and squeezed it into a ball. "Mind if I say something personal to you, Charlie?"

Charlie didn't speak. The milk seemed to have clotted in his throat like blood.

Forster mistook silence for assent. "That old trouble of yours, you mustn't let it interfere with your happiness. It's all over and done with, people have forgotten it. Why, it was so long ago you were hardly more than a boy. Now you're living a clean, decent life, you're just as good as the next man and don't you be thinking otherwise."

Please stop, Charlie thought. *Please stop him, God, somebody, anybody, make him be quiet. It's worse than listening to Ben. They don't know, neither of them, they don't know—*

"Maybe it's not in such good taste, dragging it up like this, but I want you to understand how I feel. You're going to do fine, Charlie. You deserve a little happiness. Living with a brother is all right when it's necessary, but what the heck, a man needs a wife and family of his own. When's the big day?"

"I don't know. Louise—it's her decision."

"Don't leave all the deciding to the lady, Charlie. They like to be told once in a while, makes them feel feminine. You want me to charge the aspirin?"

"Yes."

"Right. Well, all the best to you and the little lady, Charlie."

"Thank you, Mr. Forster."

"And bear in mind what I said. The town's getting so filled up with strangers that only a few old-timers like myself know you ever had any trouble. You just forget it, Charlie. It's water under the bridge, it's spilled milk. You ever tried to follow a drop of water down to the sea? Or pour spilled milk back into the bottle?"

"No. I—"

"Can't be done. Put that whole nasty business out of your head, Charlie. It's a dead horse, bury it."

"Yes. Good-bye, Mr. Forster."

Charlie began moving toward the door but Forster moved right along beside him. He seemed reluctant to let Charlie go, as if Charlie was a link with the past, which for all its cruelties was kinder than this day of strangers and freeways and super drugstores in every shopping center.

"I've got to go now, Mr. Forster. Ben's waiting for me."

"A good man, that Ben. He was a tower of strength to you in your time of need, always remember that, Charlie. He's probably quite proud of you now, eh? Considering how you've changed and everything?"

Charlie was staring down at the door handle as though he wished it would turn of its own accord and the door would open and he could escape. *Ben's not proud of me. I haven't changed. The horse isn't dead, the milk is still spilling, the same drop of water keeps passing under the bridge.*

Forster opened the door and the old-fashioned bell at the top tinkled its cheerful warning. "Well, it's been nice talking to you, Charlie. Come in again soon for another little chat. And say hello to Ben for me."

"Yes."

"By the way, that man who was in here asking for your address, he had an official bearing like he was used to ordering people around. But don't worry, Charlie. I didn't tell him a thing about that old trouble of yours. I figured it was none of his business if he wasn't an official, and if he was he'd know about it anyway. It's all on the record."

The same drop of water was passing under the bridge, only it was dirtier this time, it smelled worse, it carried more germs. Charlie leaned forward as if he meant to scoop it up with his hand and throw it away, so far away it would disintegrate, and all the dirt and smell and germs with it. But Mr. Forster was watching him, and though his smile was benevolent his eyes were wary. *You can never tell what these nuts are going to do, no matter how hard you try to be kind to them.*

"You," Charlie said, "you look like Ben, Mr. Forster."

"What?"

"You look exactly like Ben. It shows up real clear to me."

"It does, eh? You'd better go home and get some sleep. You're tired."

He was tired but he couldn't go home. The man might be there waiting for him, ready to ask him questions. He had done nothing wrong, yet he knew he wouldn't be believed. He couldn't say it with absolute conviction, the way Louise had the night she found him on Jacaranda Road: "*Nothing's happened, Charlie . . . You haven't harmed anyone. The Oakley girl is safe at home, and I believe that even if I hadn't found you when I did, she'd still be safe at home.*"

The Oakley girl was safe at home. So was the Brant girl, Jessie. Or was she? He hadn't seen her at the playground, or outside her house when he drove past. Perhaps something had happened to her and that was why the man wanted to question him. He might even have to take a lie-detector test. He had heard once that real guilt and feelings of guilt showed up almost the same on a lie-detector test. If he were asked whether he knew Jessie Brant he would say no because this was the truth. But his heart would leap, his blood pressure would rise, his voice would choke up, he would start sweating, and all these things would be recorded on the chart and brand him a liar. Even Ben would think he was lying. Only Louise would believe him, only Louise. He felt a terrible need to hear her say: "*Nothing happened, Charlie. The Oakley girl is safe at home, and the Brant girl and the other little girls, all safe at home, all snug in their beds, nothing to fear from you, Charlie. I love you, Charlie. . . .*"

He left his car in the parking lot behind the library. The lot was almost filled, mainly with cars bearing high school and city college stickers. The back door of the library was marked Employees Only, but he used it anyway because it was the shortest way to Louise.

He found himself in the filing and catalogue room, lined with steel drawers and smelling of floor wax. An old man with a push broom looked at him curiously but offered no challenge; libraries were for everybody.

"Could you," Charlie said and stopped because his voice sounded peculiar. He cleared his throat, swallowing the last of the clotted milk. "Could you tell me if Miss Lang is here?"

"I don't know one from the other," the old man answered with a shrug. "I only been on the job three nights now."

Nodding his thanks, Charlie walked the length of the room and through a corridor with an open door at the end of it. From here he could see Louise's desk behind the reference counter but Louise wasn't there. A woman about thirty was sitting in her chair. She looked familiar to Charlie though he wasn't sure he'd ever met her.

A sixth sense seemed to warn her she was being watched. She turned her head and spotted Charlie standing in the doorway. She got up immediately, as though she was expecting his arrival and had planned a welcome for him. She came toward him, smiling.

"Mr. Gowen?"

"Yes, I—yes."

"I'm Betty Albert. Louise introduced us a couple of weeks ago. Are you looking for her?"

"Yes. I thought she was working tonight."

"She was," Miss Albert said in a confidential whisper, "but some teen-agers gave her a bad time. Oh, she handled it beautifully, it was as quiet as church within ten minutes, but the strain upset her. She went home. The public doesn't realize yet that we have quite a policing problem in the library, especially on Friday nights when school's not in session and the kids don't have a football or basketball game to go to. I claim the schools should be open all year, it would give the little darlings something to do. Bored teen-agers running around loose act worse than maniacs, don't you think? . . . Mr. Gowen, wait. You're really not supposed to use that back exit. It's just for employees. Mr. Gowen—?"

Miss Albert returned to her desk, her step light, her eyes dreamy. *He must be madly in love with her*, she thought as she lowered herself into the chair, lifting her skirt a few inches at the back to prevent seat-sag. *Why, the instant he heard she'd had a bad time and gone home, he looked sick with worry, then off he tore out the wrong exit. He's probably speeding to her side right now. Louise doesn't realize how lucky she is to have a man speeding to her side. When there isn't a thing the matter with her except nerves.*

Miss Albert sat for a while, her emotions swinging between wonder and envy. When the pendulum stopped, she found herself thinking in a more practiced and realistic manner. Louise was her superior in the library, it wouldn't hurt to do her a favor and warn her that Charlie was coming. It would give her a chance to pretty up, she'd looked awfully ratty when she left.

Louise's number was listed on a staff card beside the telephone. Miss Albert dialed, humming softly as if inspired by the sound of the dial tone.

Louise herself answered. "Yes?"

"This is Betty Albert."

"Oh. Is anything wrong?"

"No. Mr. Gowen was just here asking for you. When I told him you'd gone home he rushed right out. He should be there any minute. I thought—"

"Did he tell you he was coming here?"

"Why, no. But—well, it seemed obvious from the way he tore out and used the wrong exit and everything. I thought I'd tell you so you'd have a chance to pretty up before he arrived."

"Thanks, I'll do that," Louise said. "Good night, Miss Albert."

She hung up and went back down the hall toward her bedroom. Through the open door of the kitchen she could see her parents, her father watching something boiling on the stove, her mother getting the company dinnerware out of the top cupboard. She remembered that it was her father's birthday, and to celebrate the occasion he was preparing a special potato dish his grandmother used to cook for him in Germany when he was a boy. The thought of having to eat and pretend to enjoy the thick gray gluey balls nauseated Louise.

She spoke from the doorway. "I'm going out for a drive, if you don't mind."

Her father turned around, scowling. “But I do mind. The *kloessen* are almost done and I’ve gone to a great deal of trouble over them.”

“Yes, I know.”

“You know but you don’t care. Well, that’s typical of the younger generation, lots of knowledge, no appreciation. When my grandmother was making *kloessen* you couldn’t have dragged any of us away from the house with wild horses. I don’t understand you, Louise. One minute you’re lying down half-dead and the next minute you’re going out. You’re not consistent this last while.”

“I guess I’m not.”

“It’s that man who’s responsible. He’s no good for you. He’s blinded you to—”

“A lot of blind people do very well,” Louise said. “With luck, so will I.”

“So now the man isn’t enough. You’re demanding luck too, are you?”

“No, I’m praying for it.”

“Well, I hope you get it.”

“Then *sound* as if you hope it, will you? Just for once, *sound* as if you believed in me, as if you wanted me to have a life of my own, independent of you, unprotected by you.”

“Oh, do hush up, both of you,” Mrs. Lang said, brushing some dust off a plate with her apron. “It’s hot in here. Open another window, will you, Joe? And Louise, don’t forget to take a coat. You never can tell when the fog might come in.”

The sun had gone down and stars were bursting out all over the sky like fireworks that would burn themselves out by morning and begin their infinite fall.

Charlie leaned against the side of the building. Of all the things Miss Albert had said to him, only one had registered in his mind: Louise had gone home. When he desperately needed her reassurance, she had gone where he was afraid to follow.

Home was where people went who had never done anything wrong—like Ben and Louise. For the others—the ones like him, Charlie—there wasn’t any room, no matter how large the world. There wasn't any time to rest, no matter how long the night. Whatever their course of action or inaction they were always wrong. If they called out for help they were cowards, if they didn't call they were fools. If they stayed in one place they were loitering; if they moved they were running away. "*We, the jury, find the defendant guilty of everything and sentence him to a life of nothing*—" And all the people in the crowded courtroom, all the people in the world, broke into applause.

He knew it hadn't really occurred like that. No jury would say such a thing even though it might be what they meant. Besides, there'd been no jury, only a judge who kept leaning his head first on one hand and then on the other, as if it were too heavy for his neck. And the courtroom wasn't crowded. There were just the lawyers and bailiffs and reporter and Ben and his mother sitting near Charlie, and on the other side of the room, the child's parents, who didn't even glance at him. The girl herself wasn't brought in. Charlie never saw her again. When it was all over, Charlie rode in the back of the Sheriff's car to the hospital with two other men, and Ben took his savings and his mother's, and borrowed money from the bank, and gave it to the girl's parents, who'd sued for damages. They left town and Charlie never saw them again either.

That time it had happened. Even Louise couldn't have said it didn't, that it wasn't real, that the girl was at home safe in her bed. Perhaps she would have said it anyway, knowing it wasn't true. He couldn't afford to believe her ever again. He had to find out for himself what was real and what wasn't and which children were safe at home in their beds.

18

Ellen had expected a dull evening because the Arlingtons were usually tense and quiet the night before Howard was to leave on another business trip. She was pleasantly surprised by Virginia's show of vivacity and by the sudden interest Howard was taking in Jessie.

While the others ate at the redwood picnic table, Howard sat with Jessie on the lawn swing, asking her all about school and what she was doing during the holidays. Jessie, who'd been taught to answer adults' questions but not to speak with her mouth full, compromised by keeping her answers as brief as possible. School was O.K. Natural history was best. During the holidays she played. With Mary Martha. On the jungle gym. Also climbing trees. Sometimes they went swimming.

"Oh, come now," Howard said. "Aren't you forgetting Aunt Virginia? You visit her every day, don't you?"

"I guess."

"Do you like to visit her?"

"Yes."

"You go downtown shopping with her and to the movies and things like that, eh?"

"Not often."

"Once or twice a week?"

"Maybe."

Howard took a bite of hamburger and chewed it as if his teeth hurt. Then he put his plate down on the grass, shoving it almost out of sight under the swing. "Does anyone else go along on these excursions of yours?"

"No."

"Just the two of you, eh?"

Jessie nodded uncomfortably. She didn't know why Howard was asking so many questions. They made her feel peculiar, as if she and Virginia had been doing wrong things.

"It's nice of you to keep Virginia company," Howard said pleasantly. "She's a very lonely woman. You eat quite a few meals with her, don't you?"

"Not so many."

"When you've finished eating, what then? She reads to you, perhaps, or tells you stories?"

"Yes."

"She tells me some, too. Do you believe her stories?"

"Yes, unless they're fairy tales."

"How can you be sure when they're fairy tales?"

"They begin 'Once upon a time.'"

"Always?"

"They have to. It's a rule."

"Is it now," Howard said with a dry little laugh. "I'll remember that. The ones that begin 'Once upon a time,' I won't believe. Do I have to believe all the others?"

"You should. Otherwise—"

"Otherwise, she'd be telling fibs, eh?"

"I don't think so. Grownups aren't supposed to tell fibs."

"Some of them do, though. It's as natural to them as breathing."

Although Virginia was talking to Dave and Ellen and hadn't even glanced in Howard's direction, she seemed to be aware of trouble. She rose and came toward the swing, her stole trailing behind her like some pink wisp of the past.

"Have you finished eating, Jessie?"

"Yes."

"It's getting close to your bedtime, isn't it?"

"The kid has parents," Howard said. "Let them tell her when to go to bed. It's none of your business."

"I don't *have* to be told," Jessie said with dignity, and slid off the swing, glad for once to be getting away from the company of adults. She wished Michael were at home so she could ask him why Howard and Virginia were acting so peculiar lately.

"Well," Howard said, "I suppose now the party's over for you, Virginia. Not much use sticking around after the kid goes to bed. Shall we leave?"

"I'm warning you. Don't make a scene or you'll regret it."

"Your threats are as empty as your promises. Try another approach."

"Such as begging? You'd like that, wouldn't you? The only time you ever feel good any more is when I come crawling to you for something. Well, you're going to have to think of other ways to feel good because from now on I'm not crawling and I'm not begging."

"Three days," Howard said bitterly, "I've been home three days and not for one minute have I felt welcome. I'm just a nuisance who appears every two or three weeks and disrupts your real life. The hell of it is that I don't understand what your real life is, so I can't try to fit into it or go along with it. I can only fight it because it doesn't include me. I want, I need, a place in it. I used to have one. What went wrong, Virginia?"

Dave and Ellen exchanged embarrassed glances like two characters in a play who found themselves on stage at the wrong time. Then Ellen put some dishes on a tray and started toward the house and after a second's hesitation Dave followed her. Their leaving made no more difference to the Arlingtons than their presence had.

"What's the matter, Virginia? If it's my job, I can change it. If it's the fact that we have no family, we can change that, too."

"No," she said sharply. "I no longer want a family."

"Why not? You've wept for one often enough."

"We no longer have anything to offer a child." She stared out beyond the patio walls to the horizon. The wall of fog had begun to expand. Pretty soon the city would disappear, streets would be separated from streets and people from people and everyone would be alone. "Yes, Howard, I wept, I wept buckets. I was young then. I didn't realize how cruel it would be to pass along such an ugly thing as life. Poor Jessie."

He frowned. "Why? Why poor Jessie?"

"She's only nine, she's still full of innocence and high hopes and dreams. She will lose her innocence and high hopes and dreams; she will lose them all. By the time she's my age she will have wished a thousand times that she were dead."

Twice Louise covered the entire length of Jacaranda Road, driving in second gear, looking at every parked car and every person walking along the street or waiting at bus stops. There was no sign of Charlie or his car, and the Oakley house at 319 was dark as if no one lived in it any more. She was encouraged by the dark house. If anything had happened, there would be light and noise and excitement. *Nothing's happened. Nothing whatever—*

She drove to Miria Street. Ben let her in the front door. "Hello, Louise. I thought you were working tonight."

"I was."

"Charlie's not here but come in anyway. I'm making a fresh pot of coffee. Would you like some?"

"Please." She followed him down the hall to the kitchen. He walked slowly as though his back ached, and for the first time she thought of him not as one of the Gowen brothers but as a middle-aged man.

She accepted the cup of coffee he poured her and sat down at the table. "Are you tired, Ben?"

"A little. It was Dollar Day in most of the stores downtown. What the ladies saved on hats and dresses they came in and spent on food." He sat down opposite her. "I think I've found the right place."

"Place?"

"The apartment I wanted down near the breakwater. It's furnished, so I wouldn't have to take a thing out of the house here, and the landlord told me I could keep a dog if it wasn't too big. I'll sign the lease as soon as you and Charlie name the wedding day. . . . You don't look very pleased. What's the matter?"

"I was trying to imagine this house without you in it. It's very—difficult."

"This house has seen enough of me. And vice versa."

"Charlie would like you to stay with us."

"He'd soon get over that idea. He's nervous, that's all. He's like a kid, dreading any change even if it's a good one."

"Maybe I'm a little like that, too."

"Come off it, Louise. Why, I'll bet after you've been married a few weeks you'll meet me on the street and think, *that guy looks familiar, I must have seen him before some place.*"

"That could never happen."

"A lot of things are going to happen. Good things, I mean, the kind you and Charlie deserve."

She took a sip of coffee. It was so strong and bitter she could hardly swallow it. "Did—did Charlie come home after work?"

"No. But don't worry about it. He had to go on an errand for the boss. It was an important errand, too—making a delivery to the Forest Service up the mountain. It shows the boss is beginning to trust him with bigger things. Charlie told me on the phone not to expect him before seven o'clock."

"It's nearly nine."

"He may have had some trouble with his car. I've had trouble up there myself on hot days. The engine started to boil—"

"He was at the library about an hour ago."

"There's more to this, I suppose?"

"Yes."

Ben's face didn't change expression but suddenly he pushed his chair away from the table with such violence that his coffee cup fell into the saucer. Brown fluid oozed across the green plastic cloth like a muddy stream through a meadow. "Well, don't bother telling me. I won't listen. I want one night, just this one night, to think about my own future, maybe even dream a little. Or don't I deserve a dream because I happen to be Charlie's older brother?"

"I'm sorry, Ben. I guess I shouldn't have come running to you." She rose, pulling her coat tightly around her body as if the room had turned cold. "I must learn to deal with situations like this on my own. Don't come with me, Ben. I can let myself out."

"Situations like what?"

"You don't want to hear."

"No, but you'd better tell me."

"I think I can handle it myself."

"By crying?"

"I'm not crying. My eyes always water when—when I'm under a strain. There's a certain nerve that runs from the back of the ear to the tear ducts and—"

"We'll discuss the structure of the nervous system some other time. Where is Charlie?"

"I don't know," she said, wiping her eyes with the back of one hand. "I've been looking for him ever since Miss Albert called to tell me he'd been at the library."

"You've been looking where?"

"Up and down Jacaranda Road."

"Why Jacaranda Road? You must have had a reason. What is it?"

She took a step back, as if dodging a blow.

"You've got to answer me, Louise."

"Yes. I'm trying—trying to say it in the right way."

"If it's a wrong thing, there's no right way to say it."

"I'm not sure that it's wrong. There may be nothing to it except in Charlie's imagination and now mine. I mean, he gets so full of worry that I start to worry, too."

"What about?"

She hesitated for a long time, then she spoke quickly, slurring her words as if to make them less real. "There's a child living at 319 Jacaranda Road, a little girl named Mary Martha Oakley. Charlie swears he's never even talked to her and I believe him, but he's afraid. So am I. I think he's been watching her and—well, fantasying about her. I know this isn't good because a fantasy that gets out of control can become a fact."

"How long have you known about the girl?"

"Two days."

"And you didn't level with me."

"Charlie asked me not to."

"But you're leveling now, in spite of that. Why?"

"I want you to tell me how it was the—the other time. I've got to know all about it, how he acted beforehand, if he was quiet or moody or restless, if he stayed away from the house on nights like this without telling anyone. Did he talk about the girl a lot, or didn't he mention her? How old was she? What did she look like? How did Charlie meet her?"

Ben went over to the sink and tore off a couple of sheets of paper toweling. Then he wiped the coffee off the table, slowly and methodically. His face was blank, as if he hadn't heard a word she'd said.

"Aren't you listening, Ben?"

"Yes. But I won't do what you're asking me to. It would serve no purpose."

"It might. Everybody has a pattern, Ben. Even strange and difficult people have one if you can find it. Suppose I learned Charlie's pattern so I could be alert to the danger signals—"

"It happened a long time ago. I don't remember the details, the fine points." Ben threw the used towel in the wastebasket and sat down again, his hands pressed out flat on the table in front of him, palms down. "If there were danger signals, I didn't see them. Charlie was just a nice, quiet young man, easy to have around, never asking much or getting much. He'd had two years of college. The first year he did well; the second, he had trouble concentrating—my mother suspected a love affair but it turned out she was wrong. He didn't go back for the third year because my father died. At least that was the accepted reason. After that he went to work. He held a succession of unimportant jobs. One of them was at a veterinary hospital and boarding kennels on Quila Street near the railroad tracks. Every day the girl walked along the tracks on her way to and from school. Charlie used to chase her away because he was afraid she'd get hurt by a train or by one of the winos who hung around the area. That's how it began, with Charlie trying to protect her."

Louise listened, remembering the reason Charlie had given her for wanting to find out the name of the people who lived at 319 Jacaranda Road: "*I must tell those people they've got to take better care of their little dog unless they want it to be killed by a car or something.*"

She said, "How old was the girl?"

"Ten. But she looked younger because she was so small and skinny."

"Was she pretty?"

"No."

"What color was her hair, and was it short or long?"

"Dark and short, I think. I only saw her once, but I remember one of her front teeth was chipped from a fall."

"Though it may seem like a terrible thing to say, Ben, all this sounds very promising."

"Promising?"

"Yes. You see, I've met Mary Martha. She's a plump, pretty child with a long blond ponytail, quite mature-looking for her age. She's not a bit like that other girl. Isn't that a good sign? She doesn't fit the pattern at all, Ben." Louise's pale cheeks had taken on a flush of excitement. "Now tell me about Charlie, how he acted beforehand, everything you can think of."

"I saw no difference in him," Ben said heavily. "But then I wasn't looking very hard, I'd just gotten married to Ann. Charlie could have grown another head and I might not have noticed."

"You'd just gotten married," Louise repeated. "Now Charlie's about to get married. Is this just a coincidence or is it part of the pattern?"

"Stop thinking about patterns, Louise. A whole battery of experts tried to figure out Charlie's and got nowhere."

"Then it's my turn to try. Where did you live after the wedding?"

"Here in this house. It was only supposed to be a temporary arrangement, we were going to buy a place of our own. Then Charlie was arrested and everything blew up in our faces. I didn't have enough money left to buy a tent, but by that time it didn't matter because I had no wife either."

"And now Charlie and I will be living in this house, too." Louise was looking around the room as if she were seeing it for the first time as a place she would have to call her home. "You still don't notice any pattern, Ben?"

"What if I say yes? What do I do then?"

"You mean, what do *we* do? I'm in it with you this time."

"Don't say this time. There isn't going to be a this time. It happened once, and it's not going to happen again, by God, if I have to keep him in sight twenty-four hours a day, if I have to handcuff him to me."

"That won't be much of a life for Charlie. He'd be better off dead."

"Do you suppose I haven't thought of that?" he said roughly. "A hundred times, five hundred, I've looked at him and seen him suffering, and I've thought, this is my kid brother. I love him, I'd cut off an arm for him, but maybe the best thing I could do for him is to end it all."

"You mean, kill him."

"Yes, kill him. And don't look at me with such horror. You may be thinking the same thing yourself before long."

"If you feel like that, your problems may be worse than Charlie's." She looked a little surprised at her own words as if they had come out unplanned. "Perhaps yours are much worse because you're not aware of them. When something happens to you, or inside yourself, you've always had Charlie to blame. It's made you look pretty good in the eyes of the world but it hasn't helped Charlie. He's already had more blame than he can handle. What he needs now is confidence in himself, a feeling that he'll do the right thing on his own and not because you'll force him to. You spoke a minute ago of handcuffing him to you. That might work, up to a point. Perhaps it would prevent him from doing the wrong thing but it wouldn't help him to do the right one."

"Well, that was quite a speech, Louise."

"There's more."

"I'm not sure I want to hear it."

"Listen anyway, will you, Ben?"

"Since when have you become an authority on the Gowen brothers?"

She ignored the sarcasm. "I've been trying to do some figuring out, that's all."

"And you've decided what?"

"Charlie's problem wasn't born inside him. It doesn't belong only to him, it's a family affair. Some event, some relationship, or several of both, made him not want to grow up. He let you assume the grown-up role. He remained a child, the kid brother, the baby of the family. He merely went through the motions of manhood by imitating you and doing what you told him to."

She lapsed into silence, and Ben said, "I hope you've finished."

"Almost. Did you and Ann go on a honeymoon?"

"We went to San Francisco for a week. I can't see what that—"

"How soon after you got back did the trouble happen between Charlie and the girl?"

"A few days. Why?"

"Perhaps," she said slowly, "Charlie was only trying, in his mixed-up way, to imitate you by 'marrying' the girl."

Jessie had turned off her light and closed her door tightly to give her parents the impression that she'd gone to sleep. But both her side and back windows were wide open and she missed very little of what was going on.

She heard Virginia and Howard quarreling in the patio, and later, the gate opening and slamming shut again, and Howard's car racing out of the driveway and down the street. Virginia started to cry and Dave took her home and then set out in his car to look for Howard. Jessie lay in the darkness, staring up at the ceiling and wondering how adults could get away with doing such puzzling things without any reason. She herself had to have at least one good reason, and sometimes two, for everything she did.

Shortly before ten o'clock Ellen paused outside Jessie's door for a few seconds, then continued on down the hall.

Jessie called out, "I'm thirsty."

"All right, get up and pour yourself a glass of water."

"I'd rather you brought me one."

"All *right*." Ellen's voice was cross, and when she came into the bedroom with the glass of water she looked tired and tense. "Why aren't you ever thirsty during the day?"

"I don't have time then to think about it."

"Well, drink up. And if you need anything else get it *now*. I have a headache, I'm going to take a sleeping capsule and go to bed."

"May I take one, too?"

"Of course not. Little girls don't need sleeping capsules."

"Mrs. Oakley gives Mary Martha one sometimes."

"Mrs. Oakley is a— Well, anyway, you close your eyes and think pleasant thoughts."

"Why did Howard and Virginia have a fight?"

"That's a good question," Ellen said dryly. "If, within the next fifty years, I come up with a good answer, I'll tell it to you. Have you finished with the water?"

"Yes."

Ellen reached for the glass, still nearly full. "Now this is the final good night, Jessie. You understand that? Absolutely *final*." When she went out she shut the door in a way that indicated she meant business.

Jessie closed her eyes and thought of butterscotch sundaes and Christmas morning and flying the box kite with her name printed in big letters on all sides. Her name was away up in the air and she was flying up in the air to join it, carried effortlessly by the wind, higher and higher. She had almost reached her name when she heard a car in the driveway. She came to earth with a bang. The descent was so real and sudden and shocking that her arms and legs ached and she lay huddled in her bed like the survivor of a plane wreck.

She heard a man's footsteps across the driveway, then Virginia's voice, sounding so cold and hard that Jessie wouldn't have recognized it if it hadn't been coming from Virginia's back porch.

"You didn't find him, I suppose."

"No," Dave said.

"Well, that suits me. Good riddance to bad rubbish, as we used to say in my youth, long since gone, long since wasted on a—"

"Talk like that will get you nowhere. Be practical. You need Howard, you can't support yourself."

"That's a wonderful attitude to take."

"It's a fact, not an attitude," Dave said. "You seem ready to quarrel with anyone tonight. I'd better go home."

"Do that."

"Virginia, listen to me—"

The voices stopped abruptly. Jessie went over to the window and peered out through the slats of the Venetian blinds. The Arlingtons' porch was empty and the door into the house was closed.

Jessie returned to bed. Lying on her back with her hands clasped behind her head, she thought about Virginia and how she needed Howard because she couldn't support herself. She wondered how much money Virginia would require if Howard never came back. Virginia had a car and a house with furniture and enough clothes to last for years and years. All she'd really have to buy would be food.

Without moving her head Jessie could see the half-open door of her clothes closet. In the closet, in the toe of one of her party shoes, were the two ten-dollar bills Howard had pressed into her hand. Although she would miss the money if she gave it back to Virginia, it would be a kind of relief to get rid of it and to be doing Virginia a favor at the same time. Twenty dollars would buy tons of food, even the butterscotch sundaes Virginia liked so much.

Once the decision was made, Jessie wasted no time. She put on a bathrobe and slippers, fished the two bills from the toe of her party shoe and tiptoed down the hall, through the kitchen and out the back door.

Moving through the darkness in her long white flowing robe, she looked like the ghost of a bride.

19

THE ILLUMINATED dial on his bedside clock indicated a few minutes past midnight when Ralph MacPherson was awakened by the phone ringing. He picked up the receiver, opening his eyes only the merest slit to glance at the clock.

"Yes?"

"It's Kate, Mac. Thank heaven you're there. I need your help."

"My dear girl, do you realize what time it is?"

"Yes, of course I realize. I should, I was asleep too when the pounding woke me up."

"All right, I'm hooked," Mac said impatiently. "What pounding?"

"At the front door. There's a man out there."

"*What* man?"

"I don't know. I came downstairs without turning on any lights. I thought that it was Sheridan, and I was going to pretend I wasn't home."

"You're sure it's not Sheridan?"

"Yes. I can see his shadow. He's too big to be Sheridan. What will I do, Mac?"

"That will depend on what the man's doing."

"He's just sitting out there on the top step of the porch making funny sounds. I think—I think he's crying. Oh God, Mac, so many crazy things have happened lately. I feel I'm lost in the middle of a nightmare. Why should a strange man come up on my front porch to cry?"

"Because he's troubled."

"Yes, but why my porch? Why here? Why *me*?"

"It's probably just some drunk on a crying jag who picked your house by accident," Mac said. "If you want to get rid of him, I suggest you call the police."

"I won't do that." There was a silence. "It gives a place a bad reputation to have police arriving with their sirens going full blast and all."

"They don't usually— Never mind. What do you want me to do, Kate?"

"If you could just come over and talk to him, Mac. Ask him why he came here, tell him to leave. He'd listen to you. You sound so authoritative."

"Well, I don't feel very authoritative at this hour of the night but I'll try my best. I'll be there in about ten minutes. Keep the doors locked and don't turn on any lights. Where's Mary Martha?"

"Asleep in her room."

"See that she stays that way," he said and hung up. One Oakley female was enough to cope with at one time.

In the older sections of town the street lights were placed only at intersections, as if what went on at night between corners was not the business of strangers or casual passers-by. The Oakley house was invisible from the road. Mac couldn't even see the trees that surrounded it but he could hear them. The wind was moving through the leaves and bough rubbed against bough in false affection.

From the back seat Mac took the heavy flash-and-blinker light he'd kept there for years in case of emergency. A lot of emergencies had occurred since then but none in which a flashlight was any use. He switched it on. Although the beam wasn't as powerful as it had been, it was enough to illumine the flagstone path to the house.

The steps of the front porch were empty and for one very bad moment he thought Kate had imagined the whole thing. Then he saw the man leaning over the porch railing. His head was bent as though his neck had been broken. He turned toward the beam of the flashlight, his face showing no reaction either to the light or to Mac's presence. He was a tall, heavily built man about forty. He wore blue jeans and a sweatshirt, both stained with blood, and he kept one hand pressed against his chest as if to staunch a wound.

Mac said, "Are you hurt?"

The man's mouth moved but no sound came out of it.

Mac tried again. "I'm Ralph MacPherson. Mrs. Oakley, who lives in this house, called me a few minutes ago to report a man pounding on her door. That was you?"

The man nodded slightly though he looked too dazed to understand the question.

"What are you doing here?"

"My dau—dau—"

"Your dog? You've lost your dog, is that it?"

"Dog?" He covered his face with his hands and Mac saw that it was his right hand that was bleeding. "Not dog. Daughter. *Daughter*."

"You're looking for your daughter?"

"Yes."

"What makes you think she might be here?"

"Her best—best friend lives here."

"Mary Martha?"

"Yes."

Mac remembered his office conversation with Kate about Mary Martha's best friend. "You're Jessie Brant's father?"

"Yes. She's gone. Jessie's gone."

"Take it easy now, Brant. How did you hurt yourself?"

"Don't bother about me. Jessie—"

"You're bleeding."

"I was running and I fell. I don't care about me. Don't you understand? My daughter is missing. *She is missing from her bed*."

"All right, don't get excited. We'll find her."

Mac crossed the porch and rapped lightly on the front door. "Kate, turn on the light and open the door."

The porch light went on and the door opened almost instantly as if Kate had been standing in the hall waiting for someone to tell her what to do. She had on fresh make-up that seemed to have been applied hastily and in the dark. It didn't cover the harsh lines that scarred her face or the anxiety that distorted her eyes.

"Mac?"

"Kate, you remember Mr. Brant, don't you?"

She glanced briefly at Dave and away again. "We're acquainted. That hardly gives him the right to come pounding at—"

"Be quiet and pay attention, Kate. Mr. Brant is here looking for Jessie. Have you seen her?"

"Why no, of course not. It's after midnight. What would Jessie be doing out at a time like this? He has blood on him," she added, staring up into Mac's face. "Tell him to go away. I hate the sight of blood. I won't allow him inside my house."

Dave pressed his hands together tightly to prevent them from reaching out and striking her. His voice was very quiet. "I won't come inside your house, Mrs. Oakley. I wouldn't be here at all if I could have gotten you on the phone."

"I have an unlisted number."

"Yes. I tried to call you."

"People have no right to call others at midnight," she said, as if she herself wouldn't dream of doing such a thing. "Mary Martha and I keep early hours. She was asleep by 8:30 and I shortly afterward."

"Your daughter is in bed asleep, Mrs. Oakley?"

"Why yes, of course."

"Well, *mine isn't.*"

"What do you mean?" She turned to Mac, touching his coat sleeve with her hand like a child pleading for a favor. "What does he mean, Mac? All little girls ought to be in bed at this time of night."

"Jessie is missing," Mac said.

"I'm sure she won't be missing for long. She's probably just playing a trick on her parents. Jessie's full of ideas and she truly loves to be the center of attention. She'll turn up any minute with one of her preposterous stories and everything will be fine. Won't it? Won't it, Mac?"

"I don't know. When did you see her last?"

"This afternoon. She dropped in to invite Mary Martha to go swimming with her. I didn't allow Mary Martha to go. I've been supervising her extra carefully ever since I received that anonymous letter."

Mac had forgotten the letter. He put his hand in the left pocket of his coat. There were other papers in the pocket but the letter was unmistakable to the touch. One corner of the envelope bulged where the paper had been folded and refolded until it was no more than an inch square. Mac remembered enough of the contents of the letter to make him regret not taking it immediately to his friend, Lieutenant Gallantyne. Gallantyne had a collection of anonymous letters that spanned thirty years of police work.

Mac said, "Will you describe Jessie to me, Mr. Brant?"

"I have pictures of her at home." He almost broke down at the word *home.* His face started to come apart and he turned it toward the darkness beyond the porch railing. "I must get back to my wife. She's expecting me to—to bring Jessie home with me. She was so sure Jessie would be here."

Kate was clutching her long wool bathrobe around her as though somebody had just threatened to tear it off. "I don't know why she was sure Jessie would come here. I'm the last person in the world who'd be taken in by one of Jessie's fancy schemes. I would have telephoned Mrs. Brant immediately. Wouldn't I, Mac?"

"Of course you would, Kate," Mac said. "You'd better go back in the house now and see if you can get some sleep."

"I won't be able to close my eyes. There may be some monster loose in the neighborhood and no child is safe. He won't stop with just Jessie. Mary Martha might be next."

"Shut up, Kate."

"Oh, Mac, please don't go. Don't leave me alone."

"I have to. I'm driving Mr. Brant home."

"Everybody leaves me alone. I can't stand—"

"I'll talk to you in the morning."

The door closed, the porch light went off. The two men began walking in slow, silent unison down the flagstone path, following the beam of Mac's flashlight as if it were a dim ray of hope.

Inside the car Mac said, "Where do you live, Brant?"

"Cielito Lane."

"That's in the Peppertree tract, isn't it?"

"Yes."

The car pulled away from the curb.

"Have you called the police?"

"Virginia—Mrs. Arlington did. She lives next door. She and Jessie are very good friends. My wife thought that if Jessie were in any kind of trouble or even just playing a trick on us, she'd go to the Arlingtons' house first. We searched all through it and the garage twice. Jessie wasn't there. Virginia called the police and I set out for Mrs. Oakley's. I couldn't think of any other place Jessie would go late at night. We haven't lived in town long and we have no relatives here."

"You'll forgive me for asking this," Mac said, "but is Jessie a girl who often gets into trouble?"

"No. She never does. Leaving her bicycle in the middle of the sidewalk, coming home late for meals, things like that, yes, but nothing more serious."

"Has she ever run away from home?"

"Of course not."

"Runaways are picked up by the police every day, Brant."

"She didn't run away," Dave said hoarsely. "I wish to God I could believe she had."

"Why can't you?"

"She had no money, and the only clothes missing from her closet are the pajamas she wore to bed and a bathrobe and a pair of slippers. Jessie's a sensible girl, she'd know better than to try and run away without any money and wearing an outfit that would immediately attract everybody's attention."

That might be the whole point, Mac thought, but all he said was, "Can you think of any recent family scene or event that might make her want to run away?"

"No."

"Has she been upset about something lately?"

Dave turned and looked out the window. The night seemed darker than any he could ever remember. It wasn't the ordinary darkness, an absence of light; it was a thick, soft, suffocating thing that covered the whole world. No morning could ever penetrate it.

"Has something upset her?" Mac repeated.

"I'm trying to answer. I—she's been talking a lot about divorce, fathers deserting their families like Sheridan Oakley. Obviously Mary Martha's fed her a lot of stuff and Jessie's taken it perhaps more seriously than it deserves. She's a funny kid, Jessie. She puts on a big front about not caring but she feels everything deeply, especially where Mary Martha is concerned. The two girls have been very close for almost a year now, in fact almost inseparable."

Mac remembered the opening sentence of the letter he was carrying in his pocket: *Your daughter takes too dangerous risks with her delicate body*. He said, "Do you consider Jessie a frail child, that is, delicate in build?"

"That's an odd question."

"I have good reasons for asking it which I can't divulge right now."

"Well, Jessie might look delicate to some people. Actually, she's thin and wiry like her mother, and extremely healthy. The only times she's ever needed a doctor were when she's had accidents."

"Accidents such as?"

"Falls, stings, bites. The normal things that happen to kids plus a few extra. Right now her hands are badly blistered from overuse of the jungle gym at the school playground."

"Does she often play at the school playground?"

"I don't know. I'm at work all day."

"Would you say she goes there twice a week? Five times? Seven?"

"All the neighborhood kids go there. Why shouldn't they?" Dave added defensively, "It's well supervised, there are organized games and puppet shows and things not available in the ordinary backyard. Just what were you implying?"

"Nothing. I was merely—"

"No. I think you know something that you're not telling me. You're holding out on me. Why?"

"I have no knowledge at present," Mac said, "that would be of any value or comfort to you."

"That's only a fancy way of saying you won't tell me." There was a silence, filled with sudden distrust and uneasiness. "Who are you, anyway? What are you? How did you get into this?"

"I gave you my name, Ralph MacPherson. I'm a lawyer and an old friend of Mrs. Oakley's."

"She didn't waste much time contacting a lawyer. Why?"

"She called me as a friend, not a lawyer. I've known her since she was Jessie's age. . . . Let's see, I take the next turn, don't I?"

"Yes."

All the houses in the block were dark except for two. In the driveway that separated the two, a black Chrysler sedan was parked. Mac recognized it as one of the unmarked police cars used for assignments requiring special precautions.

Except for the number of lights burning in the two houses, there was no sign that anything had happened. The streets were deserted, and if the immediate neighbors were curious, they were keeping their curiosity behind closed drapes in dark rooms.

Mac braked the car, leaving the engine running. "I'd be a damned fool if I said I'm glad to have met you, Brant. So I'll just say I hope we meet again under more pleasant circumstances."

"Aren't you coming inside?"

"It didn't occur to me that you might want me to."

"I can't face Ellen alone."

"I don't see that I'll be of much help. Besides, you won't be alone with her, the police are there."

"I won't—I can't walk into that house and tell her I didn't find Jessie. She was so full of hope. How can I go in there and take it all away from her?"

"She has to be told the truth, Brant. Come on, I'll go with you."

The two men got out of the car and began walking toward the house. Mac had no thought of involving himself in the situation. He felt that he was merely doing his duty, helping a person in trouble, and that the whole thing—or at least his part in it—would be over in a few minutes. He could afford a few minutes, some kind words.

Suddenly the front door opened and a woman rushed out. It was as if a violent explosion had taken place inside the house and blown the door open and tossed the woman out.

She said, "Jessie?" Then she stopped dead in her tracks, staring at Mac. "Where's Jessie?"

"Mrs. Brant, I—"

"I know. You must be the doctor. It happened the way I thought. Jessie was on her way to Mary Martha's by the short cut and she fell crossing the creek. And she's in the hospital and you've come to tell me she'll be all right, it's nothing serious, she'll be home in a—"

"Stop it, Mrs. Brant. I'm a lawyer, not a doctor."

"Where is Jessie?"

"I'm sorry, I don't know."

Dave said, "She didn't go to Mary Martha's, Ellen. I haven't found her."

"Oh God. Please, God, help her. Help my baby."

Dave took her in his arms. To Mac it was not so much an embrace as a case of each of them holding the other up. He felt a deep pity but he realized there was nothing further he could do for them now. He started back to his car. The letter in his pocket seemed to be getting heavier, like a stone to which things had begun to cling and grow and multiply.

He had almost reached the curb when a voice behind him said, "Just a minute, sir."

Mac turned and saw a young man in a dark gray suit and matching fedora. The fedora made him look like an undergraduate dressed up for a role in a play. "Yes, what is it?"

"May I ask your name, sir?"

"MacPherson."

"Do you have business here at this time of night, Mr. MacPherson?"

"I drove Mr. Brant home."

"I'm sure you won't mind repeating that to the lieutenant, will you?"

"Not," Mac said dryly, "if the lieutenant wants to hear it."

"Oh, he will. Come this way, please."

As they walked down the driveway Mac saw that there was another police car parked outside the garage. Its searchlight had been angled to shine on the window of a rear bedroom. A policeman was examining the window; a second one stood just outside the periphery of the light. All Mac could see of him was his gray hair, which was cut short and stood up straight on his head like the bristles of a brush. It was enough.

"Hello, Gallantyne."

Gallantyne stepped forward, squinting against the light. He was of medium height with broad, heavy shoulders, slightly stooped. His posture and his movements all indicated a vast impatience just barely kept under control. He always gave Mac the impression of a well-trained and very powerful stallion with one invisible saddle sore which mustn't be touched. No one knew where this sore was but they knew it was there and it paid to be careful.

"What are you doing here, Mac?" Gallantyne said.

"I was invited. It seems I come under the heading of suspicious characters seen lurking in the neighborhood."

"Well, were you?"

"I was seen, I don't believe I was lurking," Mac said. "Unless perhaps I have a natural lurk that I'm not aware of. May I return the question? What are you doing here, Gallantyne? I thought you were tied to a desk."

"They untie me once in a while. Salvadore's on vacation and Weber has bursitis. Come inside. I want to talk to you."

For reasons he didn't yet understand, Mac felt a great reluctance to enter the house. He didn't want the missing child to seem any more real to him than she did now; he didn't want to see the yard where she played, the table she ate at, the room she slept in. He wanted her to remain merely a name and a number, Jessie Brant, aged nine. He said, "I'd prefer to stay out here."

"Well, I prefer different."

Gallantyne turned and walked through an open gate into a patio. He didn't bother looking back to see if he was being followed. It was taken for granted that he would be, and he was.

The back door of the house had been propped open with a flowerpot filled with earth containing a dried-out azalea. A policeman in uniform was dusting the door and its brass knob for fingerprints. There was no sign that the door had been forced or the lock tampered with.

The kitchen contained mute evidence of a family going through a crisis: cups of half-consumed coffee, overflowing ashtrays, a bottle of aspirin with the top off, a wastebasket filled with used pieces of tissue and the empty box they'd come in.

Gallantyne said, "Sit down, Mac. You look nervous. Are you the family lawyer?"

"No."

"An old friend, then?"

"I've known Brant about an hour, his wife for five minutes." He explained briefly about responding to Kate's phone call and meeting Brant on the porch of her house.

"It sounds crazy," Gallantyne said.

"Anything involving Mrs. Oakley has a certain amount of illogic in it. She's a nervous woman and she's been under a great strain, especially for the past few days."

"Why the past few days?"

"Two reasons that I know of, though there may be more. She thinks the husband she's divorcing has hired someone to spy on her. And this week she received an anonymous letter warning her to take better care of her daughter."

Gallantyne's thick gray eyebrows leaped up his forehead. "Have you read it?"

"Yes. Mrs. Oakley brought it to my office right away. She'd pretty well convinced herself that Mr. Oakley had written it to harass her. I didn't believe it. In fact, I didn't really take the whole thing seriously. Now I'm afraid, I'm very much afraid, that I made a bad mistake."

"Why?"

"Here, see for yourself." Mac took the envelope out of his pocket. He was appalled at the severe trembling of his hands. It was as if his body had acknowledged his feelings of guilt before his mind was conscious of them. "I realize now that I should have shown this to you right away. Oh, I have the customary excuses: I was busy, I was fed up with Kate Oakley's shenanigans, and so on. But excuses aren't good enough. If I—"

"You're too old for the if-game," Gallantyne said and took the letter out of the envelope. "Was it folded like this when Mrs. Oakley received it?"

"Yes."

"Well, that's a switch anyway." He read the letter through, half aloud. "'Your daughter takes too dangerous risks with her delicate body. Children must be guarded against the cruel hazards of life and fed good, nourishing food so their bones will be padded. Also clothing. You should put plenty of clothing on her, keep arms and legs covered, etc. In the name of God please take better care of your little girl.'"

Gallantyne reread the letter, this time silently, then he tossed it on the table as though he wanted to get rid of it as quickly as possible. The grooves in his face had deepened and drops of sweat appeared on his forehead, growing larger and larger until they fell of their own weight and were lost in his eyebrows. "All I can say is, I'm damn glad this wasn't sent to the Brants. As it is, I figure the kid decided to throw a scare into her parents by running away. Probably one of the patrol cars has picked her up by now. . . . Why the hell are you staring at me like that?"

"I think the letter was intended for Mrs. Brant."

"You said it was addressed to Mrs. Oakley."

"Jessie Brant and the Oakley girl, Mary Martha, are best friends. According to Brant, they're inseparable, which no doubt involves a lot of visiting back and forth in each other's houses. Mary Martha's a tall girl for her age, a trifle overweight, and inclined to be cautious. The writer of the letter wasn't describing Mary Martha. He, or she, was describing Jessie."

"You can't be sure of that."

"I can be sure of two things. Mary Martha's at home with her mother and Jessie isn't."

Gallantyne stood in silence for a minute. Then he picked up the letter, refolded it and put it in his pocket. "We won't tell anybody about this right now, not the parents or the press or anyone else."

20

HOWARD ARLINGTON woke up at dawn in a motel room. Seen through half-closed eyes the place looked the same as a hundred others he'd stayed in, but gradually differences began to show up: the briefcase Virginia had given him years ago was not on the bureau where he always kept it, and the luggage rack at the foot of the bed was empty. When he turned his head his starched collar jabbed him in the neck and he realized he was still fully dressed. Even his tie was knotted. He loosened it but the tightness in his throat didn't go away. It was as if, during the night, he'd tried to swallow something too large and too fibrous to be swallowed.

He got up and opened the drapes. Fog pressed against the window like the ectoplasm of lost spirits seeking shelter and a home. He closed the drapes again and turned on a lamp. Except for the outline of his body on the chenille bedspread, the room looked as though it hadn't been occupied. The clothes closet was empty, the ashtrays unused, the drinking glasses on the bureau still wrapped in wax paper.

He couldn't remember checking into the motel; yet he knew he must have registered, given his name and address and car license number, and paid in advance because he had no luggage. His last clear recollection was of Virginia standing in the Brants' patio saying she didn't want a child any more: "*We no longer have anything to offer a child. . . . How cruel it would be to pass along such an ugly thing as life. Poor Jessie. . . . She will lose her innocence and high hopes and dreams; she will lose them all. By the time she's my age she will have wished a thousand times that she were dead.*"

He'd quarreled with Virginia and he was in a motel. These were the only facts he was sure of. Where the motel was, in what city, how he'd reached it and why, he didn't know. He spent so much of his life driving from one city to another and checking in and out of motels that he must have acted automatically.

He left the room key on top of the bureau and went out to his car. On the front seat there was an empty pint bottle of whiskey and a hole half an inch wide burned in the upholstery by a cigarette. *Fact three*, he thought grimly, *I was drunk*. He put the bottle in the glove compartment and drove off.

The first street sign he came to gave him another fact: he was still in San Felice, down near the breakwater, no more than four miles from his own house.

The lights in the kitchen were on when he arrived. It was too early for Virginia to be awake and he wondered whether she'd left them on, expecting him home, or whether she'd forgotten to turn them off. She often forgot, or claimed to have forgotten. Sometimes he thought she kept them on deliberately because she was afraid of the dark but didn't want to admit it. He parked his car beside hers in the garage, then crossed the driveway and walked up the steps of the back porch. The door was unlocked.

Virginia was sitting at the kitchen table with the big retriever lying beside her chair. Neither of them moved.

Howard said, "Virginia?"

The dog opened his eyes, wagged his tail briefly and perfunctorily, and went back to sleep.

"At least the dog usually barks when I get home," he said. "Don't I even rate that much any more?"

Virginia turned. Her eyes were bloodshot, the lids blistered by the heat of her tears and surrounded by a network of lines Howard had never seen before. She spoke in a low, dull voice.

"The police are looking for you."

"The police? Why in heaven's name did you call them in? You knew I'd be back."

"I didn't. Didn't know, didn't call them."

"What's going on around here anyway? What have the police got to do with my getting drunk and spending the night in a motel?"

"Is that what you did, Howard?"

"Yes."

"Can you prove it?"

"Why should I have to prove it?"

She covered her face with her hands and started to weep again, deep, bitter sobs that shook her whole body. The dog rose to a sitting position and put his head on her lap, watching

Howard out of the corner of his eye, as if he considered Howard responsible for the troubled sounds.

He blames me for everything, Howard thought, *just the way she does. Only this time I don't even know what I'm being blamed for. Did I do something while I was drunk that I don't remember? I couldn't have been in a fight. There are no marks on me and my clothes aren't torn.*

"Virginia, tell me what happened."

"Jessie—Jessie's gone."

"Gone where?"

"Nobody knows. She—she just disappeared. Ellen took her a glass of water about ten o'clock and that's the last anyone saw of her except—" She stopped, pressing the back of her hand against her trembling mouth.

"Except who?" Howard said.

"Whoever made her disappear."

Howard stared at her, confused and helpless. He wasn't sure whether she was telling the truth or whether she'd imagined the whole thing. She'd been acting and talking peculiarly last night, standing in the dichondra patch saying she was a tree.

She saw his incredulity and guessed the reason for it. "You think I've lost my mind. Well, I wish I had. It would be easier to bear than this, this terrible thing." She began to sob again, repeating Jessie's name over and over as if Jessie might be somewhere listening and might respond.

Howard did what he could, brought her two tranquilizer pills and poured her some ice water from the pitcher in the refrigerator. She choked on the pills and the water spilled down the front of her old wool bathrobe. Its coldness was stinging and shocking against the warm skin between her breasts. She let out a gasp and clutched the bathrobe tightly around her neck. Her eyes were resentful but they were no longer wild or weeping.

"So the police are looking for me," Howard said. "Why?"

"They're questioning everyone, friends, neighbors, anyone who knew—who knows her. They said in cases like this it's often a relative or a trusted friend of the family."

"Cases like what?"

She didn't answer.

"When did she disappear, Virginia?"

"Between ten and eleven. Ellen tucked her in bed at ten o'clock, then she took a sleeping capsule and went to bed herself. Dave was out looking for you. Ellen said she'd locked the back door but when Dave came back it was unlocked. He checked Jessie's bedroom to see if she was sleeping. She was gone. He searched the house, calling for her, then he woke Ellen up. They came here to our house. We looked all over but we couldn't find Jessie. I called the police and Dave set out for Mary Martha's house, using the path along the creek that the girls always took."

"Kids have run away before."

"The only clothes missing are the pajamas she was wearing, a bathrobe and a pair of slippers. Besides, she had no motive and no money."

"She had the twenty dollars I gave her the other night."

"Why, of course." Virginia's face came alive with sudden hope. "Why, that would seem like a fortune to Jessie. We've got to tell—"

"We tell no one, Virginia."

"But we must. It might throw a whole new light on everything."

"Including me," Howard said sharply. "The police will ask me why I gave the kid twenty dollars. I'll tell them because I was sore at you and wanted to get back at you. But will they believe it?"

"It's the truth."

"It might not strike them that way."

She didn't seem to understand what he was talking about. When he spelled it out for her, she looked appalled. "They couldn't possibly think anything like that about you, Howard."

"Why not?"

"You're a respectable married man."

"Coraznada State Hospital is full of so-called respectable married men." He took out a handkerchief and wiped his neck. "Did the police question you?"

"Yes. A Lieutenant Gallantyne did most of the talking. I don't like him. Even when I was telling the truth he made me feel that I was lying. There was another man with him, a Mr. MacPherson. Every once in a while they'd put their heads together and whisper. It made me nervous."

"Who's MacPherson?"

"Dave said he's a lawyer."

"Whose lawyer?"

"Mrs. Oakley's."

"How did Mrs. Oakley get into this?"

"I don't *know*. Stop bullying me, I can't stand it."

She seemed on the verge of breaking up again. Howard got up, put some water and coffee in the percolator and plugged it in. After a time he said, "I'm not trying to bully you, Virginia. I simply want to find out what you told the police about last night so I can corroborate it. It wouldn't be so good—for either of us—if we contradicted each other."

She was looking at him, her eyes cold under their blistered lids. "You don't care that Jessie has disappeared, do you? All you care about is saving your own skin."

"And yours."

"Don't worry about mine. Everybody knows how I love the child."

"That's not quite accurate, Virginia," he said quietly. "Everybody knows that you love her, but not how you love her."

The coffee had begun to percolate, bubbling merrily in the cheerless room. Virginia turned and looked at the percolator as if she hoped it would do something unexpected and interesting like explode.

She said, "Where did you go after you left the Brants' last night?"

"To a liquor store and then down to the beach. I ended up at a motel."

"You were alone, of course?"

"Yes, I was alone."

"What motel?"

"I don't remember, I wasn't paying much attention. But I could find it again if I had to."

"Ellen told the police," she said, turning to face him, "that you were jealous of my relationship with Jessie."

"That was neighborly of her."

"She had to tell the truth. Under the circumstances you could hardly expect her to lie to spare your feelings."

"It's not my feelings I'm worried about. It is, as you pointed out, my skin. What else was said about last night?"

"Everything that happened, how we quarreled, and the funny way you talked to Jessie as if you were half-drunk when you only had two beers; how you tore off in the car and Dave tried to find you and couldn't."

"I didn't realize what loyal friends I had. It moves me," he added dryly. "It may move me right into a cell. Or was that the real objective?"

"You don't understand. We were forced to tell the whole truth, all of us. A child's life might be at stake. Gallantyne said every little detail could be vitally important. He made us go over and over it. I couldn't have lied to protect you even if I'd wanted to."

"And the implication is, you didn't particularly want to?"

She was staring at him in incredulity, her mouth partly open. "It still hasn't come through to you yet, has it? A child is missing, a nine-year-old girl has disappeared. She may be dead, and you don't seem to care. Don't you feel *anything*?"

"Yes. I feel somebody's trying to make me the goat."

Between four and seven in the morning Ellen Brant slept fitfully on the living-room couch beside the telephone. She'd dreamed half a dozen times that the phone was ringing and had wakened up to find herself reaching for it. She finally got up, washed her face and ran a comb through her hair, and put on a heavy wool coat over her jeans and T-shirt. Then she went into the bedroom to see if Dave was awake and could hear the telephone if it rang.

He was lying on his back, peering up at the ceiling. He turned and looked at her, the question in his eyes dying before it had a chance to be born. "There's been no news, of course."

"No. I'm going over to the Oakleys'. I want to ask Mary Martha some questions."

"The lieutenant will do that."

"She might talk to me more easily. She and her mother freeze up in front of strangers."

"What's it like outside?"

"Cold and foggy."

She knew he was thinking the same thing she was, that somewhere in that cold fog Jessie might be wandering, wearing only her cotton pajamas and light bathrobe. Biting her underlip hard to keep from breaking into tears again, she went out to the garage and got into the old Dodge station wagon. The floorboard of the front seat was covered with sand from yesterday's trip to the beach. It seemed to have happened a long time ago and in a different city, where the sun had been shining and the surf was gentle and the sand soft and warm. She had a feeling that she would never see that city again.

She backed out of the driveway, tears streaming down her face, warm where they touched her cheeks, already cold when they reached the sides of her neck. She brushed them angrily away with the sleeve of her coat. She couldn't afford to cry in front of Mary Martha, it might frighten her into silence, or worse still, into lying. She had seen Mary Martha many times after an emotional scene at home. The effect on her was always the same—blank eyes, expressionless voice: no, nothing was the matter, nothing had happened.

Mary Martha answered the door herself, first opening it only as far as the chain would allow. Then, recognizing Ellen, she unfastened the chain and opened the door wide. In spite of the earliness of the hour she was dressed as if for a visit to town in pink embroidered cotton and newly whitened sandals. Her ponytail was neat and so tightly fastened it raised her eyebrows slightly. She looked a little surprised to see Ellen, as though she might have been expecting someone else.

She said, "If you want my mother, she's in the kitchen making breakfast."

"I prefer to talk to you alone, Mary Martha."

"I'd better get my mother's permission. She's kind of nervous this morning, I don't know why. But I have to be careful."

"She hasn't told you anything?"

"Just that Mac was coming over with a soldier and we were all going to have a chat."

"A soldier?"

"He's a lieutenant. I'm supposed to remember to call him that so I'll make a good impression." Mary Martha looked down at her dress as if to reassure herself that it was still clean enough to make a good impression. "Do you want to come in?"

"Yes."

"I guess it'll be all right."

She was just closing the door when Kate Oakley's voice called out from the kitchen, "Mary Martha, tell Mac I'll be there in a minute."

"It's not Mac," the child said. "It's Jessie's mother."

"Jessie's—?" Kate Oakley appeared at the far end of the hall. She began walking toward them very rapidly, her high heels ticking on the linoleum like clocks working on different time schedules, each trying to catch up with the other. Her face was heavily made up to look pink and white but the gray of trouble showed through. She placed one arm protectively around Mary Martha's shoulders. "You'd better go and put the bacon in the warming oven, dear."

"I don't care if it gets cold," Mary Martha said. "It tastes the same."

"You mustn't be rude in front of company, lamb. That's understood between us, isn't it?"

"Yes, ma'am."

"Off you go."

Mary Martha started down the hall.

"But I want to talk to her," Ellen said desperately. "I've got to. She might know something."

"She knows nothing. She's only a child."

"*Jessie's only a child, too.*"

"I'm sorry. I really am sorry, Mrs. Brant. But Mary Martha isn't supposed to talk to anyone until our lawyer arrives."

"You haven't even told her about Jessie, have you?"

"I didn't want to upset her."

"She's got to be told. She may be able to help. She might have seen someone, heard something. How can we know unless we ask her?"

"Mac will ask her. He can handle these—these situations better than you or I could."

"Is that all it is to you, a situation to be handled?"

Kate shook her head helplessly. "No matter what I said to you now, it would seem wrong because you're distraught. Further conversation is pointless. I must ask you to leave." She opened the heavy oak door. "I'm truly sorry, Mrs. Brant, but I think I'm doing the right thing. Mac will talk to Mary Martha. She feels freer with him than she would with you or me."

"Even though he has a policeman with him?"

"Did she tell you that?"

"I figured it out."

"Well, it won't make any difference. Mary Martha adores Mac and she's not afraid of policemen."

But the last word curled upward into a question mark, and when Ellen looked back from the bottom of the porch steps, Kate was hanging on to the oak door as if for support.

When breakfast was over, Mary Martha sat on the window seat in the front room with the cat, Pudding, on her lap. She wasn't supposed to get her hands dirty or her dress wrinkled but she needed the comfort of the cat, his warm body and soft fur, his bright eyes that seemed to be aware of so many things and not to care about any of them very much.

In a little while she saw Mac and the lieutenant emerge from the fog and come up the front steps. She heard her mother talking to them in the hall, at first in the low, careful voice she used when meeting strangers, later in a higher, less restrained and more natural voice. She sounded as if she was protesting, then arguing, and finally, losing. After a time the two men came into the front room alone, and Mac closed the door.

"Hello, Mary Martha," Mac said. "This is Lieutenant Gallantyne."

Still holding the cat, Mary Martha got up and executed a brief, formal curtsy.

Gallantyne bowed gravely in return. "That's a pretty cat you have there, Mary Martha. What's his name?"

"Pudding. He has other names too, though."

"Really? Such as?"

"Geronimo, sometimes. Also King Arthur. But when he's bad and catches a bird, I call him Sheridan." She switched the cat from her left shoulder to her right. It stopped purring and made a swift jab at her ponytail. "Do you have any medals?"

Gallantyne raised his bushy eyebrows. "Well now, I believe I won a few swimming races when I was a kid."

"I mean real medals like for killing a hundred enemies."

The men exchanged glances. It was as if they were both thinking the same thing, that it seemed a long and insane time ago that men were given medals for killing.

"Lieutenant Gallantyne is not in the army," Mac said. "He's a policeman. He's also a good friend of mine, so you needn't be afraid of him."

"I'm not. But why does he want to see me instead of my mother?"

"He'll talk to your mother later. Right now you're more important."

She seemed pleased but at the same time suspicious. "Why am I?"

"We hope," Gallantyne said, "that you'll be able to help us find your friend, Jessie."

"Is she hiding?"

"We're not sure."

"She's an awfully good hider. Being so skinny she can squeeze behind things and under things and between."

"You and Jessie play together a lot, do you?"

"All the time except when one of us is being punished."

"And you tell each other secrets, I suppose?"

"Yes, sir."

"Do you promise each other never to reveal these secrets to anyone else?"

Mary Martha nodded and said firmly, "And I'm not going to, either, because I crossed my heart and hoped to die."

"Oh, I'm sure you can keep a secret very well," Gallantyne said. "But I want you to imagine something now. Suppose you, Mary Martha, were in a dangerous situation in a place nobody knew about except you and Jessie. You're frightened and hungry and in pain and you want desperately to be rescued. Under those circumstances, wouldn't you release Jessie from her promise to keep the name of that place a secret?"

"I guess so, only there isn't any place like that."

"But you have other secrets."

"Yes."

Gallantyne was watching her gravely. "I believe that if Jessie could communicate with you right now, she'd release you from all your promises."

"Why can't she comm—communicate?"

"Nobody's seen her since last night at ten o'clock. We don't know where she is or why she left or if she left by herself or with someone else."

In a spasm of fear Mary Martha clutched the cat too tightly. He let out a yowl, unsheathed his claws and fought his way out of her grasp, onto the floor. She stood, very pale and still, one hand pressed to her scratched shoulder. "He hurt me," she said in a shocked voice. "Sheridan hurt me."

"I'm sure he didn't mean to."

"He always means to. I hate him."

"You can cry if you like," Gallantyne said. "That might help."

"*No.*"

"All right, then, we'll go on. Is that O.K.?"

"I guess so."

"Did you and Jessie ever talk about running away together? Perhaps just in fun, like, *let's run away and join the circus.*"

"That would be plain silly," she said in a contemptuous voice. "Circuses don't even come here."

"Times have changed since I was a boy. The only thing that made life bearable when I was mad at my family was the thought of running away and joining the circus. Did Jessie often get mad at her family?"

"Sometimes. Mostly at Mike, her older brother. He bosses her around, he's awfully mean. We think a bad witch put a curse on him when he was born."

"Really? What kind of curse?"

"I'm not sure. But I made one up that sounds as if it might work."

"Tell it to me."

"'Abracadabra,
Purple and green,
This little boy
Will grow up mean.'

"It should be said in a more eerie-like voice, only I don't feel like it right now."

Gallantyne pursed his lips and nodded. "Sounds pretty authentic to me just the way it is. Do you know any more?"

"'Abracadabra,
Yellow and brown,
Uncle Howard's the nastiest
Man in town.'

"That one," she added anxiously, "isn't so good, is it?"

"Well, it's not so much a curse as a statement. Uncle Howard's the nastiest man in town, period. By the way, who's Uncle Howard?"

"Mr. Arlington."

"Why do you think he's so nasty, Mary Martha?"

"I don't. I only talked to him once and he was real nice. He gave me fifty cents."

"Then why did you make up the curse about him?"

"Jessie asked me to. We were going to make up curses about all the people we hate and she wanted to start with Uncle—with Mr. Arlington."

"Who was next on the list?"

"Nobody. We got tired of the game, and anyway my mother came to pick me up."

"I wonder," Gallantyne said softly, "why Jessie felt that way about Mr. Arlington. Do you have any idea?"

"No, sir. That was the first day she ever told me, when we were at the playground with Mike."

"What day was that?"

"The day my mother and I went downtown to Mac's office."

"Thursday," Mac said.

Gallantyne thanked him with a nod and turned his attention back to Mary Martha. "Previous to Thursday, you thought Jessie and the Arlingtons were good friends?"

"Yes, on account of the Arlingtons were always giving her presents and making a big fuss over her."

"Both of the Arlingtons?"

"Well—" Mary Martha studied the toes of her shoes. "Well, I guess it was mostly Aunt Virginia, him being away so much on the road. But Jessie never said anything against him until Thursday."

"Let's assume that something happened, on Wednesday perhaps, that changed her opinion of him. Did you see Jessie on Wednesday?"

"Yes, I went over to her house and we sat on the porch steps and talked."

"What about?"

"Lots of things."

"Name one."

"The book Aunt Virginia gave her. It was all about glaciers and mountains and rivers and wild things. It sounded real interesting. Only Jessie had to give it back because it cost too much money and her parents wouldn't let her keep it. *My* mother," she added virtuously, "won't let me accept anything. When Sheridan sends me parcels, I'm not even allowed to peek inside. She sends them right back or throws them away, bang, into the garbage can."

Gallantyne looked at the cat. "I gather you're referring to another Sheridan, not this one."

"Cats can't send parcels," Mary Martha said with a faint giggle. "That's silly. They don't have any money and they can't wrap things or write any name and address on the outside."

Gallantyne thought, wearily, of the anonymous letter. He'd been up all night, first with the Brants and Mrs. Arlington, and later in the police lab examining the letter. He was sure now that it had been written by a man, young, literate, and in good physical health. The description fitted hundreds of men in town. The fact that Howard Arlington was one of them meant nothing in itself.

He said, "Mary Martha, you and Jessie spend quite a lot of time at the school grounds, I'm told."

"Yes. Because of the games and swings and jungle gym."

"Have you ever noticed anyone watching you?"

"The coach. That's his job."

"Aside from the coach, have you seen any man hanging around the place, or perhaps the same car parked at the curb several days in a row?"

"No." Mary Martha gave him a knowing look. "My mother told me all about men like that. They're real nasty and I'm supposed to run home right away when I see one of them. Jessie is, too. She's a very good runner."

Perhaps not quite good enough, Gallantyne thought grimly. "How are you going to recognize these men when you see them?"

"Well, they offer you things like gum or candy or even a doll. Also, a ride in their car."

"And nothing like this ever happened to you and Jessie?"

"No. We saw a mean-looking man at the playground once, but it was only Timmy's father, who was mad because Timmy missed his appointment at the dentist. Timmy wears braces."

One corner of Gallantyne's mouth twitched impatiently. *So Timmy wears braces, and he has a mean-looking father and I am getting exactly nowhere.* "Do you know the story of Tom Sawyer, Mary Martha?"

"Our teacher told us some of it in school."

"Perhaps you remember the cave that was the secret hide-out. Do you and Jessie have somewhere like that? Not a cave, particularly, but a special private place where you can meet or leave notes for each other and things like that?"

"No."

"Think carefully now. You see, I and a great many other people have been searching for Jessie all night."

"She wouldn't hide all night," Mary Martha said thoughtfully. "Not unless she took lots of sandwiches and potato chips along."

"There's no evidence that she did."

"Then she's not hiding. She'd be too hungry. Her father says he should get a double tax exemption for her because she eats so much. What's a tax exemption?"

"You'll find out soon enough." Gallantyne turned to Mac, who was still standing beside the door as if on guard against a sudden intrusion by Kate Oakley. "Have you any questions you'd like to ask her?"

"One or two," Mac said. "What time did you go to bed last night, Mary Martha?"

"About eight o'clock."

"That's pretty early for vacation time and daylight saving."

"My mother and I like to go to bed early and get up early. She doesn't—we don't like the nights."

"Did you go to sleep right away?"

"I must have. I don't remember doing anything else."

"That seems like logical reasoning," Mac said with a wry smile. "Did you get up during the night?"

"No."

"Not even to go to the bathroom?"

"No, but you're not supposed to talk about things like that in front of strangers," Mary Martha said severely.

"Lieutenant Gallantyne is a friend of mine."

"Well, he's not mine or my mother's."

"Let's see if we can change that," Gallantyne said. "Ask your mother to come in here, will you?"

"Yes, sir. Only—well, you better not keep her very long."

"Why not?"

"She might cry, and crying gives her a headache."

"We mustn't let that happen, must we?"

"No, sir." Mary Martha executed another of her stiff little curtsies, picked up the cat and departed.

"She's a funny kid," Gallantyne said. "Is she always like that?"

"With adults. I've never seen her in the company of other children."

"That's odd. I understand you're the old family friend."

"I'm the old family friend when things go wrong," Mac said dryly. "When things are going right, I think I must be the old family enemy."

"Exactly why did you invite yourself to come with me this morning, Mac?"

"Oh, let's just say I'm curious."

"Let's not."

"All right. The truth is that Kate Oakley's a very difficult and very vulnerable woman. Because she is difficult, she can't ask for or accept help the way an ordinary vulnerable person might. So I'm here to lend her moral support. I may criticize her and give her hell occasionally but she knows I'm fond of her."

"How fond?"

"She's twenty years younger than I am. Does that answer your question?"

"Not quite."

"Then I'll lay it on the line. There's no secret romance going on between Kate Oakley and myself. I was her father's lawyer when he was alive, and when he died I handled his estate, or rather the lack of it. I am officially Mary Martha's godfather, and unofficially I'm probably Kate's, too. That's the whole story."

"The story hasn't ended yet," Gallantyne said carefully. "Surely you're not naïve enough to believe we can write our own endings in this world."

"We can do a little editing."

"Don't kid yourself."

Mac wanted to argue with him but he heard Kate's footsteps in the hall. He wondered what her reaction would have been to Gallantyne's insinuations: shock, displeasure, perhaps even amusement. He could never tell what she was actually thinking. When she was at her gayest, he could feel the sadness in her, and when she was in despair he sensed that it, too, was not real. Everything about her seemed to be hidden, as if at a certain period in her life she had decided to go underground where she would be safe.

He thought about the wild creatures in the canyon behind his house. The foxes, the raccoons, the possums, the chipmunks, they could all be lured out of their winter refuge by the promise of food and the warmth of a spring sun. There was no spring sun for Kate, no hunger that could be satisfied by food. He watched her as she came in, thinking, *what do you want, Kate? Tell me what you want and I'll give it to you if I can.*

She hesitated in the doorway, looking as though she were trying to decide how to act.

Before she had a chance to decide, Gallantyne spoke to her in a quiet, confident manner, "Please sit down, Mrs. Oakley. We're hoping you'll be able to help us."

"I hope so, too. I was—I'm very fond of Jessie. If anything's happened to her, it will be a terrible blow to Mary Martha. Do you suppose it could have been a kidnaping?"

"There's no evidence of it. The Brants are barely getting by financially, and they've received no ransom demand. We're pretty well convinced that Jessie walked out of the house voluntarily."

"How can you know that for sure?"

"There were no signs of a struggle in Jessie's bedroom, the Arlingtons' dog didn't bark as he certainly would have if he'd heard a stranger, and the back door was unlocked. It's one of the new kinds of lock built into the knob—push the knob and it locks, pull and it unlocks. We think Jessie unlocked the door, accidentally or on purpose, when she went out. I'm inclined to believe that she unlocked it deliberately with the intention of returning to the house. Someone, or something, interfered with that intention."

He paused to light a cigarette, cupping his hands around the match as though he were outside on a windy day. "We'll assume, then, that she left the house under her own power and for a reason we don't know yet. The two likeliest places she might have gone are the Arlingtons' next door, or this house. Mrs. Arlington claims she didn't see her and you claim you didn't."

"Of course I didn't," she said stiffly. "I would have phoned her mother immediately."

"What I want you to consider now is the possibility that she might somehow have gotten into the house without your seeing her, that she might have hidden some place and fallen asleep."

"There's no such possibility."

"You seem very sure."

"I am. This house is Sheridan-proof. My ex-husband acquired the cunning habit of breaking in during my absences and helping himself to whatever he fancied—liquor, furniture, silver, and more liquor. I had a special lock put on every door and window. When I go out or retire for the night, I check them all. It would be as much as my life is worth to miss any of them."

"Jessie knew about these locks, of course?"

"Yes. She asked me about them. It puzzled her that a house should have to be secured against a husband and father. . . . No, Lieutenant, Jessie could never have entered this house without my letting her in."

That leaves the Arlingtons, he thought, *or someone on the street between here and the Arlingtons' house.* "Would you call Jessie a shy child, Mrs. Oakley?"

"No. She has—had quite a free and easy manner with people."

"Does that include strangers?"

"It included everyone."

"Have you had any strangers hanging around here recently?"

She gave Mac a quick, questioning look. He responded with a nod that indicated he'd already told Gallantyne about the man in the green coupé.

"Yes," she said, "but I never connected him with Jessie or Mary Martha."

"Do you now?"

"I don't know. It seems odd that he'd show himself so openly if he were planning anything against Jessie or Mary Martha."

"Perhaps he wasn't actually planning anything, he was merely waiting. And when Jessie walked out of that house by herself, she provided what he was waiting for, an opportunity."

A spot of color, dime-sized, appeared suddenly on her throat and began expanding, up to her ear tips, down into the neckline of her dress. The full realization of Jessie's fate seemed to be spreading throughout her system like poison dye. "It could just as easily have been Mary Martha instead of Jessie. Is that what you're telling me?"

"Think about it."

"I won't. It's unthinkable. Mary Martha wouldn't leave the house without my permission, and she'd certainly never enter the car of a strange man."

"Some pretty powerful inducements can be offered a child her age who's lonely and has affection going to waste. A puppy, for instance, or a kitten—"

"No, no!" But even the sound of her own voice shouting denials could not convince her. She knew the lieutenant was right. She knew that Mary Martha had left the house without permission just a few nights before. She'd run over to Jessie's using the short cut across the creek. Suppose she'd gone out the front, the way she often did. The man had been parked across the street at that very moment. "No, no," she repeated. "I've taught Mary Martha what it took me years of torment to learn, that you can't trust men, you can't believe them. They're liars, cheats, bullies. Mary Martha already knows that. She won't have to find it out the hard way as I did, as Jessie—"

"Be quiet, Kate," Mac said in a warning tone. "The lieutenant is too busy to listen to your theories this morning."

She didn't even glance in his direction. "Poor Jessie, poor misguided child with all her prattle about her wonderful father. She believed it, and that fool mother of hers actually encouraged her to believe it even though she must have been aware what was going on."

Gallantyne raised his brows. "And what was going on, Mrs. Oakley?"

"Plenty."

"Who was involved?"

"I must caution you, Kate," Mac said, "not to make any statements you're not able and willing to substantiate."

"In other words, I'm to shut up?"

"Until you've consulted your attorney."

"All my attorney ever does for me is tell me to shut up."

"Rumors and gossip are not going to solve this case."

"No, but they might help," Gallantyne said mildly. "Now, you were going to give me some new information about Jessie's father."

Kate looked from Gallantyne to Mac, then back to Gallantyne, as if she were trying to decide which one of them was the lesser evil. "It can hardly be called new. It goes back to Adam. Brant's a man and he's been availing himself of the privilege, deceiving his wife, cheating his children out of their birthright. Oh, he puts on a good front, almost as good as Sheridan when he's protesting his great love for Mary Martha."

"You're implying that Brant is having an affair with another woman?"

"Yes."

"Who is she?"

"Virginia Arlington."

Both men were watching her, Mac painfully, Gallantyne with cool suspicion.

"It's true," she added, clenching her fists. "I can't prove it, I don't have pictures of them in bed together. But I know it's a fact."

"Facts, Mrs. Oakley, are often what we choose to believe."

"I have nothing against Mrs. Arlington, I have no reason for wanting to believe bad things about her. She's probably just a victim like me, hoodwinked by a man, taken in by his promises. Oh, you should have heard Sheridan in the heyday of his promises. . . . But then you very likely know all about promises, Lieutenant. I bet you've made lots of them."

"A few."

"And they weren't kept?"

"Some weren't."

"That makes you a liar, doesn't it, Lieutenant? No better than the rest of them—"

"Please be quiet, Kate," Mac said. "You're not doing yourself any good or Jessie any good."

He touched Gallantyne lightly on the arm and the two men walked over to the far corner of the room and began talking in whispers. Though she couldn't distinguish any words, she was sure they were talking about her until Gallantyne finally raised his voice and said, "I must ask you not to mention Charlie Gowen to anyone, Mrs. Oakley."

"Charlie Gowen? I don't even know who—"

"The man in the green coupé. Don't tell anyone about him, not your friends or relatives or reporters or any other policeman. As far as you're concerned, Charlie Gowen doesn't even exist."

21

When Charlie arrived home at 5:30, he was so tired he could hardly get out of his car and cross the patch of lawn that separated the driveway from the house. He had worked very hard all day in the hope that his boss, Mr. Warner, would notice, and approve of him. He especially needed Mr. Warner's approval because Ben was angry with him for staying out too late the previous night. Although he knew Mr. Warner and Ben were entirely different people, and pleasing one didn't necessarily mean placating the other, he couldn't keep from trying. In his thoughts they weighed the same, and in his dreams they often showed up wearing each other's faces.

At the bottom of the porch steps he stooped to pick up the evening *Journal*. It lay under the hibiscus bush, fastened with an elastic band and folded so he could see only the middle third of the oversized headline: U SEEN TH

Usually, Charlie waited for the *Journal* until after Ben had finished with it because Ben liked to be the first to discover interesting bits of news and pass them along. But tonight he didn't hesitate. He tore off the elastic band and unfolded the paper. Jessie's face was smiling up at him. It didn't look the way it had the last time he'd seen her, shocked and frightened, but she was wearing the same clothes, a white bathrobe over pajamas.

The headline said HAVE YOU SEEN THIS GIRL?—and underneath the picture was an explanation of it: "This is a composite picture made from a snapshot of Jessie Brant's face superimposed on one of a child of similar height and build wearing clothes similar to those missing from Jessie's wardrobe. The *Journal* is offering $1,000 reward for information leading to the discovery of Jessie Brant's whereabouts."

For a long time Charlie stood looking at the girl who was half-Jessie, half-stranger. Then he turned and stumbled up the porch steps and into the house, clutching the newspaper against his chest as though to hide from the neighbors an old wound that had reopened and started to bleed again. In his room, with the door locked and the blinds drawn, he read the account of Jessie's disappearance. It began with a description of Jessie herself; of her father, a technician with an electronics firm; her brother, Michael, who hadn't learned the news until he'd been picked off a fishing boat by the Coast Guard cutter; her mother, the last member of her family to see Jessie alive at ten o'clock.

The official police announcement was issued by Lieutenant D. W. Gallantyne: "The evidence now in our possession indicates that Jessie departed from her house voluntarily, using the back door and leaving it unlocked so she would be able to return. What person, or set of circumstances, prevented her return? We are asking the public to help us answer that question. There is a strong possibility that someone noticed her leaving the house or walking along the street, and that that person can give us further information, such as what direction she was going and whether she was alone. Anyone who saw her is urged to contact us immediately. Jessie's grief-stricken parents join us in this appeal."

The light in the room was very dim. Narrowing his eyes to keep them in focus, Charlie reread the statement by Gallantyne. It was wrong, he knew it was wrong. It hadn't happened like that. Somebody should tell the lieutenant and set him straight.

He lay down on the bed, still holding the newspaper against his chest. The ticking of his alarm clock sounded extraordinarily loud and clear. He'd had the clock since his college days. It was like an old friend, the last voice he heard at night, the first voice in the morning: *tick it, tick it, tick it.* But now the voice began to sound different, not friendly, not comforting.

Wicked wicked, wicked sicked, wicked sicked.

"I'm not," he whispered. "I'm not. I didn't touch her."

Wicked sicked, pick a ticket, try and kick it, wicked wicked, buy a ticket, buy a ticket, buy a ticket.

Ben called out, "Charlie? You in there?" When he didn't get an answer he tried the door and found it locked. "Listen, Charlie, I'm not mad at you any more. I realize you're a grown man now and if you want to stay out late, well, what the heck, that's your business. Right?"

"Yes, Ben."

"I've got to stop treating you like a kid brother who's still wet behind the ears. That's what Louise says and by golly, it makes sense, doesn't it?"

"I guess so."

"She'll be over pretty soon. You don't want her to catch you sulk—unprepared."

"I'm preparing, Ben."

"Good. I couldn't find the *Journal*, by the way. Have you got it in there?"

"No."

"The delivery boy must have missed us. Well, I hate to report him so I think I'll go pick one up over at the drug store. I'll be back in a few minutes."

"All right."

"Charlie, listen, you're O.K., aren't you? I mean, everything's fine?"

"I am not sicked."

"What? I didn't hear what you—"

"I am not sicked."

The unfamiliar word worried Ben. As the worry became larger and larger, chunks of it began dropping off and changing into something he could more easily handle—anger. By the time he reached the drug store he'd convinced himself that Charlie had used the word deliberately to annoy him.

Mr. Forster was standing outside his drug store. Though his face looked grave, there was a glint of excitement in his eyes as though he'd just found out that one of his customers had contracted a nonfatal illness which would require years of prescriptions.

"Well, well, it's Benny Gowen. How's the world treating you, Benny?"

"Fine. Nobody calls me Benny any more, Mr. Forster."

"Don't they now. Well, that puts me in a class by myself. What can I do for you?"

"I'd like a *Journal*."

"Sorry, I'm all sold out." Mr. Forster was watching Ben carefully over the top of his spectacles. "Soon as I put them out here on the stand this afternoon people began picking them up like they were ten-dollar bills. Nothing sells papers like a real nasty case of murder or whatever it was. But I guess you know all about it, being you work downtown in the hub of things."

"I don't have a chance to read when I'm on the job," Ben said. "Who was murdered?"

"The police don't claim it was murder. But I figure it must have been. The kid's gone, nobody's seen hide nor hair of her since last night."

"Kid?"

"A nine-year-old girl named Jessie Brant. Disappeared right from in front of her own house or thereabouts. Now, nobody can tell me a nine-year-old kid wearing nightclothes wouldn't have been spotted by this time if she were still alive. It's not reasonable. Mark my words, she's lying dead some place and the most they can hope for is to find the body and catch the man responsible for the crime. You agree, Benny?"

"I know nothing about it."

Mr. Forster took off his spectacles and began cleaning them with a handkerchief that was dirtier than they were. "How's Charlie, by the way?"

He is not sicked. "He's all right. He's been all right for a long time now, Mr. Forster."

"Reason I asked is, he came in here yesterday with a bad headache. He bought some aspirin, but shucks, taking aspirin isn't getting to the root of anything. A funny thing about headaches, some doctors think they're mostly psychological, you know, caused by emotional problems. In Charlie's case I'm inclined to agree. Look at the record, all that trouble he's had and—"

"That's in the past."

"Being in the past and being over aren't necessarily the same thing." Mr. Forster replaced his spectacles with the air of a man who confidently expected new knowledge from increased vision. "Now don't get me wrong. *I* think Charlie's O.K. But I'm a friend of his, I'm not the average person reading about the kid and remembering back. There's bound to be talk."

"I'm sure you'll do your share of it." Ben turned to walk away but Mr. Forster's hand on his arm was like an anchor. "Let go of me."

"You must have misunderstood me, Ben. I *like* Charlie, I'm on his side. But I can't help feeling there's something wrong again. It probably doesn't involve the kid at all because it started yesterday afternoon before anything happened to her. Are you going to be reasonable and listen to me, Ben?"

"I'll listen if you have anything constructive to say."

"Maybe it's constructive, I don't know. Anyhow, a man came in here yesterday asking where Charlie lived. He gave me a pretty thin story about forgetting to look up the house number. I pretended to go along with it but I knew damned well he was trying to pump me."

"About Charlie?"

"Yes."

"What'd you tell him?"

"All the right things. Don't worry about that part of it, I gave Charlie a clean bill of health, 100 percent. Only—well, it's been on my mind ever since. The man looked like an official of some kind, why was he interested in Charlie?"

"Why didn't you ask him?"

"Heck, it would have spoiled the game. I was supposed to be taken in, see. I was playing the part of—"

"Playing games isn't going to help Charlie."

Mr. Forster's eyes glistened with excitement. "So now you're leveling with me, eh, Ben? There *is* something wrong, Charlie needs help again. Is that it?"

"We all need help, Mr. Forster," Ben said and walked away, this time without interference. He knew Mr. Forster would be watching him and he tried to move naturally and easily as though he couldn't feel the leaden chains attached to his limbs. He had felt these chains for almost his entire life; attached to the other end of them was Charlie.

He stopped at the corner, aware of the traffic going by, the people moving up and down and across the streets, the clock in the courthouse tower chiming six. He wanted to quiet the clock so he would lose consciousness of time; he wanted to join one of the streams of strangers, anonymous people going to unnamed places. Whoever, wherever, whenever, was better than being Ben on his way home to Charlie to ask him about a dead child.

*

Louise's little sports car was parked at the curb in front of the house. Ben found her in the living room, leafing through the pages of a magazine. She smiled when she looked up and saw him in the doorway, but he could tell from the uneasiness in her eyes that she'd read about the child and had been silently asking the same questions that Mr. Forster was asking out loud.

He said, trying to sound cheerful and unafraid, "Hello, Louise. When did you arrive?"

"About ten minutes ago."

"Where's Charlie?"

"In his room getting dressed."

"Oh. Are you going out some place? I thought—well, it's turning kind of cold out, it might be a nice night to build a fire and all three of us sit around and talk."

Louise smiled again with weary patience as if she was sick of talk and especially the talk of children, young or old. "I don't know what Charlie has in mind. When he answered the door he simply told me he was getting dressed. I'm not even sure he wanted me to wait for him. But I'm waiting, anyway. It's becoming a habit." She added, without any change in tone, "What time did he come home last night?"

"It must have been pretty late. I was asleep."

"You went to *sleep* with Charlie still out wandering around by himself? How could you have?"

"I was tired."

"You led me to understand that you'd go on looking for him. You said if I went home for some rest that you'd take over. And you didn't."

"No."

"Why not?"

"Because I started thinking about the conversation we had earlier," Ben said with deliberation. "You gave me the business about how I should trust Charlie, let him have a chance to grow up, allow him to reach his own decisions. You can't have it both ways, Louise. You can't tell me one minute to treat him like a responsible adult and the next minute send me out chasing after him as if he was a three-year-old. You can't accuse me of making mistakes in dealing with him and then an hour later beg me to make the same mistakes. Be honest, Louise. Where do you stand? What do you really think of Charlie?"

"Keep your voice down, Ben. He might hear you."

"Is that how you treat a responsible adult, you don't let him overhear anything?"

"I meant—"

"You meant what you said. The three-year-old shut up in the bedroom isn't supposed to hear what Mom and Pop are talking about in the living room."

"I wouldn't want Charlie to think we're quarreling, that's all."

"But we *are* quarreling. Why shouldn't he think so? If he's a responsible adult—"

"Stop repeating that phrase."

"Why? Because it doesn't fit him, and you can't bear listening to the truth?"

"Stop it, Ben, please. This isn't the time."

"This is the very time," he said soberly. "Right now, this minute, you've got to figure out how you really feel about Charlie. Sure, you love him, we both do. But you're not committed to him the way I am, or to put it bluntly, you're not stuck with him. You still have a chance to change your mind, to get away. Do it, Louise."

"I can't."

"For your own sake, you'd better try. Walk out of here now and don't look back. For nearly a year you've been dreaming, and I've been letting you. Now the alarm's ringing, it's time to wake up and start moving. Beat it, Louise."

"You don't know what you're asking."

"I'm asking," he said, "that one out of this trio gets a chance to survive. It won't be Charlie and it can't be me. That leaves you, Louise. Use your chance, for my sake if not your own. I'd like to think of you as being happy in the future, leading a nice, uncomplicated life."

"There's no such thing."

"You won't leave?"

"No."

"Then God help you." He went over to the window and stood with his back to Louise so she wouldn't see the tears welling in his eyes. "A little girl disappeared last night. One person in this neighborhood has already mentioned Charlie in connection with the crime. There'll be others, not just common gossips like Forster, but men with authority. Whatever Charlie has or hasn't done, it's going to be rough on him, and on you, too, if you stick around."

"I'm sticking."

"Yes, I was afraid you would. Why? Do you want to be a martyr?"

"I want to be Charlie's wife."

"It's the same thing."

"Don't try to destroy my confidence completely, Ben," she said. "It would be easy, I don't have very much. But what I have may help Charlie and perhaps you, too, in the days to come."

"Days? You're thinking in terms of *days*? What about the months, years—"

"They're composed of days. I choose to think of them in that way. Now," she added in a gentler voice, "do I get your blessing, Ben?"

"You get everything I have to offer."

"Thank you."

She turned toward the doorway, hearing Charlie's step in the hall. It sounded brisk and lively as if he'd had an abrupt change of mood in the past ten minutes. When he came in she noticed that he was freshly shaved and wearing his good suit and the tie she'd given him for his birthday. He looked surprised when he saw that she was still there, and she wondered whether he'd expected her to leave, and if so, why he'd taken the trouble to get all dressed up. He was carrying the evening newspaper. It was crumpled and torn as though it had been used to swat flies.

He put it down carefully on the coffee table, his eyes fixed on Ben. "I found it after all, Ben. Right after you left to buy one I decided to go out and search for it again, and sure enough there it was, hidden behind that shrub with the pink flowers. Remember what we used to call it when we were kids, Ben? High biscuits. I used to think that it actually had biscuits on it but they were up so high I couldn't see them."

"I looked under the hibiscus," Ben said.

"You must have missed it. It was there."

"It wasn't there."

"You—you could have made a mistake, Ben. You were complaining about your eyes last week. Anyway, it's such a small thing, we shouldn't be raising all this fuss about it in front of Louise."

"Louise better get used to it. And if it's such a small thing, why are you lying about it?"

"Well, I—well, maybe it didn't happen *exactly* like that." The muscles of Charlie's throat were working, as if he was trying to swallow or unswallow something large and painful and immovable. "When I got home I picked up the paper and took it into my room to read."

"Why? You're not usually interested."

"I saw the headline about the little girl, and the picture. I wanted to study it, to make sure before—before going to the police."

Ben stared at him in silence for a moment, then he repeated, "Before going to the police. Is that what you said?"

"Yes. I'm sure now—the face, the clothes, her name and address. I'm very sure. That's why I got dressed up, so I'll make a good impression at headquarters. You've always told me how necessary a good impression is. Do I look O.K.?"

"You look dandy. You'll make a dandy impression. . . . Jesus Godalmighty, what are you trying to do to me, to yourself? It isn't enough that—"

"But I'm only doing what I have to, Ben. The paper said any witnesses should come forward and tell what they know. And I'm a witness. That's funny, isn't it? I always wanted to be somebody and now I finally am. I'm a witness. That's pretty important, according to the paper. I may even be the only one in the whole city, can you beat that?"

"No. I don't think anyone can. This time you've really done it, you've set a new high."

Charlie's smile was strained, a mixture of pride and anxiety.

"Well, I didn't actually *do* anything, I just happened to be there when she came out of the house. The police are wrong about which house she came out of. It wasn't her own, the way the paper said. It was the one—"

"You just happened to be there, eh, Charlie?"

"Yes."

"In your car?"

"Yes."

"Was the car parked?"

"I—I'm not sure but I think I may have been only passing by, very slowly."

"Very, *very* slowly?"

"I think so. I may have stopped for a minute when I saw her on account of I was surprised. It was so late and she shouldn't have been out. Her parents should have taken better care of her, not letting her run wild on the streets past ten o'clock, no one to protect her."

"Did you offer to protect her, Charlie?"

"Oh no."

"Did you talk to her at all?"

"No. I may have sort of spoken her name out loud because I was so surprised to see her, it being late and cold and lonely." He broke off suddenly, frowning. "You're mixing me up with your questions. You're getting me off the subject. That's not the important part, how I happened to be there and what I did. The important thing is, she didn't come out of her own house. The police think she did, so it's my duty to straighten them out. I bet they'll be very glad to have some new evidence."

"I just bet they will," Ben said. "Go to your room, Charlie."

"What?"

"You heard me. Go to your room."

"I can't do that. I'm a witness, they need me. They *need* me, Ben."

"Then they'll have to come and get you."

"You're interfering with justice. That's a very wrong thing to do."

"Justice? What kind of justice do you think is in store for you, when you can't even tell them what you were doing outside the girl's house, or whether you were parked there or just passing by?"

"You've got it all wrong, Ben. They're not after me, I didn't do anything."

Ben turned away. He wanted to hit Charlie with his fist, he wanted to weep or to run shrieking out into the street. But all he could do was stand with his face to the wall, wishing he were back on the street corner where he could pretend he was anyone, going any place, at any hour of the day or night.

The only sound in the room was Charlie's breathing. It

was ordinary breathing, in and out, in and out, but to Ben it was the sound of doom. "Maybe I ought to go ahead and let you ruin yourself," he said finally. "I can't do that, though. Not yet, anyway. So I'm asking you to stay in your room for tonight and we'll discuss this in the morning."

"Ben may be right, Charlie," Louise said. It was the first time she'd spoken since Charlie came into the room. She used her library voice, very quiet but authoritative. "You need time to get your story straight."

Charlie shook his head stubbornly. "It's not a story."

"All right then, you need time to remember the facts. You can't claim to have been at the scene without giving some plausible reason why you were there and what you were doing."

"I wanted some fresh air."

"Other streets, other neighborhoods, have fresh air. The police will ask you why you picked that one."

"I didn't. I was driving around everywhere, just driving around, breathing the free—the fresh air."

"The way you did the other night?"

"Other night?"

"When I found you on Jacaranda Road."

"Why do you bring that up?" he said violently. "You know nothing happened that night. You told me, you were the one who convinced me. You said, *nothing's happened, Charlie. Nothing whatever has happened, it's all in your mind.* Why aren't you saying that now, Louise?"

"I will, if you want me to."

"Not because you believe it?"

"I—believe it." She clung to his arm, half-protectively, half-helplessly.

He looked down at her as if she were a stranger making an intimate demand. "Don't touch me, woman."

"Please, Charlie, you mustn't talk to me like that. I love you."

"No. You spoil things for me. You spoiled my being a witness."

He jerked his arm out of her grasp and ran toward the hall. A few seconds later she heard the slam of his bedroom door. There was a finality about it like the closing of the last page of a book.

It's over, she thought. *I had a dream, the alarm rang, I woke up and it's over.*

She could still hear the alarm ringing in her ears, and above it, the sound of Ben's voice. It sounded very calm but it was the calmness of defeat.

"I should have forced you to leave. I would have, if I'd known what was going on in his mind. But this witness bit, how could I have called that?" He looked out the window. It was getting dark and foggy. The broad, leathery leaves of the loquat tree were already dripping and the street lights had appeared wearing their gauzy gray nightgowns. "Either the whole thing's a fantasy, or he's telling the truth but not all of it."

"All of it?"

"That he attacked the child and killed her."

"Stop it. I'll never believe that, never."

"You half believed it when you walked in this door. You came here for reassurance. You wanted to be told that Charlie arrived home early last night, that he and I had a talk and then he went to bed. Well, he didn't, we didn't. This isn't a very good place to come for reassurance, Louise. It's a luxury we don't keep in stock."

"I didn't come here for reassurance. I wanted to see Charlie, to tell him that I love him and I trust him."

"You trust him, do you?"

"Yes."

"How far? Far enough to allow him to go to the police with his story?"

"Naturally I'd like him to get the details straight first, before he exposes himself to—to their questions."

"You make it sound very simple, as if Charlie's mind is a reference book he can open at will and look up the answers. Maybe you're right, in a way. Maybe his mind is a book, but it's written in a language you and I can't understand, and the pages aren't in order and some of them are glued together and some are missing entirely. Not exactly a perfect place to find answers, is it, Louise?"

"Stop badgering me like this," she said. "It's not fair."

"If you don't like it, you can leave."

"Is that all I ever get from you any more, an invitation to leave, walk away, don't come back?"

"That's it."

"Why?"

"I told you before, one of the three of us should have a

chance, just a chance." He was still watching the fog pressing at the window like the gray facelessness of despair. "Charlie's my problem, now more than ever. I'll look after him. He won't go to the police tonight or any other night. He'll do what I tell him to do. I'll see that he gets to work in the morning and that he gets home safely after work. I'll stay with him, talk to him, listen to him, play the remember-game with him. He likes that —*remember when we were kids, Ben?*—he can play it for hours. It won't be a happy life or a productive one, but the most I can hope for Charlie right now is that he's allowed to survive at all. He's a registered sex offender. Sooner or later he's bound to be questioned about the child's disappearance. I only hope it's later so I can try and push this witness idea out of his head."

"How will you do that?"

"I'll convince him that he wasn't near the house, he didn't see the child, he didn't see anything. He was at home with me, he dozed off in an armchair, he had a nightmare."

"Don't do it, Ben. It's too risky, tampering with a mind that's already confused about what's real and what isn't."

"If he doesn't know what's real," Ben said, "I'll have to tell him. And he'll believe me. It will be like playing the remember-game. *Remember last night, Charlie, when you were sitting in the armchair? And you suddenly dozed off, you cried out in your sleep, you were having a nightmare about a house, a child coming out of a house. . . .*"

He had to write the letter very quickly because he knew Ben would be coming in soon to talk to him. He folded the letter six times, slipped it into an envelope, addressed the envelope to Police Headquarters and put it in the zippered inside pocket of his windbreaker. Then he returned to his desk. The desk had been given to him when he was twelve and it was too small for him. He had to hunch way down in order to work at it but he didn't mind this. It made him feel big, a giant of a man; a kindly giant, though, who used his strength only to protect, never to bully, so everyone respected him.

When Ben came in, Charlie pretended to be studying an advertisement in the back pages of a magazine.

"Dinner's ready," Ben said. "I brought home some chicken pies from the cafeteria and heated them up."

"I'll eat one if you want me to, Ben, but I'd just as soon not."

"Aren't you hungry?"

"Not very. I had chicken pie last night."

"We had ravioli last night. Don't you remember? I cut myself opening the can. Look, here's the cut on my finger."

Charlie looked at the cut with polite interest. "That's too bad. You must be more careful. I wasn't here last night for dinner."

"Yes, you were. You ate too much and later you dozed off in Father's armchair in the front room."

"No, Ben, that was a lot of other nights. Last night was different, it was very different. First I took that delivery to the Forest Service. All that heat and dust up in the mountains gave me a headache so I went to the drug store for some aspirin."

"The aspirin made you sleepy. That's why you dozed—"

"I wasn't a bit sleepy, I was hungry. I was going to take Louise some place to eat—I don't mean eat *her*," he added earnestly. "I mean, where we could both eat some food. Only she wasn't at the library so I went by myself and had a chicken pie."

"Where?"

"The cafeteria you manage. It wouldn't be loyal to go anywhere else."

"You picked a hell of a time to be loyal," Ben said. "Did anyone see you?"

"They must have. There I was."

"Did you speak to anyone?"

"The cashier. I said hello."

"Did she recognize you?"

"Oh yes. She made a joke about how everyone had to pay around that joint, even the boss's brother."

That fixes it, Ben thought. *If he'd planned every detail in advance he couldn't have done a better job of lousing things up.* "What time were you there?"

"I don't know. I hate watching the clock, it watches me back."

"What did you do after you finished eating?"

"Drove around, I told you that. I wanted some fresh air to clear the dust out of my sinuses."

"You were home by ten o'clock."

"No, I couldn't have been. It was after ten when I saw—"

"You saw nothing," Ben said harshly. "You were home with me by ten o'clock."

"I don't remember seeing you when I came in."

"You didn't. I was in bed. But I knew what time it was because I'd just turned out the light."

"You couldn't be mistaken, like about the ravioli?"

"The ravioli business was simply a device to get at the truth. I knew you'd been to the drug store and the library but I wanted you to recall those things for yourself. You did."

"Not this other, though."

"You were home by ten. I wasn't asleep yet, I heard you come in. If anyone asks you, that's what you're to say. Say it now."

"Please leave—leave me alone, Ben."

"I can't." Ben leaned over the desk, his face white and contorted. "You're in danger and I'm trying to save you. I'm going to save you in spite of yourself. Now say it. Say you were home by ten o'clock."

"Will you leave me alone, then?"

"Yes."

"You promise?"

"*Yes.*"

"I was home by ten o'clock," Charlie repeated, blinking. "You cut yourself opening a can of ravioli. You were bleeding, you were bleeding all over the bloody kitchen. Let me see your cut again. Does it still hurt, Ben?"

"No."

"Then what are you crying for?"

"I have a—a pain."

"You shouldn't eat highly spiced foods like ravioli."

"No, that was a mistake." Ben's voice was a rag of a whisper torn off a scream. "I'll try to make it up to you, Charlie."

"To me? But it's your pain."

"We share it. Just like in the old days, Charlie, when we shared everything. Remember how my friends used to kid me about my little brother always tagging along? I never minded, I liked having you tag along. Well, it will be like that again, Charlie. I'll drive you to work in the morning, you can walk over to the cafeteria and have lunch with me at noon—"

"I have my own car," Charlie said. "And sometimes Louise and I prefer to have lunch together."

"Louise's lunch hour is going to be changed. It probably won't jibe with yours any more."

"She didn't tell me that."

"She will. As for the car, it seems wasteful to keep two of them running when I can just as easily drive you wherever you want to go. Let's try it for a while and see how it works out. Maybe we can save enough money to take a trip somewhere."

"Louise and I are going to take a trip on our honeymoon."

"That might not be for some time."

"Louise said September, next month."

"Well, things are a little hectic at the library right now, Charlie. There's a chance she might not—she might not be able to get away."

"Why does Louise tell you stuff before she tells me? Explain it to me, Ben."

"Not tonight."

"Because of your pain?"

"Yes, my pain," Ben said. "I want you to give me your car keys now, Charlie."

Charlie put his left hand in the pocket of his trousers. He could feel the outline of the keys, the round one for the trunk, the pointed one for the ignition. "I must have left them in the car."

"I've warned you a dozen times about that."

"I'm sorry, Ben. I'll go and get them."

"*No.* I will."

Charlie watched him leave. He hadn't planned it like this, in fact he had planned nothing beyond the writing of the letter. But now that he saw his opportunity he couldn't resist it any more than a caged animal could resist an open gate. He picked up his windbreaker and went quietly through the kitchen and out of the back door.

22

Ralph MacPherson was preparing for an early bedtime when the telephone rang. He reached for it quickly, afraid that it would be Kate calling and afraid that it wouldn't. He hadn't heard from her all day and her parting words that morning had been hostile as if she hadn't forgiven him for doubting her story about Brant and Mrs. Arlington.

"Hello."

"This is Gallantyne, Mac."

"Don't you ever sleep?"

"I had a couple of hours this afternoon. Don't worry about me."

"I'm worried about me, not you. I was just going to bed. What's up?"

"I'm calling to return a favor," Gallantyne said. "You let me read the anonymous letter Kate Oakley received, so I'll let you read one that was brought to me tonight if you'll come down to my office."

"I've had more tempting offers."

"Don't bet on it. The two letters were written by the same man."

"I'll be right down," Mac said and hung up.

Gallantyne was alone in the cubicle he called an office. He showed no signs of the fatigue that Mac felt weighing down his limbs and dulling his eyes.

The letter was spread out on the desk with a goosenecked lamp turned on it. It was printed, like the one Kate Oakley had received, and it had been folded in the same way, many times, as though the writer was unconsciously ashamed of it and had compressed it into as small a package as possible. An envelope lay beside it, with the words Police Department printed on it. It bore no stamp.

Mac said, "How did you get hold of this?"

"It was dropped in the mail slot beside the front door of headquarters about two hours ago. The head janitor was just coming in to adjust the hot-water heater and he saw the man who put the letter in the slot. He gave me a good description."

"Who was it?"

"Charles Gowen," Gallantyne said. "Surprised?"

"I'm surprised at the crazy chances he took, delivering the letter himself, making no effort to alter his printing or the way he folded the paper."

"What kind of people take chances like that, Mac?"

"The ones who want to be caught."

Gallantyne leaned back in his chair and looked up at the ceiling. In the center of it, the shadow of the lampshade was like a black moon in a white sky. "I checked his record. It goes back a long way and he's been treated since then, both at Coraznada State Hospital and privately. But a record's a record. When a man's had cancer, the doctors can't ignore his medical history. Well, this is cancer, maybe worse. Gowen's had it, and I think he has it again. Read the letter."

It was briefer than the first one.

> To the Police:
>
> I was driving along Cielito Lane last night at 10:30 and I know you are Bad about which house Jessie came out of. It was the house next door on the west side. They will keep me a prisoner now so I can never tell you this in person but it is True.
>
> A Witness
>
> P.S. Jessie is my fiend.

Mac read it again, wondering who "they" were; the brother, probably, and the woman Mr. Forster the druggist had mentioned, Gowen's fiancée.

Gallantyne was watching him with eyes as hard and bright as mica.

"Interesting document, wouldn't you say? Notice the capitalizations, Bad and True. And the postscript."

"I suppose he intended to write 'friend' and omitted the 'r.'"

"I think so."

"And by 'Bad' I gather he means wrong."

"Yes. The house next door on the west side belongs to the Arlingtons." Gallantyne leaned forward and moved the lamp to one side, twisting the shade. The black moon slid down the white sky and disappeared. "As soon as the letter came, I sent Corcoran over to Gowen's house. The brother was there, Ben, and Gowen's girl friend, Louise Lang. Gowen was missing. The brother and girl friend claimed they didn't know where he'd gone, but according to Corcoran, they were extremely nervous and what they weren't saying, they were thinking. Anyway, I gave the word for Gowen to be picked up for questioning."

"Do you believe what he said in his letter about Jessie coming out of the Arlingtons' house?"

"Well, it seems to fit in with Mrs. Oakley's story that Mrs. Arlington and Brant were something more than neighbors."

"I've told you before, you can't afford to take Kate too seriously. She frequently thinks the worst of people, especially if they have any connection in her mind with Sheridan."

"The letter tends to support her statement."

"I don't see it."

"Then you're not looking. And the reason you're not looking is obvious—Kate Oakley. You're doing your best, in a quiet way, to keep her out of this case."

"That's a false conclusion," Mac said. "When a statement in a letter showing certain signs of disturbance is supported by the word of a woman who shows similar signs, it doesn't mean both are right because they agree. It could mean that neither is right."

"You want more evidence? O.K., let's gather some." Gallantyne got up, the swivel chair squawking in protest at the sudden, violent movement. "I'm going to talk to Brant. Coming with me?"

"No. I prefer to get some sleep."

"Sleep is for babies."

"Look, I don't want to be dragged into this thing any further."

"You dragged yourself in, Mac. You didn't come here tonight out of idle curiosity or because anyone forced you. You're here on the chance that you might be able to help Kate Oakley. Why don't you admit it? Every time you mention her name, I see it in your face and hear it in your voice, that anxious, protective—"

"It's none of your business."

"Maybe not, but when I'm working with somebody I want to be sure he's working with me and not against me on behalf of a woman he's in love with."

"Now you're telling me I'm in love with her."

"I figure somebody should. You're a little slow about some things, Mac. No hard feelings, I hope?"

"Oh no, nothing like that."

"Then let's go."

The Brant house was all dark except for a light above the front door and a lamp burning behind the heavily draped windows of the living room.

Gallantyne pressed the door chime and waited. For the first time since Mac had known him, he looked doubtful, as if he'd just realized that he was about to do something he wouldn't approve of anyone else doing, dealing another blow to a man already reeling.

"Sure, it's a dirty business," he said, as much to himself as to Mac. "But it's got to be done. It's my job to save the kid, not spare the feelings of the family and the neighbors. And by God, I think the whole damn bunch of them have been holding out on me."

"If the only way you can handle this situation is to get mad," Mac said, "all right, get mad. But watch your step. The fact that Brant's daughter is missing doesn't deprive him of his rights, both legal and human."

"How I feel now is nobody has any rights until that kid is found alive and kicking."

"That's dangerous talk coming from a policeman. If you ignore Brant's rights, or Gowen's, you're giving people an invitation to ignore yours."

Gallantyne pressed the door chime again, harder and longer this time, although the answering tinkle was no louder and no faster. "I'm sick of a little lie here and a little lie there. Gowen's in the picture all right, but he's only part of it. I want the rest, the whole works in living color. Why did Mrs. Arlington claim the kid didn't go to her house?"

"Gowen might be the one who's lying, or mistaken."

"I repeat, his statement jibes with Kate Oakley's."

"It's not necessary to drag Kate into—"

"Mrs. Oakley dragged herself in, the same way you did. She volunteered that information about Brant. Nobody asked her, nobody had to pump it out of her. She's in, Mac, and she's in because she wanted to be in."

"Why?"

"Who knows? Maybe she needs a little excitement in her life—though that should be your department, shouldn't it?"

"That's a crude remark."

"So I'm having a crude night. It happens in my line of work, you get a lot of crude nights."

A light went on in the hall and a few seconds later Dave Brant opened the door. He was still wearing the clothes he'd had on the previous night, jeans and a sweatshirt, dirty and covered with bloodstains now dried to the color of chocolate. The hand he'd injured in a fall was covered with a bandage that looked as though he'd put it on himself.

He was gray-faced, gray-voiced. "Is there any news?"

Gallantyne shook his head. "Sorry. May we come in?"

"I guess so."

"You remember Mr. MacPherson, don't you?"

"Yes."

"I'd like to talk to you for a few minutes, Mr. Brant."

"I've told you everything."

"There may be one or two little items you forgot." Gallantyne closed the door. "Or overlooked. Are you alone in the house?"

"I sent my son Michael to spend the night with a friend. My wife is asleep. The doctor was here half an hour ago and gave her a shot."

"Did he give you anything?"

"Some pills. I didn't take any of them. I want to be alert in case—in case they find Jessie and she needs me. I may have to drive somewhere and pick her up, perhaps several hundred miles away."

"I suggest you take the pills. Any picking up can be done by the police—"

"No. I'm her father."

"—in fact, must be done by the police. If Jessie turns up now, at this stage, it won't simply be a matter of putting her to bed and telling her to forget the whole thing."

"You mean she will be questioned?"

"She will be questioned if she's physically and mentally able to answer."

"Don't say that, don't—"

"You asked."

Gallantyne hesitated, glancing uneasily at Mac. The hesitation, and the doubt in his eyes, made it clear to Mac why he'd been invited to come along. Gallantyne needed his support; he was getting older, more civilized; he'd learned to see both sides of a situation and the knowledge was destroying his appetite for a fight.

"Perhaps we'd all better go in the living room and sit down," Mac said. "You must be tired, Mr. Brant."

"No. No, I'm alert, I'm very alert."

"Come on."

The single lamp burning in the living room was behind an imitation leather chair. On the table beside the chair, pictures of Jessie were spread out: a christening photograph taken when she was a baby, classroom pictures, snaps of Jessie with Michael, with her parents, with the Arlingtons' dog; Mary Martha and Jessie, arms self-consciously entwined, standing on a bridge; Jessie on the beach, on her bicycle, in a hammock reading a book.

Silently, Dave bent down and began gathering up the pictures as if to shield Jessie from the eyes of strangers. Gallantyne waited until they were all returned to their folders. Then he said, "You asked me before, Mr. Brant, if I had any news. I told you I hadn't, and that's true enough. I do have something new, though. A man claims to have seen Jessie at 10:30 last night."

"Where?"

"Coming out of the Arlingtons' house. Would you know anything about that, Mr. Brant?"

"Yes."

"What, for instance?"

"It's not—not true."

"Now why do you say that? You weren't anywhere around at that time, were you? I understand you were out searching for Mr. Arlington, who'd left here after a quarrel with his wife."

"Yes."

"Where did you go?"

"A few bars, some cafés."

"And after that?"

"Home."

"Whose home?"

Dave turned his head away. "Well, I naturally had to check in at Virg—at Mrs. Arlington's house to tell her I hadn't been able to find Howard."

"This checking in," Gallantyne said softly, "was it pretty involved? Time-consuming?"

"I told her the places where I had looked for Howard."

"It took you exactly two seconds to tell me."

"We discussed a few other things, too. She was worried about Howard, he'd been acting peculiarly all evening."

"In what way?"

"He seemed jealous of the attention Virginia paid to Jessie."

"Did he have any other cause for jealousy?"

"I don't know what you're getting at."

"It's a simple enough question, surely."

"Well, I can't answer it. I don't know what was going on in Howard's mind."

"I'm talking about *your* mind, Mr. Brant."

"I've—I've forgotten the question. I'm—you're confusing me."

"Sorry," Gallantyne said. "I'll put it another way. How did you feel when Mr. Arlington walked out of here last night?"

"We were all upset by it. Howard had never done anything like that before."

"What time did he leave?"

"Between 9:30 and ten."

"What happened after that?"

"I took Virginia home. Then I decided I'd better try and find Howard."

"You decided, not Mrs. Arlington?"

"It was my idea. She was too depressed to be thinking clearly."

"Depressed. I see. Did you attempt to cheer her up in any way?"

"I went looking for her husband."

"And you returned to her house at what time?"

"I'm not sure. I wasn't wearing a watch."

"Well, let's try and figure it out, shall we? You know what time you discovered Jessie missing from her room."

"Eleven. She has a clock beside her bed."

"Very well. At ten, your wife retired for the night. Half an hour later Jessie was seen leaving the Arlington house."

Dave kept shaking his head back and forth. "No, I told you that's not true. It's a—a terrible impossibility."

"Impossibilities can't be terrible, Mr. Brant. By definition, they don't exist. Possibilities are a different matter. They can happen, and they can be quite terrible, like the one you're seeing now."

"No. I don't, I *won't*."

"You have to," Gallantyne said. "I suggest that Jessie went over to the Arlingtons' place between ten and 10:30. The house was always open to her, she could come and go as she liked, according to Mrs. Arlington. She entered by the back door—"

"No. It was locked, it must have been locked."

"Did you lock it yourself?"

"No."

"That was a pretty serious mistake, wasn't it, Brant? Or are you so casual about that sort of thing you don't mind an onlooker?"

"She didn't see us, she couldn't—"

"I think she did. She saw her father, and the woman she called her aunt, in an attitude that shocked and frightened her so badly that she dashed out into the street. I don't know what was in her mind, perhaps nothing more than a compulsion to escape from that scene. I do know there was a man waiting for her in a car. Perhaps he'd been waiting a long time, and for many nights previously, but that was the night that counted because Jessie's guard was down. She was in a highly emotional state, she didn't have sense enough to cry out or to run away when the man accosted her."

Dave's body was bent double, his forehead touching his knees, as though he was trying to prevent himself from fainting.

Mac crossed the room and leaned over him. "Are you all right, Brant?"

"Aaah." It was not a word, merely a long, painful sigh of assent: he was all right, he wished he were dead but he was all right.

"Listen, Brant. It didn't necessarily happen the way Lieutenant Gallantyne claims it did."

"Yes. My fault, all my fault."

"Tell him, Gallantyne."

Gallantyne raised his eyebrows in a show of innocence. "Tell him what?"

"Can't you see he's in a bad way and needs some kind of reassurance?"

"All right, I'll give him some." Gallantyne's voice was quiet, soothing. "You're a real good boy, Brant. You had nothing to do with your daughter's disappearance. A little hanky-panky with the dame next door; well, Jessie was nine, old enough to know about such things. She shouldn't have been shocked or scared or confused. Don't they teach these matters in the schools nowadays? The birds and the bees, Daddy and Aunt Virginia . . . Now, you want to tell me about it?"

Slowly and stiffly, Dave raised his head. "There's nothing to tell except it—it happened."

"Not for the first time?"

"No, not for the first time."

"Did you plan on divorcing your wife and marrying Mrs. Arlington?"

"I had no plan at all."

"What about Mrs. Arlington?"

"If she had one, I wasn't the important part of it."

"Who was?"

"Jessie. Jessie seems to be a projection of herself. She's the child Virginia was and all the children Virginia will never have."

"When did you find this out?"

"Today. I started thinking about it today."

"A bit late, weren't you?" Gallantyne said. "Too late to do Jessie any good."

"You—are you trying to tell me Jessie is—that she's dead?"

"The man who was waiting for her in the car has a history of sexual psychopathy. I can't offer you much hope, Brant." *Not any hope except that the other child in his history managed to survive.*

23

HE WAS moving toward the sea as inevitably as a drop of water. There were stops for traffic lights, detours to avoid passing places where Ben or Louise sometimes went; there were backtrackings when he found himself on a strange street. These things delayed him but they didn't alter his destination.

He passed the paper company where he worked. A light was burning in the office and he went over and peered into the window, hoping to see Mr. Warner sitting at his desk. But the office was empty, the light burning only to discourage burglars. Charlie was disappointed. He would have liked to talk to Mr. Warner, not about anything in particular, just a quiet, calm conversation about the ordinary things which ordinary people discussed. To Mr. Warner he wasn't anyone special; such a conversation was possible. But Mr. Warner wasn't there.

Charlie went around the side of the building to the loading zone, which was serviced by a short spur of railroad track. He followed the spur for no reason other than that it led somewhere. He took short, quick steps, landing on every tie and counting them as he moved. At the junction of the spur and the main track he stopped, suddenly aware that he was not alone. He raised his head and saw a man coming toward him, walking in the dry, dusty weeds beside the track. He looked like one of the old winos who hung around the railroad jungle, waiting for a handout or an empty boxcar or an even break. He was carrying a paper bag and an open bottle of muscatel.

He said, "Hey, chum, what's the name of this place?"

"San Felice."

"San Felice, well, what do you know? I thought it seemed kinda quiet for L.A. It's California, though, ain't it?"

"Yes."

"Not that it matters none. I been in them all. They're all alike, except California has the grape." He touched the bottle to his cheek. "The grape and me, we're buddies. Got a cigarette and a light?"

"I don't smoke but I think I have some matches." Charlie rummaged in the pocket of his windbreaker and brought out a book of matches. On the outside cover an address was written: 319 Jacaranda Road. He recognized the handwriting as his own but he couldn't remember writing it or whose address it was or why it should make him afraid, afraid to speak, afraid to move except to crush the matches in his fist.

"Hey, what's the matter with you, chum?"

Charlie turned and began to run. He could hear the man yelling something after him but he didn't stop until the track rounded a bend and a new sound struck his ears. It was a warning sound, the barking of dogs; not just two or three dogs but a whole pack of them.

The barking of the dogs, the bend in the tracks, the smell of the sea nearby, they were like electric shocks of recognition stinging his ears, his eyes, his nose. He knew this place. He hadn't been anywhere near it for years, but he remembered it all now, the boarding kennels behind the scraggly pittosporum hedge and the grade school a few hundred yards to the south. He remembered the children taking the back way to school because it was shorter and more exciting, teetering along the tracks with flailing arms, waiting until the final split second to jump down into the brush before the freight train roared past. It was a game, the bravest jumped last, and the girls were often more daring than the boys. One little girl in particular seemed to have no fear at all. She laughed when the engineer leaned out of his cab and shook his fist at her, and she laughed at Charlie's threats to report her to the principal, to tell her parents, to let some of the dogs loose on her.

"*You can't, ha ha, because they're not your dogs and they wouldn't come back to you and a lot of them would have babies if they got away. Don't you even know that, you dumb old thing?*"

"*I know it but I don't talk about it. It's not nice to talk about things like that.*"

"*Why not?*"

"*You get off those tracks right away.*"

"*Come and make me.*"

For nearly an hour Virginia had been standing at the window with one corner of the drape pulled back just enough so that she had a view of the front of the Brant house and the curb where the black Chrysler was parked. She had seen Gallantyne and the lawyer getting out of it and had stayed at the window watching hopefully for some sign of good news. Minute by minute the hope had died but she couldn't stop watching.

She could hear Howard moving around in the room behind her, picking up a book, laying it down, straightening a picture, lighting a cigarette, sitting, standing, making short trips to the kitchen and back. His restless activity only increased her feeling of coldness and quietness.

"You can't stand there all night," Howard said finally. "I've fixed you a hot rum. Will you drink it?"

"No."

"It might help you to eat something."

"I don't want anything."

"I can't let you starve."

For the first time in an hour she turned and glanced at him. "Why not? It might solve your problems. It would certainly solve mine."

"Don't talk like that."

"Why not? Does it hurt your ego to think that your wife would rather die than go on living like this?"

"It hurts me all over, Virginia. Without you I have nothing."

"That's nonsense. You have your work, the company, the customers—you see more of them than you do of me."

"I have in the past. The future's going to be different, Virginia."

"Future," she repeated. "That's just a dirty word to me. It's like some of the words I picked up when I was a kid. I didn't know what they meant but they sounded bad so I said them to shock my aunt. I don't know what future means either but it sounds bad."

"I promise you it won't be. I called the boss in Chicago this morning while you were still in bed. I didn't mention it to you because I would have liked the timing to be right but I guess I can't afford to wait any longer. I resigned, Virginia. I told him my wife and I were going to—to adopt a baby and I wanted to spend more time at home with them."

"What made you say a crazy thing like that?"

"I hadn't planned to, it just popped out. When I heard myself saying it, it didn't seem crazy. It seemed right, exactly right, Virginia."

"No. You mustn't—"

"He offered me a managerial position in Phoenix. I'd be on a straight salary, no bonuses for a big sale or anything like that, so it would mean less money actually. But I'd be working from nine to five like anybody else and I'd be home Saturdays and Sundays. I told him I'd think about it and let him know by the end of the week."

She had turned back to the window so he couldn't see her face or guess what was passing through her mind.

"Maybe you wouldn't like Phoenix, Virginia. It's a lot bigger than San Felice and it's hot in the summers, really hot, and of course there's no ocean to cool it off."

"No—no fog?"

"No fog."

"I'd like that part of it. The fog makes me so lonely. Even when the sun's shining bright I find myself looking out towards the sea, wondering when that gray wall will start moving towards me."

"I guarantee no fog, Virginia."

"You sound so hopeful," she said. "Don't. Please don't."

"What's wrong with a little hope?"

"Yours isn't based on anything."

"It's based on you and me, our marriage, our life together."

She took a long, deep breath that made the upper part of her body shudder. "We don't have a marriage any more. Remember the nursery rhyme, Howard, about the young woman who 'sat on a cushion and sewed a fine seam, and fed upon strawberries, sugar and cream'? Well, the sitting bored her, the cream made her fat, the strawberries gave her hives and her fine seams started getting crooked. Then Jessie came to live next door. At first her visits were a novelty to me, a break in a dull day. Then I began to look forward to them more and more, finally I began to depend on them. I was no longer satisfied to be the friend next door, the pseudo-aunt. I wanted to become her mother, her legal mother. . . . Do you understand what I'm trying to tell you, Howard?"

"I think so."

"I saw only one way to get what I wanted. That was through Dave."

"Don't say any more."

"I have to explain how it happened. I was—"

"Even if Phoenix is hot in the summer, we can always buy an air-conditioned house. We could even build one from scratch if you'd like."

"Howard, listen—"

"We'll look around for a good-sized lot, make all our own blueprints or hire an architect. They say it's cheaper in the long run to hire an architect and let him decide what we need on the basis of what kind of life we want and what kind of people we are."

"And what kind of people are we, Howard?"

"Average, I guess. Luckier than most in some things, not so lucky in others. We can't ask for more than that. . . . I've forgotten exactly what the phoenix was. Do you recall, Virginia?"

"A bird," she said. "A bird with gorgeous bright plumage, the only one of his kind. He burned himself to death and then rose out of his own ashes as good as new to begin life again." She turned away from the window, letting the drape fall into place. "Lieutenant Gallantyne is leaving the Brants' house. Ask him to come in here, will you, Howard?"

"Why?"

"I want to tell him everything I didn't tell him before, about Jessie and my plans for her, about Dave, even about the twenty dollars you gave Jessie. We can't afford to hide things any more, from other people or each other. Will you ask the lieutenant to come in, Howard?"

"Yes."

"It will be a little bit like burning myself to death but I can stand it if you can."

She sat down on the davenport to wait, thinking how strange it would be to get up every morning and fix Howard's breakfast.

The girl was coming toward him around the bend in the tracks. She was taller than Charlie remembered, and she wasn't skipping nimbly along on one rail in her usual manner. She was walking on the ties between the rails slowly and awkwardly, pretending the place was strange to her. She had a whole bundle of tricks but this was one she'd never pulled before. The night made it different, too. She couldn't be on her way to or from school; she must have come here deliberately looking for him, bent on mischief and not frightened of anything—the dark, the dogs, the winos, the trains, least of all Charlie. She knew when and where the trains would pass, she knew the dogs were confined and the winos wanted only to be left alone and Charlie's threats were as empty as the cans and bottles littering both sides of the tracks. She always had an answer for everything: he didn't own the tracks, he wasn't her boss, it was a free country, she would do what she liked, so there, and if he reported her to the police she'd tell them he'd tried to make a baby in her and that would fix him, ha ha.

He was shocked at her language and confounded by her brashness, yet he was envious too, as if he wanted to be like her sometimes: *It's a free country, Ben, and I'm going to do what I like. You're not my boss, so there—* He could never speak the words, though. They vanished on his tongue like salt, leaving only a taste and a thirst.

He stood still, watching the girl approach. He was surprised at how fast she had grown and how clumsy her growth had made her. She staggered, she stumbled, she fell on one knee and picked herself up. No, this could not be pretense. The nimble, fearless, brash girl was becoming a woman, burdened by her increasing body and aware of what could happen. Danger hid in dark places, winos could turn sober and ugly dogs could escape, trains could be running off schedule and Charlie must be taken seriously.

"Charlie?"

During her time of growing she had learned his name. He felt pleased by this evidence of her new respect for him, but the change in her voice disquieted him. It sounded so thin, so scared.

He said, "I won't hurt you, little girl. I would never hurt a child."

"I know that."

"How did you find out? I never told you."

"You didn't have to."

"What's your name?"

"Louise," she said. "My name is Louise."

*

Gallantyne let Mac off in the parking lot behind police headquarters.

Mac unlocked his car and got in behind the wheel. The ugliness of the scene with Brant, followed by Virginia Arlington's completely unexpected admissions, had left him bewildered and exhausted.

"Go home and get some sleep," Gallantyne said. "I don't think you were cut out for this line of work."

"I prefer to function in the more closely regulated atmosphere of a courtroom."

"Like a baby in a playpen, eh?"

"Have it your way."

"The trouble with lawyers is they get so used to having everything spelled out for them they can't operate without consulting the rule book. A policeman has to play it by ear."

"Well, tonight's music was lousy," Mac said. "Maybe you'd better start taking lessons."

"So you don't approve of the way I handled Brant."

"No."

"I got through to him, didn't I?"

"You broke him in little pieces. I suggest you buy yourself a rule book."

"I have a rule book. I just keep it in my Sunday pants so it doesn't get worn out. Now let's leave it like that, Mac. We're old friends, I don't want to quarrel with you. You take things too seriously."

"Do I."

"Good night, Mac. Back to the playpen."

"Good night." Mac yawned, widely and deliberately. "And if you come up with any more hot leads, don't bother telling me about them. My phone will be off the hook."

He pulled out of the parking lot, hoping the yawn had looked authentic and that it wouldn't enter Gallantyne's head that he was going anywhere but home.

The clock in the courthouse began to chime the hour. Ten o'clock. Kate would be asleep inside her big locked house from which everything had already been stolen. He would have to awaken her, to talk to her before Gallantyne had a chance to start thinking about it: how could she have known about the affair between Brant and Virginia Arlington? She didn't exchange gossip with the neighbors, she didn't go to parties or visit bars, she had no friends. That left one way, only one possible way she could have found out.

He expected the house to be dark when he arrived, but there were lights on in the kitchen, in one of the upstairs bedrooms and in the front hall. He pressed the door chime, muted against Sheridan as the doors were locked against Sheridan and the blinds pulled tight to shut him out. *Yet he's here*, Mac thought. *All the steps she takes to deny his existence merely reinforce it. If just once she would forget to lock a door or pull a blind, it would mean she was starting to forget Sheridan.*

Mary Martha's voice came through the crack in the door. "Who's there?"

"Mac."

"Oh." She opened the door. She didn't look either sleepy or surprised. Her cheeks were flushed, as if she'd been running around, and she had on a dress Mac had never seen before, a party dress made of some thin, silky fabric the same blue as her eyes. "You're early. But I guess you can come in anyway."

"Were you expecting me, Mary Martha?"

"Not really. Only my mother said I was to call you at exactly eleven o'clock and invite you to come over."

"Why?"

"I didn't ask her. You know what? I never stayed up until eleven o'clock before in my whole, entire life."

"Your mother must have had a reason, Mary Martha. Why didn't you ask her?"

"I couldn't. She was nervous, she might have changed her mind about letting me stay up and play."

"Where is she now?"

"Sleeping. She had a bad pain so she took a bunch of pills and went to bed."

"When? When did she take them? What kind of pills?"

The child started backing away from him, her eyes widening in sudden fear. "I didn't do anything, I didn't do a single thing!"

"I'm not accusing you."

"You are so."

"No. Listen to me, Mary Martha." He forced himself to speak softly, to smile. "I know you didn't do anything. You're a very good girl. Tell me, what were you playing when I arrived?"

"Movie star."

"You were pretending to be a movie star?"

"Oh no. I was her sister."

"Then who was the movie star?"

"Nobody. Nobody real, I mean," she added hastily. "I used to have lots of imaginary playmates when I was a child. Sometimes I still do. You didn't notice my new dress."

"Of course I noticed. It's very pretty. Did your mother make it for you?"

"Oh no. She bought it this afternoon. It cost an enormous amount of money."

"How much?"

She hesitated. "Well, I'm not supposed to broadcast it but I guess it's O.K., being as it's only you. It cost nearly twenty dollars. But my mother says it's worth every penny of it. She wanted me to have one real boughten dress in case a special occasion comes up and I meet Sheridan at it. Then he'll realize how well she takes care of me and loves me."

In case I meet Sheridan. The words started a pulse beating in Mac's temple like a drumming of danger. He knew what the special occasion would have to be, Kate had told him a dozen times: "*He'll see Mary Martha over my dead body and not before.*"

"Louise?" Charlie peered at her through the darkness, shielding his eyes with one hand as though from a midday sun. "No. You don't look like Louise."

"It's dark. You can't see me very well."

"Yes, I can. I know who you are. You get off these tracks immediately or I'll tell your parents, I'll report you to the school principal."

"Charlie—"

"Please," he said. "Please go home, little girl."

"The little girls are all at home, Charlie. I'm here. Louise."

He sat down suddenly on the edge of one of the railroad ties, rubbing his eyes with his fists like a boy awakened from sleep. "How did you find me?"

"Is that important?"

"Yes."

"All right then. I could see you were troubled, and sometimes when you're troubled you go down to the warehouse. You feel secure there, you know what's expected of you and you do it. I saw you looking in the window of the office as if you wanted to be inside. I guess the library serves the same purpose for me. We're not very brave or strong people, you and I, but we can't give up now without a fight."

"I have nothing to fight for."

"You have life," she said. "Life itself."

"Not for long."

"Charlie, please—"

"Listen to me. I saw the child last night, I spoke to her. I don't—I can't swear what happened after that. I might have frightened her. Maybe she screamed and I tried to shut her up and I did."

"We'll find out. In time you'll remember everything. Don't worry about it."

"It seemed so clear to me a couple of hours ago. I was the witness then. It felt so good being the witness, with the law on my side, and the people, the nice people. But of course that couldn't last."

"Why not?"

"Because they're not on my side and never will be. I can hear them, in my ears I can hear them yelling, *get him, get him good, he killed her, kill him back*."

She was silent. A long way off a train wailed its warning. She thought briefly of stepping into the middle of the tracks and standing there with Charlie until the train came. Then she reached down and took hold of his hand. "Come on, Charlie. We're going home."

Even before Mac opened the door he could hear Kate's troubled breathing. She was lying on her back on the bed, her eyes closed, her arms outstretched with the palms of her hands turned up as if she were begging for something. Her hair was carefully combed and she wore a silky blue dress Mac had never seen before. The new dress and the neatness of the room gave the scene an air of unreality as if Kate had intended at first only to play at suicide but had gone too far. On the bedside table were five empty bottles, which had contained pills, and a sealed envelope. The envelope bore no name and Mac assumed the contents were meant for him since he was the one Mary Martha had been told to call at eleven o'clock.

"Kate. Can you hear me, Kate? There's an ambulance on the way. You're going to be all right." He pressed his face against one of her upturned palms. "Kate, my dearest, please be all right. Please don't die. I love you, Kate."

She moved her head in protest and he couldn't tell whether she was protesting the idea of being all right or the idea of his loving her.

She let out a moan and some words he couldn't understand.

"Don't try to talk, Kate. Save your strength."

"Sheridan's—fault."

"Shush, dearest. Not now."

"Sheridan—"

"I'll look after everything, Kate. Don't worry."

The ambulance came and went, its siren loud and alien in the quiet neighborhood. Mary Martha stood on the front porch and watched the flashing red lights dissolve into the fog. Then she followed Mac back into the house. She seemed more curious than frightened.

"Why did my mother act so funny, Mac?"

"She took too many pills."

"Why?"

"We don't know yet."

"Will she be gone one or two days?"

"Maybe more than that. I'm not sure."

"Who will take care of me?"

"I will."

She gave him the kind of long, appraising look that he'd seen Kate use on Sheridan. "You can't. You're only a man."

"There are different kinds of men," Mac said, "just as there are different kinds of women."

"My mother doesn't think so. She says men are all alike. They do bad things like Sheridan and Mr. Brant."

"Do you know what Mr. Brant did?"

"Sort of, only I'm not supposed to talk about the Brants, ever. My mother and I made a solemn pact."

Mac nodded gravely. "As a lawyer, I naturally respect solemn pacts. As a student of history, though, I'm aware that some of them turn out badly and have to be broken."

"I'm sleepy. I'd better go to bed."

"All right. Get your pajamas on and I'll bring you up some hot chocolate."

"I don't like hot chocolate—I mean, I'm allergic to it. Anyway, we don't have any."

"When someone gives me three reasons instead of one, I'm inclined not to believe any of them."

"I don't care," she said, but her eyes moved anxiously around the room. "I mean, it's O.K. to tell a little lie now and then when you're keeping a solemn and secret pact."

"But it isn't a secret any more. I know about it, and pretty soon Lieutenant Gallantyne will know and he'll come here searching for Jessie. And I think he'll find her."

"No. No, he won't."

"Why not?"

"Because."

"He's a very good searcher."

"Jessie's a very good hider." She stopped, clapping both hands to her mouth as if to force the words back in. Then she began to cry, watching Mac carefully behind her tears to see if he was moved to pity. He wasn't, so she wiped her eyes and said in a resentful voice, "Now you've spoiled everything. We were going to be sisters. We were going to get a college education and good jobs so we wouldn't always be waiting for the support check in the mail. My mother said she would fix it so we would never have to depend on bad men like Sheridan and Mr. Brant."

"Your mother wasn't making much sense when she said that, Mary Martha."

"It sounded sensible to me and Jessie."

"You're nine years old." *So is Kate*, he thought, picturing the three of them together the previous night: Jessie in a state of shock, Mary Martha hungry for companionship, and Kate carried away by her chance to strike back at the whole race of men. That first moment of decision, when Jessie had appeared at the house with her story about Virginia Arlington and her father, had probably been one of the high spots in Kate's life. It was too high to last. Her misgivings must have grown during the night and day to such proportions that she couldn't face the future.

There was, in fact, no future. She had no money to run away with the two girls and she couldn't have hidden Jessie for more than a few days. Even to her disturbed mind it must have been clear that when she was caught Sheridan would have enough evidence to prove her an unfit mother.

The three conspirators, Kate, Mary Martha, Jessie, all innocent, all nine years old; yet Mac was reminded of the initial scene of the three witches in *Macbeth—When shall we three meet again?*—and he thought, with a terrible sorrow, *Perhaps never, perhaps never again.*

He said, "You'd better go and tell Jessie I'm ready to take her home."

"She's sleeping."

"Wake her up."

"She won't want to go home."

"I'm pretty sure she will."

"You," she said, "you spoil everything for my mother and me."

"I'm sorry you feel that way. I would like to be your friend."

"Well, you can't be, ever. You're just a man."

When she had gone, he took out the letter he'd picked up from Kate's bedside table before the ambulance attendants had arrived. She had written only one line: "You always wanted me dead, this ought to satisfy you."

He realized immediately that it was intended for Sheridan, not for him. She hadn't even thought of him. First and last it was Sheridan.

He stood for a long time with the piece of paper in his hand, listening to the old house creaking under the weight of the wind. Over and beyond the creaking he thought he heard the sound of Sheridan's footsteps in the hall.

DOLL

Ed McBain

This, too is for
Dodie and Ray Crane

The city in these pages is imaginery.
The people, the places are all fictitious.
Only the police routine is based on established investigatory techniques.

I

THE CHILD Anna sat on the floor close to the wall and played with her doll, talking to it, listening. She could hear the voices raised in anger coming from her mother's bedroom through the thin separating wall, but she busied herself with the doll and tried not to be frightened. The man in her mother's bedroom was shouting now. She tried not to hear what he was saying. She brought the doll close to her face and kissed its plastic cheek, and then talked to it again, and listened.

In the bedroom next door, her mother was being murdered.

Her mother was called Tinka, a chic and lacquered label concocted by blending her given name, Tina, with her middle name, Karin. Tinka was normally a beautiful woman, no question about it. She'd have been a beautiful woman even if her name were Beulah. Or Bertha. Or perhaps even Brunhilde. The Tinka tag only enhanced her natural good looks, adding an essential gloss, a necessary polish, an air of mystery and adventure.

Tinka Sachs was a fashion model.

She was, no question about it, a very beautiful woman. She possessed a finely sculptured face that was perfectly suited to the demands of her profession, a wide forehead, high pronounced cheekbones, a generous mouth, a patrician nose, slanted green eyes flecked with chips of amber; oh, she was normally a beauty, no question about it. Her body was a model's body, lithe and loose and gently angled, with long slender legs, narrow hips, and a tiny bosom. She walked with a model's insinuating glide, pelvis tilted, crotch cleaving the air, head erect. She laughed with a model's merry shower of musical syllables, painted lips drawing back over capped teeth, amber eyes glowing. She sat with a model's carelessly draped ease, posing even in her own living room, invariably choosing the wall or sofa that best offset her clothes, or her long blond hair, or her mysterious green eyes flecked with chips of amber; oh, she was normally a beauty.

She was not so beautiful at the moment.

She was not so beautiful because the man who followed her around the room shouting obscenities at her, the man who stalked her from wall to wall and boxed her into the narrow passage circumscribed by the king-sized bed and the marble-topped dresser opposite, the man who closed in on her oblivious to her murmuring, her pleading, her sobbing, the man was grasping a kitchen knife with which he had been slashing her repeatedly for the past three minutes.

The obscenities spilled from the man's mouth in a steady unbroken torrent, the anger having reached a pitch that was unvaried now, neither rising nor falling in volume or intensity. The knife blade swung in a short, tight arc, back and forth, its rhythm as unvaried as that of the words that poured from the man's mouth. Obscenities and blade, like partners in an evil copulation, moved together in perfect rhythm and pitch, enveloping Tinka in alternating splashes of blood and spittle. She kept murmuring the man's name pleadingly, again and again, as the blade ripped into her flesh. But the glittering arc was relentless. The razor-sharp blade, the monotonous flow of obscenities, inexorably forced her bleeding and torn into the far corner of the room, where the back of her head collided with an original Chagall, tilting it slightly askew, the knife moving in again in its brief terrifying arc, the blade slicing parallel bleeding ditches across her small breasts and moving lower across the flat abdomen, her peignoir tearing again with a clinging silky blood-sotted sound as the knife blade plunged deeper with each step closer he took. She said his name once more, she shouted his name, and then she murmured the word "Please," and then she fell back against the wall again, knocking the Chagall from its hook so that a riot of framed color dropped heavily over her shoulder, falling in a lopsided angle past the long blond hair, and the open red gashes across her throat and naked chest, the tattered blue peignoir, the natural brown of her exposed pubic hair, the blue satin slippers. She fell gasping for breath, spitting blood, headlong over the painting, her forehead colliding with the wide oaken frame, her blond hair covering the Chagall reds and yellows and violets with a fine misty golden haze, the knife slash across her throat pouring blood onto the canvas, setting her hair afloat in a pool of red that finally overspilled the oaken frame and ran onto the carpet.

Next door, the child Anna clung fiercely to her doll.

She said a reassuring word to it, and then listened in terror as she heard footfalls in the hall outside her closed bedroom door. She kept listening breathlessly until she heard the front door to the apartment open and then close again.

She was still sitting in the bedroom, clutching her doll, when the superintendent came up the next morning to change a faucet washer Mrs. Sachs had complained about the day before.

April is the fourth month of the year.

It is important to know that—if you are a cop, you can sometimes get a little confused.

More often than not, your confusion will be compounded of one part exhaustion, one part tedium, and one part disgust. The exhaustion is an ever present condition and one to which you have become slowly accustomed over the years. You know that the department does not recognize Saturdays, Sundays or legal holidays, and so you are even prepared to work on Christmas morning if you have to, especially if someone intent on committing mischief is inconsiderate enough to plan it for that day—witness General George Washington and the unsuspecting Hessians, those drunks. You know that a detective's work schedule does not revolve around a fixed day, and so you have learned to adjust to your odd waking hours and your shorter sleeping time, but you have never been able to adjust to the nagging feeling of exhaustion that is the result of too much crime and too few hours, too few men to pit against it. You are sometimes a drag at home with your wife and children, but that is only because you are tired, boy what a life, all work and no play, wow.

The tedium is another thing again, but it also helps to generate confusion. Crime is the most exciting sport in the world, right? Sure, ask anybody. Then how come it can be so boring when you're a working cop who is typing reports in triplicate and legging it all over the city talking to old ladies in flowered house dresses in apartments smelling of death? How can the routine of detection become something as proscribed as the ritual of a bullfight, never changing, so that even a gun duel in a nighttime alley can assume familiar dimensions and be regarded with the same feeling of ennui that accompanies a routine request to the B.C.I.? The boredom is confusing as hell. It clasps hands with the exhaustion and makes you wonder whether this is January or Friday.

The disgust comes into it only if you are a human being. Some cops aren't. But if you are a human being, you are sometimes appalled by what your fellow human beings are capable of doing. You can understand lying because you practice it in a watered-down form as a daily method of smoothing the way, helping the machinery of mankind to function more easily without getting fouled by too much truth-stuff. You can understand stealing because when you were a kid you sometimes swiped pencils from the public school supply closet, and once a toy airplane from the five and ten. You can even understand murder because there is a dark and secret place in your own heart where you have hated deeply enough to kill. You can understand all these things, but you are nonetheless disgusted when they are piled upon you in profusion, when you are constantly confronted with liars, thieves and slaughterers, when all human decency seems in a state of suspension for the eight or twelve or thirty-six hours you are in the squadroom or out answering a squeal. Perhaps you could accept an occasional corpse—death is only a part of life, isn't it? It is corpse heaped upon corpse that leads to disgust and further leads to confusion. If you can no longer tell one corpse from another, if you can no longer distinguish one open bleeding head from the next, then how is April any different from October?

It was April.

The torn and lovely woman lay in profile across the bloody face of the Chagall painting. The lab technicians were dusting for latent prints, vacuuming for hairs and traces of fiber, carefully wrapping for transportation the knife found in the corridor just outside the bedroom door, and the dead girl's pocketbook, which seemed to contain everything but money.

Detective Steve Carella made his notes and then walked out of the room and down the hall to where the little girl sat in a very big chair, her feet not touching the floor, her doll sleeping across her lap. The little girl's name was Anna Sachs—one of the patrolmen had told him that the moment Carella arrived. The doll seemed almost as big as she did.

"Hello," he said to her, and felt the old confusion once again, the exhaustion because he had not been home since

Thursday morning, the tedium because he was embarking on another round of routine questioning, and the disgust because the person he was about to question was only a little girl and her mother was dead and mutilated in the room next door. He tried to smile. He was not very good at it. The little girl said nothing. She looked up at him out of very big eyes. Her lashes were long and brown, her mouth drawn in stoic silence beneath a nose she had inherited from her mother. Unblinkingly, she watched him. Unblinkingly, she said nothing.

"Your name is Anna, isn't it?" Carella said.

The child nodded.

"Do you know what my name is?"

"No."

"Steve."

The child nodded again.

"I have a little girl about your age," Carella said. "She's a twin. How old *are* you, Anna?"

"Five."

"That's just how old my daughter is."

"Mmm," Anna said. She paused a moment, and then asked, "Is Mommy killed?"

"Yes," Carella said. "Yes, honey, she is."

"I was afraid to go in and look."

"It's better you didn't."

"She got killed last night, didn't she?" Anna asked.

"Yes."

There was a silence in the room. Outside, Carella could hear the muted sounds of a conversation between the police photographer and the m.e. An April fly buzzed against the bedroom window. He looked into the child's upturned face.

"Were you here last night?" he asked.

"Um-huh."

"Where?"

"Here. Right here in my room." She stroked the doll's cheek, and then looked up at Carella and asked, "What's a twin?"

"When two babies are born at the same time."

"Oh."

She continued looking up at him, her eyes tearless, wide, and certain in the small white face. At last she said, "The man did it."

"What man?" Carella asked.

"The one who was with her."

"Who?"

"Mommy. The man who was with her in her room."

"Who was the man?"

"I don't know."

"Did you see him?"

"No. I was here playing with Chatterbox when he came in."

"Is Chatterbox a friend of yours?"

"Chatterbox is my *dolly*," the child said, and she held up the doll and giggled, and Carella wanted to scoop her into his arms, hold her close, tell her there was no such thing as sharpened steel and sudden death.

"When was this, honey?" he asked. "Do you know what time it was?"

"I don't know," she said, and shrugged. "I only know how to tell twelve o'clock and seven o'clock, that's all."

"Well . . . was it dark?"

"Yes, it was after supper."

"This man came in after supper, is that right?"

"Yes."

"Did your mother know this man?"

"Oh, yes," Anna said. "She was laughing and everything when he first came in."

"Then what happened?"

"I don't know." Anna shrugged again. "I was here playing."

There was another silence.

The first tears welled into her eyes suddenly, leaving the rest of the face untouched; there was no trembling of lip, no crumbling of features, the tears simply overspilled her eyes and ran down her cheeks. She sat as still as a stone, crying soundlessly while Carella stood before her helplessly, a hulking man who suddenly felt weak and ineffective before this silent torrent of grief.

He gave her his handkerchief.

She took it wordlessly and blew her nose, but she did not dry her eyes. Then she handed it back to him and said, "Thank you," with the tears still running down her face endlessly, sitting stunned with her small hands folded over the doll's chest.

"He was hitting her," she said. "I could hear her crying, but I was afraid to go in. So I . . . I made believe I didn't hear.

And then . . . then I *really* didn't hear. I just kept talking with Chatterbox, that was all. That way I couldn't hear what he was doing to her in the other room."

"All right, honey," Carella said. He motioned to the patrolman standing in the doorway. When the patrolman joined him, he whispered, "Is her father around? Has he been notified?"

"Gee, I don't know," the patrolman said. He turned and shouted, "Anybody know if the husband's been contacted?"

A Homicide cop standing with one of the lab technicians looked up from his notebook and said, "He's in Arizona. They been divorced for three years now."

Lieutenant Peter Byrnes was normally a patient and understanding man, but there were times lately when Bert Kling gave him a severe pain in the ass. And whereas Byrnes, being patient and understanding, could appreciate the reasons for Kling's behavior, this in no way made Kling any nicer to have around the office. The way Byrnes figured it, psychology was certainly an important factor in police work because it helped you to recognize that there were no longer any villains in the world, there were only disturbed people. Psychology substituted understanding for condemnation. It was a very nice tool to possess, psychology was, until a cheap thief kicked you in the groin one night. It then became somewhat difficult to imagine the thief as a put-upon soul who'd had a shabby childhood. In much the same way, though Byrnes completely understood the trauma that was responsible for Kling's current behavior, he was finding it more and more difficult to accept Kling as anything but a cop who was going to hell with himself.

"I want to transfer him out," he told Carella that morning.

"Why?"

"Because he's disrupting the whole damn squadroom, that's why," Byrnes said. He did not enjoy discussing this, nor would he normally have asked for consultation on any firm decision he had made. His decision, however, was anything but final, that was the damn thing about it. He liked Kling, and yet he no longer liked him. He thought he could be a good cop, but he was turning into a bad one. "I've got enough bad cops around here," he said aloud.

"Bert isn't a bad cop," Carella said. He stood before Byrnes's cluttered desk in the corner office and listened to the sounds of early spring on the street outside the building, and he thought of the five-year-old girl named Anna Sachs who had taken his handkerchief while the tears streamed down her face.

"He's a surly shit," Byrnes said. "Okay, I know what happened to him, but people have died before, Steve, people have been killed before. And if you're a man you grow up to it, you don't act as if everybody's responsible for it. We didn't have anything to do with his girl friend's death, that's the plain and simple truth, and I personally am sick and tired of being blamed for it."

"He's not blaming you for it, Pete. He's not blaming any of us."

"He's blaming the *world*, and that's worse. This morning, he had a big argument with Meyer just because Meyer picked up the phone on his desk. I mean, the goddamn phone was ringing, so instead of crossing the room to his own desk, Meyer picked up the closest phone, which was on Kling's desk, so Kling starts a row. Now you can't have that kind of attitude in a squadroom where men are working together, you can't have it, Steve. I'm going to ask for his transfer."

"That'd be the worst thing that could happen to him."

"It'd be the best thing for the squad."

"I don't think so."

"Nobody's asking your advice," Byrnes said flatly.

"Then why the hell did you call me in here?"

"You see what I mean?" Byrnes said. He rose from his desk abruptly and began pacing the floor near the meshed-grill windows. He was a compact man and he moved with an economy that belied the enormous energy in his powerful body. Short for a detective, muscular, with a bullet-shaped head and small blue eyes set in a face seamed with wrinkles, he paced briskly behind his desk and shouted, "You see the trouble he's causing? Even you and I can't sit down and have a sensible discussion about him without starting to yell. That's *just* what I mean, that's *just* why I want him out of here."

"You don't throw away a good watch because it's running a little slow," Carella said.

"Don't give me any goddamn similes," Byrnes said. "I'm running a squadroom here, not a clock shop."

"Metaphors," Carella corrected.

"What*ever*," Byrnes said. "I'm going to call the Chief tomorrow and ask him to transfer Kling out. That's it."

"Where?"

"What do you mean *where*? What do I care where? Out of here, that's all."

"But *where*? To another squadroom with a bunch of strange guys, so he can get on *their* nerves even more than he does ours? So he can—"

"Oh, so you admit it."

"That Bert gets on my nerves? Sure, he does."

"And the situation isn't improving, Steve, you know that too. It gets worse every day. Look, what the hell am I wasting my breath for? He goes, and that's it." Byrnes gave a brief emphatic nod, and then sat heavily in his chair again, glaring up at Carella with an almost childish challenge on his face.

Carella sighed. He had been on duty for close to fifty hours now, and he was tired. He had checked in at eight-forty-five Thursday morning, and been out all that day gathering information for the backlog of cases that had been piling up all through the month of March. He had caught six hours' sleep on a cot in the locker room that night, and then been called out at seven on Friday morning by the fire department, who suspected arson in a three-alarm blaze they'd answered on the South Side. He had come back to the squadroom at noon to find four telephone messages on his desk. By the time he had returned all the calls—one was from an assistant m.e. who took a full hour to explain the toxicological analysis of a poison they had found in the stomach contents of a beagle, the seventh such dog similarly poisoned in the past week—the clock on the wall read one-thirty. Carella sent down for a pastrami on rye, a container of milk, and a side of French fries. Before the order arrived, he had to leave the squadroom to answer a burglary squeal on North Eleventh. He did not come back until five-thirty, at which time he turned the phone over to a complaining Kling and went down to the locker room to try to sleep again. At eleven o'clock Friday night, the entire squad, working in flying wedges of three detectives to a team, culminated a two-month period of surveillance by raiding twenty-six known numbers banks in the area, a sanitation project that was not finished until five on Saturday morning. At eight-thirty A.M., Carella answered the Sachs squeal and questioned a crying little girl. It was now ten-thirty A.M., and he was tired, and he wanted to go home, and he didn't want to argue in favor of a man who had become everything the lieutenant said he was, he was just too damn weary. But earlier this morning he had looked down at the body of a woman he had not known at all, had seen her ripped and lacerated flesh, and had felt a pain bordering on nausea. Now—weary, bedraggled, unwilling to argue—he could remember the mutilated beauty of Tinka Sachs, and he felt something of what Bert Kling must have known in that Culver Avenue bookshop not four years ago when he'd held the bullet-torn body of Claire Townsend in his arms.

"Let him work with me," he said.

"What do you mean?"

"On the Sachs case. I've been teaming with Meyer lately. Give me Bert instead."

"What's the matter, don't you like Meyer?"

"I *love* Meyer, I'm tired, I want to go home to bed, will you please let me have Bert on this case?"

"What'll that accomplish?"

"I don't know."

"I don't approve of shock therapy," Byrnes said. "This Sachs woman was brutally murdered. All you'll do is remind Bert—"

"Therapy, my ass," Carella said. "I want to be with him, I want to talk to him, I want to let him know he's still got some people on this goddamn squad who think he's a decent human being worth saving. Now, Pete, I *really* am very very tired and I don't want to argue this any further, I mean it. If you want to send Bert to another squad, that's your business, you're the boss here, I'm not going to argue with you, that's all. I mean it. Now just make up your mind, okay?"

"Take him," Byrnes said.

"Thank you," Carella answered. He went to the door. "Good night," he said, and walked out.

2

SOMETIMES A case starts like sevens coming out.

The Sachs case started just that way on Monday morning when Steve Carella and Bert Kling arrived at the apartment building on Stafford Place to question the elevator operator.

The elevator operator was close to seventy years old, but he was still in remarkable good health, standing straight and tall, almost as tall as Carella and of the same general build. He had only one eye, however—he was called Cyclops by the superintendent of the building and by just about everyone else he knew—and it was this single fact that seemed to make him a somewhat less than reliable witness. He had lost his eye, he explained, in World War I. It had been bayoneted out of his head by an advancing German in the Ardennes Forest. Cyclops—who up to that time had been called Ernest—had backed away from the blade before it had a chance to pass completely through his eye and into his brain, and then had carefully and passionlessly shot the German three times in the chest, killing him. He did not realize his eye was gone until he got back to the aid station. Until then, he thought the bayonet had only gashed his brow and caused a flow of blood that made it difficult to see. He was proud of his missing eye, and proud of the nickname Cyclops. Cyclops had been a giant, and although Ernest Messner was only six feet tall, he had lost his eye for democracy, which is as good a cause as any for which to lose an eye. He was also very proud of his remaining eye, which he claimed was capable of twenty/twenty vision. His remaining eye was a clear penetrating blue, as sharp as the mind lurking somewhere behind it. He listened intelligently to everything the two detectives asked him, and then he said, "Sure, I took him up myself."

"You took a man up to Mrs. Sachs's apartment Friday night?" Carella asked.

"That's right."

"What time was this?"

Cyclops thought for a moment. He wore a black patch over his empty socket, and he might have looked a little like an aging Hathaway Shirt man in an elevator uniform, except that he was bald. "Must have been nine or nine-thirty, around then."

"Did you take the man *down*, too?"

"Nope."

"What time did you go off?"

"I didn't leave the building until eight o'clock in the morning."

"You work from when to when, Mr. Messner?"

"We've got three shifts in the building," Cyclops explained. "The morning shift is eight A.M. to four P.M. The afternoon shift is four P.M. to midnight. And the graveyard shift is midnight to eight A.M."

"Which shift is yours?" Kling asked.

"The graveyard shift. You just caught me, in fact. I'll be relieved here in ten minutes."

"If you start work at midnight, what were you doing here at nine P.M. Monday?"

"Fellow who has the shift before mine went home sick. The super called me about eight o'clock, asked if I could come in early. I did him the favor. That was a long night, believe me."

"It was an even longer night for Tinka Sachs," Kling said.

"Yeah. Well, anyway, I took that fellow up at nine, nine-thirty, and he still hadn't come down by the time I was relieved."

"At eight in the morning," Carella said.

"That's right."

"Is that usual?" Kling asked.

"What do you mean?"

"Did Tinka Sachs usually have men coming here who went up to her apartment at nine, nine-thirty and weren't down by eight the next morning?"

Cyclops blinked with his single eye. "I don't like to talk about the dead," he said.

"We're here precisely so you *can* talk about the dead," Kling answered. "And about the living who visited the dead. I asked a simple question, and I'd appreciate a simple answer. Was Tinka Sachs in the habit of entertaining men all night long?"

Cyclops blinked again. "Take it easy, young fellow," he said. "You'll scare me right back into my elevator."

Carella chose to laugh at this point, breaking the tension. Cyclops smiled in appreciation.

"You understand, don't you?" he said to Carella. "What Mrs. Sachs did up there in her apartment was *her* business, not anyone else's."

"Of course," Carella said. "I guess my partner was just wondering why you weren't suspicious. About taking a man up who didn't come down again. That's all."

"Oh." Cyclops thought for a moment. Then he said, "Well, I didn't give it a second thought."

"Then it *was* usual, is that right?" Kling asked.

"I'm not saying it was usual, and I'm not saying it wasn't. I'm saying if a woman over twenty-one wants to have a man in her apartment, it's not for me to say how long he should stay, all day or all night, it doesn't matter to me, sonny. You got that?"

"I've got it," Kling said flatly.

"And I don't give a damn what they do up there, either, all day or all night, that's their business if they're old enough to vote. You got that, too?"

"I've got it," Kling said.

"Fine," Cyclops answered, and he nodded.

"Actually," Carella said, "the man didn't *have* to take the elevator down, did he? He could have gone up to the roof, and crossed over to the next building."

"Sure," Cyclops said. "I'm only saying that neither me nor anybody else working in this building has the right to wonder about what anybody's doing up there or how long they're taking to do it, or whether they choose to leave the building by the front door or the roof or the steps leading to the basement or even by jumping out the window, it's none of our business. You close that door, you're private. That's my notion."

"That's a good notion," Carella said.

"Thank you."

"You're welcome."

"What'd the man look like?" Kling asked. "Do you remember?"

"Yes, I remember," Cyclops said. He glanced at Kling coldly, and then turned to Carella. "Have you got a pencil and some paper?"

"Yes," Carella said. He took a notebook and a slender gold pen from his inside jacket pocket. "Go ahead."

"He was a tall man, maybe six-two or six-three. He was blond. His hair was very straight, the kind of hair Sonny Tufts has, do you know him?"

"Sonny *Tufts*?" Carella said.

"That's right, the movie star, him. This fellow didn't look at all like him, but his hair was the same sort of straight blond hair."

"What color were his eyes?" Kling asked.

"Didn't see them. He was wearing sunglasses."

"At night?"

"Lots of people wear sunglasses at night nowadays," Cyclops said.

"That's true," Carella said.

"Like masks," Cyclops added.

"Yes."

"He was wearing sunglasses, and also he had a very deep tan, as if he'd just come back from down south someplace. He had on a light grey raincoat; it was drizzling a little Friday night, do you recall?"

"Yes, that's right," Carella said. "Was he carrying an umbrella?"

"No umbrella."

"Did you notice any of his clothing under the raincoat?"

"His suit was a dark grey, charcoal grey, I could tell that by his trousers. He was wearing a white shirt—it showed up here, in the opening of the coat—and a black tie."

"What color were his shoes?"

"Black."

"Did you notice any scars or other marks on his face or hands?"

"No."

"Was he wearing any rings?"

"A gold ring with a green stone on the pinky of his right hand—no, wait a minute, it was his left hand."

"Any other jewelry you might have noticed? Cuff links, tie clasp?"

"No, I didn't see any."

"Was he wearing a hat?"

"No hat."

"Was he clean-shaven?"

"What do you mean?"

"Did he have a beard or a mustache?" Kling said.

"No. He was clean-shaven."

"How old would you say he was?"

"Late thirties, early forties."

"What about his build? Heavy, medium, or slight?"

"He was a big man. He wasn't fat, but he was a big man, muscular. I guess I'd have to say he was heavy. He had very big hands. I noticed the ring on his pinky looked very small for his hand. He was heavy, I'd say, yes, very definitely."

"Was he carrying anything? Briefcase, suitcase, attaché—"

"Nothing."

"Did he speak to you?"

"He just gave me the floor number, that's all. Nine, he said. That was all."

"What sort of voice did he have? Deep, medium, high?"

"Deep."

"Did you notice any accent or regional dialect?"

"He only said one word. He sounded like anybody else in the city."

"I'm going to say that word several ways," Carella said. "Would you tell me which way sounded most like him?"

"Sure, go ahead."

"Ny-un," Carella said.

"Nope."

"Noin."

"Nope."

"Nahn."

"Nope."

"Nan."

"Nope."

"Nine."

"That's it. Straight out. No decorations."

"Okay, good," Carella said. "You got anything else, Bert?"

"Nothing else," Kling said.

"You're a very observant man," Carella said to Cyclops.

"All I do every day is look at the people I take up and down," Cyclops answered. He shrugged. "It makes the job a little more interesting."

"We appreciate everything you've told us," Carella said. "Thank you."

"Don't mention it."

Outside the building, Kling said, "The snotty old bastard."

"He gave us a lot," Carella said mildly.

"Yeah."

"We've really got a good description now."

"*Too* good, if you ask me."

"What do you mean?"

"The guy has one eye in his head, and one foot in the grave. So he reels off details even a trained observer would have missed. He might have been making up the whole thing, just to prove he's not a worthless old man."

"Nobody's worthless," Carella said mildly. "Old or otherwise."

"The humanitarian school of criminal detection," Kling said.

"What's wrong with humanity?"

"Nothing. It was a human being who slashed Tinka Sachs to ribbons, wasn't it?" Kling asked.

And to this, Carella had no answer.

A good modeling agency serves as a great deal more than a booking office for the girls it represents. It provides an answering service for the busy young girl about town, a baby-sitting service for the working mother, a guidance-and-counseling service for the man-beleaguered model, a *pied-à-terre* for the harried and hurried between-sittings beauty.

Art and Leslie Cutler ran a good modeling agency. They ran it with the precision of a computer and the understanding of an analyst. Their offices were smart and walnut-paneled, a suite of three rooms on Carrington Avenue, near the bridge leading to Calm's Point. The address of the agency was announced over a doorway leading to a flight of carpeted steps. The address plate resembled a Parisian street sign, white enameled on a blue field, 21 Carrington, with the blue-carpeted steps beyond leading to the second story of the building. At the top of the stairs there was a second blue-and-white enameled sign,

Paris again, except that this one was lettered in lowercase and it read: the cutlers.

Carella and Kling climbed the steps to the second floor, observed the chic nameplate without any noticeable show of appreciation, and walked into a small carpeted entrance foyer in which stood a white desk starkly fashionable against the walnut walls, nothing else. A girl sat behind the desk. She was astonishingly beautiful, exactly the sort of receptionist one would expect in a modeling agency; if she was only the receptionist, my God, what did the *models* look like?

"Yes, gentlemen, may I help you?" she asked. Her voice was Vassar out of finishing school out of country day. She wore eyeglasses with exaggerated black frames that did nothing whatever to hide the dazzling brilliance of her big blue eyes. Her makeup was subdued and wickedly innocent, a touch of pale pink on her lips, a blush of rose at her cheeks, the frames of her spectacles serving as liner for her eyes. Her hair was black and her smile was sunshine. Carella answered with a sunshine smile of his own, the one he usually reserved for movie queens he met at the governor's mansion.

"We're from the police," he said. "I'm Detective Carella; this is my partner, Detective Kling."

"Yes?" the girl said. She seemed completely surprised to have policemen in her reception room.

"We'd like to talk to either Mr. or Mrs. Cutler," Kling said. "Are they in?"

"Yes, but what is this in reference to?" the girl asked.

"It's in reference to the murder of Tinka Sachs," Kling said.

"Oh," the girl said. "Oh, yes." She reached for a button on the executive phone panel, hesitated, shrugged, looked up at them with radiant blue-eyed innocence, and said, "I suppose you have identification and all that."

Carella showed her his shield. The girl looked expectantly at Kling. Kling sighed, reached into his pocket, and opened his wallet to where his shield was pinned to the leather.

"We never get detectives up here," the girl said in explanation, and pressed the button on the panel.

"Yes?" a voice said.

"Mr. Cutler, there are two detectives to see you, a Mr. King and a Mr. Coppola."

"Kling and Carella," Carella corrected.

"Kling and Capella," the girl said.

Carella let it go.

"Ask them to come right in," Cutler said.

"Yes, sir." The girl clicked off and looked up at the detectives. "Won't you go in, please? Through the bull pen and straight back."

"Through the what?"

"The bull pen. Oh, that's the main office, you'll see it. It's right inside the door there." The telephone rang. The girl gestured vaguely toward what looked like a solid walnut wall, and then picked up the receiver. "The Cutlers," she said. "One moment, please." She pressed a button and then said, "Mrs. Cutler, it's Alex Jamison on five-seven, do you want to take it?" She nodded, listened for a moment, and then replaced the receiver. Carella and Kling had just located the walnut knob on the walnut door hidden in the walnut wall. Carella smiled sheepishly at the girl (blue eyes blinked back radiantly) and opened the door.

The bull pen, as the girl had promised, was just behind the reception room. It was a large open area with the same basic walnut-and-white decor, broken by the color of the drapes and the upholstery fabric on two huge couches against the left-hand window wall. The windows were draped in diaphanous saffron nylon, and the couches were done in a complementary brown, the fabric nubby and coarse in contrast to the nylon. Three girls sat on the couches, their long legs crossed. All of them were reading *Vogue*. One of them had her head inside a portable hair dryer. None of them looked up as the men came into the room. On the right-hand side of the room, a fourth woman sat behind a long white Formica counter, a phone to her ear, busily scribbling on a pad as she listened. The woman was in her early forties, with the unmistakable bones of an ex-model. She glanced up briefly as Carella and Kling hesitated inside the doorway, and then went back to her jottings, ignoring them.

There were three huge charts affixed to the wall behind her. Each chart was divided into two-by-two-inch squares, somewhat like a colorless checkerboard. Running down the extreme left-hand side of each chart was a column of small photographs. Running across the top of each chart was a listing for every working hour of the day. The charts were covered with plexiglass panels, and a black crayon pencil hung on a cord to the right of each one. Alongside the photographs, crayoned onto the charts in the appropriate time slots, was a record and a reminder of any model's sittings for the week, readable at a glance. To the right of the charts, and accessible through an opening in the counter, there was a cubbyhole arrangement of mailboxes, each separate slot marked with similar small photographs.

The wall bearing the door through which Carella and Kling had entered was covered with eight-by-ten black-and-white photos of every model the agency represented, some seventy-five in all. The photos bore no identifying names. A waist-high runner carried black crayon pencils spaced at intervals along the length of the wall. A wide white band under each photograph, plexiglass-covered, served as the writing area for telephone messages. A model entering the room could, in turn, check her eight-by-ten photo for any calls, her photo-marked mailbox for any letters, and her photo-marked slot on one of the three charts for her next assignment. Looking into the room, you somehow got the vague impression that photography played a major part in the business of this agency. You also had the disquieting feeling that you had seen all of these faces a hundred times before, staring down at you from billboards and up at you from magazine covers. Putting an identifying name under any single one of them would have been akin to labeling the Taj Mahal or the Empire State Building. The only naked wall was the one facing them as they entered, and it—like the reception-room wall—seemed to be made of solid walnut, with nary a door in sight.

"I think I see a knob," Carella whispered, and they started across the room toward the far wall. The woman behind the counter glanced up as they passed, and then pulled the phone abruptly from her ear with a "Just a second, Alex," and said to the two detectives, "Yes, may I help you?"

"We're looking for Mr. Cutler's office," Carella said.

"Yes?" she said.

"Yes, we're detectives. We're investigating the murder of Tinka Sachs."

"Oh. Straight ahead," the woman said. "I'm Leslie Cutler. I'll join you as soon as I'm off the phone."

"Thank you," Carella said. He walked to the walnut wall, Kling following close behind him, and knocked on what he supposed was the door.

"Come in," a man's voice said.

Art Cutler was a man in his forties with straight blond hair like Sonny Tufts, and with at least six feet four inches of muscle and bone that stood revealed in a dark blue suit as he rose behind his desk, smiling, and extended his hand.

"Come in, gentlemen," he said. His voice was deep. He kept his hand extended while Carella and Kling crossed to the desk, and then he shook hands with each in turn, his grip firm and strong. "Sit down, won't you?" he said, and indicated a pair of Saarinen chairs, one at each corner of his desk. "You're here about Tinka," he said dolefully.

"Yes," Carella said.

"Terrible thing. A maniac must have done it, don't you think?"

"I don't know," Carella said.

"Well, it *must* have been, don't you think?" he said to Kling.

"I don't know," Kling said.

"That's why we're here, Mr. Cutler," Carella explained. "To find out what we can about the girl. We're assuming that an agent would know a great deal about the people he repre—"

"Yes, that's true," Cutler interrupted, "and especially in Tinka's case."

"Why especially in her case?"

"Well, we'd handled her career almost from the very beginning."

"How long would that be, Mr. Cutler?"

"Oh, at least ten years. She was only nineteen when we took her on, and she was . . . well, let me see, she was thirty in February, no, it'd be almost *eleven* years, that's right."

"February what?" Kling asked.

"February third," Cutler replied. "She'd done a little modeling on the coast before she signed with us, but nothing very impressive. We got her into all the important magazines, *Vogue*, *Harper's*, *Mademoiselle*, well, you name them. Do you know what Tinka Sachs was earning?"

"No, what?" Kling said.

"Sixty dollars an hour. Multiply that by an eight- or ten-hour day, an average of six days a week, and you've got somewhere in the vicinity of a hundred and fifty thousand dollars a year." Cutler paused. "That's a lot of money. That's more than the president of the United States earns."

"With none of the headaches," Kling said.

"Mr. Cutler," Carella said, "when did you last see Tinka Sachs alive?"

"Late Friday afternoon," Cutler said.

"Can you give us the circumstances?"

"Well, she had a sitting at five, and she stopped in around seven to pick up her mail and to see if there had been any calls. That's all."

"Had there?" Kling asked.

"Had there what?"

"Been any calls?"

"I'm sure I don't remember. The receptionist usually posts all calls shortly after they're received. You may have seen our photo wall—"

"Yes," Kling said.

"Well, our receptionist takes care of that. If you want me to check with her, she may have a record, though I doubt it. Once a call is crayoned onto the wall—"

"What about mail?"

"I don't know if she had any or . . . wait a minute, yes, I think she did pick some up. I remember she was leafing through some envelopes when I came out of my office to chat with her."

"What time did she leave here?" Carella asked.

"About seven-fifteen."

"For another sitting?"

"No, she was heading home. She has a daughter, you know. A five-year-old."

"Yes, I know," Carella said.

"Well, she was going home," Cutler said.

"Do you know where she lives?" Kling asked.

"Yes."

"Where?"

"Stafford Place."

"Have you ever been there?"

"Yes, of course."

"How long do you suppose it would take to get from this office to her apartment?"

"No more than fifteen minutes."

"Then Tinka would have been home by seven-thirty . . . *if* she went directly home."

"Yes, I suppose so."

"Did she say she was going directly home?"

"Yes. No, she said she wanted to pick up some cake, and *then* she was going home."

"Cake?"

"Yes. There's a shop up the street that's exceptionally good. Many of our mannequins buy cakes and pastry there."

"Did she say she was expecting someone later on in the evening?" Kling asked.

"No, she didn't say what her plans were."

"Would your receptionist know if any of those telephone messages related to her plans for the evening?"

"I don't know, we can ask her."

"Yes, we'd like to," Carella said.

"What were *your* plans for last Friday night, Mr. Cutler?" Kling asked.

"*My* plans?"

"Yes."

"What do you mean?"

"What time did *you* leave the office?"

"Why would you possibly want to know *that*?" Cutler asked.

"You were the last person to see her alive," Kling said.

"No, her *murderer* was the last person to see her alive," Cutler corrected. "And if I can believe what I read in the newspapers, her *daughter* was the *next*-to-last person to see her alive. So I really can't understand how Tinka's visit to the agency or *my* plans for the evening are in any way germane, or even related, to her death."

"Perhaps they're not, Mr. Cutler," Carella said, "but I'm sure you realize we're obliged to investigate every possibility."

Cutler frowned, including Carella in whatever hostility he had originally reserved for Kling. He hesitated a moment and then grudgingly said, "My wife and I joined some friends for dinner at *Les Trois Chats*." He paused and added caustically, "That's a French restaurant."

"What time was that?" Kling asked.

"Eight o'clock."

"Where were you at nine?"

"Still having dinner."

"And at nine-thirty?"

Cutler sighed and said, "We didn't leave the restaurant until a little after ten."

"And then what did you do?"

"Really, is this necessary?" Cutler said, and scowled at the detectives. Neither of them answered. He sighed again and said, "We walked along Hall Avenue for a while, and then my wife and I left our friends and took a cab home."

The door opened.

Leslie Cutler breezed into the office, saw the expression on her husband's face, weighed the silence that greeted her entrance, and immediately said, "What is it?"

"Tell them where we went when we left here Friday night," Cutler said. "The gentlemen are intent on playing cops and robbers."

"You're joking," Leslie said, and realized at once that they were not. "We went to dinner with some friends," she said quickly. "Marge and Daniel Ronet—she's one of our mannequins. Why?"

"What time did you leave the restaurant, Mrs. Cutler?"

"At ten."

"Was your husband with you all that time?"

"Yes, of course he was." She turned to Cutler and said, "Are they allowed to do this? Shouldn't we call Eddie?"

"Who's Eddie?" Kling said.

"Our lawyer."

"You won't need a lawyer."

"Are you a new detective?" Cutler asked Kling suddenly.

"What's that supposed to mean?"

"It's supposed to mean your interviewing technique leaves something to be desired."

"Oh? In what respect? What do you find lacking in my approach, Mr. Cutler?"

"Subtlety, to coin a word."

"That's very funny," Kling said.

"I'm glad it amuses you."

"Would it amuse you to know that the elevator operator at 791 Stafford Place gave us an excellent description of the man he took up to Tinka's apartment on the night she was killed? And would it amuse you further to know that the description fits you to a tee? How does *that* hit your funny bone, Mr. Cutler?"

"I was nowhere near Tinka's apartment last Friday night."

"Apparently not. I know you won't mind our contacting the friends you had dinner with, though—just to check."

"The receptionist will give you their number," Cutler said coldly.

"Thank you."

Cutler looked at his watch. "I have a lunch date," he said. "If you gentlemen are finished with your—"

"I wanted to ask your receptionist about those telephone messages," Carella said. "And I'd also appreciate any information you can give me about Tinka's friends and acquaintances."

"My wife will have to help you with that." Cutler glanced sourly at Kling and said, "I'm not planning to leave town. Isn't that what you always warn a suspect not to do?"

"Yes, don't leave town," Kling said.

"Bert," Carella said casually, "I think you'd better get back to the squad. Grossman promised to call with a lab report sometime this afternoon. One of us ought to be there to take it."

"Sure," Kling said. He went to the door and opened it. "My partner's a little more subtle than I am," he said, and left.

Carella, with his work cut out for him, gave a brief sigh, and said, "Could we talk to your receptionist now, Mrs. Cutler?"

3

When Carella left the agency at two o'clock that Monday afternoon, he was in possession of little more than he'd had when he first climbed those blue-carpeted steps. The receptionist, radiating wide-eyed helpfulness, could not remember any of the phone messages that had been left for Tinka Sachs on the day of her death. She knew they were all personal calls, and she remembered that some of them were from men, but she could not recall any of the men's names. Neither could she remember the names of the women callers —yes, some of them were women, she said, but she didn't know exactly how many—nor could she remember why *any* of the callers were trying to contact Tinka.

Carella thanked her for her help, and then sat down with Leslie Cutler—who was still fuming over Kling's treatment of her husband—and tried to compile a list of men Tinka knew. He drew another blank here because Leslie informed him at once that Tinka, unlike most of the agency's mannequins (the word "mannequin" was beginning to rankle a little) kept her private affairs to herself, never allowing a date to pick her up at the agency, and never discussing the men in her life, not even with any of the other mannequins (in fact, the word was beginning to rankle a lot). Carella thought at first that Leslie was suppressing information because of the jackass manner in which Kling had conducted the earlier interview. But as he questioned her more completely, he came to believe that she really knew nothing at all about Tinka's personal matters. Even on the few occasions when she and her husband had been invited to Tinka's home, it had been for a simple dinner for three, with no one else in attendance, and with the child Anna asleep in her own room. Comparatively charmed to pieces by Carella's patience after Kling's earlier display, Leslie offered him the agency flyer on Tinka, the composite that went to all photographers, advertising agency art directors, and prospective clients. He took it, thanked her, and left.

Sitting over a cup of coffee and a hamburger now, in a luncheonette two blocks from the squadroom, Carella took the composite out of its manila envelope and remembered again the way Tinka Sachs had looked the last time he'd seen her. The composite was an eight-by-ten black-and-white presentation consisting of a larger sheet folded in half to form two pages, each printed front and back with photographs of Tinka in various poses. Only the last page bore any printed matter.

Carella studied the composite from first page to last:

TINKA
SACHS
SIZE 10-12
HEIGHT (S/F) 5'8"
BUST 34
WAIST 23
HIPS 34
HAIR BLONDE
EYES GREEN
SHOE 7-½AA
GLOVE 7
HAT 22
The Cutlers
21 CARRINGTON ST.

TINKA
SACHS
Jan 15 Vogue, COVER–
Jan Bazaar, p 65–
Feb 1 Vogue, p 115TR,
130, 131, 133–
Feb Glamour, p 11–
Mar Mlle., p 17–
Mar Seventeen, p 36,

The only thing the composite told him was that Tinka posed fully clothed, modeling neither lingerie nor swimwear, a fact he considered interesting, but hardly pertinent. He put the composite into the manila envelope, finished his coffee, and went back to the squadroom.

Kling was waiting and angry.

"What was the idea, Steve?" he asked immediately.

"Here's a composite on Tinka Sachs," Carella said. "We might as well add it to our file."

"Never mind the composite. How about answering my question?"

"I'd rather not. Did Grossman call?"

"Yes. The only prints they've found in the room so far are the dead girl's. They haven't yet examined the knife, or her pocketbook. Don't try to get me off this, Steve. I'm goddamn good and sore."

"Bert, I don't want to get into an argument with you. Let's drop it, okay?"

"No."

"We're going to be working on this case together for what may turn out to be a long time. I don't want to start by—"

"Yes, that's right, and I don't like being ordered back to the squadroom just because someone doesn't like my line of questioning."

"Nobody ordered you back to the squadroom."

"Steve, you outrank me, and you told me to come back, and that was *ordering* me back. I want to know why."

"Because you were behaving like a jerk, okay?"

"I don't think so."

"Then maybe you ought to step back and take an objective look at yourself."

"Damnit, it was *you* who said the old man's identification seemed reliable! Okay, so we walk into that office and we're face to face with the man who'd just been *described* to us! What'd you expect me to do? Serve him a cup of tea?"

"No, I expected you to accuse him—"

"Nobody accused him of anything!"

"—of murder and take him right up here to book him," Carella said sarcastically. "*That's* what I expected."

"I asked perfectly reasonable questions!"

"You asked questions that were snotty and surly and hostile and amateurish. You treated him like a criminal from go, when you had no reason to. You immediately put him on the defensive instead of disarming him. If I were in his place, I'd have lied to you just out of spite. You made an enemy instead of a friend out of someone who might have been able to help us. That means if I need any further information about Tinka's professional life, I'll have to beg it from a man who now has good reason to hate the police."

"He fit our description! Anyone would have asked—"

"Why the hell couldn't you ask in a civil manner? And *then* check on those friends he said he was with, and *then* get tough if you had something to work with? What did you accomplish your way? Not a goddamn thing. Okay, you asked me, so I'm telling you. I had work to do up there, and I couldn't afford to waste more time while you threw mud at the walls. *That's* why I sent you back here. Okay? Good. Did you check Cutler's alibi?"

"Yes."

"*Was* he with those people?"

"Yes."

"And *did* they leave the restaurant at ten and walk around for a while?"

"Yes."

"Then Cutler couldn't have been the man Cyclops took up in his elevator."

"Unless Cyclops got the time wrong."

"That's a possibility, and I suggest we check it. But the checking should have been done *before* you started hurling accusations around."

"I didn't accuse anybody of anything!"

"Your entire approach did! Who the hell do you think you are, a Gestapo agent? You can't go marching into a man's office with nothing but an idea and start—"

"I was doing my best!" Kling said. "If that's not good enough, you can go to hell."

"It's not good enough," Carella said, "and I don't plan to go to hell, either."

"I'm asking Pete to take me off this," Kling said.

"He won't."

"Why not?"

"Because I outrank you, like you said, and *I* want you on it."

"Then don't ever try that again, I'm warning you. You embarrass me in front of a civilian again and—"

"If you had any sense, you'd have been embarrassed long before I asked you to go."

"Listen, Carella—"

"Oh, it's *Carella* now, huh?"

"I don't have to take any crap from you, just remember that. I don't care what your badge says. Just remember I don't have to take any crap from you."

"Or from anybody."

"Or from anybody, right."

"I'll remember."

"See that you do," Kling said, and he walked through the gate in the slatted railing and out of the squadroom.

Carella clenched his fists, unclenched them again, and then slapped one open hand against the top of his desk.

Detective Meyer Meyer came out of the men's room in the corridor, zipping up his fly. He glanced to his left toward the iron-runged steps and cocked his head, listening to the angry clatter of Kling's descending footfalls. When he came into the squadroom, Carella was leaning over, straight-armed, on his desk. A dead, cold expression was on his face.

"What was all the noise about?" Meyer asked.

"Nothing," Carella said. He was seething with anger, and the word came out as thin as a razor blade.

"Kling again?" Meyer asked.

"Kling again."

"Boy," Meyer said, and shook his head, and said nothing more.

On his way home late that afternoon, Carella stopped at the Sachs apartment, showed his shield to the patrolman still stationed outside her door, and then went into the apartment to search for anything that might give him a line on the men Tinka Sachs had known—correspondence, a memo pad, an address book, anything. The apartment was empty and still. The child Anna Sachs had been taken to the Children's Shelter on Saturday and then released into the custody of Harvey Sadler—who was Tinka's lawyer—to await the arrival of the little girl's father from Arizona. Carella walked through the corridor past Anna's room, the same route the murderer must have taken, glanced in through the open door at the rows of dolls lined up in the bookcase, and then went past the room and into Tinka's spacious bedroom. The bed had been stripped, the blood-stained sheets and blanket sent to the police laboratory. There had been blood stains on the drapes as well, and these too had been taken down and shipped off to Grossman. The windows were bare now, overlooking the rooftops below, the boats moving slowly on the River Dix. Dusk was coming fast, a reminder that it was still only April. Carella flicked on the lights and walked around the chalked outline of Tinka's body on the thick green carpet, the blood soaked into it and dried to an ugly brown. He went to an oval table serving as a desk on the wall opposite the bed, sat in the pedestal chair before it, and began rummaging through the papers scattered over its top. The disorder told him that detectives from Homicide had already been through all this and had found nothing they felt worthy of calling to his attention. He sighed and picked up an envelope with an airmail border, turned it over to look at the flap, and saw that it had come from Dennis Sachs—Tinka's ex-husband—in Rainfield, Arizona. Carella took the letter from the envelope, unfolded it, and began reading:

Tuesday, April 6

My darling Tinka—

Here I am in the middle of the desert, writing by the light of a flickering kerosene lamp, and listening to the howl of the wind outside my tent. The others are all asleep already. I have never felt farther away from the city—or from you.

I become more impatient with Oliver's project every day of the week, but perhaps that's because I know what you are trying to do, and everything seems insignificant beside your monumental struggle. Who cares whether or not the Hohokam traversed this desert on their way from Old Mexico? Who cares whether we uncover any of their lodges here? All I know is that I miss you enormously, and respect you, and pray for you. My only hope is that your ordeal will soon be ended, and we can go back to the way it was in the beginning, before the nightmare began, before our love was shattered.

I will call East again on Saturday. All my love to Anna...

...and to you.

Dennis

Carella refolded the letter and put it back into the envelope. He had just learned that Dennis Sachs was out in the desert on some sort of project involving the Hohokam, whoever the hell they were, and that apparently he was still carrying the torch for his ex-wife. But beyond that, Carella also learned that Tinka had been going through what Dennis called a "monumental struggle" and "ordeal." What ordeal? Carella wondered. What struggle? And what exactly was the "nightmare" Dennis mentioned later in his letter? Or was the nightmare the struggle itself, the ordeal, and not something that predated it? Dennis Sachs had been phoned in Arizona this morning by the authorities at the Children's Shelter, and was presumably already on his way East. Whether he yet realized it or not, he would have a great many questions to answer when he arrived.

Carella put the letter in his jacket pocket and began leafing through the other correspondence on the desk. There were bills from the electric company, the telephone company, most of the city's department stores, the Diners' Club, and many of the local merchants. There was a letter from a woman who had done house cleaning for Tinka and who was writing to say she could no longer work for her because she and her family were moving back to Jamaica, B.W.I. There was a letter from the editor of one of the fashion magazines, outlining her plans for shooting the new Paris line with Tinka and several other mannequins that summer, and asking whether she would be available or not. Carella read these cursorily, putting them into a small neat pile at one edge of the oval table, and then found Tinka's address book.

There were a great many names, addresses, and telephone numbers in the small red leather book. Some of the people listed were men. Carella studied each name carefully, going through the book several times. Most of the names were run-of-the-mill Georges and Franks and Charlies, while others were a bit more rare like Clyde and Adrian, and still others were pretty exotic like Rion and Dink and Fritz. None of them rang a bell. Carella closed the book, put it into his jacket pocket and went through the remainder of the papers on the desk. The only other item of interest was a partially completed poem in Tinka's handwriting:

When I think of what I am
And of what I might have been,
I tremble.
I fear the night.
Throughout the day,
I perish from dragons conjured in the dark
Why were they not

He folded the poem carefully and put it into his jacket pocket together with the address book. Then he rose, walked to the door, took a last look into the room, and snapped out the light. He went down the corridor toward the front door. The last pale light of day glanced through Anna's windows into her room, glowing feebly on the faces of her dolls lined up in rows on the bookcase shelves. He went into the room and gently lifted one of the dolls from the top shelf, replaced it, and then recognized another doll as the one Anna had been holding in her lap on Saturday when he'd talked to her. He lifted the doll from the shelf.

The patrolman outside the apartment was startled to see a grown detective rushing by him with a doll under his arm. Carella got into the elevator, hurriedly found what he wanted in Tinka's address book, and debated whether he should call the squad to tell where he was headed, possibly get Kling to assist him with the arrest. He suddenly remembered that Kling had left the squadroom early. His anger boiled to the surface again. The *hell* with him, he thought, and came out into the street at a trot, running for his car. His thoughts came in a disorderly jumble, one following the next, the brutality of it, the goddamn stalking animal brutality of it, should I try making the collar alone, God that poor kid listening to her mother's murder, maybe I ought to go back to the office first, get Meyer to assist, but suppose my man is getting ready to cut out, why doesn't Kling shape up, oh God, slashed again and again. He started the car. The child's doll was on the seat beside him. He looked again at the name and address in Tinka's book. Well? he thought. Which? Get help or go it alone?

He stepped on the accelerator.

There was an excitement pounding inside him now, coupled with the anger, a high anticipatory clamor that drowned out whatever note of caution whispered automatically in his mind. It did not usually happen this way, there were usually weeks or months of drudgery. The surprise of his windfall, the idea of a sudden culmination to a chase barely begun, unleashed a wild energy inside him, forced his foot onto the gas pedal more firmly. His hands were tight on the wheel. He drove with a recklessness that would have brought a summons to a civilian, weaving in and out of traffic, hitting the horn and the brake, his hands and his feet a part of the machine that hurtled steadily downtown toward the address listed in Tinka's book.

He parked the car, and came out onto the sidewalk, leaving the doll on the front seat. He studied the name plates in the entrance hallway—yes, this was it. He pushed a bell button at random, turned the knob on the locked inside door when the answering buzz sounded. Swiftly he began climbing the steps to the third floor. On the second-floor landing, he drew his service revolver, a .38 Smith & Wesson Police Model 10. The gun had a two-inch barrel that made it virtually impossible to snag on clothing when drawn. It weighed only thirty-two ounces and was six and seven-eighths of an inch long, with a blue finish and a checked walnut Magna stock with the familiar S&W monogram. It was capable of firing six shots without reloading.

He reached the third floor and started down the hallway. The mailbox had told him the apartment number was 34. He found it at the end of the hall, and put his ear to the door, listening. He could hear the muted voices of a man and a woman inside the apartment. Kick it in, he thought. You've got enough for an arrest. Kick in the door, and go in shooting if necessary—he's your man. He backed away from the door. He braced himself against the corridor wall opposite the door, lifted his right leg high, pulling back the knee, and then stepped forward and simultaneously unleashed a piston kick, aiming for the lock high on the door.

The wood splintered, the lock ripped from the jamb, the door shot inward. He followed the opening door into the room, the gun leveled in his right hand. He saw only a big beautiful dark-haired woman sitting on a couch facing the door, her legs crossed, a look of startled surprise on her face. But he had heard a man from outside. Where—?

He turned suddenly. He had abruptly realized that the apartment fanned out on both sides of the entrance door, and that the man could easily be to his right or his left, beyond his field of vision. He turned naturally to the right because he was right-handed, because the gun was in his right hand, and made the mistake that could have cost him his life.

The man was on his left.

Carella heard the sound of his approach too late, reversed his direction, caught a single glimpse of straight blond hair like Sonny Tufts, and then felt something hard and heavy smashing into his face.

4

THERE WAS no furniture in the small room, save for a wooden chair to the right of the door. There were two windows on the wall facing the door, and these were covered with drawn green shades. The room was perhaps twelve feet wide by fifteen long, with a radiator in the center of one of the fifteen-foot walls.

Carella blinked his eyes and stared into the semidarkness.

There were nighttime noises outside the windows, and he could see the intermittent flash of neon around the edges of the drawn shades. He wondered what time it was. He started to raise his left hand for a look at his watch, and discovered that it was handcuffed to the radiator. The handcuffs were his own. Whoever had closed the cuff onto his wrist had done so quickly and viciously; the metal was biting sharply into his flesh. The other cuff was clasped shut around the radiator leg. His watch was gone, and he seemed to have been stripped as well of his service revolver, his billet, his cartridges, his wallet and loose change, and even his shoes and socks. The side of his face hurt like hell. He lifted his right hand in exploration and found that his cheek and temple were crusted with dried blood. He looked down again at the radiator leg around which the second cuff was looped. Then he moved to the right of the radiator and looked behind it to see how it was fastened to the wall. If the fittings were loose—

He heard a key being inserted into the door lock. It suddenly occurred to him that he was still alive, and the knowledge filled him with a sense of impending dread rather than elation. *Why* was he still alive? And was someone opening the door right this minute in order to remedy that oversight?

The key turned.

The overhead light snapped on.

A big brunette girl came into the room. She was the same girl who had been sitting on the couch when he'd bravely kicked in the front door. She was carrying a tray in her hands, and he caught the aroma of coffee the moment she entered the room, that and the overriding scent of the heavy perfume the girl was wearing.

"Hello," she said.

"Hello," he answered.

"Have a nice sleep?"

"Lovely."

She was very big, much bigger than she had seemed seated on the couch. She had the bones and body of a showgirl, five feet eight or nine inches tall, with firm full breasts threatening a low-cut peasant blouse, solid thighs sheathed in a tight black skirt that ended just above her knees. Her legs were long and very white, shaped like a dancer's with full calves and slender ankles. She was wearing black slippers, and she closed the door behind her and came into the room silently, the slippers whispering across the floor.

She moved slowly, almost as though she were sleepwalking. There was a current of sensuality about her, emphasized by her dreamlike motion. She seemed to possess an acute awareness of her lush body, and this in turn seemed coupled with the knowledge that whatever she might be—housewife or whore, slattern or saint—men would try to do things to that body, and succeed, repeatedly and without mercy. She was a victim, and she moved with the cautious tread of someone who had been beaten before and now expects attack from any quarter. Her caution, her awareness, the ripeness of her body, the certain knowledge that it was available, the curious look of inevitability the girl wore, all invited further abuses, encouraged fantasies, drew dark imaginings from hidden corners of the mind. Rinsed raven-black hair framed the girl's white face. It was a face hard with knowledge. Smoky Cleopatra makeup shaded her eyes and lashes, hiding the deeper-toned flesh there. Her nose had been fixed once, a long time ago, but it was beginning to fall out of shape so that it looked now as if someone had broken it, and this too added to the victim's look she wore. Her mouth was brightly painted, a whore's mouth, a doll's mouth. It had said every word ever invented. It had done everything a mouth was ever forced to do.

"I brought you some coffee," she said.

Her voice was almost a whisper. He watched her as she came closer. He had the feeling that she could kill a man as readily as kiss him, and he wondered again why he was still alive.

He noticed for the first time that there was a gun on the tray, alongside the coffee pot. The girl lifted the gun now, and pointed it at his belly, still holding the tray with one hand. "Back," she said.

"Why?"

"Don't fuck around with me," she said. "Do what I tell you to do when I tell you to do it."

Carella moved back as far as his cuffed wrist would allow him. The girl crouched, the tight skirt riding up over her thighs, and pushed the tray toward the radiator. Her face was dead serious. The gun was a super .38-caliber Llama automatic. The girl held it steady in her right hand. The thumb safety on the left side of the gun had been thrown. The automatic was ready for firing.

The girl rose and backed away toward the chair near the entrance door, the gun still trained on him. She sat, lowered the gun, and said, "Go ahead."

Carella poured coffee from the pot into the single mug on the tray. He took a swallow. The coffee was hot and strong.

"How is it?" the girl asked.

"Fine."

"I made it myself."

"Thank you."

"I'll bring you a wet towel later," she said. "So you can wipe off that blood. It looks terrible."

"It doesn't feel so hot, either," Carella said.

"Well, who invited you?" the girl asked. She seemed about to smile, and then changed her mind.

"No one, that's true." He took another sip of coffee. The girl watched him steadily.

"Steve Carella," she said. "Is that it?"

"That's right. What's *your* name?"

He asked the question quickly and naturally, but the girl did not step into the trap.

"Detective second/grade," she said. "87th Squad." She paused. "Where's that?"

"Across from the park."

"What park?"

"Grover Park."

"Oh, yeah," she said. "That's a nice park. That's the nicest park in this whole damn city."

"Yes," Carella said.

"I saved your life, you know," the girl said conversationally.

"Did you?"

"Yeah. *He* wanted to kill you."

"I'm surprised he didn't."

"Cheer up, maybe he will."

"When?"

"You in a hurry?"

"Not particularly."

The room went silent. Carella took another swallow of coffee. The girl kept staring at him. Outside, he could hear the sounds of traffic.

"What time is it?" he asked.

"About nine. Why? You got a date?"

"I'm wondering how long it'll be before I'm missed, that's all," Carella said, and watched the girl.

"Don't try to scare me," she said. "Nothing scares me."

"I wasn't trying to scare you."

The girl scratched her leg idly, and then said, "There're some questions I have to ask you."

"I'm not sure I'll answer them."

"You will," she said. There was something cold and deadly in her voice. "I can guarantee that. Sooner or later, you will."

"Then it'll have to be later."

"You're not being smart, mister."

"I'm being very smart."

"How?"

"I figure I'm alive only because you don't know the answers."

"Maybe you're alive because I *want* you to be alive," the girl said.

"Why?"

"I've never had anything like you before," she said, and for the first time since she'd come into the room, she smiled. The smile was frightening. He could feel the flesh at the back of his neck beginning to crawl. He wet his lips and looked at her, and she returned his gaze steadily, the tiny evil smile lingering on her lips. "I'm life or death to you," she said. "If I tell him to kill you, he will."

"Not until you know all the answers," Carella said.

"Oh, we'll get the answers. We'll have plenty of time to get the answers." The smile dropped from her face. She put one hand inside her blouse and idly scratched her breast, and then looked at him again, and said, "How'd you get here?"

"I took the subway."

"That's a lie," the girl said. There was no rancor in her voice. She accused him matter-of-factly, and then said, "Your car was downstairs. The registration was in the glove compartment. There was also a sign on the sun visor, something about a law officer on a duty call."

"All right, I drove here," Carella said.

"Are you married?"

"Yes."

"Do you have any children?"

"Two."

"Girls?"

"A girl and a boy."

"Then that's who the doll is for," the girl said.

"What doll?"

"The one that was in the car. On the front seat of the car."

"Yes," Carella lied. "It's for my daughter. Tomorrow's her birthday."

"He brought it upstairs. It's outside in the living room." The girl paused. "Would you like to give your daughter that doll?"

"Yes."

"Would you like to see her ever again?"

"Yes."

"Then answer whatever I ask you, without any more lies about the subway or anything."

"What's my guarantee?"

"Of what?"

"That I'll stay alive."

"*I'm* your guarantee."

"Why should I trust you?"

"You have to trust me," the girl said. "You're mine." And again she smiled, and again he could feel the hairs stiffening at the back of his neck.

She got out of the chair. She scratched her belly, and then moved toward him, that same slow and cautious movement, as though she expected someone to strike her and was bracing herself for the blow.

"I haven't got much time," she said. "He'll be back soon."

"Then what?"

The girl shrugged. "Who knows you're here?" she asked suddenly.

Carella did not answer.

"How'd you get to us?"

Again, he did not answer.

"Did somebody see him leaving Tinka's apartment?"

Carella did not answer.

"How did you know where to come?"

Carella shook his head.

"Did someone identify him? How did you trace him?"

Carella kept watching her. She was standing three feet away from him now, too far to reach, the Llama dangling loosely in her right hand. She raised the gun.

"Do you want me to shoot you?" she asked conversationally.

"No."

"I'll aim for your balls, would you like that?"

"No."

"Then answer my questions."

"You're not going to kill me," Carella said. He did not take his eyes from the girl's face. The gun was pointed at his groin now, but he did not look at her finger curled inside the trigger guard.

The girl took a step closer. Carella crouched near the radiator, unable to get to his feet, his left hand manacled close to the floor. "I'll enjoy this," the girl promised, and struck him suddenly with the butt of the heavy gun, turning the butt up swiftly as her hand lashed out. He felt the numbing shock of metal against bone as the automatic caught him on the jaw and his head jerked back.

"You like?" the girl asked.

He said nothing.

"You *no* like, huh, baby?" She paused. "How'd you find us?"

Again, he did not answer. She moved past him swiftly, so that he could not turn in time to stop the blow that came from behind him, could not kick out at her as he had planned to do the next time she approached. The butt caught him on the ear, and he felt the cartilage tearing as the metal rasped downward. He whirled toward her angrily, grasping at her with his right arm as he turned, but she danced out of his reach and around to the front of him again, and again hit him with the automatic, cutting him over the left eye this time. He felt the blood start down his face from the open gash.

"What do you say?" she asked.

"I say go to hell," Carella said, and the girl swung the gun again. He thought he was ready for her this time. But she was only feinting, and he grabbed out at empty air as she moved swiftly to his right and out of reach. The manacled hand threw him off balance. He fell forward, reaching for support with his free hand, the handcuff biting sharply into his other wrist. The gun butt caught him again just as his hand touched the floor. He felt it colliding with the base of his skull, a two-pound-six-and-a-half-ounce weapon swung with all the force of the girl's substantial body behind it. The pain shot clear to the top of his head. He blinked his eyes against the sudden dizziness. Hold on, he told himself, hold on, and was suddenly nauseous. The vomit came up into his throat, and he brought his right hand to his mouth just as the girl hit him again. He fell back dizzily against the radiator. He blinked up at the girl. Her lips were pulled back taut over her teeth, she was breathing harshly, the gun hand went back again, he was too weak to turn his head aside. He tried to raise his right arm, but it fell limply into his lap.

"Who saw him?" the girl asked.

"No," he mumbled.

"I'm going to break your nose," she said. Her voice sounded very far away. He tried to hold the floor for support, but he wasn't sure where the floor was any more. The room was spinning. He looked up at the girl and saw her spinning face and breasts, smelled the heavy cloying perfume and saw the gun in her hand. "I'm going to break your nose, mister."

"No."

"Yes," she said.

"No."

He did not see the gun this time. He felt only the excruciating pain of bones splintering. His head rocked back with the blow, colliding with the cast-iron ribs of the radiator. The pain brought him back to raging consciousness. He lifted his right hand to his nose, and the girl hit him again, at the base of the skull again, and again he felt sensibility slipping away from him. He smiled stupidly. She would not let him die, and she would not let him live. She would not allow him to become unconscious, and she would not allow him to regain enough strength to defend himself.

"I'm going to knock out all of your teeth," the girl said.

He shook his head.

"Who told you where to find us? Was it the elevator operator? Was it that one-eyed bastard?"

He did not answer.

"Do you want to lose all your teeth?"

"No."

"Then tell me."

"No."

"You have to tell me," she said. "You *belong* to me."

"No," he said.

There was a silence. He knew the gun was coming again. He tried to raise his hand to his mouth, to protect his teeth, but there was no strength in his arm. He sat with his left wrist caught in the fierce biting grip of the handcuff, swollen, throbbing, with blood pouring down his face and from his nose, his nose a throbbing mass of splintered bone, and waited for the girl to knock out his teeth as she had promised, helpless to stop her.

He felt her lips upon him.

She kissed him fiercely and with her mouth open, her tongue searching his lips and his teeth. Then she pulled away from him, and he heard her whisper, "In the morning, they'll find you dead."

He lost consciousness again.

On Tuesday morning, they found the automobile at the bottom of a steep cliff some fifty miles across the River Harb, in a sparsely populated area of the adjoining state. Most of the paint had been burned away by what must have been an intensely hot fire, but it was still possible to tell that the car was a green 1961 Pontiac sedan bearing the license plate RI 7-3461.

The body on the front seat of the car had been incinerated. They knew by what remained of the lower portions that the body had once been a man, but the face and torso had been cooked beyond recognition, the hair and clothing gone, the skin black and charred, the arms drawn up into the typical pugilistic attitude caused by post-mortem contracture of burned muscles, the fingers hooked like claws. A gold wedding band was on the third finger of the skeletal left hand. The fire had eaten away the skin and charred the remaining bones and turned the gold of the ring to a dull black. A .38 Smith & Wesson was caught in the exposed springs of the front seat, together with the metal parts that remained of what had once been a holster.

All of the man's teeth were missing from his mouth.

In the cinders of what they supposed had been his wallet, they found a detective's shield with the identifying number 714-5632.

A call to headquarters across the river informed the investigating police that the shield belonged to a detective second/grade named Stephen Louis Carella.

5

TEDDY CARELLA sat in the silence of her living room and watched the lips of Detective Lieutenant Peter Byrnes as he told her that her husband was dead. The scream welled up into her throat, she could feel the muscles there contracting until she thought she would strangle. She brought her hand to her mouth, her eyes closed tight so that she would no longer have to watch the words that formed on the lieutenant's lips, no longer have to see the words that confirmed what she had known was true since the night before when her husband had failed to come home for dinner.

She would not scream, but a thousand screams echoed inside her head. She felt faint. She almost swayed out of the chair, and then she looked up into the lieutenant's face as she felt his supporting arm around her shoulders. She nodded. She tried to smile up at him sympathetically, tried to let him know she realized this was an unpleasant task for him. But the tears were streaming down her face and she wished only that her husband were there to comfort her, and then abruptly she realized that her husband would never be there to comfort her again, the realization circling back upon itself, the silent screams ricocheting inside her.

The lieutenant was talking again.

She watched his lips. She sat stiff and silent in the chair, her hands clasped tightly in her lap, and wondered where the children were, how would she tell the children, and saw the lieutenant's lips as he said his men would do everything possible to uncover the facts of her husband's death. In the meantime, Teddy, if there's anything I can do, anything I can do personally I mean, I think you know how much Steve meant to me, to all of us, if there's anything Harriet or I can do to help in any way, Teddy, I don't have to tell you we'll do anything we can, anything.

She nodded.

There's a possibility this was just an accident, Teddy, though we doubt it, we think he was, we don't think it was an accident, why would he be across the river in the next state, fifty miles from here?

She nodded again. Her vision was blurred by the tears. She could barely see his lips as he spoke.

Teddy, I loved that boy. I would rather have a bullet in my heart than be here in this room today with this, with this information. I'm sorry. Teddy I am sorry.

She sat in the chair as still as a stone.

Detective Meyer Meyer left the squadroom at two P.M. and walked across the street and past the low stone wall leading into the park. It was a fine April day, the sky a clear blue, the sun shining overhead, the birds chirping in the newly leaved trees.

He walked deep into the park, and found an empty bench and sat upon it, crossing his legs, one arm stretched out across the top of the bench, the other hanging loose in his lap. There were young boys and girls holding hands and whispering nonsense, there were children chasing each other and laughing, there were nannies wheeling baby carriages, there were old men reading books as they walked, there was the sound of a city hovering on the air.

There was life.

Meyer Meyer sat on the bench and quietly wept for his friend.

Detective Cotton Hawes went to a movie.

The movie was a western. There was a cattle drive in it, thousands of animals thundering across the screen, men sweating and shouting, horses rearing, bullwhips cracking. There was also an attack on a wagon train, Indians circling, arrows and spears whistling through the air, guns answering, men screaming. There was a fight in a saloon, too, chairs and bottles flying, tables collapsing, women running for cover with their skirts pulled high, fists connecting. Altogether, there was noise and color and loud music and plenty of action.

When the end titles flashed onto the screen, Hawes rose and walked up the aisle and out into the street.

Dusk was coming.

The city was hushed.

He had not been able to forget that Steve Carella was dead.

*

Andy Parker, who had hated Steve Carella's guts when he was alive, went to bed with a girl that night. The girl was a prostitute, and he got into her bed and her body by threatening to arrest her if she didn't come across. The girl had been hooking in the neighborhood for little more than a week. The other working hustlers had taken her aside and pointed out all the Vice Squad bulls and also all the local plainclothes fuzz so that she wouldn't make the mistake of propositioning one of them. But Parker had been on sick leave for two weeks with pharyngitis and had not been included in the girl's original briefing by her colleagues. She had approached what looked like a sloppy drunk in a bar on Ainsley, and before the bartender could catch her eye to warn her, she had given him the familiar "Wanna have some fun, baby?" line and then had compounded the error by telling Parker it would cost him a fin for a single roll in the hay or twenty-five bucks for all night. Parker had accepted the girl's proposition, and had left the bar with her while the owner of the place frantically signaled his warning. The girl didn't know why the hell he was waving his arms at her. She knew only that she had a John who said he wanted to spend the night with her. She didn't know the John's last name was Law.

She took Parker to a rented room on Culver. Parker was very drunk—he had begun drinking at twelve noon when word of Carella's death reached the squadroom—but he was not drunk enough to forget that he could not arrest this girl until she exposed her "privates." He waited until she took off her clothes, and then he showed her his shield and said she could take her choice, a possible three years in the jug, or a pleasant hour or two with a very nice fellow. The girl, who had met very nice fellows like Parker before, all of whom had been Vice Squad cops looking for fleshy handouts, figured this was only a part of her normal overhead, nodded briefly, and spread out on the bed for him.

Parker was very very drunk.

To the girl's great surprise, he seemed more interested in talking than in making love, as the euphemism goes.

"What's the sense of it all, would you tell me?" he said, but he did not wait for an answer. "Son of a bitch like Carella gets cooked in a car by some son of a bitch, what's the sense of it? You know what I see every day of the week, you know what we *all* of us see every day of the week, how do you expect us to stay human, would you tell me? Son of a bitch gets cooked like that, doing his job is all, how do you expect us to stay human? What am I doing here with you, a two-bit whore, is that something for me to be doing? I'm a nice fellow. Don't you know I'm a nice fellow?"

"Sure, you're a nice fellow," the girl said, bored.

"Garbage every day," Parker said. "Filth and garbage, I have the stink in my nose when I go home at night. You know where I live? I live in a garden apartment in Majesta. I've got three and a half rooms, a nice little kitchen, you know, a nice apartment. I've got a hi-fi set and also I belong to the Classics Club, I've got all those books by the big writers, the important writers. I haven't got much time to read them, but I got them all there on a shelf, you should see the books I've got. There are nice people living in that apartment building, not like here, not like what you find in this crumby precinct, how old are you anyway, what are you nineteen, twenty?"

"I'm twenty-one," the girl said.

"Sure, look at you, the shit of the city."

"Listen, mister—"

"Shut up, shut up, who the hell's asking you? I'm *paid* to deal with it, all the shit that gets washed into the sewers, that's my job. My neighbors in the building know I'm a detective, they respect me, they look up to me. They don't know that all I do is handle shit all day long until I can't stand the stink of it any more. The kids riding their bikes in the courtyard, they all say, 'Good morning, Detective Parker.' That's me, a detective. They watch television, you see. I'm one of the good guys. I carry a gun. I'm brave. So look what happens to that son of a bitch Carella. What's the sense?"

"I don't know what you're talking about," the girl said.

"What's the sense, what's the sense?" Parker said. "People, boy, I could tell you about people. You wouldn't believe what I could tell you about people."

"I've been around a little myself," the girl said drily.

"You can't blame me," he said suddenly.

"What?"

"You can't blame me. It's not my fault."

"Sure. Look, mister, I'm a working girl. You want some of this, or not? Because if you—"

"Shut up, you goddamn whore, don't tell me what to do."

"Nobody's—"

"I can pull you in and make your life miserable, you little slut. I've got the power of life and death over you, don't forget it."

"Not quite," the girl said with dignity.

"Not quite, not quite, don't give me any of that crap."

"You're drunk," the girl said. "I don't even think you can—"

"Never mind what I am, I'm not drunk." He shook his head. "All right, I'm drunk, what the hell do you care what I am? You think I care what *you* are? You're *nothing* to me, you're *less* than nothing to me."

"Then what are you doing here?"

"Shut up," he said. He paused. "The kids all yell good morning at me," he said.

He was silent for a long time. His eyes were closed. The girl thought he had fallen asleep. She started to get off the bed, and he caught her arm and pulled her down roughly beside him.

"Stay where you are."

"Okay," she said. "But look, you think we could get this over with? I mean it, mister, I've got a long night ahead of me. I got expenses to meet."

"Filth," Parker said. "Filth and garbage."

"Okay, already, filth and garbage, do you want it or not?"

"He was a good cop," Parker said suddenly.

"What?"

"He was a good cop," he said again, and rolled over quickly and put his head into the pillow.

6

AT SEVEN-THIRTY Wednesday morning, the day after the burned wreckage was found in the adjoining state, Bert Kling went back to the apartment building on Stafford Place, hoping to talk again to Ernest Cyclops Messner. The lobby was deserted when he entered the building.

If he had felt alone the day that Claire Townsend was murdered, if he had felt alone the day he held her in his arms in a bookshop demolished by gunfire, suddenly bereft in a world gone cold and senselessly cruel, he now felt something curiously similar and yet enormously different.

Steve Carella was dead.

The last words he had said to the man who had been his friend were angry words. He could not take them back now, he could not call upon a dead man, he could not offer apologies to a corpse. On Monday, he had left the squadroom earlier than he should have, in anger, and sometime that night Carella had met his death. And now there was a new grief within him, a new feeling of helplessness, but it was coupled with an overriding desire to set things right again—for Carella, for Claire, he did not really know. He knew he could not reasonably blame himself for what had happened, but neither could he stop blaming himself. He had to talk to Cyclops again. Perhaps there was something further the man could tell him. Perhaps Carella had contacted him again that Monday night, and uncovered new information that had sent him rushing out to investigate alone.

The elevator doors opened. The operator was not Cyclops.

"I'm looking for Mr. Messner," Kling told the man. "I'm from the police."

"He's not here," the man said.

"He told us he has the graveyard shift."

"Yeah, well, he's not here."

"It's only seven-thirty," Kling said.

"I know what time it is."

"Well, where is he, can you tell me that?"

She spoke with a pronounced Riverhead accent that somehow marred her clean good looks. She was a tall girl, perhaps nineteen years old, wearing a dark-grey suit and a white blouse, her auburn hair brushed back behind her ears, the lobes decorated with tiny pearl earrings.

"There are some things I want to ask him," Kling said.

"About the Tinka Sachs murder?"

"Yes."

"He was telling me about that just recently."

"When was that?"

"Oh, I don't know. Let me think." They walked out of the lobby and into the street. Marjorie had long legs, and she walked very swiftly. Kling, in fact, was having trouble keeping up with her. "What's today, anyway?"

"Wednesday," Kling said.

"Wednesday, mmm, boy where does the week go? It must have been Monday. That's right. When I got home from the movies Monday night, he was downstairs putting out his garbage. So we talked awhile. He said he was expecting a detective."

"A detective? Who?"

"What do you mean?"

"Did he say *which* detective he was expecting? Did he mention a name?"

"No, I don't think so. He said he'd talked to some detectives just that morning—that was Monday, right?—and that he'd got a call a few minutes ago saying another detective was coming up to see him."

"Did he say that exactly? That *another* detective was coming up to see him? A *different* detective?"

"Oh. I don't know if he said just that. I mean, it could have been one of the detectives he'd talked to that morning. I really don't know for sure."

"Does the name Carella mean anything to you?"

"No." Marjorie paused. "Should it?"

"Did Mr. Messner use that name when he was talking about the detective who was coming to see him?"

"No, I don't think so. He only said he'd had a call from a detective, that was all. He seemed very proud. He told me they probably wanted him to describe the man again, the one he saw going up to her apartment. The dead girl's. Brrrr, it gives you the creeps, doesn't it?"

"Yes," Kling said. "It does."

They were approaching the elevated station now. They paused at the bottom of the steps.

"This was Monday afternoon, you say?"

"No. Monday night. Monday *night*, I said."

"What time Monday night?"

"About ten-thirty, I guess. I told you, I was coming home from the movies."

"Let me get this straight," Kling said. "At ten-thirty Monday night, Mr. Messner was putting out his garbage, and he told you he had just received a call from a detective who was on his way over? Is that it?"

"That's it." Marjorie frowned. "It *was* kind of late, wasn't it? I mean, to be making a business visit. Or do you people work that late?"

"Well, yes, but . . ." Kling shook his head.

"Listen, I really have to go," Marjorie said. "I'd like to talk to you, but—"

"I'd appreciate a few more minutes of your time, if you can—"

"Yes, but my boss—"

"I'll call him later and explain."

"Yeah, you don't *know* him," Marjorie said, and rolled her eyes.

"Can you just tell me whether Mr. Messner mentioned anything about this detective the next time you saw him. I mean, *after* the detective was there."

"Well, I haven't seen him since Monday night."

"You didn't see him at *all* yesterday?"

"Nope. Well, I usually miss him in the morning, you know, because I'm gone before he gets home. But sometimes I drop in at night, just to say hello, or he'll come in for something, you know, like that. And I told you about the television. We just didn't hear it. My mother commented about it, as a matter of fact. She said Cyclops was probably—that's what we call him, Cyclops, everybody does, he doesn't mind—she said Cyclops was probably out on the town."

"Does he often go out on the town?"

"Well, I don't think so—but who knows? Maybe he felt like having himself a good time, you know? Listen, I really have to—"

"All right, I won't keep you. Thank you very much, Marjorie. If you'll tell me where you work, I'll be happy to—"

"Oh, the hell with him. I'll tell him what happened, and he can take it or leave it. I'm thinking of quitting, anyway."

"Well, thank you again."

"Don't mention it," Marjorie said, and went up the steps to the platform.

Kling thought for a moment, and then searched in his pocket for a dime. He went into the cafeteria on the corner, found a phone booth, and identified himself to the operator, telling her he wanted the listing for the lobby phone in Tinka's building on Stafford Place. She gave him the number, and he dialed it. A man answered the phone. Kling said, "I'd like to talk to the superintendent, please."

"This is the super."

"This is Detective Kling of the 87th Squad," Kling said. "I'm investigating—"

"Who?" the superintendent said.

"Detective Kling. Who's this I'm speaking to?"

"I'm the super of the building. Emmanuel Farber. Manny. Did you say this was a detective?"

"That's right."

"Boy, when are you guys going to give us some rest here?"

"What do you mean?"

"Don't you have nothing to do but call up here?"

"I haven't called you before, Mr. Farber."

"No, not you, never mind. This phone's been going like sixty."

"Who called you?"

"Detectives, never mind."

"Who? Which detectives?"

"The other night."

"When?"

"Monday. Monday night."

"A detective called you Monday night?"

"Yeah, wanted to know where he could reach Cyclops. That's one of our elevator operators."

"Did you tell him?"

"Sure, I did."

"Who was he? Did he give you his name?"

"Yeah, some Italian fellow."

Kling was silent for a moment.

"Would the name have been Carella?" he asked.

"That's right."

"Carella?"

"Yep, that's the one."

"What time did he call?"

"Oh, I don't know. Sometime in the evening."

"And he said his name was Carella?"

"That's right, Detective Carella, that's what he said. Why? You know him?"

"Yes," Kling said. "I know him."

"Well, you ask him. He'll tell you."

"What time in the evening did he call? Was it early or late?"

"What do you mean by early or late?" Farber asked.

"Was it before dinner?"

"No. Oh no, it was after dinner. About ten o'clock, I suppose. Maybe a little later."

"And what did he say to you?"

"He wanted Cyclops' address, said he had some questions to ask him."

"About what?"

"About the murder."

"He said that specifically? He said, 'I have some questions to ask Cyclops about the murder?'"

"About the Tinka Sachs murder, is what he actually said."

"He said, 'This is Detective Carella, I want to know—'"

"That's right, this is Detective Carella—"

"'—I want to know Cyclops Messner's address because I have some questions to ask him about the Tinka Sachs murder.'"

"No, that's not it exactly."

"What's wrong with it?" Kling asked.

"He didn't say the name."

"You just said he *did* say the name. The Tinka Sachs murder. You said—"

"Yes, that's right. That's not what I mean."

"Look, what—?"

"He didn't say Cyclops' name."

"I don't understand you."

"All he said was he wanted the address of the one-eyed elevator operator because he had some questions to ask him about the Tinka Sachs murder. That's what he said."

"He referred to him as the one-eyed elevator operator?"

"That's right."

"You mean he didn't know the name?"

"Well, I don't know about that. He didn't know how to *spell* it, though, that's for sure."

"Excuse me," the telephone operator said. "Five cents for the next five minutes, please."

"Hold on," Kling said. He reached into his pocket, and found only two quarters. He put one into the coin slot.

"Was that twenty-five cents you deposited, sir?" the operator asked.

"That's right."

"If you'll let me have your name and address, sir, we'll—"

"No, forget it."

"—send you a refund in stamps."

"No, that's all right, operator, thank you. Just give me as much time as the quarter'll buy, okay?"

"Very well, sir."

"Hello?" Kling said. "Mr. Farber?"

"I'm still here," Farber said.

"What makes you think this detective couldn't spell Cyclops' name?"

"Well, I gave him the address, you see, and I was about to hang up when he asked me about the spelling. He wanted to know the correct spelling of the name."

"And what did you say?"

"I said it was Messner, M-E-S-S-N-E-R, Ernest Messner, and I repeated the address for him again, 1117 Gainesborough Avenue in Riverhead."

"And then what?"

"He said thank you very much and hung up."

"Sir, was it your impression that he did not know Cyclops' name until you gave it to him?"

"Well, I couldn't say that for sure. All he wanted was the correct spelling."

"Yes, but he asked for the address of the one-eyed elevator operator, isn't that what you said?"

"That's right."

"If he knew the name, why didn't he use it?"

"You got me. What's *your* name?" the superintendent asked.

"Kling. Detective Bert Kling."

"Mine's Farber, Emmanuel Farber, Manny."

"Yes, I know. You told me."

"Oh. Okay."

There was a long silence on the line.

"Was that all, Detective Kling?" Farber said at last. "I've got to get these lobby floors waxed and I'm—"

"Just a few more questions," Kling said.

"Well, okay, but could we—?"

"Cyclops had his usual midnight-to-eight-A.M. shift Monday night, is that right?"

"That's right, but—"

"When he came to work, did he mention anything about having seen a detective?"

"He *didn't*," Farber said.

"He didn't mention a detective at all? He didn't say—"

"No, he didn't come to work."

"What?"

"He didn't come to work Monday nor yesterday, either," Farber said. "I had to get another man to take his place."

"Did you try to reach him?"

"I waited until twelve-thirty, with the man he was supposed to relieve taking a fit, and finally I called his apartment, three times in fact, and there was no answer. So I phoned one of the other men. Had to run the elevator myself until the man got here. That must've been about two in the morning."

"Did Cyclops contact you at all any time yesterday?"

"Nope. You think he'd call, wouldn't you?"

"Did he contact you today?"

"Nope."

"But you're expecting him to report to work tonight, aren't you?"

"Well, he's due at midnight, but I don't know. I hope he shows up."

"Yes, I hope so, too," Kling said. "Thank you very much, Mr. Farber. You've been very helpful."

"Sure thing," Farber said, and hung up.

Kling sat in the phone booth for several moments, trying to piece together what he had just learned. Someone had called Farber on Monday night at about ten, identifying himself as Detective Carella, and asking for the address of the one-eyed elevator operator. Carella knew the man was named Ernest Messner and nicknamed Cyclops. He would not have referred to him as the one-eyed elevator operator. But more important than that, he would never have called the superintendent at all. Knowing the man's name, allegedly desiring his address, he would have done exactly what Kling had done this morning. He would have consulted the telephone directories and found a listing for Ernest Messner in the Riverhead book, as simple as that, as routine as that. No, the man who had called Farber was not Carella. But he had known Carella's name, and had made good use of it.

At ten-thirty Monday night, Marjorie Gorman had met Cyclops in front of the building and he had told her he was expecting a visit from a detective. That could only mean that "Detective Carella" had already called Cyclops and told him he would stop by. And now, Cyclops was missing, had indeed been missing since Monday night.

Kling came out of the phone booth, and began walking back toward the building on Gainesborough Avenue.

The landlady of the building did not have a key to Mr. Messner's apartment. Mr. Messner has his own lock on the door, she said, the same as any of the other tenants in the building, and she certainly did not have a key to Mr. Messner's lock, nor to the locks of any of the other tenants. Moreover, she would *not* grant Kling permission to try his skeleton key on the door, and she warned him that if he forced entry into Mr. Messner's apartment, she would sue the city. Kling informed her that if she cooperated, she would save him the trouble of going all the way downtown for a search warrant, and she said she didn't *care* about his going all the way downtown, suppose Mr. Messner came back and learned she had let the police in there while he was away, *who'd* get the lawsuit then, would he mind telling her?

Kling said he would go downtown for the warrant.

Go ahead then, the landlady told him.

It took an hour to get downtown, twenty minutes to obtain the warrant, and another hour to get back to Riverhead again. His skeleton key would not open Cyclops' door, so he kicked it in.

The apartment was empty.

7

DENNIS SACHS seemed to be about forty years old. He was tall and deeply tanned, with massive shoulders and an athlete's easy stance. He opened the door of his room at the Hotel Capistan, and said, "Detective Kling? Come in, won't you?"

"Thank you," Kling said. He studied Sachs's face. The eyes were blue, with deep ridges radiating from the edges, starkly white against the bronzed skin. He had a large nose, an almost feminine mouth, a cleft chin. He needed a shave. His hair was brown.

The little girl, Anna, was sitting on a couch at the far end of the large living room. She had a doll across her lap, and she was watching television when Kling came in. She glanced up at him briefly, and then turned her attention back to the screen. A give-away program was in progress, the m.c. unveiling a huge motor launch to the delighted shrieks of the studio audience. The couch was upholstered in a lush green fabric against which the child's blond hair shone lustrously. The place was oppressively overfurnished, undoubtedly part of a suite, with two doors leading from the living room to the adjoining bedrooms. A small cooking alcove was tucked discreetly into a corner near the entrance door, a screen drawn across it. The dominant colors of the suite were pale yellows and deep greens, the rugs were thick, the furniture was exquisitely carved. Kling suddenly wondered how much all this was costing Sachs per day, and then tried to remember where he'd picked up the notion that archaeologists were poverty-stricken.

"Sit down," Sachs said. "Can I get you a drink?"

"I'm on duty," Kling said.

"Oh, sorry. Something soft then? A Coke? Seven-Up? I think we've got some in the refrigerator."

"Thank you, no," Kling said.

The men sat. From his wing chair, Kling could see through the large windows and out over the park to where the skyscrapers lined the city. The sky behind the buildings was a vibrant blue. Sachs sat facing him, framed with the light flowing through the windows.

"The people at the Children's Shelter told me you got to the city late Monday, Mr. Sachs. May I ask where in Arizona you were?"

"Well, part of the time I was in the desert, and the rest of the time I was staying in a little town called Rainfield, have you ever heard of it?"

"No."

"Yes. Well, I'm not surprised," Sachs said. "It's on the edge of the desert. Just a single hotel, a depot, a general store, and that's it."

"What were you doing in the desert?"

"We're on a dig, I thought you knew that. I'm part of an archaeological team headed by Dr. Oliver Tarsmith. We're trying to trace the route of the Hohokam in Arizona."

"The Hohokam?"

"Yes, that's a Pima Indian word meaning 'those who have vanished.' The Hohokam were a tribe once living in Arizona, haven't you ever heard of them?"

"No, I'm afraid I haven't."

"Yes, well. In any case, they seem to have had their origins in Old Mexico. In fact, archaeologists like myself have found copper bells and other objects that definitely link the Hohokam to the Old Mexican civilization. And, of course, we've excavated ball courts—an especially large one at Snaketown—that are definitely Mexican or Mayan in origin. At one site, we found a rubber ball buried in a jar, and it's our belief that it must have been traded through tribes all the way from southern Mexico. That's where the wild rubber grows, you know."

"No, I didn't know that."

"Yes, well. The point is that we archaeologists don't know what route the Hohokam traveled from Mexico to Arizona and then to Snaketown. Dr. Tarsmith's theory is that their point of entry was the desert just outside Rainfield. We are now excavating for archaeological evidence to support this theory."

"I see. That sounds like interesting work."

Sachs shrugged.

"Isn't it?"

"I suppose so."

"You don't sound very enthusiastic."

"Well, we haven't had too much luck so far. We've been out

there for close to a year, and we've uncovered only the flimsiest sort of evidence, and . . . well, frankly, it's getting a bit tedious. We spend four days a week out on the desert, you see, and then come back into Rainfield late Thursday night. There's nothing much in Rainfield, and the nearest big town is a hundred miles from there. It can get pretty monotonous."

"Why only *four* days in the desert?"

"Instead of five, do you mean? We usually spend Fridays making out our reports. There's a lot of paperwork involved, and it's easier to do at the hotel."

"When did you learn of your wife's death, Mr. Sachs?"

"Monday morning."

"You had not been informed up to that time?"

"Well, as it turned out, a telegram was waiting for me in Rainfield. I guess it was delivered to the hotel on Saturday, but I wasn't there to take it."

"Where were you?"

"In Phoenix."

"What were you doing there?"

"Drinking, seeing some shows. You can get very sick of Rainfield, you know."

"Did anyone go with you?"

"No."

"How did you get to Phoenix?"

"By train."

"Where did you stay in Phoenix?"

"At the Royal Sands."

"From when to when?"

"Well, I left Rainfield late Thursday night. I asked Oliver—Dr. Tarsmith—if he thought he'd need me on Friday, and he said he wouldn't. I guess he realized I was stretched a little thin. He's a very perceptive man that way."

"I see. In effect, then, he gave you Friday off."

"That's right."

"No reports to write?"

"I took those with me to Phoenix. It's only a matter of organizing one's notes, typing them up, and so on."

"Did you manage to get them done in Phoenix?"

"Yes, I did."

"Now, let me understand this, Mr. Sachs . . ."

"Yes?"

"You left Rainfield sometime late Thursday night . . ."

"Yes, I caught the last train out."

"What time did you arrive in Phoenix?"

"Sometime after midnight. I had called ahead to the Sands for a reservation."

"I see. When did you leave Phoenix?"

"Mr. Kling," Sachs said suddenly, "are you just making small talk, or is there some reason for your wanting to know all this?"

"I was simply curious, Mr. Sachs. I knew Homicide had sent a wire off to you, and I was wondering why you didn't receive it until Monday morning."

"Oh. Well, I just explained that. I didn't get back to Rainfield until then."

"You left Phoenix Monday morning?"

"Yes. I caught a train at about six A.M. I didn't want to miss the jeep." Sachs paused. "The expedition's jeep. We usually head out to the desert pretty early, to get some heavy work in before the sun gets too hot."

"I see. But when you got back to the hotel, you found the telegram."

"That's right."

"What did you do then?"

"I immediately called the airport in Phoenix to find out what flights I could get back here."

"And what did they tell you?"

"There was a TWA flight leaving at eight in the morning, which would get here at four-twenty in the afternoon—there's a two-hour time difference, you know."

"Yes, I know that. Is that the flight you took?"

"No, I didn't. It was close to six-thirty when I called the airport. I might have been able to make it to Phoenix in time, but it would have been a very tight squeeze, and I'd have had to borrow a car. The trains out of Rainfield aren't that frequent, you see."

"So what *did* you do?"

"Well, I caught American's eight-thirty flight, instead. Not a through flight; we made a stop at Chicago. I didn't get here until almost five o'clock that night."

"That was Monday night?"

"Yes, that's right."

"When did you pick up your daughter?"

"Yesterday morning. Today is Wednesday, isn't it?"

"Yes."

"You lose track of time when you fly cross-country," Sachs said.

"I suppose you do."

The television m.c. was giving away a fourteen-cubic-foot refrigerator with a big, big one-hundred-and-sixty-pound freezer. The studio audience was applauding. Anna sat with her eyes fastened to the screen.

"Mr. Sachs, I wonder if we could talk about your wife."

"Yes, please."

"The child . . ."

"I think she's absorbed in the program." He glanced at her, and then said, "Would you prefer we discussed it in one of the other rooms?"

"I thought that might be better, yes," Kling said.

"Yes, you're right. Of course," Sachs said. He rose and led Kling toward the larger bedroom. His valise, partially unpacked, was open on the stand alongside the bed. "I'm afraid everything's a mess," he said. "It's been hurry up, hurry up from the moment I arrived."

"I can imagine," Kling said. He sat in an easy chair near the bed. Sachs sat on the edge of the bed and leaned over intently, waiting for him to begin. "Mr. Sachs, how long had you and your wife been divorced?"

"Three years. And we separated a year before that."

"The child is how old?"

"Anna? She's five."

"Is there another child?"

"No."

"The way you said 'Anna,' I thought—"

"No, there's only the one child. Anna. That's all."

"As I understand it, then, you and your wife separated the year after she was born."

"That's right, yes. Actually, it was fourteen months. She was fourteen months old when we separated."

"Why was that, Mr. Sachs?"

"Why was what?"

"Why did you separate?"

"Well, you know." Sachs shrugged.

"No, I don't."

"Well, that's personal, I'm afraid."

The room was very silent. Kling could hear the m.c. in the living room leading the audience in a round of applause for one of the contestants.

"I can understand that divorce is a personal matter, Mr. Sachs, but—"

"Yes, it is."

"Yes, I understand that."

"I'd rather not discuss it, Mr. Kling. Really, I'd rather not. I don't see how it would help you in solving . . . in solving my wife's murder. Really."

"I'm afraid *I'll* have to decide what would help us, Mr. Sachs."

"We had a personal problem, let's leave it at that."

"What sort of a personal problem?"

"I'd rather not say. We simply couldn't live together any longer, that's all."

"Was there another man involved?"

"Certainly not!"

"Forgive me, but I think you can see how another man might be important in a murder case."

"I'm sorry. Yes. Of course. Yes, it would be important. But it wasn't anything like that. There was no one else involved. There was simply a . . . a personal problem between the two of us and we . . . we couldn't find a way to resolve it, so . . . so we thought it best to split up. That's all there was to it."

"What was the personal problem?"

"Nothing that would interest you."

"Try me."

"My wife is dead," Sachs said.

"I know that."

"Any problem she might have had is certainly—"

"Oh, it was *her* problem then, is that right? Not yours?"

"It was *our* problem," Sachs said. "Mr. Kling, I'm not going to answer any other questions along these lines. If you insist that I do, you'll have to arrest me, and I'll get a lawyer, and we'll see about it. In the meantime, I'll just have to refuse to cooperate if that's the tack you're going to follow. I'm sorry."

"All right, Mr. Sachs, perhaps you can tell me whether or not you mutually agreed to the divorce."

"Yes, we did."

"Whose idea was it? Yours or hers?"

"Mine."

"Why?"

"I can't answer that."

"You know, of course, that adultery is the only grounds for divorce in this state."

"Yes, I know that. There was no adultery involved. Tinka went to Nevada for the divorce."

"Did you go with her?"

"No. She knew people in Nevada. She's from the West Coast originally. She was born in Los Angeles."

"Did she take the child with her?"

"No. Anna stayed here with me while she was gone."

"Have you kept in touch since the divorce, Mr. Sachs?"

"Yes."

"How?"

"Well, I see Anna, you know. We share the child. We agreed to that before the divorce. Stuck out in Arizona there, I didn't have much chance to see her this past year. But usually, I see quite a bit of her. And I talk to Tinka on the phone, I *used* to talk to her on the phone, and I also wrote to her. We kept in touch, yes."

"Would you have described your relationship as a friendly one?"

"I loved her," Sachs said flatly.

"I see."

Again, the room was silent. Sachs turned his head away.

"Do you have any idea who might have killed her?" Kling asked.

"No."

"None whatever?"

"None whatever."

"When did you communicate with her last?"

"We wrote to each other almost every week."

"Did she mention anything that was troubling her?"

"No."

"Did she mention any of her friends who might have had reason to . . . ?"

"No."

"When did you write to her last?"

"Last week sometime."

"Would you remember exactly when?"

"I think it was . . . the fifth or the sixth, I'm not sure."

"Did you send the letter by air?"

"Yes."

"Then it should have arrived here before her death."

"Yes, I imagine it would have."

"Did she usually save your letters?"

"I don't know. Why?"

"We couldn't find any of them in the apartment."

"Then I guess she didn't save them."

"Did *you* save *her* letters?"

"Yes."

"Mr. Sachs, would you know one of your wife's friends who answers this description: Six feet two or three inches tall, heavily built, in his late thirties or early forties, with straight blond hair and—"

"I don't know who Tinka saw after we were divorced. We led separate lives."

"But you still loved her."

"Yes."

"Then why did you divorce her?" Kling asked again, and Sachs did not answer. "Mr. Sachs, this may be very important to us . . ."

"It isn't."

"Was your wife a dyke?"

"No."

"Are you a homosexual?"

"No."

"Mr. Sachs, *whatever* it was, believe me, it won't be something new to us. Believe me, Mr. Sachs, and please trust me."

"I'm sorry. It's none of your business. It has nothing to do with anything but Tinka and me."

"Okay," Kling said.

"I'm sorry."

"Think about it. I know you're upset at the moment, but—"

"There's nothing to think about. There are some things I will never discuss with anyone, Mr. Kling. I'm sorry, but I owe at least that much to Tinka's memory."

"I understand," Kling said, and rose. "Thank you for your time. I'll leave my card, in case you remember anything that might be helpful to us."

"All right," Sachs said.

"When will you be going back to Arizona?"

"I'm not sure. There's so much to be arranged. Tinka's lawyer advised me to stay for a while, at least to the end of the month, until the estate can be settled, and plans made for Anna . . . there's so much to do."

"*Is* there an estate?" Kling asked.

"Yes."

"A sizable one?"

"I wouldn't imagine so."

"I see." Kling paused, seemed about to say something, and then abruptly extended his hand. "Thank you again, Mr. Sachs," he said. "I'll be in touch with you."

Sachs saw him to the door. Anna, her doll in her lap, was still watching television when he went out.

At the squadroom, Kling sat down with a pencil and pad, and then made a call to the airport, requesting a list of all scheduled flights to and from Phoenix, Arizona. It took him twenty minutes to get all the information, and another ten minutes to type it up in chronological order. He pulled the single sheet from his machine and studied it:

AIRLINE SCHEDULES FROM PHOENIX AND RETURN

EASTBOUND:

Frequency	Airline & Flt.		Departing Phoenix	Arriving Here	Stops	
Exc. Sat.	American	#946	12:25 AM	10:45 AM	(Tucson	12:57 AM- 1:35 AM
					(Chicago	6:35 AM- 8:00 AM
Daily	American	# 98	7:25 AM	5:28 PM	(Tucson	7:57 AM- 8:25 AM
					(El Paso	9:10 AM- 9:40 AM
					(Dallas	12:00 PM–12:30 PM
Daily	TWA	#146	8:00 AM	4:20 PM	Chicago	12:58 PM- 1:30 PM
Daily	American	# 68	8:30 AM	4:53 PM	Chicago	1:27 PM- 2:00 PM
Daily	American	# 66	2:00 PM	10:23 PM	Chicago	6:57 PM- 7:30 PM

WESTBOUND:

Frequency	Airline & Flt.		Departing Here	Arriving Phoenix	Stops	
Exc. Sun.	American	#965	8:00 AM	11:05 AM	Chicago	9:12 AM- 9:55 AM
Daily	TWA	#147	8:30 AM	11:25 AM	Chicago	9:31 AM-10:15 AM
Daily	American	#981	4:00 PM	6:55 PM	Chicago	5:12 PM- 5:45 PM
Daily	TWA	#143	4:30 PM	7:40 PM	Chicago	5:41 PM- 6:30 PM
Daily	American	# 67	6:00 PM	10:10 PM	(Chicago	7:12 PM– 7:45 PM
					(Tucson	9:08 PM– 9:40 PM

It seemed entirely possible to him that Dennis Sachs could have taken either the twelve-twenty-five flight from Phoenix late Thursday night, or any one of three flights early Friday morning, and still have been here in the city in time to arrive at Tinka's apartment by nine or nine-thirty P.M. He could certainly have killed his wife and caught an early flight back the next morning. Or any one of four flights on Sunday, all of which—because of the time difference—would have put him back in Phoenix that same night and in Rainfield by Monday to pick up the telegram waiting there for him. It was a possibility—remote, but a possibility nonetheless. The brown hair, of course, was a problem. Cyclops had said the man's hair was blond. But a commercial dye or bleach—

One thing at a time, Kling thought. Wearily, he pulled the telephone directory to him and began a methodical check of the two airlines flying to Phoenix. He told them he wanted to know if a man named Dennis Sachs, or any man with the initials D.S., had flown here from Phoenix last Thursday night or Friday morning, and whether or not he had made the return flight any time during the weekend. The airlines were helpful and patient. They checked their flight lists. Something we don't ordinarily do, sir, is this a case involving a missing person? No, Kling said, this is a case involving a murder. Oh, well in that case, sir, but we don't ordinarily do this, sir, even for the police, our flight lists, you see . . . Yes, well I appreciate your help, Kling said.

Neither of the airlines had any record of either a Dennis Sachs or a D.S. taking a trip from or to Phoenix at any time before Monday, April 12th. American Airlines had him listed as a passenger on Flight 68, which had left Phoenix at eight-thirty A.M. Monday morning, and had arrived here at four-fifty-three P.M. that afternoon. American reported that Mr. Sachs had not as yet booked return passage.

Kling thanked American and hung up. There was still the possibility that Sachs had flown here and back before Monday, using an assumed name. But there was no way of checking that—and the only man who could make any sort of a positive identification had been missing since Monday night.

*

The meeting took place in Lieutenant Byrnes's office at five o'clock that afternoon. There were five detectives present in addition to Byrnes himself. Miscolo had brought in coffee for most of the men, but they sipped at it only distractedly, listening intently to Byrnes as he conducted the most unorthodox interrogation any of them had ever attended.

"We're here to talk about Monday afternoon," Byrnes said. His tone was matter-of-fact, his face expressed no emotion. "I have the duty chart for Monday, April twelfth, and it shows Kling, Meyer and Carella on from eight to four, with Meyer catching. The relieving team is listed as Hawes, Willis and Brown, with Brown catching. Is that the way it was?"

The men nodded.

"What time did you get here, Cotton?"

Hawes, leaning against the lieutenant's filing cabinet, the only one of the detectives drinking tea, looked up and said, "It must've been about five."

"Was Steve still here?"

"No."

"What about you, Hal?"

"I got here a little early, Pete," Willis said. "I had some calls to make."

"What time?"

"Four-thirty."

"Was Steve still here?"

"Yes."

"Did you talk to him?"

"Yes."

"What about?"

"He said he was going to a movie with Teddy that night."

"Anything else?"

"That was about it."

"I talked to him, too, Pete," Brown said. He was the only Negro cop in the room. He was sitting in the wooden chair to the right of Byrnes's desk, a coffee container clasped in his huge hands.

"What'd he say to you, Art?"

"He told me he had to make a stop on the way home."

"Did he say where?"

"No."

"All right, now let's get this straight. Of the relieving team, only two of you saw him, and he said nothing about where he might have been headed. Is that right?"

"That's right," Willis said.

"Were you in the office when he left, Meyer?"

"Yes. I was making out a report."

"Did he say anything to you?"

"He said good night, and he made some joke about bucking for a promotion, you know, because I was hanging around after I'd been relieved."

"What else?"

"Nothing."

"Did he say anything to you at any time during the afternoon? About where he might be going later on?"

"Nothing."

"How about you, Kling?"

"No, he didn't say anything to me, either."

"Were you here when he left?"

"No."

"Where were you?"

"I was on my way home."

"What time did you leave?"

"About three o'clock."

"Why so early?"

There was a silence in the room.

"Why so early?" Byrnes said again.

"We had a fight."

"What about?"

"A personal matter."

"The man is dead," Byrnes said flatly. "There are no personal matters any more."

"He sent me back to the office because he didn't like the way I was behaving during an interview. I got sore." Kling paused. "That's what we argued about."

"So you left here at three o'clock?"

"Yes."

"Even though you were supposed to be working with Carella on the Tinka Sachs case, is that right?"

"Yes."

"Did you know where he was going when he left here?"

"No, sir."

"Did he mention anything about wanting to question anyone, or about wanting to see anyone again?"

"Only the elevator operator. He thought it would be a good idea to check him again."

"What for?"

"To verify a time he'd given us."

"Do you think that's where he went?"

"I don't know, sir."

"Have you talked to this elevator operator?"

"No, sir, I can't locate him."

"He's been missing since Monday night," Meyer said. "According to Bert's report, he was expecting a visit from a man who said he was Carella."

"Is that right?" Byrnes asked.

"Yes," Kling said. "But I don't think it *was* Carella."

"Why not?"

"It's all in my report, sir."

"You've read this, Meyer?"

"Yes."

"What's your impression?"

"I agree with Bert."

Byrnes moved away from his desk. He walked to the window and stood with his hands clasped behind his back, looking at the street below. "He found something, that's for sure," he said, almost to himself. "He found *something* or *somebody*, and he was killed for it." He turned abruptly. "And not a single goddamn one of you knows where he was going. Not even the man who was allegedly working this case with him." He walked back to his desk. "Kling, you stay. The rest of you can leave."

The men shuffled out of the room. Kling stood uncomfortably before the lieutenant's desk. The lieutenant sat in his swivel chair, and turned it so that he was not looking directly at Kling. Kling did not know where he was looking. His eyes seemed unfocused.

"I guess you know that Steve Carella was a good friend of mine," Byrnes said.

"Yes, sir."

"A good friend," Byrnes repeated. He paused for a moment, still looking off somewhere past Kling, his eyes unfocused, and then said, "Why'd you let him go out alone, Kling?"

"I told you, sir. We had an argument."

"So you left here at three o'clock, when you knew goddamn well you weren't going to be relieved until four-forty-five. Now what the hell do you call that, Kling?"

Kling did not answer.

"I'm kicking you off this goddamn squad," Byrnes said. "I should have done it long ago. I'm asking for your transfer, now get the hell out of here."

Kling turned and started for the door.

"No, wait a minute," Byrnes said. He turned directly to Kling now, and there was a terrible look on his face, as though he wanted to cry, but the tears were being checked by intense anger.

"I guess you know, Kling, that I don't have the power to suspend you, I guess you know that. The power rests with the commissioner and his deputies, and they're civilians. But a man can be suspended if he's violated the rules and regulations or if he's committed a crime. The way I look at it, Kling, you've done *both* those things. You violated the rules and regulations by leaving this squadroom and heading home when you were supposed to be on duty, and you committed a crime by allowing Carella to go out there alone and get killed."

"Lieutenant, I—"

"If I could personally take away your gun and your shield, I'd do it, Kling, believe me. Unfortunately, I can't. But I'm going to call the Chief of Detectives the minute you leave this office. I'm going to tell him I'd like you suspended pending a complete investigation, and I'm going to ask that he recommend that to the commissioner. I'm going to *get* that suspension, Kling, if I have to go to the mayor for it. I'll get departmental charges filed, and a departmental trial, and I'll get you dismissed from the force. I'm *promising* you. Now get the hell out of my sight."

Kling walked to the door silently, opened it, and stepped into the squadroom. He sat at his desk silently for several moments, staring into space. He heard the buzzer sound on

Meyer's phone, heard Meyer lifting the instrument to his ear. "Yeah?" Meyer said. "Yeah, Pete. Right. Right. Okay, I'll tell him." He heard Meyer putting the phone back onto its cradle. Meyer rose and came to his desk. "That was the lieutenant," he said. "He wants me to take over the Tinka Sachs case."

8

THE MESSAGE went out on the teletype at a little before ten Thursday morning:

> MISSING PERSON WANTED FOR QUESTIONING CONNECTION HOMICIDE XXX ERNEST MESSNER ALIAS CYCLOPS MESSNER XXX WHITE MALE AGE 68 XXX HEIGHT 6 FEET XXX WEIGHT 170 LBS XXX COMPLETELY BALD XXX EYES BLUE LEFT EYE MISSING AND COVERED BY PATCH XXXXX LAST SEEN VICINITY 1117 GAINESBOROUGH AVENUE RIVERHEAD MONDAY APRIL 12 TEN THIRTY PM EST XXX CONTACT MISPERBUR OR DET/2G MEYER MEYER EIGHT SEVEN SQUAD XXXXXXXXXX

A copy of the teletype was pulled off the squadroom machine by Detective Meyer Meyer who wondered why it had been necessary for the detective at the Missing Persons Bureau to insert the word "completely" before the word "bald." Meyer, who was bald himself, suspected that the description was redundant, overemphatic, and undoubtedly derogatory. It was his understanding that a bald person had no hair. None. Count them. None. Why, then, had the composer of this bulletin (Meyer visualized him as a bushy-headed man with thick black eyebrows, a black mustache and a full beard) insisted on inserting the word "completely," if not to point a deriding finger at all hairless men everywhere? Indignantly, Meyer went to the squadroom dictionary, searched through balas, balata, Balaton, Balboa, balbriggan, and came to:

> **bald** (bôld) adj. 1. lacking hair on some part of the scalp: *a bald head or person.* 2. destitute of some natural growth or covering: *a bald mountain.* 3. bare; plain; unadorned: *a bald prose style.* 4. open; undisguised: *a bald lie.* 5. *Zool.* having white on the head: *bald eagle.*

Meyer closed the book, reluctantly admitting that whereas it was impossible to be a little pregnant, it was not equally impossible to be a little bald. The composer of the bulletin, bushy-haired bastard that he was, had been right in describing Cyclops as "completely bald." If ever Meyer turned up missing one day, they would describe him in exactly the same way. In the meantime, his trip to the dictionary had not been a total loss. He would hereafter look upon himself as a person who lacked hair on his scalp, a person destitute of some natural growth, bare, plain and unadorned, open and undisguised, having white on the head. Hereafter, he would be known zoologically as The Bald Eagle—Nemesis of All Evil, Protector of the Innocent, Scourge of the Underworld!

"Beware The Bald Eagle!" he said aloud, and Arthur Brown looked up from his desk in puzzlement. Happily, the telephone rang at that moment. Meyer picked it up and said, "87th Squad."

"This is Sam Grossman at the lab. Who'm I talking to?"

"You're talking to The Bald Eagle," Meyer said.

"Yeah?"

"Yeah."

"Well, this is The Hairy Ape," Grossman said. "What's with you? Spring fever?"

"Sure, it's such a beautiful day out," Meyer said, looking through the window at the rain.

"Is Kling there? I've got something for him on this Tinka Sachs case."

"I'm handling that one now," Meyer said.

"Oh? Okay. You feel like doing a little work, or were you planning to fly up to your aerie?"

"Up *your* aerie, Mac," Meyer said, and burst out laughing.

"Oh boy, I see I picked the wrong time to call," Grossman said. "Okay. Okay. When you've got a minute later, give me a ring, okay? I'll—"

"The Bald Eagle *never* has a minute later," Meyer said. "What've you got for me?"

"This kitchen knife. The murder weapon. According to the tag, it was found just outside her bedroom door, guy probably dropped it on his way out."

"Okay, what about it?"

"Not much. Only it matches a few other knives in the girl's kitchen, so it's reasonable to assume it belonged to her. What

I'm saying is the killer didn't go up there with his own knife, if that's of any use to you."

"He took the knife from a bunch of other knives in the kitchen, is that it?"

"No, I don't think so. I think the knife was in the bedroom."

"What would a knife be doing in the bedroom?"

"I think the girl used it to slice some lemons."

"Yeah?"

"Yeah. There was a pitcher of tea on the dresser. Two lemons, sliced in half, were floating in it. We found lemon-juice stains on the tray, as well as faint scratches left by the knife. We figure she carried the tea, the lemons, and the knife into the bedroom on that tray. Then she sliced the lemons and squeezed them into the tea."

"Well, that seems like guesswork to me," Meyer said.

"Not at all. Paul Blaney is doing the medical examination. He says he's found citric-acid stains on the girl's left hand, the hand she'd have held the lemons with while slicing with the right. We've checked, Meyer. She was right-handed."

"Okay, so she was drinking tea before she got killed," Meyer said.

"That's right. The glass was on the night table near her bed, covered with her prints."

"Whose prints were covering the knife?"

"Nobody's," Grossman said. "Or I should say *everybody's.* A whole mess of them, all smeared."

"What about her pocketbook? Kling's report said—"

"Same thing, not a good print on it anywhere. There was no money in it, you know. My guess is that the person who killed her also robbed her."

"Mmm, yeah," Meyer said. "Is that all?"

"That's all. Disappointing, huh?"

"I hoped you might come up with something more."

"I'm sorry."

"Sure."

Grossman was silent for a moment. Then he said, "Meyer?"

"Yeah?"

"You think Carella's death is linked to this one?"

"I don't know," Meyer said.

"I liked that fellow," Grossman said, and hung up.

*

Harvey Sadler was Tinka Sachs's lawyer and the senior partner in the firm of Sadler, McIntyre and Brooks, with offices uptown on Fisher Street. Meyer arrived there at ten minutes to noon, and discovered that Sadler was just about to leave for the Y.M.C.A. Meyer told him he was there to find out whether or not Tinka Sachs had left a will, and Sadler said she had indeed. In fact, they could talk about it on the way to the Y, if Meyer wanted to join him. Meyer said he wanted to, and the two men went downstairs to catch a cab.

Sadler was forty-five years old, with a powerful build and craggy features. He told Meyer he had played offensive back for Dartmouth in 1940, just before he was drafted into the army. He kept in shape nowadays, he said, by playing handball at the Y two afternoons a week, Mondays and Thursdays. At least, he *tried* to keep in shape. Even handball twice a week could not completely compensate for the fact that he sat behind a desk eight hours a day.

Meyer immediately suspected a deliberate barb. He had become oversensitive about his weight several weeks back when he discovered what his fourteen-year-old son Alan meant by the nickname "Old Crisco." A bit of off-duty detective work uncovered the information that "Old Crisco" was merely high school jargon for "Old Fat-in-the-Can," a disrespectful term of affection if ever he'd heard one. He would have clobbered the boy, naturally, just to show who was boss, had not his wife Sarah agreed with the little vontz. You *are* getting fat, she told Meyer; you should begin exercising at the police gym. Meyer, whose boyhood had consisted of a series of taunts and jibes from Gentiles in his neighborhood, never expected to be put down by vipers in his own bosom. He looked narrowly at Sadler now, a soldier in the enemy camp, and suddenly wondered if he was becoming a paranoid Jew. Worse yet, an *obese* paranoid Jew.

His reservations about Sadler and also about himself vanished the moment they entered the locker room of the Y.M.C.A., which smelled exactly like the locker room of the Y.M.H.A. Convinced that nothing in the world could eliminate suspicion and prejudice as effectively as the aroma of a men's locker room, swept by a joyous wave of camaraderie,

Meyer leaned against the lockers while Sadler changed into his handball shorts, and listened to the details of Tinka's will.

"She leaves everything to her ex-husband," Sadler said. "That's the way she wanted it."

"Nothing to her daughter?"

"Only if Dennis predeceased Tinka. In that case, a trust was set up for the child."

"Did Dennis know this?" Meyer asked.

"I have no idea."

"Was a copy of the will sent to him?"

"Not by me."

"How many copies did you send to Tinka?"

"Two. The original was kept in our office safe."

"Did she *request* two copies?"

"No. But it's our general policy to send two copies of any will to the testator. Most people like to keep one at home for easy reference, and the other in a safe deposit box. At least, that's been our experience."

"We went over Tinka's apartment pretty thoroughly, Mr. Sadler. We didn't find a copy of any will."

"Then perhaps she *did* send one to her ex-husband. That wouldn't have been at all unusual."

"Why not?"

"Well, they're on very good terms, you know. And, after all, he *is* the only real beneficiary. I imagine Tinka would have wanted him to know."

"Mmm," Meyer said. "How large an estate is it?"

"Well, there's the painting."

"What do you mean?"

"The Chagall."

"I still don't understand."

"The Chagall painting. Tinka bought it many years ago, when she first began earning top money as a model. I suppose it's worth somewhere around fifty thousand dollars today."

"That's a sizable amount."

"Yes," Sadler said. He was in his shorts now, and he was putting on his black gloves and exhibiting signs of wanting to get out on the court. Meyer ignored the signs.

"What about the rest of the estate?" he asked.

"That's it," Sadler said.

"That's what?"

"The Chagall painting *is* the estate, or at least the substance of it. The rest consists of household furnishings, some pieces of jewelry, clothing, personal effects—none of them worth very much."

"Let me get this straight, Mr. Sadler. It's my understanding that Tinka Sachs was earning somewhere in the vicinity of a hundred and fifty thousand dollars a year. Are you telling me that all she owned of value at her death was a Chagall painting valued at fifty thousand dollars?"

"That's right."

"How do you explain that?"

"I don't know. I wasn't Tinka's financial adviser. I was only her lawyer."

"As her lawyer, did you ask her to define her estate when she asked you to draw this will?"

"I did."

"How did she define it?"

"Essentially as I did a moment ago."

"When was this, Mr. Sadler?"

"The will is dated March twenty-fourth."

"March twenty-fourth? You mean just last month?"

"That's right."

"Was there any specific reason for her wanting a will drawn at that time?"

"I have no idea."

"I mean, was she worried about her health or anything?"

"She seemed in good health."

"Did she seem frightened about anything? Did she seem to possess a foreknowledge of what was going to happen?"

"No, she did not. She seemed very tense, but not frightened."

"Why was she tense?"

"I don't know."

"Did you ask her about it?"

"No, I did not. She came to me to have a will drawn. I drew it."

"Had you ever done any legal work for her prior to the will?"

"Yes. Tinka once owned a house in Mavis County. I handled the papers when she sold it."

"When was that?"

"Last October."

"How much did she get for the sale of the house?"

"Forty-two thousand, five hundred dollars."

"Was there an existing mortgage?"

"Yes. Fifteen thousand dollars went to pay it off. The remainder went to Tinka."

"Twenty . . ." Meyer hesitated, calculating. "Twenty-seven thousand, five hundred dollars went to Tinka, is that right?"

"Yes."

"In cash?"

"Yes."

"Where is it, Mr. Sadler?"

"I asked her that when we were preparing the will. I was concerned about estate taxes, you know, and about who would inherit the money she had realized on the sale of the house. But she told me she had used it for personal needs."

"She had spent it?"

"Yes." Sadler paused. "Mr. Meyer, I only play here two afternoons a week, and I'm very jealous of my time. I was hoping . . ."

"I won't be much longer, please bear with me. I'm only trying to find out what Tinka did with all this money that came her way. According to you, she didn't have a penny of it when she died."

"I'm only reporting what she told me. I listed her assets as she defined them for me."

"Could I see a copy of the will, Mr. Sadler?"

"Certainly. But it's in my safe at the office, and I won't be going back there today. If you'd like to come by in the morning . . ."

"I'd hoped to get a look at it before—"

"I assure you that I've faithfully reported everything in the will. As I told you, I was only her lawyer, not her financial adviser."

"Did she *have* a financial adviser?"

"I don't know."

"Mr. Sadler, did you handle Tinka's divorce for her?"

"No. I began representing her only last year, when she sold the house. I didn't know her before then, and I don't know who handled the divorce."

"One last question," Meyer said. "Is anyone else mentioned as a beneficiary in Tinka's will, other than Dennis or Anna Sachs?"

"They are the only beneficiaries," Sadler said. "And Anna only if her father predeceased Tinka."

"Thank you," Meyer said.

Back at the squadroom, Meyer checked over the typewritten list of all the personal belongings found in Tinka's apartment. There was no listing for either a will or a bankbook, but someone from Homicide had noted that a key to a safety deposit box had been found among the items on Tinka's workdesk. Meyer called Homicide to ask about the key, and they told him it had been turned over to the Office of the Clerk, and he could pick it up there if he was interested and if he was willing to sign a receipt for it. Meyer was indeed interested, so he went all the way downtown to the Office of the Clerk, where he searched through Tinka's effects, finding a tiny red snap-envelope with the safety deposit box key in it. The name of the bank was printed on the face of the miniature envelope. Meyer signed out the key and then—since he was in the vicinity of the various court buildings, anyway—obtained a court order authorizing him to open the safety deposit box. In the company of a court official, he went uptown again by subway and then ran through a pouring rain, courtesy of the vernal equinox, to the First Northern National Bank on the corner of Phillips and Third, a few blocks from where Tinka had lived.

A bank clerk removed the metal box from a tier of similar boxes, asked Meyer if he wished to examine the contents in private, and then led him and the court official to a small room containing a desk, a chair, and a chained ballpoint pen. Meyer opened the box.

There were two documents in the box. The first was a letter from an art dealer, giving an appraisal of the Chagall painting. The letter stated simply that the painting had been examined, that it was undoubtedly a genuine Chagall, and that it could be sold at current market prices for anywhere between forty-five and fifty thousand dollars.

The second document was Tinka's will. It was stapled inside a lawyer's blueback, the firm name Sadler, McIntyre and

Brooks printed on the bottom of the binder, together with the address, 80 Fisher Street. Typewritten and centered on the page was the legend LAST WILL AND TESTAMENT OF TINKA SACHS. Meyer opened the will and began reading:

LAST WILL AND TESTAMENT
of
TINKA SACHS

I, Tinka Sachs, a resident of this city, county, and state, hereby revoke all wills and codicils by me at any time heretofore made and do hereby make, publish and declare this as and for my Last Will and Testament.

FIRST: I give, devise and bequeath to my former husband, DENNIS R. SACHS, if he shall survive me, and, if he shall not survive me, to my trustee, hereinafter named, all of my property and all of my household and personal effects including without limitation, clothing, furniture and furnishings, books, jewelry, art objects, and paintings.

SECOND: If my former husband Dennis shall not survive me, I give, devise and bequeath my said estate to my Trustee hereinafter named, IN TRUST NEVERTHELESS, for the following uses and purposes:

(1) My Trustee shall hold, invest and reinvest the principal of said trust and shall collect the income therefrom until my daughter, ANNA SACHS, shall attain the age of twenty-one (21) years, or sooner die.

(2) My Trustee shall, from time to time; distribute to my daughter ANNA before she has attained the age of twenty-one (21) so much of the net income (and the net income of any year not so distributed shall be accumulated and shall, after the end of such year, be deemed principal for purposes of this trust)

and so much of the principal of this trust as my Trustee may in his sole and unreviewable discretion determine for any purposes deemed advisable or convenient by said Trustee, provided, however, that no principal or income in excess of an aggregate amount of Five Thousand Dollars ($5,000) in any one year shall be used for the support of the child unless the death of the child's father, DENNIS R. SACHS, shall have left her financially unable to support herself. The decision of my Trustee with respect to the dates of distribution and the sums to be distributed shall be final.

(3) If my daughter, ANNA, shall die before attaining the age of twenty-one (21) years, my Trustee shall pay over the then principal of the trust fund and any accumulated income to the issue of my daughter, ANNA, then living, in equal shares, and if there be no such issue then to those persons who would inherit from me had I died intestate immediately after the death of ANNA.

THIRD: I nominate, constitute and appoint my former husband, DENNIS R. SACHS, Executor of this my Last Will and Testament. If my said former husband shall predecease me or shall fail to qualify or cease to act as Executor, then I appoint my agent and friend, ARTHUR G. CUTLER, in his place as successor or substitute executor and, if my former husband shall predecease me, as TRUSTEE of the trust created hereby. If my said friend and agent shall fail to qualify or cease to act as Executor or Trustee, then I appoint his wife, LESLIE CUTLER, in his place as successor or substitute executor and/or trustee, as the case may be. Unless otherwise provided by law, no bond or other security shall be required to permit any Executor or Trustee to qualify or act in any jurisdiction.

The rest of the will was boilerplate. Meyer scanned it quickly, and then turned to the last page where Tinka had signed her name below the words "IN WITNESS WHEREOF, I sign, seal, publish and declare this as my Last Will and Testament" and where, below that, Harvey Sadler, William McIntyre and Nelson Brooks had signed as attesting witnesses. The will was dated March twenty-fourth.

The only thing Sadler had forgotten to mention—or perhaps Meyer hadn't asked him about it—was that Art Cutler had been named trustee in the event of Dennis Sachs's death.

Meyer wondered if it meant anything.

And then he calculated how much money Tinka had earned in eleven years at a hundred and fifty thousand dollars a year, and wondered again why her only possession of any real value was the Chagall painting she had drenched with blood on the night of her death.

Something stank.

9

HE HAD checked and rechecked his own findings against the laboratory's reports on the burned wreckage, and at first only one thing seemed clear to Paul Blaney. Wherever Steve Carella had been burned to death, it had not been inside that automobile. The condition of the corpse was unspeakably horrible; it made Blaney queasy just to look at it. In his years as medical examiner, Blaney had worked on cases of thermic trauma ranging from the simplest burns to cases of serious and fatal exposure to flame, light, and electric energy—but these were the worst fourth-degree burns he had ever seen. The body had undoubtedly been cooked for hours: The face was unrecognizable, all of the features gone, the skin black and tight, the single remaining cornea opaque, the teeth undoubtedly loosened and then lost in the fire; the skin on the torso was brittle and split; the hair had been burned away, the flesh completely gone in many places, showing dark red-brown skeletal muscles and charred brittle bones. Blaney's internal examination revealed pale, cooked involuntary muscles, dull and shrunken viscera. Had the body been reduced to its present condition inside that car, the fire would have had to rage for hours. The lab's report indicated that the automobile, ignited by an explosion of gasoline, had burned with extreme intensity, but only briefly. It was Blaney's contention that the body had been burned elsewhere, and then put into the automobile to simulate death there by explosion and subsequent fire.

Blaney was not paid to speculate on criminal motivation, but he wondered now why someone had gone to all this trouble, especially when the car fire would undoubtedly have been hot enough to eliminate adequately and forever any intended victim. Being a methodical man, he continued to probe. His careful and prolonged investigation had nothing to do with the fact that the body belonged to a policeman, or even to a policeman he had known. The corpse on the table was not to him a person called Steve Carella; it was instead a pathological puzzle.

He did not solve that puzzle until late Friday afternoon.

*

Bert Kling was alone in the squadroom when the telephone rang. He lifted the receiver.

"Detective Kling, 87th Squad," he said.

"Bert, this is Paul Blaney."

"Hello, Paul, how are you?"

"Fine, thanks. Who's handling the Carella case?"

"Meyer's in charge. Why?"

"Can I talk to him?"

"Not here right now."

"I think this is important," Blaney said. "Do you know where I can reach him?"

"I'm sorry, I don't know where he is."

"If I give it to you, will you make sure he gets it sometime tonight?"

"Sure," Kling said.

"I've been doing the autopsy," Blaney said. "I'm sorry I couldn't get back to you people sooner, but a lot of things were bothering me about this, and I wanted to be careful. I didn't want to make any statements that might put you on the wrong track, do you follow?"

"Yes, sure," Kling said.

"Well, if you're ready, I'd like to trace this for you step by step. And I'd like to say at the onset that I'm absolutely convinced of what I'm about to say. I mean, I know how important this is, and I wouldn't dare commit myself on guesswork alone—not in a case of this nature."

"I've got a pencil," Kling said. "Go ahead."

"To begin with, the comparative conditions of vehicle and cadaver indicated to me that the body had been incinerated elsewhere for a prolonged period of time, and only later removed to the automobile where it was found. I now have further evidence from the lab to support this theory. I sent them some recovered fragments of foreign materials that were embedded in the burned flesh. The fragments proved to be tiny pieces of wood charcoal. It seems certain now that the body was consumed in a *wood* fire, and not a gasoline fire such as would have occurred in the automobile. It's my opinion that the victim was thrust headfirst into a fireplace."

"What makes you think so?"

"The upper half of the body was severely burned, whereas most of the pelvic region and all of the lower extremities are virtually untouched. I think the upper half of the body was pushed into the fireplace and kept there for many hours, possibly throughout the night. Moreover, I think the man was murdered *before* he was thrown into the fire."

"Before?"

"Yes, I examined the air passages for possible inhaled soot, and the blood for carboxyhemoglobin. The presence of either would have indicated that the victim was alive during the fire. I found neither."

"Then how *was* he killed?" Kling asked.

"That would involve guesswork," Blaney said. "There's evidence of extradural hemorrhage, and there are also several fractures of the skull vault. But these may only be postmortem fractures resulting from charring, and I wouldn't feel safe in saying the victim was murdered by a blow to the head. Let's simply say he was dead before he was incinerated, and leave it at that."

"Then why was he thrown into the fire?" Kling asked.

"To obliterate the body beyond recognition."

"Go on."

"The teeth, as you know, were missing from the head, making dental identification impossible. At first I thought the fire had loosened them, but upon further examination, I found bone fragments in the upper gum. I now firmly believe that the teeth were knocked out of the mouth before the body was incinerated, and I believe this was done to further prevent identification."

"What are you saying, Blaney?"

"May I go on? I don't want any confusion about this later."

"Please," Kling said.

"There was no hair on the burned torso. Chest hair, underarm hair, and even the upper region of pubic hair had been singed away by the fire. Neither was there any hair on the scalp, which would have been both reasonable and obvious had the body been thrust into a fireplace head first, as I surmise it was. But upon examination, I was able to find surviving hair roots in the subcutaneous fat below the dermis on the torso and arms, even though the shaft and epithelial sheath had been destroyed. In other words, though the fire had consumed whatever hair had once existed on the torso and arms, there was nonetheless evidence that hair *had been growing* there. I could find no such evidence on the victim's scalp."

"What do you mean?"

"I mean that the man who was found in that automobile was bald to begin with."

"What?"

"Yes, nor was this particularly surprising. The atrophied internal viscera, the distended aorta of the heart, the abundant fatty marrow, large medullary cavities, and dense compact osseous tissue all indicated a person well on in years. Moreover, it was my initial belief that only one eye had survived the extreme heat—the right eye—and that it had been rendered opaque whereas the left eye had been entirely consumed by the flames. I have now carefully examined that left socket and it is my conclusion that there had not been an eye in it for many many years. The optic nerve and tract simply do not exist, and there is scar tissue present which indicates removal of the eye long before—"

"Cyclops!" Kling said. "Oh my God, it's Cyclops!"

"Whoever it is," Blaney said, "it is *not* Steve Carella."

He lay naked on the floor near the radiator.

He could hear rain lashing against the window panes, but the room was warm and he felt no discomfort. Yesterday, the girl had loosened the handcuff a bit, so that it no longer was clamped so tightly on his wrist. His nose was still swollen, but the throbbing pain was gone now, and the girl had washed his cuts and promised to shave him as soon as they were healed.

He was hungry.

He knew that the girl would come with food the moment it grew dark; she always did. There was one meal a day, always at dusk, and the girl brought it to him on a tray and then watched him while he ate, talking to him. Two days ago, she had showed him the newspapers, and he had read them with a peculiar feeling of unreality. The picture in the newspapers had been taken when he was still a patrolman. He looked very young and very innocent. The headline said he was dead.

He listened for the sound of her heels now. He could hear nothing in the other room; the apartment was silent. He wondered if she had gone, and felt a momentary pang. He glanced again at the waning light around the edges of the window shades. The rain drummed steadily against the glass. There was the sound of traffic below, tires hushed on rainswept streets. In the room, the gloom of dusk spread into the corners. Neon suddenly blinked against the drawn shades. He waited, listening, but there was no sound.

He must have dozed again. He was awakened by the sound of the key being inserted in the door lock. He sat upright, his left hand extended behind him and manacled to the radiator, and watched as the girl came into the room. She was wearing a short silk dressing gown belted tightly at the waist. The gown was a bright red, and she wore black high-heeled pumps that added several inches to her height. She closed the door behind her, and put the tray down just inside the door.

"Hello, doll," she whispered.

She did not turn on the overhead light. She went to one of the windows instead and raised the shade. Green neon rainsnakes slithered along the glass pane. The floor was washed with melting green, and then the neon blinked out and the room was dark again. He could hear the girl's breathing. The sign outside flashed again. The girl stood near the window in the red gown, the green neon behind her limning her long legs. The sign went out.

"Are you hungry, doll?" she whispered, and walked to him swiftly and kissed him on the cheek. She laughed deep in her throat, then moved away from him and went to the door. The Llama rested on the tray alongside the coffeepot. A sandwich was on a paper plate to the right of the gun.

"Do I still need this?" she asked, hefting the gun and pointing it at him.

Carella did not answer.

"I guess not," the girl said, and laughed again, that same low throaty laugh that was somehow not at all mirthful.

"Why am I alive?" he said. He was very hungry, and he could smell the coffee deep and strong in his nostrils, but he had learned not to ask for his food. He had asked for it last night, and the girl had deliberately postponed feeding him, talking to him for more than an hour before she reluctantly brought the tray to him.

"You're not alive," the girl said. "You're dead. I showed you the papers, didn't I? You're dead."

"Why didn't you really kill me?"

"You're too valuable."

"How do you figure that?"

"You know who killed Tinka."

"Then you're better off with me dead."

"No." The girl shook her head. "No, doll. We want to know how you found out."

"What difference does it make?"

"Oh, a lot of difference," the girl said. "He's very concerned about it, really he is. He's getting very impatient. He figures he made a mistake someplace, you see, and he wants to know what it was. Because if *you* found out, chances are somebody else will sooner or later. Unless you tell us what it was, you see. Then we can make sure nobody else finds out. Ever."

"There's nothing to tell you."

"There's plenty to tell," the girl said. She smiled. "You'll tell us. Are you hungry?"

"Yes."

"Tch," the girl said.

"Who was that in the burned car?"

"The elevator operator. Messner." The girl smiled again. "It was my idea. Two birds with one stone."

"What do you mean?"

"Well, I thought it would be a good idea to get rid of Messner just in case he was the one who led you to us. Insurance. And I also figured that if everybody thought you were dead, that'd give us more time to work on you."

"If Messner was my source, why do you have to work on me?"

"Well, there are a lot of unanswered questions," the girl said. "Gee, that coffee smells good, doesn't it?"

"Yes," Carella said.

"Are you cold?"

"No."

"I can get you a blanket if you're cold."

"I'm fine, thanks."

"I thought, with the rain, you might be a little chilly."

"No."

"You look good naked," the girl said.

"Thank you."

"I'll feed you, don't worry," she said.

"I know you will."

"But about those questions, they're really bothering him, you know. He's liable to get bugged completely and just decide the hell with the whole thing. I mean, I like having you and all, but I don't know if I'll be able to control him much longer. If you don't cooperate, I mean."

"Messner was my source," Carella said. "He gave me the description."

"Then it's a good thing we killed him, isn't it?"

"I suppose so."

"Of course, that still doesn't answer those questions I was talking about."

"What questions?"

"For example, how did you get the name? Messner may have given you a description, but where did you get the name? Or the address, for that matter?"

"They were in Tinka's address book. Both the name *and* the address."

"Was the description there, too?"

"I don't know what you mean."

"You know what I mean, doll. Unless Tinka had a *description* in that book of hers, how could you match a name to what Messner had told you?" Carella was silent. The girl smiled again. "I'm *sure* she didn't have descriptions of people in her address book, did she?"

"No."

"Good, I'm glad you're telling the truth. Because we found the address book in your pocket the night you came busting in here, and we know damn well there're no descriptions of people in it. You hungry?"

"Yes, I'm very hungry," Carella said.

"I'll feed you, don't worry," she said again. She paused. "How'd you know the name and address?"

"Just luck. I was checking each and every name in the book. A process of elimination, that's all."

"That's another lie," the girl said. "I wish you wouldn't lie to me." She lifted the gun from the tray. She held the gun loosely in one hand, picked up the tray with the other, and then said, "Back off."

Carella moved as far back as the handcuff would allow. The girl walked to him, crouched, and put the tray on the floor.

"I'm not wearing anything under this robe," she said.

"I can see that."

"I thought you could," the girl said, grinning, and then rose swiftly and backed toward the door. She sat in the chair and crossed her legs, the short robe riding up on her thighs. "Go ahead," she said, and indicated the tray with a wave of the gun.

Carella poured himself a cup of coffee. He took a quick swallow, and then picked up the sandwich and bit into it.

"Good?" the girl asked, watching.

"Yes."

"I made it myself. You have to admit I take good care of you."

"Sure," Carella said.

"I'm going to take even better care of you," she said. "Why'd you lie to me? Do you think it's nice to lie to me?"

"I didn't lie."

"You said you reached us by luck, a process of elimination. That means you didn't know who or what to expect when you got here, right? You were just looking for someone in Tinka's book who would fit Messner's description."

"That's right."

"Then why'd you kick the door in? Why'd you have a gun in your hand? See what I mean? You knew who he was *before* you got here. You knew he was the one. How?"

"I told you. It was just luck."

"Ahh, gee, I wish you wouldn't lie. Are you finished there?"

"Not yet."

"Let me know when."

"All right."

"I have things to do."

"All right."

"To *you*," the girl said.

Carella chewed on the sandwich. He washed it down with a gulp of coffee. He did not look at the girl. She was jiggling her foot now, the gun hand resting in her lap.

"Are you afraid?" she asked.

"Of what?"

"Of what I might do to you."

"No. Should I be?"

"I might break your nose all over again, who knows?"

"That's true, you might."

"Or I might even keep my promise to knock out all your teeth." The girl smiled. "*That* was my idea, too, you know, knocking out Messner's teeth. You people can make identifications from dental charts, can't you?"

"Yes."

"That's what I thought. That's what I told him. *He* thought it was a good idea, too."

"You're just *full* of good ideas."

"Yeah, I have a lot of good ideas," the girl said. "You're not scared, huh?"

"No."

"I would be, if I were you. Really, I would be."

"The worst you can do is kill me," Carella said. "And since I'm already dead, what difference will it make?"

"I like a man with a sense of humor," the girl said, but she did not smile. "I can do worse than kill you."

"What can you do?"

"I can corrupt you."

"I'm incorruptible," Carella said, and smiled.

"Nobody's incorruptible," she said. "I'm going to make you *beg* to tell us what you know. Really. I'm warning you."

"I've told you everything I know."

"Uh-uh," the girl said, shaking her head. "Are you finished there?"

"Yes."

"Shove the tray away from you."

Carella slid the tray across the floor. The girl went to it, stooped again, and picked it up. She walked back to the chair and sat. She crossed her legs. She began jiggling her foot.

"What's your wife's name?" she asked.

"Teddy."

"That's a nice name. But you'll forget it soon enough."

"I don't think so," Carella said evenly.

"You'll forget her name, and you'll forget her, too."

He shook his head.

"I promise," the girl said. "In a week's time, you won't even remember your *own* name."

The room was silent. The girl sat quite still except for the jiggling of her foot. The green neon splashed the floor, and then blinked out. There were seconds of darkness, and then the light came on again. She was standing now. She had left the gun on the seat of the chair and moved to the center of the room. The neon went out. When it flashed on again, she had moved closer to where he was manacled to the radiator.

"What would you like me to do to you?" she asked.

"Nothing."

"What would you like to do to me?"

"Nothing," he said.

"No?" she smiled. "Look, doll."

She loosened the sash at her waist. The robe parted over her breasts and naked belly. Neon washed the length of her body with green, and then blinked off. In the intermittent flashes, he saw the girl moving—as though in a silent movie—toward the light switch near the door, the open robe flapping loose around her. She snapped on the overhead light, and then walked slowly back to the center of the room and stood under the bulb. She held the front of the robe open, the long pale white sheath of her body exposed, the red silk covering her back and her arms, her fingernails tipped with red as glowing as the silk.

"What do you think?" she asked. Carella did not answer. "You want some of it?"

"No," he said.

"You're lying."

"I'm telling you the absolute truth," he said.

"I could make you forget her in a minute," the girl said. "I know things you never dreamed of. You want it?"

"No."

"Just try and get it," she said, and closed the robe and tightened the sash around her waist. "I don't like it when you lie to me."

"I'm not lying."

"You're naked, mister, don't tell *me* you're not lying." She burst out laughing and walked to the door, opening it, and then turned to face him again. Her voice was very low, her face serious. "Listen to me, doll," she said. "You are *mine*, do you understand that? I can do whatever I want with you, don't you forget it. I'm promising you right here and now that in a week's time you'll be crawling on your hands and knees to me, you'll be licking my feet, you'll be *begging* for the opportunity to tell me what you know. And once you tell me, I'm going to throw you away, doll, I'm going to throw you broken and cracked in the gutter, doll, and you're going to wish, believe me, you are just going to *wish* it was you they found dead in that car, believe me." She paused. "Think about it," she said, and turned out the light and went out of the room.

He heard the key turning in the lock.

He was suddenly very frightened.

"Is it fogging?" Willis said.

"No, it's okay."

Brown closed the outlet valve with two fingers and exhaled, clearing the mask. "Okay," he said, and began walking toward the house. He was a huge man, six feet four inches tall and weighing two hundred and twenty pounds, with enormous shoulders and chest, long arms, big hands. His skin was very dark, almost black, his hair was kinky and cut close to his scalp, his nostrils were large, his lips were thick. He looked like a Negro, which is what he was, take him or leave him. He did not at all resemble the white man's pretty concept of what a Negro *should* look like, the image touted in a new wave of magazine and television ads. He looked like himself. His wife Caroline liked the way he looked, and his daughter Connie liked the way he looked, and—more important—*he* liked the way he looked, although he didn't look so great at the moment with a mask covering his face and hoses running to the canister resting at the back of his neck. He walked into the house and paused just inside the door. There were parallel marks on the floor, beginning at the jamb and running vertically across the room. He stooped to look at the marks more closely. They were black and evenly spaced, and he recognized them immediately as scuff marks. He rose and followed the marks to the fireplace, where they ended. He did not touch anything in or near the open mouth of the hearth; he would leave that for the lab boys. But he was convinced now that a man wearing shoes, if nothing else, had been dragged across the room from the door to the fireplace. According to what they'd learned yesterday, Ernest Messner had been incinerated in a wood-burning fire. Well, there had certainly been a wood-burning fire in this room, and the stink he and Willis had encountered when entering was sure as hell the stink of burned human flesh. And now there were heel marks leading from the door to the fireplace. Circumstantially, Brown needed nothing more.

The only question was whether the person cooked in this particular fireplace was Ernest Messner or somebody else.

He couldn't answer that one, and anyway his eyepieces were beginning to fog. He went outside, took off the mask, and suggested to Willis that they drive into either Middlebarth or York to talk to some real estate agents about who owned the house with the smelly fireplace.

*

Elaine Hinds was a small, compact redhead with blue eyes and long fingernails. Her preference ran to small men, and she was charmed to distraction by Hal Willis, who was the shortest detective on the squad. She sat in a swivel chair behind her desk in the office of Hinds Real Estate in Middlebarth, and crossed her legs, and smiled, and accepted Willis's match to her cigarette, and graciously murmured, "Thank you," and then tried to remember what question he had just asked her. She uncrossed her legs, crossed them again, and then said, "Yes, the house on 407."

"Yes, do you know who owns it?" Willis asked. He was not unaware of the effect he seemed to be having on Miss Elaine Hinds, and he suspected he would never hear the end of it from Brown. But he was also a little puzzled. He had for many years been the victim of what he called the Mutt and Jeff phenomenon, a curious psychological and physiological reversal that made him irresistibly attractive to very big girls. He had never dated a girl who was shorter than five-nine in heels. One of his girl friends was five-eleven in her stockinged feet, and she was hopelessly in love with him. So he could not now understand why tiny little Elaine Hinds seemed so interested in a man who was only five feet eight inches tall, with the slight build of a dancer and the hands of a Black Jack dealer. He had, of course, served with the Marines and was an expert at judo, but Miss Hinds had no way of knowing that he was a giant among men, capable of breaking a man's back by the mere flick of an eyeball—well, almost. What then had caused her immediate attraction? Being a conscientious cop, he sincerely hoped it would not impede the progress of the investigation. In the meantime, he couldn't help noticing that she had very good legs and that she kept crossing and uncrossing them like an undecided virgin.

"The people who own that house," she said, uncrossing her legs, "are Mr. and Mrs. Jerome Brandt, would you like some coffee or something? I have some going in the other room."

"No, thank you," Willis said. "How long have—"

"Mr. Brown?"

"No, thank you."

"How long have the Brandts been living there?"

"Well, they haven't. Not really."

"I don't think I understand," Willis said.

Elaine Hinds crossed her legs, and leaned close to Willis, as though about to reveal something terribly intimate. "They bought it to use as a summer place," she said. "Mavis County is a marvelous resort area, you know, with many many lakes and streams and with the ocean not too far from any point in the county. We're supposed to have less rainfall per annum than—"

"When did they buy it, Miss Hinds?"

"Last year. I expect they'll open the house after Memorial Day, but it's been closed all winter."

"Which explains the broken hasp on the front door," Brown said.

"Has it been broken?" Elaine said. "Oh, dear," and she uncrossed her legs.

"Miss Hinds, would you say that many people in the area knew the house was empty?"

"Yes, I'd say it was common knowledge, do you enjoy police work?"

"Yes, I do," Willis said.

"It must be terribly exciting."

"Sometimes the suspense is unbearable," Brown said.

"I'll just *bet* it is," Elaine said.

"It's my understanding," Willis said, glancing sharply at Brown, "that 407 is a pretty isolated road, and hardly ever used. Is that correct?"

"Oh, yes," Elaine said. "Route 126 is a much better connection between Middlebarth and York, and of course the new highway runs past both towns. As a matter of fact, most people in the area *avoid* 407. It's not a very good road, have you been on it?"

"Yes. Then, actually, anyone living around here would have known the house was empty, and would also have known the road going by it wasn't traveled too often. Would you say that?"

"Oh, yes, Mr. Willis, I definitely *would* say that," Elaine said.

Willis looked a little startled. He glanced at Brown, and then cleared his throat. "Miss Hinds, what sort of people are the Brandts? Do you know them?"

"Yes, I sold the house to them. Jerry's an executive at IBM."

"And his wife?"

"Maxine's a woman of about fifty, three or four years younger than Jerry. A lovely person."

"Respectable people, would you say?"

"Oh, yes, *entirely* respectable," Elaine said. "My goodness, of *course* they are."

"Would you know if either of them were up here Monday night?"

"I don't know. I imagine they would have called if they were coming. I keep the keys to the house here in the office, you see. I have to arrange for maintenance, and it's necessary—"

"But they didn't call to say they were coming up?"

"No, they didn't." Elaine paused. "Does this have anything to do with the auto wreck on 407?"

"Yes, Miss Hinds, it does."

"Well, how could Jerry or Maxine be even *remotely* connected with that?"

"You don't think they could?"

"Of course not. I haven't seen them for quite some time now, but we did work closely together when I was handling the deal for them last October. Believe me, you couldn't find a sweeter couple. That's unusual, especially with people who have their kind of money."

"Are they wealthy, would you say?"

"The house cost forty-two thousand five hundred dollars. They paid for it in cash."

"Who'd they buy it from?" Willis asked.

"Well, you probably wouldn't know her, but I'll bet your wife would."

"I'm not married," Willis said.

"Oh? *Aren't* you?"

"Who'd they buy it from?" Brown asked.

"A fashion model named Tinka Sachs. Do you know her?"

If they had lacked, before this, proof positive that the man in the wrecked automobile was really Ernest Messner, they now possessed the single piece of information that tied together the series of happenings and eliminated the possibility of reasonable chance or coincidence:

1) Tinka Sachs had been murdered in an apartment on Stafford Place on Friday, April ninth.

2) Ernest Messner was the elevator operator on duty there the night of her murder.
3) Ernest Messner had taken a man up to her apartment and had later given a good description of him.
4) Ernest Messner had vanished on Monday night, April twelfth.
5) An incinerated body was found the next day in a wrecked auto on Route 407, the connecting road between Middlebarth and York, in Mavis County.
6) The medical examiner had stated his belief that the body in the automobile had been incinerated in a wood fire elsewhere and only later placed in the automobile.
7) There was only one house on Route 407, five and a half miles from where the wrecked auto was found in the gravel pit.
8) There had been a recent wood fire in the fireplace of that house, and the premises smelled of burned flesh. There were also heel marks on the floor, indicating that someone had been dragged to the fireplace.
9) The house had once been owned by Tinka Sachs, and was sold only last October to its new owners.

It was now reasonable to assume that Tinka's murderer knew he had been identified, and had moved with frightening dispatch to remove the man who'd seen him. It was also reasonable to assume that Tinka's murderer knew of the empty house in Mavis County and had transported Messner's body there for the sole purpose of incinerating it beyond recognition, the further implication being that the murderer had known Tinka at least as far back as last October when she'd still owned the house. There were still a few unanswered questions, of course, but they were small things and nothing that would trouble any hard-working police force anywhere. The cops of the 87th wondered, for example, who had killed Tinka Sachs, and who had killed Ernest Messner, and who had taken Carella's shield and gun from him and wrecked his auto, and whether Carella was still alive, and where?

It's the small things in life that can get you down.

Those airline schedules kept bothering Kling.

He knew he had been taken off the case, but he could not stop thinking about those airline schedules, or the possibility that Dennis Sachs had flown from Phoenix and back sometime between Thursday night and Monday morning. From his apartment that night, he called Information and asked for the name and number of the hotel in Rainfield, Arizona. The local operator connected him with Phoenix Information, who said the only hotel listing they had in Rainfield was for the Major Powell on Main Street, was this the hotel Kling wanted? Kling said it was, and they asked if they should place the call. He knew that if he was eventually suspended, he would lose his gun, his shield and his salary until the case was decided, so he asked the operator how much the call would cost, and she said it would cost two dollars and ten cents for the first three minutes, and sixty-five cents for each additional minute. Kling told her to go ahead and place the call, station to station.

The man who answered the phone identified himself as Walter Blount, manager of the hotel.

"This is Detective Bert Kling," Kling said. "We've had a murder here, and I'd like to ask you some questions, if I may. I'm calling long distance."

"Go right ahead, Mr. Kling," Blount said.

"To begin with, do you know Dennis Sachs?"

"Yes, I do. He's a guest here, part of Dr. Tarsmith's expedition."

"Were you on duty a week ago last Thursday night, April eighth?"

"I'm on duty *all* the time," Blount said.

"Do you know what time Mr. Sachs came in from the desert?"

"Well, I couldn't rightly say. They usually come in at about seven, eight o'clock, something like that."

"Would you say they came in at about that time on April eighth?"

"I would say so, yes."

"Did you see Mr. Sachs leaving the hotel at any time that night?"

"Yes, he left, oh, ten-thirty or so, walked over to the railroad station."

"Was he carrying a suitcase?"

"He was."

"Did he mention where he was going?"

"The Royal Sands in Phoenix, I'd reckon. He asked us to

make a reservation for him there, so I guess that's where he was going, don't you think?"

"Did you make the reservation for him personally, Mr. Blount?"

"Yes, sir, I did. Single with a bath, Thursday night to Sunday morning. The rates—"

"What time did Mr. Sachs return on Monday morning?"

"About six A.M. Had a telegram waiting for him here, his wife got killed. Well, I guess you know that, I guess that's what this is all about. He called the airport right away, and then got back on the train for Phoenix, hardly unpacked at all."

"Mr. Blount, Dennis Sachs told me that he spoke to his ex-wife on the telephone at least once a week. Would you know if that was true?"

"Oh, sure, he was always calling back east."

"How often, would you say?"

"At least once a week, that's right. Even more than that, I'd say."

"How much more?"

"Well . . . in the past two months or so, he'd call her three, maybe four times a week, something like that. He spent a hell of a lot of time making calls back east, ran up a pretty big phone bill here."

"Calling his wife, you mean."

"Well, not only her."

"Who else?"

"I don't know who the other party was."

"But he *did* make calls to other numbers here in the city?"

"Well, *one* other number."

"Would you happen to know that number offhand, Mr. Blount?"

"No, but I've got a record of it on our bills. It's not his wife's number because I've got that one memorized by heart, he's called it regular ever since he first came here a year ago. This other one is new to me."

"When did he start calling it?"

"Back in February, I reckon."

"How often?"

"Once a week, usually."

"May I have the number, please?"

"Sure, just let me look it up for you."

Kling waited. The line crackled. His hand on the receiver was sweating.

"Hello?" Blount said.

"Hello?"

"The number is SE—I think that stands for Sequoia—SE 3-1402."

"Thank you," Kling said.

"Not at all," Blount answered.

Kling hung up, waited patiently for a moment with his hand on the receiver, lifted it again, heard the dial tone, and instantly dialed SE 3-1402. The phone rang insistently. He counted each separate ring, four, five, six, and suddenly there was an answering voice.

"Dr. Levi's wire," the woman said.

"This is Detective Kling of the 87th Squad here in the city," Kling said. "Is this an answering service?"

"Yes, sir, it is."

"Whose phone did you say this was?"

"Dr. Levi's."

"And the first name?"

"Jason."

"Do you know where I can reach him?"

"I'm sorry, sir, he's away for the weekend. He won't be back until Monday morning." The woman paused. "Is this in respect to a police matter, or are you calling for a medical appointment?"

"A police matter," Kling said.

"Well, the doctor's office hours begin at ten Monday morning. If you'd care to call him then, I'm sure—"

"What's his home number?" Kling asked.

"Calling him there won't help you. He really is away for the weekend."

"Do you know where?"

"No, I'm sorry."

"Well, let me have his number, anyway," Kling said.

"I'm not supposed to give out the doctor's home number. I'll try it for you, if you like. If the doctor's there—which I know he isn't—I'll ask him to call you back. May I have your number, please?"

"Yes, it's Roxbury 2, that's RO 2, 7641."

"Thank you."

"Will you please call me in any event, to let me know if you reached him or not?"

"Yes, sir, I will."

"Thank you."

"What did you say your name was?"

"Kling, Detective Bert Kling."

"Yes, sir, thank you," she said, and hung up.

Kling waited by the phone.

In five minutes' time, the woman called back. She said she had tried the doctor's home number and—as she'd known would be the case all along—there was no answer. She gave him the doctor's office schedule and told him he could try again on Monday, and then she hung up.

It was going to be a long weekend.

Teddy Carella sat in the living room alone for a long while after Lieutenant Byrnes left, her hands folded in her lap, staring into the shadows of the room and hearing nothing but the murmur of her own thoughts.

We now know, the lieutenant had said, that the man we found in the automobile definitely wasn't Steve. He's a man named Ernest Messner, and there is no question about it, Teddy, so I want you to know that. But I also want you to know this doesn't mean Steve is still alive. We just don't know anything about that yet, although we're working on it. The only thing it *does* indicate is that at least he's not for certain dead.

The lieutenant paused. She watched his face. He looked back at her curiously, wanting to be sure she understood everything he had told her. She nodded.

I knew this yesterday, the lieutenant said, but I wasn't sure, and I didn't want to raise your hopes until I had checked it out thoroughly. The medical examiner's office gave this top priority, Teddy. They still haven't finished the autopsy on the Sachs case because, well, you know, when we thought this was Steve, well, we put a lot of pressure on them. Anyway, it isn't. It isn't Steve, I mean. We've got Paul Blaney's word for that, and he's an excellent man, and we've also got the corroboration—what? Corroboration, did you get it? the corroboration of the chief medical examiner as well. So now I'm sure, so I'm telling you. And about the other, we're working on it, as you know, and as soon as we've got anything, I'll tell you that, too. So that's about all, Teddy. We're doing our best.

She had thanked him and offered him coffee, which he refused politely, he was expected home, he had to run, he hoped she would forgive him. She had shown him to the door, and then walked past the playroom, where Fanny was watching television, and then past the room where the twins were sound asleep and then into the living room. She turned out the lights and went to sit near the old piano Carella had bought in a secondhand store downtown, paying sixteen dollars for it and arranging to have it delivered by a furniture man in the precinct. He had always wanted to play the piano, he told her, and was going to start lessons—you're never too old to learn, right, sweetheart?

The lieutenant's news soared within her, but she was fearful of it, suspicious: Was it only a temporary gift that would be taken back? Should she tell the children, and then risk another reversal and a second revelation that their father was dead? "What does that mean?" April had asked. "Does dead mean he's never coming back?" And Mark had turned to his sister and angrily shouted, "Shut up, you stupid dope!" and had run to his room where his mother could not see his tears.

They deserved hope.

They had the right to know there was hope.

She rose and went into the kitchen and scribbled a note on the telephone pad, and then tore off the sheet of paper and carried it out to Fanny. Fanny looked up when she approached, expecting more bad news, the lieutenant brought nothing but bad news nowadays. Teddy handed her the sheet of paper, and Fanny looked at it:

Wake the children.
Tell them their father
may still be alive.

Fanny looked up quickly.

"Thank God," she whispered, and rushed out of the room.

II

THE PATROLMAN came up to the squadroom on Monday morning, and waited outside the slatted rail divider until Meyer signaled him in. Then he opened the gate and walked over to Meyer's desk.

"I don't think you know me," he said. "I'm Patrolman Angieri."

"I think I've seen you around," Meyer said.

"I feel funny bringing this up because maybe you already know it. My wife said I should tell you, anyway."

"What is it?"

"I only been here at this precinct for six months, this is my first precinct, I'm a new cop."

"Um-huh," Meyer said.

"If you already know this, just skip it, okay? My wife says maybe you don't know it, and maybe it's important."

"Well, what is it?" Meyer asked patiently.

"Carella."

"What about Carella?"

"Like I told you, I'm new in the precinct, and I don't know all the detectives by name, but I recognized him later from his picture in the paper, though it was a picture from when he was a patrolman. Anyway, it was him."

"What do you mean? I don't think I'm with you, Angieri."

"Carrying the doll," Angieri said.

"I still don't get you."

"I was on duty in the hall, you know? Outside the apartment. I'm talking about the Tinka Sachs murder."

Meyer leaned forward suddenly. "Yeah, go ahead," he said.

"Well, he come up there last Monday night, it must've been five-thirty, six o'clock, and he flashed the tin, and went inside the apartment. When he come out, he was in a hell of a hurry, and he was carrying a doll."

"Are you telling me Carella was at the Sachs apartment last Monday night?"

"That's right."

"Are you sure?"

"Positive." Angieri paused. "You *didn't* know this, huh? My wife was right." He paused again. "She's *always* right."

"What did you say about a doll?"

"A doll, you know? Like kids play with? Girls? A big doll. With blond hair, you know? A *doll*."

"Carella came out of the apartment carrying a child's doll?"

"That's right."

"Last Monday night?"

"That's right."

"Did he say anything to you?"

"Nothing."

"A doll," Meyer said, puzzled.

It was nine A.M. when Meyer arrived at the Sachs apartment on Stafford Place. He spoke briefly to the superintendent of the building, a man named Manny Farber, and then took the elevator up to the fourth floor. There was no longer a patrolman on duty in the hallway. He went down the corridor and let himself into the apartment, using Tinka's own key, which had been lent to the investigating precinct by the Office of the Clerk.

The apartment was still.

He could tell at once that death had been here. There are different silences in an empty apartment, and if you are a working policeman, you do not scoff at poetic fallacy. An apartment vacated for the summer has a silence unlike one that is empty only for the day, with its occupants expected back that night. And an apartment that has known the touch of death possesses a silence unique and readily identifiable to anyone who has ever stared down at a corpse. Meyer knew the silence of death, and understood it, though he could not have told you what accounted for it. The disconnected humless electrical appliances; the unused, undripping water taps; the unringing telephone; the stopped unticking clocks; the sealed windows shutting out all street noises; these were all a part of it, but they only contributed to the whole and were not its sum and substance. The real silence was something only felt, and had nothing to do with the absence of sound. It touched something deep within him the moment he stepped through the door. It seemed to be carried on the air itself, a shuddering reminder that death had passed this way, and that some of its frightening grandeur was still locked inside these rooms. He paused with his hand on the doorknob, and then sighed and closed the door behind him and went into the apartment.

Sunlight glanced through closed windows, dust beams silently hovered on the unmoving air. He walked softly, as though reluctant to stir whatever ghostly remnants still were here. When he passed the child's room, he looked through the open door and saw the dolls lined up in the bookcase beneath the windows, row upon row of dolls, each dressed differently, each staring back at him with unblinking glass eyes, pink cheeks glowing, mute red mouths frozen on the edge of articulation, painted lips parted over even plastic teeth, nylon hair in black, and red, and blond, and the palest silver.

He was starting into the room when he heard a key turning in the front door.

The sound startled him. It cracked into the silent apartment like a crash of thunder. He heard the tumblers falling, the sudden click of the knob being turned. He moved into the child's room just as the front door opened. His eyes swept the room —bookcases, bed, closet, toy chest. He could hear heavy footsteps in the corridor, approaching the room. He threw open the closet door, drew his gun. The footsteps were closer. He eased the door toward him, leaving it open just a crack. Holding his breath, he waited in the darkness.

The man who came into the room was perhaps six feet two inches tall, with massive shoulders and a narrow waist. He paused just inside the doorway, as though sensing the presence of another person, seemed almost to be sniffing the air for a telltale scent. Then, visibly shrugging away his own correct intuition, he dismissed the idea and went quickly to the bookcases. He stopped in front of them and began lifting dolls from the shelves, seemingly at random, bundling them into his arms. He gathered up seven or eight of them, rose, turned toward the door, and was on his way out when Meyer kicked open the closet door.

The man turned, startled, his eyes opening wide. Foolishly, he clung to the dolls in his arms, first looking at Meyer's face, and then at the Colt .38 in Meyer's hand, and then up at Meyer's face again.

"Who are you?" he asked.

"Good question," Meyer said. "Put those dolls down, hurry up, on the bed there."

"What . . . ?"

"Do as I say, mister!"

The man walked to the bed. He wet his lips, looked at Meyer, frowned, and then dropped the dolls.

"Get over against the wall," Meyer said.

"Listen, what the hell . . . ?"

"Spread your legs, bend over, lean against the wall with your palms flat. Hurry up!"

"All right, take it easy." The man leaned against the wall. Meyer quickly and carefully frisked him—chest, pockets, waist, the insides of his legs. Then he backed away from the man and said, "Turn around, keep your hands up."

The man turned, his hands high. He wet his lips again, and again looked at the gun in Meyer's hand.

"What are you doing here?" Meyer asked.

"What are *you* doing here?"

"I'm a police officer. Answer my—"

"Oh. Oh, okay," the man said.

"What's okay about it?"

"I'm Dennis Sachs."

"Who?"

"Dennis—"

"Tinka's husband?"

"Well, her ex-husband."

"Where's your wallet?"

"Right here in my—"

"Don't reach for it! Bend over against that wall again, go ahead."

The man did as Meyer ordered. Meyer felt for the wallet and found it in his right hip pocket. He opened it to the driver's license. The name on the license was Dennis Robert Sachs. Meyer handed it back to him.

"All right, put your hands down. What are you doing here?"

"My daughter wanted some of her dolls," Sachs said. "I came back to get them."

"How'd you get in?"

"I have a key. I used to live here, you know."

"It was my understanding you and your wife were divorced."

"That's right."

"And you still have a key?"

"Yes."

"Did she know this?"

"Yes, of course."

"And that's all you wanted here, huh? Just the dolls."

"Yes."

"Any doll in particular?"

"No."

"Your daughter didn't specify any particular doll?"

"No, she simply said she'd like some of her dolls, and she asked if I'd come get them for her."

"How about *your* preference?"

"*My* preference?"

"Yes. Did *you* have any particular doll in mind?"

"Me?"

"That's right, Mr. Sachs. You."

"No. What do you mean? Are you talking about *dolls*?"

"That's right, that's what I'm talking about."

"Well, what would I want with any *specific* doll?"

"That's what *I'd* like to know."

"I don't think I understand you."

"Then forget it."

Sachs frowned and glanced at the dolls on the bed. He hesitated, then shrugged and said, "Well, is it all right to take them?"

"I'm afraid not."

"Why not? They belong to my daughter."

"We want to look them over, Mr. Sachs."

"For what?"

"I don't know for what. For *anything*."

Sachs looked at the dolls again, and then he turned to Meyer and stared at him silently. "I guess you know this has been a pretty bewildering conversation," he said at last.

"Yeah, well, that's the way mysteries are," Meyer answered. "I've got work to do, Mr. Sachs. If you have no further business here, I'd appreciate it if you left."

Sachs nodded and said nothing. He looked at the dolls once again, and then walked out of the room, and down the corridor, and out of the apartment. Meyer waited, listening. The moment he heard the door close behind Sachs, he sprinted down the corridor, stopped just inside the door, counted swiftly to ten, and then eased the door open no more than an inch. Peering out into the hallway, he could see Sachs waiting for the elevator. He looked angry as hell. When the elevator did not arrive, he pushed at the button repeatedly and then began pacing. He glanced once at Tinka's supposedly closed door, and then turned back to the elevator again. When it finally arrived, he said to the operator, "What took you so long?" and stepped into the car.

Meyer came out of the apartment immediately, closed the door behind him, and ran for the service steps. He took the steps down at a gallop, pausing only for an instant at the fire door leading to the lobby, and then opening the door a crack. He could see the elevator operator standing near the building's entrance, his arms folded across his chest. Meyer came out into the lobby quickly, glanced back once at the open elevator doors, and then ran past the elevator and into the street. He spotted Sachs turning the corner up the block, and broke into a run after him. He paused again before turning the corner. When he sidled around it, he saw Sachs getting into a taxi. There was no time for Meyer to go to his own parked car. He hailed another cab and said to the driver, just like a cop, "Follow that taxi," sourly reminding himself that he would have to turn in a chit for the fare, even though he knew Petty Cash would probably never reimburse him. The taxi driver turned for a quick look at Meyer, just to see who was pulling all this cloak and dagger nonsense, and then silently began following Sachs's cab.

"You a cop?" he asked at last.

"Yeah," Meyer said.

"Who's that up ahead?"

"The Boston Strangler," Meyer said.

"Yeah?"

"Would I kid you?"

"You going to pay for this ride, or is it like taking apples from a pushcart?"

"I'm going to pay for it," Meyer said. "Just don't lose him, okay?"

It was almost ten o'clock, and the streets were thronged with traffic. The lead taxi moved steadily uptown and then crosstown, with Meyer's driver skillfully following. The city was a bedlam of noise—honking horns, grinding gears, squealing tires, shouting drivers and pedestrians. Meyer leaned forward and kept his eye on the taxi ahead, oblivious to the sounds around him.

"He's pulling up, I think," the driver said.

"Good. Stop about six car lengths behind him." The taxi meter read eighty-five cents. Meyer took a dollar bill from his wallet, and handed it to the driver the moment he pulled over to the curb. Sachs had already gotten out of his cab and was walking into an apartment building in the middle of the block.

"Is this all the city tips?" the driver asked. "Fifteen cents on an eighty-five-cent ride?"

"The city, my ass," Meyer said, and leaped out of the cab. He ran up the street, and came into the building's entrance alcove just as the inner glass door closed behind Sachs. Meyer swung back his left arm and swiftly ran his hand over every bell in the row on the wall. Then, while waiting for an answering buzz, he put his face close to the glass door, shaded his eyes against the reflective glare, and peered inside. Sachs was nowhere in sight; the elevators were apparently around a corner of the lobby. A half-dozen answering buzzes sounded at once, releasing the lock mechanism on the door. Meyer pushed it open, and ran into the lobby. The floor indicator over the single elevator was moving, three, four, five—and stopped. Meyer nodded and walked out to the entrance alcove again, bending to look at the bells there. There were six apartments on the fifth floor. He was studying the names under the bells when a voice behind him said, "I think you're looking for Dr. Jason Levi."

Meyer looked up, startled.

The man standing behind him was Bert Kling.

Dr. Jason Levi's private office was painted an antiseptic white, and the only decoration on its walls was a large, easily readable calendar. His desk was functional and unadorned, made of grey steel, its top cluttered with medical journals and books, X-ray photographs, pharmaceutical samples, tongue depressors, prescription pads. There was a no-nonsense look about the doctor as well, the plain face topped with leonine white hair, the thick-lensed spectacles, the large cleaving nose, the thin-lipped mouth. He sat behind his desk and looked first at the detectives and then at Dennis Sachs, and waited for someone to speak.

"We want to know what you're doing here, Mr. Sachs," Meyer said.

"I'm a patient," Sachs said.

"Is that true, Dr. Levi?"

Levi hesitated. Then he shook his massive head. "No," he said. "That is not true."

"Shall we start again?" Meyer asked.

"I have nothing to say," Sachs answered.

"Why'd you find it necessary to call Dr. Levi from Arizona once a week?" Kling asked.

"Who said I did?"

"Mr. Walter Blount, manager of the Major Powell Hotel in Rainfield."

"He was lying."

"Why would he lie?"

"I don't *know* why," Sachs said. "Go ask *him*."

"No, we'll do it the easy way," Kling said. "Dr. Levi, *did* Mr. Sachs call you from Arizona once a week?"

"Yes," Levi said.

"We seem to have a slight difference of opinion here," Meyer said.

"Why'd he call you?" Kling asked.

"Don't answer that, Doctor!"

"Dennis, what are we trying to hide? She's dead."

"You're a doctor, you don't have to tell them anything. You're like a priest. They can't force you to—"

"Dennis, she is dead."

"Did your calls have something to do with your wife?" Kling asked.

"No," Sachs said.

"Yes," Levi said.

"Was *Tinka* your patient, Doctor, is that it?"

"Yes."

"Dr. Levi, I *forbid* you to tell these men anything more about—"

"She was my patient," Levi said. "I began treating her at the beginning of the year."

"In January?"

"Yes. January fifth. More than three months ago."

"Doctor, I swear on my dead wife that if you go ahead with this, I'm going to ask the A.M.A. to—"

"Nonsense!" Levi said fiercely. "Your wife is dead! If we can help them find her killer—"

"You're not helping them with anything! All you're doing is dragging her memory through the muck of a criminal investigation."

"Mr. Sachs," Meyer said, "whether you know it or not, her memory is already in the muck of a criminal investigation."

"Why did she come to you, Doctor?" Kling asked. "What was wrong with her?"

"She said she had made a New Year's resolution, said she had decided once and for all to seek medical assistance. It was quite pathetic, really. She was so helpless, and so beautiful, and so alone."

"I *couldn't* stay with her any longer!" Sachs said. "I'm not made of iron! I couldn't handle it. That's why we got the divorce. It wasn't my fault, what happened to her."

"No one is blaming you for anything," Levi said. "Her illness went back a long time, long before she met you."

"What was this illness, Doctor?" Meyer asked.

"Don't tell them!"

"Dennis, I *have* to—"

"You *don't* have to! Leave it the way it is. Let her live in everyone's memory as a beautiful exciting woman instead of—"

Dennis cut himself off.

"Instead of what?" Meyer asked.

The room went silent.

"Instead of what?" he said again.

Levi sighed and shook his head.

"Instead of a drug addict."

12

IN THE silence of the squadroom later that day, they read Dr. Jason Levi's casebook:

January 5

The patient's name is Tina Karin Sachs. She is divorced, has a daughter aged five. She lives in the city and leads an active professional life, which is one of the reasons she was reluctant to seek assistance before now. She stated, however, that she had made a New Year's resolution, and that she is determined to break the habit. She has been a narcotics user since the time she was seventeen, and is now addicted to heroin.

I explained to her that the methods of withdrawal which I had thus far found most satisfactory were those employing either morphine or methadone, both of which had proved to be adequate substitutes for whatever drugs or combinations of drugs my patients had previously been using. I told her, too, that I personally preferred the morphine method.

She asked if there would be much pain involved. Apparently she had once tried cold-turkey withdrawal and had found the attempt too painful to bear. I told her that she would experience withdrawal symptoms—nausea, vomiting, diarrhea, lacrimation, dilation of pupils, rhinorrhea, yawning, gooseflesh, sneezing, sweating—with either method. With morphine, the withdrawal would be more severe, but she could expect relative comfort after a week or so. With methadone, the withdrawal would be easier, but she might still feel somewhat tremulous for as long as a month afterward.

She said she wanted to think it over, and would call me when she had decided.

January 12

I had not expected to see or hear from Tinka Sachs again, but she arrived here today and asked my receptionist if I could spare ten minutes. I said I could, and she was shown into my private office, where we talked for more than forty-five minutes.

She said she had not yet decided what she should do, and wanted to discuss it further with me. She is, as she had previously explained, a fashion model. She receives top fees for her modeling and was now afraid that treatment might entail either pain or sickness which would cause her to lose employment, thereby endangering her career. I told her that her addiction to heroin had made her virtually careerless anyway, since she was spending much of her income on the purchase of drugs. She did not particularly enjoy this observation, and quickly rejoindered that she thoroughly relished all the fringe benefits of modeling—the fame, the recognition, and so on. I asked her if she really enjoyed anything but heroin, or really thought of anything but heroin, and she became greatly agitated and seemed about to leave the office.

Instead, she told me that I didn't know what it was like, and she hoped I understood she had been using narcotics since she was seventeen, when she'd first tried marijuana at a beach party in Malibu. She had continued smoking marijuana for almost a year, never tempted to try any of "the real shit" until a photographer offered her a sniff of heroin shortly after she'd begun modeling. He also tried to rape her afterwards, a side effect that nearly caused her to abandon her beginning career as a model. Her near-rape, however, did not dissuade her from using marijuana or from sniffing heroin every now and then, until someone warned her that inhaling the drug could damage her nose. Since her nose was part of her face, and her face was part of what she hoped would become her fortune, she promptly stopped the sniffing process.

The first time she tried injecting the drug was with a confirmed addict, male, in a North Hollywood apartment. Unfortunately, the police broke in on them, and they were both arrested. She was nineteen years old at the time, and was luckily released with a suspended sentence. She came to this city the following month, determined never to fool with drugs again, hoping to put three thousand miles between herself and her former acquaintances. But she discovered, almost immediately upon arrival, that the drug was as readily obtainable here as it was in Los Angeles. Moreover, she began her association with the Cutler Agency several weeks after she got here, and found herself in possession of more money than she would ever need to support both herself *and* a narcotics habit. She began injecting the drug under her skin, into the soft tissue of her body. Shortly afterwards, she abandoned the subcutaneous route and began shooting heroin directly into her veins. She has been using it intravenously ever since, has for all intents and purposes been hopelessly hooked since she first began skin-popping. How, then, could I expect to cure her? How could she wake up each morning without knowing that a supply of narcotics was available, in fact accessible? I explained that hers was the common fear of all addicts about to undergo treatment, a reassurance she accepted without noticeable enthusiasm.

I'll think about it, she said again, and again left. I frankly do not believe she will ever return again.

January 20

Tinka Sachs began treatment today.

She has chosen the morphine method (even though she understands the symptoms will be more severe) because she does not want to endanger her career by a prolonged withdrawal, a curious concern for someone who has been endangering her career ever since it started. I had previously explained that I wanted to hospitalize her for several months, but she flatly refused hospitalization of any kind, and stated that the deal was off if that was part of the treatment. I told her that I could not guarantee lasting results unless she allowed me to hospitalize her, but she said we would have to hope for the best because she wasn't going to admit herself to any damn hospital. I finally extracted from her an agreement to stay at home under a nurse's care at least during the first several days of withdrawal, when the symptoms would be most severe. I warned her against making any illegal purchases and against associating with any known addicts or pushers. Our schedule is a rigid one. To start, she will receive ¼ grain of morphine four times daily—twenty minutes before each meal. The doses will be administered hypodermically, and the morphine will be dissolved in thiamine hydrochloride.

It is my hope that withdrawal will be complete within two weeks.

January 21

I have prescribed Thorazine for Tinka's nausea, and belladonna and pectin for her diarrhea. The symptoms are severe. She could not sleep at all last night. I have instructed the nurse staying at her apartment to administer three grains of Nembutal tonight before Tinka retires, with further instructions to repeat 1½ grains if she does not sleep through the night.

Tinka has taken excellent care of her body, a factor on our side. She is quite beautiful and I have no doubt she is a superior model, though I am at a loss to explain how photographers can have missed her obvious addiction. How did she keep from "nodding" before the cameras? She has scrupulously avoided marking either her lower legs or her arms, but the insides of her thighs (she told me she does not model either lingerie or bathing suits) are covered with hit marks.

Morphine continues at ¼ grain four times daily.

January 22

I have reduced the morphine injections to ¼ grain twice daily, alternating with ⅛ grain twice daily. Symptoms are still severe. She has canceled all of her sittings, telling the agency she is menstruating and suffering cramps, a complaint they have apparently heard from their models before. She shows no desire to eat. I have begun prescribing vitamins.

January 23

The symptoms are abating. We are now administering ⅛ grain four times daily.

January 24

Treatment continuing with ⅛ grain four times daily. The nurse will be discharged tomorrow, and Tinka will begin coming to my office for her injections, a procedure I am heartily against. But it is either that or losing her entirely, and I must go along.

January 25

Started one grain codeine twice daily, alternating with ⅛ grain morphine twice daily. Tinka came to my office at eight-thirty, before breakfast, for her first injection. She came again at twelve-thirty, and at six-thirty. I administered the last injection at her home at eleven-thirty. She seems exceptionally restless, and I have prescribed ½ grain of phenobarbital daily to combat this.

January 26

Tinka Sachs did not come to the office today. I called her apartment several times, but no one answered the telephone. I did not dare call the modeling agency lest they suspect she is undergoing treatment. At three o'clock, I spoke to her daughter's governess. She had just picked the child up at the play-school she attends. She said she did not know where Mrs. Sachs was, and suggested that I try the agency. I called again at midnight. Tinka was still not home. The governess said I had awakened her. Apparently, she saw nothing unusual about her employer's absence. The working arrangement calls for her to meet the child after school and to spend as much time with her as is necessary. She said that Mrs. Sachs is often gone the entire night, in which case she is supposed to take the child to school in the morning, and then call for her again at two-thirty. Mrs. Sachs was once gone for three days, she said.

I am worried.

February 4

Tinka returned to the office again today, apologizing profusely, and explaining that she had been called out of town on an assignment; they were shooting some new tweed fashions and wanted a woodland background. I accused her of lying, and she finally admitted that she had not been out of town at all, but had instead spent the past week in the apartment of a friend from California. After further questioning, she conceded that her California friend is a drug addict, is in fact the man with whom she was arrested when she was nineteen years old. He arrived in the city last September, with very little money, and no place to live. She staked him for a while, and allowed him to live in her Mavis County house until she sold it in October. She then helped him to find an apartment on South Fourth, and she still sees him occasionally.

It was obvious that she had begun taking heroin again.

She expressed remorse, and said that she is more than ever determined to break the habit. When I asked if her friend expects to remain in the city, she said that he does, but that he has a companion with him, and no longer needs any old acquaintance to help him pursue his course of addiction.

I extracted a promise from Tinka that she would never see this man again, nor try to contact him.

We begin treatment again tomorrow morning. This time I insisted that a nurse remain with her for at least two weeks.

We will be starting from scratch.

February 9

We have made excellent progress in the past five days. The morphine injections have been reduced to ⅛ grain four times daily, and tomorrow we begin alternating with codeine.

Tinka talked about her relationship with her husband for the first time today, in connection with her resolve to break the habit. He is, apparently, an archaeologist working with an expedition somewhere in Arizona. She is in frequent touch with him, and in fact called him yesterday to say she had begun treatment and was hopeful of a cure. It is her desire, she said, to begin a new life with him once the withdrawal is complete. She knows he still loves her, knows that had it not been for her habit they would never have parted.

She said he did not learn of her addiction until almost a year after the child was born. This was all the more remarkable since the baby—fed during pregnancy by the bloodstream of her mother, metabolically dependent on heroin—was quite naturally an addict herself from the moment she was born. Dennis, and the family pediatrician as well, assumed she was a colicky baby, crying half the night through, vomiting, constantly fretting. Only Tinka knew that the infant was experiencing all the symptoms of cold-turkey withdrawal. She was tempted more than once to give the child a secret fix, but she refrained from doing so, and the baby survived the torment of force withdrawal only to face the subsequent storm of separation and divorce.

Tinka was able to explain the hypodermic needle Dennis found a month later by saying she was allergic to certain dyes in the nylon dresses she was modeling and that her doctor had prescribed an antihistamine in an attempt to reduce the allergic reaction. But she could not explain the large sums of money that seemed to be vanishing from their joint bank account, nor could she explain his ultimate discovery of three glassine bags of a white powder secreted at the back of her dresser drawer. She finally confessed that she was a drug addict, that she had been a drug addict for close to seven years and saw nothing wrong with it so long as she was capable of supporting the habit. He goddamn well knew she was earning most of the money in this household, anyway, so what the fuck did he want from her?

He cracked her across the face and told her they would go to see a doctor in the morning.

In the morning, Tinka was gone.

She did not return to the apartment until three weeks later, disheveled and bedraggled, at which time she told Dennis she had been on a party with three colored musicians from a club downtown, all of them addicts. She could not remember what they had done together. Dennis had meanwhile consulted a doctor, and he told Tinka that drug addiction was by no means incurable, that there were ways of treating it, that success was almost certain if the patient— Don't make me laugh, Tinka said. I'm hooked through the bag and back, and what's more I like it, now what the hell do you think about that? Get off my back, you're worse than the monkey!

He asked for the divorce six months later.

During that time, he tried desperately to reach this person he had taken for a wife, this stranger who was nonetheless the mother of his child, this driven animal whose entire life seemed bounded by the need for heroin. Their expenses were overwhelming. She could not let her career vanish because without her career she could hardly afford the enormous amounts of heroin she required. So she dressed the part of the famous model, and lived in a lavishly appointed apartment, and rode around town in hired limousines, and ate at the best restaurants, and was seen at all the important functions—while within her the clamor for heroin raged unabated. She worked slavishly, part of her income going toward maintaining the legend that was a necessary adjunct of her profession, the remainder going toward the purchase of drugs for herself and her friends.

There were always friends.

She would vanish for weeks at a time, lured by a keening song she alone heard, compelled to seek other addicts, craving the approval of people like herself, the comradeship of the dream society, the anonymity of the shooting gallery where scars were not stigmata and addiction was not a curse.

He would have left her sooner but the child presented a serious problem. He knew he could not trust Anna alone with her mother, but how could he take her with him on archaeological expeditions around the world? He realized that if Tinka's addiction were allowed to enter the divorce proceedings, he would be granted immediate custody of the child. But Tinka's career would automatically be ruined, and who knew what later untold hurt the attendant publicity could bring to Anna? He promised Tinka that he would not introduce the matter of her addiction if she would allow him to hire a responsible governess for the child. Tinka readily agreed. Except for her occasional binges, she considered herself to be a devoted and exemplary mother. If a governess would make Dennis happy and keep this sordid matter of addiction out of the proceedings, she was more than willing to go along with the idea. The arrangements were made.

Dennis, presumably in love with his wife, presumably concerned about his daughter's welfare, was nonetheless content to abandon one to eternal drug addiction, and the other to the vagaries and unpredictabilities of living with a confirmed junkie. Tinka, for her part, was glad to see him leave. He had become a puritanical goad, and she wondered why she'd ever married him in the first place. She supposed it had had something to do with the romantic notion of one day kicking the habit and starting a new life.

Which is what you're doing now, I told her.

Yes, she said, and her eyes were shining.

February 12

Tinka is no longer dependent on morphine, and we have reduced the codeine intake to one grain twice daily, alternating with ½ grain twice daily.

February 13

I received a long-distance call from Dennis Sachs today. He simply wanted to know how his wife was coming along and said that if I didn't mind he would call once a week—it would have to be either Friday or Saturday since he'd be in the desert the rest of the time—to check on her progress. I told him the prognosis was excellent, and I expressed the hope that withdrawal would be complete by the twentieth of the month.

February 14

Have reduced the codeine to ½ grain twice daily, and have introduced thiamine twice daily.

February 15

Last night, Tinka slipped out of the apartment while her nurse was dozing. She has not returned, and I do not know where she is.

February 20

Have been unable to locate Tinka.

March 1

Have called the apartment repeatedly. The governess continues to care for Anna—but there has been no word from Tinka.

March 8

In desperation, I called the Cutler Agency today to ask if they have any knowledge of Tinka's whereabouts. They asked me to identify myself, and I said I was a doctor treating her for a skin allergy (Tinka's own lie!). They said she had gone to the Virgin Islands on a modeling assignment and would not be back until the twentieth of March. I thanked them and hung up.

March 22

Tinka came back to my office today.

The assignment had come up suddenly, she said, and she had taken it, forgetting to tell me about it.

I told her I thought she was lying.

All right, she said. She had seized upon the opportunity as a way to get away from me and the treatment. She did not know why, but she had suddenly been filled with panic. She knew that in several days, a week at most, she would be off even the thiamine—and then what would there be? How could she possibly get through a day without a shot of *something*?

Art Cutler had called and proposed the St. Thomas assignment, and the idea of sun and sand had appealed to her immensely. By coincidence, her friend from California called that same night, and when she told him where she was going he said that he'd pack a bag and meet her down there.

I asked her exactly what her connection is with this "friend from California," who now seems responsible for two lapses in her treatment. What lapse? she asked, and then swore she had not touched anything while she was away. This friend was simply *that*, a good friend.

But you told me he is an addict, I said.

Yes, he's an addict, she answered. But he didn't even *suggest* drugs while we were away. As a matter of fact, I think I've kicked it completely. That's really the only reason I came here, to tell you that it's not necessary to continue treatment any longer. I haven't had anything, heroin or morphine or *anything*, all the while I was away. I'm cured.

You're lying, I said.

All right, she said. If I wanted the truth, it was her California friend who'd kept her out of prison those many years ago. He had told the arresting officers that he was a pusher, a noble and dangerous admission to make, and that he had forced a shot on Tinka. She had got off with the suspended sentence while he'd gone to prison; so naturally she was indebted to him. Besides, she saw no reason why she shouldn't spend some time with him on a modeling assignment, instead of running around with a lot of faggot designers and photographers, not to mention the Lesbian editor of the magazine. Who the hell did I think I was, her keeper?

I asked if this "friend from California" had suddenly struck it rich.

What do you mean? she said.

Well, isn't it true that he was in need of money and a place to stay when he first came to the city?

Yes, that's true.

Then how can he afford to support a drug habit and also manage to take a vacation in the Virgin Islands? I asked.

She admitted that she paid for the trip. If the man had saved her from a prison sentence, what was so wrong about paying his fare and his hotel bill?

I would not let it go.

Finally, she told me the complete story. She had been sending him money over the years, not because he asked her for it, but simply because she felt she owed something to him. His lie had enabled her to come here and start a new life. The least she could do was send him a little money every now and then. Yes, she had been supporting him ever since he arrived here. Yes, yes, it was she who'd invited him along on the trip; there had been no coincidental phone call from him that night. Moreover, she had not only paid for *his* plane fare and hotel bill, but also for that of his companion, whom she described as "an extremely lovely young woman."

And no heroin all that while, right?

Tears, anger, defense.

Yes, there had been heroin! There had been enough heroin to sink the island, and she had paid for every drop of it. There had been heroin morning, noon, and night. It was amazing that she had been able to face the cameras at all, she had blamed her drowsiness on the sun. That needle had been stuck in her thigh constantly, like a glittering glass cock! Yes, there had been heroin, and she had loved every minute of it! What the hell did I want from her?

I want to cure you, I said.

March 23

She accused me today of trying to kill her. She said that I have been trying to kill her since the first day we met, that I know she is not strong enough to withstand the pains of withdrawal, and that the treatment will eventually result in her death.

Her lawyer has been preparing a will, she said, and she would sign it tomorrow. She would begin treatment after that, but she knew it would lead to her ultimate death.

I told her she was talking nonsense.

March 24

Tinka signed her will today.

She brought me a fragment of a poem she wrote last night:

When I think of what I am
And of what I might have been,
I tremble.
I fear the night.
Throughout the day,
I rush from dragons conjured in the dark.
Why will they not

I asked her why she hadn't finished the poem. She said she couldn't finish it until she knew the outcome herself. What outcome do you want? I asked her.

I want to be cured, she said.

You *will* be cured, I told her.

March 25

We began treatment once more.

March 27

Dennis Sachs called from Arizona again to inquire about his wife. I told him she had suffered a relapse but that she had begun treatment anew, and that we were hoping for complete withdrawal by April 15th at the very latest. He asked if there was anything he could do for Tinka. I told him that the only person who could do anything for Tinka was Tinka.

March 28

Treatment continues.

¼ grain morphine twice daily.

⅛ grain morphine twice daily.

March 30

⅛ grain morphine four times daily.

Prognosis good.

March 31

⅛ grain morphine twice daily.

One grain codeine twice daily.

April 1

Tinka confessed today that she has begun buying heroin on the sly, smuggling it in, and has been taking it whenever the nurse isn't watching. I flew into a rage. She shouted "April Fool!" and began laughing.

I think there is a chance this time.

April 2

One grain codeine four times daily.

April 3

One grain codeine twice daily.

½ grain codeine twice daily.

April 4

½ grain codeine four times daily.

April 5

½ grain codeine twice daily, thiamine twice daily.

April 6

Thiamine four times daily. Nurse was discharged today.

April 7

Thiamine three times daily.
We are going to make it!

April 8

Thiamine twice daily.

April 9

She told me today that she is certain the habit is almost kicked. This is my feeling as well. The weaning from hypodermics is virtually complete. There is only the promise of a new and rewarding life ahead.

That was where the doctor's casebook ended because that was when Tinka Sachs was murdered.

Meyer glanced up to see if Kling had finished the page. Kling nodded, and Meyer closed the book.

"He took two lives from her," Meyer said. "The one she was ending, and the one she was beginning."

That afternoon Paul Blaney earned his salary for the second time in four days. He called to say he had completed the postmortem examination of Tinka Sachs and had discovered a multitude of scars on both upper front thighs. It seemed positive that the scars had been caused by repeated intravenous injections, and it was Blaney's opinion that the dead girl had been a drug addict.

13

SHE HAD handcuffed both hands behind his back during one of his periods of unconsciousness, and then had used a leather belt to lash his feet together. He lay naked on the floor now and waited for her arrival, trying to tell himself he did not need her, and knowing that he needed her desperately.

It was very warm in the room, but he was shivering. His skin was beginning to itch but he could not scratch himself because his hands were manacled behind his back. He could smell his own body odors—he had not been bathed or shaved in three days—but he did not care about his smell or his beard, he only cared that she was not here yet, what was keeping her?

He lay in the darkness and tried not to count the minutes.

The girl was naked when she came into the room. She did not put on the light. There was the familiar tray in her hands, but it did not carry food any more. The Llama was on the left-hand side of the tray. Alongside the gun were a small cardboard box, a book of matches, a spoon with its handle bent back toward the bowl, and a glassine envelope.

"Hello, doll," she said. "Did you miss me?"

Carella did not answer.

"Have you been waiting for me?" the girl asked. "What's the matter, don't you feel like talking?" She laughed her mirthless laugh. "Don't worry, baby," she said. "I'm going to fix you."

She put the tray down on the chair near the door, and then walked to him.

"I think I'll play with you awhile," she said. "Would you like me to play with you?"

Carella did not answer.

"Well, if you're not even going to talk to me, I guess I'll just have to leave. After all, I know when I'm not—"

"No, don't go," Carella said.

"Do you want me to stay?"

"Yes."

"Say it."

"I want you to stay."

"That's better. What would you like, baby? Would you like me to play with you a little?"

"No."

"Don't you like being played with?"

"No."

"What do you like, baby?"

He did not answer.

"Well, you have to tell me," she said, "or I just won't give it to you."

"I don't know," he said.

"You don't know what you like?"

"Yes."

"Do you like the way I look without any clothes on?"

"Yes, you look all right."

"But that doesn't interest you, does it?"

"No."

"What *does* interest you?"

Again, he did not answer.

"Well, you *must* know what interests you. Don't you know?"

"No, I don't know."

"Tch," the girl said, and rose and began walking toward the door.

"Where are you going?" he asked quickly.

"Just to put some water in the spoon, doll," she said soothingly. "Don't worry. I'll be back."

She took the spoon from the tray and walked out of the room, leaving the door open. He could hear the water tap running in the kitchen. Hurry up, he thought, and then thought, No, I don't need you, leave me alone, goddamn you, leave me alone!

"Here I am," she said. She took the tray off the seat of the chair and then sat and picked up the glassine envelope. She emptied its contents into the spoon, and then struck a match and held it under the blackened bowl. "Got to cook it up," she said. "Got to cook it up for my baby. You getting itchy for it, baby? Don't worry, I'll take care of you. What's your wife's name?"

"Teddy," he said.

"Oh my," she said, "you still remember. That's a shame." She blew out the match. She opened the small box on the tray, and removed the hypodermic syringe and needle from it. She affixed the needle to the syringe, and depressed the plunger to squeeze any air out of the cylindrical glass tube. From the same cardboard box, which was the original container in which the syringe had been marketed, she took a piece of absorbent cotton, which she placed over the milky white liquid in the bowl of the spoon. Using the cotton as a filter, knowing that even the tiniest piece of solid matter would clog the tiny opening in the hypodermic needle, she drew the liquid up into the syringe, and then smiled and said, "There we are, all ready for my doll."

"I don't want it," Carella said suddenly.

"Oh, honey, please don't lie to me," she said calmly. "I *know* you want it, what's your wife's name?"

"Teddy."

"Teddy, tch, tch, well, well," she said. From the cardboard box, she took a loop of string, and then walked to Carella and put the syringe on the floor beside him. She looped the piece of string around his arm, just above the elbow joint.

"What's your wife's name?" she asked.

"Teddy."

"You want this, doll?"

"No."

"Oooh, it's very good," she said. "We had some this afternoon, it was very good stuff. Aren't you just aching all over for it, what's your wife's name?"

"Teddy."

"Has she got tits like mine?"

Carella did not answer.

"Oh, but that doesn't interest you, does it? All that interests you is what's right here in this syringe, isn't that right?"

"No."

"This is a very high-class shooting gallery, baby. No eye-droppers here, oh no. Everything veddy veddy high-tone. Though I don't know how we're going to keep ourselves in junk now that little Sweetass is gone. He shouldn't have killed her, he really shouldn't have."

"Then why did he?"

"I'll ask the questions, doll. Do you remember your wife's name?"

"Yes."

"What is it?"

"Teddy."

"Then I guess I'll go. I can make good use of this myself." She picked up the syringe. "Shall I go?"

"Do what you want to do."

"If I leave this room," the girl said, "I won't come back until tomorrow morning. That'll be a long long night, baby. You think you can last the night without a fix?" She paused. "Do you want this or not?"

"Leave me alone," he said.

"No. No, no, we can't leave you alone. In a little while, baby, you are going to tell us everything you know, you are going to tell us exactly how you found us, you are going to tell us because if you don't we'll leave you here to drown in your own vomit. Now what's your wife's name?"

"Teddy."

"No."

"Yes. Her name is Teddy."

"How can I give you this if your memory's so good?"

"Then don't give it to me."

"Okay," the girl said, and walked toward the door. "Goodnight, doll. I'll see you in the morning."

"Wait."

"Yes?" The girl turned. There was no expression on her face.

"You forgot your tourniquet," Carella said.

"So I did," the girl answered. She walked back to him and removed the string from his arm. "Play it cool," she said. "Go ahead. See how far you get by playing it cool. Tomorrow morning you'll be rolling all over the floor when I come in." She kissed him swiftly on the mouth. She sighed deeply. "Ahh," she said, "why do you force me to be mean to you?"

She went back to the door and busied herself with putting the string and cotton back into the box, straightening the book of matches and the spoon, aligning the syringe with the other items.

"Well, good night," she said, and walked out of the room, locking the door behind her.

*

Detective Sergeant Tony Kreisler of the Los Angeles Police Department did not return Meyer's call until nine o'clock that Monday night, which meant it was six o'clock on the Coast.

"You've had me busy all day long," Kreisler said. "It's tough to dig in the files for these ancient ones."

"Did you come up with anything?" Meyer asked.

"I'll tell you the truth, if this hadn't been a homicide you're working on, I'd have given up long ago, said the hell with it."

"What've you got for me?" Meyer asked patiently.

"This goes back twelve, thirteen years. You really think there's a connection?"

"It's all we've got to go on," Meyer said. "We figured it was worth a chance."

"Besides, the city paid for the long-distance call, right?" Kreisler said, and began laughing.

"That's right," Meyer said, and bided his time, and hoped that *Kreisler's* city was paying for *his* call, too.

"Well, anyway," Kreisler said, when his laughter had subsided, "you were right about that arrest. We picked them up on a violation of Section 11500 of the Health and Safety Code. The girl's name wasn't Sachs then, we've got her listed as Tina Karin Grady, you suppose that's the same party?"

"Probably her maiden name," Meyer said.

"That's what I figure. They were holed up in an apartment in North Hollywood with more than twenty-five caps of H, something better than an eighth of an ounce, not that it makes any difference out here. Out here, there's no minimum quantity constituting a violation. Any amount that can be analyzed as a narcotic is admissible in court. It's different with you guys, I know that."

"That's right," Meyer said.

"Anyway, the guy was a mainliner, hit marks all over his arms. The Grady girl looked like sweet young meat, it was tough to figure what she was doing with a creep like him. She claimed she didn't know he was an addict, claimed he'd invited her up to the apartment, got her drunk, and then forced a shot on her. There were no previous marks on her body, just that one hit mark in the crook of her el—"

"Wait a minute," Meyer said.

"Yeah, what's the matter?"

"The *girl* claimed he'd forced the shot on her?"

"That's right. Said he got her drunk."

"It wasn't the *man* who alibied her?"

"What do you mean?"

"Did the man claim he was a pusher and that he'd forced a fix on the girl?"

Kreisler began laughing again. "Just catch a junkie who's willing to take a fall as a pusher. Are you kidding?"

"The girl told her doctor that the man alibied her."

"Absolute lie," Kreisler said. "*She* was the one who did all the talking, convinced the judge she was innocent, got off with a suspended sentence."

"And the man?"

"Convicted, served his time at Soledad, minimum of two, maximum of ten."

"Then *that's* why she kept sending him money. Not because she was indebted to him, but only because she felt guilty as hell."

"She deserved a break," Kreisler said. "What the hell, she was a nineteen-year-old kid. How do you know? Maybe he *did* force a blast on her."

"I doubt it. She'd been sniffing the stuff regularly and using pot since she was seventeen."

"Yeah, well, we didn't know that."

"What was the man's name?" Meyer asked.

"Fritz Schmidt."

"Fritz? Is that a nickname?"

"No, that's his square handle. Fritz Schmidt."

"What's the last you've got on him?"

"He was paroled in four. Parole Office gave him a clean bill of health, haven't had any trouble from him since."

"Do you know if he's still in California?"

"Couldn't tell you."

"Okay, thanks a lot," Meyer said.

"Don't mention it," Kreisler said, and hung up.

There were no listings for Fritz Schmidt in any of the city's telephone directories. But according to Dr. Levi's casebook, Tinka's "friend from California" had only arrived here in September. Hardly expecting any positive results, Meyer dialed the

Information operator, identified himself as a working detective, and asked if she had anything for a Mr. Fritz Schmidt in her new listings.

Two minutes later, Meyer and Kling clipped on their holsters and left the squadroom.

The girl came back into the room at nine-twenty-five. She was fully clothed. The Llama was in her right hand. She closed the door gently behind her, but did not bother to switch on the overhead light. She watched Carella silently for several moments, the neon blinking around the edges of the drawn shade across the room. Then she said, "You're shivering, baby."

Carella did not answer.

"How tall are you?" she asked.

"Six-two."

"We'll get some clothes to fit you."

"Why the sudden concern?" Carella asked. He was sweating profusely, and shivering at the same time, wanting to tear his hands free of the cuffs, wanting to kick out with his lashed feet, helpless to do either, feeling desperately ill and knowing the only thing that would cure him.

"No concern at all, baby," she said. "We're dressing you because we've got to take you away from here."

"Where are you taking me?"

"Away."

"Where?"

"Don't worry," she said. "We'll give you a nice big fix first."

He felt suddenly exhilarated. He tried to keep the joy from showing on his face, tried not to smile, hoping against hope that she wasn't just teasing him again. He lay shivering on the floor, and the girl laughed and said, "My, it's rough when a little jolt is overdue, isn't it?"

Carella said nothing.

"Do you know what an overdose of heroin is?" she asked suddenly.

The shivering stopped for just a moment, and then began again more violently. Her words seemed to echo in the room, do you know what an overdose of heroin is, overdose, heroin, do you, do you?

"Do you?" the girl persisted.

"Yes."

"It won't hurt you," she said. "It'll *kill* you, but it won't hurt you." She laughed again. "Think of it, baby. How many addicts would you say there are in this city? Twenty thousand, twenty-one thousand, what's your guess?"

"I don't know," Carella said.

"Let's make it twenty thousand, okay? I like round numbers. Twenty thousand junkies out there, all hustling around and wondering where their next shot is coming from, and here we are about to give you a fix that'd take care of seven or eight of them for a week. How about that? That's real generosity, baby."

"Thanks," Carella said. "What do you think," he started, and stopped because his teeth were chattering. He waited. He took a deep breath and tried again. "What do you think you'll . . . you'll accomplish by killing me?"

"Silence," the girl said.

"How?"

"You're the only one in the world who knows who we are or where we are. Once you're dead, silence."

"No."

"Ah, *yes*, baby."

"I'm telling you no. They'll find you."

"Uh-uh."

"Yes."

"How?"

"The same way I did."

"Uh-uh. Impossible."

"If *I* uncovered your mistake—"

"There *was* no mistake, baby." The girl paused. "There was only a little girl playing with her doll."

The room was silent.

"We've got the doll, honey. We found it in your car, remember? It's a very nice doll. Very expensive, I'll bet."

"It's a present for my daughter," Carella said. "I told you—"

"You weren't going to give your daughter a *used* doll for a present, were you? No, honey." The girl smiled. "I happened to look under the doll's dress a few minutes ago. Baby, it's all over for you, believe me." She turned and opened the door. "Fritz," she yelled to the other room, "come in here and give me a hand."

*

The mailbox downstairs told them Fritz Schmidt was in apartment 34. They took the steps up two at a time, drawing their revolvers when they were on the third floor, and then scanning the numerals on each door as they moved down the corridor. Meyer put his ear to the door at the end of the hall. He could hear nothing. He moved away from the door, and then nodded to Kling. Kling stepped back several feet, bracing himself, his legs widespread. There was no wall opposite the end door, nothing to use as a launching support for a flat-footed kick at the latch. Meyer used Kling's body as the support he needed, raising his knee high as Kling shoved him out and forward. Meyer's foot connected. The lock sprang and the door swung wide. He followed it into the apartment, gun in hand, Kling not three feet behind him. They fanned out the moment they were inside the room, Kling to the right, Meyer to the left.

A man came running out of the room to the right of the large living room. He was a tall man with straight blond hair and huge shoulders. He looked at the detectives and then thrust one hand inside his jacket and down toward his belt. Neither Meyer nor Kling waited to find out what he was reaching for. They opened fire simultaneously. The bullets caught the man in his enormous chest and flung him back against the wall, which he clung to for just a moment before falling headlong to the floor. A second person appeared in the doorway. The second person was a girl, and she was very big, and she held a pistol in her right hand. A look of panic was riding her face, but it was curiously coupled with a fixed smile, as though she'd been expecting them all along and was ready for them, was in fact welcoming their arrival.

"Watch it, she's loaded!" Meyer yelled, but the girl swung around swiftly, pointing the gun into the other room instead, aiming it at the floor. In the split second it took her to turn and extend her arm, Kling saw the man lying trussed near the radiator. The man was turned away from the door, but Kling knew instinctively it was Carella.

He fired automatically and without hesitation, the first time he had ever shot a human being in the back, placing the shot high between the girl's shoulders. The Llama in her hand went off at almost the same instant, but the impact of Kling's slug sent her falling halfway across the room, her own bullet going wild. She struggled to rise as Kling ran into the room. She turned the gun on Carella again, but Kling's foot struck her extended hand, kicking the gun up as the second shot exploded. The girl would not let go. Her fingers were still tight around the stock of the gun. She swung it back a third time and shouted, "Let me *kill* him, you bastard!" and tightened her finger on the trigger.

Kling fired again.

His bullet entered her forehead just above the right eye. The Llama went off as she fell backward, the bullet spanging against the metal of the radiator and then ricocheting across the room and tearing through the drawn window shade and shattering the glass behind it.

Meyer was at his side.

"Easy," he said.

Kling had not cried since that time almost four years ago when Claire was killed, but he stood in the center of the neon-washed room now with the dead and bleeding girl against the wall and Carella naked and shivering near the radiator, and he allowed the hand holding the pistol to drop limply to his side, and then he began sobbing, deep bitter sobs that racked his body.

Meyer put his arm around Kling's shoulders.

"Easy," he said again. "It's all over."

"The doll," Carella whispered. "Get the doll."

14

THE DOLL measured thirty inches from the top of her blond head to the bottoms of her black patent-leather shoes. She wore white bobby sox, a ruffled white voile dress with a white nylon underslip, a black velveteen bodice, and a ruffled lace bib and collar. What appeared at first to be a simulated gold brooch was centered just below the collar.

The doll's trade name was Chatterbox.

There were two D-size flashlight batteries and one 9-volt transistor battery in a recess in the doll's plastic belly. The recess was covered with a flesh-colored plastic top that was kept in place by a simple plastic twist-lock. Immediately above the battery box, there was a flesh-colored, open plastic grid that concealed the miniature electronic device in the doll's chest. It was this device after which the doll had been named by its creators. The device was a tiny recorder.

The brooch below the doll's collar was a knob that activated the recording mechanism. To record, a child simply turned the decorative knob counterclockwise, waited for a single beep signal, and began talking until the beep sounded again, at which time the knob had to be turned once more to its center position. In order to play back what had just been recorded, the child had only to turn the knob clockwise. The recorded message would continue to play back over and over again until the knob was once more returned to the center position.

When the detectives turned the brooch-knob clockwise, they heard three recorded voices. One of them belonged to Anna Sachs. It was clear and distinct because the doll had been in Anna's lap when she'd recorded her message on the night of her mother's murder. The message was one of reassurance. She kept saying over and over again to the doll lying across her lap, "Don't be frightened, Chatterbox, please don't be frightened. It's nothing, Chatterbox, don't be frightened," over and over again.

The second voice was less distinct because it had been recorded through the thin wall separating the child's bedroom from her mother's. Subsequent tests by the police laboratory showed the recording mechanism to be extremely sensitive for a device of its size, capable of picking up shouted words at a distance of twenty-five feet. Even so, the second voice would not have been picked up at all had Anna not been sitting very close to the thin dividing wall. And, of course, especially toward the end, the words next door had been screamed.

From beep to beep, the recording lasted only a minute and a half. Throughout the length of the recording, Anna talked reassuringly to her doll. "Don't be frightened, Chatterbox, please don't be frightened. It's nothing, Chatterbox, don't be frightened." Behind the child's voice, a running counterpoint of horror, was the voice of Tinka Sachs, her mother. Her words were almost inaudible at first. They presented only a vague murmur of faraway terror, the sound of someone repeatedly moaning, the pitiable rise and fall of a voice imploring—but all without words because the sound had been muffled by the wall between the rooms. And then, as Tinka became more and more desperate, as her killer followed her unmercifully around the room with a knife blade, her voice became louder, the words became more distinct. "Don't! Please don't!" always behind the child's soothing voice in the foreground, "Don't be frightened, Chatterbox, please don't be frightened," and her mother shrieking, "Don't! Please don't! Please," the voices intermingling, "I'm bleeding, please, it's nothing, Chatterbox, don't be frightened, Fritz, stop, please, Fritz, stop, stop, oh please, it's nothing, Chatterbox, don't be frightened."

The third voice sounded like a man's. It was nothing more than a rumble on the recording. Only once did a word come through clearly, and that was the word "Slut!" interspersed between the child's reassurances to her doll, and Tinka's weakening cries for mercy.

In the end, Tinka shouted the man's name once again, "Fritz!" and then her voice seemed to fade. The next word she uttered could have been a muted "please," but it was indistinct and drowned out by Anna's "Don't cry, Chatterbox, try not to cry."

The detectives listened to the doll in silence, and then watched while the ambulance attendants carried Carella out on one stretcher and the still-breathing Schmidt out on another.

"The girl's dead," the medical examiner said.

"I know," Meyer answered.

"Who shot her?" one of the Homicide cops asked.

"I did," Kling answered.

"I'll need the circumstances."

"Stay with him," Meyer said to Kling. "I'll get to the hospital. Maybe that son of a bitch wants to make a statement before he dies."

I didn't intend to kill her.

She was happy as hell when I came in, laughing and joking because she thought she was off the junk at last.

I told her she was crazy, she would never kick it.

I had not had a shot since three o'clock that afternoon, I was going out of my head. I told her I wanted money for a fix, and she said she couldn't give me money any more, she said she wanted nothing more to do with me or Pat, that's the name of the girl I'm living with. She had no right to hold out on me like that, not when I was so sick. She could see I was ready to climb the walls, so she sat there sipping her goddamn iced tea, and telling me she was not going to keep me supplied any more, she was not going to spend half her income keeping me in shit. I told her she owed it to me. I spent four years in Soledad because of her, the little bitch, she owed it to me! She told me to leave her alone. She told me to get out and leave her alone. She said she was finished with me and my kind. She said she had kicked it, did I understand, she had kicked it!

Am I going to die?

I

I picked

I picked the knife up from the tray.

I didn't intend to kill her, it was just I needed a fix, couldn't she see that? For Christ's sake, the times we used to have together. I stabbed her, I don't know how many times.

Am I going to die?

The painting fell off the wall, I remember that.

I took all the bills out of her pocketbook on the dresser, there was forty dollars in tens. I ran out of the bedroom and dropped the knife someplace in the hall, I guess, I don't even remember. I realized I couldn't take the elevator down, that much I knew, so I went up to the roof and crossed over to the next building and got down to the street that way. I bought twenty caps with the forty dollars. Pat and me got very high afterwards, very high.

I didn't know Tina's kid was in the apartment until tonight, when Pat accidentally tipped to that goddamn talking doll.

If I'd known she was there, I might have killed her, too. I don't know.

Fritz Schmidt never got to sign his dictated confession because he died seven minutes after the police stenographer began typing it.

The lieutenant stood by while the two Homicide cops questioned Kling. They had advised him not to make a statement before Byrnes arrived, and now that he was here they went about their routine task with dispatch. Kling could not seem to stop crying. The two Homicide cops were plainly embarrassed as they questioned him, a grown man, a cop no less, crying that way. Byrnes watched Kling's face, and said nothing.

The two Homicide cops were called Carpenter and Calhoun. They looked very much alike. Byrnes had never met any Homicide cops who did not look exactly alike. He supposed it was a trademark of their unique specialty. Watching them, he found it difficult to remember who was Carpenter and who was Calhoun. Even their voices sounded alike.

"Let's start with your name, rank, and shield number," Carpenter said.

"Bertram Kling, detective/third, 74-579."

"Squad?" Calhoun said.

"The Eight-Seven." He was still sobbing. The tears rolled down his face endlessly.

"Technically, you just committed a homicide, Kling."

"It's excusable homicide," Calhoun said.

"Justifiable," Carpenter corrected.

"Excusable," Calhoun repeated. "Penal Law 1054."

"Wrong," Carpenter said. "Justifiable, P.L. 1055. 'Homicide is justifiable when committed by a public officer in arresting a person who has committed a felony and is fleeing from justice.' *Just*ifiable."

"Was the broad committing a felony?" Calhoun asked.

"Yes," Kling said. He nodded. He tried to wipe the tears from his eyes. "Yes. Yes, she was." The tears would not stop.

"Explain it."

"She was . . . she was ready to shoot Carella. She was trying to kill him."

"Did you fire a warning shot?"

"No. Her back was turned to me and she was . . . she was leveling the gun at Carella, so I fired the minute I came into the room. I caught her between the shoulders, I think. With my first shot."

"Then what?"

Kling wiped the back of his hand across his eyes. "Then she . . . she started to fire again, and I kicked out at her hand, and the slug went wild. When she . . . when she got ready to fire the third time, I . . . I . . ."

"You killed her," Carpenter said flatly.

"Justifiable," Calhoun said.

"Absolutely," Carpenter agreed.

"I said so all along," Calhoun said.

"She'd already committed a felony by abducting a police officer, what the hell. And then she fired two shots at him. If that ain't a felony, I'll eat all the law books in this crumby state."

"You got nothing to worry about."

"Except the Grand Jury. This has to go to the Grand Jury, Kling, same as if you were an ordinary citizen."

"You still got nothing to worry about," Calhoun said.

"She was going to kill him," Kling said blankly. His tears suddenly stopped. He stared at the two Homicide cops as though seeing them for the first time. "Not again," he said. "I couldn't let it happen again."

Neither Carpenter nor Calhoun knew what the hell Kling was talking about. Byrnes knew, but he didn't particularly feel like explaining. He simply went to Kling and said, "Forget those departmental charges I mentioned. Go home and get some rest."

The two Homicide cops didn't know what the hell *Byrnes* was talking about, either. They looked at each other, shrugged, and chalked it all up to the eccentricities of the 87th.

"Well," Carpenter said. "I guess that's that."

"I guess that's that," Calhoun said. Then, because Kling seemed to have finally gotten control of himself, he ventured a small joke. "Stay out of jail, huh?" he said.

Neither Byrnes nor Kling even smiled.

Calhoun and Carpenter cleared their throats and walked out without saying good night.

She sat in the darkness of the hospital room and watched her sedated husband, waiting for him to open his eyes, barely able to believe that he was alive, praying now that he would be well again soon.

The doctors had promised to begin treatment at once. They had explained to her that it was difficult to fix the length of time necessary for anyone to become an addict, primarily because heroin procured illegally varied in its degree of adulteration. But Carella had told them he'd received his first injection sometime late Friday night, which meant he had been on the drug for slightly more than three days. In their opinion, a person psychologically prepared for addiction could undoubtedly become a habitual user in that short a time, if he was using pure heroin of normal strength. But they were working on the assumption that Carella had never used drugs before and had been injected only with narcotics acquired illegally and therefore greatly adulterated. If this was the case, anywhere between two and three weeks would have been necessary to transform him into a confirmed addict. At any rate, they would begin withdrawal (if so strong a word was applicable at all) immediately, and they had no doubt that the cure (and again they apologized for using so strong a word) would be permanent.

They had explained that there was none of the addict's usual psychological dependence evident in Carella's case, and then had gone on at great length about personality disturbances, and tolerance levels, and physical dependence—and then one of the doctors suddenly and quietly asked whether or not Carella had ever expressed a prior interest in experimenting with drugs.

Teddy had emphatically shaken her head.

Well, fine then, they said. We're sure everything will work out fine. We're confident of that, Mrs. Carella. As for his nose, we'll have to make a more thorough examination in the morning. We don't know when he sustained the injury, you see, or whether or not the broken bones have already knitted. In any case, we should be able to reset it, though it may involve an operation. Please be assured we'll do everything in our power. Would you like to see him now?

She sat in the darkness.

When at last he opened his eyes, he seemed surprised to see her. He smiled and then said, "Teddy."

She returned the smile. She touched his face tentatively.

"Teddy," he said again, and then—because the room was dark and because she could not see his mouth too clearly—he said something which she was sure she misunderstood.

"That's your name," he said. "I didn't forget."

RUN MAN RUN

Chester Himes

I

HERE IT was the twenty-eighth of December and he still wasn't sober. In fact, he was drunker than ever.

An ice-cold, razor-edged wind whistled down Fifth Avenue, billowing his trench coat open and shaving his ribs. But it didn't occur to him to button his coat. He was too drunk to give a damn.

He staggered north toward 37th Street, in the teeth of the wind, cursing a blue streak. His lean hawk-shaped face had turned blood-red in the icy wind. His pale blue eyes looked buck wild. He made a terrifying picture, cursing the empty air.

When he came to 37th Street he sensed that something had changed since he'd passed before. How long before he couldn't remember. He glanced at his watch to see if the time would give him a clue. The time was 4:38 A.M. No wonder the street was deserted, he thought. Every one with any sense was home in bed, snuggled up to some fine hot woman.

He realized the lights had been turned off in the Schmidt and Schindler luncheonette on the corner where the porters had been working when he had passed before, whenever that was. He distinctly remembered the ceiling lights being on for the porters to work. And now they were off.

He was instantly suspicious. He tried the plate-glass doors set diagonally in the corner. But they were locked. He pressed his face against the plate-glass window at front. Light from the Lord & Taylor Christmas tree was reflected by the stainless-steel equipment and plastic counters. His searching gaze probed among the shining coffee urns, steam soup urns, grills, toasters, milk and fruit juice cisterns, refrigerated storage cabinets and along the linoleum floor on both sides of the counter. But there was no sign of life.

He hammered on the door and shook the knob. "Open this goddamned door!" he shouted.

No one appeared.

He lurched around the corner toward the service entrance on 37th Street.

He saw the Negro at the same time the Negro saw him. The Negro was wearing a tan cotton canvas duster overtop a blue cotton uniform, white work gloves and a dark felt hat. He held something in his hand.

He knew immediately that the Negro was a porter. But sight of a Negro made him think that his car had been stolen instead of lost. He couldn't have said why, but he was suddenly sure of it.

He stuck his right hand inside of his trench coat and staggered forward.

The Negro's reaction was just as sudden but different. Upon seeing the drunken white man staggering in his direction, he thought automatically, Here comes trouble. Every time I get ready to put out the garbage, some white mother-raper comes by here drunk and looking for trouble.

He was alone. The other porter, Jimmy, who was helping him with the garbage, was down in the basement stacking the cans onto the lift. And the third porter, Fat Sam, would be in the refrigerator in the pantry getting some chickens to fry for their breakfast. From there, even with the blower turned off, he wouldn't be able to hear a call for help. And he doubted if Jimmy could hear him down in the basement. And here was this white mother-raper already making gun motions, like an Alabama sheriff. By the time he could get any help he could be stone cold dead.

He looped the heavy wire cable attached to the metal switch box once around his wrist, fashioning a weapon to defend himself. If this mother-raper draws a gun on me, I'm gonna whip his head 'till it ropes like okra, he thought.

But another look at the white man changed his thoughts. This makes the third time a white mother-raper has drawed a gun on me down here, his second thoughts ran. I'm gonna quit this job, if I live and nothin' don't happen, and get me a job in a store where there's lots of other people working, as sure as my name is Luke Williams.

Because this white man looked dangerous. Not like those other white drunks who were just chicken-shit meddlers. This white man looked mean. He looked like he'd shoot a colored man just for the fun. A snapbrim hat hung precariously on the back of his head and his yellow hair flagged low over his forehead. Even from a distance Luke could see that this face was flushed and his eyes had an unfocused maniacal look.

The white man staggered to a stop at point-blank range and stood weaving back and forth on widespread legs. He kept his hand inside of his coat. He didn't speak. He just stared at Luke through unfocused eyes. Whiskey fumes spewed from his half-open mouth.

Luke began to sweat, despite the fact he wore only a cotton duster. Working twenty years on the night shift had taught him anything could happen to a colored man downtown at night.

"Look, man, I don't want no trouble," he said in a placating voice.

"Don't move!" the white man blurted thickly. "If you move you're dead."

"I ain't gonna move," Luke said.

"What's that you're holding in your hand?"

"It's just a switch for the elevator," Luke said nervously.

The white man drew a revolver slowly from beneath his coat and aimed it at Luke's stomach. It was a regulation .38-caliber police special.

Luke's voice went desperate. "I just came out here to bring the elevator up with the garbage. This is just the safety switch."

The white man glanced briefly at the folded iron doors on which he was standing. Luke made a slight motion, pointing to the female plug in the wall. The white man looked up in time to catch the motion.

"Don't move!" he repeated dangerously.

Luke froze, afraid to bat an eye.

"Drop it!" the white man ordered.

Gooseflesh rippled down Luke's spine. With infinite caution he detached the cable from his wrist and dropped the switch to the iron doors. The metallic clang shattered his nerves.

"I ought to gut-shoot you, you thieving son of a bitch," the white man said in a threatening voice.

Luke had seen a night porter shot by a stickup man. He had been shot three times in the stomach. He recalled how the porter had grabbed his guts with both hands and doubled over as though attacked by sudden cramps. Sweat leaked into the corner of his eyes. He felt his own knees buckle and his legs begin to tremble, as though he had already been shot.

"I ain't got no money, I swear, mister." His voice began to whine with pleading. "There ain't none in the store neither. When they close this place at nine they take—"

"Shut up, you son of a bitch," the white man cut him off. "You know what I'm talking about. You came out here an hour ago, using that switch as a blind, and watched out while your buddy stole my car."

"Stole your car!" Luke exclaimed in amazement. "Nawsuh, mister, you got me wrong."

"Where is the garbage then?"

Luke realized suddenly the man was serious. He became extremely careful with his words. "My buddy is down in the basement stacking the cans on the elevator. When he's got it loaded he'll rap for me to bring it up. I plugs in the cable and pushes the switch. That way can't nobody get hurt."

"You're lying, you were out here before."

"Nawsuh, mister, I swear 'fore God. This is the first time I've been outside all night. I ain't even seen your car."

"I know all about you night porters," the white man said nastily. "You're nothing but a bunch of finger men and look-outs for those uptown Harlem thieves."

"Look, mister, please, why don't you call the police and report your car stolen," Luke pleaded. "They'll tell you that we porters here are all honest."

The white man dug into his left pants pocket and brought out the velvet-lined leather folder containing his detective badge.

"Take a good look," he said. "I'm the police."

"Oh no," Luke moaned hopelessly. "Look, boss, maybe you parked your car on 35th or 39th Street. They both run the same way as this street. It's easy to make a mistake."

"I know where I parked my car—right across from here. And you know what happened to it," the detective charged.

"Boss, listen, maybe Fat Sam knows something about it," Luke said desperately. "Fat Sam is the mopping porter." He figured Fat Sam could handle a drunk cop better than himself. Fat Sam had a soft line of Uncle Tom jive and white folks who were distrustful of a lean Negro like himself were always convinced of Fat Sam's honesty. "He was mopping the floor on the side and he might have seen something." Anyway, once the cop got inside and Fat Sam got some hot coffee into him, maybe he'd come to his senses.

"Where's this Fat Sam?" the detective asked suspiciously.

"He's in the icebox," Luke said. "You go in through the door here and it's on the other side of the pantry. The door might be closed—the icebox door that is—but he'll be inside."

The detective gave him a hard look. He knew the Harlem expression. "By way of Fat Sam," meant by way of the undertaker, but the Negro looked too scared to pull a gag. So all he said was, "He'd better know something."

2

THE PANTRY had white enamel walls and a red brick floor. All available space was occupied by the latest of equipment needed for a big fast turnover in short orders, but it was so expertly arranged there were ample passages from the outside and the basement and into the lunchroom.

Racks of glassware and dishes, stacked eight feet high, sat on roller coasters. Fitted tin trays, empty now to be returned, on which cooked items came fresh each morning from the factory, were stacked six feet high. Heavy metal trays filled with freshly polished silver were stacked beside the silver polishing machine. Everything was spic and span and in readiness for the rapid service which would begin at breakfast.

An atmosphere of sterilized order prevailed, such as in a hospital. It was so typical of all New York stores and offices after the night's cleaning the detective experienced a definite feeling of doubt as he silently crossed the red brick floor to the refrigerator.

He paused momentarily beneath the red light above the closed door that indicated there was someone inside. The feeling was so strong that he was making a mistake he debated whether to turn around and leave. But he decided to scare the Negroes anyway. It'd be good for them. If they were innocent it'd help keep them that way. He pulled open the door.

The fat black man in a blue denim porter's uniform, holding an armful of frying chickens, gave such a start a chicken flew from his arms as though it were alive. His eyes popped. Then he recovered himself and said testily, "Jesus Christ, white folks, don't scare me like that."

"What'd you jump for?" the detective asked accusingly.

"Force of habit," Fat Sam confessed, grinning sheepishly. "I always jumps when somebody slips up on me while I'm handling chickens."

"You're a goddamned liar," the detective accused. "You jumped because you're guilty."

Fat Sam drew himself up and got on his dignity. "Guilty of what? Who the hell are you to come in here accusing me of something?"

"You were mopping the floor along the 37th Street side," the detective charged. "You could see everything happening on the street."

"What the hell you got to do with it?" Fat Sam asked while picking up the fallen chicken. "I could see everything happening inside too. I could see all over. Are you one of the firm's spies?"

Slowly and deliberately, the detective flashed his badge, watching Sam's face for a sign of guilt.

But Fat Sam looked unimpressed. "Oh, so you're one of them. What's that got to do with me? You think I'm stealing from the company?"

"There was a car stolen from across the street while you were working on that side," the detective said in a browbeating voice.

Fat Sam laughed derisively. "So you think I stole a car? And hid it here in this icebox, I suppose?" He looked at the detective pityingly. "Come on in and look, Master Holmes. You won't find nothing in here but us perishables—meat, milk, juices, eggs, lettuce and tomatoes, soup stock, leftovers, and me—all perishables. No automobiles, Master Holmes. You been looking too long through your magnifying glass. That ain't no automobile you see, that's a cockroach. Haw-haw-haw."

For a moment the detective looked as though he had swallowed some castor oil. "You're so funny you'd get the stiffs laughing in the morgue," he said sourly.

"Hell, what's funnier than you looking in here for an automobile?" Fat Sam said.

"I'll tell you how you did it," the detective said in a blurred, uncertain voice. "You came back here from out front and used that telephone by the street door. Your buddy was working and he didn't notice." By now the detective had got his eyes focused on Fat Sam's face and they looked dangerous. "You telephoned up to Harlem to a car thief and told him to come down and lift it. That's right, ain't it, wise guy?"

Fat Sam was astonished into speechlessness. The cracker's even got it all figured out, he was thinking.

"What was his name?" the detective asked suddenly.

And suddenly Fat Sam realized the man was serious. He felt cold sweat break out on his skull beneath his short kinky hair.

"I don't know any car thief in Harlem or anywhere else," he said solemnly.

"You stood out there toward the front of the counter, faking with your mop, where you could watch both Fifth Avenue and 37th Street at the same time and give a signal if you saw a police car come in sight," the detective hammered as though trying to get a confession.

Covertly Fat Sam studied his face. Bright red spots burned on the high cheekbones and the lick of hair hung down like a curled horn. He couldn't make out whether the white man's eyes were blue or gray; they had a reddish tinge and glowed like live coals. The thought came to him that white folks could believe anything, no matter how foolish or impossible, where a Negro was concerned.

In a careful voice he said, "Take it easy, chief. Let me fix you a good hot cup of coffee. You drink some hot coffee and give this problem some study. Then you won't believe the first thing pops in your mind, 'cause you'll see that I couldn't 'a had anything to do with stealing a car."

"The hell you didn't," the detective accused bluntly and illogically.

He and Fat Sam were about the same height, a little over six feet, and his stare bored into Fat Sam with a diabolical malevolence.

"As God be my secret judge—" Fat Sam began eloquently but the detective cut him off.

"Don't hand me that Uncle Tom shit. I'll bet you're a preacher."

Fat Sam was touched to the quick. "What if I have been a preacher?" he challenged hotly. "You think I've been a porter all my life?"

"A chicken-stealing preacher like you is just the type to be a lookout for car thieves," the detective said brutally.

"Just because I've been a preacher don't mean I stole any chickens, or cars either," Fat Sam replied belligerently.

"What's that you got in your hands?" the detective asked pointedly.

"Chickens," Fat Sam admitted. "But I ain't stealing these chickens," he denied. "I'm just taking them. There's a difference between stealing and taking. We're allowed to take anything we want to eat. I'm taking these out to fry them on the grill. Okay?"

The detective reached beneath his coat and drew his service revolver. With slow deliberation he aimed it at Fat Sam's stomach.

"You'd better tell me who the car thief is or you'll never eat fried chicken again," he threatened.

Fat Sam felt his intestines cramp. "Listen, chief, as God be my secret judge, I'm as innocent as a baby," he said in the gentle tone one uses on a vicious dog. "You've been drinking kind of heavy and naturally you're upset because someone lifted a car on your beat. But it happens all the time. You're going about it like it's your own personal problem."

"It is personal," the detective said flatly. "It's my car."

"Oh no," Fat Sam cried. He tried to stem his laughter but couldn't. "Haw-haw-haw!" His mouth stretched open, showing all his teeth, and his fat belly rocked. "Haw-haw-haw! Here you is, a detective like Sherlock Holmes, pride of the New York City police force, and you've gone and got so full of holiday cheer you've let some punk steal your car. Haw-haw-haw! So you set out and light on the first colored man you see. Haw-haw-haw! Find the nigger and you've got the thief. Haw-haw-haw! Now, chief, that crap's gone out of style with the flapper girl. It's time to slow down, chief. You'll find yourself the last of the rednecks. Haw-haw-haw!"

Fat Sam's laughter had authority. It touched the white man on the raw. He stared at Fat Sam's big yellow teeth and broke out with frustrated rage. Instead of scaring these Negroes they were laughing at him.

"And when I find who stole my car he's going out of style too," he threatened. "Out of style and out of sight and out of life. And if you had anything to do with it you're going to wish you'd never been born."

Fat Sam wanted to tell the detective that he wasn't frightened by his threats, but it didn't look like the time to tell this white man anything. The detective had gone off again as though in a maniacal trance and his shoulders rose as though he were heaving.

"Control yourself, chief," Fat Sam urged desperately. "You're gonna find your car. It ain't like you lost your life."

Slowly the detective returned the service revolver to its holster. Fat Sam breathed with relief; but the relief was short-lived for the detective drew another revolver from his trench coat pocket. Fat Sam felt his throat tighten; it got too small to swallow. Hot sweat broke out beneath the cold sweat on his body, giving him the itch. But he was afraid to scratch. He watched the detective through white-walled eyes.

"Take a good look," the detective said, waving the pistol in front of him.

It was a .32-caliber revolver with a silencer attached. To Fat Sam it looked as big as a frontier Colt.

"This pistol was taken off a dead gangster," the detective went on in his strange unemotional voice. "The serial number has been filed off. The ballistic record is in the dead file. This pistol doesn't exist. I can kill you and the son of a bitch who helped you steal my car and go down the street and buy a drink. No one can ever prove who did it because the weapon will never be found. The weapon doesn't exist. Got it, Sambo?"

A chicken slipped from Fat Sam's trembling hands. His shiny black skin began turning ashy.

"What're you thinking about, chief?" he asked in a terrified whisper.

"You wait, you'll see. First I'm going to knock the bastard down." He went into a frenzy of rage and began jumping about, demonstrating just how he would do it. "Then I'm going to kick out his teeth. I'm going to break his jaw and kick out his eyes" . . . Fat Sam watched the antics of the raving madman in fascinated terror . . . "then I'm going to kick him in the nuts until he's spayed like a dog." He was talking through gritted teeth as he jumped about. A tiny froth of saliva had collected in each corner of his mouth.

Fat Sam had never seen a white man go insane like this. He had never realized that the thought of Negroes could send a white man out his head. He wouldn't have believed it. He had thought it was all put on. And now this sight of violence unleashed because of race terrified him as though he had come face to face with the devil, whom he'd never believed in either.

"Then I'm going to shoot the son of a bitch in his belly until his guts run out," the detective raged on in a deadly voice.

Three sounds followed one behind another like a cold motor coughing.

Fat Sam's eyes widened slowly in ultimate surprise. "You shot me," he said in an incredulous voice.

The chickens slipped one by one from his nerveless fingers.

The detective looked down in shock at the gun in his hand. A thin wisp of smoke curled from the muzzle and the smell of cordite grew strong in the small cold room.

"Jesus Christ!" he exclaimed in a horrified whisper.

Fat Sam grabbed the handle of the tray to support himself. He could feel the sticky mess pouring from his guts.

"God in heaven!" he whispered.

He fell forward, pulling the tray from the rack along with him. Thick, cold, three-day-old turkey gravy poured over his kinky head as he landed, curled up like a fetus, between a five-gallon can of whipping cream and three wooden crates of iceberg lettuce.

"Have mercy, Jesus," he moaned in a voice that could scarcely be heard. "Call an ambulance, chief, you done shot me for nothing."

"Too late now," the detective said in a voice gone stone cold sober.

"Ain't too late," Fat Sam begged in a fading whisper. "Give me a chance."

"It was an accident," the detective said. "But no one will believe it."

"I'll believe it," Fat Sam said as though it were his last chance, but his voice didn't have any sound.

The detective raised the pistol again, took aim at Fat Sam's gravy-coated head, and pulled the trigger.

As the gun coughed, Fat Sam's body gave a slight convulsion and relaxed.

The detective bent over and vomited on the floor.

3

THE SOUND of a laboring truck caught the detective's attention. He experienced a shock of fear. A shudder ran through his body and he suddenly felt the cold. He listened intently in an effort to identify the vehicle. When convinced it was not a police van he felt a vague relief, even though he knew it was only his sense of guilt that conjured up such an idea.

It sounded like the motor of a hydraulic lift. He thought of the lift from the basement, but that would be electric and could scarcely be heard from his position.

For an instant he experienced a sense of someone standing behind him, watching his movements, and was overcome with a wild, raw panic. He wheeled toward the open door, pointing the cocked revolver, prepared to shoot on sight.

Then he realized the sound came from a garbage truck outside. There was no other sound like it. Breath flowed from his stiff lips in a soft hissing sound.

He pocketed the revolver and stepped quickly into the pantry. There was no one in sight. He quickly crossed to the street door and locked it on the inside. He didn't stagger but his legs felt wobbly. Sweat trickled into his eyes and his head felt burning hot. Drops of sweat formed in his armpits despite the chill of his body and trickled down his ribs.

Seeing the mop sink on that side of the refrigerator, adjoining the silver polishing machine, he took off his hat, ran cold water over his face and head and dried himself on a cleaning cloth spread over the side of the sink.

He felt less panicky.

Of all the rotten luck, he thought.

He returned to the refrigerator to close the door. He saw his own filth on the wooden floor and smelled the putrid whiskey stink and lingering cordite fumes. His stomach ballooned into his mouth and he had to bite down a return of nausea.

His gaze lit on the gravy-crowned body of Fat Sam. His thoughts became fuddled again. He felt only pity for the man he'd killed.

Poor bastard, he thought. Dead in the gravy he loved so well.

He turned out the refrigerator light from the switch panel beside the door and pulled the door shut softly, like closing the lid of a coffin.

Fat Sam went by way of Fat Sam, he thought.

He was breathing heavily, but he couldn't control it. He felt spent. A couple of glasses of milk was what he needed, he thought. He didn't know there was milk in the containers in the lunchroom. He thought it was kept in the refrigerator and he could not open the door again.

Suddenly his stomach fell from hunger. He had to eat something or he would be sick again, he knew. He went over and foraged in the food trays stacked along the outside wall. He found half of a cold broiled chicken and ate a leg ravenously. It made him think of Fat Sam with his arms filled with the chickens he had intended to fry. He thought of him as he had seen him living, a big black man with popping eyes who might have been jolly. A man you could have sat down with and eaten fried chicken and talked about life. A man who would have known a lot about women. Maybe a funny man. Women always love a funny man, he thought.

The realization of what he'd done exploded inside of him like a dynamite blast. He hadn't intended to shoot him but the hole in his head made it murder. He might have gotten away with it if he hadn't shot him in the head. That and the illegal gun. He knew he couldn't talk his way out of that.

He was scared more than he'd ever been in all his life. Scared of the law he'd sworn to uphold. Scared of the court where he would be tried. Scared of the pure and simple process of justice. . . . But he was no longer panic-stricken. It was the Negro who was dead. He was still alive. There was no reason why he couldn't keep alive if he didn't go haywire. There were no witnesses. And the gun didn't exist.

His nerves drew taut and his mind got sharp and cunning. The only thing to do now is to clean it up, he thought. Wipe the slate clean.

He went out into the lunchroom where he could watch the loading of the garbage truck. On that side were two great plate-glass windows with long cushioned seats beneath, where clients could wait for a place at the counter. But he didn't sit down. He stood far back in the shadow where he could see without being seen.

The truck was backed at an angle to the curb and two porters were rolling the big galvanized garbage cans from the lift. He recognized Luke but the other porter he hadn't seen.

The motor of the truck was running noisily. It gave him a sense of reassurance. Noise wouldn't disturb the people in this neighborhood, no matter what happened.

The driver stood on the pavement behind the truck and took the cans as they were passed to him and dumped them over the loading lip of the intake compartment. When it was filled he worked a lever that brought down the big steel plate that pressed out the water and packed the garbage into the body of the truck. He worked the truck alone.

He was a big, rangy, slow-motioned man of about sixty. He had a lined brown face and kinky gray hair that showed beneath a greasy cap. The easy manner in which he handled the heavy cans gave the impression of great strength.

Automatically the detective counted the cans; there were fifteen in all. They have a hell of a lot of garbage for a place of this size, he thought.

When they had finished with the cans, wooden crates containing empty tin cans were loaded in the same manner. But when it came to the cardboard cartons, the driver flattened them out and stored them into a separate compartment.

He must sell them to some paper mill, the detective thought. Every mother's son has got himself some kind of racket to go along with the job.

He could see that the three men were talking and laughing as they worked, although he couldn't hear what they said. He looked at the second porter for some time. He was a younger man than the others and he looked different, more educated; he seemed to listen mostly although he laughed with the two others.

When they'd finished loading, Luke gave the driver a carton of leftover sandwiches. It was the policy of the firm to throw day-old sandwiches into the garbage, but the porters saved them for the garbage man. The detective had no way of knowing this, and he thought they were selling them. He smiled indulgently.

The driver climbed into his seat, waved a hand and drove off. The detective was relieved; for a moment he had feared the porters might invite him inside for coffee. It was better they hadn't.

He had forgotten Fat Sam other than as a motive and a vague sense of guilt. Most of the scare had left him. He now felt sad. There was something sad about killing a man in the midst of so much food, he thought. Maybe *ironical* was the word.

He watched the two porters load the empty cans back onto the lift. Their breath made geysers of steam in the cold air. He saw the young porter get into the lift with the empties and Luke pick up the switch box and push the DOWN button. As the elevator descended, the young porter's head disappeared with the garbage cans and the heavy steel doors closed slowly above him on the steel arch at the top of the lift. A moment after the doors had become level with the sidewalk, Luke removed his finger from the button and pulled the cable from the plug.

The detective hastened back into the pantry and unlocked the street door. Then he stood to one side so he could block Luke's retreat once he had entered. His right hand was stuck into his trench coat pocket.

Luke caught a glimpse of the detective standing beside the door when he opened it. He stopped stock-still, suddenly apprehensive. The detective's strange expression gave him a shock. He had been telling Jimmy and the garbage man about the drunken detective losing his car. But he hadn't expected to find him standing beside the doorway in such a threatening attitude; he'd expected to see him talking amicably to Fat Sam and having coffee and sandwiches.

"Er-er, didn't Fat Sam know anything about your car, chief?" he asked hesitantly, standing before the open door dangling the cable foolishly. He was afraid to enter.

"No, he didn't, George," the detective said strangely. "I guess I made a mistake."

Luke did a double take. The detective's face was blue-white with huge red splotches, but he looked sober enough. Sam's got him sobered up, Luke thought with relief. Grinning widely, he stepped inside and hung the cable on a hook beside the door.

"It happens," he said philosophically. "My name's Luke though, not George."

The detective drew his hand from his pocket and wiped it hard down over his face. "Yeah, Luke, it happens," he agreed. "Even the best of detectives can make mistakes sometimes."

Luke threw him another quick searching look. He was startled by the difference in the man's expression. He don't look like the same man, he thought. He looks sad. Fat Sam must have been quoting the Bible to him.

"I'm supposed to be one of the best of detectives and how I made that mistake I don't know," the detective said slowly. He sounded tired.

"Ain't nothing to worry about," Luke said encouragingly. "I knew just as soon as you got a little coffee inside of you to combat all that good bourbon you've been drinking you'd remember where you parked your car."

"It's not my car I'm thinking about, it's my coming in here meddling with you colored men," the detective confessed. "You were only doing your work and attending to your business."

Luke's eyes popped. Sam must have really given him the works, to get a city dick talking like a convert at a revival meeting, he thought.

"Aw, forget it, chief," he said. "We're used to that kind of thing. White folks get to drinking and the first thing they think about is colored folks stealing something from them. You're from the South, ain't you?"

"That's the hell of it," the detective said. "I was born and raised in Jackson Heights on Long Island and I've never lived outside of New York City in my life. I never had nothing against colored people. I don't know what made me think like that—suspecting you porters. I guess I must have just picked it up."

Luke batted his eyes. He didn't know just what to say. The man made him uncomfortable. He didn't want to agree that being a Negro made him automatically suspect. But he didn't want to rile the man, now that he had quieted down.

"Well, anyway, you're gentleman enough to admit you were wrong, which the average white man in your case wouldn't do," he said diplomatically. But he felt uneasy, nevertheless; he wasn't accustomed to white people admitting they were wrong. "Takes a man to admit up that he's wrong," he added compulsively, annoyed with himself because he felt he had to support this mother-raper. He wanted to pass but the detective stood in such a way he couldn't get by. "Excuse me," he said finally. "I want to see how Fat Sam is coming along."

But the detective wouldn't let him pass.

"Listen, Luke, I want to tell you what happened to me tonight," he said. "I owe it to you boys." He sighed. "I was working my beat, Times Square, when I saw a rumble taking place in the Broadway Automat. A drunk claimed he'd been rolled by some floozie he'd picked up. I caught her as she was turning into 47th Street and he made a positive identification. I should have taken her in but she was a good-looking whore and it was a good chance to score. So I propositioned her if she'd kick back his money and take me on, I'd let her go. I'd already been guzzling the booze or I wouldn't have done it."

He ran his hand down over his face again and Luke stared at him in growing horror. Something about this white detective's confession filled him with a sense of dread. Perhaps it was the way this white man referred to a white woman, talking to a Negro. It wasn't natural for a white man to talk like that to a colored man. But he gave a sickly grin and tried not to show what he was feeling.

Unnoticing, the detective talked on. "We stopped in several bars on the way. Then I got the bright idea to park my car on a side street where it wouldn't be spotted by the lieutenant. I went up to her pad with her and killed another half bottle. Then I had a blackout. The next thing I knew I was outside on Fifth Avenue and I couldn't find my car. I didn't even know what street I'd parked it on. I started to go back and ask her where I'd parked it, but I couldn't find the house. I couldn't remember what the entrance looked like, or even what street it was on. It could have been on any of these side streets from 39th to 35th. I couldn't even remember the whore's name. Then when I looked into my wallet I found she'd clipped me for my last hundred and twenty bucks."

Luke whistled in amazement, as was expected. But he wished to hell the detective hadn't told him all that. He didn't know why, but it put a burden on him, a sort of unspoken responsibility, for what he didn't know. But he kept the note of agreement in his voice and said, "No wonder you felt mad with the world. I wondered what was troubling you. I suspect I'd felt the same way. But I swear, ain't none of us had anything to do with stealing your car—if it was stolen."

"I know that now," the detective admitted.

Luke tried again to get past him, but he seemed extremely reluctant to let him go.

"Wait, Luke, listen—you know one thing? I've blown my career, destroyed it, just like that," he said, snapping his fingers.

"Aw, it ain't that bad," Luke said reassuringly. He felt he just had to reassure this white man who had suspected him, as if it were an obligation; he couldn't let him down. "You just feel bad because you made a mistake and you've got a hangover. Everything looks worse than it really is when you got a hangover."

"No, it's finished," the detective stated. "I'll keep on being a cop but I won't feel the same. I won't have any pride left. Listen, Luke, I'm thirty-two years old and a bachelor. A woman chaser."

"Hell, chief, all young policemen are women chasers," Luke said. "Ain't nothing strange in that. It's natural, being around so many women and getting it for free."

"Matt Walker's the name," the detective said suddenly, sticking out his hand. "Just call me Matt, Luke."

Luke stared at the outstretched hand. Suddenly he realized he was supposed to shake it. He shook it as though with enthusiasm. "Matt," he said experimentally.

"That's right—Matt," Walker said. "But I don't mean what you're thinking, Luke. About the women, I mean. It's not women that's my downfall. Listen, I graduated from New York City College. I was a guard on the basketball team and had a chance to turn pro. But I had to go into service for two years and when I came out I was rusty. So I joined the force. I spent five years in uniform, the last three driving a patrol car. Meanwhile I was going to the school for detectives and I graduated with honors. I'm a marksman with a pistol. I've been in plainclothes for two years, on the Times Square beat, the really big time."

Suddenly Luke lost all sympathy. These people, he thought. These mother-raping people with all their chances.

"What you need is some of Fat Sam's fried chicken," he said with forced enthusiasm.

"Fried chicken," Walker echoed strangely.

He acts like a sick man, Luke thought. Like a man on his deathbed. But he kept on with his bogus jubilance and said, "Yes sir, fried chicken is good for what ails you. It ought to be ready now, and I'm sure there'll be plenty for you too. That is if you don't mind eating downstairs with us. We wouldn't have any objection to your eating at the counter, but the firm don't allow us to feed anybody in here. And sometimes the super sits in his car across the street and watches us through the windows to see what we're doing."

That information gave Walker a turn but he only said, "I'm not really hungry, Luke."

"It won't be any trouble," Luke insisted. He finally got up the nerve to push past the detective. "I'll tell Fat Sam," he said as he crossed the pantry toward the lunchroom door.

"I wouldn't bother him about it," Walker said curiously.

But Luke didn't pay him any attention. He opened the door into the lunchroom and called, "Fat Sam! Hey, Fat Sam!"

But the lunchroom was dark and deserted. Fat Sam was not at the grill frying chicken. Luke turned and looked at Walker in surprise. "He must have finished and taken it downstairs," he said lamely, but he was thinking it was strange the detective hadn't mentioned it.

"He's in the icebox," Walker said.

Luke glanced at the switch panel beside the refrigerator door. The lights were off.

"What's he doing in there with the lights off?" he asked suspiciously. "He can't see."

The detective's face contorted in a crooked grimace that was meant for a smile. "Take a look," he said.

A sixth sense warned Luke against opening the door. He glanced covertly at the detective, thinking there was something very strange about the way he looked and talked. It gave him the creeps.

"Go ahead," the detective said.

Luke was suddenly overcome by a terrifying premonition.

But there was nothing he could do about it. He was like a bird charmed by a snake. As though controlled by the white man's thoughts, he switched on the lights.

"Open the door," the detective said.

Luke wanted to refuse. He wanted to tell the white man to open the door himself. But one glance into the detective's opaque, hypnotic eyes and his will flowed away like water. With infinite dread he slowly opened the door and looked inside with dazed eyes. He saw Fat Sam's body crouched down between the crates of lettuce and a can of whipping cream.

"He's hurt!" he exclaimed, moving quickly to Fat Sam's assistance. He slipped in the vomit which he hadn't noticed and looked down. "He was sick," he said. "He must have fallen." Kneeling down beside Fat Sam, he took hold of an arm and asked, "Sam, are you hurt? Are you—" He saw the blood oozing from the gravy that covered the back of Fat Sam's head and his voice stuck in his throat. Finally his voice came out in a whisper, "He's been shot."

He knew the detective was standing behind him, watching him. He knew the detective had shot Fat Sam in the back of his head, that was why he'd been acting so strangely. He wanted to turn around and accuse the detective. But he couldn't move his head.

"You don't believe I could have killed him accidentally, do you?" the detective asked from behind his back.

Luke looked again at the bullet wound in the back of Sam's head and knew it couldn't have been an accident.

But he said, "Sure," in a weak, sick voice, then tried again to make it sound more convincing, "Sure." That didn't sound convincing enough and he added in a louder tone, "You were just pointing your pistol at him like you was doing with me outside and it just went off accidentally. Yes sir, anybody could see that right away."

"No, you don't believe it," the detective said regretfully. "Nobody would believe it. A colored man shot with a hot gun by a drunken white cop. Who's going to believe it was an accident? Nobody."

"Me, boss, I believes you," Luke said in a voice that sounded like a prayer.

"Nobody," Walker contradicted. "Neither the judge nor the jury nor the public nor anybody. You can see it for yourself—me standing in court saying it was an accident—and nobody on God's green earth believing it. Maybe if this was Mississippi they'd let me off even if they didn't believe it. But this is New York State, and here they'll fry me."

"No they won't, boss," Luke said in that prayerlike voice. "I'll tell 'em it was an accident. I'll tell 'em I saw it. I'll say Fat Sam jumped on you and all you did was shoot him in self-defense. I'll say he had a carving knife . . ." His voice petered out in futility. "But I swear before God that I believe you," he whispered.

"It's a dirty shame," the detective said.

Slowly, as though it were manipulated by invisible strings, Luke's head pivoted until he faced the doorway. But tears filled his eyes, blurring the vision of the detective standing there with the pistol pointing at him. He couldn't tell there was a silencer attached to the pistol because all he could see of it was the round hole of the muzzle.

He knew it would come out of that little round hole and there wasn't anything he could do to stop it.

It caught him directly between the eyes.

4

"I looked over Jordan and what did I see
Comin' for to carry me home . . ."

Jimmy sang the verse of the sweet old spiritual in a low bass voice as he washed the garbage cans and stacked them against the wall beside the lift. He took the cans from the lift and held them upside down over the washing machine which spurted jets of boiling water up inside of them, washing and sterilizing at the same time.

The garbage cans, empty milk cans, cleaning utensils and empty tins were kept in a basement room beneath the 37th Street sidewalk.

As a rule Luke helped with this chore while Fat Sam cooked their breakfast. But he knew that Luke was detained by the drunken cop. He didn't have any complaint. Luke was the boss, more or less, by reason of being the longest employed.

Anyway, it wasn't a hard job for Jimmy. The cans were heavy, but he handled them with the tireless ease of a man who didn't know his strength.

His size was deceptive also. He was six feet tall and weighed one hundred and eighty-two pounds, but he looked much smaller. He had the big-boned, broad-shouldered, flat-chested, muscular build of the southern farmhand accustomed to heavy plowing, coupled with the sleepy-type, sepia-colored good looks that Joe Louis had at the age of twenty-four. His eyes were alert and intelligent.

As always when he worked with his hands, his mind was crowded with numerous thoughts. He was thinking with amusement about all the modern labor-saving equipment used by the Schmidt and Schindler chain such as the garbage can washers; in some stores they even had refrigerated garbage rooms to keep the garbage from stinking—like all those deodorants for the working class. And yet they couldn't get along without the old "muscle grease" supplied by the likes of him.

And he was also thinking about the company's custom of calling the *automats* "stores," and the central kitchen the "factory." There were more than a hundred stores throughout New York City but only three or four *luncheonettes* with counters served by waitresses like this one.

While in the back of his mind was a knot of irritation imposed by the drunken cop. He was hungry but reluctant to go upstairs and see what was holding up Luke and Fat Sam. He didn't want to get embroiled in some stupid argument with a drunken white man. Fat Sam and Luke could take it, but he was too quick-tempered. Lots of folks attributed his temper to the fact that he was young. But it wasn't that, he thought. He just wanted to be treated like a man, was all.

He smiled as he recalled some of the run-ins he'd had with various superintendents. Once he'd accused the company of withholding too much tax from overtime pay, and in the course of the argument he and two of the top superintendents had begun shouting at each other. Finally one of the supers had said, "You argue too much, I can't do anything for you." And he had shouted in reply, "Then what the goddamn hell are you talking to me for?"

The only reason they hadn't fired him was because they couldn't get anyone else who could do his work. It was his job to polish all the stainless steel in the lunchroom, and one had to have a sort of genius for that kind of work to keep it from streaking. It tickled him to think how much abuse American bosses took from the workers in order to get the work done. Evolution of the profit system, he thought. Years ago the boss kicked the worker in the pants and threatened to fire him if he didn't toe the line. Nowadays with the unions and federal relations boards and specialized work, the boss kept his goddamn mouth shut.

He was laughing to himself as he finished sweeping the floor, took up the trash and put away the broom.

Cop or no cop, he was going up and get his breakfast, he resolved. As hungry as he was he could eat two fried chickens by himself. And because he'd been made to wait so long he'd also have a bowl of cereal with heavy cream, a pint of fresh orange juice, six pieces of buttered toast, some whipped potatoes and fresh green peas, a lettuce and tomato salad, a package of vanilla ice cream with a can of sliced peaches in heavy syrup for dessert. He'd make the company pay for the white son of a bitch meddling them. Anyway, the superintendents were always pointing out they were privileged to eat all they wanted. And he always did. Although it'd be cheaper for the company to double his pay than feed him, he was thinking as he left the garbage room and went into the other part of the basement.

He stopped in the storeroom where the seasonings, condiments, canned goods and soaps were kept and hung up his tan canvas duster which he shared with the day porters, then went next door into the men's locker room and put his cap and gloves in his locker.

Next door was the waitresses' locker room, but they didn't come to work until seven o'clock and he'd only seen a few of them at night when they were going off work as he was coming on.

The main hall held the steam-heated soup kettles, a bread-slicing machine, a meat slicer and a big old-fashioned refrigerator packed with a variety of sliced cold meats.

He stuffed three slices of boiled ham into his mouth and went to the end of the hall, past the engineer's control room, and ascended the stairs.

There was a landing halfway up where the staircase made a right-angle turn. He was looking up as he made the turn. That was when he saw the detective for the first time.

Walker had just closed the refrigerator door after having shot Luke between the eyes and had started down to the basement to finish off the third porter. But the murder of Luke had shaken him and he had halted for a moment to get himself together and reload. He was standing at the head of the stairs with his left side toward Jimmy and the revolver with the silencer attached dangling loosely from his right hand.

"Went out like a light," he was muttering to himself when he sensed Jimmy's presence and jerked about to face him.

The first thought that struck Jimmy's mind when he saw Walker's flushed, taut, skeletonized face was, My God, the Phantom of the Opera! Seen from below, Walker looked inhuman and nine feet tall. His trench coat hung open like a ragged opera cape and blond hair flagged down over red-tinted eyes that looked completely insane.

The son of a bitch is crazy drunk, Jimmy thought. Fat Sam hasn't been able to handle him.

His guts tightened into a knot but he didn't stop. He wasn't going to let the son of a bitch think he was afraid of him.

Walker's teeth bared like a vicious dog's and the pistol came up level in his right hand. He didn't speak.

Jimmy ducked from reflex an instant before Walker fired. The bullet burned a crease along Jimmy's left ribs. Rage exploded in his brain as though all his emotions and sensations had gone off in one big blast. For one brief instant his mind became oversensitized, as at the moment of death. He saw Walker's face as though it were magnified a hundred times; saw the tracery of capillaries in the maniacal eyes; saw the sweat drops oozing from skin pores as big as whiskey glasses; saw the blond hair stubble growing from hard white jaws like wheat stalks on a snow-covered field; saw distinctly the outlines of the amalgam fillings in Walker's uneven yellow-stained teeth. The picture was burned on his memory with the acid fire of fury.

It lasted but an instant and his body had never stopped its violent reflex motion.

Charge the mother-raper! one part of his insensate mind urged. *Get his gun and beat his brains to a pulp!*

But the other part of his mind screamed the warning, RUN, MAN, RUN!

His panic-stricken muscles were straining in incredible frenzy like a wild stallion in a fit of stone-blind terror. Before Walker could shoot again he had turned on the staircase, as though performing a grotesque ballet step, and started down.

The second shot creased the back of his neck, burned through his fury like a red-hot iron and lighted a fuze of panic in his enraged brain. He was in an awkward position, his left leg crossed over his right onto the stair below, left arm raised in reflexive defense, right arm groping forward, and his body doubled over in a downward slant like an acrobat beginning a twisting somersault. But his corded muscles moved as fast as a striking snake. His taut legs propelled him in a burst of power across the landing and his right side slammed into the wall, bruising him from shoulder to hip.

"Mother-raper!" he cursed, gasping through gritted teeth, and came off the wall turning, pushing with his right leg and right arm and right hip simultaneously, spinning like a whirling dervish, moving so fast he was around the corner and out of range before Walker's third shot dug a hole in the white plaster wall where a fraction of an instant before, the shadow of his head had been.

He went down the bottom stairs in a somersault. It was started and he couldn't stop it, like doing an exercise in gym, so he took it, catching the third stair with the palms of both hands and making the circle, landing on his feet in a squatting position on the concrete floor of the front hall in the basement, his body still in the act of propulsion.

Walker charged down the top stairs, teetering as though half blind. He missed the last stair before the landing, slammed sidewise into the wall and fell to his hands and knees.

"Wait a minute, you black son of a bitch!" he screamed unthinkingly.

Jimmy heard him and came up from his squatting position with a mighty push.

The minds of both were sealed, each in its compelling urge, one to kill and one to live, so that neither registered the humor in Walker calling to Jimmy to wait and get himself killed.

Jimmy turned the corner into the garbage room, thinking vaguely of escaping through the lift, leaning to one side for greater leverage. His rubber-soled shoes slipped on a greasy spot on the concrete floor and he crashed against the doorjamb in passing, bruising his left leg from ankle to hip. He was out of range before Walker could take aim again but he could hear him coming down the stairs in a shower of footsteps. Then he realized he couldn't get the heavy lift doors raised without the lift being in motion.

He had turned out the lights in there on leaving and the idea came to him to trap Walker in the dark. But light shone in from the hall through the open door and he'd have to double back and shut it. He skidded to a stop and whirled about but he had gone too far. Walker was already entering the doorway, running in a careful manner, holding the pistol forward ready to snap a shot.

Jimmy had lost precious seconds by his last maneuver and was caught like a sitting duck. There was no place to hide, no time to dodge, nothing to grab and throw. The galvanized two-gallon bucket containing the rags, sponge and soap which he used to clean the stainless steel sat on the floor to his right.

From sheer instinctive reflex, the blind unthinking compulsion of a man to defend his life, he kicked the bucket as though he were kicking a field goal, drove it in a straight incline toward the leveled gun.

Walker fired an instant later and the bullet went through the galvanized bucket in midair and caught Jimmy in the chest, above the heart. The bucket had lessened its force so that it didn't go deep enough to kill, but it hit him like a fist, catching him off balance from the kick, and knocked him down.

The bucket struck Walker in the chest and knocked him down at the same time.

Jimmy turned over quickly on all fours and started running again before getting to his feet. He could feel himself bleeding in the chest. He didn't know how badly he was hit but he knew he had to hurry. He knew the bucket had knocked Walker down and he knew he had to escape before Walker had time to get to his feet again and take aim.

Out of the corner of one eye he noticed the stack of freshly cleaned garbage cans. Spinning about in the same running motion he snatched two cans from on top and threw them back toward Walker just as he was clambering to his feet. The cans knocked his feet out from underneath him again and Jimmy kept turning in a circle and threw two more. The cans rocketing on the concrete floor made noise enough to wake the dead and Jimmy couldn't tell whether Walker was shooting again or not. It was terrifying in the half-dark room with the ear-shattering noise where he wouldn't have been able to hear the silenced shots.

But Walker hadn't had a chance to shoot again. He was fighting off the cans with his arms and elbows, his face livid with rage. "Get away, goddammit!" he shouted, mouthing unintelligible curses, as though the cans had life and could hear him.

Then he saw Jimmy heading for another door at the end of the room but it was a risky shot in the almost-dark with the garbage cans still banging about. There was only one more shell left in the pistol with the silencer and he couldn't take the time to reload. He stumbled after the fleeing Negro, knocking his shins against the frisky cans, cursing in a blue streak.

Jimmy hit the frail wooden door with his right shoulder without waiting to see whether it was unlocked or not. The rusted lock broke and the door banged open against the wall of a narrow, pitch-dark corridor beneath the adjoining building on 37th Street.

He knew the corridor led into other corridors that connected all the basements of the buildings in that block. Somewhere there must be a janitor awake, or a building superintendent, ran his desperate thoughts. Above in the high stone buildings there must be some living people, charwomen or night porters, watchmen with guns, some human eyes to witness his plight and tell his story. But there seemed only himself and the mad cop with the silenced gun in a world of black dark horror.

He ran through the dark in a blind line, trusting to luck, sobbing unknowingly, feeling the blood flowing down his chest and collecting in a warm sticky band above his belt.

Walker ran after him, ricocheting from one wall to the other, cursing steadily and relentlessly. He had to fight down the compelling urge to draw his service revolver and spray the dark with .38-caliber slugs.

Jimmy ran full tilt into a wall, striking his forehead against the calcimined bricks. He slumped to the floor, stunned but not unconscious.

Walker heard him groan and stopped, peering into the dark for the gleam of eyes. He'd always heard that a Negro's eyes shone in the dark like an animal's and he held the pistol ready to fire at anything that gleamed. He could hear the Negro moving but he couldn't see a thing.

Jimmy climbed slowly to his feet. His body felt as though he'd been beaten with a length of heavy iron chain and only the will to live started him running again.

Suddenly he was running off into space. The corridor had made a right turn and dropped three steps. He landed on his knees and the palms of his hands, scraping off the skin on the rough concrete floor. The sharp sudden pain acted as a stimulant; it got him up and going again.

But the pause in the dark had rendered Walker's thoughts rational again. He groped into his inside coat pocket and found a fountain pen torch. The tiny beam showed him the turn in the corridor and the descending steps. But by then Jimmy had turned another corner and was out of sight.

For a moment Walker considered reloading the pistol. He had felt the loose empties in his pocket when searching for the torch and thought some of them to be good. But he couldn't risk taking the time, what with this maze of corridors and the Negro was already out of sight.

Jimmy was running now with his left hand dragging the wall and his right held straight out in front. He turned two corners in the dark and came out suddenly in a short lighted corridor. He'd lost sound of the pursuing footsteps. He felt a surge of hope. He saw a closed door to his right, opened it and looked in. There was an unmade bed, cigarette-scarred dressing table, dirty clothes hanging over chairs, an empty pint whiskey bottle and glass atop an oilcloth-covered table. But no occupant. He supposed it was the room of a janitor's helper.

As he closed the door to leave he heard footsteps somewhere behind him.

"Help!" he yelled, plunging ahead. "Help! Somebody help!"

No one answered.

He turned at the far end of the corridor as Walker turned into the corridor at the near end, and went into another corridor. A glance to the left showed a long expanse of brightly lit whitewashed walls and a clean concrete floor. He turned right. Before him was a heavy oak door. He could hear the footsteps plainly. There wasn't time to turn back to the corner and grapple with the mad killer. If the door wouldn't open he was dead.

"Hey!" he heard a voice call. "Hey!"

He didn't look around. All it meant to him was death. Son of a bitch calling, Hey, let me kill you. His stomach was tied in a knot as small as a pea and nausea came up into his mouth like week-old vomit.

He reached out his hand for the doorknob.

This is where Mrs. Johnson's young black son loses sight on the world, he thought with a flash of that bitter self-corroding irony which white people call "Negro humor."

He turned the knob. It turned. He pushed the door and it opened.

"Hey! Hey there!" he heard the voice again.

Hey yourself, he thought.

Light shone briefly through the open door on what looked like rows of electric sewing machines, spinning in a slow circular movement about a large square room. He felt so lightheaded it seemed as though he were floating after them. When he turned to close the door he fell heavily against it. His stomach drew in from the effort to keep erect and he felt the warm sticky blood flow down his leg. He thought he was urinating on himself.

In a daze he groped for the lock without realizing what he was doing. It was a Yale lock and he pushed down the button releasing the catch and the bolt snapped shut.

He didn't hear the voice calling, "Hey! Who the hell's that hollering?" Nor the sound of shuffling footsteps down the corridor, approaching the door. He didn't hear the man try the knob and shake the door and shout in an irritated, half-drunken voice, "Open that door and come out of there, who-ever in the hell you are. I gotta finish cleaning up."

He was unconscious before he hit the floor.

5

AT 5:22 A.M. the window washer appeared. He was a slight, dark-haired, incommunicative man of Italian extraction. He wore a leather jacket over a blue pullover, army surplus pants, shearling-lined boots and a logger's cap with earmuffs. He carried his pail, brush, sponge, chamois and squeegees with him, but had handles stored in each of the places he served.

He entered through the back door on 37th Street. Without announcing his presence, he stood on the edge of the sink and took down two sections of a telescoped handle from the top of the refrigerator, then filled his pail with clear cold water from the tap.

He started on the inside of the front windows, first removing the vase of gladiolas from the polished oak window ledge. Attaching the soft wash brush to the long handle, he washed the top of the windows, using a minimum of water so that not a drop splashed on the stainless-steel window frames. Then with half the handle he did the middle section, and washed the bottom by hand. In the same manner he used the squeegee in quick downward strokes, catching the dirty water at the bottom of the pane in the sponge with a quick flip of the wrist. Lastly he wiped the window frames with a damp chamois and moved on. He never looked back.

He worked rapidly and automatically with sure deft motions. He was proud of his skill and the work absorbed him completely.

The absence of the porters was unusual, but he scarcely noticed it. He supposed they were downstairs eating and hadn't heard him arrive. Anyway, it didn't concern him. He had his work to do and didn't like to waste time jawing with colored philosophers. He'd come to the conclusion that all colored porters were philosophers, deep down. There must be something about the job. With him it was different. He was his own boss. He had his own clients: shoe stores, notion stores, haberdasheries, clothing stores, restaurants, all within walking distance. He cleaned their windows once every working day, inside and out, for which he got a stated weekly fee. From there he would go to the cafeteria at the corner of 36th Street, S & S's nearest competitor, then down across 34th Street. He had to be through with them all by 7:30 at the latest. He didn't have time to discuss the problems of life. Maybe colored porters had more problems of life than himself. Colored porters were great on discussing the problems of life. But the only problem he had was when it got so cold the water froze to the panes before he could squeegee it down. And talking about it couldn't help it. He worked from three to four hours a day and grossed $177 weekly. That wasn't bad, he was thinking.

He was finished on the inside in eight minutes. He stopped at the sink to change water and went outside. His breath made vapor geysers, but he didn't feel the cold.

He had finished the front on Fifth Avenue and had begun on the 37th Street side when the milk truck drove up.

"How goes it, Tony?" the milkman greeted.

"Fine," Tony said without breaking motion.

"Everything's always fine with you," the milkman complained.

"Why not?" Tony said.

The milkman grunted and looked about for the empties. He went to the back door and stuck his head inside and called, "Hey, Luke . . . Sam . . . hey fellows."

No one answered.

Turning back to Tony, he asked, "Where the hell's everybody?"

Tony shrugged. "I haven't seen them."

The milkman knew where the empties were kept. It wouldn't have taken him but a minute to go down to the basement and get them, but it was the age of specialized work and it wasn't his job to bring them up to the sidewalk.

Expressing his disapproval by the preciseness of his actions, he unloaded three five-gallon cans of milk with pump lids, a five-gallon can of coffee cream and a three-gallon can of heavy cream with plain lids, and lined them against the wall beside the elevator doors.

He got into his truck, started the motor and drove off.

Tony didn't look around. When he'd finished he emptied his pail, squeezed out the sponge and chamois, put the handle back on top of the refrigerator and went down the street to the next job.

He was still washing the inside of the windows of the 36th Street cafeteria when the S & S factory truck came down 37th Street from Madison Avenue, and he didn't see it. The driver circled out from the curb and backed in at an angle before the pantry door. He climbed down, slapping his gloved hands together, opened the pantry door and bellowed, "All right, lovers, the chow's here!"

No one answered. He didn't expect an answer. Unloading the truck was a sore point for the night porters. They were due off at six o'clock, but he seldom arrived before ten minutes to six and most times later. Usually they were dressed and ready to go home, waiting impatiently with the canvas jumpers worn over their street clothes. He turned back to the truck, expecting them to appear behind him, silent and evil.

The factory trucks were especially constructed with red lacquered, airtight wooden bodies, bearing the S & S crest in gold letters, not unlike the mail trucks of England.

The driver pulled down the tailgate which became an elevator platform, and opened the double doors. The platform was lowered hydraulically to the street by a lever inside the body. He stepped onto it and ascended to the floor of the truck, went inside and began checking the items for delivery to that store.

Still no porters appeared.

Hell, he didn't give a damn, he told himself. It wasn't his job to unload it.

He had four trays of chicken pies, three of baked macaroni, three of baked beans and frankfurters—those were the casserole items. There were two stacks of trays of cakes and pastries, and another smaller stack containing five trays of raw hamburger patties and two trays of raw minute steaks. In addition there were two large enclosed aluminum racks of pies, two five-gallon cans of soup stock, two five-gallon cans of concentrated hot chocolate, a box of S & S bacon, a carton of S & S coffee, a package of cold boiled ham, two packages of sandwich cheese, two aluminum baskets of sandwich bread, a basket of rolls and a crate of oranges. They'd have to get whatever else they needed from the second and third deliveries during the day.

He pushed the racks onto the platform at the back and peered around for the porters.

Where the hell are those boys? he thought with growing irritation. That goddamn little fat manager ought to be here too by now.

He looked at his watch. Six minutes to six.

He heard someone whistling in high shrill notes the rhythm of "Rock Around the Clock" and poked his head around the side of the truck. Well, here come two rocks, anyway, he thought.

Two colored day porters approached from the direction of the 35th Street exit of the Independent Subway's 6th Avenue line, which came down from Harlem.

One was clad in a light tan camel's hair overcoat, dark brown narrow brim hat with a gay feather in the band, and a silk foulard muffler with a deep maroon background. His young brown face looked excessively good-humored for so early an hour on a cold miserable morning. His companion, who was older, wore a blue Chesterfield overcoat with a velvet collar, black bowler hat, and a white silk knitted muffler. Both wore black shoes, dark trousers, and suede gloves to match their coats.

They'd been recounting their amorous adventures of the night past and unaccountably the young man had broken into rhythm. The older man looked at him indulgently.

"Come on, sports, let's move this chow," the truck driver greeted them as they came up.

"Where're the night porters?" the older porter asked. "That's their job."

"They've already left," the driver said. "And this stuff can't wait."

The older porter pulled back his sleeve and looked at his watch. "It ain't six o'clock yet, just three minutes to six," he protested.

The young man consulted his watch. "I got five minutes to six."

"You better take that thing back to the Jew," the older porter said.

The driver looked at his watch again. He had four and one half minutes to six but he said, "I got six o'clock on the head, and I just set mine by Western Union."

At that moment a short fat apparition rounded the corner, head bowed into the wind. He was bundled up so completely in a dark tweed ulster, dark plaid muffler and a black slouch hat that only the steamy lenses of his horn-rimmed glasses were visible.

"Here's the boss now," the young porter said. "What time you got, boss?"

"What's going on here, boss man?" the driver asked in a condescending voice. "I can't get my wagon unloaded." The truck drivers felt more important than the store managers and liked to rub it in.

The manager eased off his glasses and took in the situation. "Where's Luke?" he demanded.

"They gone home," the older porter said.

"Goddamn son of a bitch to hell!" the manager said.

"Who you mean by that?" the porter challenged.

The manager stormed into the pantry without replying. He was late and weary and irritated almost beyond control. His wife had kept him up until two o'clock playing bridge and he'd lost nine dollars, then she'd had cramps all the rest of the night from something she'd eaten and he'd been nursing her with hot-water bottles until he'd had to leave for work.

"Bastard son of a bitch to all hell and gone," he raved to himself as he hung his hat and coat on the hooks inside the door. Then controlling himself, he opened the door wide and hooked it open and said in a placating voice, as though choking on every word, "Come on, boys, let's get the food inside."

The porters didn't argue. Without stopping to change their clothes, they took down the grappling hooks and dragged the stacks of empty trays outside for loading when the truck was unloaded, then carried out the four-wheeled dollies to bring in the stacks of food from the factory.

"That man just don't come to work evil some mornings," the young porter said of the manager. "He comes to work evil every morning. His wife must beat him."

"It's this job what's beating him," the older porter said.

The manager had come out to give a hand just in time to hear what they said about him. He turned around and went back inside.

Grinning broadly, the driver lowered the loaded platform to the level of the sidewalk.

"That ain't no way to talk about your boss," he said.

"Hell, he ain't going to be here long," the older porter said.

They talked as they worked. Grappling the handles of the bottom tray, they drew the stacks onto the dollies with accustomed skill and wheeled them inside and down the inclined floor, stacking them about the staircase railing and along the wall. They looked like comic opera figures performing these chores in their good clothes.

"Where you guys get the money to buy such fine clothes?" the driver asked enviously.

"You're like all the white laborers I've ever seen," the older porter replied. "You think we've got to be doing something illegal just 'cause we dress decently."

The driver shut up. He didn't like to be called a laborer and that wasn't what he meant.

Another two expensively dressed porters appeared and pitched in without being ordered. They stacked the cans of soup stock and spinach alongside the refrigerator and the pie racks in the corner. All of them made derisive comments about the food selected for the day's menu.

It was the manager's duty to make up the menus, but he chose to ignore their remarks as he checked the deliveries. He went about with his list, poking into trays, uncovering cans, examining the pastries and pies. The only comment he had to offer was, "Goddamn son of a bitch!"

The white sandwich man and one of the white short-order cooks arrived together, looking like tramps in their worn overcoats and weather-beaten hats, although they earned much more than the porters. After them, a few minutes late, the other help straggled in.

One of the porters went down to the basement and brought up the lift for the bread baskets. The sandwiches were made in the basement hall.

"Man, you ought to see how they left them garbage cans," he said in a loud voice to everyone. "They look like they been fighting down there."

The manager's ears perked up. "Goddamn sons of bitches!" he said.

Several of the men turned to look at him. He bent over suddenly to peer into the creamed spinach. He didn't have any authority over the night porters. But by God this was carrying it too far, he thought angrily. He'd have something to say to the superintendent about them leaving before time.

Everyone began conjecturing on the reasons the night crew left before time.

"They must have all got drunk," someone offered.

"Maybe they got hold of some chicks."

"It ain't like Luke to walk off the job."

The others agreed.

"Now that Fat Sam might do anything if he's juiced. And that other boy, Jimmy what's-his-name, I don't know nothing about him. But you're right about Luke."

Jimmy was relatively new on the job and he held himself aloof. He never saw any of the others after working hours except by accident and they felt that he was a little uppish. He wasn't well liked. They didn't say anything bad about him; they just didn't say anything good.

Finally most of them went down into the locker room and left the porters to finish the unloading. They were still talking about it as they changed into their starched white working uniforms.

"Fatty's gonna complain to the superintendent, that much's for sure," the colored dishwasher remarked.

They all agreed with him.

Every man had a locker of his own with his own personal lock. Judging from the size of the locks, they didn't trust one another.

The sandwich man finished changing his clothes and began slicing the cheese. The dishwasher went upstairs and turned on the steam in the dishwashing machine. It was too soon to start the dishwashing machine and the manager rushed in from the pantry and shouted, "Goddamn son of a bitch!"

The dishwasher gave him such a black evil look he scurried back into the pantry.

By then the porters had finished unloading. At the instant the manager came in from the lunchroom where the dishwashing machine was located, the young porter in the tan coat playfully scooted a heavy iron dolly across the floor. The steel edge caught the manager on the anklebone and he turned pea green with pain.

Grabbing his injured foot in both his hands he hopped about on the other foot and raved in earnest, "Goddamn son of a bitch to hell of a bitch bitching son of a bitching hell of a bitching black bastards!"

All of the colored porters gave him threatening looks but he continued to rave, "Goddamn son of a bitching bitch of a bitching—"

The cereal cook had just gone into the refrigerator to check the orange juice on hand before juicing the crate of oranges. He came dashing out as though he'd suddenly gone crazy and ran into the manager, knocking him down.

"They's daid!" he screamed in a high keening voice. "They's daid! Both of 'em! They's in there daid!"

"Who in the goddamn son of a bitching hell is dead?" the manager screamed back, rolling about on the floor with his bruised ankle clutched in both hands.

The help came running from all directions to see the cause of the commotion.

"W-w-w-who's daid?" the gray-faced cook screamed, his eyes bucking whitely with indignation. "Both of 'em's daid, thass who! Luke and Fat Sam both! They's shot in the haid and both of 'em is in there stone cold daid!"

For a moment the tableau held, mouths open, eyes stretched, breath held.

Then the manager got up, standing on one leg like a crane, and said quietly, "I'll call the police," and hopped one-legged toward the telephone.

6

WHEN DETECTIVE Walker saw the janitor's helper approaching down the brightly lit corridor his first thought was, Now I've got to kill another one.

He had almost caught up with the Negro porter. He had had him cornered, ready for the kill. And now this drunken imbecile had to appear on the scene.

Walker watched the janitor's helper as he staggered down the corridor to the dead-end room where the porter had taken refuge. He stood back of the corner, peering with one eye. He had him limned in the bright light against the painted tin sign at the far end of the corridor which read APEX DRESSES with an arrow pointing toward the closed oak door.

The janitor's helper would have seen him if he had been more observant but his attention was focused on the door. No doubt a broken-down alcoholic, a wino, Walker thought; he looked like one in his filthy rags and run-over shoes. A dirty bastard, repulsive to the sight. Dirtying up the world. Walker's thoughts began justifying the murder before he had committed it. Probably the bastard had just been on the job for a couple of weeks. In another week he'd be fired for drunkenness. He'd be back on Skid Row in the Bowery, drinking the squeezings of canned heat and bay rum, sitting with other crum-bums around a bonfire in the gutter made from packing crates, a burden to the city. The kind of bastard who'd be better off dead; the world would be a better place without him. Furthermore, it would confuse the issue. The murders of the three Negro porters could be attributed to a single motive, but that of a white janitor's helper in another building at the same time would look like the actions of a maniac. No one would ever think of him as a maniac.

He backed out of sight to reload. But he found only empties in his pocket. . . . He stood there tallying up the bullets he had used. He always loaded a six-shooter with five bullets, resting the hammer on the empty chamber; and he always carried five spares. So he'd shot the first one—that was Fat Sam—three times, and then a fourth . . . The sound of the janitor's helper hammering on the locked door distracted him. The goddamned imbecile, he thought. Why the hell doesn't he unlock it? He must have a key, or at least he could get hold of one. . . . Fat Sam four times . . . He felt like shouting, Cut out that racket so I can think! . . . And then the second one just once. Right between the eyes. That one had been Luke. And this last one, he'd shot at him three times on the stairway and once in the basement. He must have hit him one of those times at least; he never had missed a target with four shots in a row. But he needed two bullets to finish it—one for this white scum and one for the Negro. And he didn't have but one.

The janitor's helper gave up and turned back down the corridor to call the superintendent. Walker listened to his shuffling footsteps. Suddenly he had the bright idea of beating him to death. That would solve the problem. He reversed the pistol in his hand and gripped it by the silencer. One quick rap on his temple and he'd never know what hit him.

He was stopped by another voice calling from somewhere above, "What the hell's going on down there, Joe?" The voice held an unmistakable note of authority.

"There's a burglar in the Apex sewing room," the helper replied.

Walker glanced around the corner at the ceiling of the corridor and noticed a ventilator duct. Beside it, painted on the whitewashed ceiling, a green arrow pierced the green-lettered word, EXIT.

"You keep out of the way, I'll call the police," the authoritative voice directed.

Walker realized his position if he was caught. For an instant he contemplated turning back toward the S & S luncheonette. Then he had the brightest idea of all.

The janitor's helper had turned the far corner and Walker heard the sound of an elevator door opening and closing. He ran silently in the direction indicated by the green exit arrow until he came to another. He passed the elevator door. The green arrows took him through a maze of corridors until he came to a sheet-iron double door with a bar handle opening onto a utility passageway to the sidewalk.

When he came out to the street it took him a few seconds to get orientated, then he realized he was on 36th Street between

Fifth and Madison avenues. The building he had just left fronted on Fifth Avenue.

He found the entrance adjoining the 36th Street cafeteria. It was a commercial building occupied by small manufacturers of toys and dresses. There was a directory flanking the doorway listing the nameplates of the occupants. He found Apex Dresses at the bottom of the list. He looked inside through the heavy glass-paneled door.

A charwoman was scrubbing the tiled floor of the entrance hall. He tried the door and found it locked. The murder pistol hung heavy in his right coat pocket. There was no point in trying to get rid of it. He had to use it again, for one thing. And it was safer in his pocket. No one was going to search him.

He knocked on the locked door. The charwoman looked up stupidly. He beckoned. She shook her head and went on working. He knocked again and showed her his badge through the glass panel. She clambered slowly to her feet and came grudgingly to the door.

"What do you want?" she asked in a harsh voice.

"Open up, I'm the police," he shouted.

"I ain't got the key."

"Go get the superintendent. He phoned for the police."

She looked at him suspiciously and turned and shambled toward an inside door. She was met by the janitor's helper, who came forward swinging a heavy ring of keys.

The detective saw them exchanging words. The janitor's helper looked at him suspiciously. Then he came forward slowly and shouted through the locked door, "Let's see your badge."

Walker held his badge close to the glass panel. The janitor's helper bent close to peer at it. He looked up at Walker and finally unlocked the door.

"You're taking mighty goddamn long to get this door open," Walker said. "The superintendent phoned for the police."

"You got here mighty fast," the janitor's helper said suspiciously. "He just got through phoning."

"I know when he phoned," Walker said.

The janitor's helper blinked, trying to assimilate that information. He was saved from replying by the superintendent, who came hurrying forward.

"There's a burglar down there in one of the sewing rooms," the superintendent said. Then on second thought he asked, "You're from the police, aren't you?"

Again Walker flashed his badge.

"All right, this way," the superintendent said, ushering him toward the elevator.

The janitor's helper followed. The charwoman made as if to follow too, but the superintendent said, "You get back to work."

They rode down two floors and in a moment Walker found himself back in the dead-end corridor which led to the sewing room.

"Give me the key," he ordered.

The superintendent took a ring of keys and selected one. "Be careful, officer, he might be armed," he cautioned.

"You two stand back," Walker said, drawing his .38-caliber service revolver.

He went forward with drawn pistol, unlocked the door and gave it a quick hard push. It opened a few inches and was stopped by a soft, heavy obstruction. Walker put his shoulder to it and pushed it inward.

The unconscious body of the porter lay in a pool of blood. Walker leaned over quickly, picked up the limp left arm and fingered the pulse. He found the pulsebeat strong and regular.

The goddamned son of a bitch is still alive, he thought angrily, and drew back his foot to kick him over the heart. Three or four swift kicks ought to finish him and no one would ever know how he got the bruises. But he was arrested by a voice at his elbow.

"My God, he's wounded!" the superintendent exclaimed.

"Either that or dead," Walker said. "He looks more like he's dead. You'd better phone the precinct station and tell them to send an ambulance."

"Joe, you phone," the superintendent ordered his helper, who was peering from the doorway. "I'll stay here and help the officer."

"You'd better phone yourself," Walker said. "And take Joe with you, he'll just be in the way."

"No, let him do it," the superintendent said. "Go ahead, Joe."

He looked down at the unconscious figure and exclaimed spontaneously, "Hell, this is a porter from the Schmidt and Schindler lunch counter." His voice held a note of surprise. "He isn't a burglar. But what the hell's he doing in here shot?" He bent down and felt the pulse. "God's fire, he's alive still."

Walker could scarcely contain his displeasure. "All right, let's get him straightened out and see if we can stop the bleeding," he grated, clutching the body beneath the armpits and dragging it brutally across the floor.

"Jesus Christ!" the superintendent protested. "What the hell you trying to do? You don't want to kill him, do you?"

Without replying, Walker ripped open the porter's uniform. Buttons scattered over the floor. The chest wound had opened again and was bleeding profusely.

Walker looked about the room, as though searching for something. It held only rows of big operator's sewing machines and the special-made operator's chairs.

"Just don't stand there!" he shouted at the superintendent. "Go get some water."

The superintendent was a small elderly man with a thin ascetic face and graying hair. His cheeks glowed with two red spots of anger.

"Let him alone," he said in a tight, furious voice. "Wait for the ambulance. What kind of officer are you? You ought to know enough not to minister to a wounded man. For the way you're treating this man, I could have you suspended."

Walker stood up and looked at the superintendent with an opaque gaze. He would have killed the superintendent instantly if he could have thought of a suitable explanation. Even if he'd had enough bullets for the illegal gun he would have killed him on the spot, finished the porter and shot the helper dead the moment he returned. But then he'd have to kill the charwoman too. That could have been managed also, he thought, but he didn't have the bullets.

"It was best to lay him on his back," he said in a slow, careful voice. "And I advise you to let me take the responsibility. You're going to have a lot of explaining to do yourself."

"Nonsense," the superintendent snapped.

Walker knelt quickly beside the body and began searching the pockets. The porters wore only thin underwear beneath their cotton uniforms, for it was hot all night in the steam-heated restaurant, and they carried everything they needed in their uniform pockets.

In addition to handkerchiefs, scraps of soap and a dustcloth, a ring of keys and two small screws, Walker found only a green Schmidt and Schindler worker's identification card, giving Jimmy's name, employment number and home address. He transferred the card to his own pocket and would have taken the keys too, but the superintendent looked on disapprovingly. He heard people approaching outside and started to straighten up.

At that moment Jimmy opened his eyes. At sight of Walker bending over him, his eyes stretched wide in terror. Instinctively he reached up and clutched Walker's arm, trying to pull him down so he could grapple with him. He was frightened for his life.

Walker jerked his arm loose from Jimmy's hand, the quick, savage motion lifting Jimmy from the floor and throwing him aside so that when he fell back, his head struck the floor. Saliva drooled from the corners of his mouth.

"Take it easy, boy," the superintendent said, drawing near. "He's a detective, he's going to protect you now."

The new face swam into Jimmy's dazed vision. Relief overcame him at the thought of being saved, but the killer was still there, standing over him. "He shot me," he said in a blurred voice. He felt himself growing faint, sinking down into unconsciousness again. He had to tell the other man before he went out. "He's the one who shot me."

The superintendent didn't understand. He bent over to hear better. "Who did you say shot you, boy?" he asked.

Jimmy's face tightened from the effort to speak. "You got to believe me, mister, he's the one who shot me. He did it himself." He saw the disbelief on the man's face and became desperate. "Search him," he whispered. "He's got the pistol in his pocket." Then he lost consciousness.

The superintendent looked at Walker with slowly growing horror.

"He's delirious," Walker said sadly.

Two patrol car cops came into the room ahead of the janitor's helper. Walker exhibited his badge.

"This man's been shot," he said authoritatively, taking command of the situation. "The ambulance has been called for. One of you stay here and the other come with me. Maybe the gunman's still on the premises."

"I'll stay," one of the cops volunteered. "Where shall I tell them to take him?"

"Better send him to the Bellevue psychiatric ward," Walker said. The cop's eyebrows went up. "He's off his nut," Walker explained. "He was conscious for a minute and talking crazy."

"He accused the detective of shooting him," the superintendent said.

The cops were startled. Their suddenly blank indrawn stares went from the superintendent to the detective and back again.

"That's what I mean," Walker said.

"He claimed that the detective still has the pistol," the superintendent persisted stubbornly.

With a quick, angry gesture Walker drew his service revolver and thrust it into the first cop's hand. "Does that look like I've shot anyone?"

The cop turned the revolver over and handed it back. "This gun hasn't been fired," he said flatly.

The superintendent walked away.

"All right, come on," Walker said harshly to the cop who'd accompany him. "Let's get to work and try to find out who did shoot him."

They went through the corridors with drawn revolvers. Walker led the way. He went in a roundabout way back to the passage where he had chased the porter. When they came to the unlighted corridors, he let the cop lead the way with his torch. They found the basement room where the Schmidt and Schindler garbage cans were stored. It was full of cops.

"What's happened here?" Walker asked.

"Double murder," a harness cop replied. "Two colored porters shot dead in the icebox."

The cop accompanying Walker whistled softly. "Jesus Christ!" he exclaimed.

"Who's in charge?" Walker asked.

"A sergeant from homicide now," the harness cop replied. "But the big brass ain't far behind."

Walker ran upstairs and found the homicide sergeant trying to establish order in the back room.

"You're looking for the third porter," he greeted.

The sergeant eyed him with hostility. He resented precinct detectives butting in. "Who are you?" he asked.

Walker showed his badge. All right, he wasn't a precinct detective, the sergeant noted. So what? It didn't diminish his hostility.

"You know Brock?" Walker said.

"Yeah," the sergeant admitted grudgingly.

"He's my brother-in-law," Walker said.

Brock was another sergeant in homicide. His name worked like a card of admission. "That so?" the sergeant said. "Yeah, we're looking for him," he admitted.

"I found him shot in the basement of the building next door."

"Yeah? Dead?"

"Not yet. I had him sent to Bellevue."

"Good. Now we got an eyewitness. None of these jokers here want to admit knowing anything about it."

"He won't be much help," Walker said. "He's off his nut."

The sergeant grunted. "It's a nutty business."

Walker moved over to the refrigerator and opened the door and fiddled with the light switches, planting his fingerprints all around.

"Watch out! You're leaving fingerprints," the sergeant warned.

Walker snatched his hand away. "I doubt if they'll figure with all these people around."

"They sure won't if you keep smearing yours over all the others," the sergeant said. Then suddenly he grinned. "Don't mind me, just be careful is all."

Walker grinned back.

7

NOW IT WAS II A.M.

Big hard flakes of snow drifted from a low gray sky, diminishing visibility. Traffic crawled through the streets. But nothing had changed. In all the places in the city where crimes had not been committed during the night, business went on as usual.

The circus performed by the police and the citizens was just about over. This circus had been staged a thousand, a hundred thousand, a million or more times. It scarcely changed and almost never solved anything.

For a fleeting moment Sergeant Brock of homicide wondered why they did it, what did they expect to accomplish, whom did they expect to fool? The moment of doubt passed as quickly as it had come and he was a cop again, sworn to uphold the law and assigned to solve murders.

He was assisting Lieutenant Baker of the homicide department in the preliminary investigation which was the circus of his mind. There was a big silent young man from the D.A.'s office following them around and sitting in on all questioning, as was his duty. His sharp brown eyes behind rimless spectacles saw all but he said nothing. Lieutenant Baker conducted all the interrogations.

He had begun with the day porters, questioning them separately, seeking a shape to the life the murdered men had lived. It came out that Luke was a home man with a wife and eleven children and if he had a vice no one knew of it. Fat Sam was just the opposite. He lived with a big sloppy woman who looked quite like him and they spent most of their time boozing around bars and having street scenes. None admitted knowing anything about Jimmy.

The white men had been questioned next. As with one mind they all declared they didn't know the night porters; they were not acquainted with them. Of course they had seen them around but none admitted to ever seeing one of them off duty.

The waitresses were all white and they didn't know anything about anything. Although when they were asking about

Jimmy, Sergeant Brock distinctly heard a little blond waitress say, "He's cute." But when he looked at her she was looking away and didn't appear interested.

While the lieutenant was questioning the help who were being detained in the locker rooms, the assistant medical examiner arrived and pronounced the bodies of Luke Williams and Samuel Jenkins "dead on arrival." He filled in two tags with vital statistics provided by their S&S identity cards and when the bodies had been photographed, tagged the toes and had them taken to the morgue.

By then the place was swarming with Schmidt and Schindler superintendents, upsetting the fingerprint crew and setting Lieutenant Baker's teeth on edge with their gratuitous advice. Finally Lieutenant Baker herded them into the women's locker room—they refused to go into the men's—with the suggestion, "All right, gentlemen, stay here and have an orgy while we go on with our work." There was a lot of giggling but the lieutenant firmly shut the door and posted a guard.

The police had a few minutes of respite. The fingerprint men dusted all the surfaces in the pantry, lunchroom and basement and all the doorknobs and collected so many different prints they were appalled. That necessitated fingerprinting all of the help, including the superintendents.

While they were thus engaged, the three interrogators—Lieutenant Baker, Sergeant Brock and the assistant D.A.—went into the building next door where the wounded porter had been found, and questioned the superintendent and his helper, Joe. The superintendent told them of being informed of a burglar by his helper, of calling the precinct station, of the detective arriving almost immediately following his phone call. He had taken the detective to the basement and they had found the wounded porter in the Apex Company sewing room, lying unconscious in a pool of blood. He had recognized the S&S uniform the porter had been wearing and had realized instantly he wasn't a burglar. He had had to caution the detective about handling the wounded man so roughly. And then when the porter had regained consciousness, he had accused the detective of being the man who had shot him.

Both detectives assumed that blank, indrawn look of all police when a brother officer is accused of a crime. But they did not attempt to discredit the superintendent's statement. The assistant D.A. asked the superintendent to come to his office later and make a formal statement, which the superintendent agreed to do.

The helper's story was practically the same. He had heard someone in the basement and on investigation he had found the door to the sewing room locked. No, it was not usually locked at that time, he still had to mop the floor. No, there was nothing to steal but the sewing machines and they were bolted to the tables. He would have taken a look, he declared, but the super had told him to leave it alone while he called the police. He had been suspicious when the detective had arrived so quickly after the super had telephoned; the super had just finished telephoning and he was just coming from his office when the detective was hammering on the front door. No, he hadn't noticed anything strange about the detective other than he looked drunk, but that wasn't strange for a detective at that hour in the morning. No, he hadn't heard the porter accuse the detective of shooting him, he hadn't been there, he had gone to let in the patrol car cops and when he got back the porter looked unconscious just like he had left him.

The assistant D.A. told him he'd better come down to his office and make a formal statement too.

"At the same time with the super?" he asked.

"No," both the assistant D.A. and the superintendent said in unison.

On second thought the assistant D.A. asked him if he had heard any shooting previous to his discovery of someone in the sewing room. No, he hadn't heard anything that sounded like shooting. The superintendent remembered that the porter had said the detective still carried the gun, but on examination by the patrol car police the detective's pistol proved to have been unfired. No, they hadn't heard the porter make the accusation, he had told them about it.

"Well, that finishes us here," Lieutenant Baker said.

When they returned to the Schmidt and Schindler luncheonette they found a number of newspaper reporters collected in the cold on 37th Street, clamoring for the details of the murders. But first the lieutenant telephoned homicide and asked to have detective Walker report to him. Then he telephoned

Bellevue and ordered Jimmy transferred to the hospital ward of the county jail downtown. He was informed that the porter was still unconscious from loss of blood and that it would be dangerous to transfer him at the time.

"All right, as soon as you can," he said.

Finally he went outside and issued a statement to the press to the effect that the murders were a mystery and they had discovered no leads but expected to uncover some when the investigation moved into Harlem.

He ordered the help released from the locker rooms and rounded up his crew and left.

Authority was returned to the Schmidt and Schindler superintendents. Orders were issued thick and fast. The women were set to cleaning the already spotless counters. The men were put to cleaning the inside of the refrigerator where the porters had been murdered. All the shelves and containers were emptied and every scrap of food was put into the garbage. Then all the empty shelves and containers which were not discarded were scoured and rinsed with boiling water. The wooden, ribbed floor where the bodies had lain were scraped, scrubbed and washed down with scalding water spurting from a plastic hose. It was as though they were trying to wash away the deed itself.

Two police cars were stationed in the street to keep away the curious and the morbid and the regular sightseers who collect at the scene of a murder.

By eleven A.M. the murder had been expertized, efficiently, unemotionally, thoroughly, and as far as was discernible the slight pinprick on the skin of the city had closed and congealed.

8

LIEUTENANT BAKER had intended for the assistant D.A. to assist him in the interrogation of detective Walker and for Sergeant Brock to go up to Harlem and question the victims' relatives. But it didn't work out that way.

Brock asked to sit in on the questioning of Walker, who was his wife's brother. The lieutenant hadn't known this; he was embarrassed. But he consented for Brock to sit in.

"Just keep quiet is all," the assistant D.A. demanded.

Then Walker wasn't there. The lieutenant telephoned his house and when no one answered, telephoned the bureau of the special detail out of which Walker worked. But no one had seen or heard from him. So the lieutenant had broadcast a reader for him to be picked up. Then they sat down to wait.

"It's incredible to think a detective shot those men," the assistant D.A. said. "What possible motive could he have?"

The lieutenant sucked at his pipe and said nothing. The assistant D.A. looked pointedly at Brock. He seemed to be seeking confirmation of his own conclusion. Brock realized he was on a spot. But he refused to be drawn into prejudgment.

"Let's wait and hear what he has to say," he said.

Almost imperceptibly, the lieutenant nodded approval.

"I think they were killed by someone from Harlem," the assistant D.A. said. "Although that's just between us. Legally my mind is open."

Brock examined a blank spot on the wall.

Finally the lieutenant admitted, "It's a possibility we're going to look into."

"Maybe they belonged to some terrorist group and were executed for some reason or other, perhaps for refusing to bomb the luncheonette."

Both detectives looked at him.

"It does sound foolish," he admitted. "But this is a foolish business."

"It is that," the lieutenant agreed wholeheartedly.

They were saved from further discussion by the arrival of detective Walker.

Walker wore the same clothes he had worn all night. His face was redder and his eyes were red-rimmed. He gave Brock an accusing look but nodded dutifully, then turned toward the lieutenant and asked, "You want to talk here?"

A uniformed cop who had entered with Walker placed a chair for him facing the lieutenant's desk.

"Sit down, Walker," the lieutenant said.

A stenographer came in with a notebook and stylo and took a seat at the end of the desk. The assistant D.A. sat flanking the lieutenant on the other side. Brock sat apart.

"Tell us all you remember about last night," the lieutenant ordered Walker. "And don't leave anything out."

"Only the commissioner has the right to cross-examine me," Walker said but he was pleasant enough.

"In most instances," the lieutenant agreed. "But in this instance you have been accused of homicide and that's in our province."

Walker smiled. "Right, Lieutenant, I have no objections."

He leaned back in his chair and closed his eyes and began to speak. "As you know, my tour of duty is from eight to four in the Times Square district. I deal chiefly with prostitutes and pickpockets but occasionally there are shootings and robberies in the district—"

"You're on a special assignment?" the assistant D.A. asked.

Walker looked at him and smiled. He appeared rather boyish. "Not exactly," he replied. "It was formerly called the vice squad. Now we're just ordinary detectives, based in the central police station."

He paused to see if the assistant D.A. was satisfied and the lieutenant said, "Go on."

"Last night, shortly before going off duty, I took a final check on the Broadway Automat to see if there were any wanteds inside or any prostitutes working. There wasn't anybody in there but bums—"

"How could you tell?" the assistant D.A. asked.

Walker looked at him again but this time he didn't smile. "Bums look like bums," he said flatly. "What else you expect them to look like?"

"Go on," the lieutenant said shortly.

"When I came out I saw a prostitute running toward me—that was south—from 47th Street." He looked at the assistant D.A. defiantly and said, "I knew she was a prostitute because she looked like a prostitute."

The lieutenant gave an almost imperceptible nod.

"A big man in a dark overcoat without any hat was chasing her. I cut in front of her and seized her, then I moved to seize the man. But I saw he had an open knife in his hand and I let go the woman to stop him. He tried to get around me to get at the woman and I had to sap him to subdue him."

"You struck him with your pistol?" the assistant D.A. asked. Everyone looked at him, all of them wondering what he was trying to get at.

"I sapped him with my sap," Walker said shortly. "He fell to the ground and when I looked around for the prostitute she was running around the end of the old Times building headed down Broadway toward 42nd Street. I knew I'd never catch her on foot and I couldn't leave the man lying in the street so I ran around the corner on 46th Street and got my car and stopped to put the man in the back and then went after her."

"Did you have an official car?" the lieutenant asked.

"It was my own personal car," Walker said.

"What kind of car?"

"A Buick Riviera."

"That's a lot of car for a detective first grade," the lieutenant remarked.

"It's my money," Walker flared.

"He's a bachelor," Brock intervened.

"Go on," the lieutenant said mildly.

"I didn't see her in either direction on 42nd Street so I drove on down Broadway to 34th Street without seeing a single living soul. I turned in Herald Square and came back up Sixth Avenue to 42nd Street again—"

"What was happening to your prisoner?" the lieutenant interrupted.

"He was still out—"

"It didn't worry you?"

"I didn't stop to think. I wanted to find that whore—"

"Why the urgency? What was the charge?"

"Oh, I forgot to tell you. He said she had robbed him."

The lieutenant nodded.

"I turned over to Fifth Avenue, still without seeing a soul, and again I drove down to 34th Street—"

"Hadn't it occurred to you she might have gone into a house by then?" the assistant D.A. asked.

"She could have," Walker admitted. "But I wasn't thinking." Again all three officials looked at him sharply. "I just wanted to catch that thieving whore." The bright red spots stood out on Walker's cheeks and his eyes began looking wild.

The lieutenant and the assistant D.A. regarded him curiously, but Brock looked away in embarrassment.

The next instant Walker had gotten himself under control and by way of explanation for his outburst said, "I don't like the hookers; it seems unjust for a prostitute to steal a sucker's money when he intends to pay her."

The homicide men were not impressed by his opinion, and the assistant D.A. didn't quite understand. But they all passed it.

"Anyway, I turned again on 34th Street over to Madison," Walker continued. "I was going north on Madison when I saw this woman coming south from the direction of 42nd Street. She must have seen my car at the same time for she ran around the corner on 36th Street heading toward Fifth Avenue. It's an eastbound street—36th—and I couldn't drive into it—"

"Why not?" the lieutenant asked. "There was no traffic about and you were on police business."

"I wasn't thinking," Walker said. "I just parked on Madison at the corner and got out and ran after her. I had to cross Madison and just as I turned into 36th Street she ran up the steps of a house way down the block and disappeared. When I got there the entrance was locked. I tried to find some way into the back entrance but all those houses are adjoining—"

"Did you take the number of the house?" the lieutenant asked.

"No, but I—"

"Where is the house in relation to the building on the corner where the porter was found wounded?"

"I think it's the second house—"

"You *think*?"

"It was the second house," Walker flared.

For a moment no one spoke, then the lieutenant said mildly, "Go on."

Walker seemed to be getting his thoughts together. Finally he said, "That was when I saw the Negro."

A pregnant silence followed. All three regarded him with steady speculation.

"What Negro?" the lieutenant asked softly.

Walker shrugged. "I don't know. I heard someone behind me and there was a Negro coming toward me—"

"Which direction had you been facing?"

"Madison. The Negro came from toward Fifth—"

"From the direction of the building on the corner?"

"Yes. My first thought was that he was a prowler—"

"Why?" the lieutenant asked.

"Why what?" Walker was genuinely puzzled.

"What made you think he was a prowler?"

"Oh, that. Hell, why else would a Negro be in that neighborhood?"

"There are Negro janitors and porters and some might even live there."

"This one was a porter."

Again there was a pregnant silence. But no one broke it.

"When I moved to apprehend him," Walker continued, "he said if I was a policeman I was just the man he was looking for. He said there was a burglar hiding in the basement of the corner building. It was then I noticed he was wearing a Schmidt and Schindler porter's uniform—"

"You hadn't noticed before?"

"There hadn't been any before. I had just seen the Negro." Walker seemed to wait for another question.

But all the lieutenant said was, "Go on, you had just seen that the Negro was wearing a uniform."

Walker gave him a searching look, but he was well under control. "I asked him for some identification and he produced a Schmidt and Schindler worker's identity card," he continued. "He said the burglar had first been discovered in the Schmidt and Schindler luncheonette on 37th Street and had escaped through the basement—"

"What did this Negro look like?" the lieutenant asked.

"Look like? Like a Negro, what was he supposed to look like?"

"Was he tall, short, fat, slim?" the lieutenant questioned patiently. "Black, yellow, brown? Young, old, middle-aged?"

"I didn't notice, he just looked like a Negro. I didn't study him. If I was going to catch this burglar I didn't have much time—"

"That's not much to go on," the lieutenant said mildly.

"Well, I remember seeing the name *Wilson* on his identity card—"

"Have a reader put out for a Negro Schmidt and Schindler porter named Wilson," the lieutenant directed the stenographer, who sat scribbling at the end of his desk. The stenographer started to get up, but the lieutenant said, "Not now. Just make a note of it. Or a Negro named Wilson masquerading as a porter."

"Yes sir."

"Go on," he said to Walker.

"I went with the Negro to the entrance of the building on Fifth Avenue. There was a charwoman scrubbing the front hall floor. I knocked. She was so stupid it took me some time to get across to her that I was a detective. She went for the superintendent and when I looked around, the Negro had disappeared."

"You didn't look for him?"

"No, I figured he had gone back to the Schmidt and Schindler luncheonette. And then the janitor's helper in the building came staggering to the door with the keys and acting all suspicious because the superintendent had just telephoned for the police and I had arrived too soon."

"You told him that the Schmidt and Schindler porter had brought you?"

"I told him nothing. He was just a stupid wino and it would have probably taken him all night to figure it out."

The lieutenant gave an almost imperceptible nod. Walker glanced at him suspiciously.

"You told the superintendent about your informant?"

"He didn't ask. I just followed him down to the basement where they thought the burglar was hiding."

"Instead, you found another Negro Schmidt and Schindler porter," the lieutenant supplied. "This one was wounded."

"That's right."

"And he accused you to your face of shooting him?"

"That's right."

"How do you account for that?" the assistant D.A. asked.

Walker looked at him. Slowly he spread his hands. His breath came out in a sigh. "I don't know," he confessed. "It'll take a psychiatrist to figure it out. That's why I had him sent to Bellevue." He paused in thought for a moment. "The way I figure it, I was the first person he saw on regaining consciousness and he thought I was the one who had shot him. Or maybe he didn't even think about it, maybe the image of the one who had shot him was still in his mind—he went out seeing it and came to imagining he was seeing the same one—his mind didn't allow for the time gap. Or maybe he was just having hallucinations. Maybe he never saw the one who shot him—"

"He was shot from in front," the lieutenant said.

"Anyway, I couldn't have shot him unless I was two people. At the time he was shot I had a prisoner in my car and I was chasing this whore who I'm sure knows me—by sight anyway."

"We'll find the prostitute all right," the lieutenant said. "But you haven't told us what you did with the man."

"I haven't got to it."

"All right, go ahead."

"Just a minute," the assistant D.A. said. "You think then that the wounded porter was delirious?"

"Definitely. The man who shot him was probably a Negro too."

"Then the Negro porter you met on the street—the informant—might very likely be the murderer himself?" the lieutenant suggested.

"Very likely," Walker said. "At least I think so now."

"But it didn't occur to you at the time?"

"I wasn't thinking and I didn't know about the murders until afterwards."

"Did you look at the bodies?"

"I was going to, but the sergeant in command stopped me."

"Ump!" the lieutenant grunted. "Well now, let's get on to your prisoner."

"I had gone next door to the Schmidt and Schindler luncheonette and had found the men from homicide there, and that was how I learned about the murders. The sergeant cautioned me about leaving fingerprints—"

"Yes, they found your prints all over."

"That's what he said, I was leaving them all over. Then suddenly I remembered my car and prisoner—"

"What made you remember them all of a sudden?"

"How the hell do I know? I just remembered them, that was all. I went down 37th Street to Madison and when I looked for my car across the street at the corner of 36th Street it was gone and the prisoner was gone. I felt like I was going crazy and having hallucinations myself. I'd lost the whore, I'd been accused of shooting a strange Negro, I'd lost my prisoner and my car—"

"You'd also lost the Negro porter who had informed you of the burglary," the lieutenant reminded him.

"Yes, him too. I called in and reported my car stolen—you can check for yourself—"

"I believe you."

"I didn't mention the prisoner because I hadn't taken his name. Then I went back to the lunchroom to tell about the Negro I'd met on the street, or maybe find him if he was there. But all of you were interrogating the superintendent in the other building and the homicide men wouldn't let me enter—"

"Why didn't you come around to the other building and ask for us?"

"I didn't think."

The lieutenant gave him a long, critical look. "For a first-grade detective you don't seem to have your thoughts very well organized," he said.

Suddenly Walker wilted, he cupped his burning face in his hands. "It's been a rough night," he confessed.

He's been drinking heavily, the lieutenant thought, and Sergeant Brock, his brother-in-law, thought, He's blind drunk, but he doesn't show it.

"All right," the lieutenant said, not unkindly, "some time today take a look at the colored workers in the restaurant and try to spot your man, and if you don't see him there take a look at the bodies of the two murdered porters in the morgue and see if either of them is the one."

Walker composed himself and straightened up. "May I go now?"

"Take a seat out in the hall until the stenographer transcribes his copy. Then you can come in and read it and sign it and I'll witness it. Okay?"

"Then go and get some sleep," Brock said.

He and the lieutenant looked across at one another as Walker left the room.

9

IT WAS 3 P.M. and it had stopped snowing but fog was closing in. The upper stories of the midtown skyscrapers had disappeared as though being slowly swallowed by the cephalopodan sky. The brightly lighted storefronts were scattered oases in the gloom, faintly luminous, and car lights of the congested traffic made a slowly spinning pageantry, vaguely seen. Pedestrians walked with care.

New York City.

Already the snow removers were out on Fifth Avenue and gloved and overcoated laborers were shoveling piles of snow from the sidewalks into waiting trucks.

As Brock drove slowly in the stream of northbound traffic he had a fleeting image of a city in the stomach of a cloud. It was a clean and peaceful and orderly city being slowly consumed.

But when he came into Harlem at 110th Street and turned west on 113th Street the image suddenly changed, and now it was the image of a city already consumed with only bits of brick and mortar left to remind one that there had ever been a city.

Brock wasn't given to imagination and he felt as though his mind was playing tricks on him. He realized, of course, his mind was making a block to keep him from thinking about Walker. But he was too old and tough a cop to feel that he had to think about Walker now. There would be plenty of time after all the facts were in to begin thinking about Walker. Now was the time to try to find a motive.

Meanwhile as he drove down the slum street he was assailed with a feeling of disgust. At least they could clean the goddamned streets, he thought as his car skidded from side to side over weeks' accumulation of snow.

The crosstown streets in Harlem which did not serve through traffic or bus lines were seldom cleaned of snow all winter, and piles of frozen garbage now covered with a mantel of snow lay along the curbs.

Brock firmly closed his mind.

Already news of the murders had spread in Harlem and the few Negroes he saw on the street eyed him with hostility. He didn't let it worry him. He could take care of himself. Physically, he was a tremendous man built like a telephone booth and about the same size. He had a cube-shaped head with a weather-reddened face and small, colorless eyes that remained cold and inscrutable. He wore a look of joviality which did not show in his eyes at all.

The building in which Luke Williams had lived was a scabby tenement near Eighth Avenue, with the outside walls flaking away and a number of broken panes in evidence replaced with yellowing newspaper. Before entering he locked his car securely and cased the street.

The dark damp hallway was unlighted and the stink of urine and salted pork bones being cooked in too old cabbage hit him in the face. He hesitated an instant at the bottom of the stairs and debated whether he should draw his pistol. A black man could stand unseen in the dark and cut his head off.

Then he put the thought from his mind as ridiculous and started up the stairs. What was happening to him? he asked himself. This was the best policed, the richest, the most civilized city in the world, and here he was, a police detective sergeant of the Homicide Bureau, experiencing trepidation on entering this residence of supposedly law-abiding, respectable people—at least it had the approval of the city. He'd better get his thoughts straightened out, he told himself, and get his subconscious rid of Walker. It affected his whole point of view.

He stopped before the door of the third-floor-front apartment and knocked. The door was cracked on a chain and a dark-skinned woman with streaks of gray in her straightened hair peered at him. Suddenly her eyes filled with repugnance.

"I suppose you're from the police," she said in a flat, resigned voice. "After he was killed."

The last was like a curse. He fumbled for the leather folder holding his badge and tried to keep the guilty feeling from his voice, "Yes. Sergeant Brock. And you're Mrs. Williams. May I come in? I have to ask you a few questions about your husband."

Silently she unchained the door and opened it. He quickly noticed she was a big woman, big-boned, with distinct African features. She looked very strong. There was more bitterness in her expression than grief.

She wore a black cardigan over a long, blue woolen dress and the backs of her hands were almost the same color as her sweater.

Then his quick glance surveyed the room. In the center was a large oval table holding an ashtray and table lamp and surrounded by a number of straight-backed chairs in various stages of repair. To one side stood a potbellied coal stove on a tin plate flanked by a worn, grease-slicked armchair. Luke's chair, he supposed. On the other a double bed covered with a maroon cotton chenille spread was pushed into the corner.

The black faces of many wide-eyed children peering around the frame of an inside door looked like a stack of disembodied heads. Their mother went over and closed the door in their faces, still without speaking, and then came back and turned on the table lamp.

"Sit you down, sir," she bade the detective, and seated herself on the edge of the bed.

Brock sat on a straight-backed chair and put his hat on the table and took out his notebook and stylo. He looked at her. The whites of her brown eyes were clear with no hint that she had been crying. She sat erect with her hands in her lap. She seemed bitterly resigned as though she had transferred the burden of her grief and worry to someone else.

There was no need of any preparatory talk. She had heard of Luke's murder on the one o'clock news broadcast and she had telephoned his sister and asked her to go down to the morgue and identify the body. She had gone to the PS and brought the younger children home and that's as far as she had got. She supposed someone from the company would come up to see her later. And she hadn't heard anything from the three older ones. Her eldest, a nineteen-year-old girl, worked as a sales girl in the 72nd Street Automat and she would be at work. She must have heard about it, but she hadn't telephoned. She didn't have a telephone herself, and had to use Mrs. Soames' next door. Her eighteen-year-old son was in the army at a camp in Augusta, Georgia, and she didn't know whether he had heard or not. But he would be coming home to help her soon as he heard. And her seventeen-year-old son —she didn't know where he was, just somewhere in Harlem. He and his father had never got along and she didn't know what he would do; she had heard he was living with a woman.

"Can you think of any connection he might have had with the murders?" Brock asked with his stylo poised. "Anything, a chance remark, a seemingly innocent question, anything?"

"Lord, no, he's not a mean boy, just wild. Once he got away from here I doubt if he's ever thought of his father."

"I'll take his name anyway."

"Melvin Douglas."

They had eight younger children and all were living at home and went to school.

"We have four rooms," she said in reply to Brock's look. "It's crowded but we managed."

Their fifteen-year-old son slept in the kitchen and the four girls had one bedroom and the three boys had the other. The youngest still slept in a crib and she and Luke had slept in there in the sitting room, where they all ate, too, when they ate together.

They had come from Marion, Georgia, right after they'd been married, twenty years ago. Luke had come back for her after he'd got his job with Schmidt and Schindler and all their children had been born in Harlem. He had been a good father and a good provider, although she had done day work from time to time, still did, but she'd never had to. He had never done anything really bad in his life, she would swear to it on her mother's grave. Of course she knew he'd been going to see another woman during the past three years, after she had given birth to her eleventh, but that was just male nature.

"Do you know who this woman is?"

"Sure, her name is Beatrice King, she belongs to the same church we do, the Church of God in Christ on 116th Street, but she ain't got nothing to do with this, I'm sure. She's a widow and she's not mean, she just frisky."

He wrote down the name and asked curiously, "Aren't you ever pinched for money? Luke didn't earn enough from his salary to take care of all of you."

"'Course, after all the children came, naturally we been hard up for money, like all colored people are, but Luke makes —made—more than twice as much as he did when we got married."

The children helped each other. They trusted in the Lord. But she didn't know what they were going to do now.

"Luke had some life insurance?"

"I suppose so. With the company."

The company was their father, only next to God, Brock understood.

Brock was very seldom depressed. A sergeant on homicide couldn't afford to have emotions. But when he left Mrs. Williams and walked down the dark stinking stairs out into the narrow dirty street, he was shaken. He had the feeling that something had gone wrong somewhere. Maybe it had happened just last night or maybe it had happened a long time ago. But somewhere the whole mechanism of the American way of life had slipped a cog, or maybe it was the heart. The heart had missed a beat and had never caught up.

Well, there was nothing he could do about it, he told himself.

He drove north on Eighth Avenue to an address near 144th Street and climbed to the fifth floor. He knocked at the door of what was listed as a kitchenette on the mailbox in the entrance.

A big sloppy light-complexioned woman in a flannel wrapper flung open the door. Her recently straightened hair was in curlers and smelled like a singed pig. Her breath smelled of gin. He looked quickly past her and saw the dirty, unmade bed with two pillows which had large black grease spots where greasy heads had rested.

"Mrs. Jenkins?" he asked.

"No, I'm Gussie, there ain't no Mrs. Jenkins. Why, you from the police?"

Suddenly he felt better, less guilty. He could think of no reason he should feel less guilty on finding a hurt bad colored woman than on finding a hurt good colored woman, but there it was. He felt more at ease. He flashed his badge.

"Lord, what's that man done now?" Gussie asked theatrically. "You got him in jail? He should have been here hours ago."

"He hasn't done anything we know of," Brock said. "But get himself killed."

She flung up her hands automatically, in the gesture of the scandalized, prepared to be scandalized at whatever he had done. It was the traditional attitude. Colored women appear scandalized before the white man at anything bad their men have done. Suddenly she froze, went rigid, in a grotesque posture like a petrified clown. Her light skin paled, her full-blown face sagged with shock. She looked suddenly twenty years older.

"Killed?" Her voice had sunk to a whisper.

"I'm afraid so."

"Whoever'd want to kill Sam? He wouldn't hurt nobody. He wasn't nothing but talk."

"That's what we're trying to find out. May I come in?"

She opened the door wider. "'Scuse me, I been jarred out of my manners. Was he stabbed?"

He entered the one room and looked about for a place to sit. There was a square wooden table across from the bed, flanked with two overstuffed armchairs, and two straight-backed chairs beside the bed, but all contained articles of clothing and soiled dishes. She removed the clothes from one of the armchairs beside the table and he sat down and put his hat on the table and she sat on the bed facing him. He wondered briefly if there was any reason these women sat on their beds, but quickly dismissed the thought.

"Just tell me in your own words all you knew about Sam Jenkins," he commenced.

All she knew about Fat Sam did not supply him with the slightest motive of why he had been shot. She had met him in a bar where she had been working as barmaid five years before and she'd been living with him ever since. He was a jolly man who liked his liquor and his fun, and that had suited her fine. For the past three years she hadn't been working; he had earned enough to support them both.

Brock got the idea that she did a little hustling on the side, but he doubted if Fat Sam had known, or whether he would have cared.

She seemed certain that Fat Sam was not mixed up with any racket that would have caused him to be shot; first he was too lazy and secondly he didn't care about possessions. He had hit the numbers several times to her knowledge, once for enough to buy a car, but he had thrown his money away on liquor and good times. He had often told her when he died he didn't want to leave anything behind for someone else to enjoy.

"Did he steal from the company?" he asked just to have something to ask her.

"Not enough for anybody to really mind. He brought home a little food from time to time, ham hocks and the ends of roasts that were going in the garbage anyway. 'Course it was against the rules but if anybody had ever suspected him they'd never said anything."

He got the picture of an amoral, petty-thieving Negro, the usual stereotype. She was the same. He didn't realize this was the reason he felt at ease with her.

When he got up to leave he said, "Well, thank you, Gussie."

"I hope I been some help."

"You've been of great help," he lied. "Would you like to go down to the morgue and identify his body, or does he have some relatives who would want to go?"

"I'll go. If he's got any relatives, I don't know 'em."

Next he drove to the apartment building at the corner of 149th Street and Broadway where Jimmy Johnson, the wounded porter, roomed. He parked before the entrance on 149th Street.

It was a six-story building of light-colored firebrick, in reasonably good repair. One look was enough to tell him that Negroes had not occupied it very long. The front steps and tiled floor of the front hall were clean and the glass panes of the front door were clean and unbroken. But a sprinkling of graffito already marred the light gray walls and a drawing of huge male genitals had been scratched on the elevator door.

It was an automatic elevator, slow, but it worked. He rode up to the fifth floor and knocked at the door of the apartment where Johnson roomed. The door was opened by a middle-aged West Indian who wore a perpetual frown. The West Indian introduced himself as Mr. Desilus and invited Brock to enter, stopping to lock all of the locks on the front door before showing Brock into a parlor that looked out on Broadway.

They were joined immediately by Mrs. Desilus, a very proper dark-skinned woman wearing a black satin dress that reached to her ankles and a glossy black pompadour, and their thirteen-year-old daughter, a bushy-haired girl named Sinette.

Without waiting to learn of Brock's errand, Mr. Desilus assumed the position of a persecuted man. "I'll not have it," he shouted. "We're respectable God-fearing people. I'll have to ask that young fellow to move. We can't have the police coming to our house. What will people think? What effect will it have on our young daughter here?"

Brock was confounded. First, he couldn't understand Mr. Desilus, who spoke with a pronounced accent; secondly, he didn't know where the daughter came into it. He had remained standing as he hadn't been asked to sit down, and now concluding that Mr. Desilus was more concerned about his reputation than the murders or his wounded roomer, he was ready to leave.

"I take it you've heard about the luncheonette murders?" he asked anyway.

Mr. Desilus gave him a pitying look. "We have a radio and a television set. We're not living in the backwoods here."

"Well, I won't bother you again," Brock promised. "But I have to ask you a few questions about your roomer, Johnson."

"I don't know anything about that young fellow, and I don't want to know," he said. "'Cepting he's always got his head buried in books."

"He goes to college," Sinette said.

"You speak when you're spoken to," her mother reprimanded.

"You better go talk to his girl friend," Mr. Desilus said, washing his hands of the whole business. "She lives on the third floor. She knows more about him than we do; we just gave the poor fellow a place to stay."

Brock stifled a sigh. "Will you give me her name then?"

"I don't know her name," Mr. Desilus said angrily.

Brock looked at him, wondering what he was so angry about.

"Linda Lou Collins," Sinette said, defying her mother. "She's a singer."

"Well, I'll go see Miss Collins," Brock said to Mr. Desilus, "if you'll just let me out."

Mr. Desilus led him to the door and as he was unlocking the many locks he muttered, "I'm going to put that boy out of my house."

Brock counted four locks, one with a bar attached to the floor.

"Don't do that, please, Mr. Desilus, I beg you," he said. "I'd hate to think I was the reason for him losing his room. He's perfectly innocent of any crime, I assure you. No censure will be attached to you in any event. And I'm sure your daughter has nothing to fear."

Sinette wouldn't have liked that last remark.

Mr. Desilus' frown certainly wasn't indicative of sympathy but he grudgingly consented to give the boy another chance, being as they were Christians.

"I thought you would," Brock said and started to add more, but thought it best to leave it at that.

He paused for a moment in the corridor outside the door, attracted by the sound of Mr. Desilus meticulously locking all four locks. Then he took the elevator down to the third floor.

No one answered Miss Collins' door. That was that. He got in his car and drove back to the Homicide Bureau. He had to do some thinking.

10

THE TURNKEY let her into the cell and locked the door behind her.

"Oh, daddy," she cried, half sobbing, her high heels beating a tattoo on the concrete floor as she went swiftly to his cot. "What are they doing to you?"

"Baby!" he exclaimed. "Oh, baby, I wondered when you'd come. It's been all of four days and I'm going crazy."

Her Persian lamb coat smelled of outdoors and damp perfume as she leaned over to kiss him. Her damp resilient lips fused against his dry chapped lips and her fingers dug desperately into his shoulders. Finally she drew back and looked at him. Their gazes locked and each felt the shock of sudden desire.

"Don't talk for a moment," she said. "Just let me look at you."

"You smell so good," he said. "They say the badder the woman the gooder she smell. You must be a bad, bad woman, baby."

The smile started around her mouth and spread quickly all over her face.

"I came and I came," she said, sighing, and sat sidewise on the cot, looking at him as though she couldn't believe he was alive. Her feet scuffled a newspaper which had fallen unnoticed to the floor. Suddenly she giggled. "Sounds naughty, doesn't it?"

He laughed. The morning light slanted through the barred window high up in the east wall, pearling the melted snowdrops on her black felt hat, and suddenly they were somewhere else, enclosed by love. A deep rose glow suffused her caramel-colored skin and her huge brown eyes glowed like liquid light.

"Linda, you sure are a beautiful girl."

"Hug me, hug me, then!"

"You'll have to do all the work," he said ruefully.

Frantically her quick strong fingers explored the outline of his body beneath the covers.

"Jimmy!" she exclaimed in a horrified voice. "Where are your arms?"

He grinned sheepishly. "They've put me in a straitjacket. They don't like me because I accused one of their white detectives of shooting me. They say I'm crazy."

A shadow came over her face. "The dirty bastards," she said but she sounded insincere.

He tried to catch her gaze but she looked away. "You think so too, don't you?"

Instead of replying she jumped to her feet and slipped out of her coat. Her broad-shouldered, narrow-hipped body with low pointed breasts was dramatized by a turtleneck sweater-dress of tan cashmere. Flinging the coat across the foot of the cot, she leaned over quickly and kissed him again, then sat on the edge of the cot but avoided his gaze.

"So that's why they let me see you without a guard?"

"Because you think I'm crazy too?"

"Don't be silly. The straitjacket."

"Oh, that. No one's been allowed to see me except the district attorney and a bunch of cops."

She turned and smiled at him again, postponing what she'd intended to say. "You're all right now?"

"I'm fine as can be expected, just locked up and can't move is all, like the way they say to keep a woman faithful."

"God, I was frantic when I'd heard you were shot!" she exclaimed, shuddering involuntarily. "I was dead asleep and Sinette kept banging on the door until I answered and she said you were dying in Bellevue. They'd just got it over the radio."

He grinned cynically. "I suppose Mr. Desilus had conniptions worrying about his reputation."

"Sinette was worried about you. Are you sure you're all right?"

"It's just a flesh wound, the one in the chest. I had lost a lot of blood is all. The others were just scratches."

"God, it must have been awful."

"Don't let anybody ever tell you they weren't scared when they were being shot at. You don't know, baby, you don't know."

She shivered.

"Are you cold?"

"Just scared," she confessed.

"Anyway, I'm still alive."

"Let's count our blessings."

"Bullshit," he said. "Just kiss me and you'll feel warmer."

She leaned over again and kissed him.

"Feel warmer?"

She glanced at him through the corners of her eyes and laughed.

"If I could use my arms I'd hug you and that'd make you warmer still," he said, but it didn't have the intended effect.

Her face clouded again.

"Daddy, why did you do it?"

"Do what?"

She picked up the newspaper that had dropped to the floor and held it spread out before him. The front page carried a banner headline: WOUNDED PORTER FINGERS VICE COP AS LUNCHEONETTE KILLER.

He looked at the headline woodenly. "So the papers finally got it. That'll get the lead out of their pants."

"Now you've made everybody mad," she said accusingly.

"If they're mad, then goddamn them!" he cried angrily. "No one wants to believe my story. I told them the truth: A goddamn drunken crazy cop murders two porters and tries to murder me too and I'm not supposed to talk about it because he's white and it might prejudice the civil rights movement. They've got me locked up as though I'm the crazy one, while the maniac runs free. Let them be mad. If they get mad enough maybe they'll try to get at the truth instead of trying to shut me up."

She looked at him with pity and distress. "They are investigating, daddy, they're doing all they can—"

"So they've been brainwashing you too?"

She was hurt. "Believe me, Jimmy, the district attorney and the commissioner and everyone's on your side."

"I haven't got any side," he raved, squirming beneath the covers as though trying to free himself. "I've got a hole in my front side where that maniac shot me."

"They want to find the killer as badly as you do," she went on, trying to keep calm.

"I told them who the killer was."

"But they don't have any evidence. It's just your word against his. They can't take it to court without more evidence."

"They don't want any evidence."

"He told them another story and they can't prove—"

"I know what he told them," he interrupted rudely. "They read me his statement. He said he was looking for a whore, some whore he'd arrested in Times Square. He claims she got away from him and he was looking for her way down on 36th Street—as if she had wings—when all of a sudden a colored man dressed like a Schmidt and Schindler porter—get that now—another colored Schmidt and Schindler porter appeared out of thin air and told him about a burglar in the basement of the commercial building on the corner. Another Schmidt and Schindler porter—colored porter. He had already murdered two, and had chased me into the basement of that building, and the fourth colored Schmidt and Schindler porter, whom nobody has ever seen before or since, suddenly appears and tells him about a burglar. Do you believe that shit?"

"They know he's lying, Jimmy honey," she said in a soothing voice. "The district attorney told me that—"

"Then why don't they arrest him?"

"They know he's lying but they can't prove he's involved in the murders."

"The hell they can't! The garbage man told them what Luke told him and me about the drunken white detective he'd sent inside to talk to Fat Sam. He ain't got no reason to lie. He doesn't even work for the city; Schmidt and Schindler uses a private garbage-collection company."

"They admit his story is credible," she said. "But he didn't see the detective—he just had Luke's word for it—and Luke is dead."

"What the hell! Do they think there were two drunken white detectives wandering around in the area at that time of morning?"

"I told you, daddy, they believe he was inside the restaurant. They believe that part of your story—"

"Thank them for nothing."

"But they haven't got any proof. Didn't anyone else see him. Both the window washer and the milk truck driver and everybody said they didn't see anyone or hear any shooting."

"They told you an awful goddamn lot. Did they tell you about his fingerprints. They didn't find his fingerprints, I suppose. And what about the garbage cans? What about the bullets that landed in the wall? Ballistics will show what pistol they were fired from."

"They haven't found the pistol; they don't even have any record of the pistol the bullets came from."

"Now goddammit they're going to say there wasn't any pistol, much less a white murderer. I suppose they're going to say the bullets came from an unknown source!"

"And they did find his fingerprints," she went on doggedly. "But he'd been all over the restaurant after you and the—the others were found and he'd left his fingerprints all over everything. I mean when he was in there then."

"Goddamn right! He was alibi-ing for the fingerprints he'd left there when he'd committed the murders—"

"Jimmy darling, listen. They admit your story could be true. They say if it isn't true it shows a vivid and logical imagination. What they think—"

"I know what they think! They think I'm crazy! At least that's what they want everybody else to think."

"No, they don't, honey. I know they don't. I've talked to them—the district attorney and the commissioner and the inspectors and all of them. They don't think you're crazy at all. The district attorney has been in touch with Durham since the first day. He's had your entire past investigated. He's talked with the chief of police and the sheriff and the president of North Carolina College. He knows you graduated with honors. He's talked with your mother and sister in Durham. He knows your sister works in the bank of the North Carolina Mutual Insurance Company—he even knows it's the biggest Negro-owned insurance company in the world. He says there's hardly a white student in Harvard who wouldn't envy your clean record. He even knows that you chose to come to New York and enroll in the law school at Columbia University rather than try to force your way into the white university at Chapel Hill and cause your family a lot of grief and worry. They've even got a statement from your old boss out at the Chesterfield factory—he said he'd take your sworn word against that of all the detectives in New York City. They know all about your studies at Columbia and where you've lived and what you've done since you came to New York. And the Schmidt and Schindler Company is behind you one hundred percent. Don't you think for a minute that anyone believes you're crazy."

"I suppose this isn't a straitjacket they've got me wrapped up in. I suppose I'm just lying here with my arms folded because I don't want to hug you."

"Listen, honey, Jimmy, they want to help you. I know. I'm not easy to fool. You know yourself I never get taken in by what white people say unless I know they're sincere. It isn't that. What they think is that you've got it in for him and are trying to frame him—maybe he did something when he was in the restaurant the first time that made you want to frame him for the murders—"

"They think I committed the murders and shot myself and I'm trying to frame him for it? Is that it?"

"—did something to hurt you in some kind of way," she went on.

"Goddamn right he did! He shot me and tried to kill me."

"I mean what they think is, if he isn't the murderer, then what have you got against him personally?"

"Listen, when he started shooting at me, I didn't even know that he'd already killed Luke and Fat Sam. All I knew he was trying to kill me and I didn't have time to think of anything else. All I accused him of at first was shooting at me."

"They know that too. That's what they can't understand. The superintendent of the other building said that when you came to, the first thing you did was accuse him of shooting you. He said you told him positively that the detective had shot you and that you appeared to him to be in your right senses and know exactly what you were saying. That's what puzzles them."

"Goddamn right! I'm shot by a killer and when I point out the killer who shot me, they're puzzled. What the hell am I supposed to say? That I haven't even been shot? That I was just running through all those basements for my health and then I lay down on the floor and a hole burst open in my chest and the blood started leaking out? Is that what they want me to say?"

"They don't want you to say anything public at this time. All you're doing by talking to the newspapers is making sympathy for him."

"I haven't talked to any newspapers."

"They're saying that maybe you've got a persecution complex."

"Goddamn right! Anytime a Negro accuses a white man of injuring him in any way, the first thing they say is he's got a persecution complex. He's blaming it on the power structure. Bullshit! I suppose it was a persecution complex that got old Luke and Fat Sam shot full of holes."

Sweat had beaded on her upper lip from her effort to reason with him, and her eyes were beginning to look sick.

"Jimmy, daddy, honey, do something for me," she begged. "You know I wouldn't ask you to do anything dishonorable. If I didn't know it was for your own good—"

He saw it coming and tried to head it off. "Linda baby, you believe me, don't you?"

"Of course I believe you, daddy." He saw the doubt in her averted gaze. "Of course I believe you. It isn't that—" He saw the lines of exasperation crease her tight moist brow. "But why would he want to kill all of you? Especially you? You say you hadn't even talked to him, hadn't even seen him. . . ."

He saw the doubt harden into disbelief. He felt crushed inside. Now no one believed him.

"You want me to tell you why he did it?" he asked in a flat, toneless voice.

She looked up quickly with hope in her eyes.

"I don't know why," he said. "He just did it. That's all I know."

The hope went out of her eyes.

"I don't suppose you'll do it, but I wish you would," she said hopelessly. "For your own good, daddy."

"Do what, Linda?"

"Take it back."

He hadn't expected her to ask that. It felt like a sneak punch in the guts. "You mean tell the newspapers what I said about the detective isn't true?"

"You don't have to go that far. You can just give them a statement that you didn't mean it the way they put it. You can say the detective is lying about not being in the restaurant before the murders—"

"But I told you, baby, I haven't talked to any newspapers. They got the story from someone else. No one's been allowed to see me but you."

"But you'll be allowed to see the reporters now."

"If I say the story isn't true?"

She didn't reply immediately.

"Did they ask you to get me to do that?" he pressed her. "The district attorney and the commissioner and the others?"

"Not exactly. They just explained how it would make it easier for them to catch the real killer if you don't—didn't—start off smearing the police department. I mean if you just wouldn't make a positive accusation—if you would just leave room for doubt. Even if he shot at you—"

"Even *if* he did?"

"Well, then, he did shoot at you. But you don't know for an absolute certainty that he murdered Luke and Fat Sam."

"No, not any more than I know that I'm lying here."

"Don't you see, honey, if they let him go, he'll do something to trip himself up—"

"Such as kill me."

"—otherwise they might never get the proof."

He lay looking at her through dull eyes, unable to move.

"Won't you do it, honey?"

"Not as long as I am black."

"We've got to work with them, honey; they're our only hope, even if they are white—"

"I'm going to keep on saying the son of a bitch shot me and murdered Luke and Fat Sam until I am dead," he said.

II

JIMMY WAS dressed and waiting when the lawyer was shown into his cell.

"I'm Mr. Hanson," said the slim young man, pink-cheeked and dapper in a Homburg and a Chesterfield overcoat. "I'm from the legal firm that represents Schmidt and Schindler. I've arranged for your release."

Shaking hands, Jimmy looked big and country in his duffel coat and snapbrim hat beside this small neat figure.

"Yes sir, that's what the jailer told me."

Hanson looked curiously about the cell. All this was new to him: prison cells and violent men. His firm handled only civil cases. He looked back at the big solemn Negro. They're a lost people, he thought.

"How do you feel, Jim? Does the wound trouble you still?"

"No sir, I just want to get out of here."

Hanson smiled understandingly. "I can appreciate that."

They left the cell and followed the turnkey through cell blocks of meddlesome prisoners, arriving at the guards' room. Hanson presented some papers to the chief warder which got the barred gates opened.

Outside, Jimmy asked, "What's my status, Mr. Hanson? Am I out on bail, or what?"

"You're free, Jim. No bail, no restrictions. You can go and come as you please. However, you mustn't leave town."

"I'm not thinking of that."

They took an express elevator and rode down in silence, then pushed their way through the crowded corridor toward the westside doorways.

"Are you going home now?" Hanson asked.

"I think I'll stop by the store on my way uptown and let them know I'll be back tonight."

"No, no, don't do that," Hanson advised. "Just report on duty at nine o'clock as usual. But if I were you, I would take several days off, a week or more. Perhaps it would be better if you remained home until your wounds are completely healed. Your pay continues as usual."

"Well, in that case I think I will," Jimmy said gratefully. "I want to catch up on my studies."

"Do that then."

They came out on the broad concrete steps facing the square. Below, taxis were lined along the curb and cars streamed past, worming down the stone canyons beneath an overcast sky. People streamed past them, entering and leaving the court building. It was a busy hour of morning; traffic court was in session.

"If you have any trouble, Jim, resulting from this affair, come directly to me," Hanson suggested, giving Jimmy his card. "Don't discuss it with anyone before talking to me. And I'd further suggest that you don't discuss this affair at all. Okay?"

"Okay," Jimmy said.

While they were shaking hands, Jimmy stiffened. Blood drained from his face, leaving it putty gray. Suddenly in the crowd on the sidewalk below, a face stood out he'd never forget.

Walker was standing to the right of the steps in the stream of pedestrian traffic, his trench coat flaring open in the wind and both hands stuck into his pockets, staring up at Jimmy through opaque blue eyes. This was the way Jimmy had first seen him, impassive, unspeaking, seemingly without thought or emotion; the difference was that then he had been looking down at him with a drawn revolver in his right hand, and an instant later, without one word being spoken, there had been the first silenced shot and the open look at death.

He shuddered involuntarily.

Hanson whirled about, following his terrified gaze, and saw a man standing on the sidewalk. The man looked as dangerous as a man can look.

"Oh, that's Walker, the detective you—" He broke off.

"Yes sir, that's him. I'd remember him in hell."

He looked back at Jimmy's stricken face.

"I wouldn't be frightened of him, if I were you," he said calmly.

"No sir," Jimmy agreed. "I wouldn't if I were you either. He didn't try to kill you."

Hanson frowned. "I can't discuss that. But my advice to you is to ignore him, don't give any attention to what he might say or do; and keep away from him. The police have him under surveillance. They know what they are doing."

"I sure hope so," Jimmy said. "That's all I want to do, I promise you, keep away from him as far as possible. But I'd feel easier if he was locked up."

"That might happen yet," Hanson said. "But in the meantime, don't let him worry you. He has no authority to approach you; he has been suspended during the period of the investigation."

"Well," Jimmy said slowly, "that doesn't help me much."

Hanson appeared embarrassed. He didn't know what to say. It wasn't as if Negroes were like other people. You had to give them special assurances, and he had already given all the assurances he could give.

Jimmy noticed his embarrassment and said, "Well, I guess I'll be going." But he hesitated as though afraid to go alone.

Hanson took out his wallet and extracted a five-dollar bill. "Here, you'd better take a taxi."

Jimmy shook his head. "Thanks just the same, sir, but I'll be all right on the bus. I live at 149th Street and Broadway and the bus stops at 145th Street. Nothing can happen to me in that crowded neighborhood."

Hanson looked at him doubtfully, but said nothing.

Jimmy walked quickly away without looking in Walker's direction.

Hanson watched him cross the park and walk down Centre Street toward Chambers and Broadway where he'd catch the bus. Then he turned and watched Walker to see what he would do.

But Walker gave no sign of further interest in the boy. He kept looking up toward the entrance as though waiting for someone. A moment later another man who looked like another detective rushed from the building and hailed him, "Hey, Matt!" and ran down the steps to join him. They shook hands and talked briefly and then the man took Walker by the arm and they went down the street in the opposite direction taken by the boy.

He's not giving the boy a thought, Hanson concluded and signaled for a taxi.

Jimmy sat beside a gray-haired white woman in the only vacant seat on the bus and tried not to think. What good was thinking? he asked himself. It'd only be a form of self-torture. He couldn't do anything himself and no one believed him anyway.

Across from him a blear-eyed soul brother was talking in a loud voice to another soul brother. "You just got to tell those mothers, man, don't be scared of 'em. . . ." The listening soul brother looked ashamed of him.

I'm alive, Jimmy told himself. That's something.

The bus went slowly up Broadway by fits and starts. It passed Canal Street, which looked for all the world like a stationary carnival. It passed Third Avenue at Cooper Square. It passed Fourth Avenue at Union Square. Jimmy glanced at Klein's, a famous outlet store, and recalled the story about a sale they had on mink coats which had caused a traffic jam of chauffeur-driven Rolls Royces. He wondered what the Communist orators who held forth on the Square had thought of that. It crossed Fifth Avenue at Madison Square. It crossed Sixth Avenue at Herald Square, made famous by the cut-rate department stores, Gimbel's, Macy's and Sak's 34th Street. It crossed Seventh Avenue at Times Square, the world renowned hurdy-gurdy of movie theatres and restaurants built around the old triangular Times building. It crossed Eighth Avenue at Columbus Circle, where naked children bathed in the fountain at the entrance to Central Park and were chased across the grass by red-faced, embarrassed cops. Cutting Manhattan on the bias.

Jimmy watched the city scene go past, he looked at the faces of the people, white faces mostly, sprinkled with a few black and brown faces everywhere, and wondered how many of them were scared too.

He tried not to think. He didn't want to think. But he couldn't help himself. The street scenes faded from his vision as he relived those minutes of terror. What had happened between Walker and the fellows? he wondered. What could they have done or said to make him mad enough to kill them? Was the man a homicidal maniac? Or had he just been in a homicidal rage? All he knew was what he had been told by his examiners, and that was nothing.

He was overcome by such a sense of dread that he began to shiver. The gray-haired woman sitting beside him asked in alarm, "Are you sick, young man?"

He looked at her stupidly, he'd forgotten her presence. He tried to smile. "No, ma'am, just a foot stepped on my grave." He saw she didn't understand and explained, "It's an expression when one shivers suddenly."

She seemed relieved.

He tried to keep himself under control. But he was still in a daze of dread when he alighted at 145th Street. At the corner of 149th Street there was a bar-restaurant which catered mostly to colored people, called Bell's. He stopped at the lunch counter for coffee and toast. Even that early in the morning jokers were playing the jukebox in the adjoining bar and putting out their big loud voices: "Maaan, listen here to me, I worked them mother-raping dice 'til they come red-hot," crowed one voice and another voice, "An' w'en I ate up the last foot, my old lady jumped salty. . . ."

He listened and slowly relaxed. Everything was sane and normal as he knew it. His appetite grew. He ordered more coffee and a stack of flapjacks. Another customer was having fried country sausage so he ordered some too. He ate ravenously, cleaning his plate. Still he wasn't filled. He ate a slice of apple pie and a scoop of vanilla ice cream and told himself that was enough.

He paid and went outside. Something drew his gaze. He saw detective Walker standing on the far corner of 149th Street, hands in his trench coat pockets, watching him from his opaque blue eyes. His stomach turned over and all the good food he'd just eaten went suddenly sour. Panic exploded in him. He felt as he had when Walker had first shot at him, naked and defenseless. One part of his mind urged him to run as it had done then. It took all of his will to fight down the impulse and reason with himself. This was in the street, he told himself; there were people going and coming. The man wouldn't dare shoot. But then maybe the son of a bitch was crazy, his mind whispered. Maybe he was shell-shocked, one of those war psychos. Maybe he was a member of some rape-fiend racist group, dedicated to violence. White men had murdered those civil rights workers in Mississippi, bludgeoned them into pieces. But this was New York City. Hell, what difference did that make? his mind asked. There had been that psycho over in some city in New Jersey who had taken an automatic army rifle and had gone down the street, shooting people he had never seen before. He had killed thirteen before the police disarmed him. White cops were always shooting some Negro in Harlem. This was a violent city, these were violent people. Read any newspaper any day. What protection did he have?

He broke out into a cold sweat. But he forced himself to walk normally toward the entrance to his building. He cut diagonally across 149th Street to avoid Walker as far as possible. Walker watched him, unmoving. His body felt as fragile as spun glass, his feet seemed nailed to the ground.

He got into the entrance hall without looking around. The hall was deserted. He pushed the button for the elevator. He was afraid to take the stairs, afraid he couldn't make it, afraid the detective would catch him on them, shoot him down. No one would hear the silenced shots; few people ever used the stairway, it was closed off from the hallways and the doors were kept shut. He stuck his thumb against the button and held it. The elevator had been at the top; it came slowly. . . . Come on, mother-raper, he raved in desperate silence. Come on, goddammit, do you want me to be killed? . . . Over his shoulder he watched the entrance, expecting Walker at any instant. Usually when he wanted the elevator there were so many residents waiting they couldn't all get on. Now it was just his luck—

A shadow fell across the glass-paneled front door. A man entered, wearing a trench coat. Jimmy's heart tripped; the air froze in his lungs like a drawing coldness passing through his chest. His stomach constricted in a small ball of terror. Then he saw the black face looking out from beneath the pushed-back hat. His bones wilted as he sucked in air. Relief gagged him. There had never been a black face more welcome.

The elevator came and he got on; the colored man followed. He felt his heart beating sluggishly. He felt the man looking at him. He started making up a story. But the man got off at the third floor.

He tightened up again the instant he was alone. He was trembling by the time he reached the fifth floor. His hands shook as though he had the palsy as he fumbled with the keys to his apartment. He kept looking over his shoulder down the empty hall. Finally he got the door open, got inside, and stood for a moment in the dark hall to regain his composure.

Once he had been amused by Mr. Desilus' distrust of the colored people of Harlem, as though he lived in fear of someone breaking into his apartment. What did they have that anyone would want to steal? he had asked himself. But now he was infinitely grateful for all the locks on his front door. There was a lock at the top and one at the bottom and two in the middle. One of the middle locks had a chain and the other was attached to a long bar anchored to the floor.

He locked all four locks. They could be opened with keys from the outside. But he hesitated before fastening the bolts at the top and bottom edges of the door because the family was out—Mr. and Mrs. Desilus were at work and Sinette was in school—and he didn't want them to come home and find themselves bolted out. But on second thought he fastened the bolts too. They'd just have to understand.

He went through the gloomy hall to his front corner bedroom. It was a large room furnished with a bedroom suite of oak veneer—a specialty of the credit stores—which consisted of a double bed, dressing table, chest of drawers, two small bed tables and a green imitation leather ottoman thrown in. Mrs. Desilus had given him a large deal table for a desk. It held his books and papers and an old-fashioned upright typewriter. There was a large rag rug on the polished oak floor.

He paid fifteen dollars a week rent.

His girl, Linda Lou, had added feminine touches: two stringy black Topsy dolls flanking the dressing table mirror, which she had dared him to remove; clear nylon see-through curtains and flowered paper drapes to brighten the room and give more light; a chintz cover for his armchair and a foam rubber cushion for his desk chair.

It was a light, pleasant room with windows on both Broadway and 149th Street. On clear days he could look down the steep incline of 149th Street to Riverside Drive, the Hudson River, and the New Jersey shoreline in the murky distance. But there was nothing pleasant about it at the moment.

He closed and locked the door on the inside. Now there was no way for the killer to reach him. Neither of his windows opened onto fire escapes and only a bird or an insect could get at him. He sighed deeply and slowly the panic and the terror left him. At least he was safe there, if only temporarily.

But that was all he could think of at the moment, just to stay alive.

He threw his hat on the bed and hung his duffel coat in the closet. Then he remembered it was bad luck to put your hat on the bed. He moved it onto the table. He only drank alcoholic drinks at what he called "social occasions" and never kept liquor in his room, but he wished at the moment he had something to drink. He needed something to blunt his thoughts, they kept too near the edge of panic. But there was nothing to relieve them and he tried to assess his predicament realistically.

I've got to give this situation some thought, he told himself. I'm in a dangerous position. What could have stopped that maniac from coming inside down there and shooting me dead and walking off without anyone seeing him?

He strolled to the window looking out on Broadway as he racked his brain trying to recall every detail of the minutes when Walker had been shooting at him, trying to surprise a clue. But he couldn't think of a single acceptable reason for the murders.

Absently he drew aside the nylon curtains and looked down at the small drab park running up the center of Broadway. An old woman was sitting on a green iron bench, feeding bread crumbs to a flock of pigeons on the crusted snow. Suddenly he felt a taste of bile in his mouth as though his gall bladder had burst.

Walker stood to one side of the old woman, his open trench coat flaring in the wind, both hands stuck into his pockets, hat pushed back from his maniacal face, staring up at the front of the building with a steady intensity. He stood with his feet wide apart and his shoulders hunched. He appeared statuesque in his immobility.

Jimmy dropped the curtains as though they had turned red-hot, stepped back from the window, gasping for breath, trying to subdue his shock. Now he knew for certain, knew beyond all doubt, that the detective was shadowing him, searching for an opportunity to murder him. The dread and the terror came up in him in waves and he felt too weak to stand.

He dropped into the armchair, twisting his head to watch the immobile figure in the park below.

What could he do? He didn't feel safe anymore. Should he telephone the police? What would they do? What could he tell them? They hadn't believed anything he had said. Why would they believe him now?

Then he thought of Hanson, the attorney. He went to the closet and fished Hanson's card from his duffel coat. The telephone was in the master bedroom and Mr. Desilus did not permit him to make outside calls, only to receive calls and that grudgingly. But this was an emergency and besides, Mr. Desilus was not there.

He unlocked his room door and went down the hall. For an instant his stomach went hollow for fear the bedroom might be locked, and he didn't dare leave the apartment. The bedroom door was open but the telephone was locked by a padlock on the dial.

"These goddamn people don't even trust themselves," he muttered bitterly.

He found a bowl of hairpins on the dressing table and took one and tried to pick the lock. But it bent out of shape. He tried another. It was a cheap lock and he got it open with his sixth hairpin. The room was tightly closed with the curtains drawn and the windows barred and felt almost airless. By the time he got the lock open he felt as though he were suffocating.

Finally he got Hanson on the phone.

"This is James Johnson, Mr. Hanson. You told me to call you if there was any trouble—"

"Yes, Jim, what is it now! What kind of trouble are you having now?" His voice was brisk and impatient.

"That detective, Walker—"

"The one you pointed out this morning? What about him now?"

"He's following me. He's waiting to get a chance to kill me. He's—"

"I think you're exaggerating, Jim. I watched him this morning after you had left. He showed no sign of any interest in you. He did not follow you and he did not—"

"Maybe he didn't follow me but he was up here at the corner of 149th Street when I got home. I kept away from him as you advised—"

"Are you certain it was Walker whom you saw? You're not imagining all of this? When I saw Walker last he was leaving the courthouse in the company of another detective."

"That could be so, but I'm certain of this. I'm not imagining it. He's still up here. I got inside the building and came up to my apartment and locked myself in. Then for some reason or other I looked out the window—I have a window overlooking Broadway—and I saw him down there in the park staring up at the building."

"You are certain of this? You're not leading me on any wild-goose chase?"

"Yes sir, there's no way I can be mistaken."

A sigh came over the phone. "All right, Jim, don't be alarmed. There's nothing he can do to you. Remain in your room and ignore him." Hanson paused.

Jimmy was silent. He didn't know what to say.

"What was he doing?" Hanson asked. "Was there anything threatening in his behavior?"

"There never was. The first time he shot at me there wasn't anything threatening in his behavior; he just aimed at me and fired."

"All right, all right," Hanson said as though he didn't want to hear about it. "Now what is he doing?"

"Nothing. He's just standing down in the park staring up at the front of this building. But I'm scared. What's to stop him—"

"All right, I'll tell you what I'll do. I'll have the commissioner's office send someone up there to find out what he's doing."

"Yes sir, but they won't believe me."

"There won't be any need for them to talk to you at all. I will tell them what you have reported to me and ask them to investigate. You go right ahead with your studies or whatever you're doing as though nothing had happened. Okay?"

"I may as well tell you, Mr. Hanson. I know the man is waiting to kill me."

"All right, Jim, all right. But you're safe. Nothing is going to happen to you, so try to take it easy. And give me your telephone number. I will phone you when I hear from the commissioner's office and tell you what they have found out."

Jimmy thanked him and read the telephone number from the dial. He hung up, relocked the padlock and went back to his room to keep an eye on Walker until the men from the commissioner's office arrived, whoever they might be.

But Walker was nowhere in sight. His frantic gaze searched the park and the other side of the street, then with growing alarm he raised the window and leaned out to search the sidewalk below. But the dreaded figure had disappeared. He was more terrified by Walker's disappearance than he had been by his presence.

He went back to the front door to make certain it was locked and bolted. Then he went into Sinette's room, which opened onto the fire escape, to see that the iron grille over the window was closed and locked. When he returned to his room he locked his own door again. He sat at the table and opened a textbook and tried to force his mind to concentrate on the printed page. But the print blurred in his vision and he saw only a tall demoniac white man standing at the top of some stairs, aiming a pistol at his heart and firing without warning, without a change of expression in the tight angular face.

What did a man do when he knew someone was going to kill him? Kill the killer first? That was what men did in the western movies. But this wasn't a movie. Not even a gangster film. This was real life.

He got up and started pacing the floor. His legs kept buckling, his mind felt dead, beaten to death by his fear. But he forced himself to keep moving. At least the movement helped contain his panic.

Finally, he didn't know how much later, the telephone rang. He unlocked his door, went cautiously through the hall to the master bedroom and answered it.

"Mr. Hanson?"

"Yes . . . Jim?"

"Yes sir? Did the commissioner's men find him? When I got back to my room after telephoning you, he was gone."

"I see. . . . The telephone is in another room and you cannot see the street from that room?"

"No sir, it's a back room that looks out over the courtyard. My room is on the front."

"I see. . . ." There was a long silence. Jimmy swallowed and waited. "The commissioner sent two members of his staff uptown to your vicinity," Hanson finally went on. "They drove up and down Broadway on both sides several times, then toured all the side streets. But they didn't see Walker."

"Then he must have seen me standing at the window at the same time I saw him. Then he came into the building. He must be hiding somewhere in the building. Did they search the building?"

"No, they returned to headquarters and put out a police call to have Walker picked up. Walker heard the broadcast and telephoned the commissioner's office. He had been in the detectives' room at the Homicide Bureau on Leonard Street since shortly after we both saw him on Centre Street this morning. Another detective had been with him all of the time and several other detectives, passing through, had exchanged greetings with him."

"But that's impossible," Jimmy said.

Hanson remained silent.

"I don't mean I doubt your word. But there's something very strange going on. I saw him. I know I saw him. He was up here. It was just like I said. He was standing in the park down on Broadway staring up at this building . . ." Jimmy knew that he sounded hysterical. But he couldn't help it. He felt hysterical. "Listen, Mr. Hanson, I'm being framed. Everything I've said about that detective is true."

"*You're* being framed?" Hanson echoed. "No one has accused you of anything. You are doing all the accusing."

"I mean there's some sort of conspiracy to make it sound as though I'm crazy."

Hanson let the silence run until it revealed his disbelief. Then he said with a flat unemotional deliberation, "Johnson, if I were you I wouldn't make that charge in public." His voice sounded strange to Jimmy, as though he were talking through a pipe or from under water. "I wouldn't charge the police with conspiring to show that you're insane. I wouldn't touch that angle if I were you. My advice to you is to drop all these accusations against detective Walker until you have incontrovertible proof. You have put yourself in an indefensible position. It's regrettable from both your position and ours that you made the last charge against Walker. . . . Okay?"

"But he was here!" Jimmy said, almost sobbing. "I saw him standing at the corner of 149th Street. I came from the restaurant. He was standing there. I cut across the street to avoid passing close to him. And I saw him later standing down there in the park on Broadway when I looked out of the window. That's the God's truth, Mr. Hanson."

"The difficulty is, Johnson, that he has proof that he was someplace else. He has reliable witnesses." Hanson's voice sounded very strange to Jimmy; it sounded more pitying than anything else. "In fact, Johnson, his claim that he was in the detectives' room at homicide when you claim to have seen him uptown is irrefutable."

"Yes sir," Jimmy said. "Irrefutable." The receiver had grown so heavy in his hand he could barely hold it. "I'll take your advice. Thank you for letting me know."

"Don't mention it," Hanson said.

It was a relief for Jimmy to put the heavy receiver down.

12

LINDA LOU was washing lingerie in the kitchen when the doorbell rang.

"Shit!" she exclaimed irritably.

She was wearing an old nubbly maroon bathrobe she wouldn't have been caught dead in, over a cotton flannel gown she wore only to sleep in privately, and a pair of worn-out mules. She had scarcely awakened and hadn't as yet washed her face. Her short crisp hair looked more kinky than curly and her face bore the stolid, slightly sullen look of early morning stupidity. She glanced at the kitchen clock and saw that it was past three in the afternoon but didn't take the trouble to notice how many minutes past three. She hadn't even had coffee. She'd gotten up and started washing lingerie as she always did after a troubled night. Jimmy worried her.

The doorbell rang again, long and insistently.

Maybe it's the numbers man, she thought, adding mentally, I hope.

She had a small two-room apartment on the third floor rear. She wiped her hands on her robe as she went through the living room to open the front door, her hips moving with a lazy roll.

Jimmy stood in the doorway.

"Oh, honey, it's you!" she exclaimed, half in exasperation and half in joy. Her hands flew quickly to her matted curls but one feel was enough to know they were hopeless. She laughed fatalistically, and moved aside. "Well, come on in."

Jimmy entered and started past her. His face bore the fixed expression of a sleepwalker.

"I know I look like hell, but you can kiss me, can't you?" she complained. "Just for old times' sake."

He kissed her absently, frowning at his thoughts.

"Well!" she said, put out. "I asked for it." Then she noticed his expression. "My God, what's happened? You haven't broken out of jail, have you?"

He didn't smile. "No, I was released this morning."

"I was just going down to see you when I'd finished washing."

"Well, you're shut of that chore," he said bitterly. "They let me out. They decided I wasn't the murderer after all."

"Hush," she said, putting her hand over his mouth. "Come on back to the kitchen while I make coffee."

"I don't want any coffee," he said.

"Well, I do," she said irritably, turning toward the kitchen.

"I'm sorry, I wasn't thinking," he apologized, following her meekly. "I'm kind of upset."

She pushed him down into a straight-backed chair beside the table. "You just sit there and tell mama about it."

In age she was but a year older, but in experience she was his mother.

"I know you're going to think I'm crazy—" he began, but she stopped him.

"Well, if it's like that you'd better wait until I've had some coffee 'cause otherwise I can't do any kind of thinking."

He relaxed a little. "This is a dangerous city," he said, sighing. "Dangerous and indifferent and cynical."

"You just think too much," she said, dumping coffee from a can into the strainer of a battered aluminum percolator. "New York is not for thinkers, it's for stinkers. You're too nice to be a stinker. You let it get you down. You haven't learned yet to take it as it comes." She moved about as she talked, running water into the pot through the spout, saying apologetically, "I do everything ass backwards, don't I?" She put the pot on the stove and turned on the gas, then reached for the matches and found the box empty. "Shit!" she said and turned off the gas until she found a book of paper matches on the shelf over the stove.

It was a small compact kitchen, incredibly dirty, with cosmetics and curling irons and half-eaten sandwiches lying about with dirty dishes, empty milk bottles and cans. The white enameled stove and refrigerator came with the apartment, but the tubular steel table with the yellow plastic-bottomed chairs belonged to her.

She caught him looking at her and said defensively, "I know I look sloppy and talk sloppy. My mother always told me Never let your sweetheart see you in the morning before you get dressed up in your airs—"

"You look fine," he said.

"Fine," she mimicked. "Shit!"

He'd been thinking how sane and normal life appeared in that dirty little kitchen. Dripping wet stockings hung from the clothes rack lowered from the ceiling; the rest of the washing was in the sink. Outside, across the gloomy courtyard, was the grimy brick wall of another wing of the building with the dirty windows shut against the cold afternoon. It looked so safe and peaceful it seemed incredible that there was a maniac walking the streets bent on killing him.

"I mean it," he insisted.

She laughed deprecatingly. "Who're you kidding? If I looked that fine you'd have thrown me on the bed."

"I'm just worried," he said.

"I know, baby, I'm just kidding." She rubbed his head.

The pot started percolating, filling the room with the tantalizing coffee scent.

"I think I'll have some coffee after all," he said.

"I thought you would," she said, searching for two clean cups in the cupboard. She got a half-used can of condensed milk from the refrigerator and placed it on the table alongside a bowl of sugar cubes. Then she served a carton of cinnamon toast and a stick of butter wrapped in tinfoil. "Well, I guess that's enough for afternoon tea," she chattered on. "So let me sit my big ass down."

"Don't talk so vulgarly," he said. "You're always trying to be hard-boiled."

"Listen to the man!" she exclaimed as she poured the coffee. "You think I'm trying to shock you? I'm just rattled, that's all. You come in here and catch me looking like the morning after and expect me to be beautiful and demure."

She knew he was going to tell her something she didn't want to hear and she was trying to head him off.

But it was seething in his mind and came out with a bang.

"That detective is trying to kill me," he said.

She had her coffee cup almost to her lips. Her hand froze and her eyes brimmed with tears. "Well, you might have let me drink my coffee," she said. "At least get the first sip in peace."

He jumped to his feet, looking like a hurt child. "I'm sorry I bothered you. I should have known better. You don't believe me either. No one believes me. The only way anyone will believe me is for me to wind up dead."

She put down her cup, sloshing coffee over the table, jumped up and ran around the table, knocking over a chair, and gripped him by the arms. She had a wire-tight, bone-dry look of fury.

"Sit down!" she shouted, wrestling with him, trying to force him back into the chair. "You're going to sit down and drink your coffee if I'm going to have to make you beat me up."

"If you're not going to believe me what's the use—"

"Shut up!" she fumed and kept struggling until she got him seated again. "You're a hundred percent imbecile and baby on top of that. I feel like killing you myself."

"I just got to talk to somebody about it," he said. "I got to make somebody believe me."

She kissed him on top of the head and went back to her own seat, righting the overturned chair on the way.

"I believe you," she said, looking steadily into his eyes across the table. "Now tell me what it is that I believe."

He gave the first little smile. "No, go ahead and drink your coffee," he said. "In peace."

When they had finished he told her about seeing the detective on 149th Street and in the park on Broadway and his conversation with the lawyer, Mr. Hanson.

"But why!" she exclaimed. "Why does he want to kill you?"

"Because I'm the only one who knows he killed the others. I'm the only witness against him. He's afraid I'll find some proof."

She nodded understandingly. "If you just knew why he killed the others."

"That's what really worries me. I can't think of any reason on earth why he'd kill either Luke or Fat Sam. Unless he's a real psychopathic. And that's what I think he is, a homicidal maniac. That's what scares me most. If he's a psycho, he didn't need any reason to kill them."

"But how can you be so sure of that? There might have been an argument or a fight. They might have attacked him for some reason or other. You said he was drunk—"

"No, there wasn't any sign of a struggle of any kind."

"Well, maybe not a real fight. But if he was drunk like you say, there could have been a real dirty argument. You know how some white men are toward colored men when they get drunk; they get dirty and abusive and start saying things the average colored man up North won't take—"

"No, neither Luke nor Fat Sam were like that," he contended.

"How do you know what they were like? You've only been working with them for a little over four months. You just saw them on the job. You never saw them away from work. You don't know how they'd react in that kind of situation. You never saw them being cursed out by a drunken white man."

"But I'd be willing to bet my life neither one of them would have gotten into a serious fuss with a white detective. Both of them were kind of Uncle Toms in different ways. Luke was one of those even-tempered slow-thinking kind of people—"

"He'd be just the one to blow his top when he really got mad," she argued.

"Maybe. But I doubt it. Luke had been working for Schmidt and Schindler too long to lose his head with a white drunk. He'd been with the firm more than twenty years, and in that time he must have come up against scores of white drunks who were abusive."

"Well, what about Fat Sam? You told me he'd been a preacher. And you and I both know preachers who've got the temper of a devil. I once knew a preacher back home who'd beat the living hell out of every man he thought was a sinner; he'd knock them down in the street, kick them unconscious. He sent more than one suspected sinner to the hospital—"

"I know, but Fat Sam wasn't that kind. He wasn't a devil-fighting preacher. He was a chicken-season preacher, one of those jive ministers. He only preached when the chickens were fat or during hog-killing time. A drunken white man couldn't have made him mad enough to fight, no matter what he said. He'd pop his eyes and quote the Scriptures and if the white man kept on he'd start ducking and dodging like a minstrel man."

"Anyway, it was Fat Sam the detective saw first, you said."

"After he went into the store."

"That's what I mean. You don't know what happened between them."

"I doubt if anything—"

"But you don't know. Maybe he'd already killed Fat Sam when Luke went inside. You couldn't have heard anything outside, loading the garbage truck, could you?"

"No, but—"

"Then maybe Luke found Fat Sam dead and he killed Luke too. You said you went down to the basement on the elevator. You couldn't have heard the shots, could you?"

"If it had been a regular pistol. But I figured it out afterwards he had a silencer on his pistol. That's why I couldn't hear when he shot at me. At first I thought I was just too scared to hear—"

"Do the police know he used a silencer?"

"Oh sure. They know the pistol had a silencer. And they know it was the same pistol that shot me that killed Luke and Fat Sam. But as they told you, they can't find the pistol or any record of it. At least that's what they say!"

"A dirty cop like him could have that kind of pistol," she said. "But that doesn't help us any."

"There's another angle. Luke said he accused him of looking out while somebody stole his car. But in the statement he made to the D.A. he claims his car wasn't stolen until after he'd come into the other building and found me shot. He claims the car was stolen while he was inside helping with the investigation."

"Maybe we should talk to the D.A. about that," she said excitedly. "The D.A. told me they were convinced the detective had been in the store earlier, just like you said. Maybe if they knew he had accused you-all of stealing his car—"

"But they know all of that," he cut in bitterly.

"But that would give him the motive," she contended.

"I've told them all of that. They just won't believe me. They say there isn't any proof." He paused, then went on despondently, "It's just that he's a cop—pride of the City of New York. He's a white detective and I'm just a poor colored porter."

"But you've got Schmidt-Schindler behind you."

"They're behind me, all right. Way behind me. They're so far behind me I'm going to be dead before they catch up."

"You're not going to be dead, honey," she said, reaching across the table to capture his hand. "You just be careful and no one's going to kill you."

"Listen, baby, do you know how easy it is to kill a man?" he said. "I read all about Murder Incorporated when the story broke but I never thought anything about it until now. Do you know all a man's got to do to murder someone and go scot-free? All he's got to do is catch him alone somewhere, anywhere, and shoot him dead, stab him in the heart, knock out his brains, and just walk off—just like that maniac could have caught me alone in the hall downstairs. That's all, just kill him and walk away."

Blood drained from her face, leaving a greenish pallor beneath bloodless yellow skin, as the terror came up from her constricted stomach.

"You're not just trying to scare me, are you?" she asked in a small scared voice.

"No, I'm just trying to show you how easy it is. All that detective's got to do is just keep on following me about until he catches me alone—downstairs, upstairs outside my door, on any street between here and 116th when I go to my classes, at any time of day or night, and shoot me dead with that silenced pistol. He can wait for me any night when I get off the subway at Herald Square—"

"You never told me how you go to work."

"I take the IRT on Broadway at 145th down to 59th then change over to the Sixth Avenue Independent. I come up on 35th Street in front of Macy's and walk over to Fifth Avenue and 37th. And anywhere along that way he can shoot me down. All the stores in that section are closed by then and there are a hundred places where he can shoot me without being seen."

"Can't you get a Fifth Avenue bus on Riverside Drive and get off right in front of the store?"

"What's going to stop him from shooting me while I'm walking down 149th Street in the dark to Riverside?"

"But they'll know it was him."

"That won't help me any," he pointed out.

Her face burned with a reddish-brown blush. "That was stupid," she confessed.

"And if they can't prove a motive and can't find the weapon, what can they do to him, even if they feel certain that he killed me?"

She realized she'd been crying and wiped her cheeks with her hands. "It's hard to believe there's anyone like that loose in the world," she said.

"It's not hard for me to believe," he said. "What about that psycho over in New Jersey who shot those thirteen people? What about that colored boy in Brooklyn who went down the street with a butcher's knife and stabbed seven people to death? What about that drunk in the Bronx who shot those two couples in a booth in a crowded bar, two men and their wives, shot them to death, because they wouldn't accept drinks from him? You're telling me it's hard to believe? In this violent city? The papers are filled with stories of senseless murders every day. What's one more murder in a city like this? If they ever caught all the murderers in this one city alone they wouldn't have space in the jails for them. These people look on a killing like a circus performance. A man like him hasn't got any more compunction about killing than taking a drink of water. As long as he doesn't get caught. What cop in this city gives a good goddamn about killing somebody? I don't *believe* he's trying to kill me. I *know* he's trying to kill me. It might sound fantastic, but I know what I'm talking about. If I want to keep on living I'd better not let him catch me alone."

"Then I'll go with you whenever you have to go any place," she said.

"You can't go with me everywhere."

"Why can't I? We both work at night. I don't have to be at the club until eleven. That gives me plenty of time to go with you to work at nine and get back to 125th Street in plenty of time to eat before going to the club. Then I can pick you up at six every morning. I can wait outside the lunchroom on 37th Street."

"But you get off at four. What will you do until six?"

"Oh, the club stays open until then, sometimes until seven or eight. It's just that the acts finish at four, but you know the jazz musicians congregate there after-hours for jam sessions and they'd be glad if I stayed."

"No," he said. "I don't want you to get killed too."

"He wouldn't shoot me," she contended. "It's you he's after; he wouldn't bother me."

"You don't know this man. He's a psycho. He'd kill you as quick as he'd kill me if he got the opportunity. One more killing wouldn't make any difference to him."

"He wouldn't take the chance. A woman screams. He'd have to kill you first and I'd be screaming so loud all of New York would hear me. You've never heard me scream. You've only heard me sing. But I can scream, honey. When it comes to screaming, I can wake up the dead."

"No," he said. "I'll go alone. I'll take my chances."

"No you won't," she said. "I'll go with you."

"Well, not now. I'm going back to my room now, where it's safe."

"Wait, I'll come with you."

He grinned. "It won't be safe then."

She bridled. "Why not! You think I'm going to rape you? I'm not that hard up."

"It's just you don't know Mr. Desilus," he said.

13

WALKER SQUEEZED into the place at the jammed bar the big man in a dark gray coat and dark green hat had been holding for him.

"Thanks for covering for me, Brock," he said.

"Don't mention it," Brock said.

A bald-headed bartender with a heavily lined face and a cynical expression approached and swabbed at the bar with a damp towel.

"Rye and water and salami on rye," Walker said.

"How about another tongue on rye for me, Junior?" Brock said, then drained his glass and added, "Another bourbon on the rocks."

It was eight o'clock at Lindy's and the cocktail hour was verging into dinner. Behind them, across the expanse of crowded tables, curtained windows veiled the sight of packed pedestrians fighting for passage along the sidewalk and the dense traffic clogging Times Square. The place was filled with newspaper columnists taking a fling at kosher cuisine, Broadway racketeers, here and there a Brooklyn gangster and his retinue, and a smattering of $100 call girls making themselves available for potbellied executives from the garment industry five minutes south by taxi.

"You kept the commissioner off my ass," Walker said.

"Glad to do it," Brock said. "But I'd like to know what for. Just a matter of habit. I'm one of those inquisitive sons of bitches that want to know why I do what I do."

Walker glanced at him. "It's with that Schmidt and Schindler business where the dinge fingered me."

"Naturally." Brock showed his teeth in what was supposed to be a grin, but his eyes didn't change expression. "But all I know about that business is what I read in the newspapers."

"Oh, come off it," Walker said.

"Sure," Brock said.

The bartender served their sandwiches and Brock bit off half of his. Walker drained his glass at a gulp and tapped on the bar for a refill. The bartender reached for the bottle he'd just returned to the shelf and poured without interest. Brock finished his sandwich with his second bite.

"Well, hell," Walker said defensively. "After the other dinges were found dead, I couldn't admit having been in there, could I? What would this district attorney do with that, riding the department as he is? All he'd want is to tie some charge like that onto one of us."

"Sure," Brock said, finishing his bourbon on the rocks.

Walker glanced into the mirror behind the bar, studying the faces in the room.

"It's safe," Brock said. "That's why I chose here. Don't no one here listen to anyone but themselves."

"I know it's safe," Walker confirmed. "It's my beat. I was just looking for stoolies."

"The stoolies split when I showed," Brock said.

Walker swilled his rye and banged on the bar for another. When it came he looked into the bottom of the glass as though it were a crystal ball.

"It was just my rotten luck," he said. "Just my rotten luck. When I left that whore's pad it was the only joint close by where I could get some coffee. I just went inside to get some coffee from those dinges."

Brock looked away. "I ain't asking you for it, you know. You don't have to feel obliged to tell me anything."

"Hell, I don't mind telling you," Walker said. "I'm as innocent of any crime as a newborn babe."

"Sure," Brock said, looking at the glasses behind the bar.

"I'd have leveled with the lieutenant if that punk district attorney's assistant hadn't been there. He wouldn't have understood."

"Sure, what makes you think I'll understand?"

"Won't you?" Walker asked appealingly, looking at him with a frank, open expression.

"Well, go on then, if you want, but I ain't asking you for it."

Walker sucked air silently, as though he had been holding his breath. "I'd been with the whore, naturally—" He had a certain youthful appeal, like a college boy confessing an indiscretion.

"Naturally," Brock grunted.

Walker looked piqued for a moment as though he might challenge Brock's sarcasm, but he decided to pass it. "I'd gotten so loaded I didn't know where I was anymore. Then while

I was wandering around trying to remember where I'd left my car, I saw this joint with the dinge porters working and went in for some coffee."

"Sure."

Brock's tone of voice galled Walker but he tried not to show it. He picked up his glass and emptied it.

Brock looked at him disapprovingly. "You should eat more if you're going to drink like that," he advised.

Dutifully, Walker bit into his salami sandwich as though it were rank poison.

"Hey, Junior," Brock called to the bartender. "How about some gefüllte fish and a dill pickle!"

"Rye bread?"

"Pumpernickel." He thumped his glass. "And a refill."

"Right, boss."

"All right, all right, I'm a goy." Brock acknowledged the slur. "I like gefüllte fish, so what?"

"So nothing, boss."

Brock snorted. Walker seemed absorbed in his thoughts. They waited in silence until he was served. He cut off a slice of gefüllte fish, slapped it onto a slice of pumpernickel and bit it off. Then he bit into the dill pickle.

"How do you figure the porter fingering you?" he asked Walker through a mouthful of food.

"Just rotten luck, that's all. Just my rotten luck. The bastard recognized me."

Brock looked steadily ahead, chewing like a camel, and kept silent.

Walker threw him another quick look but his blunt profile told him nothing. "I've been playing with his gal," he went on. "A little brown piece who does a gig up in the Big Bass Club in Harlem."

"Sure, I see how it is," Brock lied. "But he didn't know your name, so he said."

"It don't figure that she was going to tell him either," Walker said. "But he knew me all right. He'd seen me up there in the club and he knew how it went."

"Sure, I see that much," Brock lied. "But after that I'm blind."

"Well, hell, after I got my coffee I left," Walker said irritably. "Those killings took place after that. The bit about the Negro dressed as a porter sending me in there to look for the burglar is straight."

"Sure," Brock said. "It sounds screwy enough to be straight."

"Maybe he's the one who did it. I'd know him again if I saw him, that's for sure."

"Sure. But you didn't remember what he looked like when Lieutenant Baker questioned you. How is that?"

Walker's gaze moved around a bit and he swallowed. "I didn't think it was important then," he said. "Anyway, he didn't ask."

"Well, maybe he didn't," Brock had to admit. "I don't remember."

Walker relaxed. "I don't remember, either, to tell you the truth. But I've been thinking about it a lot since. And the only way it adds up, it's a home job, strictly a dinge affair."

Brock looked up. "A dinge with a silencer on his rod?" he questioned with raised brows.

"Why not?" Walker argued. "These folks are getting modernized. Sawed-off shotguns and Molotov cocktails. But any way you figure it, it must have been someone from uptown. Might have been gal trouble—"

"With a silencer?"

"Well, maybe not," Walker conceded. "When a dinge shoots another about his gal, he wants to hear the gun go off. But it might have been anything. You can never tell nowadays about a Harlem affair. It might have been something to do with the numbers, a religious wingding; maybe some cat took a powder with a payoff—they might have been running a numbers' drop in there."

"Sure," Brock said. "For the ghosts in that area?"

"Hell, it wasn't any ghost that shot 'em."

"That's for sure."

"The man we're looking for is good and goddamn alive. And a goddamn smart son of a bitch or else he'd left a clue."

Brock stared at him without expression. "Whoever killed those porters is a maniac," he said.

"Maybe," Walker said, appearing to think about it. "Maybe not. There might be something behind those killings bigger than we think."

"Such as?"

"Well, one of 'em might have been a connection for the H-ring. It's an ideal setup. They could keep the shit there for distribution to the pushers. One of 'em could have done it without the others knowing anything about it. Or they all could have been in it together." He showed a certain youthful ebullience as he enthusiastically developed his theory. "It would have been easy as pie. Whatever it was, that dinge knows who made the hits. He *knows* him," he contended dramatically. "You can bet on that. And he's scared to name him. He's scared if he names him his own number is up—"

"He named you," Brock reminded mildly.

Walker brushed it off with a gesture, and went on: "He's so scared he's shitting in his pants. So he fingers the first man he sees. And that happened to be me," he finished with a spread of his hands.

"Sure," Brock said admiringly. "You oughta been on the stage."

"You don't believe me?" Walker asked with genuine astonishment.

Brock looked at him curiously. "Sure. It's just that you said a moment ago he fingered you because of his gal."

Walker flew into a rage. Red spots burned in his cheeks and his blue eyes went opaque. "What the hell, goddammit, are you conducting an investigation?"

Brock shrugged his massive shoulders. "I told you I wasn't asking for it."

Walker rapped for another drink, gulped it down, and relaxed. "Good old Brock. Forget it. I'm just touchy. Can't blame me for that, can you? All this brass riding my ass. I'm telling you just how it was. It was just a coincidence. I was coming out the whore's pad, just like I told you, and ran into this Negro dressed like a porter, and when I stopped him to question him, he says he's looking for a cop because there was a burglar in the basement."

"I remember you saying you'd just left her pad when you stopped in the lunchroom for some coffee, and all the porters were alive then; or is my memory just bad?"

Walker put on a sheepish look. "I didn't tell you all of it," he confessed. "You see, the whore had clipped me for a couple of C's and I had gone back for it."

"Sure. I see," Brock lied. "But I keep thinking you said you didn't remember where she lived."

"Well, hell goddammit, you think I was going to admit knocking off a piece while I was supposed to be on duty and being clipped like a lain to boot? That's why I went with the Negro to look for the burglar, to give myself an alibi for being off duty half the night."

"Sure, I see," Brock lied. "That was when your car was stolen?"

"Some time during then. I didn't miss it until after the bodies were discovered and I went back to look for it where I'd parked it on 36th Street. Just like I told the lieutenant—if you remember."

"You sure hit a jackpot of coincidences," Brock said.

"Don't you believe in coincidences?" Walker challenged.

"Why not?" Brock conceded. "They always figure in murder cases. We're working on the same angle ourselves."

"What angle?"

"Coincidences."

Walker shot him a quick, baffled look. "I was just going to ask what you homicide men were working on, but if it's top secret and all that—"

"I told you. Coincidences. And speaking of coincidences, like I said before, I'm still wondering what you wanted me to cover you for this morning."

"Oh that." Walker shrugged it off. "I've been shadowing that third dinge. Someone killed those other two dinges—"

"Like I said, that's for sure."

"And I figure whoever did it is going to kill this third one and level it off. So I'm keeping tab on him. More for my own sake than for his. If the killer comes out into the open, I've got him. And if it's the one I'm thinking, I'll know him. I'm going to have to get him to get clear myself."

"Sure. We figured that angle too. About the killer coming out into the open to get the third man."

"Well, if you homicide men are shadowing him too, then I can let up," Walker said.

"We're not shadowing him, if that's what you want to know," Brock said. "We're just at the figuring stage right now." He looked at Walker inquiringly. "You were shadowing him this morning when he went home?"

"Yeah. He must have spotted me and reported to the Schmidt and Schindler shyster. I figured he saw me when he looked out of his window. That's why I rushed downtown and looked for you. But you were out. So I telephoned you. I figured the commissioner was going to get in touch with you."

"I see you've been doing a lot of figuring too."

"What the hell's the matter with you!" Walker exclaimed angrily. "I'm in a jam. I've got to figure. And all you can do is be sarcastic."

"I want to help you," Brock said.

"Why don't you act like it?"

"I am acting like it. I'm just curious about how you knew his window."

"That bastard has fingered me for murder. Remember?" Walker said flatly. "I know everything there is to know about a bastard who fingers me for murder."

"Sure," Brock said. "Including his gal. So what do you want me to do? You said when you phoned you had another favor to ask."

"I want you to find the whore I picked up that morning so I can get an alibi for the first time I went into the joint."

"I thought you just said you knew where she lived."

"I didn't say any such a goddamned thing."

Brock thought that over for a moment and decided finally he was wrong. That hadn't been what Walker had said. "You think she'll give you an alibi?" he asked.

"She'd better," Walker said.

"Sure," Brock said. "How you want me to go about it?"

"Just put some pressure on these pimps around here and make them spill. Some of them know where she's holed up. They all know I've lost my shield for now, and I don't want to have to hurt any of 'em."

"How long are you suspended for?"

"Until the investigation is over."

"That might be forever," Brock said. "A murder investigation is never over until the murderer has been brought to trial."

"You don't have to tell me."

"All right, Matt, maybe I can help you," Brock said. "We're looking for her too."

Walker glanced up sharply. "What for?" he asked suspiciously.

"Just a coincidence. We want to give you an alibi too," Brock admitted. "What are you going to give me to go on?"

Walker strained at his memory. "Not much," he confessed. "All I draw is a blank from the time we had our first drink over at the Carnival bar."

"Did she slip you a Mickey?"

"No. I just changed from rye to Pernod."

"I see. I thought you went back to get the money she clipped you for?"

"I didn't find her. She had already split."

"I see."

"All I remember about her is she's new on the stem. Too tony for a Times Square hustler. Felt at home in the plush joints. Called herself Cathy. Dyed blonde, brown eyes, five feet four-or-five inches, about one hundred and twenty, twenty-five pounds, twenty-eight to thirty years old, slightly bucked teeth, molars full of amalgam fillings of recent date, scar from Caesarean on belly—no other marks."

Brock studied him curiously. "You looked at her good enough," he remarked dryly. "That'll help if we find her corpse."

"I think of them as corpses," Walker said.

"Sure," Brock said, commenting idly. "She must have lived a fairly decent life until she got into the trade."

"Must have," Walker conceded indifferently. "I know she wasn't from New York. Probably from London. She spoke English."

"What about her place, apartment, room, whatever it was?"

"I keep thinking of a room, but it doesn't have to be *her* room. You know how whores' pads run together in your mind after a time, like a bad dream. You can't remember them apart anymore."

"You're a real gay dog, aren't you?"

"Well, hell, you know how it goes on my beat."

"Sure. All the vice you want for free. So what do you want me to do when we find her?"

"I want to talk to her first."

"Maybe I can arrange that, if I'm the one who finds her."

"Well, thanks, Brock." Walker called the bartender and settled his bill. "How is Jenny?" he asked Brock.

"Fine. Did you ever find your car?"

"I thought you knew. They found it the next day. Down by the Armory on 34th Street. The thief must have used it for a job and ditched it there."

"An accommodating thief, wasn't he? Brought it right back to the vicinity where he lifted it."

Walker shrugged carelessly.

"Was it locked?" Brock asked.

"I forgot to ask," Walker said indifferently. He turned to leave. "Give my love to Jenny."

"Right." Brock looked at him blankly, thinking, It's a damn good thing you're my brother-in-law. But he only said, "Take it easy, Matt. Watch out for coincidences." It was all he could do to keep the disgust from his voice. He beckoned to the bartender. "What you got for a bellyache, Junior?"

14

WALKER NOTICED that it was 9:15 when he emerged onto the street. He should have stayed with Brock longer, he realized, until 10 at least, but he had let Brock get on his nerves with all his sly insinuations. Well, to hell with that. Brock was all right, he told himself. Good old Brock. He was going to find it damn difficult to digest that story of his. But if he had to plead insanity, Brock would make a good witness.

Times Square was lit up. The lights filled him with a pricklish titillation. All these thousands of people searching for a thrill. I've got your thrill, dear, he said silently to a good-looking woman who passed. Ah well, he thought. That's life.

His car was parked in a *no-parking* zone at the curb. It was a big silver-gray coupé. During a vacation in Germany several summers before he had heard the big American cars referred to as Land Cruisers. Those envious Krauts, he thought. He was reminded fleetingly of Lieutenant Baker's pointed reference to its cost—"a lot of car for a first-grade detective." Well hell, did anyone think he bought it out of his salary? He just played the angles, that was all. If whores wanted to sell pussy and there were men who wanted to buy it, they had to pay the law-enforcement officers. That was no more than right and just. People couldn't expect their vice for free, that was illogical.

There was a traffic violation ticket tucked beneath the windshield wiper. He plucked it off and stuck it carelessly into his trench coat pocket. Then he got in and eased into the northbound traffic on Broadway, thinking, Now I'm in the Manhattan fleet.

He kept up Broadway to Columbus Circle and took Central Park West to 110th Street and followed Convent Avenue up to 145th Street, passing through the campus of New York City College, his old home grounds, on the way. He was feeling melancholy when he turned over to pick up Broadway again. He made a U-turn at 150th Street, easing to the curb across from the apartment building where the porter lived, and sat studying the window.

The shades were drawn but slivers of light showed about the edges. The bird hasn't flown, he thought.

He got out and went into a corner bar run by people of Italian descent. A couple of colored prostitutes with dyed red hair sat at the bar, but all the male customers were white. He kept on through to the back and looked in the telephone directory. He found a Linda Lou Collins at the right address, put a dime in the slot and dialed the number.

"Hello . . . Jimmy?" He heard a note of anxiety in the contralto voice and it made him sad.

He hung up without answering.

When he came out he noticed how the neighborhood had changed since his school days at City College. Colored people were moving in and it was getting noisy. Already Harlem had taken over the other side of the street. This side, toward the river, was still white, but there was nothing to stop the colored people from walking across the street.

His thoughts intensified his feeling of melancholy. Poor colored people, soon they'd have to live on riverboats, he thought.

He drove slowly south on Broadway. South of 145th Street the Puerto Ricans were taking over, crowding out the Germans and the French, who'd gotten there first. It was like a dark cloud moving over Manhattan, he thought. But it wasn't his problem; he'd leave it to the city planners, to Commissioner Moses and his men.

The red light caught him at 125th Street. To his right was a ferryboat moving away from the pier bound for the New Jersey coast across the Hudson River. Looking eastward was Harlem, extending across the island to the Triborough Bridge. Those poor colored people; they had a hard life, he thought. They'd be better off dead, if they only knew it. Hitler had the right idea.

The light changed and he shook off the thought and continued down beside the iron stanchions of the subway where it had come out of the ground at 129th Street.

They weren't dead, he thought, and that was a fact.

On sudden impulse he turned west off Broadway at 121st Street and went up the hill past International House. He came out on the winding Riverside Drive and passed the Greek letter fraternity houses of the Columbia University students and farther down, the modern apartment buildings interspersing the old stone houses of a former grandiloquence.

He felt as sad as he had ever felt in all his life.

But when he passed the Yacht Club basin at 77th Street the sadness began to leave him, and when he turned on 72nd Street and came to Broadway again, it was gone. He was back among the pimps and the prostitutes, the racketeers and the horseplayers, the has-been actors and actresses, cheap hotels and cheap people, the tag-end of Times Square. He began feeling like the Cock of the Walk.

Now he was a man of purpose again; a man with a purpose.

He kept down Broadway to Madison Square and turned east on 23rd Street to First Avenue, and south into the landscaped streets of Peter Cooper Village. He parked in front of a modern red brick apartment building which looked much the same as any other building in the Village and went inside.

He was feeling sorry for himself, thinking how unlucky he was. If he hadn't accidentally pulled the trigger and killed Fat Sam, the whole incident would have been just a joke. Now it was double murder; and that wasn't the end.

He rode up in the big silent elevator to the third floor, unlocked the polished pine corridor door of an apartment, and passed through a right-angled alcove into a large pleasant sitting room, the outside wall of which was one glass window closed off by bright yellow drapes. Handwoven scatter rugs decorated the polished pine floor, and the maple furniture was made to order.

A woman lay stretched out at full length on a long divan, watching a color television program on a built-in screen between two modernistic bookcases filled with books in the French and German languages. She wore a man's purple silk dressing gown and red pumps with heels like the stems of champagne glasses. In the soft white light from a parchment-shaded reading lamp, her skin had the dull gleam of polished ivory and her long black hair hung loosely over her shoulders like the folds of a mantilla.

"What is the trouble with you?" she greeted Walker. "You have gotten your mouth pulled down like the mouth of a fish." She spoke textbook English with a European accent. Her eyes were eloquent with passion, but she didn't move.

"You're a gorgeous piece, Eva," he said, looking at her with unveiled lust.

"Am I not?" she said. "But you did not answer me."

"I feel blue and depressed," he said. "Let's go to bed."

"Oh la-la." Her green eyes smiled indulgently. "You are like the men from my native Yugoslavia," she said, sitting up with slow, indolent movements. "Always sad and passionate. But you do not look like them, you look more Germanic and tortured, like the characters from Wagner's operas."

As though angered by the allusion, he said roughly, "You talk too much." He took her hand and pulled her savagely to her feet. "Go get undressed."

"You are too rough," she protested.

"Goddammit!" he exclaimed, dragging her into the bedroom. "Just be my whore and shut up."

He began stripping off his clothes as though in a blind rage, tossing them to the floor about the room. She was so frightened she undressed quickly also. But he was nude and groping for her before she had time to arrange herself beneath the bedcovers. He handled her brutally, taking her as though in a raging fury, gritting his teeth and mouthing obscenities while making love, as though any instant he might choke her to death.

His behavior terrified her. She could scarcely breathe. Afterwards they lay panting and exhausted, without tenderness or rapport.

"You hate me when you make love to me," she accused. "Why is that?"

He didn't reply. He closed his eyes and turned away from her.

"You rape me each time," she said. "I think always you are going to murder me."

Suddenly she realized he was asleep. He had gone to sleep instantly.

Sighing, she got up and went into the big modernistic bathroom adjoining. She ran a hot bath and lay in it, thinking, I'd better get away from him. There is something wrong with him. He is not quite human.

He slept for about fifteen minutes and awakened abruptly, refreshed and alert. He heard her splashing in the tub and leaped from bed nude and went into the bathroom to take a shower. He was in the best of spirits, humorous and charming and almost playful.

"Don't get your hair wet," he said. "It feels funny when I kiss you."

She tied her hair into a ball atop her head but the ends were already wet.

"You are a funny man," she said.

"What's funny about me?" he asked in genuine surprise.

"Strange."

"Mm. . . . But you like me?"

"Sometimes."

He laughed and went into the glass-enclosed shower which was separate from the tub. He turned on needles of hot water and then cold. When he stepped out he was pink-skinned and goose-pimply. She was drying herself with a big wrap-around towel.

"Don't you have any *bidets* in America?" she asked. "Anywhere?"

"I don't know," he confessed, laughing. "I've never seen any."

She thought he was joking. "What do women do?" she asked.

"Get in the tub, I suppose."

"Every time?"

"There are not all that many times," he said.

"But suppose it is day and they do not have much time? Or they are in the man's place?"

"Wear contraceptives, I suppose."

"It is not for that, I ask. How do they clean themselves?"

He laughed so hard she began to laugh too. But after a moment, seeing him strap on his service revolver, she became sober and frightened again.

"You are not permitted to wear that anymore," she objected. "You will get into trouble."

"Who said so?" He spoke offhandedly as he continued dressing.

"You do not have your badge. You told me so yourself, and I also read about it in the newspaper, that you have been suspended."

"I've been reinstated," he said airily. He reached into his pants pocket and took out a duplicate badge. "See, here's my shield."

She looked at it suspiciously, suspecting a trick. She never knew when he was serious, and his strange, mirthful mood made her apprehensive. It frightened her badly to realize how much she feared him.

While putting on his trench coat he said, "Get the package I asked you to keep for me."

"Is it not too late?" she questioned. "You told me it was evidence, and you have taken it out before."

He stood stock-still and looked at her with speculation. The opaqueness had closed over his blue eyes and there were bright red spots on each of his high cheekbones.

But he said only, "You must remember I work at night."

"But of course," she quickly conceded and went into a small adjoining dressing room.

He stepped out into the sitting room to wait and relaxed by practicing drawing his service revolver. Then he realized she was taking too long. Soundlessly he opened her bedroom door and slipped inside.

She stood beside the unmade bed in the dressing gown she had put back on after her bath, her shoulders hunched, her head cocked slightly to one side. Hearing him in back of her she gave a violent start, and turned involuntarily to look at him. Her face was stark white and pure terror looked out from her wide green eyes. She began trembling from head to foot.

His gaze went directly to the unwrapped package on the bed. The long blue steel .32-caliber revolver with the silencer attached gleamed dully in the dim light from the single bed lamp.

He smiled at her sadly. "You looked," he said. "Like Lot's wife."

She backed slowly to the distant wall.

"Oh God," she whispered sobbingly. "You are the one who killed those men. You shot them with this pistol."

"You shouldn't have looked," he said and began moving toward her.

She would have run but she found herself cornered and the strength went out of her bones. She opened her mouth to scream and her lips worked convulsively but no sound came forth.

"I'm sorry you looked," he said.

He put out his left hand slowly and clutched her by the lapels of the dressing gown. She didn't resist; she didn't have the strength to raise her arms. She was immobilized, like a bird charmed by a snake, rendered powerless by the look of pure malevolence in his distorted face.

He began slapping her with his right hand; her left cheek with his open palm, her right cheek with the back of his hand. He slapped her steadily, as though in a dream; with an expression of detachment he watched her terror-stricken face pivot back and forth, as though it might have been a punching bag.

She kept her eyes open; she was too terrified to close them; and slowly they became senseless. Her head rang with a continuous tolling sound and her face became numb. She lost her sense of balance and the room began to rock. But he held her upright and kept on slapping her as though he'd forgotten what he was doing.

Finally she found enough voice to whisper, "You are going to kill me."

The words shocked him back to his senses. He released her abruptly and stepped back, exclaiming, "I don't want to hurt you."

She crumbled to the carpet, but still kept her gaze on him. His tall figure wavered in her vision and the floor seemed to rock wildly beneath her. But she didn't care anymore.

"You must kill me," she said in a faint, lisping voice. "Because I am going to tell that you killed those men."

He looked at her reproachfully. "If you do that, I will tell them that you're a Communist spy," he said.

She tried to laugh but couldn't. "They know I am not a spy," she lisped. "They have investigated me so often they know I am not a spy. But you are a murderer and I am going to tell them."

"Then I will tell your compatriots that you are a capitalist spy," he said. "You speak seven languages and you have often been seen with me. If I tell them you are a capitalist spy, they will believe me. Your people will believe you are a capitalist spy quicker than my people will believe that I have murdered two dinges. It's just a matter of what people want to believe. Do you want to believe me?"

She began to cry, her prone body convulsed with sobs. "Kill me," she begged in her faint lisping voice. "Please kill me. You will be safe then. Do not accuse me please of being a spy. It will make much trouble for me with everyone."

"I can guess," he said sadly.

"Please," she begged. "I will not tell. I will do anything you say. I am not a brave person. Please do not say I am a spy. I will not tell on you."

"I didn't think you would," he said matter-of-factly, looking at his watch.

It was midnight.

He picked up the silenced revolver from the bed, examined it to see that it was loaded, slipped it carelessly into his trench coat pocket and gave her a sad smile.

"You shouldn't have looked."

She sobbed without replying.

"I'll be back later," he said.

She didn't answer.

He went out through the sitting room and the front hall and walked down the corridor toward the elevator. His vision was slightly out of focus but he felt sober physically. It was his mind that felt drunk. He was going to kill the third dinge and go scot-free. If he had to plead insanity, she'd make another witness for his defense. But the beautiful part of it was if he could just keep his nerve he could do it in such a way that it could never be proved against him. Everyone might think he had killed them, but no one would be able to prove it. And he'd go right back on the police force as though nothing had happened. Because they wouldn't fire him if they couldn't prove him guilty.

15

THE BIG BASS CLUB was on 125th Street near Eighth Avenue, right in the heart of Harlem. It had the likeness of a bass violin inlaid in the tiled front wall identifying itself. In the glass-enclosed frame beside the entrance doorway there were numerous glamour photos of the entertainers. In her picture, Linda Lou Collins looked so much like Pearl Bailey as to arouse suspicions of the management's integrity.

The entrance opened into a public room with a bar curved like the side of a bass viol and booths along the opposite wall. The murals were composed of eight bars of various blues hits painted on the walls.

A curtained doorway at the back led to the private club where money was the only requisite for admission. It was another world, a Harlem nightclub for home folks, like nothing else on earth.

The atmosphere was both sensual and animal, thick, dense, odorous, pungent and perfumed. Bulls herded their cows. They were domesticated bulls but they were dangerous. Every man had his knife and wore his scars of conflict. Every bull had his cow with heavy udders filled with sex, smelling of the breeding pen, cows that had been topped again and again and wanted to be topped again indefinitely. Most times they were as orderly as bulls packed into any corral. But violence always lay cocked and ready in the smoke-filled, whiskey-fumed air.

It was a hangout for people whose business was vice—pimps, gamblers, racketeers, madames and prostitutes. Aside from the Negro middle class, they were the only ones who could afford it. The prices were too high for working people. However, Negroes of the middle class—businessmen and professionals, doctors, lawyers, dentists and morticians—came when they were in the mood for slumming. The entertainment was good, but it was adapted for colored people. It had to be good.

The guests just sat and drank and listened and ate fried chicken when they got hungry and were entertained. There was no provision made for dancing. If they wanted to dance, the manager told them to go to the Savoy Ballroom where they had the space for it.

No one flirted with other men's women or other women's men. It was not a place to change partners, make dates or play eyesie and footsie with former bedmates. Everyone kept their passions in their own backyard and tended strictly to their own business. Yet sex was the most predominant factor of the overall atmosphere.

When Walker pushed through the curtained doorway, Linda Lou was singing: "*Come to me, my melancholy baby, cuddle up and don't you cry . . .*"

She was standing in a baby blue spotlight beside a white baby grand piano at which sat a slim dark man with shiny conked hair, making the soft run of notes sound like falling rain.

She was singing in that copyrighted Negro woman's blues voice which lies between soprano and contralto, and is husky on the deep notes and plaintive on the high notes, and has that slightly whiny sexy intake between breaths.

She wore a show-through scarlet evening dress that looked violet in the blue-tinted light; underneath, her wide-shouldered voluptuous body shook as though held in a passionate embrace.

She was singing directly to Jimmy, who sat enthralled at a ringside table beside a numbers banker—a squat dark man—and an overdressed "showgirl" who were complete strangers to him.

Her gaze flickered briefly to the white man seen dimly in the entrance, but he didn't interest her. Lots of white people visited there, musicians, racketeers and thrill-seekers, but they went unnoticed.

The manager was a big black rugged man who had formerly been a policeman. He went over toward the curtain to head off Walker. He didn't welcome unescorted white men who were strange to him.

"If you're looking for girls, friend, you won't find nothing here but trouble," he greeted. "Why don't you try the Braddock or Apollo bars?"

Walker smiled and showed his shield. "It's a free country, isn't it?"

The manager studied his face.

"Looking for anybody in particular?"

"I just want to see the show, buddy boy," Walker said. "Is there any law against that?"

"Nope. Go ahead and enjoy yourself," the manager said evenly. "Just don't call me *buddy boy* is all."

Walker stepped past him and looked over the room. A girl showing a lot of skinny brown shoulders combined with an overpainted mouth in a way she thought was sexually exciting leaned from a cubbyhole and said musically, "Check you hat and coat, kind sir?"

He looked at her. Her eyes got bright with promise. He looked away without replying and the promise left her eyes. When he had spotted Jimmy, he moved toward the back, still wearing his hat and trench coat.

The manager beckoned to his bouncer, a big black man bigger than himself, who looked exceptionally hard-used for his size. "Keep an eye on that chappie," he ordered.

"Shamus?" the bouncer asked.

"No, a city dick, but he's got a sad look, and I don't trust cops with a sad look about them. They ain't sad for nothing."

"That's no lie," the bouncer said.

Walker noticed them whispering and smiled to himself. He could damn near guess what they were saying. He kept moving along the back wall until he reached a place where it was almost dark and stood leaning back against the wall with his hands in his trench coat pocket, gently patting the silenced revolver. The people at nearby tables glanced up at him briefly, then paid him no further attention.

Linda had seen the whole play. Her attention had been drawn again when the manager spoke to the white man, and she had noticed his exchange with his bouncer. She watched the white man through the corners of her eyes. When her act was finished there was a smattering of applause. She knew it didn't mean they didn't like her singing; these people just didn't believe in applause.

During her break she went over and sat beside Jimmy. The Jive Fingers, a rhythm group, took over.

Without asking their permission, the numbers banker ordered champagne for all four of them and tried to start a conversation.

"You sounded mighty good, Miss Linda Lou."

"Why don't you catch this act?" Linda said coolly, giving him the brush-off. "They're good."

"'Scuse me," he said. "I didn't mean nothing."

Jimmy couldn't tell whether it was an apology or a rebuke. But Linda put her finger to her lips for silence, then leaned over and whispered in Jimmy's ear, "There's a strange-looking white man standing in back—against the wall. He keeps looking at us. Wait for a moment, then look around and see if you know him."

Jimmy felt his intestines knot. His voice stuck in his throat like a bone. He knew who it was without looking around. He started to look anyway, his head pivoting involuntarily, but she stopped him. "Not now! He's watching us."

"Let him watch!" he whispered fiercely.

But she clutched his arm, restraining him, alerted by her intuition. "No, don't let him see that you've seen him."

"Goddamn, Linda," he muttered, but obeyed her.

The numbers banker had his ears cocked, trying to follow their conversation. Linda caught him and gave him a furious look. He took a sudden interest in the act.

A waiter approached Walker and asked him to sit down. "It's against the rules to stand up in here, chief," he said.

When Walker turned his head to reply, Linda whispered, "Now!"

Jimmy gave a quick look, his gaze stabbing the dark shadows with the beginning of panic. He felt foolish and cowardly at the same time for being influenced by Linda to peep. But the instant he saw Walker's profile, he turned away quickly and was overcome by a strange sense of resignation that left him unnaturally relaxed.

"It's him," he said, forgetting to whisper, relapsing into a state of fatalism.

The numbers banker had resumed his interest in their affair and was peering toward the rear to see the man in question. But neither of them noticed. Jimmy had drawn into himself and sat with bowed shoulders and downcast eyes. He had built up such apprehension at seeing Walker again, he was left with a sense of letdown by his fatalistic mood.

"It's him all right," he repeated tonelessly. "The maniac."

"Listen," Linda whispered tensely. "Will you do what I tell you?"

"Why not?" he said.

"Then I want you to get up as though you haven't seen him. Kiss me good-bye, then stop at the checkroom and get your coat and hat as though you were going home. Then take a seat out at the bar. You'll be safe there. I want to see if he follows you."

Jimmy looked at her for a long moment. "You never have believed me, have you?"

"Oh, daddy, let's don't quarrel. I've got a plan."

"All right." Jimmy stood up and leaned over and kissed her. "I hope your plan works—whatever it is," he said and left her.

But the numbers banker had finally got the man spotted. He turned to Linda and said, "I don't want to interfere in your business, Miss Linda Lou, but if it's that white sport back there what's bothering you and your gentleman friend, I'll take care of him for you."

Linda watched Jimmy stop at the checkroom for his coat and hat, turning over possibilities in her mind. She decided to confront him and get it straight to her satisfaction once and for all.

"If you want to do me a big favor," she said to the numbers banker, "let me have this table for a while."

"Sure thing," he said, standing. "But I'll be around."

"Where am I going to sit?" his showgirl friend complained petulantly.

"Sit on you thumb, baby," he said, laughing at his joke.

She gave him an evil look but she got up to follow him. "You ain't as funny as you think you is," she said.

The next instant Linda had forgotten them. She turned back to watch Walker and saw him move casually toward the exit as though the show was boring him. She looked around and located the manager and when she caught his eye beckoned to him. He came over to her table.

"Who's the white man who just left?" she asked.

"A city dick. Is he bothering you?"

"Not me. He's shadowing my boyfriend. I want to talk to him."

He looked around. Walker was nowhere in sight. "He's gone."

"No he isn't. He's outside at the bar. He thought Jimmy had left but I told Jimmy to stop at the bar."

"Okay, little sister, I'll give him over to you," he said. "But if you can't handle him, give him back to me."

She gave him her glad smile reserved for special friends. "Thanks, General."

When Walker found Jimmy sitting at the bar, he was momentarily confused. All the seats at the bar were taken and the booths were occupied. He stood in the center of the aisle and let the black people move around him.

General came from the club and said, "A lady wants to talk to you, friend."

Walker was beginning to feel drunk. "What lady?" he asked thickly.

"The lady who sings. Linda Lou."

Jimmy heard him and it required all of his willpower to keep from looking around. Walker glanced once in his direction, then suddenly came to a decision.

"Right," he said and followed the manager back into the club to Linda's table.

"Sit down," she ordered.

He sat down and looked at her with a sympathetic expression. The manager still lingered. The Jive Fingers began harmonizing on one of their own songs called "Don't Blow Joe," and all over the place big and little feet began patting time.

Satisfied that Linda had the situation under control the manager left them.

"Take off you hat," Linda said to Walker.

He looked surprised but removed his hat obediently. His rumpled blond hair gave him a youthful, devil-may-care look.

She studied him openly, torn between curiosity and loathing.

"Why don't you let him alone?" she said in a tense, furious voice. "If you did it, like he says, you've already got away with it. So just let him alone."

"I don't know what you mean," he said.

"The hell you don't!" she flared. "You're following him about. He thinks you're trying to kill him too."

"Don't get excited," he said.

"Don't try to scare me too," she warned in a blinding rage. "I'm covered. Look around you. If you try to hurt either one of us you'll wind up dead. These people in here don't give a hoot in hell for who you are. If I tell them you're trying to hurt me they'll cut your throat and leave your carcass in some dirty gutter." She stared at him challengingly, breathing hard. "Don't you believe me?"

"I believe you," he said sadly. "That's what it all comes down to. Who believes who."

"Then get wise to yourself!" she raved. "Get up off of him. If you just hurt so much—" She caught herself. "What was that you said?"

"I said that's all it is, who believes who," he repeated dutifully. "You believe him. He says I'm tryin to kill him. So you believe him. You're his girl. Why not? What kind of girl friend would you be if you disbelieved him? But have you thought of the possibility that he might be lying?"

"He's not lying," she denied automatically.

He just looked at her. The voices of the Jive Fingers filled the silence: "*I'm gonna sit right down and write myself a letter, and make believe it came from you . . .*"

"Did you hear that?" he asked. "That's all it amounts to—*make believe*."

"Shit!" she rejected scornfully. "Those two men are making believe they're dead?"

"But you're worrying about *who* shot *him*," he argued. She stared at him without replying. "Someone right up here in Harlem," he said.

The suggestion jarred her but she rejected it from a sense of racial loyalty. "I don't believe it."

He sensed that he had shaken her. He pressed his advantage, "Look at it objectively. I'm the first person he saw when he regained consciousness after being shot. The first thing he said was that I shot him. *Me!* I had just come into the building from the street. One of the janitors unlocked the door to let me in. The charwoman saw me enter. The building superintendent was standing right there when I came inside. They took me down into the basement of a strange building and showed me into a room. A man I had never seen before was lying unconscious in a pool of blood. The first thing he says on opening his eyes was, 'That's the man who shot me.' I doubt if he could even see me distinctly, he had lost so much blood. And you believe him. Does that sound reasonable?"

"Why couldn't you have shot him before?" she asked. "That's the way he tells it."

"That would have been impossible," he said evenly. "I was with a woman when he was shot. The police know this. The woman will swear to it. And there are other witnesses. Do you think I would be free if what he said were true? Do you think the police are imbeciles?"

He saw the doubt flicker in her eyes. "Then what are you following him around for?" she asked.

"I'm trying to keep him from getting killed." He sounded sincere.

She wore a puzzled frown when the manager came to tell her she was on again.

"Wait 'til I come back," she told Walker.

The manager followed her backstage. "How's it going?" he asked with concern.

"I don't know," she confessed.

She began with an old favorite, "*If this ain't love it'll have to do . . .*" Jimmy heard her over the amplifier in the bar and went back into the club to listen. But he saw Walker sitting alone at her table and stopped beside the checkroom, numbed by a strange bewilderment. He felt lost in a situation which he did not understand. What did she have to say to him? What was he telling her? He felt his legs trembling. He listened to Linda's twangy voice and watched her shaking body, but he couldn't meet her eyes. She looked at him from across the floor and tried to capture his gaze to tell him that she loved him with her eyes. But she couldn't reach him; he had turned away from her. Tears leaked into her voice.

The checkroom girl thought he was being two-timed and looked at him pityingly, but the next moment she was staring longingly at Walker's angular profile. That's life, she thought.

Someone in the audience cried for "Rocks in My Bed" and she took it and gave out. When she'd finished her act, she tried once more to find Jimmy's eyes but couldn't find them, and went slowly back to the table where Walker waited.

Jimmy turned away and went back to his seat at the bar. The manager came out and patted him on the shoulder. "Brace yourself, pops," he encouraged. "She's in there pitching for you."

Jimmy felt flooded with shame. She'd made it a goddamn community project, he thought bitterly.

Inside the club, Walker greeted Linda on her return, "Listen, lady. What do you know about him? What do you really know? How do you know he wasn't pushing H, or fingering for car thieves, or picking up for prowlers? How do you know what he was doing down there all night?"

"He wasn't doing nothing but working," she said. "I know him."

"How long have you known him?" he pressed.

She hesitated for an instant, then said defiantly, "Almost ever since he's been in New York."

"How long has that been?"

"He came up here the first of July," she answered reluctantly.

"A little over six months," he said derisively. "You haven't even known him for a year."

"I know him just the same," she declared. "It doesn't take long to know a man—if you ever know him. And I know he wasn't involved in anything crooked."

"Maybe *he* wasn't," he conceded. "But what about the other two? What do you know about them? Can you truthfully tell yourself that they weren't involved in some kind of dangerous activity?"

"Maybe, but I don't believe it," she argued.

"All right, say you don't believe it. That's what I told you at first. It's just a matter of what you want to believe." He sounded so earnest and sincere she found herself sympathizing with him, but she quickly put it from her mind and his next words brought back her suspicion. "But consider the possibility. They were involved in some racket. Someone from up here went down there for a showdown. Whoever it was shot them. Your friend witnessed the shooting, or accidentally appeared at the wrong time—"

"How do you know that?" She caught him up quickly.

"I'm just imagining," he said. "Whoever it was had to kill your friend because he was an eyewitness. But your friend got away. Whoever it was, your friend knows him. But he's scared to name him. He knows the minute he names him, his number is up. It might be someone sitting right here in this room."

His intense voice made Linda look about at the familiar colored faces: pimps, gangsters, numbers men, thieves. Could any of them be the murderer? She knew several men present who were reputed to have killed someone.

Doubt grew slowly in the back of her mind, and with it his image slowly changed. He looked so fresh and boyish in that atmosphere of crime and sex. He smelled of out of doors. She visualized him with a sweetheart somewhere. She'd be a nice girl who thought of marrying him. She'd rumple his shiny blond hair and caress him. But she mustn't be sentimental about him, she told herself sternly. Only it was so difficult to think in that atmosphere.

An instrumental trio—piano, bass and drums—had taken over and were knocking themselves out with a vulgar, old-time tune . . . "Yass-yass-yass!" some loud-mouthed drunken madam shouted. The joint began rocking and jumping, reeling and rolling. . . . It didn't make sense that this rawboned, bright-eyed young white man wanted to kill her Jimmy, or that he had murdered those other two colored porters in cold blood, Linda thought. . . . The instruments thundered and another drunken woman screamed uncontrollably, "It's your ass-ass-ass!" . . . It didn't make sense.

Wearily she brought her suspicion back into force. "Then what are you following him around for?" she asked.

"I could say what I told you before, I'm trying to keep him from getting killed," he said. "But I'd be lying. Look at it from my point of view. Your friend put the finger on me. He got me suspended from my job. He's put me under suspicion. If I was Jesus Christ from heaven, I couldn't love him. I hate him. But I don't want to hurt him. All I want to do is catch the killer. Look at it reasonably. I've *got* to catch the killer. Until I catch the killer, I'll be under suspicion. I'll never be reinstated on the force. There will always be people who'll think I'm a murderer. So I'm going to keep on following him until the killer shows himself. And the killer's going to try to kill him the first opportunity he gets. You can bet your sweet life on that."

The fear came up into her loins like sexual torture. Because if that was the way it was, she knew she couldn't help him. Someone had to help. Suddenly Walker appeared to be her friend.

"What can he do?" she asked desperately, tears welling into her eyes. "He can't just go on like this and get himself killed."

"The only thing he can do to help himself is to tell who the killer is," he said in a positive tone of voice.

Her face clouded again with suspicion and perplexity. "He'll only just say it was you."

"That will get him killed for sure," he said.

She put her face in her hands to hide her terror. "If only I knew what to believe," she sobbed.

The colored guests studiedly ignored them. The girl was in trouble, they concluded; that was obvious. That was the only reason a white man could make her cry. But it wasn't their business. Never butt in on an argument between a colored woman and a white man, was their maxim. The woman might turn on you.

Walker leaned forward and gently removed her hands from her face. He looked into her eyes intently and said in an intense, sincere voice, "Listen, Linda, you're the only one outside of himself who can help him. Make him tell you who the killer is. Swear to secrecy if you have to. Do anything you have to do, but make him tell. Then you tell me."

"Oh, I couldn't do that," she said spontaneously.

He drew back. "It's his funeral."

She gasped sobbingly. "But what will you do?"

"I'll fix him so you won't have to worry."

"If it was that easy he'd have already told," she argued.

"You're missing the picture," he said earnestly. "He's scared the police can't help him. He knows if they arrest the killer, there will be someone else to do it. He figures the only chance he has is to keep buttoned up and maybe the killer will let him off. As long as he keeps fingering me, he figures he's safe. He saw the killer. Don't forget that." He hammered his statements into her mind. "He's got to name someone for the police. He can't say he didn't see the killer because the killer shot him in the chest. Do you understand that?"

She stared into his bright blue eyes as she listened to his hypnotic voice. She felt as though he were casting a spell over her.

She tried to maintain a sense of logic, to keep thinking straight. But he was such an appealing man. She felt a strange desire to touch him. And he looked so innocent.

"What will be the difference if I tell you who the killer is?" she asked.

He leaned forward again and held her gaze. "I will kill him," he said.

She shuddered with a thrill of horror. It flooded her with sexual desire. She was repulsed by him and at the same time irresistibly drawn to him. He would kill a man, she thought. She looked into his eyes and trembled from a strange bewilderment. Their eyes were locked together, his subduing hers. She felt naked and powerless before him.

"If I get him to tell, how will I get in touch with you?" she asked submissively in a small breathless voice.

"You can telephone me." He gave her a number with a SPring exchange. "If you forget, I'm in the telephone book. Matt Walker, 5 Peter Cooper Road. Phone any time of day or night. I'll come up to your apartment."

She sighed. "I just hope I'm doing the right thing," she whispered doubtfully, as though speaking to herself.

"You're trying to save your friend's life," he said. "That's all you can do."

"I hope so," she murmured.

After a moment he asked, "How are you going home, Linda?"

"I'll get someone here to drive us. The man who was sitting with us. He's a numbers banker; no one will bother us if we ride with him."

"Numbers banker!" he repeated. "How do you know he isn't the killer?"

She shivered. "Please," she protested. "I can't suspect everyone."

"That's all right," he indulged her. "I'll follow you in my car. If you still believe that I'm the killer you'll be safe with him."

"Oh no!" she cried, covering her face again.

"If it happens that he really is the killer," he continued, "then you'll be safe with me following you."

Her hands dropped into her lap, the strength gone from her arms. Her eyes told him that she put her fate in his hands.

"One more thing, Linda," he went on. "Your friend will go home with you. He'll want to know what we've been talking about, what I've said to you. Don't tell him. Continue to act as though you believe him implicitly. Do you understand?"

She nodded meekly.

"Then you start working him around to being sensible. You know how to do it. As much woman as you are, you could make any man tell you his secrets. Work on him. Put that lovely body of yours on him. You know how to do it. In the meantime I'll park across the street on Broadway. When I see a light in his room, I'll come up to your flat to see what you've found out. Okay?"

She wanted to tell him not to come, but she found herself saying, "All right," against her will.

The Jive Fingers had just come on again and were giving out in a frenzy with: "*It ain't what you do but it's the way that you do it . . .*"

16

IT WAS past five o'clock in the morning and it was close and still and very hot in her small sitting room crammed with junky furniture. She sat in a red-and-white silk upholstered imitation Louis Quinze love seat which had cost her a fortune in a Third Avenue antique shop. She hadn't changed from her working clothes but her Persian lamb coat was flung carelessly across an overstuffed chair which had come from the Salvation Army secondhand store.

He stood in the middle of the red carpeted floor with his head bowed dejectedly. He still wore his duffel coat, buttoned up despite the heat, on which snowflakes had melted into glistening water drops.

"I just wished you hadn't talked to that murdering son of a bitch," he said once again.

She had her legs tucked underneath her and her shoulders were bowed as though in resignation. But she looked at him with an expression of intolerable frustration.

"That's all you've been saying since we got home," she charged angrily. "You act as if I wanted to talk to him; as if I had enjoyed it."

"It just looks like I'm hiding behind your skirts," he said.

"Why should you care how it looks? I just did it for you."

"I know," he admitted, looking cornered as though by his own knowledge. "I know you did."

On sudden impulse he went over and knelt on the floor before her, overcome by a sudden wave of tenderness. He seized her hands and kissed them and was engulfed by the smell of woman and perfume.

"You're all I got," he said. "If you don't believe me, who will?"

"Don't say that. You have your mother and your sister. You talk as if they were dead."

"Dead to me anyway. They're in another land."

She too was overcome by a sudden wave of tenderness. She stroked his kinky hair. It felt stiff and electric to her touch, inspiring an indefinable thrill.

For a moment neither spoke. It was as though they were enclosed in a tomb. No sound came from the sleeping building or penetrated from without. The double windows opening on the back courtyard were closed and curtained with heavy green drapes.

"I believe *in* you," she said stroking his hair. "That's more important."

He got quickly to his feet.

"Listen, Linda, this isn't a matter of semantics," he said. "This man is trying to kill me and he's killed two other men besides."

She sighed feelingly. "I'm sorry I'm not as educated as you are," she said reprovingly.

"Goddamn!" he exclaimed, scrubbing his face with the palm of his hand. "Now you bring that up, as though I'm the one who's guilty."

"It'd just make it easier for us to get a case against him and get others to believe you too if he looked more like the type who'd do such a thing."

"If he *looked* like a murderer?" he exploded. "What's a murderer supposed to look like?"

"I mean if he looked vicious," she said defensively. "Like some of those Negro-hating sheriffs in the South. It'd make more sense. But he doesn't act as if he's got any prejudice at all."

"Jesus Christ, I believe he's got you half convinced I'm lying," he accused.

"That just isn't so," she flared. "You started all this just because I asked you how well you could see the man who shot at you."

"Not *shot at me*, *shot me*, you mean," he corrected angrily. "And he's *the man*. I saw him as well as I see you."

"Well, from the way you first described what happened it didn't sound as if you hardly saw him at all."

He wheeled about and stared at her.

"You mean because I ran?"

"You said he starting shooting at you before you'd hardly seen him, without giving you any warning. You were coming up the stairs and the first thing you knew somebody was shooting at you—"

"Not somebody—*him*! And let me tell you something, Linda. You don't know what it's like to have a man shoot at you without warning. There's no such thing as calling for help or shouting for the police or trying to reason with him to find out what it's all about. You don't think about justice or the courts of law or retribution or anything else like that. All you think is, *Run, man, run for your life*. But you see him all right. You see him in a way you'll never forget him."

She could just stare at him; he had almost convinced her again.

Then he added, "That legend on the county court building, *the true administration of justice is the firmest pillar of good government*, is just so much shit when a man is shooting at you."

It was something Matt might say, she thought, recalling his boyish looks, his intense voice and earnest blue eyes, and it didn't seem possible. *He'd kill the killer*, he had said, but she couldn't believe he'd murder two defenseless colored men and shoot at Jimmy without warning.

"Did he look like he looked tonight?" she asked. "You said the man who shot you didn't look angry or anything, didn't show any kind of emotion. Is that possible? For him to shoot you without any reason at all?"

"White men've been killing colored men for years for no reason you'd understand."

"In the South."

"It's still America."

"And anyway, they always had a reason—at least a reason that other white men understood, even though it didn't justify it. But no one can think of any reason for him to have done it."

"He had a reason. He's a schizophrene. Do you know what a schizophrene is?"

"Somebody with two personalities, one good and one evil."

"No. A schizophrene doesn't have any personality. He's out of contact with reality, with morality too. He could kill you in cold-blood murder and smile while he did it."

She shuddered. "If he's that far gone, wouldn't they know about it in the police department? Don't they have to pass psychiatric tests? They don't hire crazy men for policemen."

"They wouldn't have to know. That's the hell of it. He could pass the kind of tests they give. And maybe he was all right when he first went on the force. Maybe something happened to him since he's been a detective. Some of them can't take it. There are men who go crazy from the power it gives them to carry a gun. And he's on the vice squad, too. There's no telling what might happen to a man's mind who constantly associates with criminals and prostitutes."

"Wouldn't someone know? His wife, or his sweetheart if he's not married. His relatives, or somebody?"

"Not necessarily. It might have just broken out."

"I don't understand that," she confessed.

"He might have just gone crazy the night he killed Luke and Fat Sam. Something might have happened that all of a sudden sent him crazy, made him lose contact with reality. Some little thing. It didn't have to be anything big."

"Couldn't you explain that to the district attorney? Wouldn't he understand it?"

"I've already told the police of the Homicide Bureau. They think I'm too intelligent for my own good."

"Then what about the lawyer from Schmidt and Schindler? He's with a big firm. They must have a lot of influence to represent Schmidt and Schindler. Tell him what you told me. Ask him to have Matt—"

"*Matt!* You're calling him Matt now," he caught her up.

"He said that was his name," she snapped. "I'm not in the South. What difference does it make what I call him anyway? Why don't you listen to what I'm saying?"

"I am listening."

"Then ask the lawyer to have his brain examined— What do you call it when they test to see if you're crazy?"

"Psychoanalyzed. But you can't have a man psychoanalyzed against his will unless he's officially charged with a crime—and pleads insanity."

"Well, you can ask him, can't you?" she insisted. "It'll give him something to work on. All those lawyers he's with—they must be able to do something, all the gripes they have to handle for Schmidt and Schindler. You told me they serve a half a million people a day—"

"Yes, and do you know what those lawyers would say?"

"No, and you don't either."

"Listen, you know what you've told me about the white agents you've had. You ask them to try to get you into a certain spot—say the King Cole room at the St. Regis, or rather not that big, say some night spot in the Village. You think you'd be a hit; you're certain you can put it over. You have the voice, you have the experience, you have the looks and you have the personality. They know all this. It would look like they'd want to advance you for their own ten percent—"

"Twenty-five percent," she cut in. "That's what my agent takes."

"All the more reason," he went on. "But they say, no, you're a blues singer. As if a blues singer can only sing in blue joints for blue people. You say, Lena Horne sang there. They say, *Lena*, but you ain't Lena, baby, you're for the blues. You told me that you kept fighting with your agent for two years to get booked into that nightclub in the Village. It wasn't that the management didn't want to give you a trial—your agent just wouldn't book you. Two years before you could get him to do it. So after he's done it, he makes up your repertoire. You're not allowed to sing what you want, or what you sing best, or even what might make the biggest hit. No, he says, sing a spiritual, then a slave chant, the blues for an encore, then a social protest ballad, and another blues encore. Then after he's done this great thing for you, he wants you to pay him off with your body. And why? Because you're a colored singer and they think of a colored singer in just one way. They think that all a colored woman has is a voice to be directed and a body to be used. That's the way it would be if I go down and ask them to have this schizophrene psychoanalyzed. They'll think instinctively that I'm getting beyond myself, being too smart for a nigger, or that some white person put me up to do it, or that I'm trying to cover up something—my own guilt, perhaps. Chances are they'll think I don't know what I'm talking about. They'll try not to laugh in my face, and save it for a lunch table joke. You say yourself he doesn't look like a schizophrene. You don't even believe me yourself, because of how he looks—"

"That just isn't so," she denied.

"The hell it isn't so! Don't deny it. It is so! He doesn't look like a killer to you, and you're colored like me. How do you think he looks to them, who're white like he is? They'll think I'm the one who's a schizophrene. Maybe you're beginning to think so too, since you've talked to him."

"Oh God Jesus Christ!" she cried. "Are you going to harp on that all night? I've got a splitting headache."

He drew suddenly into himself. "I'll go then."

"Oh, don't be so touchy," she said, trying to control her exasperation. "I want to help you—if I can. If you'll just let me help you without keeping on throwing accusations in my face every minute."

"You could help me, if you believed me," he said solemnly.

"Don't go into that again, please," she begged. "Just tell me what to do and I'll do it."

"If I knew what to do, I'd go ahead and do it," he said. "What I thought was, maybe we could figure out some way to get him out into the open. Schizophrenes like to boast if they have a sympathetic audience. Maybe you could get him to confess to you—since you've got to know him so well. Play on his vanity. I can't tell you how, but you ought to know how, much experience as you've had."

She gave him an angry look. "Oh God, Jimmy, why don't you try being honest yourself for once?" she said.

He turned to stone. "So you think it's me who's lying?"

She felt at the end of her patience. She buried her face in her hands and stifled a sob. "I don't know what to think anymore," she confessed.

He stepped over to the lamp table and picked up his hat. He moved slowly, like an old man. He felt as though she had betrayed him.

She scrambled to her feet and clutched him by his arms, held him and made him look down into her eyes. "Stay with me, honey," she pleaded. "Hold me in your arms. I need you as much as you need me. Don't run out on me."

He held himself rigid and aloof. "I need you too, but you've already run out on me," he accused.

Tears streamed down her face. She sobbed chokingly. "You're asking too much of me. I'm not one of the strong people. I'm just a singer of the blues."

"I'm just asking you to believe me," he said.

"You don't know how I feel," she said sobbingly. "I feel as if my emotions had been taken out and beat with a stick."

"It's not how you *feel*," he said. "It's what you *believe*."

"I *want* to believe you," she declared, releasing his arms for a moment to wipe away her tears with the palms of her hands. "But we don't always believe what we want to," she added.

He stepped back out of her reach. He felt broken up inside. "I wish you hadn't said that," he said. "You've *got* to believe me—or we're finished."

"How can I believe you when what you say is so unbelievable?" she cried hysterically.

He turned and started toward the door. "Good-bye," he said.

She ran after him and clutched him about the waist, trying to hold him back. "No. Don't say good-bye like that. I'll go up to your room with you—it'll be safer."

He shook her off roughly. "Goddammit, no!" he shouted. "I'll go my way alone."

17

WALKER HAD brought the elevator up to the third floor; he had switched off the light and shut off the power. The doors could be opened but the elevator couldn't be moved.

He stood inside the darkened elevator and surveyed the darkened corridor through the Judas window. He had to stand close, with his eyes almost glued to the tiny diamond-shaped pane, in order to see the door to Linda Lou's apartment at the end of the corridor. He had been standing there for a long time. No one had appeared.

It was nearly six o'clock when he saw Jimmy rush into the corridor and slam the door behind him. He took the revolver with the silencer attached from his trench coat pocket and held it loosely in his right hand.

Jimmy headed toward the elevator, moving like a sleepwalker, looking neither to the right nor left. He felt castrated, impotent, horsewhipped. He was afraid to think, afraid of what he might do. He tried to draw in his emotions and nail them down. He was so tight inside that he felt wooden and his breath wouldn't go any deeper than his throat. But the emasculating notion persisted: His girl had turned against him for a white man, for a schizophrenic murderer who had already murdered two colored men and was trying to kill him too.

Halfway to the elevator was the green door to the service stairway. Impatience jerked him in that direction. His raging frustration wouldn't tolerate waiting for the elevator to come up from the ground floor where it always stayed that time of morning.

He snatched the door handle and jerked open the door as though he would pull it off its hinges. He was muttering curses under his breath and his head roared with such a fury of anguish and chagrin that he didn't hear the elevator doors being hastily opened.

Walker ran silently down the corridor on the balls of his feet, caught the door to the stairway before it had completely closed on its hydraulic hinge. He held the revolver shoulder high, muzzle up, in the pose of a marksman prepared to shoot at any angle.

But Jimmy had taken the stairs three at a time, goaded by his insufferable humiliation. He had turned at the landing and was already out of sight.

Walker leaped toward the stairs in headlong pursuit. He landed on the second step and tried to take the next three in one stride. His foot slipped on the iron tread and he fell to his hands on the landing. The revolver butt struck the concrete stairs with a metallic clatter.

"Goddammit!" he cursed softly.

Jimmy wheeled about on the fourth floor landing like a startled cat and looked down over the banister. For a brief, frozen moment his panic-stricken gaze locked with Walker's opaque blue stare. Again the maniacal face looked nine feet high. His mind exaggerated every sight. His eyes stretched as though they were bursting in their sockets and popping from his head. Then cold terror swept him in a freezing wave as he saw Walker swing the muzzle of the revolver up and around.

The next instant he was running. He was leaping up the stairs. He was running for his life.

He heard Walker scrambling to his feet. It urged him to greater effort. He strained his muscles to their limit. But it seemed to him as though he had never moved so slowly. He died with every step.

He rounded the corner as Walker rounded the corner below. He ran crouched over and close to the wall. The instinct to live had subdued his panic. He was cold-headed now and his thoughts came crystal clear, like scenes lit by lightning. He knew he couldn't leave the staircase to turn into the corridor. Walker could catch up and shoot him before he could reach his door and get it open. On the stairs he could keep far enough ahead to keep out of range. But the stairs ended at the door to the roof above the sixth floor. If the door was open he'd still have a chance. He'd have the rooftops to run on, the parapets to duck behind. Maybe he'd find another door to another building unlocked and be able to get down the stairs to the street. But it all depended on the door above being unlocked.

As he leaped toward the fifth floor landing the door opened from the corridor and a colored man appeared. The man was grumbling to himself. "It's the fourth time this week that elevator's been stuck in the mawning—" Jimmy burst upon him so abruptly his eyes bucked wildly with terror. But Jimmy was just as terrified. Without stopping or breaking his stride, he wrapped his arms about the man and propelled him back into the corridor.

The man wrestled instinctively to defend himself. "What you tryna do, man, what you tryna do?" he shouted as though to subdue his enemy by the loudness of his voice.

"I'm not trying to hurt you, man, I'm not trying to hurt you!" Jimmy shouted in reply, trying to reassure the man of his peaceful intentions by the loudness of his voice.

For a moment they fought silently in panic-stricken fury. The service door closed slowly on its hydraulic hinge. Walker had caught up in time to hear the desperate conflict taking place in the corridor. He stopped and let the door close while trying to make up his mind whether to kill them both or wait for another chance.

"Turn me loose, man, turn me loose!" the stranger panted threateningly. "I'll take my knife and cut your throat."

"I'm not fighting you, man," Jimmy gasped. "You got to protect me."

His words spurred the man to frantic effort. "You tryna rob me, man, I know," he gasped.

"I'm not trying to rob you!" Jimmy shouted.

"Turn me loose then!" the man demanded.

But Jimmy had wrestled him down the corridor in the direction of his own door. Now the problem was how to keep him there while he got it unlocked.

"Can't turn you loose," he hollered at the top of his voice. "Unless you promise to come inside with me."

"Come in your house?" The man was outraged. He had relaxed a little but now he got buck wild again. "I don't play that stuff!" he yelled.

"It's not like you think," Jimmy kept hollering, hoping he'd wake up the neighbors. "I just want you to stand here."

"I ain't going for that right here in this hall," the man began shouting again.

"Man, goddammit, I'm being pursued," Jimmy shouted back. "Can't you see that? I just want you to stand here and protect me until I get into my house."

"Pursued?" The man looked up and down the empty corridor. "You being pursued?" He gave Jimmy another wild look and his eyes bucked white. Then he wrenched himself free in a burst of superhuman strength and ran toward the stairs.

Frantically Jimmy got out his keys. It seemed as though he would never get all the locks unlocked. He broke out in cold sweat at the sudden thought that the door might be bolted on the inside. As he fumbled with the locks he expected Walker to appear any moment. He couldn't turn his head because the various keyholes claimed his attention. He cursed his proprietors. All those mother-raping locks would get them all killed on their threshold some day, he thought in rising panic. Then suddenly the last lock clicked and the door swung inward. He rushed inside and wheeled about and didn't pause until he had all the locks securely locked again.

Then he leaned against the wall in a state of nausea while cold sweat trickled down his hot body like sluggish worms.

Walker had returned the revolver to his trench coat pocket and leaned against the wall of the staircase, feeling letdown and intolerably thwarted. It was just his goddam rotten bad luck, he was thinking. The black son of a bitch was a bad omen, like a carrion crow.

He was still leaning in the same position when the door into the corridor was flung open and a colored man came tearing through, his eyes bucking wildly and his skin powdered with gray. At sight of him, the colored man drew up short and his eyes seemed about to fly from their sockets. The man had started down the stairs but curved in mid-motion and went up instead.

Walker heard him run out into the corridor on the sixth floor. Then after a while he heard the door being opened again cautiously. He knew the man was up there listening for a sound of movement. Probably peering furtively over the banister.

He pushed from the wall and went slowly down the stairs. May as well let the Negro get on to work, he was thinking. None of them had long to be here. On the third floor he went into the corridor and kept on back to Linda Lou's apartment door.

Linda was expecting to see Jimmy when she opened the door. She was nude underneath a sleazy kimono. She wanted him to make love to her and was afraid he might refuse again.

Her emotions were braced against another scene. At sight of Walker, her unbearable tension broke in a flood and she became instantly hysterical.

"Oh, it's you, the villain," she said in a gaspy voice.

He tensed for an instant, but relaxed when she went into a fit of hysterical laughter.

"I'm the monster," he agreed, smiling at her sadly.

He came in without being asked and closed the door behind him. His opaque eyes made a quick professional scrutiny of the junky room.

"Don't mind me," she said chokingly. "This is my natural manner. Just pull up a chair and make yourself at home."

She's light-headed, he thought.

She groped blindly toward the love seat and sat on the edge and buried her face in her hands. Her smooth brown thighs were exposed but she didn't notice. Her bowed shoulders shook convulsively.

He went and stood beside her and stroked her shaking shoulders, slowly and soothingly. He could feel her vibrant flesh beneath the flimsy nylon kimono.

"You shouldn't have quarreled with him," he said.

"*Me* quarrel with *him*! My God!" she sobbed. "I hardly had a chance to say a word."

"You should have expected it the first time," he said, continuing to stroke her shoulders. "You shouldn't get upset."

"I shouldn't get upset! It isn't every day a girl has her sweetheart walk out on her."

The heavy revolver with the silencer in his trench coat pocket bumped gently against the arm of the love seat as he soothingly stroked her shoulders. He felt his palm getting electric.

"He'll come back," he said. "He hasn't got anywhere else to go."

The thought intensified her crying.

His legs grew weak from standing and he felt himself growing dizzy in the close hot room. He looked about for a seat but her fur coat occupied the only chair which looked reliable. He saw the worn ottoman beside the television table and brought it over to sit on. He removed his hat and sat down in front of her and took her left hand and began stroking it slowly and soothingly from fingertips to wrist.

She looked down and noticed her bare thighs were exposed and drew her kimono closed.

"Did you get him to talk at all?" he asked.

"Talk! How he did talk!" she exclaimed, bursting into hysterical laughter again.

"Don't worry about that now," he said, lengthening his stroke from her fingertips up her smooth bare forearm to her elbow. "Don't think about that now. We'll find some way to save him."

She became conscious of his hand gently stroking her bare arm. It sent tingles through her body like slight electric shocks. She wiped at her cheeks with her other hand and tried to control her convulsions. But her body kept shaking as when she put sex into a song.

"If he was only more passionate," she complained, her voice still choking slightly on the words.

"You're a passionate girl," he said in a low intense voice, and began stroking the upper part of her arm and shoulder. "You've got too much passion for the average man."

He had leaned so close to her that she could smell his damp ruffled hair. Her free hand touched it involuntarily and a shock went through her body.

Suddenly his hand closed over her breast.

She shuddered spasmodically.

His lips found hers in a hot blind kiss.

She put her arms about him and pressed her breasts against his coat. She felt the room going away in a stifling flood of desire.

An arm went underneath her legs and he stood, picking her up, and carried her into her bedroom.

It was like taking candy from a baby, he thought.

She didn't pay the slightest attention when he uncoupled the shoulder holster of his service revolver. She didn't appear to see him until he stood nude, then she said, "Oh," and when he lay in her arms she said "Oh" again. Then she matched her passion against his and hers was the greater.

She was already asleep by the time he had dressed.

He staggered from the apartment, pulling the door shut on the Yale snap lock, and found the elevator as he had left it. His legs kept buckling and he felt as though he had reentered a dream he had dreamed a thousand times before. It gave him an insufferable sensation of being outside of his own emotions.

At first, when he left the building, he couldn't remember where he had parked his car. He had forgotten entirely his reason for being uptown.

He began walking up the incline toward Amsterdam Avenue. Needle-fine snow slanted against his hot face and his coat flapped open in the wind. He'd gone half the long block before he remembered having parked his car on Broadway. He turned about and retraced his steps. When he passed the entrance of the apartment house again he suddenly remembered why he had come uptown.

He began feeling unlucky again. He felt intolerably depressed when he climbed into his car and began driving south on Broadway. He kept on down to 23rd Street, intending to return to his apartment in Peter Cooper Village, but as he neared it he thought of Eva and kept on past and turned north into Roosevelt Drive on the East River. He drove up past the UN building and entered the approach to the Triborough Bridge before reaching 125th Street.

His head felt as though it were ringed in steel. The left side felt definitely heavier than the right. He had to fight down the almost overpowering inclination to steer the car to the left, into the stream of oncoming traffic. It was so strong he had to grit his teeth and grip the wheel with all his might to control it. Still he felt as though he were driving on a road that slanted to the left and he had to keep the wheels turned sharply to the right to keep from sliding off. His teeth were on edge and there was an acid taste throughout his mouth.

He kept on turning on the clover-leaf bridge, feeling as though he were sliding down a scenic railway, until he came to the exit for the Bronx River Parkway.

It was a big superhighway split down the center by a continuous park, heading straight north toward Westchester County, cutting the Bronx in half. The limit was fifty miles an hour but the north-bound traffic was light at that hour and he eased the big Buick up to ninety, a hundred. The speed relaxed his tension slightly and by the time he turned off into Bronxville his nerves had quit jerking him about.

He kept on through the winding residential streets and stopped in front of a small ranch-type house made of plate-glass panels and natural pine with a huge fieldstone fireplace jutting from one end.

A blond, blue-eyed woman of about thirty-five, wearing a flowered plastic apron over a wool tartan dress, answered his ring. Her eyes flooded with compassion at sight of him.

"You're sick, Matt!" she exclaimed.

"Not sick, Jenny, just beat," he said, entering the front hall. "I want to go to bed."

They never kissed or indulged in any gesture of affection. But their casual instinctive understanding of each other showed they were very close. She wanted to ask questions but was restrained by the same undemonstrative trait.

"Take the guest room, it's made up," she said. "I'll fix some toast and coffee while you're bathing. How do you want your eggs?"

"I don't want anything to eat," he said rudely, heading toward the bar in the sitting room. He poured a stiff drink of rye. "Where's Peter and Jeanie?"

"They're in school, of course," she answered in surprise.

"Didn't realize it was so late," he muttered, gulping another drink.

"I'll fix you something to eat anyway," she said, containing her disapproval with an effort.

"Don't want anything to eat," he said crossly, like a little boy. "My head won't stand it." Then, in an offhanded manner, he asked, "Where's Brock?"

"Oh, he hasn't been home from work," she said innocently. "He stayed in the city last night—some special detail he's on."

"You know," he said slowly and deliberately, like a little boy telling his big sister a dirty secret, "Brock believes I murdered those two dinges."

He watched the horror flood into her face.

"Oh, don't say a thing like that!" she cried. "He's going crazy trying to get you reinstated."

He smiled at her sadly. "He does though."

"I won't hear it," she said sharply. "You go on to bed. You're sick and upset. I'll bring your breakfast as quick as I can."

She turned away and hurried toward the kitchen before he could say anything else. But he had said all he wanted to say. He took the bottle of rye and kept on through the sitting room to the guest room at the other end of the house.

He put the whiskey on the night table and peeled off his trench coat. Then, on sudden impulse, he took the revolver with the silencer from his trench coat pocket and went through the connecting bathroom into the master bedroom. It contained a double clothes closet with a hat shelf. He wrapped the revolver in a handkerchief and shoved it back into the far corner of the hat shelf, behind stacks of seldom worn hats and odds and ends of summer things. Then he returned to the guest room and finished undressing.

He was asleep when she brought in his breakfast tray. He was twisting and turning and gritting his teeth as though in the thralls of a nightmare. She got a damp towel from the bathroom and wiped his sweating forehead.

Poor Matt, she thought compassionately. He should never have been a cop.

18

Where can I get a gun?

The one thought had possessed Jimmy's mind from the instant he had stood trembling behind the locked door.

Four hours had passed. He hadn't undressed; he hadn't even taken off his hat and overcoat.

He got up and left the house and went searching for a bar on Eighth Avenue which he remembered having heard was a hangout for muggers and stickup men, and where one could get a hot rod. He found the bar and kept on through to the back and sat on a stool.

A big fat black bartender with popeyes and a perpetually surprised expression came down and swabbed the bar in front of him.

"I want to buy a pistol," Jimmy said, lowering his voice.

The bartender jumped as though he'd been prodded with a shiv and his already popping eyes bugged out.

"This ain't no hardware store, man!" he exclaimed in a loud outraged voice, moving his arms theatrically. "This here is a respectable bar. We sells gin, whiskey, brandy, tequila, rum, wine, cordials, light and dark beer and ale. Nothing but alcoholic refreshments. Just name your drink and we got it." He frowned with dignity. "Now what you want to drink?"

"I'll have a Coke," Jimmy said.

The bartender looked shocked all over. "Is you come into my bar looking for trouble, man?" he asked challengingly.

"What you so mad about? What's wrong with drinking Coke?" Jimmy asked.

With silent disapproval the bartender served the drink, then stalked toward the front of the bar like an offended rooster.

Jimmy twisted about on his high wooden stool and looked for another soul-brother to approach about buying a pistol. Several ragged alcoholics stood at the front end of the long mahogany bar, nursing empty shot glasses, but the back end, where he sat among the stools reserved for the elite, was deserted. Two loafers posing as businessmen sat at a front table beneath the small, diamond-shaped, stained-glass panes, reading halves of the morning *News.* In one of the booths along the wall, a drunken prostitute slept; in another a blind beggar sat drinking cognac, his seeing-eye dog half asleep on the floor beside him. None of them appeared to him as likely hot rod peddlers.

He turned his attention back to the rows of flyspecked bottles on the mirror-backed shelves behind the bar. In the center was a faded sign reading:

DON'T ASK FOR CREDIT
HE'S DEAD

Through the corners of his eyes he noticed the bartender looking at him furtively, trying to case him.

Time passed. He sipped his Coke. The bartender started inching slowly back in his direction. He took his time. He swabbed the bar in front of imaginary customers. He wiped off a bottle and polished a glass. He tried the spigots in the sink to see if they were still working. He rinsed out his towel. He acted as though he wasn't giving his Coke-drinking customer a thought in the world. Slowly he worked his way back like a purse-snatcher stalking a sucker in a crowd. He stopped in front of Jimmy and looked down at the Coke with a jaundiced expression.

"You oughtn't to drink that stuff this early in the morning," he said. "It'll ruin your stomach."

Jimmy swished the liquid about in his glass. The bartender reminded him of a schoolteacher he'd had as a youth down South.

"What ought one to drink in the morning?" he asked dutifully.

"Gin," the bartender said. "It calms the stomach nerves."

"Okay, put some gin in it," Jimmy said.

Slowly, with a great show of hesitation, the bartender took the gin bottle and stood it on the bar.

"You don't want it in that Coke," he stated more than asked.

"Why not?"

"If it's for tonic you want to drink it, you oughtn't to mix it," the bartender informed him patiently. "Gin and Coke is an after-dinner liqueur, like all them French cognacs—fixes you up for the sport."

"What kind of sport?"

The bartender's brows shot up in a look of amazement. "*The* sport."

"Oh, you mean women," Jimmy said.

The bartender shot him a supercilious look. "What other kind of sport is there?" he asked condescendingly.

He replaced the gin bottle on the shelf and stalked off again, looking disgusted by Jimmy's ignorance. But he didn't go far this time. He only went far enough to swab an imaginary speck from the chrome-plated beer tap. Then he came back like a precinct cop giving the third degree.

"Who sent you here, fellow?"

"No one," Jimmy said. "I just heard I could get one here."

"Who told you that?"

"I don't remember."

"You ain't thinking about some other place, is you?"

"No, this is the place. This is the Blue Moon Bar, isn't it?"

"What's left of it," the bartender admitted cautiously. Again he took down the gin bottle, put two shot glasses on the bar and filled them to the brim.

"I don't want but one," Jimmy said.

The bartender's eyes popped. "Can't you see me, man, big as I is?"

"Excuse me," Jimmy said. He lifted his shot and toasted, "To your health."

The bartender picked his up and emptied it with a swallow. "Cheers," he said, smacking loudly and licking his lips. "You're new here, ain't you?"

"Yeah, practically," Jimmy admitted. "I've been here about six months. I came from Durham."

The bartender thought this over. "North Carolina?"

"Yes."

"There's a good show at the Apollo," he said. "It's a matinee today."

"What about it?" Jimmy asked.

"Good show is all," the bartender repeated noncommittally. "You ought to catch it."

"What for?"

The bartender studied him carefully. "It's got some acts what might interest a man like you from Durham, North

Carolina," he said just as carefully. "Got one act by two comedians you ought to like. One of these comedians says where can I buy a gun? Other comedian says you ought to go to the Apollo, man. First comedian says what for, man? Second comedian says you want to buy a gun, don't you? First comedian asks, they sells guns at the Apollo? Second comedian says naw, man, that's a theatre where a man can get a seat way up in the back row in the balcony, all by himself, nobody to bother you, nobody sitting on either side of you. First comedian asks how come all of that just to see a show? Second comedian says you want to buy a gun, don't you? First comedian says sure. Second comedian says that's the way I like to see shows."

The bartender looked hard at Jimmy to see if he had got it.

Jimmy had got it.

"Right," he said. "I'd like to see that show."

"I thought you would," the bartender said. "The price is right. Twenty bucks."

"Twenty bucks," Jimmy said. "That's all right."

"Best time to be there is around three-thirty," the bartender said.

"Three-thirty," Jimmy echoed.

The bartender lifted the bottle of gin. "Big or little?" he asked.

He lost Jimmy then. Jimmy looked at the shot glasses and looked at the bartender. "The same as before is all right," he said.

The bartender put down the bottle and stalked away in overwhelming disgust.

Suddenly Jimmy got it. "Hey," he called to the bartender.

The bartender returned with a great show of reluctance.

"Not too big, not too little," Jimmy said.

"That's what I always say," the bartender agreed, looking relieved. "Give a woman that's not too old and not too young. Thirty-two is the age I like best in a woman."

"You and me both," Jimmy said. He motioned toward the empty glasses. "What do I owe you?"

The bartender filled the shot glasses again without replying.

"*Salut*," Jimmy said, emptying his.

The bartender's brows shot up again. "Cheers," he said and emptied his. He licked his lips and said, "A buck, twenty."

Jimmy gave him two dollar bills, picked up a half dollar of the change. He slid from his stool and said, "I'm sure going to see that show."

The bartender smiled indulgently. "Have your sport, sport," he said.

Outside, a sand-fine snow drifted through the gray morning, stinging Jimmy's face. It wasn't yet eleven o'clock and he had to find some way to kill the time until his rendezvous. But he had decided when he left home that morning not to return until he had a pistol in his pocket.

He turned up his coat collar and walked down Eighth Avenue to 125th Street. Turning the corner toward Seventh Avenue, he came unthinkingly upon the entrance to the Big Bass Club. He was shocked by the sudden memory of the nightmare horror he had lived through since leaving there less than six hours ago. But he no longer felt helpless now that he knew he'd get a pistol.

"God helps those who helps themselves," his mother had often told him.

On passing a shoeshine parlor he turned in on sudden impulse and took a seat in the row of elevated chairs. A sign on the wall announced that shines were priced:

Regular—15¢
Special—20¢
Deluxe—25¢

"Regular," he said to the shoeshine boy.

The shoeshine boy gave him the silent treatment reserved for cheapskates and began dabbing liquid cleaner on his brown shoes as though thinking of more pleasant things.

In the back was a record shop presided over by a slim brown girl with a petulant expression. It was too early for her customers and she leaned on her elbows on the glass-topped counter, leafing through a Negro picture magazine with a bored air.

Jimmy's thoughts went to Linda as the shoeshine boy worked with the electric brush. He felt contrite for having left her as he did. She'd probably been so worried she couldn't sleep, he thought. And if she'd happened to go up to his room and found out he'd left without notifying her, she'd probably be terrified. Maybe he ought to have slept with her, he thought. She became so frustrated when she went without loving. But goddammit, she always thought she could solve all of life's problems in bed, he thought resentfully.

The shoeshine boy gave the cloth a final pop.

"*C'est fini,*" he said.

"*Vous avez fait du bon travail,*" Jimmy replied.

The shoeshine boy's dark face flowered in a sudden white smile. "You was stationed there too, hey, man? In gay Paree?"

"No, I was in Versailles," Jimmy lied. He had never been out of the States.

"That's what I like about the army," the shoeshine boy said enthusiastically. "They'd just as soon station you in them palaces as not."

Damn right, Jimmy thought. Someone else's palaces.

But he gave the boy a quarter and told him to keep the change. He hadn't eaten that morning and the two shots of gin on an empty stomach had made him light-headed and ravenous.

Frank's Restaurant was across the street, but the lunch-hour waiters were mostly white, old-timers left over from the time it was a Jim Crow place catering strictly to a white trade, and he didn't like their condescension. So he kept on walking toward Seventh Avenue, past the solid front of grocery stores, drugstores, shoe stores, hat stores, butcher shops, notion stores, and Blumstein's, the biggest department store uptown. Across the street, bars abutted bars, all selling the same liquor and all doing good business. The doors of the two theatres—the Apollo, which interspersed a B-movie between shows by big-name Negro bands, singers, and a black-face minstrel act; and Loew's 125th Street, which dished up a double feature of western and gangster films—were closed and the ticket booths empty. Loew's would open first, at one o'clock; the Apollo at two-thirty.

The Theresa Hotel occupied the corner site. On its ground floor corner was a snack bar called Chock Full O' Nuts. Jimmy passed it. He'd never decided whether it meant the place was chock full of nuts, or the food, or the customers felt as though they were chock full of nuts after eating the food. He couldn't imagine anything more disagreeable than being chock full of nuts.

He passed the hotel entrance and turned into the entrance to the hotel grill adjoining the lobby. Sitting on a high stool at the counter, he ate a breakfast of fried country sausage, scrambled eggs, hominy grits swimming in butter, two slices of buttered toast, and coffee with cream, served by a sleepy-eyed waitress. It was a good breakfast for 90¢ and he tipped the waitress a dime.

The clock over the counter read 11:30 when he'd finished. Still four hours to go.

He went out and stopped next door to read the titles of books by colored authors in the showcase of the hotel bookstore. *Black No More*, by George Schuyler, he read; *Black Thunder*, by Arna Bontemps; *The Blacker the Berry*, by Wallace Thurman; *Black Metropolis*, by Cayton and Drake; *Black Boy*, by Richard Wright; *Banana Bottom*, by Claude McKay; *The Autobiography of an Ex-Colored Man*, by James Weldon Johnson; *The Conjure-Man Dies*, by Rudolph Fisher; *Not Without Laughter*, by Langston Hughes.

Suddenly he felt safe. There, in the heart of the Negro community, he was lulled into a sense of absolute security. He was surrounded by black people who talked his language and thought his thoughts; he was served by black people in businesses catering to black people; he was presented with the literature of black people. *Black* was a big word in Harlem. No wonder so many Negro people desired their own neighborhood, he thought. They felt safe; there was safety in numbers.

The idea of a white maniac hunting him down to kill him seemed as remote as yesterday's dream. If he had seen Walker at the moment he would have walked up to him and knocked out his teeth.

It was a funny thing, he thought. He'd told the truth about the murders to a number of people. He'd told his girl; he'd told the D.A.; he'd told all the various police officials who'd questioned him; he'd told the lawyer representing Schmidt and Schindler. And none of them believed him. But he could walk up to any colored man in sight on that corner and tell him, and the man would believe him implicitly.

Looking up, he saw his silhouette reflected in the plate-glass window. Hair stuck out beneath the brim of his hat like wool beneath a sheep's ears.

"If I don't get a haircut I'll soon look like the original Uncle Tom," he said to himself, and turned in the direction of the barbershop south of 124th Street.

It was a big place with modernistic décor, six new chairs, and the latest in tonsorial equipment. It seemed specifically designed to make the customer defensive. All six chairs were occupied and most of the waiting seats were taken. The smartly uniformed barbers all had glossy straightened hair. Two manicurists were at work with their trays attached to the chair arms.

A brisk young woman in a glass cashier's cage asked, "Do you have an appointment, sir?"

"No, I don't," he confessed. "Do I need one?"

She gave him a patronizing smile, but a barber signaled that he'd take him on next, and she put away her smile.

He hung up his coat, put his hat on the rack and sat down and began absently leafing through *Ebony* Magazine. Prosperous people looked out from the pages. None looked as though they had anything to fear. Suddenly he began thinking about the killer and the horror returned. He wondered again what had happened to set him off; what had Fat Sam done or said? Or had it been Luke? The police admitted there'd been no sign of a struggle. So it had to be something that was said. But what could either one of them have said to get the both of them killed in cold blood? Jimmy knew that Walker was bent on killing him because he was the only one left to identify him. But what about them?

He was so engrossed in his thoughts the barber had to come over and get him when his chair became vacant. He slipped into the nylon gown and the barber wrapped a sheet of tissue paper about his neck.

"Just a haircut," he said.

The barber edged his hair with the electric clippers and feathered the neckline with the shears.

"Take some off the top," he said.

"You ought to have it straightened," the barber suggested. "You have just the right kind of hair; it's thick and coarse."

"You'd never get my die-hard kinks straightened out," Jimmy said, laughing.

"Oh yes," the barber said. "It'll come out soft as silk and straight as white folks' hair. I'll put a wave in it for you if you want."

Jimmy looked about at the other men with straightened hair. One man had his marcelled like a woman's. Then suddenly he thought of the detective sitting in the Big Bass Club talking to Linda, his thick blond hair shining in the dim light. Maybe it was the son of a bitch's hair that had caught Linda's fancy, he thought; maybe that was what had made her think he looked so innocent. Colored women were simple-minded about straight hair anyway, he thought.

"How much will it cost?" he asked.

"Seven dollars. That includes the cutting. But it'll last you for a couple of months," the barber said. "You'll just have to come in and have it trimmed every two weeks."

"Okay," Jimmy decided. "Give it the works."

The barber wrapped a bath towel about his neck, then daubed gobs of heavy yellow Vaseline into his hair and massaged it into the scalp.

"That's to keep from burning you," he explained as he went along. Then he took a large jar of a thick white emulsion and began applying it with a wooden spatula. "This here stuff that does the straightening job is liquid fire."

"What is it?" Jimmy asked.

"I don't know exactly," the barber admitted as he began slowly working the straightener into the Vaseline. "Some say it's made out of potato flour and lye, others say raw potatoes and lye. Anyway, it's got lye in it."

Jimmy felt his scalp begin to burn through the heavy coating of Vaseline. "Damn right," he said.

Using a fine-toothed metal comb with a wooden handle, the barber kneaded the smoldering paste slowly back and forth through Jimmy's hair until the hair was killed to the roots. Then he combed it back and forth until it became as straight as threads of silk.

When the straightening procedure was finished, he took Jimmy to one of the row of bowls at the back of the shop and washed his hair in hot soapy water until it was thoroughly clean. What had been a thick mass of kinky hair was now a mop of dull black hair so straight it stuck to his head. The barber took Jimmy back to the barber chair and massaged his hair with petroleum hair oil to give it a gloss. After that he carefully combed it and set it in big rolling waves. He tied a net about his head and put him beneath the hot-air drier to one side while he began on another customer. When his hair became dry, the barber removed the net and Jimmy had a head of sleek wavy locks. The operation had required two hours.

He stood and looked at himself in the mirror. Having straight hair gave him a strange feeling. He felt that he was handsomer, but he was vaguely ashamed, as though he'd turned traitor to his race.

The barber stood smiling, waiting for a compliment, but Jimmy couldn't meet his gaze. He tipped him a dollar from a sense of guilt, paid his check at the cashier's cage, and hurried from the shop.

But the big two-faced clock atop a pillar in front of the corner jewelry store told him there was still an hour to go before the Apollo opened. He crossed 125th Street, stopped in the United Cigar store and bought cigarettes, and kept on up Seventh Avenue.

He found that he was hungry again. He had a yen for some good home cooking, southern style: pig's feet and lye hominy; hog maws and collard greens; stewed chitterlings with black-eyed peas and rice; roasted opossum and candied yams; crackling cornbread; fried catfish and succotash; and some blackberry pie; or even just some plain buttermilk biscuits with blackstrap sorghum molasses.

He'd always heard that one could find anything and everything in Harlem, from purple Cadillacs to underwear made of unbleached flour sacks. But he hadn't found anything good to eat. The big chain cafeterias had come in and put the little restaurants out of business. All you could get in one of them was grilled chops and French fried potatoes; roasts and mashed potatoes; side dishes of creamed spinach and Harvard beets, green beans and plain boiled rice; all kinds of cockeyed salads —crab salad and tuna fish salad and chicken salad and egg salad. The salad dressing manufacturers must have started that salad craze, he thought. Tomato and lettuce salad with Thousand Island dressing. What kind of turds would that make? They'd made a salad spread where you didn't even need the salad anymore—you just spread the spread on two slices of bread and you had a salad sandwich.

He wanted some good heavy food that stuck to the linings of a man's stomach and gave you courage. He was tired of eating Schmidt and Schindler food, luncheonette-style food, no matter how good it was supposed to be.

He came to a dingy plate-glass, curtained-off storefront which held a sign reading: HOME COOKING. It looked like a letter from home. He went inside and sat at one of the five empty tables covered with blue-and-white checked oilcloth. To one side a coal fire burned in a potbellied stove. It was hot enough in there to give a white man a suntan.

He chose hog maws and turnip greens with a side dish of speckled peas. He splashed it with a hot sauce made from the seeds of chili peppers. The hot dish with the hot sauce scorched the inside of his mouth and burned his gullet as it went down. Sweat ran down his face and dripped from his chin. But after he'd finished, he felt a hundred percent better. He felt mean and dangerous and unafraid; he felt as if he could take the killer by his head and twist it off.

He sat there sweating and drinking cup after cup of boiled coffee strong enough to embalm the Devil, until it was time to go.

The doors of the Apollo were open and two uniformed colored cops were standing in the lobby when he arrived.

Only a few people came for the movie which preceded the stage show. With the exception of five teen-agers down in the front row, smoking marijuana, he had the balcony to himself.

A gangster film was showing. It looked like a grave-robbing job done on the corpse of the ancient movie, *Little Caesar*, by a drunken ghoul.

Near the end of the movie a young colored man came in and wormed down the row and took the seat beside him. He was dressed in a buttoned-up, belted trench coat and a snap-brim hat pulled low over his eyes. It was almost pitch-dark in the balcony but he wore dark sunglasses which looked as though he had glass spots in his black skin. He might have come straight out of the movie that was showing, Jimmy thought.

"You the man?" he asked in a husky whisper.

"Yeah," Jimmy replied in a whisper. "I'm the man."

He spoke so authoritatively the young man stiffened, thinking for the moment he might really be *The Man*.

"You the man what want a woman?" he asked.

The question startled Jimmy. He'd been expecting the man with the pistol. "What kind of woman?" he asked angrily.

It was the other's turn to be startled. "You *is* the man, ain't you?"

"Not if you're trying to sell me a woman," Jimmy said.

"Well, how old a woman would you buy if you was buying a woman?" the young man tried again.

"Oh," Jimmy said, getting it at last. "A thirty-two-year-old woman."

The other breathed in relief. "You is the man," he acknowledged.

With a pageantry of caution, he took a package wrapped in brown paper from beneath his coat and handed it to Jimmy.

Jimmy started fishing for his pocketbook, but the other said, "Go ahead and look at it, man."

Jimmy opened the package. A blue-steel .32-caliber revolver gleamed dully in the dim light. It had an iron butt with a corrugated grip and the replica of an owl's head imprinted on one side. Brass shells looked like dead birds' eyes staring from the cylinder chambers. It looked deadly in the dim light.

"It looks fine," Jimmy said.

"It'll kill a rock," the other said. "If you're close enough to it."

Jimmy paid him twenty dollars. The young man stored it away in some inside pocket beneath the buttoned-up trench coat and said, "See you, man," and left just before the lights came on.

Jimmy sat looking at the gun in the light. There was no one near enough to observe him. Suddenly he felt secure. He'd lay for him in the downstairs hall of his apartment house, he thought. He'd wait until the son of a bitch drew the pistol with the silencer, then he'd kill him. He wasn't apprehensive or excited. He wasn't scared of what might happen to him afterward. He looked at it objectively, as though it concerned someone else. He'd kill the son of a bitch with the pistol in his hand, and then they could all believe whatever in the hell they wanted to believe after that.

He had a pistol too now. He had evened up the difference. He stuck the pistol against his belly, underneath his belt, and buttoned up his coat. He got up to go.

19

LINDA WAS in the downstairs hall of the apartment house when Jimmy arrived. She gripped him by the arm.

"Don't scare me like that," she said tensely. She looked furious. "I've been waiting here for hours, afraid to move."

"What the hell for?" he said roughly. "You don't believe I'm in any danger."

"You fool!" she said.

He tried to move her hand from his arm. She wouldn't let go.

"No," she said. "You're coming with me."

They rode up in the elevator in silent conflict, neither looking at the other.

When the elevator stopped on the third floor, she tugged at his arm. He pulled back. She backed against the door to keep it from closing.

"Goddammit, come on!" she cried. "I'm going to put you to sleep. When I get through rocking you you'll want to go to sleep and never wake up."

"You're the one who's a fool," he said, but he let her drag him from the elevator.

She held to his arm like a cop making an arrest and didn't let go until she had her key in the lock.

It was dark in the apartment. She switched on the overhead light and closed the door. Then she turned and gripped him by both arms as though she would shake him.

"Now you listen to me—" she began. She broke off and stared at him appraisingly. "You look different," she observed. "You got a haircut. While I was worrying myself sick there you were—" She stopped. Her eyes widened. She took off his hat. "Oh, daddy, you've got new hair!" she exclaimed rapturously. She ran her fingers through his oily locks, rumpling his waves. "It's soft as silk." She gave him an adoring smile and cooed, "Daddy, you look beautiful."

Then she went as sweet as sugar candy. Her big brown eyes got limpid and her mouth got wet. Her body folded into his.

He could feel her pointed breasts through the thickness of their coats.

He pulled her tight against him. His lips melted into hers. Right then he would have given everything to be free of his horror and fear and the terrifying knowledge that a mad killer was stalking him. He peeled back her coat and buried his mouth in her neck. He could hear her gasping.

Her hands fumbled with the buttons of his overcoat as she pressed her body hard against his. She got it open and opened his suit coat. Her hand moved down from his chest. It touched the handle of the .32-caliber revolver stuck beneath his belt. She said "Oh!" Her hand closed about the grip. She said "Oh!" again in a different tone of voice.

Her body stiffened. She jerked her body from his embrace, flung open his coat, and pulled the pistol out.

"Jesus," she said in sudden cold shock.

"Give it here," he said and reached for it.

"No! No! No!" she cried, holding it out of his reach.

"Goddammit, give it here!" he shouted and lunged toward her, clutching at her wrist. "That isn't any plaything!"

"You fool!" she muttered.

She twisted sideways, holding the pistol extended, and bumped him with her hip. He grabbed her by the shoulders and tried to turn her around.

"That thing's loaded," he warned.

She wrenched loose from his grip and butted him with her solid hips, knocking his feet from under him. She tried to run but he grabbed her about the neck like a drowning man clutching at a log. She kept running and carried him halfway across the sitting room as he hung on. His weight made her stumble and fall to her knees, and she was unable to brace herself because she still held the pistol extended. He landed heavily on her back, flattening her to the carpet.

"You can't have it," she panted as she squirmed about beneath him.

He clung to her neck and tried to inch up her back. Their heavy coats hampered their movements and their bodies began to steam in the close hot room.

She made a sudden turn and rolled over beneath him. He

grabbed at the love seat with one hand, trying to get anchorage, but missed it, and she slipped from his grip. When she tried to stand up he made another sudden grab for her wrist. He got hold of her coat sleeve and pulled her down again. She kept twisting and they smashed into the spindle-legged lamp table and knocked it over. A leg broke with a crashing sound and the alabaster lamp thudded on the floor.

Her struggles ceased automatically.

"You're breaking up my furniture!" she screamed.

"Goddamn your furniture," he muttered and lunged toward her like a swimmer.

Before she could move again he had captured both of her wrists.

"Goddamn you!" she grated in a raw fury. "You broke my table."

She tried to hit him in the face but couldn't free her hand. She twisted beneath him in a blind rage, threshing about like harpooned fish. He pinned her wrists to the floor, flattening her on her back, and sat astride her stomach. She ceased struggling and spat in his face.

"I'll pay you back," she said through gritted teeth. Her face was swollen with rage.

"Let it go, goddammit," he muttered.

She released her grip on the pistol. "All right, go ahead and take it," she grated. "And I hope you get yourself killed."

He knocked the pistol out of reach and started to get up. But something about the way she lay touched off his passion like an electric shock. Her skirt had hiked up to her sky-blue nylon panties, exposing a smooth brown sheen of legs above her stockings. The violent exertion had opened her pores and a strong compelling odor of woman and perfume came up from her like scented steam. He felt his mouth fill with tongue and his stomach drain down to his groin.

"I'm going to take it all right, goddammit," he mouthed, and reached down and opened her legs.

It didn't need any force; they opened at his touch.

They made love in a sweating rage, as though trying to kill one another. They uttered strange guttural sounds as though cursing one another in a savage tongue. When they had finished, neither could move. They lay waiting for strength to return, panting for breath.

Then he stood up and buttoned his clothes and straightened his overcoat. He picked up the pistol without looking at her and stuck it back into his belt. The air was fecund with the mating smell. He didn't speak.

She stood up then and began shaking her skirt down like a pullet rustling its tail feathers. Her attention went first to the broken table. She tried to stand it up before removing her coat. But it wouldn't stand on three legs.

"You've broken my favorite antique," she said accusingly, but she didn't sound angry anymore.

"It's more of an antique now," he said unsympathetically.

She threw him a reproving look. But she was drained of rancor. She felt almost light-hearted with a warm afterglow.

"You'll have to have it fixed," she said and propped it against the wall.

"Of course," he said.

She picked up the alabaster lamp and set it on the table close to the wall so it wouldn't topple off. Then she switched it on to see if it was broken. She acted as though she'd forgotten all about the pistol.

The light came on, shining up into her face, highlighting her softly molded features in exotic relief. Sweat was beaded on her upper lip.

Finally she sighed. "Now I suppose you want to take your pistol and go out and shoot him," she said, half in derision. "Or have I got some sense into you?"

"He's got his pistol and I've got mine," he said stubbornly. "That makes us even now."

"Come on and go to bed," she said. "I'm not going to let you go until you've got some sense."

"To you that's the only thing that makes any sense," he said harshly.

"Well, isn't it?" she said.

He didn't answer.

She took off her fur coat and threw it carelessly across the armchair. "I'll make us some drinks," she said and started toward the kitchen.

"I'm not going to stay," he said.

She turned and looked at him tentatively. Then she walked up to him, cupped his face in her hands, drew it down and kissed him, forcing her tongue between his teeth.

He pushed her away and picked up his hat from the floor.

"Leave the pistol here," she pleaded.

"Hell no," he said.

"Two wrongs don't make a right," she argued. She still felt she could persuade him to give her the pistol.

But she only infuriated him. "Goddamn the morality of it!" he flared. "We can stand here and argue all night about what's right and what's wrong. You've got your opinion and I've got mine. You can't convince me and I can't convince you. People have been arguing a thousand years about right and wrong. I'm finished with that. I'm going to kill the schizophrenic bastard and keep on living myself."

The warm afterglow left her and her loins turned icy cold.

"You sound more like a crazy killer than he does," she charged. "You sure it's not you who is persecuting him, instead of the other way around?"

"I ought to slap you in the mouth for that," he said.

"Go ahead and slap me," she taunted him. "Draw your big pistol and shoot me. Everybody is persecuting mama's boy and he's got to knock everybody around. Next thing you'll be saying is that I'm trying to kill you too."

His neck swelled from holding his temper. He gave her a long, appraising look. "You know, Linda, you don't sound like a colored woman," he said thoughtfully. "You've been taking up for this white bastard ever since you talked to him."

"You don't think I'm colored do you!" she exclaimed and began tearing off her clothes in a fury of defiance. She didn't stop until she was stripped to her stockings and garter belt. "Do I look like I'm white, or do you want to see some more?"

His hair-trigger passion flared again, but he held himself in. "Listen," he said slowly. "Last night when I left you here he was laying for me in the hall outside. I took the stairs just on impulse instead of taking the elevator. I'm sure he was hiding in the elevator and if I'd stepped inside of it he'd have shot me. As it was he followed me up the stairs and if he hadn't slipped and made a lot of noise I'd be dead right now."

"He's admitted he's following you," she said without bothering to put her clothes back on. "He's just trying to trap the killer, he says. If that doesn't make sense, why hasn't he killed you before now?"

"He hasn't had a chance, that's why."

"Then why didn't he kill you last night—or this morning rather? Just because he slipped and you saw him shouldn't have made any difference, the way you tell it. He'd have been glad for you to see him shoot you, according to your story."

"Because I ran, that's why. Because I lit out and ran for my life, just like I did the first time. He had the pistol in his hand. The same one with the silencer attached. The one he killed Luke and Fat Sam with. And shot me with. Listen, I'm going to tell you just exactly how it happened."

She felt herself turn to ice all over as she listened to his story. If what he said was true, she'd slept with Matt right after he'd tried to kill him.

"I can't believe it," she said in a horrified tone of voice.

"I'm not trying to make you believe it anymore," he said and put on his hat. "And I'm not going to run anymore. I'm through with that shit."

He walked out and slammed the door behind him.

She rushed into her bedroom and snatched the telephone from the night table as though to rip out the cord. Her fingers trembled as she dialed Walker's number.

"If I find out he's telling the truth I'll stab out your heart myself," she raved, speaking aloud to herself.

Walker's number didn't answer.

Her imagination began to work. Maybe Walker was somewhere in the building still. If Jimmy ran into him he might shoot him on sight; she wasn't sure any longer what Jimmy might do. But Walker was more used to handling pistols than Jimmy. If he saw Jimmy draw, he'd beat him to the draw. She imagined them in a gun duel on the service stairway. One falling dead, rolling head over heels down the stairs. Which one?

Sudden terror sent her flying to the bathroom. Then she went into the kitchen and drank a glass of gin. She sat down but she didn't feel the cold plastic seat on her bare skin. Panic kept coming up inside of her like the taste of vomit.

Suddenly she jumped up and ran into the sitting room. She'd have to find out whether Matt was in the building. She started out of the door without realizing she was undressed. A man was coming from the apartment across the hall. His eyes bucked as though he'd hit a hundred-dollar jackpot. His gaze focused on one point of her anatomy.

She drew back and slammed the door in his face. She grabbed her clothes from where she'd thrown them on the floor. She was frantic with haste. She had started out again when she got on her dress, then stopped and slipped into her fur coat.

This coat will be worn out before I get it paid for, she thought absently.

Outside, the man from across the hall was waiting patiently. She made for the elevator. He followed her. She rode up to the top floor and walked to the service stairs. He kept following her. She started down the stairs. He closed up and took her by the arm.

"How about my apartment, sugar, it's cozier," he said.

She swatted him in the face with the palm of her hand.

He backed away and felt blood dripping from his nose. He took out his handkerchief to staunch the blood. She continued on down the stairs. He called after her, "You is crazy, sure enough. I thought you was crazy."

She kept down the stairs to the entrance foyer, walked to the back of the hall and tried the door leading to the basement stairs. It was locked. She went to the front of the hall beside the entrance and sat down on the hard wooden straight-backed bench beside the door.

People came and went. Married couples eyed her furtively: the husbands with secret longing, the wives with secret envy, each hiding it from the other. Single women eyed her jealously. Most of the single men made passes at her, and several of the single women. Some sat down beside her, but the atmosphere was too cold for comfort.

She sat there for an hour in a cold numb panic, scarcely noticing the people who spoke to her. She was watching for Walker.

Suddenly it occurred to her that Jimmy might not be in his room. He might have gone out looking for Walker.

She jumped up and took the elevator back to her apartment and telephoned Jimmy's apartment. The girl, Sinette, answered. She said she would see if Jimmy was in his room. A moment later she said, "He hasn't come back since he went out this morning. Is that you calling, Miss Collins?"

"Yes," Linda said. "When he comes home have him call me at once, please."

She started to go back to the bench beside the entrance and take up her watch again. Then she realized it would be useless. She might be able to stop it from happening for a time, but as long as Jimmy had the gun and Matt kept following him about, one of them was certain to be killed.

She felt herself going dead inside. She went back to the kitchen and swallowed four shots of gin in rapid succession. Then she went into her bedroom and dialed police headquarters.

A tired voice said, "Central Police."

"I'd like to talk to someone in the department that investigates murders," she said.

"About what?" the voice asked indifferently.

"I'd like to talk to the person who's investigating the murders at the Schmidt and Schindler luncheonette at—"

"You mean the automat murders," the voice said, taking on a slight interest. "Just hang on, I'll turn you over to homicide."

The voice from homicide told her to come down to the Homicide Bureau on Leonard Street and ask for Sergeant Peter Brock.

20

When Walker awakened, the room was dark. The shades were drawn. He had no idea what time it was.

He felt a sudden sense of danger. He became alert in every nerve, tense in every muscle. He lay still without breathing. He strained his ears to listen.

But he heard only the muted sound of the television from the adjoining sitting room. Then he heard Jeanie scream with laughter, and Peter Junior shout, "Hush!"

He knew that Jenny had told them to keep quiet because he was asleep in the guest room. He sensed that they resented his presence. But the sense of danger was something different. It was imminent, as though a reckoning were closing in upon him.

Finally he moved his arm and looked at the luminous dial of his wristwatch. The radiant hands pointed to 6:31. He had slept all day. He felt as though he had wasted precious time.

He switched on the reading light and felt along the floor for the bottle of rye. His hand encountered nothing. He turned over on his side and craned his neck to peer over the edge of the bed. He saw nothing but the dark green carpet. He leaned over to look underneath the bed. It was gone. That was more of Jenny's doings.

He felt the need of a drink bad. But there was no way of getting to the liquor cabinet in the sitting room with the children there. He damned Brock's children to hell.

With an abrupt movement he stood up. He'd slept nude but there was a fresh pair of pajamas and a bathrobe hung across the back of a chair. They were Brock's, he knew. He thought of that saying that came out of the war: Kilroy was here. Only it was Jenny who had been here.

But it wasn't that.

He put on the robe. It was too big for him. He hadn't realized Brock was so much thicker than himself.

He kept looking about the room. His sixth sense kept sounding the danger alarm. But it was something he couldn't see.

His clothes had been hung up, he noticed. His holstered service revolver had been hung from a chair back by the strap. That was strange. Jenny didn't like the sight of pistols. He knew that she had come in and straightened up while he was asleep.

But it wasn't that.

He opened the clothes closet and looked into his coat pockets for cigarettes and his lighter. His sixth sense sounded danger like a burglar alarm. He stiffened. Suddenly he knew his clothes had been searched. He didn't know how he knew it, but suddenly it was fact. The presence of the searcher was as strong as a scent.

"Brock," he muttered softly to himself. "What the hell is his game?"

He felt the danger closing in. It was as though he were being cornered by hounds of retribution.

I'll have to finish it tonight, he told himself. It can't go on any longer. I'll have to finish off the last Negro and ditch the gun.

It was as though the pistol had turned red-hot. It was the pistol that would hang him.

He went quickly into the bathroom and put his ear to the panel of the adjoining door. He could hear the muted sounds of the television, but nothing else.

They'd all be eating soon, he reckoned. They usually ate dinner at 6:30 in the winter, but they were probably waiting on him to awaken. Jenny would no doubt be in the kitchen. She fixed the meals herself and had the colored girl serve. By now Brock should be home. He always thought of Brock by his family name. But Brock would probably be downstairs in his workroom.

He knocked gently on the door panel. There was no answer. He knocked louder. He didn't expect an answer, but he wanted to make sure. Silently he turned the knob and pushed. The door didn't budge. He pushed harder, then leaned his weight against it softly.

"Bolted from the other side," he muttered.

Never to his knowledge had they locked the bathroom door.

That smart son of a bitch! he thought.

He wondered how much Brock knew. His teeth clenched

and the taut muscles rippled down his jaws. He had to fight down the rising panic. Had Brock found the gun, or was he just guessing?

There was a door from the guest room to the sitting room on one side, and to the adjoining bath on the other. Brock's and Jenny's bedroom opened into a hall that ran in back of the sitting room to the dining room and another short hall that led to the kitchen and the garage. In order to get into their bedroom with the bathroom door locked, he would have to pass through the sitting room and dining room.

"The clever bastard," he said softly.

He'd have to wait until they were all at dinner and then find some excuse to leave the table for a moment. It would have to be a good excuse because Brock would be watching him. He could act as though he were suddenly nauseated and had to rush to the toilet. That would be crude, but it would be believable.

He got under a cold shower and stayed as long as he could bear it. The tension didn't leave him but the panic subsided. While he was toweling himself he heard someone open the bedroom door. His stomach knotted.

"Matt." It was Jenny's voice. He realized he'd been holding his breath.

"Yes, Jenny."

"Hurry up. Dinner's on the table."

"Coming right away."

He heard her leave and close the door behind her.

He dressed hurriedly. He was in a frenzy of haste to see the expression in Brock's eyes.

The sitting room was empty when he passed through. Two television stools sat side by side, facing the dead screen. He kept on through to the dining room, bracing himself to meet his brother-in-law.

Everyone was seated. Brock sat at one end of the table, Jenny at the other. There was a place for him across from the two children.

A sepia-colored girl was serving grapefruit halves.

As he walked behind the children to get to his place, he rumpled Peter's hair. Peter was nine. He moved his head in a gesture of displeasure.

"'Lo, uncle Matt," he said grudgingly.

His hand moved on to Jeanie's head. She was eleven and wore her hair in pigtails. She reacted to his gesture like a kitten, smiling up at him.

He took his seat and unfolded his napkin. Finally he met Brock's gaze. There wasn't anything in Brock's eyes.

"Jenny said you were working all last night," he said.

"Yeah," Brock said. "On the automat murders."

Jenny's face contorted with revulsion. "Do we have to talk about that at the dinner table?" she said sharply.

They finished their grapefruit in silence. The girl removed the plates and brought in a leg of lamb and serving dishes containing peas and carrots, whipped potatoes and a sauce. Brock carved and served the roast and Jenny the vegetables as the plates circled the table. The girl served individual plates of mint gelatin salad. There was a napkin-covered basket of poppyseed rolls. The children drank milk with their dinner; the grownups water.

Matt forced down a mouthful of the roast.

"How do you feel now?" Jenny asked.

"Fine," he said. Then he turned to Brock and asked, "No word of my girl friend as yet?"

"Not that one," Brock said. "We ran across another one."

Matt knew the answer but he had to ask anyway. "What one was that?"

The children stared at him with silent curiosity.

"Eva Modjeska," Brock said.

"She must be a foreigner," Peter piped up.

"Children should be seen and not heard," Jenny rebuked him sharply.

Matt felt the tension growing in his chest and tried to control his breathing. "How did you run across her?" he asked between breaths.

"Coincidence," Brock said. "Somebody called homicide and said there was a murdered woman at that address."

The breath turned rock hard in Matt's chest.

"If you're going to discuss murders, you'll both have to leave this table," Jenny said angrily.

Brock showed his willingness to keep silent but Matt blurted out, "Was she dead?"

"No," Brock murmured. "Somebody beat her up bad; but she wouldn't say who."

Jenny turned furiously on Matt. "I mean it," she said.

"Uncle Matt's getting sent from the table," Peter said slyly.

Jenny wheeled on him. "Another word out of you and you'll get sent to bed."

Matt forced a grin and stood up. Now was his chance to get the pistol from her closet. "My stomach was turning flip-flops anyway," he said.

"Sit down, Matt," Brock said. It was said cordially enough but it sounded almost like an order.

Matt jerked a look of sudden rage at Brock. For an instant their eyes locked. There still wasn't anything in Brock's eyes.

Then Jenny said, "Oh, sit down and finish your dinner and quit acting like a child. You should know better than to talk about such things before the children."

Matt was caught. His face had flushed crimson but it didn't look as though it was caused by his stomach. He sat down reluctantly and riveted his gaze on his plate. He didn't want Brock to see the murderous rage in his eyes.

They were all saved from embarrassment by the telephone ringing.

Brock started to get up to answer it but Jenny stopped him. "Let the maid answer it."

The maid passed through from the kitchen to the telephone stand in the back hall.

"Mr. Peter Brock's residence," they heard her say in a proper voice. Then after a moment she said, "I will see if he is here."

Brock got up and went to the phone. "Yeah," he said. "Yeah . . . Yeah . . . Hold her, I'll be right down."

He came back into the dining room but didn't sit down. "I'm sorry, Jenny," he said, "but I have to leave. Something important has come up."

"Can't you finish your dinner first?" she said.

"No. There isn't much time," he said.

Matt winced. He felt time closing in on him.

"Want me to go along with you?" he asked in a breathless voice.

"You'd better stay here," Brock said, without giving him an opening to ask about the call.

Matt waited until he heard Brock back his car out of the drive. Jenny was saying something but he didn't know what. Then he said, "Excuse me," and got up.

"You haven't had your dessert," Jenny said.

"Another time," he said.

He went down the hall toward her and Brock's bedroom. He knew that she heard him and wondered why he went that way to get to the guest room. But it didn't matter what she thought. She wouldn't follow him and if she did, that wouldn't matter either.

He had to get the pistol and get going. Get it cleaned up. Brock was right. There wasn't much time.

21

THE NAME on the stainless-steel doorplate read: MATHEW WALKER.

Jimmy pushed the bell button and heard the distant sound of muted chimes. He felt the pistol beneath his belt pressing against his drum-tight belly. It reassured him. But there was no need drawing it now.

He waited. No one answered. There was no Judas window in the door. No one could see him from the inside. He pushed the button again.

He knew what he was going to do. He didn't feel nervous but he noticed that his hands were trembling. He breathed in short jerky gasps.

Still no one answered.

He turned and walked back down the red flagstone floor of the well-lighted corridor past other identical polished pine doors spaced along the pale blue walls. He felt his knees buckling from nerve tension.

The main thing was to keep his head, he told himself. Just don't get panicky. If Walker was at home and had spotted him through some unseen peephole in the door, then everything was fine. Walker wasn't going to shoot him in the back right there in the house in Peter Cooper Village where he lived.

A woman came from one of the doors and looked him over appraisingly. She seemed intrigued by what she saw. She appraised him further while they waited for the elevator.

She was a dark-haired woman with a bony, interesting face, dark eyes and a big mouth splashed with red. She wore a white knitted scarf over her head and a black cloth coat with an extremely wide flare. She looked about thirty-five and well-sexed.

They had the elevator to themselves. She smiled at him.

"Are you looking for someone?" she asked.

On sudden impulse he said, "Listen, if I get killed down here by someone it'll be detective Mathew Walker who did it. Remember that."

She shrank into the far corner and gave him a horror-stricken look. When the elevator stopped on the main floor she hurried out, giving him a swift frightened glance over her shoulder before disappearing toward the exit.

Jimmy didn't follow her. The elevators were situated on the corridor which ran parallel to the street. There was a pine-paneled waiting room beside the entrance.

He took a seat beside a reading table where he could see everyone who entered or left the building. Shaded wall lamps gave the room an intimate air. An artificial fire burned brightly in the English-type fireplace. A man and a woman on a nearby settee were talking in low intense voices. There was an atmosphere of quiet, genteel respectability.

Jimmy wondered how a killer like Walker fitted into that picture. But he didn't want to think about it. He didn't want to think about anything. He knew what he was going to do, and there was no need of any further thought.

The well-dressed people who had gone to work that morning were returning, singly and in pairs, with slightly wilted looks and lines of weariness in their faces. They gave Jimmy scarcely a glance.

Jimmy waited. His legs trembled. The handle of the pistol jabbed into his stomach. He cleaned his fingernails with a penknife. Time passed. White faces swam past his vision. Ordinarily he would have felt ill at ease, out of place. But he felt nothing.

Walker came in hurriedly. His hat was slanted to the back of his head and his hands were dug into the pockets of his flapping trench coat. Red spots burned in his high cheekbones and his face had a murderous expression.

He saw Jimmy and did a double take. Shock showed openly in his opaque blue eyes. Then came a flicker of fear. An instant later the opaqueness closed in again. He took a seat on the other side of the fireplace and looked at the artificial fire with a sad expression. He sat with his legs stretched out and both hands in his coat pockets as though time meant nothing to him.

He's got the pistol in his pocket, Jimmy thought. His drawn-up legs began jerking from nerve tension. He stood up and went toward the exit, walking stiff-jointed, his shoulders high and braced and his back flattened like a board.

Walker got leisurely to his feet and followed.

Jimmy stopped in the doorway and looked up and down

the street. Snow covered the plots of grass and lighted windows dotted the surrounding buildings. His plan was to make Walker follow him uptown and kill him in the hall of his own apartment house. But first he had to get safely on the bus. And it was four blocks to the nearest bus stop at the corner of First Avenue and 23rd Street.

A couple came from the building and went down the steps to the sidewalk. When they turned in the direction of First Avenue, Jimmy leaped down the steps and passed them and slowed to a walk a few paces ahead.

Walker came down and followed a few paces behind.

The couple crossed the street. Jimmy crossed ahead of them, Walker behind. They came to a side street for pedestrians only. The couple turned off and left Jimmy walking in the empty road. His heart jumped into his mouth. What was to stop Walker from shooting him in the back and turning into the next building? No one would see him; no one would hear the shot.

He wheeled about, facing Walker across the street, and sprinted after the departing couple. The man heard him approaching and turned defensively.

"Pardon me, sir," Jimmy gasped. "I'm looking for a man named Mr. Williamson." The man eyed him suspiciously. "He asked me to come down and see him about some work," he continued hurriedly. "I've been looking all over this place and I can't find the address."

They were a middle-aged couple and the man looked patient. "What address did he give you, boy?" he asked.

"He said the first house on the first walk off Peter Cooper Road, but I haven't seen anything down here but streets."

The man smiled tolerantly. "This is the first walk so it must be one of these two houses facing each other."

Jimmy saw Walker loitering in front of the house across the street. He said, "Thank you, I'll try this one."

The man waited for him to enter the building. The entrance hall was deserted. He made a show of looking at the nameplates over the mailboxes. Through the glass-paneled doors he saw the couple moving off; then Walker sauntering across the street. He unbuttoned his coat and gripped the handle of his pistol.

It was a tight spot. If he shot Walker down there and they didn't find the murder pistol on him, he could offer no defense. If Walker shot him without anyone witnessing it, there'd be no way to tie it to him.

A woman entered from the street, carrying a shopping bag. He went quickly ahead of her to the elevator. The elevator was empty and they boarded it together. She looked at him suspiciously and tightened her grip on her purse. She got off at the fourth floor. There were push buttons for eight floors. Jimmy pushed the button for the top floor. When it reached the top he opened and closed the door and pushed the button for the second floor. His plan was to get off and try to find some other way out of the building if no one had boarded it by then. But people boarded it at every floor and it was crowded by the time it reached the bottom.

Walker was standing there as though waiting for the elevator when the doors opened. Their eyes met briefly. Jimmy's brown eyes widened in a look of pure hatred; Walker's blue eyes looked dispassionate.

People started toward the exit. Jimmy followed, keeping close.

At the bottom of the steps a big man in a loud tweed ulster stopped and tipped a wide-brimmed hat to a younger woman in a fur coat.

"I hope it'll be my pleasure to see more of you, ma'am," he said. "I'd like to have the pleasure of taking you to dinner."

The woman smiled coyly. "You have my phone number, Mr. Davis. Phone me tomorrow afternoon."

"That I'll do," the big man said.

"Tomorrow afternoon, Mr. Davis."

"Just call me Jim, ma'am. Jim Davis. That's the name. I'm not used to all this formality."

"All right, Jim," the woman said in honeyed tones.

"Until then," the big man said gallantly and turned in the direction of Peter Cooper Road, the woman in the opposite direction.

Jimmy closed in beside the man. "Pardon me, sir," he said, "but can you tell me how to get to the bus stop?"

The big man stopped and looked at him. "You're new here in New York, aren't you, boy?"

"Yes sir," Jimmy replied. "Just got here last week. Been down here to see a man about some work, but I don't know how to get out of this place."

"How you like it up here?" the big man asked.

Jimmy drew his shoulders together and shivered theatrically. "Sure is cold." He found the Uncle Toming distasteful, but it was necessary.

The big man laughed. "I'm from Texas—what part of the South are you from?"

"Georgia," Jimmy lied. "Columbus, Georgia."

"This ain't like Georgia, is it?"

"No sir, wish I was back."

The big man chuckled. "Come on, I'll show you where you catch your bus."

They walked side by side toward First Avenue.

"What I hate about this city is it's full of foreigners," the big man said. "In my town there ain't nobody but Americans and colored folks and a few Mexicans—Americans all," he added grandiloquently. "Here it's just like one of those European capitals."

Small stores fronted on First Avenue and it was brightly lit. When they'd walked a block, Jimmy said, "Boss, I think we're being followed."

The big man stopped abruptly and turned about. He spotted Walker immediately. "Yeah, that fellow in the trench coat looking in that delicatessen window. I saw him when I left the house."

"Yes sir, I saw him there too, standing in the hall."

The big man looked at Jimmy thoughtfully. "Is he following you or me?"

"He ain't got no reason to be following me, boss," Jimmy said. "I ain't done nothing to nobody."

The big man chuckled. "Maybe he's one of those sissies," he conjectured, staring at Walker a moment longer. But Walker seemed absorbed in a roast turkey. "Don't worry about him," he added. "I'm a sheriff in my hometown; I know how to take care of his kind."

"I sure am glad of that," Jimmy said.

The big man walked him to the bus stop and patted him on the shoulder. "Here you are, boy. Do you know how to get home from here?"

"Yes sir, boss. Thank you, sir."

The big man crossed the street to a taxi stand and got into a taxi. Several other people were waiting for the 23rd Street bus. Walker was nowhere in sight.

But as the bus appeared, Walker came suddenly from a tobacco store across the street. Jimmy was the third one to board; Walker waited until last. It was near the start of its run and the bus was practically empty. Jimmy chose an empty seat near the middle. Walker sat in the seat across from him. Neither looked at the other. The bus filled up.

Jimmy transferred to the Broadway bus at Madison Square. Others transferred, Walker among them.

They rode standing to Columbus Circle, then found seats. Neither showed the slightest interest in the other.

Jimmy alighted at 145th Street; Walker followed.

On one corner was a big chain drugstore; on the other a cafeteria of the Bickford chain. There were subway kiosks on all the corners. The intersection was well lit and crowded with people of all races.

Jimmy walked leisurely up Broadway, past the lighted front of the Woolworth store, the lobby of the RKO movie house. He was on his home ground. He was tense but he wasn't scared. He knew that Walker intended to kill him before he could get up to his room. But he wasn't worried. He was going to kill him first.

He kept close to other people, made a point of keeping someone between himself and Walker, in the line of fire, all the time.

Pedestrian traffic thinned in the block between 148th and 149th Streets. Jimmy put himself in front of a big colored couple so that they practically walked on his heels. As he neared 149th Street, his stomach began to knot. It was like a film showing the countdown for an atom bomb. The hand was ticking off the seconds toward the zero hour. He had to get across 149th Street; then walk thirty paces on 149th Street to the entrance of the apartment house—he had counted them. Once he got inside the hallway he had to station himself so he would be out of line of fire from the street but facing the door, so he would see Walker first.

When he came to the curb he stepped out from in front of the colored couple and turned to look down the street to get Walker's exact position. He had gripped his pistol and had drawn it halfway from his belt.

Walker had disappeared. He was thunderstruck. He stood there foolishly for an instant, not knowing which way to turn. The street was momentarily empty in all directions. He was a perfect target. A sudden surge of panic shocked him into action.

Bell's Bar & Grill fronted on Broadway at the corner. Behind the curtained windows colored people crowded about the circular bar. The muted blare of the jukebox floated into the street. Parked cars lined the curb in front.

He ducked instinctively and broke toward the entrance to the bar. The bullet aimed for his heart hit him high in the left shoulder, and spun him about. He went off balance, falling in a grotesque stumble. The second bullet hit him in the back, beneath the right shoulder blade, went between two ribs and penetrated his right lung. He couldn't hear the shots and didn't know what direction they were coming from. He felt the tearing of the bullet's trajectory inside him. He tried to call for help but didn't have the breath. Nothing came from his mouth but blood. With one last desperate effort he jerked his pistol free and fired it at the pavement.

The shot hurried Walker. He was standing in the street between two parked cars. He had opened the hood of one and was bent over as though looking at the motor. His head and shoulders were shielded from view from all sides. He held the pistol with the silencer out of sight beneath the hood. He shot once more quickly, aiming at the head of the grotesquely stumbling figure, but missed.

Jimmy was unconscious when his body crashed heavily into the plate glass door of Bell's Bar.

The doors of the bar burst open and excited colored people erupted. The man in front did a hop-skip-and-jump to keep from stepping on the fallen body.

"My God!" a woman screamed, catching sight of Jimmy.

People came running from all directions, attracted by the sound of his one futile shot. From inside the bar a big bass voice blared from the jukebox.

Walker put the pistol into his trench coat pocket and sauntered calmly across the northbound traffic lane, skirted the dividing parkway, and crossed the traffic lane on the other side of Broadway. He didn't look back.

He was accustomed to scenes of violence. He knew that he wouldn't be noticed. There was always a period of from one to five minutes after a killing when the victim claimed everyone's whole attention. No one ever looked about for the killer until they had recovered from the shock.

He turned south on Broadway and continued walking casually toward the subway kiosk. He could have left the pistol in the motor of the car. That would have substantiated his story that some uptown racketeer did all three killings. But he wasn't finished with it yet. He had one more to go.

It had been a mistake to let her keep the pistol, he was thinking. He should have reckoned on a woman's curiosity. But there was no help for it now. She was the last witness who could appear against him. She had to be silenced and then it would be over. And then he would get rid of the pistol forever.

He knew it was going to look strange as hell for her to be killed with the same pistol that killed three Schmidt and Schindler Negro porters. The police might conceivably suspect him; they would know he had been often seen with her. Brock would know for sure. But that couldn't be helped. They couldn't convict him without the pistol because there wouldn't be any witnesses left. They could think whatever they goddamned well pleased.

He was going down the steps of the subway kiosk when the first of the patrol cars screamed around the corner into Broadway from 145th Street.

22

BROCK STARED thoughtfully at Linda across his desk. He fiddled with a 98¢ plastic stylo. In front of him was a memorandum pad on which he had written nothing.

"What are you holding out?" he asked.

Linda had told him, as near as she could remember, word for word, everything that Jimmy had said to her except that he had gotten hold of a pistol.

"Why do you think I'm holding something out?" she answered sullenly. "Why do you policemen always act as if everybody's guilty? You're jumping on me as if I'd done something."

"Sure," Brock said. "I'm jumping on you just because you're a defenseless little girl who wants to see justice done and got me up from my dinner table."

Linda puffed up with indignation but she couldn't meet his eyes.

Behind Brock's desk was a window reinforced by wire mesh. Through it Linda could see the picture windows of an apartment house toward the river. Lights showed in the windows. Behind the lights people could be seen, moving about, reading, watching television. White people. They looked safe and secure and protected.

"What would you say if one of those women in that big apartment house over there told you that a detective was trying to kill her husband?" she challenged.

"I'd laugh like hell," he said.

"You'd laugh like hell because you'd know it couldn't happen to a white man of his class. But Jimmy was shot. That did happen. Two other porters in the store were murdered. That happened too. And what are the police doing about it?"

"Sure," Brock said. "We're just sitting here and letting your boyfriend get murdered."

"You're doing more than that!" she flared angrily. "You're accusing me of holding something out. What do you think I'm holding out? Do you think Jimmy killed those other two men and shot himself? Maybe he swallowed the gun."

"Sure," Brock said placidly. "Somebody has swallowed the gun and that's a fact."

"You don't believe any of it?" she asked. "You don't even believe two men were murdered?"

"Two men were murdered is a fact," Brock said. "But Johnson told us practically the same thing you're telling us now. What's happened to make you get scared all of a sudden when you've had all this time to get scared in and you've been as calm as a statue."

"It was what he said happened this morning," she said. She shuddered involuntarily. "If he was telling the truth it was just by the hand of God he missed being murdered."

"Sure," Brock said. "If he was telling the truth."

"Why don't you try to find out whether he was telling the truth?"

"Suppose I believe his story," Brock said. "It's the same thing he said happened the time of the murders. The murderer laying in wait, the shot without warning, the flight down the stairs—the only thing different is the location. One thing is for sure, either your boyfriend has a single-track mind or else the murderer has."

"All right, go ahead and laugh," she said bitterly. "It's going to be even funnier if he gets killed."

"Sure," Brock said. "But what I'm trying to find out is what you're holding out that makes you so scared all of a sudden."

"I just started to believing him, is all."

Brock stared at her. "Sure," he said. "It took you quite some time to get around to believing him, didn't it?"

Her brown cheeks took on a copper-colored blush.

"It was just hard to believe at first," she said. "But I know that detective Walker was in the building this morning."

"We know that too," he admitted. "Walker claims he's following your friend Johnson to find the murderer. He's got his ready-made story just like Johnson has got his ready-made story. We're not a court of law. We can't decide on who's telling the truth and who isn't. We're just police officers. So what can we do?"

"You can stop him," she said.

"How?"

"You can hold him on suspicion or something, can't you? The police uptown are always picking up colored people on suspicion."

"Sure," Brock said. "We can hold him until his lawyers get there. That would be about an hour."

"It's horrible," she said with a sob in her voice. "Everybody's just waiting to see what he'll do next. It's just like watching a cat play with a mouse."

"If we had some charge to hold Johnson on, that would make it easier," he said. "That might give us the time we need."

"Well, you can hold him in protective custody, or something like that, can't you? You can always find a charge to hold a colored man."

"Not unless he asked for it," Brock said. "If we just picked him up, it would be the same as with Walker. We could hold him until the Schmidt and Schindler attorneys got there with a writ."

"That wouldn't help any," she admitted.

"I'm afraid not," he said. "But if I knew what you're holding out, maybe that would help."

"Don't start that again!" she exclaimed. "I'm not holding anything out."

"You women," he said bitterly. "What has Walker got that makes you women want to shield him?"

"I'm not shielding him," she denied.

"Not only you," he said; then he paused, struck by a sudden idea. "There's one thing we might try." He stood up. "I'm going to take you to see a woman."

Two other detectives at their desks looked up curiously as they passed.

He put her in his private car and drove her over to Peter Cooper Village. He parked in front of number 5, Peter Cooper Road, and they went up the short entrance hall past the waiting room with its English type fireplace where an hour before Jimmy had waited for Walker to appear. They rode up to the third floor in the big silent elevator.

The nameplate on the door said EVA MODJESKA.

Brock pushed the bell button. The muted sound of chimes came from within the apartment. He waited. No one answered. He pushed the button again. Still no one answered.

He said in his ordinary voice, “Miss Modjeska, this is detective Brock from the Homicide Bureau. I talked to you early this morning. I must talk to you again.”

From the other side of the door a thick, lisping voice with a slight foreign accent said, “Why won’t you let me alone? Why do you persecute me?”

“Either you open the door or I’ll get the building superintendent to open it,” he said.

The lock clicked and the door opened into a pitch-dark alcove.

“Pass in,” the lisping accented voice said from the dark.

Linda hesitated.

“Don’t be afraid,” Brock said, steering her around the corner into the large sitting room.

The door closed and a vague shape followed them.

“Be seated, please.”

Heavy drapes were drawn across the big front window and one dim night lamp burned on an occasional table in the far corner.

“Why don’t we sit down?” Brock said. The two women ignored him. They all remained standing.

Eva noticed Linda staring at her and turned her face away. She wore a heavy red woolen robe buttoned up to the neck. Her hair hung loosely over her shoulders in a tangled mass. Both sides of her face were so swollen that her eyes had almost disappeared and her mouth formed a lipless indentation. Her skin ranged in colors from deep purple to bright orange.

“I have told you I do not know who attacked me,” she lisped in a resigned, beaten manner. “He was a burglar. I came home unexpected and caught him in this room. He attacked me so suddenly I did not see his face.”

“Sure,” Brock said. He brought a chair and faced it toward the davenport. “Sit down.”

She sat down as though accustomed to obeying orders.

“You sit down too,” he told Linda.

Linda slowly sat on the edge of the davenport and stared down at her hands, horror overcoming her curiosity.

“Please do not humiliate me,” Eva begged.

“Miss Modjeska, this is Miss Collins,” Brock said. “Miss Collins’ boyfriend works for Schmidt and Schindler’s restaurants.”

A flicker of fear crossed Eva's face. Brock gave no sign he'd noticed it.

"Early one morning last week her boyfriend was shot," he continued. "The other two night porters who worked with him were murdered. You must have read about it in the newspapers."

A violent shudder passed over Eva's body. "I know nothing of that," she lisped in a frightened voice.

"Sure," Brock said. "That's why I brought Miss Collins along, so she could tell you something about it."

"Does she have to?" Eva pleaded.

"I'm afraid so," Brock said, then turned to Linda. "Go ahead and tell her what you told me. And don't leave anything out."

As Linda told her story, Eva wilted. From time to time she shuddered convulsively. Brock sat on the arm of the davenport and stared at her.

"So you see," he said when Linda had concluded, "this man is very dangerous."

"Yes, yes, I know," Eva lisped. "But he is sick."

"Sure," Brock said. "That's why you didn't tell me he beat you up."

"You must stop him," Eva said, leaning forward tensely. "I did not know he was planning to kill the other man too."

"That's right," Brock said. "Now go ahead and tell me that you knew all along he killed the other two men."

Eva hid her face in her hands. "I didn't know until last night," she lisped in a muffled voice.

"Sure," Brock said in a tight voice. "You knew last night but you didn't tell me when I talked to you early this morning."

"I wanted to tell you," Eva lisped sobbingly. "It was I who telephoned the police and told them there was a murdered woman at this address. I planned to tell you then but I was afraid."

"You were afraid all right," Brock said tightly. "You were afraid he was going to come back and kill you. That's why you telephoned the police. Now go ahead and spill it all," he said roughly. "How did you find out he was the murderer?"

"I saw the pistol," Eva confessed in a terrified voice. "I had read about the murders in the newspapers. It was said they were committed with a pistol that had a silencer attached.

When I saw the pistol had a silencer attached to it I knew that he was the murderer."

"Stop shuddering," Brock said savagely. "Get down to the facts. Where did you see the pistol?"

"He gave it to me to keep for him," she lisped. "It was the same day the murders were committed. I did not have any suspicions. It was wrapped in a package. He told me not to open it. He said that it contained evidence which would convict a murderer. He said that he was afraid to keep it in his own apartment because it might be searched. He said it would be safe in my apartment because I work for UN and would not be connected to a local murder case. Last night he came for it again. He was acting so strangely that I became suspicious and opened it." She shuddered again uncontrollably. "When I saw the pistol I realized at that moment that he was the murderer."

"God in heaven!" Linda exclaimed. "It was true after all. And I never did believe it entirely." She looked stunned.

"Goddammit," Brock said. "What kind of women are you two?" Then he turned on Eva and said bitterly, "He almost killed you. He left you here for dead. You were afraid he was going to come back and finish you off. And you didn't even feel it was necessary to tell the police who the murderer was. You were just going to sit here and let him murder someone else."

"Please don't say that," she sobbed. "I wanted to tell, but I was afraid. He said he would accuse me of being a spy if I told. He said they would not find the pistol and it would be my word against his. He said all that mattered was what people wanted to believe. There are people in my country who would want to believe that I am a spy."

Linda jumped to her feet and cried, "You've got to stop him. You've got to send someone up to Jimmy's room. Please hurry," she added as Brock made no move. "He might be uptown at this very minute laying somewhere for Jimmy."

"Sit down," Brock said roughly. "He's not uptown. I know where he is." Then to Eva, "Where's your telephone."

She gestured toward the bedroom. "Beside the bed."

The two women sat tensely across from one another, staring at his back as he walked heavily from the room. They listened in silence while he dialed, avoiding each other's eyes.

They heard him say, "Jenny? . . . Yeah? . . . No, everything's fine; let me talk to Matt. . . . Yeah? When? . . . He didn't say where he was going? . . . No, no. Did he go anywhere else in the house before he left? . . . Yeah . . . Yeah . . . No, nothing's wrong. . . . No, it's of no importance . . . No, I was just curious . . . No, don't wait up for me, I'll probably be late. . . . Yeah. Bye dear."

Linda was in the room before he'd finished talking. "You don't know where he is," she accused in a frightened voice.

"Now don't you start getting the wind up," Brock said. "He can't get far. I'll have him picked up in an hour, and I'll have someone go uptown and hold hands with your boy friend."

"For God's sake hurry!" she begged. "Jimmy's got a pistol too. He bought one today. If he finds Walker in the building he's going to try to kill him."

For an imperceptible instant, Brock stood frozen. The next instant he was dialing rapidly. "So that's it," he said softly as he waited for the connection. "So that's what scared you out of your pants. Women! And you expect the police— Hello," he said into the mouthpiece. "Sergeant Brock. Give me Lieutenant Baker. . . . Lieutenant—Brock. . . . Yeah, it broke. Better put a reader out for Walker. . . . No, for the automat murders . . . oh . . . yeah? When? . . . Bad? . . . Sure, but we didn't have it sooner. . . ."

His gaze went involuntarily toward Linda. She clutched him by the arm. "He's been hurt!" she cried hysterically. "He's been shot! He's been killed!"

"Just a minute," Brock said into the mouthpiece.

He turned quickly and slapped Linda with his free hand.

"Oh!" she said, and calmed down.

"Get yourself together," he said. "Your boy friend is still alive." Then he spoke into the mouthpiece again, "No, it was Johnson's girl friend; she thought something had happened to Johnson. . . . Yeah, I told her he was alive. . . . No, I'm at the apartment of Eva Modjeska in Peter Cooper— Yeah, that one. . . . Yeah. . . . Okay. . . . Send someone over to pick them up. . . . Yeah, both of them. . . . Hold them on anything; hold them as accomplices. . . . Better hurry it up. . . ."

23

THERE WAS an underground corridor connecting the basements of all the buildings in Peter Cooper Village.

Walker entered the boiler room three blocks distant from the building where his and Eva's apartments were located and entered the building by the service stairway. He stopped at Eva's back door and put his ear to the panel. He didn't hear a sound from within.

He used Eva's door key and unlocked the door silently. He pulled on the knob hard with his left hand and turned it without a sound. Holding it turned, he drew the pistol with the silencer and held it cocked in his right hand. Then he pushed the door in quickly, holding the pistol aimed straight ahead, and stepped inside. He closed the door as quickly and as silently as he had opened it.

He stood in the pitch-dark room and held his breath to listen. He didn't hear a sound.

He was in the small back laundry. He moved forward silently, his empty left hand extended in front of him. He put his ear to the kitchen door and listened again.

He didn't believe she had gone out. He doubted too if she was sleeping. It would be more like her to sit in the dark and brood, he thought.

He opened the door without a sound and groped his way silently across the kitchen. Another door led to the side of the sitting room that served as a dining room. He looked for a sign of light underneath the door but there wasn't a light in the house. That meant she had the window curtains drawn tight or there would be a dim light from the street lamps, he thought.

Again he stood with his ear to the door. He thought he heard the sound of breathing. He held his breath and didn't hear it anymore.

I hate to do this, he thought. It would be easier if I could shoot her in the dark.

He stood unmoving in the dark for several minutes, waiting for his sixth sense to warn him of any danger. But nothing came to arouse his suspicions.

He opened the door silently and groped with his left hand for the light switch. The big bright floor lamp at the end of the davenport came on before his hand touched the switch.

Brock sat in the middle of the davenport with his .38-calibre service revolver aimed at his heart.

"Drop the pistol, Matt," he said flatly.

Walker froze as though his flesh were solid stone. Slowly his fingers relaxed their grip on the pistol handle and it fell to the carpet with a thud. He smiled at Brock like a sad little boy.

"You clever bastard," he said softly.

"Sure," Brock said. "Just be careful or I'll drop you in your tracks."

"I'm wearing my service revolver too," Walker said, smiling. "Do you want that too?"

"No," Brock said, shaking his head. "You wouldn't shoot me with your service revolver."

"Don't be too sure," Walker said.

"I'll take a chance," Brock said, and put his revolver back into its holster. "Sit down."

Walker drew up a straight-backed dining room chair and sat straddling it, facing Brock. He looked at Brock with a sad steady smile.

"Eva squealed," he said.

"Sure," Brock said. "What did you think she would do, go on keeping silent forever?"

"I knew she would squeal," Walker said. "But I didn't think she would do it so soon. I thought I'd have a chance to clean the slate before."

"Sure," Brock said. "And then silence her forever."

"That would have been the only thing to do," Walker said. "Then no one would have ever known for sure."

"No," Brock said. "I knew before she squealed."

Walker stared at him contemplatively. "It was that story of mine," he conjectured. "I knew you didn't believe that. But without Eva you couldn't have known for sure."

"No," Brock said. "It wasn't that story. I didn't swallow your first story either—the one you handed the D.A. But when you told me that story at Lindy's I already knew."

Walker showed curiosity. "You clever bastard; how did you find out for sure?"

"I had found the prostitute—the one you slept with that night."

"You had? You knew where she was all the time?" Walker gave him a hurt, accusing look. "And you held out on me?"

"Sure. I wanted to keep her alive."

"What did she know?"

"She knew you had the gun. You threatened to shoot her with it too. Where did you get the gun?" Brock asked.

"I took it from the homicide museum," Walker said. "It's the rod Baby Face killed Jew Mike with."

"So that's where it came from."

"I thought you might have guessed that too," Walker said. After a moment he added, "I must have pitched a wingding that night. I wonder who else I threatened."

"We'll know that better later on," Brock said.

"Yeah, it'll all come out at the trial," Walker said in a soft sad voice. "Where did you find her?"

"In Bellevue hospital. You ruined her face. You broke it in with the same pistol. What happened to you that night?"

"I don't know. Just drinking too much I suppose."

"No," Brock said. "It was more than that."

"Maybe too many women," Walker said.

"No, not that either," Brock said. "Are you sick?" he asked.

Walker stared at him blankly for a moment. "You mean insane?"

"No, I mean sick physically," Brock said. "Syphilis or cancer or something like that."

Walker broke out in a sudden boyish laugh. "Not that I know of, unless I have syphilis of the brain."

"That could be," Brock said.

"What do you think they'll do with me?" Walker asked.

"It was a break for you that you beat up those two women," Brock said. "That will probably get you into the nut house."

"Yeah, I guess everybody will think I'm nuts," Walker said. "Does Jenny know?"

"Not yet."

Walker gave a heartfelt sigh. "Why didn't you stop me before now, Brock?"

"I wanted to give you a chance to get rid of the gun," Brock confessed.

"After I'd killed the other one?" Walker asked.

"No, I figured you'd give up on that when you became suspicious of me," Brock said. "I kept trying to tell you that I knew without just coming out and saying it. I thought you'd know I wanted you to get rid of the gun; I thought you'd have sense enough to see that."

"I thought you were against me," Walker said. "I didn't think you'd be for me."

"I wasn't for you," Brock said. "I was for Jenny."

"You were going to let me get away with it."

"Sure," Brock said. "You've never had a wife and two children. You don't know how hard it'll be on them to have a murderer for a brother and an uncle."

"Do they have to know?" Walker asked.

"It's out of my hands now," Brock said. After a moment he asked, "Why did you kill them, Matt?"

"Brock, you won't believe it," Walker said. "Nobody will believe it. But I shot the first one by pure accident. I was waving the pistol at him and it just went off. I didn't know then it had a hair trigger on it. I was more surprised than he was. But I knew the moment it happened that no one would ever believe it. So I had to finish him."

"Sure, but what started it in the first place?" Brock asked.

"I thought they had stolen my car," Walker admitted. "I was drunk and I'd forgotten where I'd parked it. And when I saw them I just thought all of a sudden they'd been up with stealing it."

"Because they were Negroes?"

"You know how you are when you're that drunk."

"Sure," Brock said. "But what about the other one?"

"Well hell, after I'd finished the first one, I couldn't stop there," Walker said. "The other one had seen me and I had to silence him too. I wouldn't have bothered the third one if he hadn't come up the stairs and seen me too." He believed what he was saying.

"I'm sorry for you," Brock said.

"I'm sorry for you too," Walker said.

"Sure," Brock said. "It's going to be tough for the family, but we'll get over that."

"It isn't that," Walker said. "It's because you didn't take my service revolver when you had the chance. I'm faster on the draw than you are."

For a long silent moment, neither of them moved. They stared into one another's eyes as though hypnotized.

Walker sat with his arms folded across the back of the chair. Brock sat with his right hand on the davenport at his side and his left hand resting loosely on his thigh.

Finally Brock said, "Sure. But you wouldn't have any way out after that. They'd exterminate you like a mad dog."

"I know," Walker said. "But it's just that I'm started now and I can't stop."

It seemed to Brock as if it took him ten thousand years to get his hand up to his shoulder holster and get his pistol out. He saw the pistol in Walker's hand before his cleared the holster and heard the shot. He was startled to hear the second shot, the one made by his own pistol. He didn't believe it when he saw the sudden small blue hole appear directly between Walker's staring blue eyes where his bullet had entered Walker's brain. He sat unmoving in a half daze and watched Walker fall forward to the back of the chair, turning the chair over beneath him as he toppled to the floor.

He got slowly to his feet and looked behind him. He saw where the bullet from Walker's revolver had gone into the back of the davenport.

"He could have shot me five times straight running," he said softly. "Poor devil. It was his only way out."

He walked heavily across the floor and into the bedroom and began dialing the telephone.

24

"FOR GOD'S SAKE, what were you trying to do? Make me drop dead?" Linda greeted him before she shrugged out of her fur coat and sat in the chair for visitors.

Jimmy looked up from his white hospital bed and tried sheepishly to smile.

Nine days had passed since he'd been shot and she was his first visitor. While he had hovered on the brink of death, she had been knocking on the gates of the nut house. It was very unrewarding. They both showed it.

Finally he got out through stiff lips, "I just wanted to kill the mother-raper and keep on living myself."

Linda's eyes stretched. It was meant to show disapproval.

"Wasn't nobody gonna believe me anyway," he muttered. "Til I was dead."

Linda put her hot perfumed hand over his dry mouth; it had an aphrodisiacal effect on both.

"The DA believed you—" she began.

"Bull shit!" he muttered.

"Sergeant Brock believed—"

"Linda baby, please—"

"Well shit then, I believed you."

"No you didn't!"

Her throat caught and she gulped guiltily. "Well for Chrissakes, what do you want a girl to do? Why didn't you let me help you? I could have lured him into the apartment and you wouldn't have had to take all those rape-fiend risks."

Agitation lifted him onto his elbows. Pain flickered through his lung but he ignored it. "Baby, I couldn't trust you." It sounded like a moan.

Suddenly her face felt like it had caught fire. "Well," she admitted slowly. "It don't take Malcolm X to see that."

"Anyway," he said defensively. "I had it all planned out."

She passed that reply and pushed him back into his pillow. "Shut up now, you don't have to explain to me."

"But I want to explain to you. You got to know. I wanted to

kill him while he had the gun in his possession. Without giving him a chance. Like he did Luke and Fats."

She tried to show her agreement. And she understood. But her smile stopped at her teeth. There was pity behind her eyes, even shock . . . My God! she thought. He doesn't realize how obvious he'd been to Walker. He's just a baby, she thought, and very lucky to be alive. But it doesn't matter now, the only thing that matters now is to keep the terror out my eyes.

It was only then he took her look for disapproval. "What's a man gonna do?" he questioned hotly. "I couldn't keep running all my mother-raping life."

"Shush!" She leaned over and sealed his mouth with her lips. They tasted hot, wet and breathless. "You just scared the living shit out of me," she confessed, quickly adding, "But I love you for it."

His eyes, which were all that could show it, lit with hope. "Then we're still engaged?"

She looked at him indignantly. "You fool, you think I'm going to lose you now? All I been through!"

THE TREMOR OF FORGERY

Patricia Highsmith

For
ROSALIND CONSTABLE
as a small souvenir
of a rather long friendship.

I

"YOU'RE SURE there's no letter for me?" Ingham asked. "Howard Ingham. I-n-g-h-a-m." He spelt it, a little uncertainly, in French, though he had spoken in English.

The plump Arab clerk in the bright red uniform glanced through the letters in the cubbyhole marked I-J, and shook his head. "*Non, m'sieur.*"

"*Merci,*" Ingham said with a smile. It was the second time he had asked, but it was a different clerk. He had asked ten minutes ago when he arrived at the Hotel Tunisia Palace. Ingham had hoped for a letter from John Castlewood. Or from Ina. He had been away from New York five days now, having flown first to Paris to see his agent there, and just to take another look at Paris.

Ingham lit a cigarette and glanced around the lobby. It was carpeted with Oriental rugs, and air-conditioned. The clientèle looked mostly French and American, but there were a few rather dark-faced Arabs in western business suits. The Tunisia Palace had been recommended by John. It was probably the best in town, Ingham thought.

He went out through the glass doors onto the pavement. It was early June, nearly 6 P.M., and the air was warm, the slanting sunlight still bright. John had suggested the Café de Paris for a pre-lunch or -dinner drink, and there it was, across the street and at the second corner, on the Boulevard Bourguiba. Ingham walked on to the boulevard, and bought a Paris *Herald-Tribune.* The rather broad avenue had a tree-bordered, cement-paved division down its middle on which people could walk. Here were the newspaper and tobacco kiosks, the shoeshine boys. To Ingham, it looked something between a Mexico City street and a Paris street, but the French had had a hand in both Mexico City and Tunis. Snatches of shouted conversation around him gave him no clue as to meaning. He had a phrase book called *Easy Arabic* in one of his suitcases at the hotel. Arabic would obviously have to be memorized, because it bore no relation to anything he knew.

Ingham walked across the street to the Café de Paris. It had pavement tables, all occupied. People stared at him, perhaps because he was a new face. There were many Americans and English, and they had the expressions of people who had been here some time and were a little bored. Ingham had to stand at the bar. He ordered a pernod, and looked at his newspaper. The place was noisy. He spotted a table and took it.

People idled along the pavement, staring at the equally blank faces in the café. Ingham watched especially the younger people, because he was on an assignment to write a film script about two young people in love, or rather three, since there was a second young man who didn't get the girl. Ingham saw no boy and girl walking along, only single young men or pairs of boys holding hands and talking earnestly. John had told Ingham about the closeness of the boys. Homosexual relationships had no stigma here, but that had nothing to do with the script. Young people of opposite sex were often chaperoned or at least spied upon. There was a lot to learn, and Ingham's job in the next week or so until John arrived was to keep his eyes open and absorb the atmosphere. John knew a couple of families here, and Ingham would be able to see inside a middle-class Tunisian home. The story was to have the minimum of written dialogue, but still something had to be written. Ingham had done some television writing, but he considered himself a novelist. He had some trepidations about this job. But John was confident, and the arrangements were informal. Ingham had signed nothing. Castlewood had advanced him a thousand dollars, and Ingham was scrupulously using the money only for business expenses. Quite a bit of it would go for the car he was supposed to hire for a month.

"*Merci, non*," Ingham said to a peddler who approached him with a long-stemmed, tightly bound flower. The oversweet scent lingered in the air. The peddler had a handful, and was pushing about among the tables yelling, "Yas-*meen*?" He wore a red fez and a limp, lavender jubbah so thin one could see a pair of whitish underpants.

At one table, a fat man twiddled his jasmine, holding the blossom under his nose. He seemed in a trance, his eyes almost crossed with his daydream. Was he awaiting a girl or only thinking of one? Ten minutes later, Ingham decided he was awaiting no one. The man had finished what looked like colorless soda pop. He wore a light gray business suit. Ingham supposed he was middle-class, even a bit upper. Perhaps he made thirty or more dinars per week, sixty-three dollars or more. Ingham had been boning up on such things for a month. Bourguiba was tactfully trying to extricate his people from the reactionary bonds of their religion. He had abolished polygamy officially, and disapproved of the veil for women. As African countries went, Tunisia was the most advanced. They were trying to persuade all French businessmen to leave, but still depended to a great extent on French monetary aid.

Ingham was thirty-four, slightly over six feet tall, with light brown hair and blue eyes, and he moved rather slowly. Although he never bothered about exercise, he had a good physique with broad shoulders, long legs and strong hands. He had been born in Florida, but considered himself a New Yorker, because he had lived in New York since the age of eight. After college—the University of Pennsylvania—he had worked for a newspaper in Philadelphia and written fiction on the side, without much luck until his first book, *The Power of Negative Thinking*, a rather flippant and juvenile spoof of positive thinking, in which his pair of negative-thinking heroes emerged covered in glory, money and success. On the strength of this, Ingham had quit journalism, and had had two or three rocky years. His second book, *The Gathering Swine*, had not been so well received as the first book. Then he had married a wealthy girl, Charlotte Fleet, with whom he had been very much in love, but he had not availed himself of her money, and her wealth in fact had been a handicap. The marriage had ended after two years. Now and again, Ingham sold a television play or a short story, and he had kept going in a modest apartment in Manhattan. This year, in February, he had had a breakthrough. His book *The Game of "If"* had been bought for a film for $50,000. Ingham suspected it had been bought more for the crazy love story in it than for its intellectual content or message (the necessity and validity of wishful thinking), but no matter, it had been bought, and for the first time Ingham was enjoying a taste of financial security. He had declined an invitation to write the film script of *The Game of "If."* He thought film scripts, even television plays, were not his forte, and *The Game* was a difficult book for him to think of in film terms.

John Castlewood's idea for *Trio* was simpler and more visual. The young man who didn't get the girl married someone else, but wreaked vengeance on his successful rival in a most horrible way, first seducing his wife, then ruining the husband's business, then seeing that the husband was murdered. Such things could scarcely happen in America, Ingham supposed, but this was in Tunisia. John Castlewood had enthusiasm, and he knew Tunisia. And John had known Ingham and had invited him to try the script. They had a producer named Miles Gallust. Ingham thought that if he felt he wasn't getting anywhere, wasn't capable, he would tell John, give back the thousand dollars, and John could find someone else. John had done two good films on small budgets, and the first, *The Grievance*, had had the better success. That had been set in Mexico. The second had been about Texas oil-riggers, and Ingham had forgotten the title. John was twenty-six, full of energy and the kind of faith that went with not knowing much about the world as yet, or so Ingham thought. Ingham felt that John had a future better, more than likely, than his own would be. Ingham was at an age when he knew his potentialities and limitations. John Castlewood did not know his as yet, and perhaps was not the type ever to think about them or recognize them, which might be all to the good.

Ingham paid his bill, and went back to his hotel room for a jacket. He was getting hungry. He glanced again at the two letters in the box marked I-J, and at the empty cubbyhole under his hanging key. "*Vingt-six, s'il vous plaît*," he said, and took the key.

Again taking John's advice, Ingham went to the Restaurant du Paradis in the Rue du Paradis, which was between his hotel and the Café de Paris. Later, he wandered around the town, and had a couple of café exprès standing at counters in cafés where there were no tourists. The patrons were all men in these places. The barmen understood his French, but Ingham did not hear anyone else speaking French.

He had thought to write a letter to Ina when he got back to his hotel, but he felt too tired, or perhaps uninspired. He went to bed and read some in a William Golding novel that he had brought from America. Before he fell asleep, he thought of the girl who had flirted with him—mildly—in the Café de Paris. She had been blond, a trifle chubby, but very attractive. Ingham had thought she might be German (the man with her could have been anything), and he had felt pleased when he had heard her talking French with the man as they went out. Vanity, Ingham thought. He should be thinking about Ina. She was certainly thinking about him. At any rate, Tunisia was going to be a splendid place not to think any more about Lotte. Thank God, he had almost stopped. It had been a year and six months since his divorce, but sometimes to Ingham it seemed like only six months, or even two.

2

THE NEXT morning, when there was again no letter for him, it occurred to Ingham that John and Ina might have written to him at the Hotel du Golfe in Hammamet, where John had suggested he should stay. Ingham had not yet made a reservation there, and he supposed he should for the 5th or 6th of June. John had said, "Look around Tunis for a few days. The characters are going to live in Tunis . . . I don't think you'd like to work there. It'll be hot, and you can't swim unless you go to Sidi Bou Said. We'll work in Hammamet. Terrific beach for an afternoon swim, and no city noises . . ."

After a whole day of walking and driving about Tunis, enduring also the long closure of everything except restaurants from noon or 12:30 until 4, Ingham was ready to go to Hammamet tomorrow. But he thought as soon as he got to Hammamet, he would reproach himself for not having seen enough of Tunis, so he decided to stay on two more days. On one of those days, he drove to Sidi Bou Said, sixteen kilometers away, had a swim and took lunch at a rather chic hotel, as there were no independent restaurants. It was a very clean town of chalk-white houses and bright blue shutters and doors.

There had been no room free at the Golfe when Ingham had telephoned the day before, but the manager had suggested another hotel in Hammamet. Ingham went to the other hotel, which he found too Hollywood in atmosphere, and at last put himself up at a hotel called La Reine de Hammamet. All the hotels had beaches on the Gulf of Hammamet, but were set back fifty yards or more from the water. The Reine had a large main building, gardens of lime and lemon and bougainvillea, and also fifteen or twenty bungalows of varying sizes, each given privacy by the leaves of citrus trees. The bungalows had kitchens, but Ingham was not in a mood to start housekeeping, so he took a room in the main building with a view on the sea. He immediately went down for a swim.

There were not many people on the beach at this hour, though the sun was still above the horizon. Ingham saw a couple of empty beach chairs. He didn't know if one had to rent them or not, but he assumed they belonged to the hotel, so he took one. He put on his sunglasses—another thought of John Castlewood, who had made him a present of these—and pulled a paperback out of his robe pocket. After fifteen minutes, he was asleep, or at least in a doze. *My God*, he thought, *my God, it's quiet and beautiful and warm . . .*

"Hello! Good evening!— You an American?"

The loud voice startled Ingham like a gunshot, and he sat up in his chair. "Yes."

"Excuse me interrupting your reading. I'm an American, too. From Connecticut." He was a man of fifty or so, grayish-haired, balding, with a slight bulge at his waistline, and with an enviable tan. He was not very tall.

"New York here," Ingham said. "I hope I haven't taken your chair."

"Ha-ha! No! But the boys'll be collecting them in another half hour or so. Have to put 'em away, or they wouldn't be here tomorrow morning!"

Lonely, Ingham thought. Or had he a wife just as chummy? But one could be lonely with that, too. The man was looking out at the sea, standing only two yards from Ingham.

"My name's Adams. Francis J. Adams." He said it as if he were proud of it.

"Mine's Howard Ingham."

"What do you think of Tunisia?" Adams asked with his friendly smile that bulged his brown cheeks.

"Very attractive. Hammamet, anyway."

"I think so. Best to have a car to get around in. Sousse and Djerba, places like that. Got a car?"

"Yes, I have."

"Good. Well—" He was backing, taking his leave. "Drop in and see me some time. My bungalow's just up the slope there. Number ten. Any of the boys can tell you which is mine. Just ask for Adams. Come in and have a drink some evening. Bring your wife, if you have one."

"Thanks very much," Ingham said. "No, I'm alone."

Ingham sat on another five minutes, then got up. He took a shower in his room, then went downstairs to the bar. It was a large bar with red Persian carpeting that covered the floor. A middle-aged couple was speaking French. Another table of three was British. There were only seven or eight people in the room, a few of them watching television in the corner.

A man came from the television set to the British table and said in a voice without excitement, "The Israelis have blasted a dozen airports."

"Where?"

"Egypt. Or maybe Jordan. The Arabs are going to be a pushover."

"That news came through in French?" asked another of the Englishmen.

Ingham stood at the bar. The war was on apparently. Tunisia was quite a distance from the fighting. Ingham hoped it wouldn't interfere with work plans. But the Tunisians were Arabs, and there was going to be some anti-western emotion, he knew, if the Arabs lost, and of course they would lose.

Ingham avoided the beach for the next couple of days, and took some drives into the country. The Israelis were mopping up the Arabs, and twenty-five airbases had been destroyed on Monday, the day the war broke out. A Paris paper reported a few cars with western licence plates overturned in a street in Tunis, and also the windows of the USIS library broken on the Boulevard Bourguiba. Ingham did not go to Tunis. He went to the town of Naboul, northeast of Hammamet, and to Bou Bir Rekba inland, and to a few other tiny towns, dusty and poor, whose names he could not remember easily. He ran into a market morning at one, and walked about among camels, pottery, baubles and pins, cotton clothing and straw mats, all spread out on coarse sheets on the ground. People jostled him, which Ingham did not like. The Arabs didn't mind human contact, and on the contrary needed it, Ingham had read. That was everywhere apparent in the souk. The jewelry in the market was shoddy, but it inspired Ingham to go to a good shop and buy a silver pin for Ina, a flat triangle which fastened with a circle. They came in all sizes. Since the box was so small for posting, Ingham bought also an embroidered red vest for her —a man's garment, but so fancy, it would look very feminine in America. He posted them the afternoon of the same day, after much time-killing, waiting for the post office in Hammamet to open at 4 P.M. The post office was open only one hour in the afternoon, according to a sign outside.

On the third day at the Reine, he wrote to John Castlewood. John lived on West Fifty-third Street in Manhattan.

8 June 19—

Dear John,

Hammamet is as pretty as you said. A magnificent beach. Are you still arriving the 13th? I am ready to get to work here, chatting with strangers at every opportunity, but the kind of people you want don't always know much French. I visited Les Arcades last night. [This was a coffeehouse a mile or so from the Reine.]

Please tell Ina to write me a line. I've written to her. Sort of lonely here with no word from home. Or maybe as you said the mail is fantastically slow . . .

And so he trailed off, and felt a little more lonely after he had written it than before. He was checking with the Golfe every day, sometimes twice a day. No letter or cable had come. Ingham drove to the post office to mail his letter, because he wasn't sure it would get off today, if he left it to the hotel. Various clerks had given him three different times for mail arrival, and he assumed they would be equally vague as to collection.

Ingham went down to the beach around 6. The beach was approached via a patch of jungle-like palm trees which grew, however, out of the inevitable sand. There was a footworn path which he followed. A few metal poles, perhaps from a children's abandoned playground, stuck up out of the sand and were encrusted near the top with small white snails fastened tightly like barnacles. The metal was so hot, he could barely touch it. He walked on, daydreaming about his novel. He intended to devote the next hour to thinking about his novel, and he had brought his notebook and pen. There was really nothing more he could do on *Trio* until John got here.

He went into the water, swam out until he felt slightly tired, then turned back. The water was shallow quite far out. There was smooth sand underfoot, which farther inshore became rocky, then sand again, until he stood upon the beach. He wiped his face on his terry-cloth robe, as he had forgotten to bring a towel. Then he sat down with his notebook. His book was about a man with a double life, a man unaware of the amorality of the way he lived, and therefore he was mentally deranged, or unbalanced, to say the least. Ingham did not like to admit this, but he had to. In his book, he had no intention of justifying his hero Dennison. He was simply a young man (twenty when the book began) who married and led a happy family life, and became a director in a bank at thirty. He appropriated funds from the bank when he could, by forgery mainly, and he was as free with giving and lending as he was in stealing. He invested some of the money with a view to his family's future, but he gave away two-thirds of it (also usually under false names) to people who needed it and to men who were trying to start their own businesses.

As often happened, Ingham's ruminations made him doze within twenty minutes, and after writing only twelve lines of notes, he was half asleep when the voice of the American woke him like a repeated dream:

"Hello, there! Haven't seen you for a couple of days."

Ingham sat up. "Good afternoon." He knew what was coming, and he knew he would go, this evening, to have a drink at Adams' bungalow.

"How long're you here for?" Adams asked.

"I don't quite know." Ingham had stood up and was putting on his robe. "Maybe another three weeks. I have a friend coming."

"Oh. Another American?"

"Yes." Ingham looked at the spear Adams was carrying, a sort of dart five feet long without apparent means of projection.

"I'm on my way back to my bungalow. Want to come along and have a cooling drink?"

Ingham at once thought of Coca-Cola. "All right. Thank you.— What do you do with that spear?"

"Oh, I aim at fish and never catch them." A chuckle. "Actually sometimes I snare up shells I couldn't reach if I were just swimming."

The sand became hot inland, but still bearable. Ingham was carrying his beach shoes. Adams had none.

"Here we are," said Adams suddenly, and turned onto a paved but gritty walk which led to his blue-and-white bungalow. The bungalow's roof was domed for coolness, in Arabian style.

Ingham glanced over his shoulder at a building he had not noticed before, a service building of some sort where several adolescent boys, waiters and clean-up boys of the hotel, he supposed, leaned against the wall chatting.

"Not much, but it's home just now," said Adams, opening his door with a key he had fished from somewhere in the top of his swimming trunks.

The inside of the bungalow was cool, the shutters closed, and it seemed dark after the sunlight. Adams evidently had an air-conditioner. He turned on a light.

"Sit ye down. What can I get you? A scotch? Beer? Coke?"

"A Coke, thanks."

They had stomped their feet carefully on the bare tiles outside the door. Adams walked briskly and squeakily across the tile floor into a short hall that led to a kitchen.

Ingham looked around. It looked like home, indeed. There were seashells, books, stacks of papers, a writing table that was obviously much used, with ink bottles, pens, a stamp box, a pencil sharpener, an open dictionary. A *Reader's Digest.* Also a Bible. Was Adams a writer? The dictionary was English-Russian, neatly covered in brown paper. Was Adams a spy? Ingham smiled at the thought. Above the desk hung a framed photograph of an American country house that looked like New England, a white farmhouse surrounded at a generous distance by a three-railed white fence. There were elm trees, a collie, but no person in the picture.

Ingham turned as Adams entered with a small tray.

Adams had a scotch and soda. "You a teetotaler?" he asked, smiling his paunchy little smile.

"No, I just felt like a Coke. How long've you been here?"

"A year," Adams said, beaming, bouncing on his toes.

Adams had high arches, high insteps and rather small feet. There was something disgusting about Adams' feet, and having looked at them once, Ingham did not look again.

"Your wife isn't here?" Ingham asked. He had seen a woman's photograph on the chest of drawers behind Adams, a woman in her forties, sedately smiling, sedately dressed.

"My wife died five years ago. Cancer."

"Oh.— What do you do to pass the time here?"

"I don't feel too lonely. I keep busy." Again the squirrel-like smile. "Once in a while someone interesting turns up at the hotel, we make acquaintances, they go on somewhere else. I consider myself an unofficial ambassador for America. I spread goodwill—I hope—and the American way of life. Our way of life."

What the hell did that mean, Ingham wondered, the Vietnam War springing at once to his mind. "How do you mean?"

"I have my ways.— But tell me about yourself, Mr. Ingham. Sit down somewhere. You're here on vacation?"

Ingham sat down in a large scooped leather chair that creaked. Adams sat on the sofa. "I'm a writer," Ingham said. "I'm waiting for an American friend who wants to do a film here. He's going to be cameraman and director. The producer is in New York. It's all rather informal."

"Interesting! A film on what subject?"

"A story about young people in Tunisia. John Castlewood —the cameraman—knows Tunisia quite well. He lived a few months here with a family in Tunis."

"So you're a film writer." Adams was putting on a colorful short-sleeved shirt.

"No, just a writer. Fiction. But my friend John wanted me to do his film with him." Ingham detested the conversation.

"What books have you written?"

Ingham stood up. He knew more questions were coming, so he said, "Four. One of them was *The Game of 'If.'* You probably haven't heard of it." Adams hadn't, so Ingham said, "Another book was called *The Gathering Swine*. Not so succesful."

"*The Gadarene Swine*?" Adams asked, as Ingham had thought he would.

"*Gathering*," Ingham said. "I meant it to sound like Gadarene, you see." His face felt warm with a kind of shame, or boredom.

"You make enough to live on?"

"Yes, with television work now and then in New York." He thought suddenly of Ina, and the thought caused a throb in his body, making Ina strangely more real than she had been since he got to Europe, or Africa. He could see Ina in her office in New York now. It would be noonish. She would be reaching for a pencil, or a sheet of typewriter paper. If she had a lunch date, she would be a little late for it.

"You're probably famous and I don't realize it," Adams said, smiling. "I don't read much fiction. Now and then, something that's condensed. Like in the *Reader's Digest*, you know. If you've got one of your books here, I'd like to read it."

Ingham smiled. "Sorry. I don't travel with them."

"When's your friend due?" Adams stood up. "Can't I freshen that? How about a scotch now?"

Ingham agreed to the scotch. "He's due Tuesday." Ingham caught a glimpse of his own face in a mirror on the wall. His face was pink from the sun and starting to tan. His mouth looked severe and a little grumpy. A sudden loud voice, shouting in Arabic just outside the shuttered windows, made him flinch, but he continued staring at himself. This is what Adams saw, he thought, what the Arabs saw, an ordinary American face with blue eyes that looked too sharply at everything, above a mouth not exactly friendly. Three creases undulated across his forehead, and the beginning of wrinkles showed under his eyes. Maybe not a very friendly face, but it was impossible to change one's expression without being phoney. Lotte had done a little damage. The best he could do, Ingham thought out of nowhere, the proper thing to do was to be neutral, neither chummy nor standoffish. Play it cool.

"What do you think about the war?" Adams asked, smiling as usual. "The Israelis have got it won."

"Can you get the news? By radio?" Ingham was interested. He must buy a transistor, he thought.

"I can get Paris, London, Marseille, Voice of America, practically anything," Adams said, gesturing toward a door, which presumably led to a bedroom. "Just scattered reports now, but the Arabs are finished."

"Since America is pro-Israel, I suppose there'll be some anti-American demonstrations?"

"A few, no doubt," said Adams, as cheerfully as if he were talking about flowers pushing up in a garden. "A pity the Arabs can't see a yard in front of their noses."

Ingham smiled. "I thought you might well be pro-Arab."

"Why?"

"Living here. Liking them, I thought." On the other hand, he read the *Reader's Digest*, which was always anti-Communist. On the other hand, what was the other hand?

"I like the Arabs. I like all peoples. I think the Arabs ought to do more with their own land. What's done is done, the creation of Israel, right or wrong. The Arabs ought to do more with their own desert and stop complaining. Too many Arabs sit around doing nothing."

That was true, Ingham thought, but since Adams read the *Reader's Digest*, he suspected anything he said, and thought about it twice. "Have you a car? Do you think the Arabs will turn it over?"

Adams chuckled comfortably. "Not here. My car's the black Cadillac convertible under the trees. Tunisia is pro-Arab, of course, but Bourguiba isn't going to allow much trouble. He can't afford it."

Adams talked about his farm in Connecticut, and about his business in Hartford. He had had a soft drinks bottling plant. Adams obviously enjoyed reminiscing. His had been a happy marriage. He had a daughter who lived in Tulsa. Her husband was a brilliant engineer, Adams said. Ingham thought, *I'm afraid to fall in love with Ina. I'm afraid to fall in love with anyone since Lotte.* It was so obvious, he wondered why he hadn't realized it before, months ago? Why should it come to him now, while talking with this ordinary little man from Connecticut? Or had he said he originally came from Indiana?

Ingham said good-bye, with a vague promise to meet Adams in the bar next day around 8, just before dinner. Adams said he sometimes took dinner at the hotel, rather than cook. As he walked back to the main building of the hotel, Ingham thought about Ina. It wasn't bad, maybe even wise, he thought, the way he felt about her. He was not out of his mind about her. He cared for her and she was important to him. He had taken his film contract for *The Game of "If"* to show her before he signed it, her approval being just as important to him as his agent's. In fact, Ina knew all about film contracts, but emotionally as well, he had wanted her approval. She was intelligent, pretty, and physically attractive to him. She was dependable and unneurotic. She had her own work, and she wasn't a bore or a drag—as Lotte had been, out of bed, he had to admit. Ina had some talent for playwriting. She'd have been better than him for this job, in fact, and Ingham wondered why John hadn't suggested her doing the script instead of him? Or maybe he had, and Ina hadn't been able to get away from New York. John and Ina had known each other a little longer than Ingham had known either of them. Ina might not mention it to him, if John had asked her to write *Trio*, Ingham thought.

Suddenly, Ingham felt happier. If there wasn't a letter from John when he got to the hotel, if there was none tomorrow, and if John didn't come on the 13th, Ingham felt he could take it in stride. Maybe he was acquiring the African tempo. *Don't be anxious. Let the days pass.* He realized that Francis J. Adams had been curiously stimulating. The *Reader's Digest* condensations! The American way of life! Adams was so plainly content with himself, with everything. It was fabulous, in these times. An Arab boy had brought fresh bathtowels while Ingham had been there, and Adams had talked with him in Arabic. The boy seemed to like Adams. Ingham tried to imagine having lived in the hotel for a year. Was Adams some kind of American agent? No, he was much too naïve. Or could that be part of his cover? One never knew these days, did one? Ingham didn't know what to make of Adams.

3

JUNE 13th came and went. There was no word from John, and what was even stranger, no word from Ina. On the 14th, inspired by a good lunch at the hotel, Ingham cabled Ina:

WHAT'S UP? WRITE ME HOTEL REINE HAMMAMET. I LOVE YOU. HOWARD.

He sent it to CBS. At least it would be there the first thing tomorrow morning, Thursday. Ingham had been in Tunisia two weeks now without a word from John or Ina. Even Jimmy Goetz, not one for writing letters, had sent him a postcard of good luck wishes. Jimmy was off to Hollywood to write a film script of someone's novel. His postcard had come to the Hotel du Golfe.

The days began to drag. They dragged for two days, then Ingham picked up mentally, or perhaps slowed down, so that he didn't mind the dragging. He was making some progress in planning his novel, and had the first three chapters clearly in mind.

Ingham was now on demi-pension, so he took lunch or dinner away from the hotel, usually at the restaurant Chez Melik in the town of Hammamet, a kilometer away. He could walk to Hammamet along the beach—more pleasant if it were evening and not so warm—or take his car. Melik's was a terrace restaurant, very cheap and informal, up some steps from the street. The terrace was shaded with grapevines, and one corner of it looked down on a strawy cattle pen, where sheep and goats sometimes stood, waiting to be slaughtered. Sometimes instead of living animals, there was a heap of bleeding sheepskins at which cats pulled, over which flies buzzed. Ingham did not always enjoy looking down there. The good thing about Melik's was the mixed cliéntèle. There were turbaned camel drivers, Tunisian or French students with fluty instruments or guitars, French tourists, occasionally some British, and ordinary men from the village who lingered over their vin rosé, picking their teeth and nibbling from plates of fruit until midnight. Once Adams came with him to Melik's. Adams had been there before, of course, and was not so fond of the place as Ingham. Adams thought it could be cleaner.

Ingham had met four or five people in his hotel, but he did not care very much for any of them. One was an American couple who had asked him to play bridge, but Ingham had told them he didn't know how to play, which was nearly true. Another was an American named Richard Messerman, a bachelor on the prowl, but having luck, he said, only at the Hotel Fourati, a mile away, where he often spent the night. Ingham did not accept Messerman's invitations to cruise the Fourati. Another was a German homosexual from Hamburg, who had luck only in Hammamet with Arab boys, but plenty of luck, he told Ingham. His name was Heinz something-or-other, and he spoke good English and French, and was usually wearing white tight trousers with colorful belts.

Oddly enough, Ingham found Adams the best company, perhaps because Adams asked nothing of him. Adams had the same affable manner with everyone—with Melik, the pharmacist, the man in the post office, the Arab boys at the hotel. Adams looked happy. Ingham feared that one day he would spring something on him like Christian Science or Rosicrucianism, but after nearly two weeks, Adams hadn't.

It was growing hotter. Ingham found himself eating less and losing a little weight.

He had sent a second cable to Ina, this one to her home in Brooklyn Heights, but still no reply had come. Three days after the second cable, Ingham tried to ring her one afternoon, when it would be morning in New York and she would be at her office. This attempt kept him waiting in the air-conditioned lobby of the hotel for more than two hours, but the hotel could not get through even to Tunis. The lines to Tunis were too crowded. Ingham had the distinct feeling that a telephone call was hopeless, unless he went to Tunis, which of course he could do; it was only sixty-one kilometers away. But he did not go, and he did not try again to telephone Ina. Instead he wrote a long letter in which he said:

> Africa is strangely good for thinking. It's like standing naked in glaring sunlight against a white wall. Somehow nothing is hidden in this bright light . . .

But his important thought, about being afraid to fall in love, and his consequently even more substantial feeling about Ina, he preferred not to write her. Maybe at some time he would mention it, or maybe it was best left unsaid, because she might not understand and think he was not enthusiastic enough about her.

> Tell John if he doesn't hurry up and get here, I'm going to start my novel. What's holding him up? It's true it's pleasant here, and it's free (if we sell this thing) but it's turning into a vacation and I don't like vacations . . . The Arabs are very friendly and informal. They loaf a lot, sitting at tables under trees, drinking coffee and wine. There is a section like the Casbah next to an old fortress which juts out to sea. There the houses are all white, full of plump jolly moms, most of them pregnant again. Never a closed door, so you can see into rooms with mats on the floor, babies crawling, brazier fires with grandma fanning them with the end of her shawl . . . Car is a Peugeot station wagon, behaving well so far . . . I wish like mad you were here. Why couldn't John have put us both on this job? . . . Could you send me a snapshot? You know I haven't a single picture of you?

She would probably send him an awful snapshot for a laugh, Ingham thought. He faced the fact that he was terribly lonely. He supposed it would take four or five days for his letter to reach Ina. That meant the 20th or 21st of June.

The Israelis had won the war, all right, a blitzkrieg, the papers called it. And as Adams had predicted, there were no serious reverberations in Hammamet, but in Tunis just enough broken glass and street fighting to make Ingham prefer to keep away. If the Arabs in Hammamet cafés were talking about the war, Ingham couldn't tell it, as he could not understand a word. Their conversations had a certain level of intensity and loudness which did not seem to vary.

Ingham had put in a request for a bungalow, and on the 19th of June, one was available. The refrigerator and stove were very new, because the bungalows in his section had been built only in the spring, Adams had said. There was a small but excellently stocked grocery store just inside one driveway of the hotel about a hundred yards from his bungalow, which sold spirits and cold beer, all kinds of canned goods, even kitchen gadgets and toothpaste. If he and John holed up here, Ingham thought, they'd hardly need to leave the bungalow except to take a swim and visit the store for provisions. His bungalow, number three, had only one big room plus kitchen and bath, but it had two single beds. John probably wouldn't want to share it for sleeping, and Ingham didn't much like the idea either, but John could sleep in the main building. The table in the bungalow was a big wooden one, splendid for working. Ingham bought salami, cheese, butter, eggs, fruit, Ritz crackers and scotch the afternoon he moved in, then he went over about 5 to invite Adams for a house-warming drink.

Adams wasn't in, and Ingham supposed he was on the beach. He found Adams lying on a straw mat on his stomach, writing something. Adams, oblivious of Ingham's approach until he was quite close, finished off his sentence or whatever with a satisfied flourish, lifting his pen in the air.

"Hello-o, Howard!" Adams said. "Got your bungalow?"

"Yes, just now."

Adams was pleased to be invited, as Ingham had known he would be. He agreed to come to number three at 6 o'clock.

Ingham went back and did some more unpacking. It was good to have a sort of "house" instead of a hotel room. He thought of his desk in his apartment on West Fourth Street, near Washington Square. He'd had the apartment only three months. It was air-conditioned and more expensive than any place he'd ever had, and he had taken it only after the film sale of *The Game of "If"* had become definite. Ina had a set of keys. He hoped she was looking in now and then, but she had taken his few plants to her Brooklyn house, and there weren't any chores for her to do except forward letters that looked important. Ina was brilliant at telling what was important and what wasn't. Ingham had of course told his agent and his publishers that he would be in Tunisia, and by now they knew he was at the Reine.

"Well!" Adams stood at the door with a bottle of wine. "Looks *very* nice!— Here, I brought you this. For the house-warming. Or for your first meal, you know."

"Oh, thanks, Francis! That's very nice of you. What'll you have?"

They had their usual scotch, Adams' with soda.

"Any news from your friend?" Adams asked.

"No, I'm sorry to say."

"Can't you send a telegram to someone who knows him?"

"I've done that." Ingham meant Ina.

The boy called Mokta, a waiter at the bungalows' bar-café, knocked on the open door, smiling his wide, friendly smile. "Good evening, messieurs," he said in French. "Is there anything you have need of?"

"I think nothing, thanks," Ingham said.

"You would like breakfast at what time, sir?"

"Oh, you serve breakfast?"

"It is not *necessary* to take it," Mokta said with a quick gesture, "but many people in the bungalows take it."

"All right, at nine o'clock, then," Ingham said. "No, eight thirty." The breakfast would probably be late.

"Nice boy, Mokta," Adams said when Mokta had left. "And they really work them here. Have you seen the kitchen in that place?" He gestured toward the low, square building that was the bungalows' café-with-terrace. "And the room where they sleep there?"

Ingham smiled. "Yes." He had had a glimpse today. The boys slept in a room that was a field of ten or twelve jammed-together beds. The sink in the kitchen had been full of dirty water and dishes.

"The drains are always stopped up, you know. I make my own breakfast. I imagine it's a little more sanitary. Mokta's nice. But that sour-puss *directrice* works him to death. She's a German, probably only hired because she can speak Arabic and French. If they're out of towels, it's Mokta who has to go to the main building and get them.— How're you doing on your book?"

"I've done twenty pages. Not as fast as my usual rate, but I can't complain." Ingham was grateful for Adams' interest. He had found out that Adams wasn't a writer or a journalist, but he still didn't know what Adams did, except study Russian in a casual way. Maybe Adams didn't do anything. That was possible, of course.

"It must be hard, writing when you think each day you'll have to drop it," Adams said.

"That doesn't bother me too much." Ingham replenished Adams' drink. He served Adams crackers and cheese. The bungalow began to seem more attractive. The waning sunlight shone through half open, pale blue shutters onto the white walls. Ingham thought that he and John might spend no more than ten days on the script. John knew someone in Tunis who could help him in finding the small cast. John wanted amateurs.

He and Adams were in good spirits when they went off in Ingham's car to have dinner at Melik's. The terrace was half full, not noisy as yet. Someone was strumming a guitar, someone else tootling a flute hesitantly at a back table.

Adams talked about his daughter Caroline in Tulsa. Her husband, the engineer, was about to be sent off to Vietnam, as he was in some kind of civilian army reserve. Caroline was due to have a baby within five months, and Adams was pleased and hopeful, because her first child had miscarried. Adams was pro-Vietnam War, Ingham had discovered early on. Ingham was sick of it, sick of discussing it with people like Adams, and he was glad Adams did not say anything else about the war that evening. Democracy and God, those were the things Adams believed in. It wasn't Christian Science or Rosicrucianism with Adams—at least not so far—but a sort of Billy Graham, all-round God with an old-fashioned moral code thrown in. What the Vietnamese needed, Adams said in appallingly plain words, was the American kind of democracy. Besides the American kind of democracy, Ingham thought, the Americans were introducing the Vietnamese to the capitalist system in the form of a brothel industry, and to the American class system by making the Negroes pay higher for their lays. Ingham listened, nodding, bored, mildly irritated.

"You've never been married?" Adams asked.

"Yes. Once. Divorced.— No children."

They were having a smoke after the couscous. Not much edible meat tonight, but the couscous and the spicy sauce had been delicious. Couscous was the name of the African millet flour, Adams had explained, granulated flour that was cooked by steaming it over a broth. It could be made also from wheat. It was tan in color, bland in flavor, and over it was spooned hot or medium hot red sauce, turnips, and pieces of stewed lamb. It was a specialty at Melik's.

"Was your wife a writer, too?" Adams asked.

"No, she didn't do anything," Ingham said, smiling a little. "A woman of leisure. Well, it's past, and it was a long time ago." He was ready to tell Adams it was longer than a year and a half ago, in case Adams asked.

"Do you think you'll marry again?"

"I don't know.— Why? Do you think it's the ideal life?"

"Oh, I think that depends. It's not the same for every man." Adams was smoking a small cigar. When his cheeks flattened out, his face looked longer, more like an ordinary face, and when he removed the cigar, the little pouches came back, like a cartoon of himself. Between the cheeks, the thin, pink mouth smiled good-naturedly. "I was certainly happy. My wife was the kind who really knew how to run a home. Put up preserves, took care of the garden, a good hostess, remembered people's birthdays, all that. Never annoyed when I got delayed at the plant.— I thought of marrying again. There was even one woman—a lot like my wife—I might've married. But it's not the same when you're not young any more."

Ingham had nothing to say. He thought of Ina and wished she were here, sitting with them now, wished he could take a walk with her on the beach tonight, after they had said good night to Adams, wished they could go back to his bungalow and go to bed together.

"Any girl in your life now?" Adams asked.

Ingham didn't like to talk to anyone about Ina, but did it matter if he talked to someone like Adams? "Yes, I suppose so. I've known her about a year. She works for CBS-TV in New York. She's written some television plays and also some short stories. Several published," he added.

The flutist was gaining strength. An Arab song began shakily, reinforced by a wailing male voice.

"How old is she?"

"Twenty-eight."

"Old enough to know her own mind."

"Um-m. She had a marriage that went wrong—when she was twenty-one or -two. So I'm sure she's in no hurry to make a mistake again. Neither am I."

"But you expect to marry?"

The music grew ever louder.

"Vaguely.— I can't see that it matters very much, unless people want children."

"Is she going to join you here in Tunisia?"

"No. I wish she were. She knows John Castlewood very well. In fact she introduced us. But she has her job in New York."

"And she hasn't written you either? About John?"

"No." Ingham warmed a little to Adams. "It's funny, isn't it? How slow can mail *get* here?"

Their dessert of yoghurt had arrived. There was also a platter of fruit.

"Tell me more about your girl. What's her name?"

"Ina Pallant.— She lives with her family in a big house in Brooklyn Heights. She has a crippled brother she's very fond of—Joey. He has multiple sclerosis, practically confined to his wheelchair, but Ina's a great help to him. He paints—rather surrealistically. Ina arranged a show for him last year. But of course he couldn't have got the show unless he was good. He sold—oh, seven or eight out of thirty canvases." Ingham disliked saying it, but he thought Adams would be interested in figures. "One picture, for instance, was of a man sitting casually on a rock in a forest, smoking a cigarette. In the foreground, a little girl is running forward, terrified, and a tree is growing out of the top of her head."

Adams leaned forward with interest. "What's that supposed to mean?"

"The terror of growing up. The man represents life and evil. He's entirely green. He just sits watching—or not even watching—with an air of having the whole situation in his power."

Melik's plump son, aged about thirteen, came and leaned on chubby hands on the table, exchanging something in Arabic with Adams. Adams was grinning. Then the boy totted up their bill. Ingham insisted on paying, because it was part of his bungalow-warming.

Downstairs, on the dusty street, Ingham noticed an old Arab whom he had seen a few times before, loitering around his car. The Arab had a short gray beard and wore a turban and classic baggy red pants held up somehow under the knees. He walked with a stick. Ingham knew he must try the car doors when he—Ingham—wasn't in sight, hoping with indefatigable patience for the day or the hour when Ingham would forget to lock everything. Now as the Arab drifted away from the big Peugeot station wagon, Ingham barely glanced at him. The Arab was becoming a fixture, like the tan fortress or the Café de la Plage near Melik's. Ingham and Adams walked a little way up the main street, but since this became dark, they turned back. The interesting corner, the only alive part of the town at this time of night was the broad sandy area in front of the Plage, where a few men sat at tables with their coffees or glasses of wine. The yellow light from the Plage's big front windows flowed out onto the sand, onto the first table legs and a few sandaled feet under them.

As Ingham looked at the front door, a man was rudely pushed out and nearly fell. Ingham and Adams stopped to watch. The man seemed a little drunk. He went directly back into the Plage, and was again shoved out. Another man came out and put an arm around him, talking to him. The drunk had a stubborn air, but let himself be sent off in the direction of the white houses behind the fortress. Ingham continued to watch the unsteady man, fascinated by whatever passion filled him. Just beyond the glow of the café's lights, the man stopped and half turned, staring defiantly at the café door. In the doorway of the Plage now, a tall man and the man who had put his arm around the drunken man were talking together and keeping an eye on the motionless, determined figure two hundred yards away.

Ingham was rapt. He wondered if they were carrying knives? Perhaps, if it was a long-standing grudge.

"Probably a quarrel about a woman," Adams said.

"Yes."

"Very jealous when it comes to women, you know."

"Yes, I'm sure," Ingham said.

They walked a little on the beach, though Ingham did not like the fine sand getting into his shoes. By the light of the moon, small children were gathering bits off the beach—the second or third wave of scavengers after their parents and elder siblings—and putting their findings away in bags that hung from their necks. Ingham had never seen such a clean beach as this one. Nothing was ever left by all the picker-uppers, not even a four-inch-long splinter of wood, because they used the wood for fires, and not even a shell, because they sold all the shells they could to tourists.

Ingham and Adams had a final coffee at the Plage. A smelly, arched doorway to their right revealed a huge "W.C." and an arrow, in black paint, on a blue wall three feet beyond. The ceiling was groined, if such a word could be used, by projecting supports ornamented with big yellow knobs that suggested stage footlights. Ingham realized that he had nothing to talk to Adams about. Adams, silent himself, must have realized the same thing in regard to Ingham. Ingham smiled a little as he drank the last of his sweet black coffee. Funny to think of someone like himself and Adams, hanging around together just because they were Americans. But their good night twenty minutes later, on the hotel grounds, was warm. Adams wished him a happy stay, as if he had moved in permanently, or as if, Ingham thought, he were a newcomer to an expedition, doomed to a different and rather lonely life for months to come. But Ingham had no duties at all except those he assigned himself, and he was free to go hundreds of miles anywhere in his car.

Before he went to bed that night, Ingham looked through his personal and his business address books, and found two people to whom he might write in regard to John. (He hadn't Miles Gallust's address, or he had left it in New York, and he reproached himself for this oversight.) The two people were William McIlhenny, an editor in the New York office of Paramount, and Peter Langland, a free-lance photographer whom John knew pretty well, Ingham remembered. Ingham thought of cabling, but decided a cable would look too dramatic, so he wrote Peter Langland a short, friendly note (they had met at a party with John, and Ingham remembered him more clearly now, a chunky blond fellow with glasses), asking him to prod John and ask John to cable, in case he had not yet written. The probably four or five days until the letter reached New York seemed an eon to wait, but Ingham tried to make himself be patient. This was Africa, not Paris or London. The letter had to get to Tunis before it could be put on a plane.

Ingham posted the letter the next morning.

4

TWO OR THREE days went by. Ingham worked.

In the mornings, Mokta brought his continental breakfast around 9:15 or 9:30. Mokta always had a question: "The refrigerator works well?" Or "Hassim has brought you enough towels?" Always Mokta asked these things with a disarming smile. He was more blond than brunette, and he had gray-blue eyes with long lashes.

Ingham supposed Mokta was popular with both women and men, and though he was only seventeen or so, he had probably had experience with both. At any rate, with his good looks and his manner, he was not going to spend the rest of his life carrying breakfast trays and stacks of towels across the sand. "Only one thing I'd like, my friend," Ingham said. "If you see a letter for me in that madhouse, would you bring it immediately?"

Mokta laughed. "*Bien sûr, m'sieur! Je regarde tout le temps —tout le temps pour vous!*"

Ingham waved a casual good-bye and poured himself some coffee, which was strong enough but not hot. Sometimes it was the other way around. He pulled on his pajama top. He slept only in the pants. The nights were warm, too. He thought of the desk in the bungalow manager's office. Dare he hope for a letter today by 10:30? 11? Ingham had been told by the hotel's main office that mail came twice a day to the bungalow headquarters and was delivered as soon as it arrived, but this was patently not so, because Ingham had seen people going to the office in the bungalow headquarters and looking through the post there, post that was sometimes sorted and sometimes not. How could he expect Arab boys, or even the harassed, ill-tempered German *directrice* to care very much about people's mail? There was never anyone at the desk. Stacks of towels filled one corner of the office—although when Ingham had asked for a clean towel, having used his for more than a week, the boy had told him he hadn't changed it because it didn't look dirty. Mysterious gray metal files stood against the walls. The absurdity of the contents of this office had given it a Kafka-like futility to Ingham. He felt that he never would, never could receive any letter of significance there. And it was maddening to Ingham to find the door sometimes locked for no apparent reason, no one around to open it, or no one with the key. This would send him forging across the sand to the main building on the off-chance that post had arrived and not yet been brought to the bungalows.

Ingham was working when Mokta came in just before 11 with a letter. Ingham seized it, automatically fishing in his pocket for some coins for Mokta.

"Hallelujah!" Ingham said. The envelope was a long business airmail, and it was postmarked New York.

"*Succès!*" said Mokta. "*Merci, m'sieur!*" He bowed and left.

The letter was from Peter Langland, strangely enough. Their letters had crossed.

June 19, 19—

Dear Mr. Ingham—or Howard,

By now you no doubt know of the sad events of over last weekend, as Ina said she would write you. John spoke to me just two days before. He was in a crise, as you probably know, or maybe you didn't know. But none of us expected anything like this. He was afraid he couldn't go through with *Trio* under the circumstances, which made him feel doubly guilty, I think, because you were already in Tunisia. Then he had his personal problems, as you probably know from Ina. But I know he would want me to write a line to you and say he is sorry, so herewith I do it. He simply couldn't stand up to everything that was on his shoulders. I liked John very much and thought very highly of him, as I think everyone did who knew him. We all believed he had a great career coming. It is a shock to all of us, but especially to those who knew him well. I suppose you'll be coming home now, and maybe you've already left, but I trust this can be forwarded to you.

Yours sincerely,
Peter Langland

John Castlewood had killed himself. Ingham walked to the window with the letter in his hand. The blue shutters were closed against the augmenting morning sun, but he stared at the shutters as if he could see through them. This was the end of the Tunisia expedition. How had John done it? A gun? Sleeping pills most likely. *What a hell of a thing*, Ingham thought. And why? Well, he hadn't known John well enough to guess. He remembered John's face—always lively, usually smiling or grinning, pale below the neat, straight black hair. Maybe a trifle weak, that face. Or was that an afterthought? A weak beard, anyway, soft, pale skin. John hadn't looked in the least depressed when Ingham had last seen him, at that last dinner in New York with Ina in a restaurant south of the Square. It had been the evening before the day Ingham caught the plane. "You know where to go in Tunis for the car rental?" John had asked, making sure of the practical things as usual, and he had asked again if Ingham had packed the street map of Tunis and the Guide Bleu for Tunisia, both of which John had lent or given him.

"For Christ's sake," Ingham muttered. He walked up and down his room, and felt shattered. An anecdote of Adams' drifted into his mind: Adams fishing on a small river (Connecticut? Indiana?) when he was ten years old, and bringing his line up with a human skull on the end of it, a skull so old "it didn't matter," Adams had said, so he had never told his parents, who he had feared wouldn't believe him, anyway. Adams had buried the skull, out of fear. Suddenly Ingham wanted the comfort of Adams' presence. He thought of going over now to tell Adams the news. He decided against it.

"Good God," Ingham said, and went to his kitchen to pour himself a scotch. The drink did not taste good at that hour, but it was a kind of rite, in Castlewood's honor.

He'd have to think now about starting home. Tell the hotel. See about a plane from Tunis to New York.

Surely he'd hear from Ina today. Ingham looked at the calendar. The weekend Peter meant was the 10th and 11th of June. What the hell was happening over in the great, fast western world? It was beginning to seem slower than Tunisia.

Ingham went out and walked in the now empty driveway that curved toward the bar-café-mail-office-supply-department of the bungalows. The sand under his tennis shoes was powdery.

He walked with his hands in the pockets of his shorts, and when he encountered a huge woman talking in French to her tiny son, who looked like a wisp beside her, Ingham turned aimlessly back. He was trying to think what he should do next. Cable Ina again, perhaps. He might stay on a day or so to get a letter from her—if she had written. Suddenly, everything seemed so doubtful, so vague.

He went back to his bungalow—which he had left unlocked against the advice of Adams who told him to lock it if he were away even one minute—took his billfold and set out, having locked the door this time, for the main building of the hotel. He would cable Ina, and take a look at the newspapers on the tables in the lobby. Sometimes the papers were several days old. There might be something about John in a Paris *Herald Tribune.* He should look for a Monday June 12th paper, he thought. Or possibly a Tuesday paper, the 13th.

A series of broad, shallow steps led from the beach up to the rear entrance of the hotel. There was an open shower for swimmers at the foot of the steps, and some corpulent Germans, a man and a woman, were yelling and screaming as they de-sanded each other's backs under the water. On going closer to them, Ingham was irked to hear that they were speaking very American American.

At the hotel desk, Ingham sent a cable to Ina:

HEARD ABOUT JOHN FROM LANGLAND. WRITE OR CABLE AT ONCE. BAFFLED. LOVE. HOWARD.

He sent it to Ina's house in Brooklyn, because she would surely get it there, whatever was happening, and she just might not be at work if her brother Joey was having a bad spell and she had to look after him. Neither on the low tables nor on the shelves at the back of the lobby could Ingham find a paper of weekend June 10–11, nor a paper in English or French for June 12th or 13th.

"If you please," Ingham said in careful French to the young Arab clerk at the desk, handing him a five-hundred-millime bill, "would you see that any letter that comes for me today is delivered at once to my bungalow? Number three. It is very important." He had printed his name on a piece of paper.

He thought of having a drink at the bar, and decided not to. He did not know what he wanted to do. Oddly enough, he felt he could work on his novel this afternoon. But logically he should make plans about leaving, speak to the hotel now. He didn't.

Ingham went back to his bungalow, put on swimming trunks, and went for a swim. He saw Adams at some distance, bearing his spear, but managed to avoid Adams' seeing him. Adams always went for a swim before lunch, he said.

That afternoon, Ingham found he could write only one paragraph. He was too anxious for a word from Ina, which he felt positive would come in the afternoon post that arrived at any time between 4:30 and 6:30. But nothing came except something from the U.S. Internal Revenue Department in a windowed envelope, forwarded by Ina. The government wanted three hundred and twenty-eight dollars more. Ingham's accountant had made a slight mistake, apparently. Ingham wrote the check and put it in an airmail envelope.

To satisfy himself, Ingham looked first in the bungalow headquarters' office—eight unclaimed letters, but none for him—then walked to the main building. Nothing there for him, either. He walked back barefoot, carrying his sandals, letting the little waves break against his ankles. The declining sun was behind him. He stared at the wet sand at his feet.

"Howard! Where've you been?" Adams stood a few yards away, his nose shiny and brown. Now he reminded Ingham of a rabbit. "Come and have a drink *chez moi*!"

"Thanks very much," Ingham said, hesitated, then asked, "when did you mean?"

"Now. I was just on my way home."

"Did you have a good day?" Ingham asked, making an effort. They were walking along.

"Very fine, thanks. And you?"

"Not too good, thanks."

"Oh? What happened?"

Ingham gestured toward Adams' house, a vague forward gesture which he had, in fact, picked up from Adams.

They walked on over the gritty cement path, past the bungalow headquarters, Adams on neat bare feet, Ingham with his heelless sandals on now, because of the heat of the sand. He felt sloppy in sandals or slippers without heels, but they were certainly the coolest footgear.

Adams hospitably set to work making scotches with ice. The air-conditioning felt wonderful to Ingham. He stepped outside the door and carefully knocked the sand from his slippers, then came in again.

"Try this," Adams said, handing Ingham his drink. "And what's your news?"

Ingham took the drink. "The man who was supposed to join me killed himself in New York about ten days ago."

"*What?*— Good heavens! When did you hear?"

"This morning. I had a letter from a friend of his."

"John, you mean.— Why did he do it? Something wrong with a love affair? Something financial?"

Ingham felt grateful for every predictable question. "I don't think because of a love affair. But I don't know. Maybe there's no reason at all—except anxiety, something like that."

"How did he do it?"

"I dunno. Sleeping pills, I suppose."

"He was twenty-six, you told me." Adams' face was full of concern. "Worried about money?"

Ingham shrugged. "He wasn't rolling, but he had enough for this project. We had a producer, Miles Gallust. We were advanced a few thousand dollars.— What's the use wondering? There're probably a lot of reasons why he did it, reasons I don't know."

"Sit down."

Adams sat down on the sofa with his drink, and Ingham took the squeaky leather chair. The closed shutters made the light in the room a pleasant dusk. A few thin bars of sun came in near the ceiling above Adams' head.

"Well," Adams said, "I suppose without John you'll be thinking of leaving here—going back to the States."

Ingham heard a gloominess in Adams' tone. "Yes, no doubt. In a few days."

"Any news from your girl?" Adams asked.

Ingham disliked the term "your girl." "Not yet. I cabled her today."

Adams nodded thoughtfully. "When did this happen?"

"The weekend of June tenth and eleventh. I'm sorry I didn't see any papers then. I think the Paris *Herald Tribune* might have mentioned it."

"I can understand that it's a blow," Adams said sympathetically. "How well did you know John?"

Platitudes.

Adams made them both a second drink. Then Ingham went to his bungalow to put on some trousers for dinner. He had fatuously hoped for a cable from Ina to be lying on the corner of his work table when he walked into his bungalow. The table was empty of messages as usual.

Melik's was lively that evening. There were two tables with wind instruments, and one guitar somewhere else. A man at another table had a well-behaved German police dog who put his ears back at the noise, but did not bark. It was too noisy to talk comfortably, and that was just as well, Ingham thought. The man with the dog was tall and slender and looked like an American. He wore levis and a blue denim shirt. Adams sat with his pouchy smile, giving an occasional tolerant shake of his head. Ingham felt like a small silent room—maybe an empty room—within a larger room where all this din came from. The American had led his dog away.

Adams shouted, for the second time, "I said, you ought to see more of this country before you take off!"

Ingham nodded his emphatic agreement.

The moon was almost full. They walked a little on the beach, and Ingham looked at the beige, floodlit fortress whose walls sloped gently back, looked at the huddled, domed white Arab houses behind it, heard the still balmy breeze in his ears, and felt far away from New York, from John and his mysterious reasons, even far away from Ina—because he resented her not having written. He hated his resentment and his small-mindedness for having it. Maybe Ina had good reasons for not having written. But if so, what were they? He was not even close to Adams, Ingham thought with a slight start of fear, or loneliness.

Where would he go? Look at the Tunisia map tomorrow, Ingham thought. Or get back to work on the book, until Ina's letter or cable came. That was the wisest thing. His bungalow with breakfast cost about six dollars a day, not that he was worried about money. But much of his Tunisian expenses would obviously have to come out of his own pocket now.

They said good night on the bungalow driveway. "My thoughts are with you," Adams said, speaking softly, because people were asleep in the nearby bungalows. "Get some rest. You've had a shock, Howard."

5

INGHAM MEANT to sleep late, but he awakened early. He went for a swim, then came back and made some instant coffee. It was still only half-past 7. He worked until Mokta brought his breakfast at 9.

"Ah, you work early this morning!" Mokta said. "Be careful you do not make the head turn." He made a circular motion with one finger near his ear.

Ingham smiled. He had noticed that Arabs were always worried about overstraining their brains. One young man he had spoken with in Naboul had told him that he was a university student, but had overstrained his brain, so he was on a vacation of several weeks on doctor's orders. "Don't forget to see if I have a letter, will you, Mokta? I shall look around eleven, but a letter may come before then."

"But today is Sunday."

"So it is." Ingham was suddenly depressed. "By the way, I can use a clean towel. Hassim took mine yesterday and forgot to bring a clean one."

"Ah, that Hassim! I am *sorry*, sir! I hope there are clean towels today. Yesterday we used them all."

Ingham nodded. Somebody was getting clean towels, anyway.

"And you know," Mokta said, leaning gracefully against the door jamb, "all the boys go to school for *five months* to learn hotel work? You would not believe it, would you?"

"No." Ingham buttered a piece of toast.

Ingham slept from 12 until 1. He had written nine pages and he was pleased with his work. He took his car and drove to Bir Bou Rekba, a tiny town about seven kilometers away, and had lunch at a simple little restaurant with a couple of tables out on the pavement. The wandering cats were skinnier, ribs showing, and all their tails were broken at a painful angle. Breaking cats' or kittens' tails was evidently a minor sport in Tunisia. Most of the cats in Hammamet had broken tails, too. Ingham heard no French. He heard nothing that he could understand. It was appropriate, this environment, he thought, as the main character in his book lived half his time in a world unknown to his family and his business associates, a world known only to himself, really, because he couldn't share with anyone the truth that he was appropriating money and forging checks with three false signatures several times a month. Ingham sat in the sun dreaming, sipping chilled rosé, wishing—but not desperately at this moment—that time would pass a little faster so that he could have a word from Ina. What would her excuse be? Or maybe a letter from her had got lost, or maybe two had. Ingham had telephoned the Hotel du Golfe the day before yesterday, but not yesterday. He was sick of being told there wasn't anything for him. And anyway, the Golfe was apparently forwarding reliably to the Reine. The sun made his face throb, and he felt as if he were being gently broiled. He had never known the sun so close and big. People farther north didn't know what the sun was like, he thought. This was the true sun, the ancient fire that seemed to reduce one's lifespan to a second and one's personal problems to a minuscule absurdity.

The dramas people invent! Ingham thought. He felt a detached disgust for the whole human race.

A scruffy, emaciated cat looked at him pleadingly, but they had taken away Ingham's plate of fish-with-fried-egg. Ingham tossed the inside of some bread onto the dusty cement. It was all he had. But the cat ate it, chewing patiently with its head turned sideways.

That afternoon, he worked again, and produced five pages.

Monday and Tuesday came and went without a letter from Ina. Ingham worked. He avoided Adams. Ingham felt morose, and knew he would be bad company. In such a mood, he was apt to say something bitter. On Wednesday, when he would have liked to have dinner with Adams, he remembered that Adams had said he always spent Wednesday evenings alone. It seemed to be a law Adams had made for himself. Ingham ate in the hotel dining room. The cruising American was still here, dining with a man tonight. Ingham nodded a greeting. He realized that he hadn't answered Peter Langland's letter. He wrote a letter that evening.

June 28, 19—

Dear Peter,

I thank you very much for your letter. I had not heard the news, as you know from my first letter, and matter of fact Ina hasn't written me as yet. I was very sorry to hear about John, as I had thought like everyone else that he was doing well. I didn't know him well, as you may know —for the past year, but not well. I had no idea he was in any kind of crisis.

In the next week, I'll probably leave and go back to the States. This is undoubtedly the strangest expedition of my life. Not a word, either, from Miles Gallust, who was to be our producer.

Forgive this inadequate letter. I am frankly still dazed by the news.

Yours,
Howard Ingham

Peter Langland lived on Jane Street. Ingham sealed the envelope. He had no stamps left. He would take the letter into Hammamet tomorrow morning.

In the bungalow fifteen feet behind Ingham's, beyond some lemon trees, some French were saying good night. Ingham could hear them distinctly through his open window.

"We'll be in Paris in three days, you know. Give us a telephone call."

"But of course! Jacques! Come along!— He's falling asleep standing up!"

"Good night, sleep well!"

"Sleep well!"

It seemed very dark beyond his window. There was no moon.

The next day passed like the one before, and Ingham did eight pages. He knocked on Adams' door at 5 P.M. to invite him for a drink, but Adams was not in. Ingham did not bother to look for him on the beach.

On the morning of 30th June, a Friday, a letter from Ina arrived in a CBS envelope. Mokta brought it. Ingham tore it open, in too much of a hurry to tip Mokta.

The letter was dated June 25th, and it said:

Howard dear,

I am sorry I have not written before. Peter Langland said he wrote you, in case you hadn't heard about John, but it was in the Times (London) and Trib in Paris, so we supposed you'd seen it in Tunisia. I am still so bouleversed, I can't write just now, really. But I will in a day or so, I hope tomorrow. That's a promise. Please forgive me. I hope you are all right.

My love,
Ina

The letter was typewritten. Ingham read it a second time. It wasn't a letter at all. It made him a little angry. What was he supposed to do, sit here another week until she felt in the mood to write? Why was she so bouleversed? "We supposed . . ." Was she so close to Peter Langland? Had she and Peter been holding John's hand in the hospital before John died? That was, assuming he had taken sleeping pills.

Ingham took a walk along the beach, plodding the same sand he had crossed so many times in quest of a letter from Ina. Maddening, he thought, her letter. She was the kind who could dash off a ten-line letter and give the facts, and perhaps say, "Details later," but here there weren't even any facts. It was unexpectedly heartless of her, Ingham felt. She might have had the imagination to realize his position, sitting miles away, waiting. And why hadn't she had time to write him in all the days before John did it? And this was the girl he intended to marry? Ingham smiled, and it was a relief. But he felt swimmy and lost, as if he floated in space. Yes, it was understood that they would marry. He had proposed in a casual way, the only way Ina would have liked. She hadn't said, "Oh, *yes*, darling!" but it was understood. They might not marry for several months. It depended on their jobs and the finding of an apartment, perhaps, because sometimes Ina had to go to California for six weeks or so, but the point was—

His thoughts trailed off, cooked by the sun on his head,

discouraged by the sheer effort of imagining New York's unwritten conventions in this torrid Arabic land. Ingham remembered a story Adams had told him: an English girl had smiled, or maybe just stared too long, at an Arab, who had followed her along a dark beach and raped her. That had been the girl's story. An Arab considered a girl's stare a green light. The Tunisian government, to keep in good odor with the west, had made a big to-do, tried the man and given him a long sentence, which had been very soon commuted, however. The story was an absurdity, and Ingham laughed, causing a surprised glance from two young men—they looked French—who were walking past with skin-diving gear just then.

In the afternoon, Ingham worked, but did only three pages. He was fidgety.

That evening, he had dinner with the man in levis. Ingham had found him in the Café de la Plage, where he went to have a drink at 8. The man spoke to him first. Again the German police dog was with him. He was a Dane and spoke excellent English with a slight English accent. His name was Anders Jensen. He said he lived in a rented apartment in a street across from Melik's. Ingham tried the *boukhah* which Jensen was drinking. It was a little like grappa or tequila.

Ingham was in a rather tight-lipped mood, so far as giving information about himself went, but Jensen did not pump him. Ingham replied, to a question from Jensen, that he was a writer and taking a month's vacation. Jensen was a painter. He looked thirty or thirty-two.

"In Copenhagen I had a breakdown," Jensen said with a tired, dry smile. He was lean and tan with light straight hair and a strangely absent, drifting expression in his blue eyes, as if he were not paying full attention to anything around him. "My doctor—a psychiatrist—told me to go somewhere in the sun. I've been here for eight months."

"Are you comfortable where you are?" Jensen had said his place was simple, and he looked capable of roughing it, so Ingham supposed the house was primitive indeed. "Good conditions for painting, I mean?"

"The light is splendid," Jensen said. "Hardly any furniture, but there never is. They rent you a house, you know, and you say, 'Where's the bed? Where's a chair? Where's a table, for Christ's sake?' They say that will come tomorrow. Or next week. The truth is, they don't use furniture. They sleep on mats and fold their clothing on the floor. Or drop it. But I have a bed at least. And I made a table out of boxes and a couple of boards I picked up on the street.— They broke my dog's leg. He's just getting over the limp."

"Really?— Why?" Ingham asked, shocked.

"Oh, they just threw a big rock. They dropped it out a window, I think. Waited their chance when Hasso was lying in the shade by a house across the street. They love to hurt animals, you know. And maybe a full-bred dog like Hasso is more tempting than an ordinary dog to them." He patted the dog who was sitting by his chair. "Hasso's still nervous from it. He hates Arabs. Crooked Arabs." Again the distant but amused smile. "I'm glad he's obedient, or he'd tear the trousers off twelve a day around here."

Ingham laughed. "There's one in red pants and a turban I'd like to paste. He haunts my car all the time. Whenever it's parked around here."

Jensen lifted a finger. "I know him. Abdullah. A real bastard. Do you know, I saw him robbing a car just two streets from here in the middle of an afternoon?" Jensen laughed with delight, but almost silently. He had handsome white teeth. "And no one does anything!"

"Was he stealing a suitcase?"

"Clothing of some kind, I think. He can always flog that in the market.— I think I shall not stay here much longer because of Hasso. If they hit him again, they may kill him. Anyway, it's an inferno of heat here in August."

They got into a second bottle of wine. Melik's was quiet. Only two other tables were occupied, by Arabs, all men.

"You like to take vacations alone?" Jensen asked.

"Yes. I suppose I do."

"So you are not writing now?"

"Well, yes, I've started a book. I've worked harder in my life, but I'm working."

By midnight, Ingham was on his way with Jensen to have a look at Jensen's apartment. It was in a small white house with a door on the street which was closed by a padlock. Jensen turned on the feeblest of electric lights, and they climbed a naked white—but grimy—stairs without a banister. There was the smell of a toilet somewhere. Jensen had the next floor, which consisted of one good-sized room, and the floor above, which had two smaller rooms. A confusion of canvases leaned against the walls and lay on tables of the box-and-board variety Jensen had described. In one of the upstairs rooms, there was a little gas stove with two burners. There was one chair which neither of them took. They sat on the floor. Jensen poured red wine.

Jensen had lit two candles which were fixed in wine bottles. He was talking about having to go to Tunis for paint supplies. He said he went by bus. Ingham looked around at the paintings. A fiery orange color predominated. They were abstract, Ingham supposed, though some of the straight lines and squares in them could have been meant to be houses. In one, a rag, maybe a paint rag, was flattened and painted onto the canvas, crumpled. It was not a light in which to make a judgement, and Ingham didn't.

"Have you got a shower here?" Ingham asked.

"Oh, I use a bucket. Down on the terrace. Or the court. It has a drain."

There was a sound of two men's voices, arguing, in the street below. Jensen lifted his head to listen. The voices passed on. The tone had been more angry than usual.

Jensen had put out some dry white cheese and some bread. Ingham did not want anything. The plate of cheese was rather pretty in the candlelight, surrounded by a halo of shadow. The dog, lying on the floor by the door, gave a deep sigh and slept.

Half an hour later, Jensen put his hand on Ingham's shoulder and asked him if he would like to spend the night. Ingham suddenly realized he was queer, or at least was making a queer pass.

"No, I have my car outside," Ingham said. "Thank you, anyway."

Jensen attempted to kiss him, missed and kissed his cheek briefly. He missed because Ingham dodged a little. Jensen was on his knees. Ingham shivered. He was in shirtsleeves.

"You never sleep with men? It's nice. No complications,"

Jensen said, rolling back on his heels, sitting down again on the floor only three feet away from Ingham. "The girls here are awful, whether they're tourists or whether they're—what shall I say—native. Then there's the danger of syphilis. They all have it, you know. They're sort of immune to it, but they pass it on."

A profound bitterness was audible in Jensen's subdued tone. Ingham was at that moment calling himself an idiot for not having realized that Jensen was homosexual. After all, as a fairly sophisticated New Yorker, he might have been a bit brighter. Ingham felt like smiling, but he was afraid Jensen might think he was smiling at him, instead of at himself, so Ingham kept a neutral expression.

"Lots of boys available here, I've heard," Ingham said.

"Oh, yes. Little thieving bastards," Jensen replied with his wistful, absent smile. Now he was reclined on the floor, on one elbow. "Nice, if you send them straight out of the house."

Now Ingham laughed.

"You said you weren't married."

"No," Ingham said. "Can I see some of your paintings?"

Jensen put on another light or two. All his lights were naked bulbs. Jensen had a few pictures with huge, distorted faces in the foreground. The red-orange in many of them gave a sense of extreme heat. They were all a trifle sloppy and undisciplined, Ingham thought. But obviously he worked hard and pursued a theme: melancholy, apparently, which he thrust forward in the form of the ravaged faces, backgrounded by chaotic Arabian houses, or falling trees, or windstorms, sandstorms, rainstorms. Ingham did not know, after five minutes, whether he was any good or not. But at least the paintings were interesting.

"You've shown your work in Denmark?" Ingham asked.

"No, only Paris," Jensen replied.

Suddenly, Ingham did not believe him. Or was he wrong? And did it really matter? Ingham looked at his watch under a light globe. 12:35. He managed to say a few complimentary things, which pleased Jensen.

Jensen was restless and shifting. Ingham sensed that he was as hungry as a wolf, maybe physically hungry, certainly emotionally starving. Ingham sensed also that he was a shadow to Jensen, just a form in the room, solid to the touch, but nothing more. Jensen knew nothing and had really asked nothing about him. Yet they might both be in the bed in the upstairs room this moment.

"I'd better be taking off," Ingham said.

"Yes. A pity. Just when it's getting nice and cool."

Ingham asked to use the toilet. Jensen came with him and put on the light. It was a hole in a porcelain floor which sloped downward. Just outside, a tap on the wall dripped slowly into a bucket. Ingham supposed Jensen tossed a bucket of water into the hole now and then.

"Good night, and thanks for letting me visit," Ingham said, holding out his hand.

Jensen gripped it firmly. "A pleasure. Come again. I'll see you at Melik's. Or the Plage."

"Or visit me. I've got a bungalow and a refrigerator. I can even cook." Ingham smiled. He was perhaps overdoing it, just because he didn't want Jensen to think he had any unfriendly feelings. "How do I get back to the main road?"

"Go left outside the door. Take the first left, then first right, and you'll come out on the road."

Ingham went out. The light from Jensen's streetlamp was of no use as soon as he turned the first corner. The street was only six feet wide, not meant for cars. The white walls on either side of him, pocked with deep-set black windows, seemed strangely silent—strangely, because there was usually some kind of noise coming from any Arabic house. Ingham had never been in a residential section so late. He tripped on something and pitched forward, catching himself on both hands just in time to avoid hitting the road with his face. It had felt like a rolled up blanket. He pushed at the thing with his foot, and realized he was slightly tight. It was a man asleep. Ingham had touched a pair of legs.

"Hell of a place to sleep," Ingham murmured.

No sound from the sleeping form.

Out of curiosity, Ingham struck a match. Coverless, the man lay with one arm crumpled under him. A black scarf was around his neck. Black trousers, soiled white shirt. Then Ingham saw that the black scarf was red, that it was blood. The match burnt his fingers, and Ingham struck another and bent closer. There was blood all over the ground under the man's head. Under his jaw was a long glistening cut.

"Hey!" Ingham said. He touched the man's shoulder, gripped it convulsively, and just as suddenly pulled his hand back. The body was cool. Ingham looked around him and saw nothing but blackness and the vague white forms of houses. His match had gone out.

He thought of going back to get Jensen. At the same time, he drifted away from the corpse, drifted on away from Jensen, toward the road. It wasn't his business.

The end of the alley showed a pale light from the streetlights of the road. His car was a hundred yards to the left, down by Melik's. When Ingham was some thirty yards away from his car, he saw the old humpbacked Arab in the baggy trousers standing by the right rear window. Ingham ran toward him.

"Get the hell away!" he yelled.

The Arab scurried with a surprising agility, hunched over, and disappeared into a black street on the right.

"Son of a bitch!" Ingham muttered.

There was no one about, except two men standing under a tree in the light that came from the Plage's front windows.

Ingham unlocked his car, and glanced into the back seat when the light came on. Hadn't his beach towel (his own, not the hotel's) and his canvas jacket been on the seat? Of course. One rear window was open three inches. The Arab had fished the things out. He cursed the Arab with a new fury. He slammed the door and went to the dark street into which the Arab had vanished.

"Son of a bitch, I hope it *kills* you!" he shouted, so angry now that his face burnt. "Bastard son of a bitch!"

That the Arab couldn't understand didn't matter at all.

6

THE NEXT MORNING, lying in bed at 9 A.M. with the sun already warm through the shutters, Ingham did not remember getting home. He did not remember anything after cursing the humped Arab with the yellow-tan, filthy turban. Then he remembered the corpse. My God, yes, a corpse. Ingham imagined it a hell of a cut, maybe the kind that nearly severed the neck, so that if he had lifted the man, the head might have fallen off. No, he wouldn't tell Ina *that* part of the evening. He wouldn't tell anyone about the corpse, he thought. People might say, "Why didn't you report it?" Ingham realized he was ashamed of himself. Regardless of the red tape that might have followed, he should have reported the thing. He still could report it. The time he saw the body might be of some significance. But he wasn't going to.

He sprang out of bed and took a shower.

When he came out of the bathroom, Mokta had set his breakfast tray on the windowsill near his bed. That was good service. Ingham ate in shorts and shirt, sitting on the edge of his chair. He was thinking of a letter he would write to Ina, and before he finished his coffee, he pushed the tray aside and began it on his typewriter.

1 July, 19—
Sat. A.M.

Darling,

A strange day yesterday. In fact all these days are strange. I was furious not to have more news from you. I'll hold this till I hear from you. Would you mind telling me *why* he killed himself and secondly why were you so thrown by it?

It seems fantastic, but I have 47 pages done on my book and I think it is going along pretty well. But I am horribly lonely. Such a new sensation for me, it's almost interesting. I thought I had been lonely many times before and I have been, but never anything like this. I've set myself a mild schedule about working, because if I hadn't that, I think I'd go to pieces. On the other hand, that's just in the last week, since hearing about John. Before that, the days were sort of empty here, thanks to no news at all from John (or from you for that matter) but since his death, the bottom has fallen out—of what? Tunisia, maybe. Not me. Of course I'll leave soon, after cruising around the country a bit, since I'm here.

Last night I had dinner with a Danish painter who turned out to be a faggot and made a mild pass. He is lonely, too, poor guy, but I am sure he can find a lot of bed-companions among the boys here. Homosexuality is not against their religion, but alcohol is, and some towns are dry. Stealing is apparently okay, too. One old bastard swiped my canvas jacket and a towel last night from the back seat of my car while I was visiting the Dane—to look at his paintings, ha! I detest this particular Arab, and I know I shouldn't. Why detest anyone? One doesn't, one just focuses a lot of emotions of a nasty kind on one person, and there you are, hating something or somebody. Darling Ina, I have focused the opposite kind of emotions on you, you are everything tangible that I like and love, so why do you make me suffer now with this ghastly long silence? The days may flit by for you, but they drag here. I can see I'm going to post this off today express, even if I don't hear from you . . .

Since he did not hear from Ina in the morning post, he sent the letter express from the post office at 4 P.M.

He had dinner with Adams in a fishing town called La Goulette, near Tunis. The town bore a funny similarity to Coney Island, not that it had amusements or hot dog stands, but it was the elongated shape of the town, the lowness of its houses, the atmosphere of the sea. It also looked rather crummy and cheap and unspoilt. Ingham's first thought was to inquire about hotels here, but the barman at the bar they visited told him there were none. The waiter and the proprietor of the restaurant where they had dinner assured Ingham of the same thing. The waiter knew of a place where they let rooms, but this sounded too sketchy to bother investigating, at least at that hour.

That evening, Adams bored Ingham to a degree. Adams was launched again on the virtues of democracy for everyone, Christian morals for everyone. ("*Everyone?*" Ingham interrupted once, so loudly that the next table turned to look at him.) He thought of the happy pagans, Christless, maybe syphilisless, too, blissful. But in fact, where were they these days? Christianity and atom-bomb testing had spread themselves just about everywhere. *I swear if he gets onto Vietnam, I'll burst a vein*, Ingham said to himself. But realizing the absurdity of his emotions against this absurd little man, Ingham controlled himself, remembered that he had enjoyed Adams' company many times, and reminded himself that he would feel like a fool to make an enemy of Adams, whom he encountered once or twice a day on the hotel grounds or on the beach. His anger was only frustration, Ingham realized, frustration in every aspect of his life just now—except perhaps in his novel-in-progress.

"You can see it in their faces, the men who have turned their back on God," Adams droned on.

Where was God, that one could turn one's back on him?

Adams' pouches became pouchier. He was smiling and chewing contentedly at once.

"Drug addicts, alcoholics, homosexuals, criminals—and even the ordinary man in the street, *if* he's forgotten the Right Way—they're all wretched. But they can be *shown* the Right Way . . ."

My God, Ingham thought, was Adams cracked? And why throw in the homosexuals?

> Oh, I come to the garden alone,
> When the dew is still on the roses.
> And the voice I hear,
> Falling on my ear,
> Is my Savior's, my Savior's alone.

Falling on your *ear*? Can't you come to the garden *sober*? The remembered schoolboy joke brought irrepressible laughter, which Ingham gulped down, though tears stood in his eyes. Fortunately, Adams didn't take his smile amiss, because

Ingham could not possibly have explained it. Adams was still smiling complaisantly himself.

"I'm sure you're right," Ingham said forcefully, hoping to wind it up. One might be friendly, but one did not make friends with people like Adams, Ingham was thinking. They were dangerous.

A few minutes later, as Adams was tapering off, though still on the subject of Our Way of Life, Ingham asked, "What about some of the things normal people do in bed? Heterosexuals. Do you disapprove of those things?"

"What things do you mean?" Adams asked attentively, and Ingham thought very likely Adams really didn't know about them.

"Well—various things. Matter of fact, the same things homosexuals do. The very same things."

"Oh. Well, they're still male and female. Man and wife," Adams said cheerfully, tolerantly.

Yes, if they happened to be married, Ingham thought. "That's true," Ingham said. If OWL preached tolerance, Ingham would not be outdone. But Ingham sensed his mind beginning to boggle, as it so often did with Adams, his own unassailable arguments seeming to turn to sand. That was what happened in brainwashing, Ingham thought. It was odd.

"Have you ever written anything," Ingham asked, "on these subjects?"

Adams' smile became a little sly.

Ingham could see that he had, or wanted to, or was writing something now.

"You're a man of letters who I think I can trust," Adams said. "I do write, in a way, yes. Come to my bungalow when we get home and I'll show you."

Ingham paid for their inexpensive dinner, because he felt he had been a little rude to Adams, and because Adams had driven him here in his Cadillac. Ingham was glad Adams had driven, because half an hour after his dinner, he began to have waves of gripes in his lower abdomen, in fact all over his abdomen, up to the ribs. In Hammamet, back at the bungalows, Ingham excused himself under pretext of getting another pack of cigarettes, and went to the toilet. Diarrhea, and pretty bad. He swallowed a couple of Entero-Vioform tablets, then went over to Adams'.

Adams showed Ingham into his bedroom. Ingham had never been in the room before. It had a double bed with a very pretty red, white and blue counterpane, which Adams must have bought. There were a few shelves of books, more pictures—all photographs—a cozy, lighted nook within reach of the head of the bed, which contained a few books, a notebook, pen, ashtray, matches.

Adams opened a tall closet with a key, and pulled out a handsome black leather suitcase, which he unlocked with a small key on his keyring. Adams opened the suitcase on the bed. There was a radio of some sort, a tape machine, and two thick stacks of manuscript, all neatly arranged in the suitcase.

"This is what *I* write," Adams said, gesturing toward the typewritten stacks of papers at one side of the suitcase. "In fact, I broadcast it, as you see. Every Wednesday night." Adams chuckled.

"Really?" So that was what Adams did on Wednesdays. "That's very interesting," Ingham said. "You broadcast in English?"

"In American. It goes behind the Iron Curtain. In fact, exclusively behind the Iron Curtain."

"You're employed then. By the Government. The Voice of America?"

Adams shook his head quickly. "If you'll swear not to tell anyone—"

"I swear," Ingham said.

Adams relaxed slightly and spoke more softly. "I'm employed by a small group of anti-Communists behind the Iron Curtain. Matter of fact, they're not a small group by any means. They don't pay me much, because they haven't got it. The money comes via Switzerland, and that's complicated enough, I understand. I know only one man in the group. I broadcast pro-American, pro-western—what shall I call it? Philosophy. Pep talks." Adams chuckled.

"Very interesting," Ingham said. "How long've you been doing this?"

"Almost a year now."

"How did they contact you?"

"I met a man on a ship. About a year ago. We were on the same ship going from Venice to Yugoslavia. He was a great cardplayer on the ship." Adams smiled reminiscently. "Not dishonest, just a brilliant bridge player. Poker, too. He's a journalist, lives in Moscow. But of course he's not allowed to write what he thinks. He sticks strictly to the party line when he writes for the Moscow papers. But he's an important man in the underground organization. He got this equipment for me in Dubrovnik and gave it to me." Adams gestured with a proud flourish at his tape recorder and sender.

Ingham looked down with, he felt, a dazed respect at the suitcase. He wondered just how much they paid Adams. And why, when Radio Free Europe and the Voice of America were booming the same kind of thing into Russia free? "Have you a special wave length or something that the Russians can't jam?"

"Yes, so I was told. I can shift the wave length, depending on the orders I have. The orders come in code to me here from Switzerland—Italy sometimes. Would you like to hear a tape?"

"I would indeed," Ingham said.

Adams lifted the tape recorder from the suitcase. From a metal box in the suitcase he took a roll of tape. "March-April inclusive. We'll try this." He fixed it in the machine and pushed a button. "I won't play it loud."

Ingham sat down on the other side of the bed.

The machine hissed, then Adams' voice came on.

"Good evening, ladies and gentlemen, Russians and non-Russians, brothers everywhere, friends of democracy and of America. This is Robin Goodfellow, an ordinary American citizen, just as many of you, listening, are ordinary citizens of your own . . ."

Adams had winked at Ingham at the name "Robin Goodfellow." He advanced the tape a bit.

". . . what many of you thought of the news that came from Vietnam today. Five American planes shot down by the Vietcong, say the Americans. Seventeen American planes shot down, say the Vietcong. The Vietcong say they lost one plane. The Americans say the Vietcong lost nine. Someone is lying. Who? Who do you think? What country discloses her failures as well as her successes when it comes to rocket take-offs? When it comes even to the *poverty* in its land—which the Americans are fighting just as hard to erase as they are fighting lies, tyranny, poverty, illiteracy and communism in Vietnam? The answer is America. All of you . . ."

Adams pushed a button which advanced the tape in jerks. "Sort of a dull section." The muted tape screamed, hiccoughed, and Adams spoke again. Ingham was aware of Adams' tense, self-satisfied smile as he sat perched on the other side of the bed, though Ingham could not look at him, but kept his eyes on the tape machine. His abdomen was contracting, getting ready for another wave of pain.

". . . comfort to us all. The *new* American soldier is a crusader, bringing not only peace—eventually—but a happier, healthier, more *profitable* way of life to whatever country he sets foot in. And unfortunately, so often that setting foot—" (Adams' voice had dropped dramatically to a hushed tone and stopped) "—that setting foot means the death of that soldier, the telegram of bad news to his family back home, *tragedy* to his young wife or sweetheart, bereavement to his children . . ."

"Again not too exciting," Adams said, though he looked very excited himself. More squeaks and gulps from the tape machine, a couple of samples which did not please Adams, then:

". . . the voice of God will prevail at last. The men who put *people* before all else will triumph. The men who put 'the *State*' first, in defiance of human values, will perish. America fights to preserve *human* values. America fights not only to preserve herself but all others who would follow in her path—in our blessed way of life. Good night, my friends."

Click. Adams turned the machine off.

Our Blessed Way of Life. OBWL. Not pronounceable. Ingham hesitated, then said, "That's very impressive."

"You like it. Good." Adams began briskly putting his equipment away, back into the closet which he again locked.

If it was all true, Ingham was thinking, *if* Adams was paid by the Russians, he was paid because it was so absurd, it was really rather good anti-American propaganda. "I wonder how many people it reaches? How many listen?"

"Upwards of six million," Adams replied. "So my friends say. I call them my friends, although I don't even know their names, except the one man I told you about. A price is on their heads, if they're found out. And they're gaining recruits all the time, of course."

Ingham nodded. "What's their final plan? I mean about—changing their government's policy and all that?"

"It's not so much a final plan as a war of attrition," Adams said with his confident, pouchy smile, and from the happy sparkle in his eyes, Ingham knew that this was where his heart lay, his *raison d'être*, in these weekly broadcasts that carried the American Way of Life behind the Iron Curtain. "The results may not even be seen in my lifetime. But if people listen, and they do, I make my effect."

Ingham felt blank for a moment. "How long are your talks?"

"Fifteen minutes.— You mustn't tell anyone here. Not even another American. Matter of fact, you're the first American I've told about it. I don't even tell my daughter, just in case it might leak out. You understand?"

"Of course," Ingham said. It was late, after midnight. He wanted to leave. It was an uncomfortable feeling, like claustrophobia.

"I'm not paid much, but to tell you the truth, I'd do it for nothing," Adams said. "Let's go in the other room."

Ingham declined Adams' offer of a coffee or a nightcap, and managed to leave in five minutes, and gracefully. But as he walked in the dark back toward his own bungalow, he felt somehow shaky. Ingham went to bed, but after a moment, his insides began churning, and he was up and in the bathroom. This time he vomited, as well. That was good, Ingham thought, in case the trouble had been the *poisson-complet*—the fried fish with fried egg—at the restaurant in La Goulette. He took more Entero-Vioform.

It became 3 A.M. Ingham tried to rest between seizures. He sweated. A cold towel on his forehead made him too cold, a sensation he had not had in a long time. He vomited again. He wondered if he should try to get a doctor—it didn't seem reasonable to endure this much discomfort for another six hours—but there was no telephone in the bungalow, and Ingham could not face, even though he had a flashlight now, trudging across the sand to the main building, where in fact he might find no one to open the door at this hour. Call Mokta? Wake him at the bungalow headquarters? Ingham could not bring himself to do that. He sweated it out until daylight.

At 6:30 or 7, people were up at the bungalow headquarters. Ingham thought vaguely of trying for a doctor, of asking for some kind of medicine more effective than Entero-Vioform. Ingham put on his robe over his pajamas, and walked in sandals to the bungalow headquarters. He was chilly and exhausted. Before he quite reached the building, he saw Adams prancing on his little arched feet out of his bungalow, briskly locking his door, briskly turning.

Adams hailed him. "Hello! What's up?"

Somewhat feebly, Ingham explained the situation.

"Oh, my goodness! You should have knocked me up—as the English say, ha-ha! Throwing up, eh? First of all, take some Pepto-Bismol. Come in, Howard!"

Ingham went into Adams' bungalow. He wanted to sit down, or collapse, but made himself keep standing. He took the Pepto-Bismol at the bathroom basin. "Ridiculous to feel so demolished." He managed a laugh.

"You think it was the fish last night? I don't know how *clean* that place is, after all."

Adams' words recalled the plate of fish soup with which they had begun their dinner, and Ingham tried to forget he had ever seen the soup.

"Some tea, maybe?" Adams asked.

"Nothing, thanks." Another trip to the toilet was imminent, but there was some consolation in the thought there could not be much of anything left in him. Ingham's head began to ring. "Look, Francis, I'm sorry to be a nuisance. I—I don't know if I should have a doctor or not. But I think I'd better get back to my house."

Adams walked over with him, not quite holding his arm, but hovering just by his side. Ingham had not locked his door. Ingham excused himself and went at once to the toilet. When he came out, Adams was gone. Ingham sat down gently on the bed, still in his bathrobe. The gripes had now become a steady ache, just severe enough to preclude sleep, Ingham knew.

Adams came in again, barefoot, light and quick as a girl. "Brought some tea. Just one hot cup with some sugar in it'll do you good. Tea *balls*." He went to Ingham's kitchen, and Ingham heard water running, a pan clatter, a match being struck. "I spoke to Mokta and told him not to bring breakfast," Adams said. "Coffee's bad."

"Thank you."

The tea did help. Ingham could not drink the whole cup.

Adams gave him a cheery good-bye and said he would look in again after his swim, and if Ingham was asleep, he would not wake him. "Don't lose heart! You're among friends," Adams said.

Ingham did lose heart. He had to bring a cooking pot from the kitchen to keep by his bed, because every ten minutes or so, he threw up a little liquid, and it was not worth going to the bathroom to do. As for pride, if Adams came in and saw the pot, Ingham had no pride left.

When Adams came back, Ingham was barely aware of it. It was nearly 10 A.M. Adams said something about not coming in earlier, because he thought Ingham might have dropped off to sleep.

Mokta knocked and came in, too, but there was nothing Ingham had in mind to ask him to do.

It was between 10 and 12, when he was alone, that Ingham experienced a sort of crisis. His abdominal pain continued. In New York, he would certainly have sent for a doctor and asked for morphine, or had a friend go to a pharmacist's to get something to relieve him. Here, Ingham was holding to Adams' advice (but did Adams know how awful he felt?) not to bother about a doctor, that he'd soon feel better. But he didn't know Adams very well, and didn't even trust him. Ingham realized during those two hours that he was very much alone, without his friends, without Ina (and he meant emotionally, too, because if she were really *with* him, she would have written several times by now, would have assured him of her love), realized that he had no real purpose in being in Tunisia—he could be writing his book anywhere—and that the country wasn't to his taste at all, that he simply didn't belong here. All these thoughts came rushing in when Ingham was at his lowest physically, emptied of strength, emptied of everything. He had been attacked, ludicrous as it might be, in the vitals, where it hurt and where it counted, and where it could kill. Now he was exhausted and unable to sleep. The tea had not stayed down. Adams was not back at 12, as he had said he would be. Adams might have forgotten. And an hour one way or the other, what would it matter to Adams? And what could Adams do, anyway?

Somehow Ingham fell asleep.

He awoke at the sound of his slightly squeaky doorknob being turned, and raised himself feebly, alert.

Adams was tiptoeing in, smiling, carrying something. "Hello! Feeling better? I've brought something nice. I looked in just after twelve, but you were asleep, and I thought you needed it." He went on to the kitchen, almost soundless, barefoot.

Ingham realized he was covered in sweat. His ribs were slippery with sweat under his pajama top, and his sheet was damp. He fell back on his pillow and shivered.

In a very short time, Adams came forth from the kitchen with a bowl of something steaming. "Try this! Just a few spoonfuls. Very plain, won't hurt you."

It was hot beef consommé. Ingham tried it. It tasted wonderful. It was like life, like meat without the fat. It was as if he sipped back his own life and strength that had for so many hours been mysteriously separated from him.

"Good?" Adams asked, pleased.

"It is *very* good." Ingham drank almost all of it, and sank back again on his bed. Ingham felt grateful to Adams, Adams whom he had so despised in his thoughts. Who else had bothered about him? He cautioned himself that his abject gratitude might not last, once he was on his feet again. And yet, Ingham knew, he would never forget this particular kindness of Adams, never forget his words of cheer.

"There's more there in a pot," Adams said, smiling, gesturing quickly toward the kitchen. "Heat it up when you wake up again. Since you missed a night's sleep, I think you ought to sleep the rest of the afternoon. Got the Entero-Vioforms handy?"

Ingham had. Adams brought him a fresh glass of water, then left. Ingham slept again.

That evening, Adams brought eggs and bread, and made a supper of scrambled eggs and toast and tea. Ingham was feeling much better. Adams took his leave before 9, so Ingham could sleep.

"Thank you *very* much, Francis," Ingham said. He could smile now. "I really feel you saved my life."

"Nonsense! A little Christian charity? It's a pleasure! Good night, Howard, my boy. See you tomorrow!"

7

A COUPLE OF days later, on the 4th of July, a Tuesday, Ingham received a long airmail envelope from a clerk at the Reine's main desk. It was from Ina, and Ingham could tell there were at least two sheets of airmail paper in it. He started to go back to his bungalow for privacy, then realized he couldn't wait, turned back to find an empty sofa to sit on, then changed his mind again and headed for the bar. No one was in the bar, not even a waiter. He sat by a window for light, but out of the sun.

June 28, 19—

Dear Howard,

At last a moment to write. In fact I am staying home from the office today, though I have homework as usual.

The events of the last month are rather chaotic. I don't know where or how to begin, so I will just plunge in. John—first of all—killed himself in your apartment. I had given him the keys once before but only to take your letters from the mailbox (mailbox key being on your ring) and he must have taken the opportunity to have some others made. Anyway, he took an overdose, and because no one thought of looking in your apartment for four days—and anyway when I went there I had no idea I'd find John—we all simply thought he had left town, maybe gone to Long Island. He was of course in a bad state. He had not lost his nerve about the Tunisia work—but he announced that he was in love with me. I was completely surprised. It had never crossed my mind. I was sympathetic. He meant it. He felt guilty because of you. Maybe I was too sympathetic. But I told him I loved *you*. John told me this in the last days of May, just after you left. He must have taken the pills the night of June 10th, a Saturday. He had told everyone he was going away for the weekend. One could say he did it to spite both of us—destroy himself in your apartment, on your bed (but not in it). I did not lead him on, but

> I admit I was sympathetic and concerned. I made no promises to him . . .

A waiter came and asked what he wanted. Ingham murmured, "*Rien, merci*," and stood up. He went out on the terrace and read standing up in the sun.

> . . . But I hope you can see why I was upset. I don't think he told anyone else of his feelings for me, at least no one that I know. I am sure a psychiatrist would say his suicide was due to other things too (I don't even know what, honestly) and that his sudden emotion for me (itself odd) tipped things the wrong way. He said he felt guilty and could not work with you because of his feelings for me. I asked him to write to you and tell you. I thought it was not for me to do . . .

The rest of her letter was about her brother Joey, about a serial she had to edit which she thought would be a winner for CBS, about packing up John's things from his apartment, assisted by a couple of friends of John's whom she had not met before. She thanked him for the Tunisian vest, and assured him there was nothing like it in New York.

Why had she had anything to do with packing up John's things, Ingham wondered. Surely John had had a lot of friends closer to him than Ina. *I did not lead him on, but I admit I was sympathetic and concerned.* What did that mean, exactly?

Ingham walked back to his bungalow. He walked steadily, and he looked down at the sand.

"Hello-o! Good morning!" It was Adams hailing him, Adams carrying his silly Neptune spear, wearing his flippers.

"Good morning," Ingham called back, forcing a smile.

"Got some news?" Adams asked, glancing at the letter in Ingham's hand.

"Not much, I'm afraid." Ingham waved the letter casually, and walked on, not stopping, not even slowing.

He felt he did not breathe until he closed the door of his little house. That glaring sun, that brightness! It was 11 o'clock. Ingham had closed the shutters. The room was rather dark for a minute. He left the shutters closed.

Killed himself in his apartment. Of all the filthy, sloppy things to do, Ingham thought. Of all vulgar dramatics! Knowing, no doubt, that he'd be found by Ina Pallant, since she was the only person with the key.

Ingham became aware that he was walking round and round his work table, and he flung himself on the bed. The bed was not yet made up. The boy was late this morning. Ingham held the letter over his head and started reading it again, but couldn't bear to finish it. It sounded as if Ina might have given John some encouragement. If she hadn't, why mention it, or say twice that she hadn't? *Sympathetic.* Wouldn't most girls have said—more or less—it's no soap, old pal, you'd better forget it? Ina wasn't the mushy, comforting type. Had she really *liked* him? John, in the last fifteen minutes, had become a loathsome weakling to Ingham. Ingham tried and failed to see what about him could have appealed to Ina. His naïveté? His rather juvenile enthusiasm, his self-confidence? But it didn't show much self-confidence to have committed suicide.

Well, what now? No reason to wait for another letter. No reason not to leave Tunisia.

It was funny, he thought, that Ina hadn't said in her letter that she loved him. She hadn't said anything reassuring in that direction. *I told him that I loved* you. That wasn't very forceful. He felt a rush of resentment against Ina, a nasty feeling quite new to him in regard to her. He would answer Ina's letter, but not now. He wished he had someone to talk to about it, but there was no one. What could Adams say, for instance?

That afternoon, though Ingham had gone for a swim and had a short nap, he found that he could not work. His last few pages were pretty smooth, he knew how he wanted to go on (his hero Dennison had just appropriated $100,000, and was about to tinker with the company books), but the words would not come to him. His mind was shattered, at least that part of it which had to do with writing fiction.

Ingham got into his car, taking a towel and swimming trunks just in case, and drove to Sousse. He arrived at 5 o'clock. It was a city, compared to Hammamet. An American warship was at anchor beside the long, entry-forbidden pier, and there were several white-uniformed sailors and officers drifting about the town, their faces sun-tanned, their expressions fixed at a certain stony neutrality, Ingham felt. Ingham avoided staring at them, though he wanted to. An Arab boy approached him, offering a carton of Camels at not a bad price, but Ingham shook his head.

He stared into shop windows. Inferior blue jeans, and lots of white trousers. Ingham laughed suddenly. A pair of blue jeans had the rectangular Levi-Strauss label counterfeited pretty well, glossy white, stapled to the pants, but the printed letters said, THIS IS A GENUINE PAIR OF LOUISE. The bottom part of the phoney label trailed off shamelessly in printer's dots. The forgers had given up.

For a while, he daydreamed about his novel. That was a situation he knew and understood. He knew the way Dennison looked, just how big his waistline was, and what made him tick. His theme was an old one, via Raskolnikov, through Nietzsche's superman: had one the right to seize power under certain circumstances? That was all very interesting, from a moral point of view. Ingham was somewhat more interested in the state of Dennison's mind, in his existence during the period in which he led two lives. He was interested in the fact that the double life at last fooled Dennison: that was what made Dennison a nearly perfect embezzler. Dennison was morally unaware that he was committing a felony, but he was aware that society and the law, for reasons that he did not even attempt to comprehend, did not approve of what he was doing. For this reason only, he took some precautions. Ingham knew the relationship of the people around Dennison, the girl Dennison had discarded when he was twenty-six and intended to pick up again (but he would not be able to). His novel was more real and definite than Ina, John or anything else. But that was to be expected, Ingham thought. Or was it?

The sight of an old Arab in baggy red pants, with turban, leaning on a stick, made Ingham draw in his breath. He had thought he was Abdullah of Hammamet, but of course he wasn't. Just a dead ringer. It was uncanny how alike some of them could look. Ingham supposed they thought the same thing about tourists.

He shuffled through a narrow, crowded passage into a souk, bumped constantly on arms and back. He felt fingers at his left hip pocket, and glanced around in time to see a boy darting to the left between shopping nets and the billowing, tan burnouses of several women. But his billfold wasn't in that pocket, it was in a left front pocket.

Ingham had a cold lemonade on the strip of pavement down the main street. He sat at a table under a big umbrella against the sun. Then he got back into his car and headed for Hammamet. The dry countryside, empty of people, was a relief. The land was a deep yellow tan. River beds were wide, cracked and quite dry. Ingham had to pause two or three times to let flocks of sheep clatter across the road. They had mud-caked behinds, and were guided by very small boys or old barefoot women with sticks.

The Reine de Hammamet's bungalows struck him as chi-chi that evening. He did not like his bungalow now, despite its cleanliness and comfort and the little stack of manuscript on the back corner of his work table. He ought to leave. The room reminded him of his plans to work here with John. The room reminded him of happy letters he had written to Ina. Ingham took a shower. He supposed he would go to Melik's for dinner. He'd had no lunch.

When he opened his closet to get his blue blazer, he didn't see it. He glanced around the room to see if he'd left it on a chair. Ingham sighed, realizing he'd been robbed. But he had locked his door today. He hadn't, however, fastened all the shutters from the inside, a fact which he verified now by a glance. Two out of four were not fastened. Ingham looked at his stack of shirts on the shelf above his clothes. The new blue linen shirt was missing. Stud box? Ingham slid a drawer open. It was gone, and an empty circle remained in a jumble of clean socks.

Oddly enough, they hadn't taken his typewriter. Ingham looked around, at his suitcase above his closet, at his shoes in the bottom of the closet. Yes, they'd taken his new pair of black shoes. What would an Arab do with English shoes, Ingham wondered. But the stud box. There'd been the nice old gold links Ina had given him before he left America, and a pair of silver ones that had belonged to Ingham's grandfather. And the tie-pin from Lotte, platinum.

"For Christ's sake," Ingham murmured. "Maybe they'll even get thirty bucks for it all, if they're sharp." And of course they were sharp. Ingham wondered if it was the old bastard in the red pants? Surely not. He wouldn't wander a kilometer from Hammamet just to rob him.

Travelers Checks? Ingham had those in the pocket of his suitcase lid. He pulled the suitcase down, and found they were still there.

Ingham went over to the bungalow headquarters to find Mokta.

Mokta was sorting towels and talking in Arabic in an explanatory way to the *directrice*. Mokta saw Ingham, and flashed a smile. Ingham indicated that he would wait outside on the terrace.

Mokta came out sooner than Ingham had expected. He swept a hand across his forehead to illustrate the ordeal he had just been through, and glanced behind him. "You want to see me, sir?"

"Yes. Someone was in my house today. A few things were stolen. Do you know who could have done it?" Ingham spoke softly, though there was no one on the terrace.

Mokta's gray eyes were wide, shocked. "But no, sir. I knew you were away this afternoon. Your car was gone. I remarked it. I was here all afternoon. I didn't see anyone around your bungalow."

Ingham told him what they had taken. "If you hear of anything—if you see any of it—tell me, will you? I'll give you five dinars if you can get anything back."

"Yes, sir.— I don't think it is any of these boys. Honestly, sir. They are honest boys."

"One of the gardeners, do you think?" He offered Mokta a cigarette, which Mokta accepted.

Mokta shrugged, but it was not an indifferent shrug. His thin body was tense with the situation. "I don't know all the gardeners. Some of them are new.— Let me look around. If you tell the *directrice*—" a flash of hands in a negative gesture "—she will attack all of us, *all* the boys."

"No, I shall not tell the *directrice* or the management. I'll leave it to you." He slapped Mokta's shoulder.

Ingham went to his car and drove to Melik's. It was late, there was not much left on the menu, but Ingham had lost what appetite he had, and sat merely for the company around him, whose conversation he could not understand. There were no English or French tonight. The Arabic talk—all male voices—sounded guttural, threatening, angry, but Ingham knew this meant nothing. They were having a perfectly ordinary evening. Melik, short, plump and smiling, came over and asked where his friend M. Ah*dam* was tonight? Melik spoke quite a good French.

"I haven't seen him today. I went to Sousse." It was of no importance, yet it was nice to say to somebody, and Arabs, Ingham knew from the sheer quantity of their speech, must say even less important things in a more verbose manner. "How's business?"

"Ah—it goes. People get afraid of the heat. But of course lots of French still come in August, the hottest time of the year."

They chatted for a few minutes. Melik's two sons, the thin one who slunk like Groucho Marx, the fat one who rolled, ministered to the two or three tables that were occupied. From below, Ingham caught a pleasant whiff of baking bread. There was a bakery just next door which functioned during the night. Ingham drank two cups of sweet coffee, not bothering to ask them to make it without sugar. During his second cup, the Dane arrived with his dog on a leash, and stood looking around from the threshold of the terrace, as if to see if a certain friend was here. He saw Ingham, and came toward him slowly, smiling.

"Good evening," Jensen said. "All by yourself tonight?"

"Evening. Yes. Have a seat." There were three empty chairs at Ingham's table.

Jensen sat down opposite, made a sound to his dog, and the dog lay down.

"How is life?" Ingham asked.

"Ah, well, excellent for working. A little boring."

Ingham thought that that was exactly the way it was. Jensen wore a fresh denim shirt. Above it, his lean face was brown, darker than his hair. His white teeth gleamed when he spoke. Jensen slumped, one elbow on the back of his chair, like a man discouraged.

"Have some wine." Ingham yelled, "*Asma!*" to empty space. Sometimes someone heard, sometimes not.

Jensen said he had a bottle of wine here, but Ingham insisted on their drinking his. The boy brought another glass.

"Are you working?" Jensen asked.

"Not today. I was in a bad mood."

"Bad news?"

"Oh, no, just a bad day," Ingham said.

"The trouble with this country is that the weather is all the same. Predictable. One has to get used to it, accept it, or it can bore one to extinction." Jensen pronounced "extinction" with clarity, like an Englishman. "Today I painted an imaginary bird in flight. He flies downward. Tomorrow I shall paint two birds in one picture, one flying up, one down. They will look like opposite tulips.— There are few basic shapes, you know, the egg which is a variation of the circle, the bird which resembles the fish, the tree and its branches which resembles its own roots and also the bronchii in the lungs. All the more complex forms, the key, the automobile, the typewriter, the tin-opener, are all man-made. But are they beautiful? No, they're as ugly as man's soul. I admit some keys are beautiful. To be beautiful, something must be stylized, that is to say streamlined, which can only be achieved through being alive for centuries of time."

Ingham found Jensen's monologue soothing. "What color are your birds?"

"Pink at present. And they'll be pink tomorrow, I suppose, because I have a lot of pink paint made up and I may as well use it." Jensen yawned, discreetly. He gave his dog an offhand slap, because the dog had growled as an Arab walked by the table. Jensen turned to look at the Arab briefly. "Would you like to come to my house for coffee?" Jensen asked.

Ingham begged off, saying that he was rather tired because he had driven to Sousse and back. What really deterred him, he thought, was the idea of walking by that particular spot in the alley where he had seen the corpse. Ingham wanted to ask Jensen if anything had happened that night, after the quarreling they had heard down in his street, but Ingham repressed it. He didn't want to hear about a corpse and try to feign surprise.

Jensen ordered coffee.

Ingham stood up and took his leave when the coffee arrived.

Back in the bungalow, Ingham thought of adding to his letter in progress to Ina. Perhaps just a paragraph—sympathetic, even commiserating, positively noble. Ingham had composed the lines in his head at Melik's. Now he read over his carefree paragraph about Our Way of Life, OWL, and his broadcasts. He couldn't send that off to Ina, even dating the remainder of his letter with the present date, because the rest of his letter would be so different. He crumpled up the page. Ina was probably not in a mood to appreciate that kind of story now, and as a matter of fact he had promised Adams not to tell anyone. What was the matter with OWL's silly illusions, anyway, if they kept him going, if they made him happy? The harm OWL did (and he might, by his absurdity, and by making nonsense of the Vietnam War, be doing some good) was infinitesimal compared to the harm done by America's foreign policy makers who actually sent people off to kill people. Perhaps it took some illusions to make people happy. Dennison was happy in his idea (not really an illusion) of doing good to the underdog, furthering his friends' businesses, bringing happiness and prosperity to several people. OWL voiced the same objectives. It was rather odd.

And here he was, Ingham thought, with both feet on the ground—presumably—and where did it get him? It got him to melancholy.

John Castlewood had been under his own illusion, because what else was a state of being "in love"? Blissful if reciprocated, tragic if it wasn't. Anyway, John had had his illusion, and then unfortunately—zip—dead. Despite her sympathy, Ina must have given him a flat no, finally.

8

THE NEXT MORNING, Ingham made a determined effort, and wrote two pages on his book. He satisfied himself that he was on the rails again. He then stopped and wrote a letter to Ina.

July 5, 19—

Dearest Ina,

Thanks for your letter which came yesterday at last, a small bang for the otherwise quiet Fourth here. I agree, there does seem to be quite a lot that needs to be explained, though maybe I should give up on suicides, at least John's, as I didn't know him at all well and feel now that I didn't know him at all. What else was he upset about besides you? I admit I am annoyed that he chose my apartment to do it in. May I say, without seeming too coarse and unfeeling, that I hope he didn't mess things up too much? I liked that apartment, until now.

It would be nice if you explained your own feelings a bit more. Just how were you sympathetic? Whatever you were, it seems to have been the wrong thing for John. Did you like or love him at all? Or do you now? Of course I can see, unless I'm wildly off the beam, that you never made him any promises (as you said) or else he would not have wanted to do away with himself. What I really can't understand, darling, is why you took so damned long to write to me. If you knew what it's like here, no old chums to talk to, too hot to work comfortably except early morning and evening, no letter for a whole month from the girl I love— It wasn't a nice month for me. What you haven't explained is why you were so upset, you couldn't write me for twenty-seven days or so, then only a note, until your letter a few days after that. I love you, I want you, I need you. Now more than ever.

I'll try it here for another week, I think. I have to think in periods of time like that, otherwise I'd feel lost—as if I don't already. But work is going reasonably well (my book) and I'd like to drive around and see some more of Tunisia, even though the days will be getting hotter, reaching a crescendo or an inferno, I am told, in August. I'll send this express. Please write me at once. I hope you'll be calmer by now, darling. I wish you were here, in this rather pretty room with me, and we could talk and —other things.

All my love, darling.
Howard

In the next days, Mokta brought no news of his missing jacket, shoes or jewelry, and Ingham gave it up. The country was vast. His minuscule possessions had been sucked up and lost forever. But as the days went on, the loss of Lotte's tie-pin, which he almost never wore, and of his grandfather's cuff-links, began to rankle. Compared to what the things meant to him, the pittance the robber would get for them was irritating to think about. Ingham had delayed reactions, heightened bitternesses (heightened joys, sometimes, too), but his realization of this did little to help. Whenever he saw the old Arab who had stolen from his car definitely, and who might have stolen from his bungalow, Ingham felt like kicking him in whatever lay in the seat of those sordid pants. As a matter of fact, the Arab now scurried away at the sight of Ingham in Hammamet, sidling like an old crab into any alley or street that was nearest. It would be even legally excusable to kick him, Ingham thought, because if a policeman arrived—there was an occasional policeman in tan shirt and trousers on the street in Hammamet—he could say with truth that he had seen Abdullah in flagrante the night of June 30–July 1. Ingham remembered the date, because it was the night he had seen the corpse also, and he had thought of speaking to the police about it. He hadn't spoken to the police, not only because he didn't relish becoming involved with them, but because he foresaw that no one would really care.

Ingham had dinner one evening with OWL at Melik's, and mentioned his robbery of a few nights before.

"One of the boys, I'm sure of it. And I'll bet I know which one," said OWL.

"Which one?"

"The short dark one."

They were all short and dark, except Mokta and Hassim.

"The one called Hammed. Has his mouth sort of open all the time." OWL demonstrated, and looked somewhat like a hare-lip, or rabbit. "Of course, I'm not sure, but I don't like his manner. He's brought my towels a couple of times. I saw him drifting around my bungalow one day, not doing anything, just drifting around looking at the windows. Did you lock your shutters tonight?"

"I did." Since the robbery, Ingham had locked them from the inside whenever he was out.

"You'll lose your lighter next, then your typewriter. A miracle they didn't take that. Obviously the robber had to get away with something he could conceal—your shoes and stud box wrapped up in the jacket, probably."

"What do you think of these people, by the way? *Their* way of life?"

"Ah-h! I don't know where to begin!" Adams chuckled. "They have their Allah, and very tolerant he must be. They're reconciled to fate. Make no great effort, that's their motto. Everything by rote in school, you know, no thinking involved. How does one change a way of life like this? Petty dishonesty is their way of life. Make a handful honest—and they'll be cheated by the majority, and go back to dishonesty as a means of self-preservation. Can you blame them?"

"No," Ingham agreed. He really did see OWL's point.

"Our country was lucky. We started out so well, with men like Tom Paine, Jefferson. What ideas they had, and they wrote them down for us! Benjamin Franklin. We may have departed now and then from them—but my goodness, they're still there, in our Constitution . . ."

Was Adams going to say it was all spoilt by Sicilians, Puerto Ricans, Polish Jews? Ingham didn't care to ask Adams what had spoilt America's idealism. He let Adams ramble on.

". . . Yes! That might be the subject of my next tape. The corruption of American idealism. You never get so far, you never make so many *friends*, you know, as when you tell the *truth*. There's always some new failure to talk about. And let's face it, our potential friends"—here Adams beamed, the happy squirrel again—"are more interested in our failures than in our successes. Failures make people human. They're jealous of us, because they think we're supermen, invincible empire-builders . . ." On and on it went.

And the curious thing, Ingham thought, was that it didn't sound so bad tonight. It sounded true, and almost liberal. No, the chief thing in which Adams was wrong, rotten even, was in saying that Communism or atheism was wrong for other people, any and all other people. Well, one rotten apple could spoil the whole barrel, Ingham thought, to use an adage which would surely please OWL. What it always came down to was the dreary fact that men were not as equal as Adams thought, that free enterprise sent certain ones to the top and certain others to the bottom, into the poverty that Adams so detested. But wasn't it possible to have a socialist system with some capacity for competition, some room for personal reward? Of course. Ingham dreamed, while Adams spun.

"Birth control! Now that's vital. A subject also that I have no fear of bringing up on my tapes. Who's more aware of it than China? And who's more aware of China than the Soviet Union? Breeders, the curse of humanity! And I don't omit the United States. Poughkeepsie is a hotbed, the biggest unemployment relief record in the States, the last I heard, mostly due to Puerto Ricans and Negroes. The biggest families, fatherless technically . . ."

Hotbed. On it went. And Ingham couldn't find a thing to deny in what Adams was saying. Of course one could cite—if one had the statistics in hand—Anglo-Saxon families guilty also of ten children, father with no job, maybe also nonexistent. But Ingham merely listened.

Jensen came in, without his dog.

"You know each other?" Ingham asked. "Mr. Jensen, Mr. Adams."

"Won't you join us?" Adams asked pleasantly.

"Have you had dinner?" Ingham asked.

"I don't care to eat," Jensen said, sitting down.

"A good day's work?" Ingham asked, feeling something was the matter with Jensen.

"No, not since noon." Jensen put his lean forearm on the table. "I think they've stolen my dog. He's missing since eleven o'clock this morning. I let him out for a pee."

"Oh, I'm sorry," Ingham said. "You looked around?"

"All over the—" Jensen might have repressed a tired curse —"neighborhood. Went around calling him everywhere."

"My goodness," said Adams. "I remember your dog. I saw him many times."

"He may be still alive," Jensen said, somewhat defiantly.

"Of course. I didn't mean to imply he wasn't," Adams said. "Is he apt to go off with strangers?"

"He's apt to tear them apart," Jensen said. "He hates crooked Arabs, and he can smell them a mile off. That's why I'm afraid they killed him already. I walked all the streets calling him—until people were yelling at me to shut up."

"Any idea who did it?" Ingham asked. Jensen took so long to answer—he looked as if he were in a daze—that Ingham asked, "You think they might be holding him for a reward?"

"I hope so. But so far nobody's told me."

"Would he be likely to eat any poisoned meat?" Adams asked.

"I don't think so. He's not a dog to gobble up putrid fish on the beach." Jensen's English was as usual eloquent and distinct.

Ingham felt very sorry for Jensen. He felt the dog was gone, dead. Ingham glanced at Adams. Adams was trying to be practical, Ingham saw, trying to suggest something Jensen might do.

"They'll toss his head in the door tomorrow morning," Jensen said. "Or maybe his tail." He laughed, grimaced, and Ingham saw his lower front teeth. "A coffee," Jensen said to the fat boy who had appeared at the table. "We shall see," Jensen said. "I am sorry to be so melancholic tonight."

They drank their coffee.

Adams said he had to be getting home. Ingham asked Jensen if he would like to go somewhere for another coffee or a drink. Adams did not care to join them.

"How about the Fourati?" Ingham asked. "It's cheerful, at least." It wasn't particularly, it was just an idea.

They got into Ingham's car. Ingham dropped Adams at the bungalows, then he and Jensen went on to the Fourati. Jensen was in levis, but his clothes were always clean, and he looked rather handsome in them. The Fourati had bright lights in its bar. Beyond the bar, people danced on a terrace to a strenuous three-piece band which was augmented unmercifully by amplifiers. Ingham and Jensen stood at the bar, looking over the dozen or so tables. Ingham felt empty, purposeless, yet not lonely. He was staring, looking at faces, simply because he had not seen them before, because they were not Arab, and because he could tell a little bit about the faces, since they were French, American, or English, and some of them German. Ingham's eyes met the eyes of a dark-haired girl in a white, sleeveless dress. After a second or two, Ingham looked down at his drink —a rum on the rocks.

"A little stuffy," Ingham said, raising his voice over the music. "The people, I mean."

"Lots of Germans, usually," Jensen said, and sipped his beer. "I saw the most beautiful boy here once. In March. He must have been having a birthday party. He looked sixteen. French. He looked at me. I never spoke to him, never saw him again."

Ingham nodded. His eyes moved again to the woman in the white dress. She had smooth brown arms. Now she smiled at him. She was with a blond, graying man in a white jacket, who might have been English, a plumpish woman in her forties, and a younger man with dark hair. Her husband? Ingham resolved not to look again at the table. He felt very attracted to the woman in the white dress. How silly could you get in a hot climate?

"Another drink?" Ingham asked.

"Coffee."

The one boy behind the counter was having a hard time keeping up with orders, so it was a while before their coffee arrived. Beyond the bar, through the open window on their left, clashing music came now from an Arabic band that was entertaining the people in the dimly lighted hotel gardens. Christ, what a hell of a noise, Ingham thought. He only hoped that the few minutes had cheered Jensen a little, and taken him away from thoughts of his dog. Ingham felt sure he would not see Hasso again. He imagined Jensen going back to Copenhagen alone, a little bitter.

Ingham invited Jensen to the bungalow. Of course, Jensen accepted. But tonight it was out of loneliness, Ingham realized, nothing to do with sex.

"Have you a big family in Denmark?" Ingham asked. They were walking along the sandy road toward the bungalow with the aid of Jensen's flashlight, which he always carried in his back pocket.

"Just a mother and father and a sister. My older brother committed suicide when I was fifteen. You know, the gloomy Danes. No, you say melancholy Danes."

"Do you write them often?" Ingham opened his door. He went tense in the darkness, before he put on a light and saw that there was no one in the room.

"Oh, often enough."

Ingham saw that his question about Jensen's family hadn't lifted Jensen's spirits in the least.

"A very nice room," Jensen said. "Simple. I like that."

Ingham brought out his scotch and glasses and ice. They both sat on Ingham's bed, beside which was a table they could use. Ingham was conscious of their respective gloominess, a gloominess for different reasons. He wasn't going to mention Ina to Jensen, and he wasn't going to mention the robbery he had had, as it seemed trivial. And perhaps Jensen's gloom was not entirely due to his dog, but to things he had no intention of telling to Ingham. What did one do in such circumstances to make life a little more bearable, Ingham wondered? Just sit, a yard or more apart, in the same room, silent? Able to speak each other's language, but still silent?

Within fifteen minutes, Ingham was uneasy and bored, though Jensen had begun to talk about a trip he had made to an inland desert town with an American friend a few months ago. They had run into sandstorms that had almost flayed the clothes off them, and they had been very cold at night, sleeping outdoors. His dog had been with them. Ingham's mind drifted. He believed, suddenly, that Ina had been in love with Castlewood, that she had slept with him. My God, maybe even in his own apartment! No, that was a bit too much. John had his own place, and he lived alone. He had thought Ina was so *solid*—solid physically in a very pleasant and attractive way, solid in her attitude toward him, in her love for him. Ingham admitted to himself that he had even been under the illusion that Ina cared more for him than he did for her. What an ass he had been! He must read her letter, her damned ambiguous letter, again tonight, after Jensen had left. He realized he had had quite enough to drink, and his glass was still half full, but he'd ponder the letter anyway and maybe a flash of intuition would enable him to understand it better, to know what had really happened. Why was Ina being so coy, so devious, if she and John had slept together? She wasn't the kind of girl to call a spade a—a what? Anyway, she called a lay a roll in the hay, or just called it going to bed with someone. She'd been quite frank with him about a couple of her affairs since her marriage.

Jensen left just before 1, and Ingham dropped him off at his street near Melik's, though Jensen had offered, even begged politely, to walk home. As he got back into his car, Ingham heard Jensen's retreating voice in his alley, calling, "Hasso! Hasso!" A whistle. A rising tone of a curse, something in Danish, a defiant yelp. Ingham remembered the corpse in that same street. A tiny street, but a street full of passion.

Ingham studied Ina's letter once more. He got no further. He went to bed vaguely angry, and decidedly unhappy.

9

IT WAS two or three days later, in the morning, that Ingham saw the brunette girl of the Fourati on the beach. She was in a beach chair, and a chair beside her was empty. A small boy was trying to sell her something out of a basket.

"*Mais non, merci. Pas d'argent aujourd'hui!*" she was saying, smiling but a bit annoyed.

Ingham had just had his noon swim, and was smoking a cigarette, walking along the edge of the water, carrying his robe. From the girl's accent, he supposed her English or American.

"Are you having trouble?" Ingham asked.

"Not really. I just can't get rid of him." She was American.

"I have no money either, but a cigarette's just as good." Ingham took two cigarettes from his pack. He thought the boy was selling seashells. The boy seized the cigarettes and ran away on bare feet.

"I thought of cigarettes, too, but I don't smoke and I haven't any." She had very dark brown eyes. Her face was smooth and tanned, her hair also smooth and pulled straight back from her forehead. *Almond* was the word that came to Ingham when he looked at her.

"I thought you were at the Fourati," Ingham said.

"I am. But a friend invited me for lunch here."

Ingham glanced up the beach toward the hotel for the friend —he assumed a man—who must be coming back at any minute. There was a yellow and white towel and a pair of sunglasses on the empty chair beside her. Suddenly Ingham knew, or at least believed, that he would see her this evening, that they would have dinner, and that they would go to bed together, somewhere. "Have you been in Hammamet long?" The usual questions, the protocol.

She had been here two weeks, and she was going on to Paris. She was from Pennsylvania. She wore no wedding ring. She was perhaps twenty-five. Ingham said he was from New York. At last—and not a moment too soon, because a man in swimming trunks and sportshirt, followed by a waiter with a tray, was walking toward them from the hotel—Ingham asked:

"Shall we have a drink some time before you leave? Are you free this evening?"

"Yes. For a drink, fine."

"I'll pick you up at the Fourati. About seven thirty?"

"All right. Oh, my name is Kathryn Darby. D-a-r-b-y."

"Mine is Howard Ingham. A pleasure. I'll see you at seven thirty." He waved a hand and went away, toward his bungalow.

The approaching man and waiter were still thirty feet away. Ingham had not glanced at the man after his first long view of him, and did not know if he was thirty years old or sixty.

Ingham worked well that afternoon. He had done four pages in the morning. He did five or six in the afternoon.

A little after 5, OWL came round and asked him to his bungalow for a drink.

"I can't tonight, thanks," Ingham said. "A date with a young lady at the Fourati. How about tomorrow here?"

"A young lady. Well! That's nice!" OWL turned into a beaming squirrel at once. "Have a good time. Yes, tomorrow would be fine. Six thirty?"

At 7:30, in a white jacket which he had had Mokta take to be washed and returned that afternoon, Ingham rang up Miss Darby from the desk at the Fourati. They sat at one of the tables in the garden and drank Tom Collinses.

She worked for her uncle in a law firm. She was a secretary, and learning a great deal about law, which she would never use, she said, because she had no intention of taking a degree. There was a warmth, a kindness—or maybe it was merely openness—about her for which Ingham was athirst. There was a naïveté, too, and a certain decorum. He was sure she didn't have affairs with just anybody, or very often, but he assumed she did sometimes, and if she happened to like him, that was his good luck, because she was very pretty.

They had dinner at the Fourati.

Ingham said, "It's a pleasure to be with you. I've been lonely here in the last month. I don't try to meet people, because I have to work. It doesn't keep me from being lonely now and then."

She asked some questions about his work. Within a few minutes, Ingham told her that the man with whom he had intended to make a film had not come. Ingham also told her he was a suicide, though he avoided mentioning John's name. He said he had decided to stay on a few weeks and to work on his own novel.

Kathryn (she had told him how to spell it) was certainly sympathetic, and it touched Ingham in a way that Adams' equally genuine sympathy had not. "What a shock it must have been. Even if you *didn't* know him well!"

Ingham changed the subject by asking her if she had seen other towns in Tunisia. She had, and she enjoyed talking about them and about the things she had bought to send and to take back home. She was on vacation alone, but had flown to Tunisia with some English friends who had been in America, and who yesterday had flown back to London.

Vague thoughts of accompanying her back to Paris, of spending a few days with her, danced in Ingham's mind. He realized they were absurd. He asked if she would like to come to his bungalow for a nightcap and a coffee. She accepted. She did not accept the nightcap, but Ingham made small, strong cups of coffee. She was pleased also at his proposal of a swim —she wearing one of his shirts. The beach was deserted. There was a half moon.

Back in his bungalow, as she sat wrapped in a large white towel, he said, "I'd like it very much if you stayed the night with me. Would you?"

"I would like it, too," she replied.

It had been simple after all.

Ingham gave her his terry-cloth robe. She disappeared into the bathroom.

Then she got into bed, naked, and Ingham slipped in beside her. There were lovely, toothpaste-flavored kisses. Ingham was more interested in her breasts. He lay gently on top of her. But after five minutes, he realized that he was not becoming excited enough to make love to her. He put this out of his mind for a moment or so, as he continued to kiss her neck, but then the realization came back. And perhaps thinking about it was fatal. She even touched him briefly, perhaps by accident. There were things he might have asked her to do, but he couldn't. Emphatically, not this girl. At last, he lay on his side, and she facing him, both locked in a tight embrace. But nothing happened. Nothing was going to, Ingham realized. It was embarrassing. It was funny. It had never happened to him before, not if he actually wished and intended to make love, as he had. Ina—she had even called him exhausting, and Ingham had been rather proud of that. He felt lost, too lost, perhaps to suffer the sense of inadequacy that he should. What was the matter? The bungalow itself? He thought not.

"You're a nice lover," she said.

He almost laughed. "You're very attractive."

Her hand on the back of his neck was pleasant, reassuring, but only vaguely exciting, and he wondered how much she minded, how much he had let her down.

Suddenly she sneezed.

"You're cold!"

"It's that swim."

He got out of bed and poured a scotch in the kitchen, came in and struggled into his robe, still holding the glass. "Do you want it neat?"

She did.

Twenty minutes later, he was driving her toward the Fourati. He had asked if she would like to stay the night, but she had said no. There was no change in her attitude toward him—alas, not as much as there might have been if he had made love to her.

"Shall we have dinner tomorrow night?" Ingham asked. "If you felt like it, we could cook something at my place. Just for a change."

"Tomorrow night I promised someone here.— Lunch tomorrow?"

"I don't make lunch dates when I'm working."

They agreed on the evening after tomorrow, again at 7:30.

Ingham went home and got at once into pajama pants. He sat on the edge of his bed. He felt utterly depressed. He could not see the bottom of his depression without actually going down there, he thought. He realized he had changed a great deal in the past month. And just how? He would know in the next few days, he thought. It was not the kind of question Ingham could answer by thinking about it.

Kathryn Darby was brighter than Lotte, Ingham thought out of nowhere. Which was not to say that anyone had to have an intellect to be brighter than Lotte. Lotte had been a mistake, a strong and powerful, long lasting mistake. Lotte had left him for another man, because she had been bored with him. The man was one who had come to their parties many times in New York, an advertising executive, witty, extrovert, the kind women always liked, Ingham had supposed, and never took seriously. Then the next thing he knew, Thomas Jeffrey had been asking for her hand, or whatever, and moreover Lotte had wanted to give it to him. Never had anything in Ingham's life, of equal importance, happened so quickly. He'd not had time even to fight, he felt. "The only time you pay attention to me is in bed," Lotte had said, more than once. It was true. She hadn't been interested in his writing, or in anyone else's books, and she had had a way, which at times had been funny, of demolishing an interesting remark by him or someone else, with a platitudinous remark of her own quite off the subject, yet well meant. Yes, he had often smiled. Though not unkindly. He had worshipped Lotte, and never had any woman had such a physical hold over him. But that was obviously not enough to keep a woman happy. No, he couldn't blame her. She had come of a wealthy family, was badly educated, spoilt, and had really no interests at all, except tennis, which she had slowly given up, perhaps out of laziness.

Or could he somehow do better, if he had another chance with Lotte? But Lotte was married now. And did he want another chance with her? Of course not. Why had he thought of it?

Ingham went to bed, still depressed, but unbothered, unconcerned even, with Kathryn Darby's scent which lingered on his pillow.

10

"HASSO," JENSEN SAID, "is probably four feet under the sand somewhere. Maybe two feet will do." Jensen looked whipped, broken, slouched over the bar of the Café de la Plage. He was drinking boukhah, and looked as if he had had several.

It was noon. Ingham had driven into Hammamet to buy a typewriter ribbon, and having tried at three likely looking stores that seemed to sell everything, had failed.

"I don't suppose," Ingham said, "you could spread the word around that you'd give a reward if somebody found him?"

"I did that the first thing. I told a couple of the kids. They'll spread it. The point is, the dog's *dead*. Or he'd come back." Jensen's voice cracked. He hunched lower over his bare forearms, and Ingham realized to his embarrassment that Jensen was on the brink of tears.

A pain of sympathy went through Ingham, and his own eyes stung. "I'm sorry. Really I am.— Bastards!"

Jensen gave a snort of a laugh and finished his little drink. "What they usually do is toss the head into one of your windows. At least they spared me that so far."

"There isn't something, maybe, that they're holding against you? Your neighbors, I mean?"

Jensen shrugged. "I don't *know* of anything. I never had any quarrels with them. I don't make any noise. I pay my landlord —in advance, too."

Ingham hesitated, then asked, "Are you thinking of leaving Hammamet?"

"I'll wait a few more days. Then—sure, for Christ's sake, I'll leave. But I'll tell you one thing, I hate the thought of Hasso's *bones* being in this goddam sand! Am I glad the Jews beat the shit out of them!"

Ingham glanced around uneasily, but as usual there was a din in the place, and probably no one near them understood any English. A couple of men, including the barman, glanced at Jensen because he was upset, but there was no hostility in their faces. "I'm with you there."

"It isn't good to hate as I do," Jensen went on, one fist clenched, the other hand clutching the tiny, empty glass, and Ingham was afraid he was going to throw it. "It isn't good."

"You'd better eat something. I'd suggest we have dinner tonight, but I've got a date. How about tomorrow night?"

Jensen agreed. They would meet at the Café de la Plage.

Ingham drove back to his bungalow, feeling wretched, as if he hadn't done enough to help Jensen. He realized he did not want to see Kathryn Darby tonight, and that he would have been less bored, even happier, with Jensen.

That afternoon, along with a letter from Ingham's mother in Florida (his parents had retired and gone there to live), came an express letter from Ina. Ina's letter said:

July 10, 19—

Dear Howard,

It's true I owe you some explanations, so I will try. First of all, why I was upset. I thought for a while that I loved John—and to continue further with the truth, I went to bed with him, twice. You may well ask "Why?" For one thing, I never thought you were madly in love with me—that is, deeply and completely. It's possible to be slightly in love, you know. Not every love is the grande passion and not every love is the kind on which to found a marriage. I was attracted to John. He was absolutely gone on me—strange as it may seem, developing suddenly, after we'd known each other for a year or so. I made him no promises. He knew about you, as you well know, and I told him you had asked me to marry you and that I had more or less agreed—in our casual way, it was on, I know. I thought John and I—if I tried to play it a bit cool with him (he was fantastically emotional) might find out if we really did or could care for each other. He was a different world to me, full of pictures in his head, which he could visualize so clearly and put into words.

Ingham thought, couldn't *he* do that, too? Or did Ina think him a lousier writer than John had been a cameraman?

Then I began to sense a certain weakness, a shakiness in John. Nothing to do with his feelings for me. That didn't seem shaky at all. It was something in his character which I did not care for, which actually frightened me. It was a weakness he should not have been *blamed* for, and I never thought of blaming him, but having seen or sensed this weakness, I knew it was no go with John and me. I tried to break it off as gently as possible—but things can never be done that way. There is always the moment when the Awful Speech must be made, because the other person won't accept the truth without it. And when I say break it off—this whole "affair" went on just about ten days. My pulling out, unfortunately, was fatal for poor John. He had five days of decline, during which I tried to help him as much as I could. The last two days, he said he didn't want to see me. I assumed he was in his own apartment. He was dead when I found him. I won't try to describe the horror of seeing him there. I don't know the right words. They don't exist.

So, dear Howard, what do you think of all this? I suspect you want to drop me. I would not blame you—and even if I did? I could have withheld this. No one knows about it but me, unless John told Peter, I mean told him everything. But I feel you have a right to know—everything. I still like you, even love you. I don't know how you feel now. When you come back, and I assume that will be very soon, we can see each other again, if you like. It is up to you.

I carry on with work, but am dead-tired. (If your employer asks for your lifeblood, give him your corpse also.) The usual amount of take-home work still. It looks like a lull in August and that's when I'll take my two weeks' vacation.

Would you write me soon, even if it's a rather grim letter?

With love,
Ina

Ingham's first reaction was one of slight contempt. What a mistake for Ina to have made! He had thought Ina was so bright. And in the letter, she was more or less begging his forgiveness, in fact pleading, or hoping, that he would take her back. It was all so god-damned silly.

It wasn't even as important as Jensen's dog, Ingham thought.

Ina was right. He wasn't "madly in love" with her, but he counted on her, he depended on her in a very important and profound way. He knew that, now that he had learned she had betrayed him. The word "betrayed" came to his mind, and he hated it. It wasn't, he thought, that he was stuffy enough to object to any affair that Ina might have had while he was gone, but the fact that she apparently had sunk so much emotion into this one. She was looking for something "real and lasting," as practically every woman in the world was, and she'd looked for it in that weak fish John Castlewood.

How he wished that Ina had written that she'd had a silly roll in the hay with Castlewood, which hadn't meant anything, and that Castlewood had taken it seriously! But Ina's letter made her sound like every feather-brained run-of-the-mill—

He wanted a drink, a drink of scotch on this. The bottle was down to the last inch. He drank this with a splash of water, not bothering with ice, then shoved his billfold in the pocket of his shorts and walked to the bungalows' grocery store. It was a quarter to 6. He'd have a couple of drinks before picking Kathryn up. Was Kathryn Darby a bore or not?

As he walked toward the store, Ingham watched a couple of camels on the edge of the main road. One of the camels was ridden by a sun-blackened wraith in a burnouse. The camels were tied together. A donkey-drawn cart, piled high with kindling and topped by a barefoot Arab, paused at the edge of the road, and someone got down. To Ingham's surprise, it was old Abdullah of the red pants. What was he doing here? Ingham watched him look in both directions, then hump across the road to the hotel side and turn in the direction of Hammamet. The cart had come from the Hammamet direction, and it went on. The Arab was lost to view by the hotel's bushes and trees. Ingham went into the grocery shop and bought eggs, scotch, and beer. The old Arab, Ingham thought, might be going to see the man who ran the curio shop a few yards down the road. And there were fruit and vegetable shops between here and Hammamet, too, run by Arabs. But his presence so near the hotel irked Ingham. Ingham realized he was living through one of the worst, therefore one of the crabbiest days of his life.

Ingham took Kathryn straight to the Café de la Plage de Hammamet for a pre-dinner drink. She had been in the Plage a couple of times with her English friends. "We adored it, but it was a little noisy. At least they said so." Kathryn was a better sport, it seemed, and obviously enjoyed the noise and the sloppiness.

Ingham looked for Jensen, hoping to see him, but Jensen was not here.

From the Plage, they went across the street to Melik's. The bakers were at work next door. One young Arab baker, lounging in shorts and a paper hat in the doorway, looked Kathryn over with interest. There was again the delicious, reassuring smell of baking bread. Melik's was loud. There were two if not three tables with flutes and stringed instruments. The canary, in a cage that hung from a horizontal ceiling pole, was accompanying the music merrily. Ingham remembered one evening when Adams had been droning away, and the canary had been asleep with its head under its wing, and Ingham had wished he might do the same. There was only one other woman besides Kathryn on the terrace. As Ingham had foreseen, the evening was a trifle boring, and yet they were not at a loss for conversation. Kathryn talked to him about Pennsylvania, which she loved, especially in autumn when the pumpkin season was on and the leaves came down. Surely, Ingham thought, she would marry a nice solid Pennsylvanian, maybe a lawyer, and settle down in a town house with a garden. But Kathryn didn't mention a man, gave no hint of one. There was something attractively independent about her. And there was no doubt at all she was very pretty. But the last thing he could have done that night was go to bed with her, the last thing in the world he wished. A nightcap at the Fourati, and the evening was over.

Ingham was pleasantly mellow on food and drink. His anger and irritability had gone, at least superficially, and for this he was grateful to Miss Kathryn Darby of Pennsylvania. What did they say there? "Shoo fly pie and apple pan dowdy."

Back in his bungalow, he read Ina's letter again, hoping now to read it without caring a damn, without a twinge of resentment. He did not quite succeed. He dropped the letter on his table, put his head back, and said:

"God, bring Jensen's dog back. *Please!*"

Then he went to bed. It was not yet midnight.

Ingham did not know what awakened him, but he pushed himself up suddenly on one elbow and listened. The room was quite dark. His doorknob gave a squeak. Ingham sprang out of bed and instinctively moved behind his work table, which was in the center of his room. He faced the door. Yes, it was opening. Ingham crouched. My God, he'd forgotten to lock it, he realized. He saw silhouetted a somewhat stooped figure: a light, the streetlight on the bungalow lane, gave a milky luminosity beyond. The figure was coming in.

Ingham seized his typewriter from the table and hurled it with all his force, shoving it with his right arm in the manner of a basketball player throwing for the basket—but the target in this case was lower. Ingham scored a direct hit against the turbaned head. The typewriter fell with a painful clatter, and there was a yell from the figure which staggered back and fell on the terrace. Ingham sprang to his door, pushed the typewriter aside with one foot, and slammed the door. The key was on the windowsill to the right. He found it, groped with fingertips for the keyhole, and locked the door.

Then he stood still, listening. He was afraid there might be others.

Still in the dark, Ingham went to his kitchen, found the scotch bottle on the drainboard, nearly knocked it over but grabbed it in time, and had a swig. If he had ever needed a drink, it was now. A second small swallow, and he slammed his palm down on the squeaking cork, replaced the bottle on the drainboard, and looked in the darkness toward his door, listening. Ingham knew the man he had hit was Abdullah. At least, he was ninety percent sure of it.

There were faint voices, coming closer. The voices were muted, excited, and Ingham could hear that they were speaking in Arabic. A small beam of light swept past his closed shutters and vanished. Ingham braced himself. Were these the man's chums—or the hotel boys investigating?

Then he heard bare feet slapping on the terrace, a grunt, the sweeping sound of something being dragged. The damned Arab, of course. They were dragging him away. Whoever they were.

Ingham heard a whispered "Mokta."

The sounds of feet faded, disappeared. Ingham stood in the kitchen at least two minutes more. He could not tell if they had spoken about Mokta, or if Mokta, with them, had been addressed. Ingham started to run out to speak to them. But was he *sure* they were the hotel boys?

Ingham gave a deep, shuddering sigh. Then he heard again soft footfalls in sand, a sound as soft as cotton. There was another faint slap, different. Someone was wiping the tiles with a rag. Wiping away blood, Ingham knew. He felt slightly sickened. The soft tread went away. Ingham waited, made himself count slowly to twenty. Then he set his reading lamp on the floor, so its light would not show much through the shutters, and turned it on. He was interested in his typewriter.

The lower front part of the frame was bent. Ingham winced at the sight of it, more for the surprising appearance of the typewriter than for the impact it must have made against the forehead of the old Arab. Even the spacer had been pushed awry, and one end stuck up. A few keys had been bent and jammed together. Ingham flicked them down automatically, but they could not fall into place. The bend in the frame went in about three inches. That was a job for Tunis, all right, the repairing.

Ingham turned his lamp out and crept between the sheets again, threw the top sheet off because it was hot. He lay for nearly an hour without sleeping, but he heard no more sounds. He put the light on again and carried his typewriter to his closet, and set it on the floor beside his shoes. He did not want Mokta or any of the boys to see it tomorrow morning.

11

INGHAM WAS interested in what Mokta's attitude would be when he brought his breakfast. But it was another boy who brought his breakfast at ten past 9, a boy Ingham had seen a couple of times, but whose name he did not know.

"*Merci*," Ingham said.

"*A votre service, m'sieur.*" Calm, inscrutable, the boy went away.

Ingham dressed to go to Tunis. The typewriter went into its case still. It crossed his mind to bring his car outside the bungalow, then put his typewriter into it, because he felt shy about being seen by one of the boys carrying his typewriter up the lane. But that was absurd, Ingham thought. How would anyone know what the old man had been hit with?

At 9.35 A.M., Ingham locked his bungalow and left it. He had put his car far up the lane, almost at Adams' bungalow, because last night he had thought to knock on Adams' door, if he had seen a light, but Adams' lights had been off. Ingham's car was on the extreme left, under a tree, and there were two other cars to the right of him, and parallel. Ingham wondered if the old Arab, not perhaps seeing his car, had assumed he was out? But how would the Arab have known what bungalow was his? Unless one of the boys told him? And that was unlikely, Ingham thought. The Arab had probably gently tried the door of every bungalow where he saw no light.

Mokta was not around.

Ingham flinched a little at the sight of Adams, coming barefoot, spear and flippers in hand, up from the beach toward his bungalow.

"Morning!" Adams called.

"Morning, Francis!" Ingham had put his typewriter in the back of his car on the floor. Now he closed the door.

"Taking off somewhere?" Adams was coming closer.

"I thought I'd go to Tunis to get a couple of typewriter ribbons and some paper." He hoped Adams wouldn't want to come along.

"Did you hear that scream last night?" Adams asked. "Around two? Woke me up."

"Yes. I heard *something.*" Ingham suddenly realized, forcibly, that he might have killed the Arab, and that this was what was making him so uneasy.

"It came from your direction. I heard a couple of the boys go out to see what was up. They didn't come back for an hour. I hear everything they do, being so close." He gestured toward his bungalow, ten yards away. "There's a little mystery there. One boy came back to the house here"—a gesture toward the headquarters building—"then ran out again after a minute."

Had he come to get the cloth, Ingham wondered. Or a shovel?

"The funny thing is, the boys won't say what it was. Maybe a fight, you know, somebody hurt. But why were they gone for an hour, eh?" Adams' face was lively with curiosity.

"I dunno what to say," Ingham said, opening his car door. "I'll ask Mokta."

"He won't tell you anything.— Are you in the mood for a drink and dinner tonight?"

Ingham was not, but he said, "Yes, fine. Come to my place for a drink?"

"Come to mine. Got something I'd like to show you." The squirrel face winked.

"All right. At six thirty," Ingham said, and got into his car.

Ingham had to go through Hammamet to get onto the Tunis road. In Hammamet he glanced around at the post office corner, at the outdoor tables of the Plage, for the old Arab in the red pants. He did not see him.

It took him forty minutes in Tunis, on foot, to find a repair shop, or the right repair shop. One or two said they could do it, but that it would take at least two weeks, and they did not sound convincing either about the repair or the time. At last, in a busy commercial street, he found a rather efficient looking shop, where the manager said it could be done in a week. Ingham believed him, but regretted the length of time.

"How did this happen?" the man asked in French.

"A maid in my hotel knocked it off a windowsill." Ingham had thought of this beforehand.

"Bad luck! I hope it didn't fall on someone's head!"

"No. On a parapet of stone," Ingham replied.

Ingham left the shop with a receipt. He felt weightless and lost without the typewriter.

On the Boulevard Bourguiba, he went to a café to have a beer and to look at the *Time* he had bought. The Israelis were standing firm with their territorial gains. It was easy to foresee a growing Arab hatred against the Jews, a worse resentment than had existed before. Things would be seething for quite a time.

He went to have lunch at a ceiling-fan-cooled restaurant on the other side of the Boulevard Bourguiba, one of the two restaurants that John Castlewood had mentioned. His scallopine milanese was well-cooked, he should have welcomed it after Hammamet fare, but he had no appetite. He was wondering if the Arab were possibly dead, if the boys had reported it to the hotel, the hotel to the police—but if so, why hadn't the police or someone from the hotel arrived early this morning? He was wondering if the boys had become frightened at finding the Arab dead, and had buried him in the sand somewhere? There were quite dense clumps of pine trees on the beach, fifty yards or so from the water. No one walked through those groves of trees. People walked around them. There was good burial ground there. Or was he being influenced by Jensen's fears about his dog?

It crossed Ingham's mind to tell Jensen about last night's adventure. Jensen, at least, would understand, Ingham thought. Ingham was now regretting that he hadn't opened the door, when he heard the boys.

He was back at the Reine by 2:45. The interior of his bungalow felt actually cool. He took off his clothes and got under a shower. The cold water was chilling, but it was also blissful. And it could not last long. Two minutes, and one became bored, shut the water off, and stepped out once more into the heat. He might ask Adams tonight how to go about getting an air-conditioner. Ingham got naked between his sheets and slept for an hour.

He awakened, and immediately thought of where he was in the chapter he was writing, a scene that was unfinished, and sat up and looked toward his typewriter. The table was empty.

He had been very soundly asleep. A week with no typewriter. To Ingham, it was like a hand cut off. He disliked writing even personal letters with a pen. He took another shower, as he was again sweaty.

Then he dressed in shorts, a cool shirt, sandals, and went out to find Mokta. One of the boys at the headquarters, languidly sweeping sand from the cement before the doorway, said that Mokta had gone on an errand to the main building. Ingham ordered a beer, sat on the terrace in the shade, and waited. Mokta came in about ten minutes, a huge stack of tied-together towels balanced on one shoulder. Mokta saw him from a distance and smiled. He was in shirtsleeves and long dark trousers. A pity, Ingham thought, that the boys weren't allowed to wear shorts in this heat.

"Mokta!— *Bon jour!* Can I speak with you a moment, when you have time?"

"*Bien sûr, m'sieur!*" There was only a brief flash of alarm in Mokta's smiling face, but Ingham had seen it. Mokta went into the office with his stack of towels. He was back at once.

"Would you like a beer?" Ingham asked.

"With pleasure, thank you, m'sieur. But I can't sit down." Mokta ran around the corner of the building to get his beer from the service door. He was back quickly with a bottle.

"I was wondering, how do I hire an air-conditioner?"

"Oh, very simple, m'sieur. I shall speak to the *directrice*, she will speak to the manager. It may take a couple of days." Mokta's smile was as broad as usual.

Ingham studied his gray eyes casually. Mokta's eyes shifted, not in a dishonest way, but simply because Mokta, Ingham thought, was alert to everything around him, even to things that weren't always there, like a shout from a superior. "Well, perhaps you can speak to her. I would like one." Ingham hesitated. He did not want to ask outright what they had done with the unconscious or dead Arab. But why wasn't Mokta bringing it up? Even if Mokta hadn't come to the bungalow with the others last night, he would have heard all about it.

Ingham offered Mokta a cigarette, which he accepted. Why didn't Mokta say something like, "Oh, m'sieur, what a *catastrophe* last night! An old beggar who tried to get into your bungalow!" Ingham could hear Mokta saying it, and yet Mokta wasn't saying it. After a minute or two, Ingham felt very uncomfortable. "It's warm today. I was in Tunis this morning," Ingham said.

"*Ah, oui?* It is always warmer in Tunis! *Mon Dieu!* I am glad I work here!"

After accepting another cigarette for the road, Mokta departed with their two beer bottles, and Ingham went back to his bungalow. He went over his notes for his chapter-in-progress, and made a few notes for the next chapter. He could have been writing an answer to Ina's last and more explanatory letter, but he did not want to think about Ina just now. It would be a letter that required some thought, unless he dashed off something that he might later regret. Ingham paper-clipped his notes and put them on a corner of his desk.

He wrote a short letter to his mother, explaining that his typewriter was undergoing a repair in Tunis. He told her that John Castlewood, whom he had not known very well, had killed himself in New York. He said he was working on a novel, and that he was going to try, despite his disappointment at the job's falling through, to gain what he could from Tunisia. Ingham was an only child. His mother liked to know what he was doing, but she was not a meddler, and did not become upset easily. His father was equally concerned, but a worse correspondent than his mother. His father almost never wrote.

Ingham still had half an hour before his appointment with OWL. He wanted very much to take a walk on the beach, past Adams' bungalow and toward Hammamet, in order to look at the sand among the trees there. He longed to find a torn-up patch that resembled a grave, he longed to be sure. But he realized that gentle rakings of sand with feet, with hands, could make a grave in the morning (or even at once) look like all the sand around it. No soil was more traceless than sand after a few minutes, even a light breeze would smooth things out, and the sun would dry any moisture that the digging might have turned up. And he didn't care to be seen peering around at the sand. And what was the Arab worth? Next to nothing, probably. That was the un-Christian thought that came to his mind, unfortunately. He locked his bungalow, and walked over to OWL's.

Adams' greeting was, as usual, hearty. "Come in! Sit ye down!"

Ingham appreciated the coolness of the room. It was like a glass of cold water when one was hot and thirsty. One drank this through the skin. What would August be like, Ingham wondered, and reminded himself that he ought to leave soon.

Adams brought an iced scotch and water.

"I got stung by a jelly-fish this afternoon," Adams said. "*Habuki*, they call them. July's the season. You can't see them in the water, you know, at least not until it's too late. Ha-ha! Got me on the shoulder. One of the boys got some salve from the office, but it didn't do any good. I went home and got some baking soda. It's still the best remedy."

"Any particular time they come out? Time of day?"

"No. It's just the season now. By the way—" Adams sat down on his sofa in his crisp khaki shorts. "I found out something more today about that yell last night. It was just outside your door. Of your bungalow."

"Oh?"

"That tallish boy—Hassim. He told me. He said Mokta was with them when they went to investigate.— You know the boy I mean?"

"Yes. He cleaned my bungalow at first." They had, for some reason, put a new boy on in the last few days.

"Hassim said it was an old Arab prowling around, and he bumped his head on something and knocked himself out. They dragged him off your terrace." Adams again chuckled, with the delight of someone who lives in a place where nothing usually ever happened, Ingham thought. "What interests me is that Mokta claims they didn't find *anyone*, though he said they looked around for an hour. Someone's lying. Maybe the old Arab did bump himself, but it could be that the boys beat him up and even killed him, and won't admit it."

"Good Lord," said Ingham, with genuine feeling, because he was imagining the boys doing just that. "By accident, you mean, beating him up too much?"

"Possibly. Because if it was a prowler they found and threw out, why should they be so cagey about it? There's a mystery there, as I said this morning.— You didn't hear anything?"

"I heard the yell. I didn't know it was so near me." He was

lying like the boys, Ingham realized, and suppose it all came out, through one of the boys, that the bump was a pretty bad fracture, a crush of the bone, and that the man was dead when they found him?

"Another thing," Adams said, "the hotels always hush up anything about thieves. Bad for business. The boys would hush anything up, because it's part of their job to keep an eye on the place and not let any prowlers in. Of course there's the watchman, as you know, but he's usually asleep and he never walks around patrolling the place."

Ingham knew. The watchman was usually asleep in his straight chair, propped against the wall, any time after 10:30 P.M. "How often does this kind of thing happen?"

"Oh—only one other time in the year I've been here. They got two Arab boys who were prowling around last November. A lot of the bungalows were empty then, and the staff was smaller. These boys were after furniture, and they broke a couple of door locks. I didn't see them, but I heard they were beaten up by the hotel boys and thrown out on the road. The Arabs are merciless with each other in a fight, you know." Adams took both their glasses, though Ingham was not quite finished. "And what do you hear from your girl?" Adams asked from the kitchen. "Ina, isn't it?"

Ingham stood up. "She wrote me.— It was she who found John Castlewood's body. He'd taken sleeping pills."

"Really! Is that so?— In his apartment, you mean?"

"Yes." Ingham hadn't told Adams that it had happened in his own apartment. Just as well.

"She's not coming over?"

"Oh, no. It's a long way. I should be getting back in a week or so. Back to New York."

"Why so soon?"

"I can't stand the heat very well.— Didn't you say you had something to show me?"

"Ah, yes. Something for you to listen to. It's short!" Adams said, holding up a finger. "But I think it's interesting. Come in the bedroom."

Another blasted tape, Ingham thought. He had hoped that Adams might have found an ancient amphora on the sea bottom, or speared a rare fish. No such luck.

Once more the suitcase on the bed, the reverently handled recording machine. "My latest," Adams said softly. "Scheduled for Wednesday next."

The tape hissed, and began:

"Good evening, friends, everywhere. This is Robin Goodfellow, bringing you a message from America, land of the . . ." Adams raced the tape, explaining that it was his usual introduction. The tape chattered and squeaked, then slowed down to ". . . what we might call democracy. It is true the Israelis have achieved a crushing victory. They are to be congratulated from a military point of view for having won over superior numbers. Two million seven hundred thousand Jews against an *Arab* population of one hundred and ten million. But who in fact struck the first blow?—I leave this, friends, to your governments to tell you. If they are honest, your governments, they will say that Israel did." (Long pause. The tape floated expectantly.) "This is an historic fact. It is not damning, not fatal to Israel's prestige, it is not going to—" (Apparently groping for a word, though Ingham was sure he had the whole thing written and rewritten before he began.) "—*blacken* Israel, at least not in the eyes of pro-Israel countries. But! Not content with mere triumph and the displacement of thousands of Arabs, the seizure of Arab territory, the Israelis now show signs of that arrogant nationalism which was the hallmark of Nazi Germany, and for which Nazi Germany at last went to her doom. I say, much as Israel was provoked by threats to her homeland, her womenfolk, and by border incidents—and there were and are incidents to the discredit of Israel that might be cited—it would be well for Israel to be magnanimous in her hour of victory, and above *all*—to guard against that overweening pride and chauvinism which has been the downfall of greater countries than she . . ."

"Or should I have said 'her'?" Adams whispered.

Ingham suppressed a crazy mirth. "I think both are okay."

". . . should not be forgotten that half the population of Israel speaks Arabic as a native tongue. This is not to say that they are always Arabs per se. The Israelis boast of having broadcast wrong directions in Arabic to Jordanian planes and tanks, implying some mental achievement. They boast of having become great farmers, now that there is no law saying they have no profession but money-lending. There is no law against their becoming farmers in the United States, but very few are. The Israeli Jews are mainly of different origin from the American Jews, who are considerably less eastern, less Arabic. The rankling Arab-Israeli antipathy shows signs of becoming one long, merciless struggle of Arab against near-Arab, fierceness against fierceness. Sanity must prevail. *Magnanimity* must prevail . . ." (Adams skipped again.) ". . . must sit down as brothers and discuss . . ."

"Oh, well," Adams said, clicking it off. "The rest is wind-up, recapitulation. What do you think?"

Ingham finally said, "I suppose the Russians will approve, since they're anti-Israel."

"The Russian *Government* is anti-*American*," Adams said, as if he were informing Ingham of something he did not know.

"Yes, but—" Ingham's mind boggled again. *Were* the Russians so anti-American, except for the Vietnam thing? "The Israeli arrogance may be only temporary, you know. After all, they've got a right to a little crowing, after what they did."

Adams gesticulated, more vigorously than Ingham had yet seen. "Temporary or not, it's dangerous while it's there, it's dangerous at any time. It's a dangerous sign."

Ingham hesitated, but could not refrain from saying, "Don't you think America's just a bit arrogant in supposing that *her* way of life is the only one in the world, the very best for everybody? Furthermore, killing people daily to foist it on them, whether they like it or not? Is that arrogance, or isn't it?" Ingham put out a half-finished cigarette, and swore to himself not to say another word on the subject. It was ludicrous, maddening, stupid.

Adams said, "America attempts to sweep away dictatorships in order to give people the freedom to vote."

Ingham did not reply. He continued to stab his cigarette gently into the ashtray. Adams was upset. This could be the end of their friendship, Ingham thought, or the end of any real liking between them. Ingham didn't care. He did not feel like saying anything mitigating. The awful thing was, there was just a grain of truth in what Adams said about Israeli nationalism.

The very countries on whom Israel was dependent had suggested she give back some of the territory she had just taken, and Israel was refusing. Both people were irritating, the Israelis and the Arabs. The only thing for any non-Jew or non-Arab to do was keep his mouth shut. If one said anything pro-Israel or pro-Arab, one ran the risk of being pounced on. It wasn't worth it. The problem was not his. He had no influence.

"I don't know what to do with the damned Arabs," Ingham said. "Why the hell don't they work more? Pardon my language.— But if a poor country's ever going to pull itself up—it shouldn't have all these hundreds of young men sitting in cafés from early morning until midnight, doing bloody nothing."

"Ah, you've got something there," Adams said, warming, smiling now.

"So between the two countries, I'm bound to say the westerner admires the Jews more, because they're not *always* on their asses. Maybe not ever, from what I hear."

"It's the climate here, it's the religion," Adams chanted, eyes to the ceiling.

"The religion, maybe. Norman Douglas concludes his book on Tunisia with a wonderful statement. He says people think the desert made the Arab what he is. Douglas says the Arab made the desert. He let the land go to hell. When the Romans were in Tunisia, there were wells, aqueducts, forests, there was the beginning of agriculture." Ingham could have gone on. His own passion surprised him. "Another thing," he said as Adams was putting away his equipment. "Oh, thank you for letting me hear the tape. I know it's possible to find the Arabs interesting, to study their fatalistic religion, admire their mosques and all that, but it all seems such whimsy, even touristy whimsy, compared to the important fact they're holding themselves back with all this nonsense. What's the use of swooning over an embroidered—houseshoe or whatever, or admiring their resignation to fate, if lots of them are begging or stealing, and from us?"

"I agree completely," Adams said, locking his closet. "And as you say, if they depend on fate, why beg from western tourists who don't believe in fate, but simply in working, in trying? Ah, some religions—" Adams abandoned his sentence in disgust.

"Let me freshen your drink. Yes, and the French and American money pouring in!"

"A half, please," Ingham said. He followed Adams into the pleasant living room, the stainless-steel kitchen. "As to funny religions, don't you think our charming west is guilty, too? Look at all the kids who come into the world entirely because the Catholic Church doesn't permit sufficient birth control. The Catholic Church ought to be *entirely* responsible for the welfare of these kids, but no, they say, let the state do it." Ingham laughed. "The Pope's nose! I wish somebody would rub it in some of the things that are going on in Ireland!"

Adams handed Ingham his drink, scrupulously one half. "All true!— There's one thing I didn't put into my tape, because it isn't very pertinent to the people behind the Iron Curtain. Or is it? I had a letter from a Jewish friend in the States just now. Now he's very much a Jew, suddenly. Before he was a Russian, or an American of Russian descent. This is what I mean by chauvinism. Let's go in and sit."

They sat down in the living room in their usual places.

"You see what I mean?" Adams said.

Ingham saw, and he hated it. He hated it because he knew it was true. Ingham might have remarked that the Russians had quite a reputation for anti-Semitism, but that, presumably, was the attitude of the Russian government, not the Russian or Communist-controlled peoples whom Adams was concerned with.

"What about the young lady at the Fourati?" Adams asked. "Is she nice?"

Adams' question sounded studiedly polite and casual, almost like a spy's, Ingham thought. He answered equally carefully, "Yes, I saw her last evening for dinner. She's from Pennsylvania. She's leaving on Wednesday."

They had scrambled eggs with fried salami and a green salad, which Adams made in his kitchen. Adams put on his radio, and they had background music of a concert from Marseille, background music, too, of a yelled conversation from the boys at the bungalow headquarters. Adams said it was nothing unusual. It was a quiet evening. But Ingham was a little on guard with Adams now. He did not like Adams' speculative eyes on him. He did not want Adams to know that his typewriter was being repaired, because Adams might guess that he had thrown it at the Arab. Ingham thought he could manage to be polite and still not invite Adams to his bungalow for the next week. Or if Adams came, he could say that he was taking a few days off from work. And presumably the typewriter would be in the closet.

12

INGHAM AWAKENED early the next morning, Sunday, to the prospect of a day without typewriter, without post, without even the consolation of a good newspaper. The Sunday papers (English, not American) arrived Tuesday or Wednesday at the main building of the hotel, a couple of copies each of the *Sunday Telegraph*, *Observer*, and the *Sunday Times*, which were maddeningly sometimes appropriated by the guests and taken up to their rooms.

There was, of course, his novel, the comforting stack of nearly a hundred pages on his desk. But he didn't care to think about it any further today, because he knew where he was going when he got his typewriter back.

And there was also Ina's letter to answer. Ingham had decided on a calm, thoughtful reply (basic tone being kindly, without reproach) which would say that he agreed with her, their feelings for each other were perhaps too vague or cool to be called love (whatever that was), and that the fact she had been so taken with John for a time proved the point. He intended to say he did not resent anything, and that he would certainly like to see her again when he returned to the States.

This mentally written letter, however, was simply diplomatic and cautious, face-saving, Ingham realized. He had been nastily stung by Ina's little affair with John. He was simply too proud to let Ina know that. And he reckoned he had nothing to lose by writing a diplomatic letter, and that he could keep his pride by doing so.

But he didn't care to spend an hour of the relatively cool morning writing it in longhand. After his breakfast—served by Mokta—Ingham drove in to Hammamet.

Again, having parked his car near Melik's, Ingham looked around for the old Arab, who was always drifting about on a Sunday morning. But not this morning. Ingham stopped for a cold rosé in the Plage. He was alert for any staring at him, but he did not think there was any. The possibility of retaliation had occurred to him, in case a few Arabs learned that he had hit, or killed, the old man. That news could certainly spread via the hotel boys. But Ingham saw and sensed nothing that suggested animosity. The retaliation might take the form of a slashed car tire, a broken windshield. He didn't anticipate a personal attack.

He went next door to the wineshop, where he bought a bottle of boukhah, then he walked through the alley toward Jensen's house. He looked at the road where he had seen the man with the cut throat. The sun was shining full on it in a bright strip, but Ingham saw no sign of blood. Then just as he was about to look away, he did see a darkish patch in the hard soil, nearly obscured by the drifting dust. That was it. But no one, not knowing, would have taken the spot for blood, he thought. Or was he wrong? Had someone dropped a bottle of wine there a couple of days ago? He went on to Jensen's.

Jensen was in, but it took some time for him to answer Ingham's knock because, he said, he had been asleep. He had wakened early, worked, then gone back to bed. He was glad to see the boukhah, but the gloom of the missing Hasso still hung about him. Jensen looked thinner. He had evidently not shaved in a couple of days. They poured the boukhah.

Ingham sat on Jensen's tousled bed. There were no sheets on it, only a thin blanket in which Jensen evidently slept.

"Still no news of Hasso?" Ingham asked.

"Nope." Jensen was stooped, washing his face in a white metal basin on the floor. Then he combed his hair.

There was no sign of his leaving, packing up, Ingham saw. He did not want to ask Jensen about that. "Can I have a glass of water with this?" Ingham asked. "Stuff's pretty fiery."

Jensen smiled his shy, naïve smile, which always came at nothing in particular. "And to think it is distilled from the sweet fig," he said sourly. He went out and reappeared with a tumbler of water. The glass was not clean, but the water looked all right. Ingham was in no mood to care.

"My typewriter's being repaired till next Saturday," Ingham said. "I was wondering if you'd like to go on a trip with me somewhere. Maybe Gabes. Three hundred and ninety-four kilometers—that is, from Tunis. In my car, I mean."

Jensen looked blank and surprised.

"We might try a camel trip somewhere. Hire a guide, maybe

—that's on me—and sleep out on the desert. Gabes is an oasis, you know, even though it's on the sea. I thought a change of scene might pick you up. I know I need it."

In the next half hour, on two or three more boukhahs, Jensen slowly brightened like a windblown candle given the shelter of a hand. "I can contribute blankets and a little cook-stove. Thermos, torch— What else do we need?"

"We'll be driving through Sfax, which looks pretty big on the map, and we can buy things there. I'd like to go to Tozour, but it looks rather far. Do you know it?" (Jensen didn't know Tozour.) "It's a famous old oasis inland, past the Chott. My map has an airport marking at Tozour." Ingham, inspired by the boukhah, was about to propose flying there, but restrained himself.

Jensen showed Ingham his latest painting, a canvas four feet high, tacked onto pieces of wood Jensen had probably found. The picture shocked Ingham. Maybe it was shockingly good, Ingham thought. It was of a disemboweled Arab, split like a steer in a butcher's shop. The Arab was screaming, not at all dead, and the red and white bowels hung down to the bottom of the canvas.

"Jesus," Ingham murmured involuntarily.

"Do you like it?"

"I *do* like it," Ingham said,

They decided to take off the next morning. Ingham would call for Jensen between a quarter of 10 and 10. Jensen was happily tight now, but at least happy for the nonce.

"Have you got some toothpaste?" Ingham asked. Jensen had some. Ingham rinsed his mouth with the remainder of his glass of water, and at Jensen's insistence spat it out the window which gave on the little court below where the toilet was. The boukhah left a powerful taste, and Ingham felt it could be smelt six feet away.

Ingham drove to the Fourati. He thought he should invite Miss Kathryn Darby for dinner tonight, and if she was not free, he would at least have been polite. She was leaving on Wednesday, and he expected to be away Wednesday. Miss Darby was not in, but Ingham left a message that he would call for her at 7:30 to go to dinner, but if she was not free, perhaps she could leave a message for him at the Reine by 5 o'clock.

Then Ingham went back to his bungalow, took a swim, had a bite of lunch from his refrigerator, and slept.

When he woke up, feeling no ill effects from the boukhah, he took his smaller suitcase from his closet and began in a happy, leisurely way to pack for the jaunt to the south. It would be even hotter, that was definite.

Mokta knocked on his door at a quarter to 5. Miss Darby was not free tonight. Ingham gave Mokta a tip.

"*Oh, merci, m'sieur!*" His face broke into his attractive smile that made him look more European than Arab to Ingham.

"I'm going away for three days," Ingham said. "I'd like you to keep an eye on the bungalow. I'll lock everything—also the closets."

"*Oui, m'sieur*. You are going on an interesting trip? Maybe to Djerba?"

"Maybe. I thought I would drive to Gabes."

"Ah, Gabes!" he said as if he knew it. "I have never been there. Big oasis." Mokta shifted on his feet, he smiled, his willing arms swung, but there was nothing for him to do. "What time will you leave? I will help you with your suitcases."

"Thanks, it's not necessary. Only one suitcase.— Have you heard anything more about the man who was prowling Friday night?"

Mokta's face went blank, and his mouth hung slightly open. "There was no *man*, m'sieur."

"Oh-h—M'sieur Adams told me Hassim said there was. The boys took him away—somewhere. I was told it was near my bungalow." Ingham was ashamed of his dishonesty, but Mokta was equally dishonest in denying the whole thing.

Mokta's hands fluttered. "The boys talk, m'sieur. They make up stories."

Ingham did not think it proper to quiz him any further. "I see. Well—let's hope there are no prowlers when I'm away."

"Ah, I *hope, m'sieur! Merci, au revoir, m'sieur*." The smile again, bow, and he went.

Ingham would never see Miss Darby again, he supposed, which mattered neither to her nor to him. He was reminded of a passage in the Norman Douglas book which he had liked, and he picked up the book and looked for it. Douglas was talking about an old Italian gardener he had met by accident somewhere in Tunisia. The passage Ingham had marked went:

> . . . He had traveled far in the Old and New Worlds; in him I recognized once again that simple mind of the sailor or wanderer who learns, as he goes along, to talk and think decently; who, instead of gathering fresh encumbrances on life's journey, wisely discards even those he set out with.

That appealed very much to Ingham now. Miss Darby was certainly not one of his encumbrances, but Ina might be. A terrible thought, in a way, because he had considered her—for a year at least—a part of his life. He had counted on her. And knowing himself, Ingham knew he had not had the whole reaction he would have, a little later, from her letter. The curious thing, the comforting thing was that Africa would help him to bear it better—if he was going to have any bad reaction. It was strange, he couldn't explain it, to be floating like a foreign particle (which he was) in the vastness of Africa, but to be absolutely sure that Africa would enable him to bear things better.

He decided not to think about his letter to Ina, the letter he would write in a few days. Let her wait, say, five or six days, ten including the time the letter would take to get there. She had made him wait a month.

Ingham went over to say good-bye to OWL.

OWL was washing his flippers in the kitchen sink. He shook his flippers neatly, like a woman shaking out a dishcloth, and stood them upside down on the drainboard. They looked seal-like, but somehow as repellent as Adams' feet.

"I'm going away for a couple of days," Ingham said.

"Going away where?"

Ingham told him. He did not mention Jensen.

"Are you giving up your bungalow?"

"No. I wasn't sure I could get it back."

"No, you're right. Would you like a drink?"

"I wouldn't mind a beer, if you have one."

"Got six, ice cold," Adams said cheerfully, and got a can from the refrigerator. Adams made himself a scotch. "You know, I found out a little something today," he said as they went into the living room. "I think—I'm pretty sure—" Adams looked around at the windows, as if for eavesdroppers, but because of the air-conditioning, his windows were all shut, even all the shutters closed except the one behind Ingham's chair where there was no sun. "I think I know who the prowler was the other night. Abdullah. The old Arab with the cane. The one you said stole your jacket or something."

"Oh. One of the boys told you?"

"No, I heard it in town," Adams said with a faintly satisfied air, as if he were in the secret service and had ferreted out something.

Ingham's heart had tripped. He hoped he did not look pale, because he felt pale.

"At the Plage," Adams continued, "they were talking about 'Abdull,' a couple of Arabs at the bar. There're lots of Abdullahs, but I saw the barman give the fellows a sign to pipe down, because of me. They know I'm at the Reine. I understood enough of what they said to know he was 'gone' or 'disappeared.' I wanted to ask them about him, because something had just made a connection in my mind. I didn't ask, I didn't want to butt in. But I remembered seeing Abdullah by the curio shop near the hotel here Friday night. It was a night I drove in to Hammamet around eight to have dinner. I'd never seen the old fellow around here before, so I remembered it. And I noticed yesterday and today, he wasn't around town. I was in Hammamet three times lately, and he wasn't around, not since Friday. It's *strange*."

Silence for a few seconds.

"Well, won't somebody report him missing?" Ingham asked. "Won't the police do something?"

"Oh—his neighbors might miss him. I presume he's got a room to sleep somewhere, probably with six other people. I doubt if he's got a wife and family. Would a neighbor go to the police?" Adams pondered this. "I doubt that. They're fatalistic. *Mektoub!* It is the will of Allah that Abdullah should disappear! *Voilà!* It's a far cry from the American Way, isn't it?"

13

JENSEN WAS punctual the next morning, standing on the road near the narrow alley, with a brown suitcase at his feet. He wore pale green cotton trousers, neatly pressed. Ingham pulled up a bit past Melik's on the other side of the road, and Jensen walked over. Ingham helped him stow the suitcase in the back of the car. They had plenty of room, even with Jensen's knapsack and dangling gear of cook-stove and pots.

"You know, Anders, you ought to put on shorts," Ingham said. "It's going to be a hot drive. You ought to save those good pants." He spoke gently, always afraid somehow to hurt Jensen's feelings.

"All right," Jensen said, like a willing, polite little boy. "I'll change up in Melik's loo." Jensen opened his suitcase and dragged out a pair of shorts made from old levis. He went up the steps to Melik's.

Ingham stood outside his car and lit a cigarette.

Jensen was back in a moment. He had lean brown legs with golden hairs. He put his trousers away carefully in his suitcase.

Ingham took the road southward, along the sea. The morning was still cool. The emptiness of the clear blue sky seemed to promise a reward, or pleasure, ahead of them. In a quarter of an hour they reached Bou Ficha, a village, and in about the same time something larger called Enfidaville. Jensen held the map. The road was good to Sousse. They did not stop at Sousse even for a coffee, but went on southward on the shorter inland route toward Sfax, where they intended to have a late lunch. Jensen reeled off the names:

"Msaken next . . . Bourdjine . . . Amphithéatre! Well! No, that's not a town, it's a fact. They have one. Probably Roman."

"I find it amazing," Ingham said, "there's so little remains of the Romans, Greeks, Turks and so forth. Carthage was a disappointment. I expected it to be so much bigger."

"No doubt it has been pillaged a thousand times," Jensen said with resignation.

In Sfax, where they lunched at a very decent restaurant with pavement tables, Jensen was of great interest to a boy of about twelve. At least that was the way Ingham saw it. He hadn't seen Jensen make a single inviting move. The boy hung around, smiling broadly, rolling big dark eyes, leaning against a metal pole some six feet away. At last the boy spoke to Jensen, and Jensen murmured something that sounded bored in Arabic. The boy giggled.

"I asked him," said Jensen, "do I look like I have a millime? Scram!"

Ingham laughed. The boy was rather handsome, but dirty.

"They don't bother you?" Jensen asked.

One had approached him in Tunis, but he said, "No, not yet."

"Little bores. Little nuisances," Jensen said, as if he spoke of a minor vice of his own which he could not shake.

Ingham anticipated that Jensen might find a boy or two on this trip. He thought it might pick Jensen up. "How much money do they want, usually?"

"Oh!" Jensen laughed. "You can get them for a packet of cigarettes. Half a packet."

They made it easily to Gabes by 6 P.M., even stopping for half an hour at a town called Cekhira for a swim. It was the hottest time of the afternoon, just after 3. They stepped out of the already ovenlike car, which had been lumbering over sandy soil toward the beach, into something worse, a bigger oven. Ingham changed as fast as possible into swimming trunks, while standing at one side of the car. There was no living thing in sight. What could have stood the heat? They ran down to the sea and jumped in. The water was refreshing to Ingham, though Jensen said the water was not cold enough. Jensen was an excellent swimmer, and could stay under water for so long that Ingham grew alarmed at one point. Jensen swam in his shorts. When they came back to the car, the door handles were too hot to touch. Ingham had to take off his trunks and use them to grip the handle. In the car, Jensen sat in his wet shorts on a towel.

Gabes was Ingham's first view of the desert, stretching inland to the west behind the town, flat and yellow-orange in the light of the setting sun. The town was quite big, but the buildings were not all jammed together as at Sousse or Sfax. There were spaces through which one could see distant palm trees with fronds stirring in the breeze. It was not so warm as Ingham had feared. They found a second-class hotel, which was respectable enough to be listed in Ingham's Guide Bleu, however. Jensen was a little proud about paying his way, and Ingham did not want to let him in for much expense. It would be odd, Ingham thought, if Jensen were really quite well off, and had simply decided to rough it for a while. That could go, Ingham supposed, as far as buying a cheap brown suitcase to begin with, and if one roughed it long enough, the suitcase could look like Jensen's at this moment. Ingham didn't care one way or the other. He found Jensen a good traveling companion, uncomplaining, interested in everything, and willing to do anything Ingham proposed.

Only Ingham's room had a toilet and shower. Jensen took a shower in Ingham's room. Then they both went out to walk around the town. The jasmine sellers were here, too. The oversweet scent had become the scent of Tunisia to Ingham—its cosmetic scent, at any rate—as certain scents evoked certain women. Lotte's had been Le Dandy. Ingham could not think of the name of Ina's now, though he had bought some for her once or twice in New York. He certainly could not recollect how it smelt. The olfactory memory might be long and primitive, antedating words, but it seemed one couldn't call up a smell in memory as one could call up a word or a line of poetry.

They went into a bar and stood. Boukhah again. Then Ingham had a scotch. The transistor, though tiny on the bar shelf, was blaring, and made talking difficult. The song whined on with no end in sight, and there was off and on singing, by a male or female voice, it was impossible to tell. When the voice stopped for a bit, the twanging, insinuating stringed instruments whammed in, as if to back up the griping vocalist with a "*Yeah! That's what I've been saying all along!*" And what were they complaining *about*? Ingham wanted to laugh.

"Good God," he said to Jensen, shaking his head.

Jensen smiled slightly, apparently able to shut out the noise.

At their feet was a swill of cigarette butts, sawdust, and spit. "Let's go somewhere else," Ingham said.

Jensen was willing.

Eventually they found a restaurant for dinner. Ingham could not eat his squid, or whatever it was, which he had ordered through a mistake of his own in the language, but at least he had the satisfaction of giving it to a grateful cat.

The next morning they paid their bill, and asked the hotel manager about camels.

"*Ah, bien sûr, messieurs!*" He quoted prices. He knew a camel driver and where to find him.

They went off with their luggage to find the camel drivers. The business took some time, because Jensen decided to wait for a driver due at 10 or 10:30, according to the other camel drivers. The drivers leaned casually, their pointed sandals crossed, against the round bodies of their camels, which were all lying around on the sand with their feet tucked in like cats. The camels looked more intelligent than their drivers, Ingham thought. It was a disturbing intelligence in their faces, a look of knowledge that could not be acquired by going to any school. All the camels regarded him and Jensen with an amused curiosity, as if to say, "Well, well, two *more* suckers!" Ingham was vaguely ashamed of his unromantic thoughts.

The awaited driver arrived on one camel, leading three others. Jensen struck the bargain. Six dinars each for overnight.

"They always make a big thing about having to feed the camels," Jensen explained to Ingham, "but the price isn't bad."

Ingham hadn't been on a camel since a certain trip to the zoo when he was a boy. He rather dreaded the lurching ride, and tried to anticipate falling off—nine feet down to the sand—so that it wouldn't hurt so much if he did. The camel jolted him up, and they were off. After a few hundred yards, it was not as bad as Ingham had feared, but the undulant movement imposed by the camel's gait made him feel silly. He would have preferred to gallop, leaning forward, in the manner of Lawrence of Arabia.

"Hey, Anders!" Ingham yelled. "What's our destination?"

"We're going toward Chenini. That little town we looked up last night." Jensen was on the camel ahead.

"Wasn't it ten kilometers away?"

"I think so." Jensen spoke to the driver, who was on the lead camel, then turned back to Ingham. "We can't walk in the desert all day, you know. We'll have to have shelter from eleven to four somewhere."

The desert was widening about them. "Where?" Ingham asked, unalarmed.

"Oh, trust him. He's no doubt making a bee-line for a shelter."

This was true, but it was 11:40 before they reached a tiny town, or cluster of houses, and Ingham was glad to stop. He had covered his head with a handkerchief. Jensen had an old canvas cap. The place had a name, but it slipped from Ingham's mind as soon as he heard it. There was a grocery store–restaurant which sold bottled drinks from a Pepsi-Cola dispenser tank, but there was no ice in the tank, only tepid water. A lunch was produced by the proprietor of the place, chick peas with lumps of inedible sausage. Jensen and Ingham ate at a tiny round table, their metal chairs slanting crazily in the sand. Ingham could not imagine why, or how, people lived here, though there was a road of sorts leading to and from the place, a ghostly trail in the sand which a jeep or a Land Rover could use, he supposed. They drank some boukhah after their lunch. Jensen had picked up a bottle somewhere. Jensen said the only thing to do was sleep for an hour or so.

"Unless you want to read. I might make a sketch." Jensen got a drawing pad from his suitcase.

There were two more stops in the course of the day. Jensen had quite a conversation with the driver, which he said was on the subject of where they would spend the night. The driver knew of a grove of palms, though it was not an oasis. They arrived there just before 7. The sun had just set. The horizon was orange, the landscape empty, but there was a cardboard carton, some old tins under the trees, which suggested that this spot might be a favorite for camel drivers to bring their customers to. Ingham was not fussy. He thought it all quite wonderful. Venus was shining.

Jensen had bought tins of beans and sardines en route from the hotel to the camels this morning. Ingham did not care if the food was hot or cold, but Jensen set up his cook-stove. He invited the driver to partake, but he declined politely, and produced his own food from somewhere. He also declined Jensen's offer of a boukhah.

Before he ate, the driver read in the failing light from a little book.

Jensen glanced at the driver and said to Ingham, "It takes imagination to enjoy a drink. There he is with the Koran, no doubt. You know, they either drink like maniacs or they're stubborn—dries. What do you call them?"

"Teetotalers," Ingham said. "He's not very friendly, is he?"

"Maybe he thinks he can't do me, because I know some Arabic. But I have the feeling he has just had a sadness of some kind."

"Really?" Ingham imagined that Arabs were more or less always the same from one day to the next, that no external event could much affect them.

After their dinner out of a mutual pot, eaten with spoons, Jensen and Ingham lay on their blankets and smoked, facing the direction in which the sun had gone down. A palm tree half sheltered them. The boukhah bottle was between them, pushed into the sand so it would stand upright. Ingham drank mostly from Jensen's canteen of water. The stars came out more and more, and became powdery with profusion. There was no sound except an occasional swish of breeze in the palm leaves.

Just as he was about to speak, Ingham saw a shooting star. It went on a long way downward in the sky—seven inches, he thought, if the sky had been a canvas and had been of a certain nearness. "Remember the night," Ingham said, "about three weeks ago, when I went to your house the first time? As I was leaving, walking toward the road, I came across a dead man. In that second stretch, after the turn. Lying in the alley."

"Really?" asked Jensen without too much surprise.

Ingham was speaking softly. "I stumbled over him. Then I lit a match. The fellow'd had his throat cut. The body was even cold. You didn't hear anything about it?"

"No, I didn't."

"What do you think happens to the body? Somebody had to remove it."

Jensen paused for a swig from the bottle. "Oh, first somebody would cover it up to hide it. Then a couple of Arabs would haul it away on a donkey, bury it in the sand somewhere. That is, if there's some reason to hide it and there usually is if a man's murdered. Excuse me a minute." Jensen got up and disappeared somewhere in the palm grove.

Ingham put his head down on his forearms. The camel driver had settled himself under robes next to one of his camels, and might have been asleep by now. He was out of hearing, and probably could not understand English, but Ingham disliked his closeness. Ingham stood up as Jensen came back. "Let's walk a little bit away," Ingham said.

Jensen took his flashlight. It was very dark when they left the cook-stove. The flashlight's beam bobbed on the irregular ripples of sand before them. Ingham imagined the ripples mountains, hundreds of feet high, imagined that he and Jensen were giants walking on the moon; or perhaps their actual size, walking on a new planet populated by tiny people to whom these ripples were mountains. They walked slowly, and both glanced behind to see how far they had gone from the palm trees. The trees were not visible, but the cook-stove glowed like a spark.

Ingham plunged in. "I had an attempted robbery at my bungalow a few nights ago."

"Oh?" said Jensen, sounding English as he did sometimes, weaving a little in the soft sand. "What happened?"

"I was asleep and I woke up when the door was being opened. I'd forgotten to lock my door. Someone started to come in. I picked up my typewriter and threw it as hard as I could. I hit the man right in the forehead." Ingham came to a stop, and so did Jensen. They faced each other without seeing each other. Jensen's torch pointed at their feet. "The thing is—I think I might've killed the man. I think he was the one they call Abdullah. You know, the old fellow with the turban and the red pants? The one who stole something out of my car?"

"Yes, sure," Jensen said attentively, as if waiting for the rest.

"Well—I'd got behind my table, you see, as soon as I heard someone coming in. Then I grabbed the first thing to hand, my typewriter. He gave a howl and fell, and I shut the door. After a minute or so, I heard some of the hotel boys come and drag the fellow away." A longer pause. Jensen wasn't saying anything. "The next morning I asked one of the boys, Mokta. He said he didn't know anything about it, which I know isn't true. The point is, I think the Arab was dead and they took him somewhere and buried him. I certainly haven't seen Abdullah since."

Jensen shrugged.

Ingham sensed the shrug without actually seeing it.

"He could be recovering somewhere." Jensen laughed a little. "When was this?"

"The night of July fourteenth-fifteenth. A Friday night. That's eleven days ago.— I'd like to know for sure, you see. It was a hell of a blow right in the forehead. It bent my typewriter frame. That's why my typewriter's being repaired."

"Oh, I see." Jensen laughed.

"Have you seen Abdullah lately?"

"I hadn't thought about it.— You know, he doesn't dare to walk in my little street, they hate him so there?"

"Really?" Ingham said weakly. He realized he did not appreciate the information. He felt a little faint. "Let's walk back. Another thing makes me think it was Abdullah. I saw him that evening around six near the hotel. And Adams also said he saw him by the gift shop on the road there. The same night." Ingham knew these details bored Jensen, but he could not stop himself from saying them.

"Did you tell this story to Adams?" Jensen asked, and Ingham could tell Jensen was smiling.

"No, I lied."

"Lied?"

"Well—Adams knows it was Abdullah. He knows since a couple of days, because of something he heard in the Plage. About Abdullah being gone, missing or something. Adams heard someone yell that night. Not only that, but one of the boys told Adams the Arab was on my terrace."

"But where did you lie?"

"I told Adams I'd heard a yell, but I said I didn't know anything about it. I didn't even admit I'd got out of bed."

"Just as well," Jensen said, and paused to light a cigarette.

What do you think'll happen if he's dead? Ingham wanted to ask, but he waited for Jensen to speak.

Jensen took so long, Ingham thought he was not going to speak, or was thinking of something else—maybe because the story was so commonplace, it did not much interest him.

"If I were you, I'd forget about it. You can't tell what happened," Jensen said.

It was vaguely comforting. Ingham realized he needed a great deal of reassurance.

"I hope you got him," Jensen said in a slow voice. "That particular Arab was a swine. I like to think you got him, because it makes up a little for my dog—just a little. However, Abdullah wasn't worth my dog."

Ingham felt suddenly better. "That's true."

They lay down again, face down, faces buried in their sweatered arms for warmth. Jensen had blown the fire out.

14

IT WAS FRIDAY, July 28th, before they got back to Hammamet. They had visited the city of Medinine and the island of Djerba. They had roughed it in a small town with no hotel, sleeping in a room above a restaurant where they had eaten. Ingham, like Jensen, had shaved every other day. In Metouia, an ancient town near Gabes where they stopped for coffee one afternoon, Jensen found a boy of about fourteen whom he liked, and went off with him, after asking Ingham if he minded waiting a few minutes. Jensen was back after only ten minutes, smiling, carrying a woolen mat with a black and red pattern. Jensen said the boy had taken him to his house, in no room of which had there been any privacy. Jensen had made him accept five hundred millimes, and the boy had stolen the mat behind his mother's back, in order to give Jensen something. The boy said his mother had woven it, but did not receive five hundred millimes from the shopkeeper to whom she sold her mats. "He's a nice boy. I'm sure he'll give the money to his mother," Jensen said. The story lingered in Jensen's mind, pleasantly. What had the mother thought of Jensen's coming home with her son, or did it happen a couple of times a day? And what did it matter if it did?

When Ingham returned to his bungalow, the neat blue and white cleanliness seemed to have a personality of its own, to be on guard, and to hold something unhappy. Absurd, Ingham thought. He simply hadn't seen anything comfortable for five solid days. But the distaste for the bungalow persisted. There were four or five letters, only two of which interested him: a contract sent by his agent for a Norwegian edition of *The Game of "If,"* and a letter from Reggie Muldaven, a friend in New York. Reggie was a freelance journalist, married, with a small daughter, and he was working on a novel. He asked Ingham how long he was going to be in Tunisia, and what was he doing there since Castlewood's suicide? *How is Ina? I haven't seen her in a month or so, and I only said hello in a restaurant that time . . .* Reggie knew Ina pretty well, however, well enough to have rung her and talked with her. Ingham was sure

Reggie was being diplomatic in saying nothing more about her. Ingham felt sure that people like Reggie would have heard about John's relationship with Ina. People always wanted to know the reasons for a suicide, and kept asking questions until they found out.

Ingham unpacked, showered and shaved. He moved slowly, thinking of other things. He was to pick up Jensen at 8 o'clock, and they were going to have dinner in the hotel dining room. It was now 6:30.

He remembered the letter he owed to Ina, and when he dressed, he sat down and began it in longhand, not that he was in the mood, but because he did not want it hanging over his head any longer.

July 28, 19—

Dear Ina,

Yes, your letter was rather a surprise. I had not known things had gone that far, shall we say. But no hard feelings here. Typewriter is being repaired, so I don't write this with my usual ease or full flow.

Of course I don't see why we shouldn't see each other again, if we both wish to. And of course I understand that, from your point of view, I perhaps seemed lukewarm. I was cautious, no doubt about that. I have a past, you're familiar with it, and it wasn't and hasn't been easy to get through—I mean this past year and a half until I met you and began to love you. And when was that? Nearly a year ago. The whole time, now a year and eight months (since my divorce) seems a sort of prolonged nightmare without sleep (matter of fact I did not sleep well for nearly a year, as I've told you, and even after meeting *you*) but I hate to think what it would have been if I had not met you at all. You at least lifted me back among the living, you lifted my morale more than I can ever say. You made me realize that someone could care for me again, and that I could care for someone. I'll always be grateful. You might even have saved my life, who knows, because even though I was able to work, always, I was going downhill mentally, losing a little weight and so forth. How long could that have lasted?

That was not bad, Ingham thought, and it was certainly sincere. He continued:

> I've just got back from a five-day trip south in the car. Gabes (oasis), camel rides, the island of Djerba. Much desert. It changes one's thinking. I think it makes people see things more clearly, or not so close up. More *simply*, perhaps. Let us not take all this so seriously. Don't feel guilty for what happened. If you'll forgive me, I must tell you that I was laughing one night at the thought that: "John sacrificed his love for Ina on the altar of Howard's bed." Somehow this had me in stitches.

He was interrupted by a knock. It was OWL.

"Well, hello! Greetings!" Ingham said as heartily as OWL usually greeted him.

"Greetings to you! When did you get back? I saw your car."

"Around five. Come in and have a drink."

"No, you're working."

"I'm only writing a letter." Ingham persuaded Adams in, then at once became aware of his absent typewriter. "Sit down somewhere. Anywhere." Ingham went into the kitchen.

"Whereabouts did you go?" Adams asked.

Ingham told him, and told about the freezing night on the desert, when he had got up at 5 A.M. and stomped around to get warm.

"By the way, I went with Anders Jensen, the Danish fellow."

"Oh, did you? Is he a nice fellow?"

Ingham didn't know what Adams meant by "nice." Maybe it included Jensen's politics. "He's good company," Ingham said. "He still can't find his dog. He's sure the Arabs got him, and he's a little bitter about that. I can't blame him."

It got to be 7:30. Ingham replenished Adams' drink, then his own. "I'm meeting Anders at eight and we're going to have dinner at the hotel. Would you like to join us, Francis?"

OWL brightened. "Why, yes, thanks."

Ingham and Jensen found Adams in the hotel bar a little after 8. They stood at the bar and had a scotch. Ingham noticed that the cash register showed the alarming figure of 480.00. A bang from a waiter, and the figure jumped to 850.00. Ingham leaned closer and saw that the register had been made in Chicago. It was registering millimes, and the dollar sign had been removed.

Jensen and OWL chatted pleasantly. Ingham had asked Jensen if everything had been all right at his house, and everything had, except that there was no news about his dog. Jensen said he had spoken to the Arab people next door, with whom he was on good terms.

Jensen ate like a starved wolf, though his table manners, in this ambience, were perfect. They had *kebab tunisien*, kidneys on a skewer. Ingham ordered a second bottle of *rosé*. The blond Frenchwoman and her small son were still here, Ingham noticed, but otherwise most of the people had changed since he had last been in the dining room.

"There's still no sign of Abdullah," Adams said to Ingham in a lull in the conversation.

"And *tant—mieux*," Jensen said firmly.

"Oh, you know about Abdullah?" Adams asked.

Ingham and Jensen were opposite each other. Adams sat at one end of the table, between them, partly in the path of waiters.

"Howard told me the story," Jensen said.

Ingham shifted and kicked Jensen deliberately with his right foot under the table, but since Adams looked quickly at Ingham at this moment, Ingham was not sure he had not kicked Adams.

"Yes, you know it happened right outside Howard's bungalow. I think the fellow was killed," Adams said to Jensen.

Jensen gave Ingham a quick, amused glance. "And so what? One less thief in this town. Plenty more to go."

"Well—" Adams tried to smile with good humor. "He was still a human being. You can't just—"

"That could be debated," Jensen said. "What makes a human being? The fact something walks on two legs instead of four?"

"Why, no. Not merely," Adams said. "There's the brain."

Jensen said calmly, buttering yet another bit of bread, "I think Abdullah used his exclusively for thinking about how to get his hands on other people's property."

Adams managed a chuckle. "That doesn't make him any less a human being."

"Any *less*? Why not? It makes him exactly that," Jensen replied.

"If we started figuring that way, we'd just kill everybody who annoyed us," Adams said. "That won't quite do, as the English say."

"The nice thing is, half the time they manage to get themselves killed, one way or another. Do you know Abdullah couldn't even walk in the little street where I live? The Arabs chased him out with stones. You call him a loss? That walking bag of rags and—" Jensen couldn't think of a word. "*Merde*," he said finally.

Ingham glanced at Jensen, trying to convey that he didn't want Jensen to go too far. Jensen knew that, of course, but Ingham could practically feel the heat of Jensen's boiling blood across the table.

"*All* people can be improved, given a chance at a new way of life," said OWL.

"If you'll forgive me, I won't be alive to see much of it, and while I'm here I prefer to trust my own experience and my own eyes," said Jensen. "When I came here about a year ago, I had quite a wardrobe. I had suitcases, cuff-links, a good easel. I was renting a private house in Sidi Bou Said, that picturesque, immaculate little village of blue and white houses—" Jensen waved a hand airily "—noted for delicately wrought birdcages, for its coffeehouses where you can't get an honest drink for love nor money, a town where you can't buy a bottle of wine in a shop. They cleaned me out there, even took a lot of my landlord's furniture. All my canvases. I wonder what they did with them? After that, I decided to live like a beatnik, and maybe I wouldn't get robbed again."

"Oh, bad luck," said Adams sympathetically. "Your dog— He didn't guard the house?"

"Hasso at that time was at a vet's in Tunis. Somebody had thrown hot water on his back. He was in pain, and I wanted to make sure the hair would grow back.— Oh, no, I don't think these mongrels would come into any house if Hasso was there. They knew he was gone for a few days."

"Good God," Ingham said. The story depressed him. No use asking if Jensen ever found out who robbed him, Ingham supposed. No one ever found out.

"You cannot fight or change an enormous tide," Jensen said with a sigh. "You must give it up, become reconciled. And yet I am human enough—yes, *human*—to be glad when one of them gets what he gave. I mean Abdullah."

OWL looked a little squelched. "Yes. Well, maybe the boys at the hotel did finish him off. But—" Adams glanced at Ingham. "That night, the boys didn't leave their bunks until they heard someone yell. I think he was killed by that one blow, whatever it was."

A blow now, not a bump. An insane amusement, perhaps caused by tension, made Ingham set his teeth.

"Maybe one of his own people stabbed him," Jensen said and gave a titter. "Maybe two Arabs were after the same house!" Now Jensen sat sideways, threw an arm over the back of his chair, and laughed. He was looking at Adams.

Adams looked surprised. "What do you know about it?" Adams asked. "Do you know something?"

"I don't think I would say if I did," Jensen said. "And do you know why? Because it just—doesn't—matter." With the last two words, he tapped a cigarette on the table, then lit it. "We speculate about Abdullah's death as if he were President Kennedy. I don't think he's quite that important."

This quietened Adams, but it was a resentful silence, Ingham could tell. Jensen daydreamed and brooded, speaking, when he did speak, in monosyllables. Ingham was sorry Jensen had made his personal resentments seem resentments against Adams. And Ingham felt that Adams had guessed that he had told Jensen something about that night that he had not told to Adams. Adams knew, too, that Ingham was essentially in accord with Jensen's outlook on life, which was not exactly OWL in nature.

They drove to the Plage in Ingham's car. Ingham had thought Adams would prefer to say good night when they left the Reine's dining room, but he did not. Jensen now stood the drinks.

"A bitter young man. It's too bad all that happened to him," Adams said when Jensen was at the bar ordering.

They were sitting at a table. Again, it was hard to talk in the place. Livened by wine and beer, the shouted conversations now and then exploded in startling whoops and roars. "I'm sure he'll get over it—when he gets back to Denmark."

Ingham had thought Jensen might ask Adams to come to his house and see his paintings, but Jensen did not. Adams would have come, Ingham was sure. They left after the single round of drinks.

"I'll be seeing you!" Ingham said to Jensen on the road.

"*À bientôt.* Thank you very much for dinner. Good night, Francis."

"Good night, good night," said Adams.

Silence as they drove back to the Reine. Ingham felt Adams' thoughts turning. Ingham put his car up near Adams' bungalow. Adams asked if he would like to come in for a nightcap.

"I think I'm a little tired tonight, thanks."

"I'd sort of like to speak with you for a minute."

Ingham came with him. The bungalow headquarters was silent and dark. The side door, where the kitchen was, stood open for air. To the left of the kitchen was the room where ten or twelve boys slept. Ingham declined another drink, but he sat down, on the edge of the sofa this time, elbows on his knees. Adams lit a cigarette and walked slowly up and down.

"I just have the feeling, if you'll forgive me—that you're not telling the truth about that night. You *needn't* forgive me for asking, if you don't want to." He smiled, not so pouchily, and in fact it was not a real smile. "I've been frank with you, you know, about my tapes. You're the only person in Tunisia who knows. Because you're a writer and an intellectual and an honest man." He cocked his head for emphasis.

Ingham disliked being called an intellectual. He was silent, and for too long, he felt.

"First of all," Adams said, ever so gently, "it's funny you wouldn't have opened your door or at least listened that night after hearing that yell. And since it was on your terrace—what am I supposed to think?"

Ingham sat back. There was a comfortable pillow to lean back against, but he did not feel comfortable. He felt he was fighting a silly duel. What Adams said was true. He couldn't continue lying without obviously lying. Ingham wished very much he could claim some kind of diplomatic immunity for the moment, put off an answer at least until tomorrow. His real problem was, he did not know the importance of whatever he might say. If he told the truth, for instance, would Adams say anything to the police? What would happen then? "I forgive you for asking," Ingham began, a statement whose falseness he realized as soon as he had uttered it. He could have gone on, *Do you mind if I reserve the right . . . After all, you're not the police.* "It happened that night as I told you. You can call me a coward for not opening the door, I suppose."

Now Adams' smile was paunchy, the shiny little squirrel again. "I simply don't believe you—if you'll forgive me," he said, even more gently. "You can trust me. I want to *know*."

Ingham felt his face grow warm. It was a combination of anger and embarrassment.

"I can see you're not telling the whole story. You'll feel better if you tell me," Adams said. "I know."

Ingham had a brief impulse to jump up and sock him. Was he a Father Confessor? Or just an old snoop? Holier-than-thou, whatever he was. "If you'll forgive me," Ingham said, "I don't see I'm under any obligation to tell you anything. Why are you quizzing me?"

Adams chuckled. "No, Howard, you're not under an obligation. But you can't throw off your American heritage just because you've spent a few weeks in Africa."

"American heritage?"

"You can't laugh it off, either. You weren't brought up like these Arabs."

"I didn't say I was."

Adams went to the kitchen.

Ingham stood up and followed him. "I really don't want a drink, thanks. If I may, I'll use your john."

"Go ahead! Just here to the right," Adams said, happy to be able to offer something. He put on the light.

Ingham had never been in Adams' bathroom before. He faced a mirror, and rather than look at himself, opened the medicine cabinet and stared into it as he made use of the toilet. Toothpaste, shaving cream, aspirin, Entero-Vioform, a lot of little bottles with yellow pills. Everything neat as an old maid. The tubes of things had American brand names like Colgate's, Squibb's and so forth. Jensen wouldn't take this load of crap, Ingham told himself, and he flushed the toilet and left the bathroom with a self-assured air. By load of crap, he meant his American heritage. Just precisely what did that mean?

Adams was seated in the straight chair at his desk, but turned sideways so that he faced Ingham, who was again on the sofa. "The reason I sound so positive," Adams began affably, smiling a little, his bluish eyes terribly alert now, "is because I talked with the people in the cottage behind you. They're French, a middle-aged couple. They heard the yell that night—and a clatter of some kind like something falling, and then they heard a door slam. Your door.— It must've been you who closed it."

Ingham shrugged. "Why not somebody in another bungalow?"

"They're positive where the sound came from." Adams was using the dogged, argumentative tone that Ingham had heard on his tapes. "Did you hit him with something that made a clatter?"

Ingham now felt only a faint warmth in his cheeks. He thought he was as deadpan as a corpse. "Is there any *purpose* in your asking me all this? Why?"

"I like to know the truth about a story. I think Abdullah's dead."

And he's not Kennedy, Ingham thought. Should he stick to his story and continue to be heckled by Adams (the alternative seemed to be to leave Hammamet), or tell the truth, suffer the shame of having lied, defy Adams to do anything about it, and at least have the satisfaction of having told the truth? Ingham chose the latter course. Or should he wait until tomorrow? He'd had a few drinks, and was he making the right decision? Ingham said, "I've told you what happened, Francis." He smiled a little at Adams. But at least it was a real smile. Ingham was amused, and as yet he did not dislike Francis J. Adams. And his smile widened as a funny possibility crossed his mind: could it be that some very rich man—of Communist persuasion—was paying OWL his stipend for his weekly broadcasts just for a joke, a joke that he could afford? Some man who didn't live in Russia? Because certainly OWL's broadcasts helped the Russians. Adams' earnestness made this possibility all the more hilarious to Ingham.

"What's amusing?" Adams asked, but he asked it pleasantly.

"Everything. Africa does turn things upside down. You can't deny that. Or are you—immune to it?" Ingham stood up. He wanted to leave.

"I'm not immune to it. It's a contrast to one's—homespun morals, shall we say. It doesn't change them or destroy them. Oh, no! If you would only realize it, it makes us hang on all the harder to our proven principles of right and wrong. They're our anchors in the storm. They're our backbone. They *cannot* be shed, even if we wished."

An anchor for a backbone! Was that one's ass? Ingham had not the faintest idea what to say, though he wanted to be polite as he left. "You're probably right.— I must go, Francis. So I'll say good night."

"Good night, Howard. And sleep well." There was no sarcasm in the "sleep well."

15

THE NEXT morning was Saturday, the day when Ingham could get his typewriter. Ingham was at the post office at a quarter of 10, and dropped Ina's letter into the box. Then he walked to Jensen's house, this time avoiding a glance at the spot where the dead Arab had lain.

Jensen was not up, but at last he stuck his head out the window. "I'll open the door!"

Ingham walked into the little cement court. "I'm going to Tunis to pick up my typewriter. Can I get anything for you?"

"No, thanks. I can't think of anything."

Jensen had bought some painting supplies in Sousse, Ingham remembered. "I was wondering if I could find a place like yours to rent in Hammamet. Do you know of anything?"

Jensen took a few seconds to let this sink in. "You mean a couple of rooms somewhere? Or a house?"

"A couple of rooms. Something Arab. Something like you've got."

"I can ask. Sure, Howard. I'll ask this morning."

Ingham said he would look in when he came back from Tunis. He wanted to tell Jensen about his conversation with Adams last night.

His typewriter was ready. They had kept the old frame, its brown paint worn at the corners down to the steel. Ingham was so pleased, he did not mind the bill, which he thought a bit excessive, seven dinars or slightly more than fourteen dollars. He tried the machine on a piece of paper in the shop. It was his old typewriter, as good as ever. Ingham thanked the man in the shop, and walked out to his car, happily weighted again.

He was back in Hammamet before 12:30. He had bought newspapers, *Time*, *Playboy*, tins of smoked oysters, potted ham, and Cross & Blackwell soups. Jensen was in the alley, straightening a bent garbage can, presumably his own, with a foot.

"Come in," Jensen said. "I've got some cold beer for us."

Jensen had the beer in a bucket of water. They sat in his bedroom.

"There's a house a quarter of a kilometer this way," Jensen

said, pointing in the Tunis direction, "but there's nothing in it, and I wouldn't trust the owner to put anything in it, no matter what he says. There's a sink, but no loo. Workmen still creeping around. Forty dinars a month, I'm sure I can get him down to thirty, but I think that's out. Now the couple of rooms below me are free. Thirty dinars a month. There's a little stove there, about like mine, and there's a sink and a sort of bed. Want to see it? I got the key from old Gamal." Gamal was Jensen's landlord.

Ingham went downstairs with Jensen. The door was just to the right of the hole-in-the-floor toilet, which projected from the wall. The larger room was next to the street, with one rather high arched window on the street. A door opposite the street led into a small square room with two windows, both on the tiny court—which had the virtue of not being overlooked, Ingham had noticed. This room had a good-sized sink and a two-burner stove on a low wooden table. The bed was a flush door, or so it appeared, with a thin mattress resting on three wooden fruit crates. Presumably white, the interior was not really white but gray with dirt, and tan in patches where the paint had been knocked off. A crumpled khaki blanket lay on the door-bed. There was an ashtray full of cigarette butts on the floor.

"Is someone sleeping here now?" Ingham asked.

"Oh, one of Gamal's nephews or something. He'll throw him out quickly enough, because he isn't paying anything. Is this all right or—is it too tatty?" Jensen asked with a facetious swish.

"I suppose it's okay. Is there any place where I could buy a table? And a chair?"

"I'm sure I can get something. I'll put the people next door onto it."

So the deal was on. Ingham was optimistic. The bedroom door had a padlock that could be switched on a chain from inside to outside. His front door key would be the same as Jensen's. They'd have the same awful john, but as Jensen pointed out, it had at least a door, which Jensen had put on himself. Ingham felt a little safer being so close to Jensen. If something went wrong, if he had an invader, at least he had an ally within shouting distance. Ingham said he would like to move in Monday, and he gave Jensen fifteen dinars to give Gamal to clinch the thing. Then Ingham drove on to the Reine.

It would be just his luck, Ingham thought, to run into OWL as he was taking his typewriter from the car to the bungalow. He even wanted to look around, from his car, and if he saw OWL to postpone removing the typewriter, but he felt ashamed of his queasiness, and at the bungalows' parking place stopped his car, and without a look around at all, opened the other door and took his typewriter out. He locked his car, then walked to his bungalow. OWL, evidently, was not around at the moment.

Monday would leave time, he thought, to give the hotel decent notice, to find a table and chair, and to write, perhaps, another ten pages on his novel. Last night, oddly enough after his disturbing conversation with Adams, Ingham had thought of a title for his book, *The Tremor of Forgery*. It was much better than two other ideas he had had. He had read somewhere, before he left America, that forgers' hands usually trembled very slightly at the beginning and end of their false signatures, sometimes so slightly the tremor could be seen only under a microscope. The tremor also expressed the ultimate crumbling of Dennison, the dual-personality, as his downfall grew imminent. It would be a profound yet unrealized crumbling, like a mountain collapsing from within, undetectable until the complete crash—because Dennison had no pangs of conscience which he recognized as such, and hardly any apprehension of danger.

Ingham went over and spoke to the hotel, and asked them to make up his bill through Sunday. Then he went back to his bungalow and answered, in a rather gay tone, Reggie Muldaven's letter. He said he didn't know what Ina was up to, and that she had shown a strange disinclination to write to him. He said he had started a novel. And of course he expressed regret at Castlewood's suicide. Then Ingham worked and did eight pages between 3 and 6, when he went for a swim. He felt, for some reason, extremely happy. It was pleasant, first of all, to have a little money, to be able to send a check for a rather expensive apartment in New York every month, to be staying at a comfortable hotel here, and to think nothing of the cost. Money wasn't everything, as OWL might say (or would he?), but Ingham had known the mind-pinching torment of being even slightly short of it.

He met Jensen by appointment at the Plage around 8, and they had a drink before going to Melik's. Jensen said the family next door had promised to find a table by tomorrow. A chair was a little more difficult, and they might have to scout the souk or buy or borrow one from Melik. Jensen had only one.

"Don't sit next to any English," Ingham said as they climbed the steps to Melik's terrace. "I'd like to talk to you."

They shared a table with two shirt-sleeved Arabs who talked constantly to each other.

Ingham said, "What do you think? Adams went on with it last night. He said the people in the bungalow behind me heard the yell, plus a clatter, plus a door being shut. Slammed. Imagine OWL going to the trouble to quiz the neighbors? Like Inspector Maigret."

Jensen smiled. "What do you call him?"

"OWL. Our way of life. The American Way. He's always preaching it, or haven't you noticed? Goodness, Godness—and democracy. They'll save the world."

The couscous looked better than usual, as to meat.

"Last night, I denied hearing anything except the yell," Ingham went on. "I denied having opened my door." Jensen so patently took Abdullah's death as no more important than a flea's death, Ingham found that he could speak more lightly of it himself now, even practically lie about it with ease.

Jensen smiled, and shook his head as if in wonderment that anyone could spend so much time on such an unimportant matter.

Ingham tried to amuse Jensen further. "Adams is trying the soft treatment, à la Porfyrivitch—or the English investigators. 'I see that you're not telling the whole truth, Howard. You'll feel better if you do, you know.'"

"What do the French people behind you say?"

"They've left. A pair of Germans there now, man and wife, I presume.— And you know, Anders, last night I was on the brink of telling OWL the truth? As you say, so what? What could he do? Gloat? Because he's solved a mystery? I don't think it would bother me."

"He couldn't do a thing, not a thing. Are you talking about

the machinery of justice? Bugger it. The last thing this country wants is to bring the thieves and the tourists face to face—in a court, that is.— Americans are funny."

The next day, Ingham moved one suitcase into his new quarters, and he and Jensen went to the souk to buy a few things, a couple of bathtowels, a broom, some cooking pots, a little mirror to hang on the wall, a few glasses, cups and saucers. The family next door had come up with a table, not very big but of the right height and sturdy. The chair was more difficult, but Jensen persuaded Melik to part with one of his for a dinar five hundred millimes.

On Monday morning, Ingham moved in. He had wiped the kitchen shelf down, so it was reasonably clean. He was not at all fussy. It was as if he had shed, suddenly, his ideas about cleanliness, spotless cleanliness, anyway, and of comfort also. A fruit crate was his night table, the ceiling light his reading light, causing him to move the head of his bed under it, if he wanted to read in bed. His second blanket, the steamer rug, rolled up, served as a pillow. Any dirty clothes, Jensen told him, could be laundered by the teenaged girl of the family next door.

On Monday and Tuesday, Ingham wrote a total of seventeen pages. Jensen lent him three canvases of Ingham's choice. Ingham had not chosen the disemboweled Arab, because Jensen seemed to like to live with it, and Ingham found it disturbing. He borrowed a picture of the Spanish fortress, very roughly painted, pale sand in foreground, blue sea and sky behind. Another picture was of a small boy in a jubbah sitting on a white doorstep, the boy looking round-eyed and abandoned. The third picture was one of Jensen's orange chaoses, and Ingham could not tell what it was, but he liked the composition.

Ingham went daily to the Reine's main desk and to the bungalow headquarters for post, though he had written his agent and Ina his new address—15 Rue El Hout. Once he saw Mokta and bought him a beer. Mokta was amused and amazed that Ingham had moved where he had. Mokta knew the street.

"All Arabs!" Mokta said.

"It is *interesting*." Ingham smiled also. "Very simple."

"Ah, I believe it!"

The air-conditioner Ingham had applied for had never appeared, Mokta had not mentioned it, so Ingham didn't.

On Wednesday, Ingham invited Adams for a drink. He gave one of Melik's boys a couple of hundred millimes in exchange for a tray of ice cubes. Ingham stood on the street to meet Adams and to guide him to the house. Adams looked around with interest as they walked through the narrow alleys. The Arabs had almost stopped staring at Ingham, but a few of them stared at Adams now.

Ingham had turned his work table into a cocktail table. His typewriter and manuscript, papers and dictionary were arranged neatly on the floor in a corner.

"Well! It's certainly simple!" Adams said, laughing. "Practically bare."

"Yes. Don't bother with compliments on the décor. I'm not expecting any." He extricated what was left of the ice from the tray, put some in a couple of glasses, and put the ice back into the metal tray because it was cooler.

"How're you going to get along without a refrigerator?" asked Adams.

"Oh, I buy things in small tins and finish them. I buy a couple of eggs at a time."

Adams was now contemplating the bed.

"Cheers," Ingham said, handing Adams his drink.

"Cheers.— Where's your friend?"

Ingham had told him his apartment was below Jensen's. "He's coming down in a few minutes. He's probably working. Sit down. On the bed, if you like."

"Is there a bathroom?"

"There's a thing outside in the court. A toilet." Ingham hoped that Adams wouldn't want to have a look at it. A few minutes ago, he wouldn't have cared, Ingham realized.

Adams sat down. "Can you work here?" he asked dubiously.

"Yes. Why not? Just as well as at the bungalow."

"You should be sure you get enough food. And *clean* food. Well—" He lifted his glass again. "I hope you'll like it here."

"Thank you, Francis."

Adams looked at Jensen's orange chaos. It was the only picture of the three that was signed. Adams smiled and jerked his head to one side. "That picture makes me hot just looking at it. What is it?"

"I don't know. You'll have to ask Anders."

Jensen came down.

"Any news of your dog?" Adams asked.

"No."

Their conversation was dull, but friendly.

Adams asked for how long Ingham had rented the rooms, and what they cost. There was no ice for their second drink. Jensen finished his second rather quickly, and excused himself, saying he was still at work upstairs.

"Any news from your girl?" Adams asked.

"No. She's just had time to get a letter of mine. Today probably."

Adams looked at his watch, and Ingham suddenly remembered that today was Wednesday, that Adams had to be home this evening for his broadcast. Ingham was a little relieved, as he did not want to go out to dinner with Adams.

"I was in Tunis yesterday," Adams said. "Saw a nasty word written in Arabic on a tailor's shop—probably a Jewish shop."

"Oh?"

Adams chuckled. "I didn't know what the word meant, but I asked an Arab. The Arab laughed. It's a word that doesn't bear repeating!"

"I'm sure the Jews have a hard time just now," Ingham said, feebly. The picture of "Arabia Aroused" in *The Observer* one Sunday had been enough to scare the hell out of anyone: a sea of open, yelling mouths, of raised fists, ready to smash anything.

Adams got up. "I should be getting back. It's Wednesday, you know." He drifted toward the door. "Howard, my boy. I don't know how long you're going to stick this out."

He was near enough to the open door to have seen the toilet, Ingham realized. Jensen had just used the toilet, and he never shut the door when he came out. "I don't find it bad at all—in this weather."

"But you can't be very comfortable. Wait till you want an ice-cold lemonade—or just a good night's sleep! You seem to be punishing yourself with this—'going native'. You're living like a man who's broke, and you're not."

So that was it. "I like a change now and then."

"There's something on your mind—something bothering you."

Ingham said nothing. Ina was maybe bothering him, vaguely. But not Abdullah, in case Adams was thinking of that.

"It's no way for a civilized man, a civilized writer to do penance," Adams said.

"Penance?" Ingham laughed. "Penance for what?"

"That's within yourself to know," he said more briskly, though he smiled. "I think you'll find all this primitiveness just a waste of time."

And who was he to talk about wasting time, Ingham thought, with his hours of fish-spearing, never catching anything? "I can't say it's that if I'm working, which I am." Ingham immediately hated that he'd begun to justify himself with Adams. Why should he?

"It's not your cup of tea. You're going against the grain."

Ingham shrugged. Wasn't the whole country against his grain, wasn't it a foreign country? And why should everything he did be *with* his grain? Ingham said pleasantly, "I'll walk down with you. It's easy to lose the way."

16

IN THE next week, Ingham's thoughts took a new and better turn in regard to his novel. He was sure his change of scene, uncomfortable as his two rooms actually were—the worst was the lack of a place to hang clothes—was responsible for the jogging of his thoughts. Dennison, being mentally odd, was not to experience a collapse when his embezzlement was discovered. And the people whom he had befriended, nearly all of whom were responsible and successful men themselves now, came to his assistance and repaid whatever money Dennison had given them. Since Dennison had himself been investing embezzled money for twenty years, his appropriations had trebled. His infuriated employers at the bank, therefore, might have lost the earnings of three-quarters of a million dollars over twenty years, but they could get the $750,000 back. What would justice do then? Therefore, the title *The Tremor of Forgery* wasn't fitting. It might almost do, but since Dennison never trembled to any extent worth mentioning, Ingham felt it wasn't right. It was Ingham's idea to leave the reader morally doubtful as to Dennison's culpability. In view of the enormous good Dennison had done in the way of holding families together, starting or helping businesses, sending young people through college, not to mention contributions to charities—who could label Dennison a crook?

Ingham was only sorry to part with the title.

Between paragraphs, Ingham often walked up and down his room in his blue terry-cloth robe, which he soaked in cold water and wrung out, over a pair of underpants. It was cooler than anything else. It also seemed less silly, in this neighborhood, than shorts and a short-sleeved shirt. None of the Arab men wore shorts, and they must know the coolest garb, Ingham thought. Jensen had kidded him: "Are you going to buy yourself a jubbah next?"

Usually Jensen had dinner with him, or he with Jensen upstairs. It didn't much matter, as they shared dishes and food, and the table situation was the same for both of them. One or the other had to clear away his work. Ingham liked eating with someone every night, it was a little thing to look forward to while he worked, and with Jensen, he did not have to make an effort, either in cooking or conversation. There were evenings when Jensen chose to say hardly a word.

Ingham had some odd moments when he would be deep in his book and get up to walk about the room in his detestable but cool heelless slippers. A transistor would be wailing somewhere, an Arab woman shouting at a child, a peddler hawking something, and now and again Ingham caught a glimpse of his own stern face in the mirror he had hung on the wall by the kitchen door. His face was darker and thinner, different. He was at these moments conscious (as he had been when suffering the gripes at the bungalow) of being alone, without friends, or a job, or any connection with anybody, unable to understand or to speak the main language of the country. Then, being more than half Dennison at these moments, he experienced something like the unconscious flash of a question: "Who am I, anyway? Does one exist, or to what extent does one exist as an individual without friends, family, anybody to whom one can relate, to whom one's existence is of the least importance?" It was strangely like a religious experience. It was like becoming nothing and realizing that one was nothing anyway, ever. It was a basic truth. Ingham remembered reading somewhere about a man from the Eastern Mediterranean who had been taken away from his village. The man had been nothing but what his family, his friends, and his neighbors had thought he was, a reflection of their opinion of him, and without them he had collapsed and had a breakdown. And whatever was right and wrong, Ingham supposed, was what people around you said it was. That was truer than all OWL's babble about the American Heritage.

It seemed to be OWL's point that one carried around a set of morals one had been brought up to believe in. But was it true? To what extent did they remain, to what extent could one act on them, if they were not the morals of the people by whom one was surrounded? And since this was not entirely off the subject of Dennison, Ingham would drift back to his typewriter and begin writing again almost at once. He had a bit more than two hundred pages. In his second week in his rooms, he enjoyed a good streak of work.

Then on a Friday, an express letter came from Ina. Ingham had not thought of her, in regard to getting a letter from her, for several days, but now he realized (rather automatically, out of habit) that she might have written him at least five days ago, if she had immediately answered his letter telling her his new address. He read:

Aug. 8, 19—

Dearest Howard,

Your change of address was a surprise. You sound as if you'll be there for some time and I suppose that is what is surprising. Anyway you mentioned a month. I'm glad, by the way, the book is going well.

I am mopey and restless and it can't be helped, or I can't help it. Anyway, I thought I would fly over to see you. I have two weeks and I'm pretty sure I can wangle three. I want very much to see you—and if we both fight like cats and dogs, or if we both say it's all off, then I can go on to Paris. But you don't seem inclined to move from that place and I do want badly to see you. I have a reservation for Pan-Am flight 807, arriving Tunis Sun. Aug. 13 at 10:30 A.M., your time. A night flight. If you want me to bring you anything, wire me.

I hope this isn't too much of a surprise. I just couldn't go off to Maine or Mexico and convince myself I'd be enjoying it. I wish I could say something amusing. But here's one New York remark in case you haven't heard it: "Some of my best friends are Arabs."

I hope to see you at the airport in Tunis. If you can't make it for some reason, I'll find my way to Hammamet.

My love, darling,
Ina

Ingham was bowled over. Ina here? In these rooms? Well, for Christ's sake, no, she'd flip. He would find her a hotel room, of course.

Sunday. Day after tomorrow. Ingham wanted to run up and tell Jensen. But Jensen had never heard of Ina.

"Damn it," Ingham said softly, and walked around the table with the letter in his hand. He thought he should go at once to the Reine to see about a room. August was a rather crowded month.

Ingham locked the street door lest the *fatma*—their vague cleaning girl who turned up more or less twice a week at any time that suited her—should come in now. He took a bucket shower in the vicinity of the toilet. The bucket was always under the tap, catching a drip. Ingham had tried to turn the tap on once, and found it so impossibly difficult, or perhaps it was already turned on full, that he had given it up.

"What's the hurry?" Jensen called from his upstairs window.

"Oh, was I hurrying?" Ingham slowed up, replaced the bucket under the tap, and walked casually into his room, drying himself.

Ingham got a room with bath at the Reine de Hammamet for Sunday afternoon. Their last one, said the clerk, but Ingham doubted that. It was a double room, two dinars eight hundred with taxes and breakfast, for one. Ingham felt slightly better with that accomplished. He walked out to his car, not even bothering to ask for any post that they might not have delivered.

That day he worked, but not with such concentration as usual.

It was Melik's that night. Ingham invited Jensen.

"Another contract?" asked Jensen.

"No. But I think I've got only two more weeks' work till I finish my first draft."

It was not difficult, after all, to say that he had a friend named Ina Pallant, aged about twenty-eight, coming on Sunday. Jensen was not the kind to ask questions like, "Is she a girl friend?"

Jensen said simply, "Oh? What's she like?"

"She works for the Columbia Broadcasting System. Television. She's a script editor, also a writer herself. Very talented. Quite nice looking, blondish."

"Has she been here before?"

"I don't think so."

Then they talked of other things. But Ingham knew it was all going to come out when Ina was here. He was too close—also physically where they lived—for Ingham to hope to keep the essentials from him.

Ingham said, "I think I told you that the man I was supposed to work with here—an American—committed suicide in New York."

"Yes. You did tell me that."

"Ina knew him, too. He was in love with her. She broke it off. So he killed himself. But they— From what Ina told me, John had been in love with her just for a couple of weeks. At least, Ina knew about it only a couple of weeks before he killed himself."

"How strange!" Jensen said. "Is she in love with you?"

"I don't know. I honestly don't."

"Are you in love with her?"

"I thought I was when I left New York. When she wrote me about John, she told me she'd been very fond of him—for a time. I don't know." It sounded like a mess, Ingham supposed. "I don't want to bore you. That's the end of it. I thought I'd tell you."

Jensen bared his front teeth and slowly extricated a fishbone. "It doesn't bore me. She must be coming here because she loves you."

Ingham smiled. "Yes, maybe. Who knows? I booked a room for her at the Reine."

"Oh. She wouldn't stay with you?"

He laughed suddenly. "I doubt it!"

17

THE TUNIS air terminal presented a confused picture. Vital direction signs vied with aspirin advertisements, the INFORMATION desk had no one at it, and several transistors, carried by people walking about, warred with louder music from the restaurant's radio on the balcony, absolutely defeating the occasional voice of a female announcer, presumably giving planes' arrival and departure times. Ingham could not even tell if the announcer was speaking in French, Arabic or English. The first three uniformed (more or less) people he asked about flight 807 from New York referred him to the bulletin board where flights were announced in lights, but ten minutes after Ina's plane was due, nothing had been said about it. It wasn't like Ina to have made a mistake, Ingham thought as he lit his third cigarette, and just then 807 flashed on: from New York, arriving at 11:10. A bit late.

Ingham had a café-cognac standing up at the bar counter of the balcony restaurant. There were some thirty white-clothed tables and a buffet table of cold cuts near the big windows which gave on the airfield. Ingham was amused to see two clusters of waiters, four in each group, chatting in corners of the room, while irate people half rose from their untended tables, clamoring for service. Ina was going to be entertained, no doubt of that!

He saw her through a half-glass fence or wall which he was not allowed to pass. Ingham raised an arm quickly. She saw him. She was in a loose white coat, white shoes, carrying a big colorful pocketbook and a sack which looked like two bottles of something. There was a passport check at booths on the left. She was only ten feet from him.

Then she rushed into his arms, he kissed her on both cheeks, then lightly on her lips. He recognized the perfume that he had forgot.

"Did you have a good trip?"

"Yes. All right. It's funny to see the sun so high."

"You haven't seen any sun till you see this one!"

"You look so brown! And thinner."

"Where's your luggage? Let's get that settled."

In less than ten minutes, they were in Ingham's car, the two suitcases stowed in back.

"Since we're in Tunis—practically," Ingham said, "I thought we'd have lunch there."

"Isn't it early? They fed us—"

"Then we'll go and have a drink somewhere. Some air-conditioned place. Do you think it's awfully hot?"

They went to the air-conditioned Hotel Tunisia Palace and had a drink in the plushy red barroom.

Ina looked well, but Ingham thought there were some new lines under her eyes. She had probably lost sleep in the last days. Ingham knew what it would be like, winding up her office work, plus her tasks in the Brooklyn Heights household, which were formidable. He watched her small, strong hands opening the pack of Pall Malls, lighting one with the strange looking matchbook from New York, dark red with an Italian restaurant's name printed on it in black.

"So you like it here?" she asked.

"I dunno. It's interesting. I've never seen a country like it.—Don't judge by this bar. It might as well be Madison Avenue."

"I'm eager to see it."

But her eyes looked eager only for him, only curious about him, and Ingham looked down at the matchbook in his fingers. Then he faced her eyes again. She had blue eyes with flecks of gray in them. Her cheekbones were a trifle broad, her jaw small, her lips well-shaped, determined, humorous, intelligent, all at once. "I took a hotel room for you in Hammamet," he said. "On the beach. Where I was first, the Reine de Hammamet. It's very pretty."

"Oh." She smiled. "Your place isn't big enough? Or are you living alone, by the way?" she added through a laugh that sounded more like her.

"Ha! Am I alone? What else? My place is small and definitely on the primitive side, as I told you. Well, you'll see."

They spoke of Joey. Joey was about the same. There was a girl called Louise, whom Ingham had never met, who came to see Joey a couple of times a week. Louise and Joey were in love, in a crazy, frightened way, Ingham gathered. It was very sad. Joey would never marry the girl, though Ina said Louise would be willing. Ina had told Ingham about Louise before. She was twenty-four, and this had been going on for two years. Now Ina only touched lightly on it, to Ingham's relief. He could not have embarked now on sympathetic remarks about Joey and Louise.

He took her to the restaurant on the other side of the Avenue Bourguiba, where the ceiling fans, and the patio beyond, gave a certain sense of coolness.

"This is one of two restaurants that John recommended," Ingham said. "His recommendations were very good, all of them."

"You must have been flabbergasted at the news," Ina said.

"Yes, I was." Ingham looked at her across the table. She had combed her hair in the hotel, and the marks of the comb showed in the dark-blond, dampened hair at her temples. "Not so flabbergasted as you, I suppose—finding him. Good God!"

She said slowly, like a confession, "The most awful moment of my life. I thought he was asleep. Not that I expected to see him there at all. Then—" She was suddenly unable to speak, but not from tears. Her throat had tightened. She looked into space somewhere beyond Ingham's shoulder.

He had never seen her like this. Surely part of it was the strain of the trip, he thought. "Don't try to talk about it. I can imagine.— Try this Tunisian starter. Turns up on every menu."

He meant the antipasto of tuna, olives, and tomatoes. Ingham had persuaded her to have scallopine, on the grounds that couscous was all too prevalent in Hammamet.

They took long over lunch, and had two coffees and many cigarettes. Ingham told her about Jensen and a little about Adams.

"And that's all the people you've met?"

"I've met others. Most of the people here are just tourists, not too interesting. Besides, I'm working."

"Did you hear from Miles Gallust, by the way?"

Gallust was the producer, the man who might have been the producer, of *Trio*. Typical of Ina to remember his name, Ingham thought. "I had a letter in early July. He regretted and all that. I only saw him once, you know. Briefly."

"So this trip is costing you something. Hiring a car and so forth."

Ingham shrugged. "But it's educational. John gave me a thousand dollars, you know, and also paid the plane fare."

"I know," said Ina, as if she knew quite well.

"The country isn't wildly expensive. Anyway, I'm not broke."

Ina smiled. "That reminds me. You know your story 'We Is All'?"

"Of course I do."

"It's winning a prize. First Prize for the O. Henry Awards. In the yearly prize story thing."

"Really? You're joking!" The story had appeared in a little quarterly somewhere, after many a rejection.

"I'm not joking. I have a friend on the committee of judges or whatever it is, and he knows I know you, so he told me on condition I wouldn't tell anyone—else, that is."

"What does that mean? A money prize or what?"

"Money? I don't know. Maybe just distinction. It *is* a good story."

Yes, it was a good story, based on Ingham's imagining the life, or the periodic crises, of one of his friends in New York who was schizophrenic. "Thank you," Ingham said quietly, but his face was warm with pride, with a shyness born of sudden glory.

"Are you sure my luggage is safe in the car?"

Ingham smiled. "Reasonably. But what a sensible question! Let's take off."

When they drove off from the restaurant, Ingham stopped and bought some day-old papers and the Saturday-Sunday edition of the Paris *Herald Tribune*. Then they drove on toward Hammamet.

"Are you tired?" he asked.

"I don't know. I should be. What is it? Nine in the morning to me, and I've been up all night, more or less."

"Get some sleep this afternoon. What do you think of this view?"

The blue gulf was on their left, in full sunlight. It spread low and wide, and looked as if it covered half the earth.

"Quite terrific! And goodness, it's warm!" She had removed her white coat. Her blouse was flower-patterned and sleeveless.

At last Ingham said, "Here's Hammamet!" and realized his joyous tone, as if he were saying, "Here's home!"

They left the wider road—a trio of camels was strolling along the verge, but Ina did not seem to notice them—and rolled onto the dusty asphalt that curved into the village.

"This doesn't look like much," he said. "The town's mainly a lot of little Arab houses and fancy hotels, but they're all on the beach, the hotels. Ahead."

"Where do you live?"

"To the left. Just here." They were passing his street. Ingham saw Jensen between their alley and the Plage, heading for the Plage, no doubt. Jensen, with his back toward Ingham and his head down, did not see him. "I'm sure you'd like to go to your hotel room before you see my place."

"Oh, I don't know."

But they were rounding the curve now toward the beach hotels.

"What a marvelous castle!" Ina said.

"That's an old fort. Built by the Spanish."

Then they were at the Reine, going through the broad gates, rolling onto crunchy gravel between tall palms, bougainvillea, and sturdy little grapefruit and lemon trees. It *was* rather spectacular. Ingham felt a surge of pride, as if he owned the place.

"This looks like an old plantation!" Ina said.

Ingham laughed. "Massa's a Frenchman. Wait till you see the beach." Ingham ran directly into Mokta as he was opening the front door. "Have you got two minutes, Mokta?"

Mokta was for once empty-handed. "*Mais oui, m'sieur!*"

Ingham introduced him to Mlle. Pallant, and explained that Mokta worked at the bungalows. Mokta got the key to number eighteen, and helped them with the luggage.

The room was lovely, with a window on the sea, and a door that went onto a good-sized whitewashed terrace with a curving white parapet.

"It's really terribly pretty!" Ina said.

The sun was sinking on their right, into the sea, and looked unnaturally huge.

"I'm dying for a shower," Ina said.

"Go ahead. Shall I—"

"Can you wait for me?" She was unbuttoning her blouse.

"Sure." He had brought the newspapers and wanted to look at them.

"So you're picking up Arabic?"

Ingham laughed. "You mean what I said to Mokta? 'Thank you, see you soon'? I don't know *anything*. What's so irritating is, words are spelled differently in different phrase books. 'Asma' is sometimes 'esma'. And 'fatma'—" Ingham laughed. "I thought at first it was our cleaning girl's name, a form of Fatima. Turns out to mean 'girl' or 'maid.' So just yell 'fatma' if you want the maid here."

"I'll remember that."

A flowery scent of soap drifted out to Ingham, but it was not steamy. No doubt she was taking a cool shower. Ingham stared at the Paris *Herald Tribune*.

Ina came out wrapped in a large white towel. "You know what I'd like to do?"

"What?"

"Go to bed."

Ingham got up. "How nice. You know that was what I was wanting, too?" He put his arms around the towel and her and kissed her. Then he went and locked the door.

He locked also the tall shutters onto the terrace.

This time it was all right. It was like former times, like all the times with Ina. It erased the silly memory of the girl from Pennsylvania, and made Ingham think that that minor mishap had been due to the fact that he loved only Ina. She adored him. She was a lovely size in bed. Why had he been so insane all these past weeks, Ingham wondered. Why had he thought he didn't love her? They smoked a cigarette, then embraced each other again. And twenty minutes after that, Ingham could have begun all over.

Ina laughed at him.

Ingham smiled, breathless and happy. "As you see, I've been saving myself for you."

"I begin to believe you."

Ingham reached for the telephone. He ordered champagne on ice, in French.

"Aren't you going to get dressed?"

"Partially. The devil with them." He got out of bed and put on his trousers. Then his shirt which he did not at once button. He had a malicious desire to ask, "Was John any good in bed?" He repressed it.

Ina looked beautiful, hands behind her head, face sleepily smiling at him, eyes half closed, satisfied. Under the sheet she spread her legs and brought them together again.

Ingham drew with contentment on his cigarette. Was this what life was all about, he wondered. Was this the most important thing? Was it even more important than writing a book?

"What are you thinking?"

Ingham fell down beside her on the bed and embraced her through the sheet. "I am thinking—you are the sexiest woman in the world."

There was a knock on the door.

Ingham got up. He tipped the waiter, then gave him a couple of dinars and a lot of change, which the waiter said would pay for the champagne.

"To you," Ingham said, as he lifted his glass.

"To you, darling—and your book. Do you like it?"

"I suppose I like it or I wouldn't be writing it. It's a theme that's been done before, but—"

"But?"

"I hope to say something else, something different.—I'm not so much interested in the story as in people's moral judgements on the hero. Dennison. I mean people in the book. Well, readers, too. And in Dennison's opinion of himself." Ingham shrugged. He didn't want to talk about it now. "It's funny, of all the books I've written, you could say this is the least original, yet it interests me as much as any of them have."

Ina set her glass on the night table, holding the top of the sheet over her breasts with the other hand. "It's what you put into it. Not how original the theme is."

That was true. Ingham didn't say anything. "I'll leave and let you sleep. We can have dinner as late as nine or so. Do you think you'd like dinner in the hotel or at a crummy—well, Arab place in the town?"

"An Arab place."

"And—would you like to meet Jensen or would you rather be alone?"

Ina smiled. She was on one elbow. She had just the beginning of a double chin, or a fullness, under her jaw, and Ingham thought it charming. "I wouldn't mind meeting Jensen."

Ingham left the Reine in a glow of happiness, on the wings of success. And he had not forgotten the prize, the kudos or whatever it was, coming to him from the O. Henry Award thing.

18

JENSEN WAS out when Ingham got home at 5:30. He was either at the Plage or taking a walk along the beach, Ingham thought. Ingham straightened up his rooms a little, gave them a sweep, then went out with the double purpose of finding Jensen and buying some flowers. Flowers in a vase, even if the vase was a glass, would look nice on his table, he thought, and he reproached himself for not having had flowers in Ina's room awaiting her. But how could he have known that the afternoon would turn out as well as it had?

Ingham was about to go into the Plage, when he saw Jensen walking slowly up from the beach, barefoot, carrying something that at first Ingham thought was a child: a long dark object which he held in both arms. Jensen plodded forward, blond and thin, like some starving Viking landed after a shipwreck. Ingham saw that what he carried was a big piece of wood.

"Hey!" Ingham called, approaching him.

Jensen lifted his head a little in acknowledgement. His mouth was open with his effort.

"What's that?"

"A log," Jensen said. "Maybe for a statue. I don't know." He gasped and set it down. It was water-logged.

Ingham had an impulse to help him, but he was in a good shirt, and his mind was on flowers.

"Not very often one finds a nice piece of wood like this. I had to go into the water for it." The legs of Jensen's levis were damp.

"I'm bringing my friend over at eight. I hope you can join us for dinner. Can you?"

"Okay. Sure. Do I have to get dressed up?"

"No. I thought we'd go to Melik's.— Do you know where I can pick up some flowers? Just a few cut flowers?"

"You can try the souk. Or maybe the jasmine guy's at the Plage." Jensen smiled.

Ingham pulled his fist back as if to hit him. "I'll be home in a few minutes," said Ingham, and walked off to the left, in hopes of seeing a flower vendor sitting on the pavement between here and the little Hammamet bank. Ingham couldn't find any flowers, and gave it up after ten minutes. He twisted off a couple of pine twigs from the trunk of a tree by the beach, and at home stuck them in a glass of water. They looked insanely nordic. Once more, he put his typewriter and papers on the floor. Then he took off his shirt and trousers and flung himself on his bed and slept.

He awakened feeling happier than when he had left the Reine, though a little dopey in the head from the heat. He took a bucket shower in the court. He was now expert at saving the right amount of water to get the soap off. He might introduce the revolutionary idea of two buckets, since the one bucket was often overflowing. He had been correct, the tap didn't come on any farther, but he could always draw water from the kitchen sink.

Ingham went to Melik's and reserved a table for between quarter of 9 and 9. Then he drove on to pick up Ina. Ina was downstairs in the Reine's lobby, sitting on a big sofa, smoking a cigarette. She was in a pink sleeveless dress with a big, cool-looking green flower printed on the dress above one breast.

"I'm not late, am I?" Ingham asked.

"No! I'm just looking over the people." She got up.

"Did you have a nap?"

"I had a swim *and* a nap. The beach is divine!"

"I forgot to say, you can get demi-pension here if you prefer. You might like lunch or dinner here, I don't know."

"I don't want to be pinned down just yet."

Ingham stopped the car in the usual place near Melik's, and asked Ina to wait a minute. He ran up the steps to the terrace. He had arranged to pick up ice. Then Ingham went back to Ina with the ice tray, locked his car, and they walked into the first narrow alley.

Ina looked around, fascinated, at everything. And the Arabs, what few there were in the alley, or leaning in doorways, looked back at her, wide-eyed and faintly smiling.

Ingham stopped at his door, a door like many others, except that his was closed and most were open.

"I must say it looks like the real McCoy!" Ina said.

Ingham was glad the toilet door was not open. "This is

where I work. And also sleep," Ingham said, letting her precede him into his room.

"*Really?*" said Ina, in a tone that sounded amazed.

"A little Robinson Crusoe, maybe, but actually I don't need any more than this." His mind was on getting her to sit down in the most comfortable place—the bed. He now had a dark red pillow that one could lean against, but only if one slumped, as the bed was rather wide.

Ina wanted to see the kitchen. "Reasonably neat," she said, still smiling, and Ingham felt that his tidying had been worthwhile. "And I suppose it's dirt cheap."

"Two dollars a day," Ingham said, coping with the ice now.

"And the john?"

"Well, that's just an outside thing. In the court. I have to wash here." The ice fell into the sink and at the same time he cut his thumb slightly on the metal grill of the tray. "Scotch and water? I have soda."

"Water's fine. Whose paintings are these?"

"Oh, those are Anders'. Do you like them?"

"I like the abstract. I'm not so fond of the little boy."

"I didn't tell him you liked painting." Ingham smiled, happy that Ina and Jensen would have something to talk about. "Here, darling."

She took her drink and sat down on the door-bed. "Oof!" she said, bouncing a little, or trying to. "Not exactly springy."

"The Arabs aren't much for beds. They sleep on mats on the floor."

Ina wore pale green earrings. Her hair was shorter. It waved naturally, and she wore it without a part. "A strange people. And just a little frightening. By the way, were there any repercussions here after the war? Or during it?"

"Yes, quite a few. Cars overturned in Tunis, windows of the American Information Service library busted right in the middle of town. I didn't—"

Jensen appeared in the doorway, and knocked. He was in his green trousers, a clean white shirt.

"Anders Jensen, Miss Pallant. Ina."

"How do you do," Ina said, looking him over, smiling, not extending a hand.

Jensen made an abortive bow. "How do you do, Miss—Ina."

He could sometimes look like an awkward, well-meaning sixteen-year-old.

"Fix you a stone," Ingham said, going to the kitchen. Jensen was amused by the adjective "stoned," and he often called a drink a stone. Ingham heard Ina ask:

"Have you been here a long time?"

Ingham brought Jensen his drink, a good big one.

They talked about Jensen's paintings. Jensen was pleased that she had noticed them, and that she liked the orange abstract. Ina did not mention her brother. Jensen said he was working now on a sand picture, inspired by the trip he and Ingham had made to Gabes.

"We slept out on the sand," Jensen said. "There wasn't any storm as in my picture, but one gets a very close view with one's eyes—at sand level."

The conversation rolled on pleasantly. Ina's quick eyes took in everything, Ingham felt, Jensen's white leather shoes, their uppers perforated, his thin hands (yellow paint under one thumbnail), his profoundly troubled face that could look tragic and merry and tragic again in a matter of seconds. Ina's forehead grew shiny with perspiration. Ingham hoped there was a breeze on Melik's terrace. She fished a gnat out of her second, iceless, drink.

"The insects here are alcoholic," Jensen said, and Ina laughed.

At Melik's, it was couscous, of course. Ina thought the place charming. The canary was in good voice. There was also a flute, not too loud, and a breeze, faint but still a breeze.

"Are women *allowed* here?" Ina asked softly, and Jensen and Ingham laughed. "They have such funny laws. Where are the women?"

"Home cooking their own dinner," Jensen said. "And these men—they've probably spent the afternoon with their girl friends, and after dinner they will visit other girl friends and finally go home—where their wives are also pregnant."

This amused Ina. "You mean, it doesn't cost much to have a lot of girl friends? These fellows don't look exactly affluent."

"I think Arab women dare not say no. I dunno. Don't ask me," said Jensen with a languid wave of a hand. He looked into space.

"Not wearing your cuff-links?" Ina said to Ingham.

Ingham was wearing very ordinary cuff-links he had bought in Tunis. "I thought I wrote you. I had a slight robbery at the Reine. In my bungalow. They took my stud box with everything I had like that—all my cuff-links, a tie pin, a couple of rings." The robbery had included his gold wedding ring, Ingham suddenly realized.

"No, you didn't mention it," Ina said.

"Also a pair of shoes," Ingham said. "I was sorry about those cuff-links. I loved them."

"I'm sorry, too."

"You'd better— Well, it's perhaps safer in the hotel where you are," Ingham said, "but if you have anything valuable, you might as well put it in one of your suitcases and lock it."

Jensen listened, expressionless.

"Thanks for the tip," Ina said. "I'm pretty lucky, usually. But then I've never been in old Araby before. They're not famous for—" She smiled and looked at Jensen. "What's the opposite of thievery?" She turned to Ingham. "You mentioned a canvas jacket you'd lost. I know you're fond of old clothes, darling, but that thing—I remember it."

"Yes. Oh, that was out of my car, a different matter." Ingham thought of the old Arab in red pants, and shifted in his chair.

"That was Abdullah," Jensen put in.

"You even know them by name?" Ina laughed. "What a place! You must point out Abdullah to me some time. He sounds like something out of the Arabian Nights."

"We hope Abdullah is no more," Jensen said.

"Oh, he got his comeuppance?" Ina asked.

"We hope so and we think so," Jensen said.

"Did somebody knife him?"

Jensen was silent for a moment, and Ingham felt relieved, because it meant Jensen at least knew he should not blurt out the bungalow story. Then he said, "It seems somebody defended their property for once, and knocked the bastard over the head."

"How fascinating!" Ina said, as if she were listening to a synopsis for a television play. "How did you hear?"

"Oh—via the grapevine." Now Jensen laughed.

"You mean he was killed?"

"He simply isn't around any more."

Ingham could feel Ina's lively interest in the story. She was about to say something else, when Adams appeared at the end of the terrace and stood looking around for a table. Ingham at once got up. "Excuse me a minute."

Ingham asked Adams to join them, and as they walked toward the table Ingham saw that Ina and Jensen were talking again.

"Ina," Ingham said, "I'd like you to meet my friend Francis Adams. Ina Pallant."

"How do you do, Mr. Adams?" Ina looked very pretty smiling up at Adams, shaking his hand.

"How do you do, Miss Pallant! How long are you going to be here?" Adams asked.

"I'm not sure. A week, perhaps," she replied.

That was cautious, Ingham thought. He signaled to one of Melik's sons to come and take Adams' order.

Adams ordered in Arabic.

"You've been here quite a while, Howard told me," Ina said.

"Yes, more than a year now. I like the climate—as long as one has air-conditioning. Ha-ha!" OWL smiled happily. "But you've got to tell me all about the States. I haven't been home for a year and a half. All I read is *Time* magazine and the *Reader's Digest* and a paper from Paris or London now and then."

"What would you like to know? I'm usually holed up in my office, then underground to Brooklyn. I'm not sure I *know* what's going on any more."

"Oh—the racial thing. And the Vietnam War. And—well—the spirit, the atmosphere. You can't get that out of a newspaper."

"Um." Ina smiled a little at Ingham, then looked back at Adams. "We're having another hot summer, as far as racial riots go. And the Vietnam War—well! I think the opponents are getting better and better organized. But I'm sure you read that, too."

"And how do you feel, just as an ordinary citizen?"

"As an ordinary citizen, I think it's a waste of time, money and people's lives," Ina said. "Not a waste of money to everybody, of course, because war always lines a few pockets."

Adams was silent for a second or two. His lamb dish was served. Ingham filled his wine glass.

"Are you in favor of the war?" Ina asked Adams.

"Oh, yes," Adams said with assurance. "I'm anti-Communist, you see."

Ingham was pleased that Ina did not bother saying, "So am I." She simply looked at Adams with mild curiosity, as if he had said he was a member of the American Legion or something—which he might well be, Ingham supposed.

Jensen yawned widely, covering it with a large thin hand, and stared off into the blackness beyond the terrace.

"Well, we'll win, of course—even if only technically. How can we lose? But to talk of something more pleasant, what are your travel plans while you're here?"

"I haven't made any yet," Ina replied. "What do you suggest?"

OWL was full of ideas. Sousse, Djerba, a camel ride on the beach, a visit to the ruins of Carthage, a lunch at Sidi Bou Said, a visit to a certain souk, in a town Ingham did not even know of, on its market day.

"I hope I can get around to some of these places by myself," Ina said. "I think Howard wants to work. He doesn't have to entertain me."

"Oh?" Adams smiled his pouchy squirrel smile at Ingham. "After all your weeks of solitude, you haven't time to show a pretty girl around the country?"

"I haven't said a thing about wanting to work," Ingham said.

"I'll be happy to drive you about a bit, if Howard's busy," Adams told her.

"And I can show you the Spanish fort," Jensen said. "My trouble is, I have no car."

Ingham was pleased that everybody was getting on well. "But tomorrow is mine," Ingham said.

They went to take coffee at the Café de la Plage. Ina loved the Plage. It looked "real," she said.

When it was time to say good night, Adams insisted that Ingham bring Ina back to his bungalow for a nightcap. Jensen went home. OWL left in his Cadillac.

"Anders is a little sad these days because of his dog," Ingham said. He told her what had happened.

"Goodness, that's too bad.— I didn't know they were mean like that."

"Just some of them," Ingham said.

Ina was enchanted with OWL's bungalow, as Ingham had thought she would be. Adams even showed her his bedroom. The closet was of course closed, and Ingham knew locked, though the key was not in the door.

"A little home away from home," Adams said. "Well, I have no home any more in the States. I still own the Connecticut house." He pointed to the photograph in the living room. "But practically everything's in storage now, so the place is empty. I suppose I'll retire there one day."

After one drink, Ina said she was exhausted and had to turn in. Adams was instantly sympathetic, and had to figure out exactly what time it would be for her—"7:15 yesterday." He almost kissed her hand as they said good night.

"Howard works too hard. Make him get out a little more. Good night, both of you!"

When they were in the car, Ingham asked, "What do you think of him?"

"Oh, a classic!" She laughed. "But he looks happy. I suppose they always are. It's the best of all possible worlds and all that."

"Yes, exactly. But I think he's a little lonely. His wife died five years ago.— I know he'd get a bang out of it if you'd spend a day with him—or part of a day, let him take you out to lunch somewhere." Ingham meant it completely, but at once he thought of OWL telling her the Abdullah incident, the events of that night, and he felt uneasy. He did not want Ina to hear the details, even the few details Adams thought he knew. What purpose would it serve? It was only depressing and ugly. Ingham drove the car onto the graveled area before the front doors.

"What's the matter, darling?"

"Nothing. Why?" Could she read his thoughts that well, Ingham wondered, in the dark?

"Maybe you're as tired as I am."

"Not quite." He kissed her in the car, then he walked with her into the lobby where she got her key. He promised to call for her tomorrow, but not before 10.

Jensen was still up when Ingham got home. "She looks like a good sport," was Jensen's comment on Ina.

That was probably pretty high praise, from Jensen, Ingham thought, and as such he appreciated it.

19

INGHAM AND Ina went to Sousse the next day, looked at the American battleship at the dock, and drank cold beer (it was frightfully hot) at the café where Ingham had once sat alone. Ina was fascinated by the souk. She wanted to buy some straw mats, but said she couldn't take them on the plane. Ingham said he would post them, so they bought four of varying sizes and design.

"Meanwhile," Ina said, "you can use them on your floors. Hang one on a wall. It'll improve the place!" She bought a big glazed earthenware vase for him, and a couple of ashtrays, and for herself a white fez.

The fez was extremely becoming.

"I won't wear it here. I'll wait till New York. Imagine! A good-looking hat for a dollar and ten cents!"

Ina's enthusiasm changed the country for Ingham. Now he enjoyed the toothy grins of the Arab shopkeepers, and the bright eyes of the kids who begged millimes from them. Ingham suddenly wished he were married to Ina. It could be, he realized. It was only for him to ask, he thought. Ina hadn't changed. John Castlewood might as well not have been.

"We could go to Djerba tomorrow," Ingham said during their lunch. He had taken her to the best restaurant he could find, as she had said she didn't want to eat at a hotel, no matter how good the food might be.

"Your friend Adams is taking me somewhere tomorrow. Tomorrow morning."

"Oh? He made a date last night?"

"He rang me up this morning just before ten."

"Oh." Ingham smiled. "Okay, I'll work tomorrow then."

"I wish you had a telephone."

"I can always ring you. From Melik's or the Plage."

"Yes—but I like to talk with you at night."

Ina had rung him a few times late at night from her house in Brooklyn. It had not always been easy, because the telephone was in the living room in Brooklyn. "I could be there in person.— Can I, tonight?"

"All night? You don't want to be there for breakfast, do you?"

Ingham said no more. He knew he would go back to her room with her tonight. And not stay for breakfast.

The day went on like a pleasant dream. There was no hurry about anything. They did not have to meet anyone. They went to the Fourati for dinner, and danced a little afterward. Ina was a good dancer, but not very fond of dancing. Two Arab men, in neat western clothes, asked Ina to dance, but she declined them both.

It was quite dark at their table on the open terrace. The only light came from the half moon. Ingham felt happy and secure. He could sense Ina's question, "Is it really the same as before? Have you really no resentments?" and yet Ingham thought it wasn't the right thing for him to make a speech about it.

"What are you thinking?" she asked. "About your book?"

"I was thinking I love you as much out of bed as in."

She laughed softly, only a nearly silent breath, or a gasp. "Let's go home. Well—to the hotel."

While Ingham was trying to catch the waiter's eye, she said: "I must get you some more cuff-links. Do you think they have any good ones here? I'd like to buy Joey some, too."

When he left Ina that night at a little after 1, Ingham wished that he was sharing her room with her. He wished there might be a second room where he could work in the daytime, of course. Then he thought of his primitive two rooms awaiting him in the Rue El Hout tonight and tomorrow, and he was glad he had those. There was time, he thought. He realized he was a little giddy with fatigue and happiness.

He worked fairly well the next day and produced eight pages. But in his short breaks from the typewriter, he did not go on thinking about his book, but about things like, "Would Ina stay on the two or three weeks she had, or would she take off for Paris after a week?" and "Ought he to pack up and go back to the States when she did? If not, why not?" Or "If he brought up the subject of marriage, just when should he do it?" and "Shouldn't they have a more serious conversation (matter of fact, they'd had none) about John Castlewood, or was it wiser never to mention Castlewood?" He came to a conclusion only about the last question: he thought it wasn't for him to bring up, but for Ina, and if she didn't, he shouldn't.

He rang her hotel from the post office at 4:30, and she was not in. Ingham left a message that he would call for her at 7:30. She should be back by then, he thought.

"You're going out tonight?" Jensen asked when Ingham got back. Jensen was washing in the court.

"Yes. Unless OWL keeps her all evening. Want to join us, Anders? I thought we might go to Tunis for a change."

Jensen hesitated as usual. "No, thanks, I—"

"Come on, what's stopping you? Let's find a crazy place in Tunis."

Jensen was persuaded.

Ingham went off at 7:15 to find Ina. He had a funny fan letter to show her which had come that day. A man in Washington State had written him about *The Game of "If,"* which he said he had borrowed from his local lending library, and he praised the book highly, but offered suggestions as to how the ending could have been improved, and his ideas utterly demolished the theme of the book.

Ina was in. She asked him to come up.

She was dressed, putting on make-up in front of the mirror. He kissed her on the cheek.

"I asked Jensen tonight. I hope you don't mind."

"No.— He's awfully quiet." She said it like a criticism.

"Not always. I'll try to make him talk tonight. He's very funny sometimes.— There was a royal wedding somewhere, I think in his own country, and he got fed up with the papers being full of it and said, 'Other people's sexual intercourse is always interesting to the public, but it's absolutely fascinating if the sheets have royal monograms.'" Ingham laughed.

Ina laughed slightly, still leaning toward the mirror.

"It's the dry way he says it. I can't do it."

"He's queer, isn't he?"

"Yes. I told you.— Is it so obvious? I didn't think so."

"Oh, women can always tell."

Because homosexuals showed no interest in them, Ingham supposed. "What'd you do with OWL today?"

"Who?"

"OWL. Our Way of Life Adams."

"Oh. We went to Carthage. Took a look at Sidi— What is it?"

"Sidi Bou Said."

"Yes." She turned from the mirror, smiling. "He certainly knows a lot. About history and things. And the coffeehouse in Sidi is fascinating! The one up the steps."

"Yes. Where they're all lounging on mats like Greeks. I hope OWL doesn't scoop me on everything there is to show you."

"Don't be silly. I didn't come here for tourism. I came to see you." She looked at him, not rushing into his arms, but it was more important to Ingham than if she had kissed him.

She was the woman he was going to marry, Ingham thought, and live with for the rest of his life. Ingham was about to break the spell—which he felt intolerably full of "destiny"—by whipping out the fan letter, when she said:

"By the way, is that story about Abdullah true? That he got killed on the hotel grounds here?"

"I don't know. Nobody's got the facts, as far as I know."

"But you heard him scream, Francis said. He said it was on your terrace."

Had OWL mentioned the slamming door? Probably. Adams had perhaps told her about the French hearing something fall, too, the clatter. "Yes, I heard it. But it was two in the morning. Dark."

"You didn't look out?"

"No."

She was looking at him questioningly. "It's interesting, because it seems the Arab disappeared since that night.— Do you think another Arab killed him?"

"Who knows?— Abdullah wasn't liked by the other Arabs. I'm sure they're great at grudge fights." He thought of telling her about the Arab with the cut throat, but decided against it, because it was a sensational story and nothing more. "I saw something odd one night by the Café de la Plage. One Arab was a bit drunk. They pushed him out the door. He stood on the sand a long while, just staring back at the door, with such a look of determination—as if he'd get the guy sometime, whoever it was. I'll never forget the way he looked."

Ina's silence after a few seconds bothered him. He thought, suppose she finds out the truth, from Jensen, for instance? Then he would be a liar, and a coward also, in her eyes. Ingham had an impulse to tell her the truth before another half minute went by. Was it so bad?

"You look worried."

"No," he said.

"How'd your work go today?"

"All right, thanks.— I love the new mats."

"No use living like an ascetic.— You know, darling, if that Arab was hacked to pieces or something, don't be afraid I'll faint. I've heard of atrocities before, mutilations and all that. Was that what happened to him?"

"I never saw the guy that night, Ina. And the hotel boys won't say what they did with him.— Maybe Adams knows something that I don't." A vague idea that he was sparing her a nasty story sustained him a little. "Let's go. I said I'd pick Anders up."

At his and Jensen's street, Ingham jumped out of the car and ran toward the house. He was some ten minutes late, though he knew Jensen wouldn't mind, and probably hadn't noticed. Ingham shouted from the court, and Jensen came down at once.

"Ina thinks you don't talk enough, so try to talk a little more tonight," Ingham said.

They went to the Plage, where scotch was available, too. Jensen had his boukhah. Ina had tried it and did not like it. Ingham thought he was stared at more than usual that evening. Or was it because he was with a pretty woman? Jensen did not seem to notice the staring. Only the plump young barman was smiling. By now he knew Ingham.

"You enjoy your visit, madame? . . . Are you here for a long time?" the barman asked Ina in French. "Not too hot?"

They were standing at the bar.

Ina seemed to appreciate his friendliness.

During dinner at Melik's, Jensen made an effort and asked Ina about her life in New York, and this got Ina onto the subject of her family. She mentioned her two cosy aunts, one widowed, one who had never married, who lived together and came to dinner on Sundays. She told him about her brother Joey, didn't dwell on his illness, but talked mainly about his painting.

"I shall remember his name," said Jensen.

Ina promised to send Jensen a catalogue from his last exhibition, and Jensen wrote his Copenhagen address for Ina, in case he was no longer in Hammamet when she sent it.

"My parents' address, but I have no flat just now," said Jensen. "I'll be in touch with Howard, in case I leave."

"I hope so," Ingham said quickly. "I'll leave before you, no doubt."

Ingham did not like the idea of parting company with Jensen. Ingham looked at Ina, who was watching them both. Ingham thought she was in a rather strange mood tonight.

"Do you go back to a job in Copenhagen?" Ina asked.

"I paint scenery sometimes for the theatres. I get along. But I'm lucky, my family can give me a little every month." He shrugged indifferently. "Well, they don't give it, it's mine from an inheritance. No hardship to anybody." He smiled at Ingham. "I shall soon see what fresh blood has flowed into our bustling little port."

Ingham smiled. He realized that with Ina gone, with Jensen gone, and with his book finished except for polishing and retyping, he would be insufferably lonely. Yet he did not want to set a date when he would leave. Unless, of course, he arranged something specific with Ina, made plans to be with her in New York. They might marry, might look for an apartment together. (His wasn't big enough for two.) It wasn't necessary for her to live forever in the Brooklyn Heights house in order to take care of Joey, Ingham thought. *Something* could be arranged there.

"Would you like to visit the fortress tomorrow morning?" Jensen asked Ina. "If you would like a walk along the beach, it is not far from the hotel, especially if we break the walk with a swim."

Jensen arranged to call for her at 11. He left after coffee.

Ingham thought Jensen had done quite well that evening, and waited for Ina to say something favorable, but she did not. "Want to take a walk along the beach?" he asked. "What kind of shoes are you wearing?" He looked under the table.

"I'll go barefoot.— Yes, I'd like that."

Ingham paid the bill. Jensen had left eight hundred millimes.

The sand on the beach was pleasantly warm. Ingham carried Ina's shoes and his own. There was no moon. They held hands, as much to stay together in the darkness as for pleasure, Ingham thought.

"You're a little triste tonight," Ingham said. "Does Anders depress you?"

"Well, he's not the soul of mirth, is he?— No, I was thinking about Joey."

"How is he—really?" It gave Ingham a twinge of pain to ask it, and yet he felt the question sounded heartless.

"He has times when he's so uncomfortable, he can't sleep. I don't mean he's any worse." Ina spoke quickly, then was silent a few seconds. "I think he should marry. But he won't."

"I understand. He's thinking of Louise.— Is she really intelligent?"

"Yes. And she knows all about the disease." Ina's steps grew more plodding in the sand, then she stopped and flexed the toes of one foot. "The funny thing—the awful thing is, he thinks he loves me."

Her grip on his hand was light, no grip at all. Ingham pressed her fingers. "How do you mean?" They were almost whispering.

"Just that. I don't know about sexually. That's ridiculous. But it seems to force anybody else out of his—affections or life or whatever. He should marry Louise. It isn't impossible that he could have children, you know."

"I'm sure," said Ingham, though he hadn't been sure.

Ina looked down at her feet. "It doesn't exactly give me the creeps, but it worries me."

"Oh, darling!" Ingham put his arm around her. "What—what does he say to you?"

"He says—oh, that he can't ever feel for another woman what he feels for me. Things like that. He's not always mopey about it. Just the opposite. He's cheerful when he says it. The thing is, I know it's true."

"You ought to get out of that house, darling.— You know, the house is big enough for you to get someone to live in, if Joey needs—"

"Oh, Mom could take care of him," Ina said, interrupting him. "Anything he needs—and it's really only making his bed. Matter of fact, he's done that several times. He can even get in and out of the tub." She laughed tensely.

Yes. Joey had his own quarters on the ground floor, Ingham remembered. "You should still get out, really, Ina.— Darling, I didn't know what was troubling you tonight, but I knew something was."

She faced him. "I'll tell you something funny, Howard. I've started going to church. Just the last two or three months."

"Well—I don't suppose it's funny," Ingham said, though he was thoroughly surprised.

"It is, because I don't believe in any of it. But it gives me comfort to see all those—grayheads, mostly, listening and singing away and getting some kind of comfort from it. You know what I mean? And it's just for an hour, every Sunday." Her voice was uncertain with tears now.

"Oh, *darling!*" Ingham held her close for a minute. A great unspeakable emotion rose in him, and he squeezed his eyes shut. "I have never," he said softly, "felt such a tenderness for anyone as I do for you—this minute."

She gave one sob against his shoulder, then pushed herself back, swept the hair back from her forehead. "Let's go back."

They began walking toward the town, toward the palely floodlit fortress—monument of some battle plainly lost, at some time, or else the Spaniards would be there.

Ingham said, "I wish you'd talk to me more about it. About everything. Whenever you feel like it. Now or any time."

But she was silent now.

She must get out of that house, Ingham thought. It was a cheerful looking house, nothing gloomy or clinging-to-the-past about it, but to Ingham it was now a most unhealthy house. It was now that he should propose something positive, he thought. But it was not the moment to ask if she would marry him. He said suddenly, stubbornly, "I wish *we* lived together somewhere in New York."

Rather to his surprise and disappointment, she made no answer at all.

Only near his car, she said, "I'm not much good tonight. Can you take me back to the hotel, darling?"

"But of course."

At the hotel, he kissed her good night, and said he would find her somewhere after her tour of the fortress with Jensen.

When he got home, Jensen's light was off, and Ingham hesitated in the court, wanting very much to waken him and speak with him. Then Jensen's light came on, as Ingham was staring at his window.

"It's me," Ingham said.

Jensen leaned on the sill. "I wasn't asleep. What time is it?" he asked through a yawn.

"About midnight. Can I see you for a minute? I'll come up."

Jensen merely pushed himself back from the sill, sleepily. Ingham ran up the outside stairs.

Jensen was in his levi shorts, which fitted his thin frame loosely. "Something happen?"

"No. I just wanted to say—or to ask—I hope you won't say anything tomorrow to Ina about Abdullah. You see, I told her the story I told Adams, that I didn't even open my door."

"No. Well, all right."

"I think it might shock her," Ingham said. "And just now she has problems of her own. Her brother—the one she was talking about who's a cripple. It's depressing for her."

Jensen lit a cigarette. "All right. I understand."

"You didn't tell her anything already, did you?"

"What do you mean?"

It was always so vague to Jensen and so clear to Ingham. "That I threw the thing that killed him—my typewriter."

"No, I didn't say that. Not at all."

In spite of Jensen's casualness, Ingham knew he could count on him, because when Jensen had said, "It just—doesn't—matter," he meant it. "The fact is—and I admit it—I'm ashamed of having done it."

"Ashamed? Nonsense. Catholic nonsense. Rather, Protestant." Jensen leaned back on his bed and swung his brown legs up on the blanket.

"But I'm not particularly a Protestant. I'm not anything."

"Ashamed yourself—or of what other people might think of you?"

There was a hint of contempt in "other people." "What other people might think," Ingham answered. The other people were only Adams and Ina, Ingham was thinking. He expected Jensen to point this out, but Jensen was silent.

"You can count on me. I won't say anything. Don't take it so seriously." Jensen put his feet on the floor in order to reach an ashtray.

Ingham left Jensen's room with the awful feeling that he had gone down in Jensen's estimation because of his weakness, his cowardice. He'd been truthful with Jensen, beginning with their talk on the desert. But it was funny how guilty he felt, how shaky with Jensen, though he knew he could trust Jensen even with a few drinks in him. Jensen was not weak. Ingham suddenly thought of the scared looking, but flirtatious and seductive Arab boy who was sometimes loitering in the alley near the house, who always said something in Arabic to Jensen. Twice Ingham had seen Jensen dismiss him with an annoyed wave of the hand. Jensen had used to go to bed with him occasionally, Jensen had said. The boy looked revolting to Ingham, mushy, unreliable, sick. Despite all that, Jensen was not weak.

20

INGHAM COULD not get to sleep. It was oppressively hot and still. After a bucket shower, he was damp with sweat again in a matter of minutes. Ingham did not mind. He was used to the discomfort by now. And his thoughts entertained him. He was thinking of Ina, and he was filled with tenderness and love for her. It was a large, all-enveloping feeling, taking in all the world, himself, all the people he knew, everyone. Ina was its center and in a way its source. He thought of her not only as an attractive woman, but in terms of her background and what had made her. She had told him she felt neglected in her childhood, because Joey, being ill from birth, had captured all her parents' affections and attentions. She had tried to do very well in school—this was in Manhattan, where the family had lived then—in order to call attention to herself. She had finally gone to Hunter College and made excellent grades, majoring in English composition. She had been in love with a Jewish boy when she was twenty, a boy more or less approved of by her family (he had been a post-graduate student of physics at Columbia, Ingham remembered), but his family had made Ina feel uncomfortable, because they strongly disapproved, at the same time saying that their son had a right to lead his own life. Nothing had come of the love but a few months of heartache for Ina, and a slightly lower mark when she graduated than she would have got, she had told Ingham, if it had not been for the break-up. Before that, at fifteen, she had had a terrible crush on a girl a little bit older, a girl who was really queer, although doing nothing about it at that time. Ingham smiled a little at that, at the bitter suffering of adolescence, the loneliness, the inability to talk to anyone. Everyone had such experiences, and somehow at twenty-five, at thirty, they became forgotten—like rocks in a stream which had to be swum over, causing pain and wounds, yet which the unconscious knew were to be expected, and so like birth pains, perhaps, the agony was not even vividly remembered. And then there was her marriage of a year and a half to that brilliant playwright Edgar something (Ingham was pleased that he had forgotten his last name) who had turned out to be a tyrant, who had drunk erratically, and had struck Ina a few times, and who had been killed in a car accident a couple of years after her divorce.

And now, Ina loved him, and she loved her brother Joey, and she had turned to the church for some moral support and perhaps for some kind of guidance. (How *much* had she turned to the church, he wondered.) But what kind of guidance did the church ever give except to counsel resignation? Stop sinning, of course, but if one were in an awful predicament with husband, family or whatever—or if the problem was poverty, for instance—the church's advice was to resign oneself to it, Ingham felt, and he was reminded of the Arabic religion, uncomfortably.

His thoughts veered away from that and returned to Ina. He was glad he and she were old enough to know the importance of tenderness, to have lost some of the selfishness and self-centeredness of youth, he hoped. They were two worlds, similar but different, complex yet able to explain themselves to each other, and he felt they had something to give each other. He recalled a few paragraphs he had written in his notebook, in preparation for the book he was writing, about the sense of identity within the individual. As it turned out, he had used none of them in his book, but it was always that way. He wanted very much to read some of these notes to Ina, to see what she would think of them, what she would say. One note, he remembered, he had copied from a book he had been reading. It concerned underprivileged children in an American primary school. The children had had no joy in life or in learning. All of them lived in crowded homes. Then the school had given each child a small mirror in which he could see himself. From then on, each child began to realize that he or she was an individual, different from everyone else, someone with a face, an identity. The world of each child had changed then.

All at once, Ingham felt acutely the pressure of Joey's tragedy on Ina now, the sadness his disease must cause in her whenever she looked at him—or thought of him—even in the best of moments. And now the mysterious and perhaps insolvable problem of Joey's attachment to her. This onus, this pain, was like something which crept up behind Ingham's back and leapt upon him, sinking its claws. He sprang out of bed.

He had an impulse to go straight to Ina now, to comfort her, to tell her that they would be married—maybe to *ask* her, but that was a technicality—to stay with her the rest of the night talking and making plans until the Tunisian dawn came up. He looked at his wristwatch. Eighteen minutes past 3. Could he even get into the hotel? Of course, if he banged on the door hard enough. Would she be annoyed? Embarrassed? But what he had to say was important enough to cause a disturbance in the night. He hesitated. Wasn't it weak, even fatal somehow, to doubt whether he should go or not?

Ingham decided that he shouldn't go at this hour. If Ina had been in a house alone, yes. It was the hotel part.

He cheered himself up by thinking about tomorrow. He would see her at lunch. He'd tell Jensen he wanted very much to see Ina alone at lunch, and Jensen wouldn't mind. And then Ingham would talk about all this, and he would talk also about their marrying. He would fly back with her, or at least very soon after she left, and they would look for an apartment in New York and maybe in less than a month from now, she would be out of that Brooklyn house and living in an apartment in Manhattan with him. That was a very exciting plan. He went back to bed, but it was at least half an hour before he fell asleep.

Ingham awakened at 9:30, and found that Jensen had already left the house. Ingham had intended to offer to drive him to the Reine, though he doubted if Jensen would have accepted. Now he would have to keep an eye out for them, if he expected to see them before lunch, Ingham supposed. He worked in the morning, mainly polishing and retyping messy pages in his manuscript, but just before 12:30, he wrote two new pages. Then he put on white dungarees and a shirt, and went down to the Café de la Plage.

He was happy to see Ina and Jensen sitting at a table over glasses of *vin rosé*. "Knock-knock," Ingham said, approaching them. "Can I crash in? Did you have a nice morning?"

They looked as if they had been talking seriously for some minutes before he arrived. Jensen dragged a chair over from another table. Ina's eyes moved all over Ingham—his face, his hands, his body—in a way that pleased him, and she was absently smiling.

"Is the fort interesting?" Ingham asked her. "I haven't been inside."

"Yes! Nobody there. We could wander around anywhere," she said.

"Not even ghosts," said Jensen.

It was soon evident Jensen was not going to leave. They went to Melik's, and all of them had yoghurt, fruit, cheese and wine, because it was too hot for anything else. Ina might enjoy a siesta, Ingham thought. He might go back with her to the hotel, and they could talk there. Jensen got the bill and asserted his right to pay it, as he wanted to take Ina to lunch. Then he excused himself.

"I'm going to work for a while—after a nap, that is. Did Fatma turn up?"

"Not this morning," Ingham said.

"Damn. If she turns up this afternoon, I think I'll send her away. Do you mind?"

"Not a bit," Ingham said.

Jensen left.

"What's your fatma like," Ina asked.

"Oh—about sixteen. Barefoot. Always a big smile. She doesn't know much French. Her favorite activity is turning the tap on the terrace. She just stands there watching the water run and run. Sometimes we give her money to buy food and wine. There's never any change from it. Whatever we give her is 'exactly enough.'" Ingham laughed.

Ina looked as if she were not listening, or was not interested.

"Tired, darling? I'll take you back to your hotel. It's so damned hot—I thought you might like a siesta. Maybe with me."

"Do you think we'd sleep?"

Ingham smiled. "I had some things I wanted to talk to you about." He wished he'd brought his notebook along, but he hadn't, and he wasn't going to the house for it. "Matter of fact, I almost came storming over to see you last night. At three thirty. I even jumped out of bed."

"A bad dream? Why didn't you come over?"

"Not a bad dream! I hadn't been to sleep. I was thinking about you.— You know, darling, you could come back to my place. We could have a nap there."

"Thanks. I think I'd rather go back to the hotel."

She'd be of course much more comfortable at the hotel, Ingham realized. But he had the feeling she disliked his place, maybe thought it sordid. He felt a vague defensiveness about his two rooms, even though she had not yet specifically attacked them. They were, after all, the sanctum of his work just now, and as such they were rather hallowed to Ingham. "All right. Let's go, darling."

He drove her to the Reine de Hammamet. The desk clerk handed her a telegram.

"That's fast communication," Ingham said, wondering whom it could be from.

"I cabled the office," Ina said. "This is from them."

Ingham waited while she read it, watched her start to frown, and saw her lips move in an inaudible "Damn."

"I've got to cable something back," she said to him. "I won't be long."

Ingham nodded, and went to look for a newspaper.

"What was it?" he asked when she was finished.

"It's about a copyright. I told them the story was in the clear, but they were still worried, so they asked me where to look. They want to check it. It's all very tedious."

Ina took a cool shower, then Ingham asked if he could do the same. The cool, not too cold water felt like heaven. It was a treat also to be able to reach for Ina's scented soap in the niche, to slip it back. There was even a huge unused white towel which he appropriated.

"Ah, delicious," he said when he came out in the towel, barefoot.

"You know, Howard—" She was lying on the bed, propped up, smoking. "It'd be nice if you had a bungalow. Why don't we take one—or two," she added, smiling.

Ingham emphatically did not want to take a bungalow. "Well, *you* could—provided they're not full up. Did you ask?"

"Not yet. But your place is so uncomfortable, darling, let's face it. That john! And you're not broke, I don't know why you do it."

"For a change. I got tired of my bungalow."

"What's there to get tired of? Good kitchen and bath, everything simple and clean. Francis says you can get an air-conditioner."

"I wanted to see how the Arabs live, buy stuff in the market and all that."

"You can see how they live without doing it. It's bloody uncomfortable the way they live. I saw a lot of them this morning, walking with Anders back of the fort."

"Isn't that a fascinating section?" Ingham smiled. "The thing is, I'm working so well now where I am. I just think of it as a place to work, you know. I wasn't intending to be there more than a month."

"Francis thinks you're punishing yourself."

"Oh? I think he said that to me, too. Sounds strangely Freudian for OWL. Anyway, he's a bit wrong. When did he say this to you, by the way?"

"I ran into him on the beach this morning. Rather he hailed me—from afar. He was out in the water. I went for an early swim. So we sat on the sand and talked for a while." She laughed. "He looks so funny with those flippers and that spear, and that waterproof cap with a *visor*. Do you know he swims with it under water?"

"Yes, I know."

She was silent a moment, then, "You know, he says you're not telling the whole story about that night Abdullah was killed. On your terrace, Francis says."

"Um-hum," Ingham said, sighing. "First of all, no one knows if he was killed or not. No one's seen a body.— Adams is acting like an old maid snoop about this. Why doesn't he call the police in, if he's so concerned?"

"Well—don't get worked up about it."

"Sorry." Ingham lit a cigarette.

"Is that why you moved?"

"Of course not.— I'm still on good terms with OWL. I moved—because of something I wanted to discuss with you, matter of fact. Or tell you about. It has to do with the book I'm writing. Essentially, it's whether a person makes his own personality and his own standards from within himself, or whether he and the standards are the creation of the society around him. It has a *little* to do with my book. But I found that since being here in Tunisia, I think about these things a lot. What I mean is—the opposite of authoritarianism. And I speak mainly of morals—I suppose. My hero Dennison makes his own, you see. But granted he's cracked."

Ina was listening in silence, watching him.

"There were moments here in Hammamet, days and weeks, in fact, when I hadn't any letters from you or from anybody, and I felt strange even to myself, as if I didn't know myself. And part of it, perhaps—I know from a moral point of view —was that the Arabs all around me had different standards, different ethics. And they were in the majority, you see. This world is theirs, not mine. You know what I mean?"

"And what did you do about it?"

He laughed. "One doesn't *do* anything. It's like a state. It's a very troubling state.— But in a way, it was quite good for my book, I think. Because it's concerned a little with the same thing."

"I don't think my moral values would change, living here. I'd really love some plain ice water."

Ingham went at once to the telephone and ordered it. Then he said, "Not necessarily change, but you might find them hard to practise if no one around you were practising them, for instance."

"Give me an example."

Ingham for some reason balked, though there was any number of examples he might have given. Petty chiseling. Or having a wife and as many mistresses as one could afford, because everyone else was enjoying the same pleasure, and to hell with what one's wife felt about it. "Well—if one's been robbed five or six times, there might be an impulse to rob back, don't you think? The one who doesn't rob, or cheat a little in business deals, comes out on the short end, if everybody else is cheating."

"Hm-m," she said dubiously. At the knock on the door, she waved a hand at him in the direction of the bathroom.

Ingham went into the bathroom. He stared at himself absently in the long mirror beside the tub, and thought he looked rather Roman. His hands were out of sight, clutching the towel from underneath. His feet looked absurd. He was thinking OWL was a bloody meddler. He had alienated Ina, just a little, from him, and for this Ingham detested OWL. If he told Ina about OWL's cockeyed broadcasts, she would know what a crack-pot he was.

"All clear," Ina called.

"Western behavior," Ingham said contemptuously as he came back. "Any woman as attractive as you ought to have five men standing around her room in the afternoons."

Ina smiled. "But why does OWL think you're not telling the whole truth about that night?" She poured water into a glass.

Ingham went to get another glass from the bathroom. "You ask him."

"As a matter of fact, I did."

"Oh?"

"He thinks you threw something or hit the Arab somehow. Did you?"

"No," Ingham said firmly, after only a second's hesitation, mainly from surprise. "I know, he's got a door slamming, boys running around, all kinds of details about that night—considering he's a fair distance from my bungalow."

"But it did happen on your terrace."

"The yell I heard was near." Ingham hated the conversation increasingly, yet he knew if he showed this, it would look a bit odd.

"He said the French people behind you heard a door shut, and they were sure it was your door."

"The French people didn't speak to me about it. Nobody spoke to anybody about Abdullah's disappearance or anything else. Nobody's talking about it except OWL."

Ina's appraising eyes on him bothered him. It was as if OWL had infected her with his own prurient curiosity, like a disease or a fever.

"That Arab might have got the *coup de grâce* from some other Arab," Ingham said, sitting down in an armchair. "OWL thinks the boys dragged him away and buried him somewhere. The hotel boys deny everything. They're hushing it—"

"Oh, no. OWL told me one boy said the Arab hit his head on something. They admitted that much."

Ingham sighed. "True. I forgot."

"You're telling me the whole story. Are you, Howard?"

"Yes."

"I have the strangest feeling you've told Anders something you haven't told me—or OWL."

Ingham laughed. "Why?"

"Oh, you're very close to Anders, face it. You practically live with him. I didn't know you got along so well with queers."

"I don't get along with them or not get along." Ina's words seemed stupid. "I never think any more about his being queer. And by the way, I haven't seen a single boy at his place since I moved in." Ingham at once regretted that. Was abstinence virtue?

She laughed. "Maybe he's in love with you."

"Oh, Ina, come off it. It's not even funny."

"He's very close to you—fond of you. You must know that."

"You're imagining. Honestly, Ina." How could they have arrived *here* in just a few minutes of conversation? He realized it was impossible to ask her this afternoon to marry him. All because of bloody OWL. "I do wish OWL would mind his own business. Has he been farting off about Anders, too?"

"No, not at all. Darling, take it easy. It's just what I see for myself."

"It's not correct. Have you got a bottle of scotch?" She had given him one bottle.

"Yes, in the closet. Back right."

Ingham got it. It had been opened, but only the neck of the bottle was gone. "Like some?" He poured some into Ina's extended glass, then poured for himself. "Anders and I get along, but there's nothing sexual about it."

"Then maybe you don't realize it."

Did she mean on his part, too? Were women *always* thinking about sex, of one kind or another? "Then it's too damned subtle for me," he said, "and if it's that subtle, what does it matter?"

"You don't seem to want to leave him—to take a bungalow."

"Oh, my God, Ina." Was it usual for women to take homosexuals so seriously, he wondered. Ingham had always thought they considered queers nothing at all. Zeros. "I've explained to you, I don't want to move, because I'm working."

"I think the bungalows have a bad association for you. Is that true?" Her voice was gentle.

"Honey—*darling*—I've never seen you like this. You're as bad as OWL! You know me—but you don't seem to understand me at all any more.— You didn't make a single comment when I was trying to explain how I'd felt in this country, this continent, since getting here. Granted, it isn't of world-shaking importance." Ingham felt his heart going faster. He was standing with his drink.

"Have you adopted the Arabian moral code, whatever that is?"

"Why do you ask that?"

"OWL said you told him that Arab's life was of no importance, because he was just a D.O.M."

That meant Dirty Old Man. "I said he was a lousy thief who a lot of people probably wanted out of the way." Ask Anders, he's eloquent on the subject, Ingham wanted to say.

"Abdullah was the one who stole your jacket out of your car, you said."

"That's true. I saw him. I just wasn't close enough to catch him."

"You didn't possibly throw something at him that night like a chair—or your typewriter," Ina said with a slight laugh.

Her smile was amused, reassuring, though Ingham knew he should not be reassured by it. "No." Ingham sighed, as if at the end of an intolerable tension. He wanted to leave. He met her eyes. Ingham felt a distance between them, a sense of separateness. He hated it and looked away.

"Was it Abdullah who took your cuff-links?"

Ingham shook his head. "That was another night. I wasn't in. I dunno who took the cuff-links.— I think I should go and let you sleep." He walked into the bathroom to dress.

She did not detain him.

When he was dressed, he sat beside her on the bed and kissed her lips. "Want a swim later? Around six?"

"I don't know. I don't think so."

"Shall I pick you up around eight? We could go to La Goulette, the fishing village."

This idea pleased her, and since it was some distance away, Ingham said he would call for her at 7.

21

INGHAM WANTED to see Adams. It was 4:45, and Adams was probably on the beach. Ingham drove his car the quarter mile to the sandy lane that led to the bungalows. The bungalows were silent and still in the sunlight, as if everyone were having a prolonged siesta. Adams' black Cadillac was parked in the usual place. Ingham put his car beside it.

He knocked on Adams' door. No answer. Ingham strolled onto the bungalow headquarters' terrace and looked down at the beach. Only three or four figures were visible, and none looked like Adams. Ingham went back to Adams' bungalow, walked to the back where it was shady, and sat down on the kitchen doorstep. Adams' gray metal garbage pail stood a couple of feet away, empty. After a moment or two, Ingham was glad OWL hadn't been in when he knocked, because he realized he had been a little angry. That wasn't the way. The way was to hint, gently, that OWL shouldn't be so prying, shouldn't be putting ideas into Ina's head, ideas that disturbed her. Ingham was cognizant of the fact *he* was lying, in taking this tack. It seemed to him that that was his business, and that no one else had a right to interfere with it. The police, of course, had a right. But the police were one thing, and Adams was another.

Ingham had been sitting, leaning against the kitchen door, perhaps fifteen minutes, when the click of a lock told him that Adams had arrived. Ingham got up quickly, and walked—slowly now—to the front of the house. Adams would no doubt have noticed his car. The front door was shut, and Ingham knocked.

The door opened. "Well, hello! Come in! I saw your car. Nice to see you!" Adams had a shopping net in his hand. He was putting things away in the kitchen. He offered Ingham a drink, or iced coffee, and Ingham asked if he had a Coke. Adams had.

"And how is Ina getting along?" Adams asked. He opened a beer can.

"I think all right." Ingham had not wanted to plunge in, but he thought, why not, so he said, "What've you been telling her about the famous night of Abdullah?"

"Why—what I know about it, that's all. She was curious, asked me all kinds of questions."

"I suppose she did, if you told her you thought I wasn't telling you the whole story. I think you've upset her, Francis." That was it, Ingham thought, knock the ball into his court for a change.

Adams was choosing his words, but it did not take him long. "I told her what I think, Howard. I've got a right to do that, even if I may be wrong." OWL said it dogmatically, as if it were a piece of gospel by which he had always lived.

"Yes. I don't deny that," Ingham said, dropping into the squeaky leather chair. "But it's too bad it upset her. Unnecessarily."

"How do you mean upset her?"

"She began asking me questions. I don't know who the Arab was that night. I never saw his face, and it seems to me only guess-work that it was Abdullah. It's based on Abdullah's apparent disappearance—and to be logical, one should leave open the possibility that he happened to disappear or leave town, and that somebody else hit himself or got hit and yelled—and that nobody at all was killed that night. You see what I mean."

OWL looked thoughtful, but unchanged. "Yes, but you know very well that isn't so."

"How do I know it? You're reasoning on circumstantial evidence and pretty thin evidence."

"Howard, you must have opened your door, at least. You must've looked out of a shutter. The yell woke you up. Anybody's interested enough to wonder where a yell comes from at two in the morning. And the French people said they were sure the door that shut was yours."

His bungalow had been quite close to theirs, Ingham realized. Their bungalow had been only twenty-five or thirty feet from his front door, albeit his front door had been on the other side of his bungalow from them.

"It's no wonder your girl is a little curious, once she knows these facts. Howard—" OWL seemed to be having difficulty, but Ingham let him struggle. "She's a nice girl, a wonderful girl. She's somebody important. It's your duty to be on the square with her."

Ingham had a sick feeling he hadn't experienced since adolescence, when he had looked into some religious books at home, dusty old things that must have belonged to great-grandparents. "Repent your sins . . . bare your soul to Christ . . ." The questions and answers had assumed that everyone had sins, apparently even from birth, but what were they? The worst Ingham had been able to think of was masturbation, but since at the same time he had been browsing in psychology books which said it was normal and natural, what was there left? Ingham didn't consider that what he had done that night had been a sin or a crime—if he had killed the Arab at all, which would always be not quite certain, until someone actually found the corpse.

Ingham said, "I've told you what I know about that night. I don't like it that Ina's bothered by what you told her, Francis. Was it necessary? To spoil part of her pleasure in her vacation like this?"

"Ah, but she knows what I mean," OWL said quietly. He had not sat down. "She's a girl with some moral convictions, you know. Oh, I don't like to use the word 'religious,' but she has some ideas about God, honesty, conscience."

It was curious to think of OWL as a preacher in a pulpit now, barefoot, barelegged, John the Baptist, swinging a copper-colored beer can. "I know what you mean. Yes. Ina's talked to me about going to church of late." Ingham didn't want to admit how little she had talked, and was annoyed that Ina—because OWL had no doubt encouraged her to speak on the subject—had probably told OWL much more than she had told him. "She has quite a cross to bear, you might say, with her crippled brother. She's very fond of him."

"She knows the value of a clear conscience."

So do I, Ingham wanted to say.

"You and Ina should marry," OWL said. "I know she loves you. But you must make peace with yourself first, Howard. Then with Ina. You think you can sweep it under the carpet, put it out of your sight—because you're in Tunisia, maybe. But you're not like that, Howard."

Now OWL was just like any one of his tapes. "Look here," Ingham said, getting up. "You seem to be accusing me of having hit that fellow that night. Maybe killed him. So why don't you just say it?"

OWL nodded, with his second variety of smile, gentle, thoughtful, alert. "All right, I'll say it. I think you hit him with something or threw something—could've been a chair, but it sounded metallic the French said, like a typewriter, for instance—and I think the man died or died later from it. I think you're ashamed to admit it. But you know something?"

Ingham let him pause dramatically, for as long as he wished.

"You're not going to be happy until you make a clean breast of it. Ina's not going to be happy either. No wonder she's troubled! She may be a sophisticated New Yorker, like you, but there's no escaping the laws of God, who rules our being. One doesn't have to be a regular church-goer to know that!"

Ingham was silent. He was a little doped by the words, perhaps.

"And one more thing," said OWL, drifting toward the closed house door, drifting back. "The problem is yours. Within you. The police need never be involved. That's what makes this case so different from most such—accidents. The problem is really yours—and Ina's."

And not yours, Ingham thought. "It's quite true the problem is my own, if there—"

"Oh, you admit—"

"—if there *were* any problem. So I wish, Francis, for my sake or for Ina's sake, you wouldn't keep on at me like this." He spoke with careful mildness. "I'd like to keep our friendship. I can't keep it, if it goes on like this."

"Well!" OWL opened his hands innocently. "I don't know why you say that, if I'm trying to do what I can to make you a happier man—a happier man with the girl who loves you, matter of fact! Ha-ha!"

Ingham suppressed his anger. Wasn't it just as silly to get angry with his words now as to get angry with his tapes? Ingham warned himself not to take it all so personally. Yet here was OWL in person, and OWL's words had been addressed to him, specifically. "I don't think I'd better talk about it any longer," Ingham said, feeling that he was exerting more control than most people would have.

"Aha. Well. That's up to you and your conscience," Adams said, like the voice of wisdom.

It was the last straw for Ingham. The bland, stupid superiority of it was more than he could excuse. He thumped his glass down with the last inch of Coke still in it. "Yes. Well, I'll be going, Francis. Thank you for the Coke."

And the way Adams let him out was also revolting. Holding the door, a slight bow, beaming on Ingham as if on a new convert-to-be whom he had just soused with propaganda, who would go home and let it sink in, and be a little more pregnable the next time. Ingham managed to turn around, smile and wave at Adams in the doorway, before he went to his car.

Now Ingham wanted to talk to Jensen. But he thought it was silly to go running from one to the other. So at home, though he heard Jensen upstairs, Ingham kept to himself. He took off his trousers and flopped on his bed, and looked at the ceiling. Adams would never let up, he thought, but he wasn't going to be forever in Tunisia. He could leave tomorrow, matter of fact, with Ina, if he simply wished to. But alas, it would look like a "retreat," he supposed, and he didn't want to give OWL even this minor satisfaction. Ingham wiped the sweat from his forehead. Just before time to see Ina, he would take a bucket shower. He could walk to the beach a couple of hundred yards away, and take a swim, but he didn't want to.

Ingham sat up with a thought. What had Ina asked Jensen this morning about Abdullah? She had seen Jensen just after her talk with OWL on the beach.

"Hey, Anders!" Ingham called.

"Yup?"

"Want to come down for a stone?"

"Two minutes." He sounded as if he were working.

Ingham got the drinks ready, and when he came back into his larger room, Jensen was standing by the table, looking rather happy. "Had a good day?"

"Pretty good. I want to work tonight."

He handed Jensen his drink. "I just had quite a session with OWL. I feel as if I've been in church."

"How so?"

Ingham remembered he couldn't tell Jensen about OWL's weekly pro-God-and-America broadcasts. That was a pity, because it would have lent humor, and also force, to his story. "He's trying to exert moral pressure on me to admit I conked Abdullah on the head. That doesn't bother me so much as the fact he's filling Ina full of it. He's saying it's got to be me who did it, because it was on my terrace, and only I"—Ingham saw Jensen shaking his head with ennui—"could have done something, and he says I'd better admit it to Ina and make peace with myself."

"Oh, merde and crap," Jensen said. "Has he nothing better to do with his time? So he gave you a sermon." Jensen leaned against the table, propped one bare foot on its toes, and laughed.

"He did, invoking God, making my peace with Him and all that.— What did Ina ask you this morning, by the way?"

"Oh, she asked me—yes—if I thought you hit the old bastard with something." Jensen looked suddenly sleepy. "I ought to take a nap before I work. This stone will help."

Ingham wanted to ask Jensen another question, but was ashamed to. He felt he was becoming as small-minded as OWL. "By the way, OWL and Ina both suggested I might have thrown my typewriter at Abdullah."

Jensen smiled. "Really? Where did you see OWL today?"

"I went to his bungalow. After I'd taken Ina to the Reine. I wanted to ask him to stop bothering Ina with all this."

"You know what you should do, my friend, take her away. I personally would tell Mr. Adams to stuff himself, but I think you are too polite."

"I did tell him to knock it off. What he's really doing is turning her against me. I don't say he means to, but—OWL keeps telling me my conscience bothers me. It doesn't."

Jensen looked unperturbed. "Go with Ina somewhere for a week or so. That's easy.— I got a package from home today. Let me show you." He went up the stairs.

In a moment, he was back with a carton. "Lots of cookies. And this." He removed the tinfoil from a foot-long gingerbread man, decorated with hat, jacket and buttons of yellow icing.

Ingham stared at it, fascinated. It was different from American gingerbread men. This one made him think of icy Scandinavian Christmases, the smell of fir trees, and of flaxen-haired children singing. "That's a work of art. What's the occasion?"

"I had a birthday last week."

"Why didn't you tell me?" Ingham accepted one of the decorated cookies. Jensen said his mother or sister had made them.

"And these," Jensen said, fishing at one side of the box. He pulled out a pair of sealskin slippers, the gray fur outside, ornamented with blue and red embroidery. "Not very appropriate for Tunisia, are they?"

Ingham suddenly had such a desire to see Jensen's part of the world, he could not speak for a moment. He held the slippers in his hand and smelled them—a fresh animal smell, of new leather, and the faintest scent of spice from the cookies they had been packed with.

The evening at La Goulette was neither a great success nor a failure. Ingham had told Ina that he had been to see OWL, because he wanted to tell her before OWL did, but even so—OWL was so quick these days—he was not sure Ina did not already know. She did not.

"I suppose you asked him—not to talk to me any more about the night of Abdullah," she said.

"Well—yes, I did. OWL knows as little about it as anybody else. Well, not *anybody*. The hotel boys know most."

"You've talked with them?"

"I thought I told you I tried to find out something from Mokta. He says he doesn't know anything—about the yell and so forth." It occurred to Ingham that Jensen, speaking his passable Arabic, might learn something from Mokta or the others. The something Ingham was interested in was whether there had been a corpse.

Ina was silent.

"Would you like to go somewhere—like Djerba? I mean, stay at a hotel there? Both of us?"

"But you say you're working—"

"That can wait. You have just a few days here." That brought up the question of whether he would leave with her, Ingham supposed. Nothing was in its right order any more. He had meant to ask her to marry him, to have that settled by now. That would have made their going on to Paris together, when she left, rather a matter of course. Should he talk to her tonight about getting married? Or was she taking that for granted? Ingham glanced around him: they were at an outdoor table of the restaurant where he had eaten the disastrous *poisson-complet.* Waiters with heavy trays yelled at peddlers and begging children to get out of their way. The light was so dim, they had hardly been able to see the menu.

Ingham did not mention marriage that evening. But he did go back with her to her hotel. They had a nightcap in her room, and they spent a couple of hours together. It was almost as wonderful as the first time after she had arrived. Ingham felt a little more serious. Was that good? And he felt a little sad and depressed when he left.

He kissed her as she lay in bed. "Tomorrow at nine thirty," he said. "We'll take a drive somewhere."

22

EIGHT O'CLOCK the next evening found Ingham where he had been the evening before, as far as Ina was concerned. She had enjoyed Sfax, had read about its eleventh-century mosque and the Roman mosaics in his Guide Bleu, but he sensed a reserve in her which took away some of his initiative, or enthusiasm. Ingham found a present for Joey, a blue leather case with loops inside to hold pencils or brushes. They had hired a rather heavy rowboat, and Ingham had rowed around a bit with her. They had gone swimming and lain in the sun.

Ingham had wanted to ask her what kind of church she was going to in Brooklyn. It wouldn't be Catholic, he was pretty sure. Her family was vaguely Protestant. But he could not get the question out. In Sfax, he had bought smoked fish, black olives and some good French wine, and he invited Ina to have dinner with him at home.

Jensen had a drink with them, but declined to stay for dinner. By now, Ingham had more dinner plates and three knives and forks. His salt was still the coarse variety, bought in haste one day, and now it was in a saucer, damp. Ingham had two candles stuck in wine bottles on the table.

He laughed. "Romantic candlelight, and it's so damned hot we have to push them to the very edge of the table!" He pinched one candle out, took a swallow of the good red wine, and said, "Ina, shall we go to Paris together?"

"When?" she asked, a little surprised.

"Tomorrow. Or the next day, anyway. Spend the last part of your vacation there.— Darling, I want to marry you. I want to be with you. I don't want you to go away from me even for a week."

Ina smiled. She was pleased, happy, Ingham was sure of that.

"You know, we could be married in Paris. Surprise everyone when we get to New York."

"Didn't you want to finish your book here?"

"Oh, that! I'm almost finished. I know I keep saying that, but I'm always slow at the end of a book. It's as if I didn't want to end it. But I know the end. Dennison goes to prison for a bit, gets psychiatric treatment, and he'll come out and do the same thing again.— That's no problem." He got up and put his arm about her shoulder. "Would you marry me, darling? In Paris?"

"Can I have a few minutes?"

Ingham released her. "Of course." He was surprised and vaguely disappointed. He felt he had to fill in the silence. "You know—I deliberately never talked to you about John. I didn't talk *much*, I hope. Because I didn't think you wanted to. Isn't that true?"

"I suppose that's true. I said it was a mistake, and a mistake it certainly was."

Ingham's brain seemed to be turning somersaults, turning over facts, choosing none. He felt whatever he might say was of great importance, and he did not want to say the wrong thing. "Do you still love him—or something?"

"No, of course not."

Ingham shrugged, embarrassed, but she might not have seen the shrug, because she was looking down at the table.

"Then what is it?— Or do you want to wait till tomorrow to talk?"

"No, I don't have to wait till tomorrow."

Ingham sat down in his place again.

"I feel that you've changed," she said.

"How?"

"You're—a little bit tough somehow. Like—" She looked up toward Jensen's rooms. "He seems to have had such an influence on you, and he's—well, the next thing to a beatnik." She was not whispering, because they both knew Jensen had gone out.

Ingham felt she was hedging from what she really wanted to say. "No, that he isn't. He doesn't come from that kind of family."

"Does that ever matter?"

"My darling Ina, I haven't known Anders very long, and I probably won't see him ever again—after a few days."

"Will you tell me exactly what happened the night that Arab— Well, what *did* he do, try to come into your house? The bungalow?"

Ingham looked away from her. He wiped his mouth with his napkin, which was a dishtowel. "I could kick Francis Adams from here to Connecticut," Ingham said. "Meddling bastard. Nothing else to do but yack."

Ina was saying nothing, watching him.

A very inward anger made Ingham silent, too. The stupidity of something like this bothering them, after all the worse things they had weathered, the John Castlewood business, his moping over Lotte which had nearly finished him even after meeting Ina—all that overcome, and now this! And Ingham was now tired of statements, speeches. He said nothing. But he realized that what Ina had said was an ultimatum. It was as if she said, "Unless you tell me what happened, or that you killed him, if you did, I won't marry you." Ingham smiled at the bizarreness of it. What did the Arab matter?

He did not go up to her hotel room with her that night. And at home, he couldn't sleep. He didn't mind. In fact he got up and reheated the coffee. Jensen had come in around 10, said hello and good night to them, and had gone upstairs. His light was now off. It was just after 1.

Ingham lay on his bed. What if he told Ina the truth? She wouldn't necessarily tell OWL. It would annoy Ingham, if she did. But hadn't he decided, days ago, not ever to tell her? But if he didn't tell her—and obviously she suspected already that he had killed the man—he would lose her, and that gave Ingham a feeling of terror. When he imagined himself without Ina, Ingham felt his morale gone, his ambition, even his self-respect somehow.

He sat up, bothered by the fact that if he told her the truth, he would be in the position of having lied, looking her straight in the eye, for the past several days. He hadn't quite succeeded with his lie, or she wouldn't still be questioning him, but he had succeeded enough to make himself a coward, and dishonest. It was a dilemma. No matter how much Jensen said, "What does the bastard matter?" the situation had come to matter quite a bit.

Or was it the lateness of the hour? He was tired.

Try to think of it objectively, he told himself. He imagined watching himself in the dark bungalow that night, being scared by the opening of his door (in fact he imagined somebody else, anybody else, being scared), having been annoyed and alarmed by a previous theft from the bungalow. Wouldn't any man have picked something up and thrown it? And then he imagined the Arab alive, flesh and bones, a person known to other people, and morally and legally speaking as important as—President Kennedy. Ingham was ninety percent sure he had killed the Arab. He had been trying to brush that aside, or minimize it by believing the Arab deserved it, or hadn't been worth anything, but suppose he had killed a Negro or a white man in the same circumstances in the States, a man with a long record of housebreaking, for instance? Something would have happened to him. A short trial or hearing and an acquittal of a charge of manslaughter, perhaps, but not just nothing—like here. He couldn't expect to find, in America, a few convenient people to whisk the body away and not mention it.

In spite of the shame of it, Ingham supposed he would have to tell Ina the truth. He would tell her his fear, also his hatred that night. He would not attempt to excuse himself for having lied. He imagined her shocked at first, but finally understanding why it had happened and excusing him, if in fact she would blame him at all. It seemed possible to Ingham that she wouldn't blame him, and that she only wanted to be satisfied that she knew the true story.

Ingham put on the light and lit a cigarette. He turned on his transistor and explored the dial for music or a human voice, and got a baritone American voice saying ". . . peace toward all." The tone was soothing. "America is a land that has *always* extended the hand of friendship and good will to *all* peoples —of whatever color or creed—the hand of *help* to any peoples who might need it—to ward off oppression—to help them to help *themselves*—win their battles against poverty . . ." Ingham thought in disgust, All right, then give the land back to the Indians! What a splendid beginning, right at home! Not a piece of lousy desert you don't want, but decent land with some value to it. Like Texas, for instance. (But no, my God, America had already taken Texas from the *Mexicans*!) Ohio, then. After all, the Indians had given the state its name, from the river there. ". . . what every man in the uniform of the American Army, Navy and Air Force *knows*—that with his privilege to *fight* for the United States of America goes a responsibility to uphold the sanctity of human justice, on *whatever* shores he may be . . ." Ingham turned the thing off so viciously that the knob came off in his hand. He hurled it to the brick floor, where it bounced and disappeared somewhere. It wasn't OWL, that steak-and-martini-filled employe of the Voice of America, or maybe the American Forces Network, but the words could have been OWL's. Did anybody fall for it, Ingham wondered. Of course not. It was just a lot of bland tripe drifting past indifferent ears, which perhaps made some Americans in Europe chuckle a little, something that people endured until the next dance record. Yet the thing must have some influence or they wouldn't keep on with it, therefore some people must be swallowing it. This was a profoundly disturbing thought to Ingham at 2:25 A.M. He thought of OWL, just a mile away, dreaming up the same stuff and actually sending it, being paid for it—OWL wouldn't lie about that. And paid by the Russians. Maybe OWL got as little as ten dollars a month for it. Ingham squirmed in his bed, and felt he was in a madhouse world, and that he might not be sane himself.

The memory of his first minute on Tunisian soil returned to him. At the airport. The sudden, shocking warmth of the air. Half a dozen Arab grease monkeys staring at the passengers, at him, under brows that Ingham had felt to be lowering and hostile, though later he had realized that that was how many Arabs' brows looked normally. Ingham had felt conspicuously, disgustingly pale, and for a few unpleasant seconds had thought, "They must hate us, these darker people. It's *their* continent, and what are we doing here? They know us, and not in a nice way, because the white man has been to Africa before." For a second or two, he had actually experienced physical fear, almost like terror. Tunisia, that tiny country, on the map not too far below Marseille (and yet how different!), which Bourguiba had described as a mere postage stamp on the vast package of Africa.

Ingham realized he was in a curiously delicate condition.

Suddenly, he had a thought: speak to Mokta before he spoke to Ina. He couldn't ask Jensen to do it. It might be useless, and yet Mokta might by this time tell him the truth, the fact —if it was a fact—that Abdullah had been killed that night. Why, Ingham thought, should he tell Ina he'd killed him if he hadn't?

23

IT WAS SATURDAY. Ingham had no appointment with Ina. He intended to call at the hotel before noon, possibly see her, or leave a message in regard to meeting her for dinner. Ingham felt she might well want to spend a day without him. But he didn't know if he was correct in assuming this. He felt no longer sure of himself about anything. He blamed part of it on a bad night's sleep, and a couple of disquietening dreams. In one dream, he had been helping to clear the colossal façade of a formerly buried Greek temple. He was with a group that was supposed to remove mud deposits from the Corinthian columns. Ingham had been upside down at the top of a column, clinging only by his knees which were soon to give out and let him drop a vast distance onto stone. He had gone on, ineffectually scraping at the wet mud with a shell-like instrument, and the dream had mercifully ended before he fell, but it lingered in his mind and was very real.

Even as he walked along the narrow alleys toward his car, he felt a clutch of fear, as if the ground might suddenly give way and drop him to a fatal depth.

It was just after 10 A.M. Ingham thought Mokta should be through with his breakfast work. He hoped he would not see Ina. It was more likely he would see OWL, whose bungalow was near.

The terrace of the bungalow headquarters had one occupied table. A man and woman in shorts lingered over the remains of breakfast. Ingham went round to the side door, which was always open. A boy was washing dishes at the sink. Another was fiddling with the big kettle on the stove.

They both looked at him in the doorway and seemed to freeze, as if waiting for their photograph to be taken.

"*Sabahkum bil'kheir*," Ingham said, meaning "Good morning," one of the few phrases he'd memorized. "Is Mokta here?"

"Ah-h." The boys looked at each other.

One said, "He is looking for the plumber. There is a W.C. broken. Lots of water."

"What bungalow, do you know?"

"That way." The boy pointed toward the hotel.

Ingham walked past OWL's Cadillac and his own car, keeping an eye out through the citrus trees for Mokta's slim, quick figure. Then Ingham heard Mokta's voice from a bungalow on his left.

Mokta appeared at the bungalow's back door, talking in Arabic to someone in the kitchen. Ingham hailed him.

"*Ah, m'sieur Eengham!*" Mokta grinned. "*Comment allez-vous?*"

Et cetera. Ingham assured him his apartment was still very agreeable. "You have a moment?"

"But certainly, m'sieur!"

Ingham did not know where they should go. He did not want to take Mokta away in his car, because that would put too much emphasis on the conversation. Almost anywhere else, they would be overheard. "Let's walk down here for a minute," Ingham said, pointing to a space between two bungalows.

Beyond, the sand dipped down toward the beach. Ingham wore his white dungarees (already too hot) and his old white sneakers into which the sand trickled unpleasantly.

"I had a question to ask you," Ingham said.

"*Oui, m'sieur,*" Mokta said attentively, his expression neutral yet braced.

"It is about that night—the night the Arab was hit on the head. The Arab they think was Abdullah." The French "*on croît*" attached no definite persons to "they." "*Was* it Abdullah?"

"M'sieur, I—I don't know anything about it." Mokta crossed his lean hands on his shirtfront.

"Ah, Mokta! You know one of the boys—Hassim—told M'sieur Adams there was a man that night. The boys took him away. What I would like to know is, was the man dead?"

Mokta's eyes widened a bit more, so that he appeared slightly frightened. "M'sieur, but if I do not even know who it *was*? I did not see the body, m'sieur."

"Then there was a body?"

"*Ah, non, m'sieur!* I do not know if there was a body. Nobody talked to me. The boys told me nothing. Nothing!"

It damned well wasn't true, Ingham thought. He looked impatiently up the sand toward the awning-bedecked bungalow headquarters. "I am not trying to get anyone into trouble, Mokta," Ingham said, and realized he would have felt silly saying this if it hadn't been Tunisia, if he hadn't been a tourist. "Do you know Abdullah?"

"No, m'sieur.— I do not know many around here. I am from Tunis, you know."

Mokta had told him that before. But Ingham knew the boys had discussed whoever it was, Abdullah or just possibly someone else, whose name they would certainly have found out. "Mokta, it is important to me. Just me. No one else. I will give you ten dinars if you tell me the truth. If there was a corpse." He thought ten dinars was a sum Mokta could understand. It was roughly half a month's wages.

Mokta's wide-eyed expression did not change, and Ingham hoped he was debating. But then came the shake of the head. "M'sieur, I could say something just to gain the money. But I do not know."

He's a decent boy, Ingham thought. He knew, but he had given some kind of word to his chums, and he was keeping it. "All right, Mokta. We won't talk any more about it." The sun was a golden weight on Ingham's head.

As Ingham walked toward the bungalow headquarters, he saw one of the boys pause in his clearing of a terrace table and stare at the two of them.

Mokta must think that it was quite important for him to have offered ten dinars, Ingham thought. He supposed Mokta would tell that to his friends, maybe increase it to twenty. It would, Ingham realized, lay him open for blackmail, because why should he have offered money? It did not bother Ingham. Was that because he intended to leave so soon, or because he didn't believe any of the boys would be clever enough to effect blackmailing? It didn't seem to be worth it to ponder this.

"You still work very hard, m'sieur?" Mokta asked as they reached level sand near the bungalow headquarters' terrace.

Ingham did not answer, because at that moment, he saw Ina coming from the direction of OWL's bungalow, Ina in a short belted robe and sandals. She looked at his car, then looked around and saw him. Ingham waved.

"Your American friend!" said Mokta. "*Au revoir, m'sieur!*" He darted for the kitchen door.

Ingham walked toward Ina. "Visiting Francis?"

"He asked me to breakfast," Ina said, smiling. "Were you taking a walk?"

"No. Came to see if there was any mail they hadn't sent on. Then I was going to call on you—or leave you a note." He stood near her now, near enough to see on her cheeks a few freckles that had come out since she had been here. But he sensed the distance between them that he had last evening. Her expression looked politely pleasant, as if she were gazing at a stranger. Ingham felt wretched.

"That's your Arab friend—that boy, isn't he?" she asked. "The one who helped me with my luggage at first?"

"Yes, Mokta. He's the one I know best. I'd very much like to talk to you. Could we possibly go to your room?"

"What's the matter, darling? You look pink around the eyes." She moved toward his car.

"I was reading late."

In the car, they said nothing. It was a very short way to the main building.

"How's Francis?" Ingham asked as he stopped the car. "His old cheery self?" Ingham wondered suddenly if OWL had shown Ina his suitcase with the tapes and made her swear to tell no one, not even him, about them. That would be funny.

"Filled to the brim with OWL-ish glee, yes," Ina said, smiling. "I wish I knew his secret."

Fantasy, Ingham thought. Illusions. He followed Ina into the hotel. She had a letter.

"From Joey," she said.

In her room, she said, "Excuse me while I get out of this suit," and went into the bathroom, taking shorts and a shirt.

Ingham stood by the closed terrace shutters, wondering how he should begin. But he never got anywhere planning the beginnings of things he had to say.

Ina came back, wearing the pale blue shirt outside her shorts. She took a cigarette. "You wanted to talk to me?"

"It's about that night. I wasn't telling you the whole story. I saw someone coming in the door, and I threw my typewriter and hit him in the head. It was very dark. I'm not sure it was Abdullah—but I think so."

"Oh. And then?"

"Then—I shut the door and locked it. The door hadn't been locked because I forgot that night. I waited to find out if there was anyone else with him. But all I heard was—some of the hotel boys coming to drag whoever it was off the terrace." Ingham went into the bathroom and drank some water from the cold tap. He was suddenly dry in the mouth.

"You mean he was dead," Ina said.

"That's what I don't know. The boys here won't tell me anything, believe it or not. I was just asking Mokta, offered him ten dinars to tell me if the man was dead. Mokta says he didn't see anything and the boys didn't tell him anything."

"That's very strange."

"It isn't. Mokta knows. He wants to deny there was *anyone* around that night." Ingham sighed, baffled and tired of the subject. "They want to hush up anything about thieving. In Tunisia, I mean. And that old Arab, let's face it, nobody's going to make a stink about *his* life—if he was killed. You see, I don't know, Ina. I know it was a hard blow."

She said nothing. Her face looked a little paler.

"There's one thing I'd like to ask, darling." He came closer to where she was standing. "Don't tell OWL this, would you? It's not his business, and he'd only gloat because he suspects something like this happened. He'd keep telling me it's on my conscience, I ought to tell the police or something, when as a matter of fact it's not on my conscience."

"Are you sure? You seem to be taking it pretty seriously."

Ingham put his hands in the pockets of his dungarees. "I may take it a bit seriously—*if* I killed him. It's not the same thing as its being on my conscience. The guy was coming into my bungalow, maybe not for the first time. I've got a right to throw something at somebody who's coming into my place at night in a stealthy manner, intending no good. It wasn't a hotel guest who'd made a mistake and walked into the wrong bungalow!"

"You could see it was an Arab?"

"I think he had a turban. He was like a black silhouette in the doorway, sort of stooped. God, I'm sick of it," Ingham said.

"I think you could do with a scotch." Ina went to her closet. She fixed his drink in the bathroom, with a splash of water.

"Don't you want to read your letter from Joey?"

"I can tell by his handwriting he's all right.— You told Anders about this?"

"Yes. Only because he knows more about Tunisia than I do. I asked him what I should do, what I should expect. He told me not to do anything."

"And that the Arab's life was worthless.— It's a funny country."

"It isn't funny. They just have their ways about things."

"I can understand another Arab throwing something, but it seems a little violent from you. A typewriter!"

The scotch was a comfort. "Maybe. I was scared.— You know, a couple of months ago, I was walking back from Anders' place in the dark, and I stumbled over a man lying in the street. I struck a match—and I saw that his throat had been cut. He was dead. An Arab."

"How awful!" She sat down on the edge of her bed.

"I wasn't going to mention it. It's just a horrible story. I suppose these things happen more often here than they do in the States. Though maybe that's debatable!" Ingham laughed.

"So what did you do?"

"That night? Nothing, I'm afraid. The street was dark, nobody around. If I'd seen a policeman, I'd have told him, but I didn't see a policeman. And—yes. That was the night Abdullah was hovering around my car, or rather he'd just fished my canvas jacket out the back window which was open a little. Anyway, I yelled at him and he scuttled away. He could scuttle like a crab!"

"You seem to think he's dead."

"I think more than likely.— But if I can't get it out of Mokta for money, even promising him I won't tell the police, do you think the police are going to get anything out of anybody?"

"Or out of you?"

"The police haven't asked me anything."

She hesitated. "I think, Howard dear, you'd go to the police in the States just by way of protecting your property. I think you don't want to here because you probably killed the man. It's no doubt awkward here if—"

"Less awkward, probably."

"Wouldn't you talk to the police in the States if you thought you'd killed someone?"

"Yes. I think so. But—you'd have to imagine chums of the thief—or maybe chums of mine—dragging the body away. I suppose it could happen in the States. But in the States it's a little hard to get rid of a body. The real point is, why should I go and announce that I've killed someone when that's not necessarily true? The point is—"

"But you said you think he's dead."

"The point is, my house was broken into. Or entered. That's worth reporting in the States, yes. But here, why bother? It happens all the time." Ingham saw that his argument irritated her. "And any corpses are just buried in the sand somewhere."

"The point is," she said, "as a member of society, you should report it. In either place. It'll bother you if you don't."

"It doesn't bother me. You sound like OWL."

"I'm sorry you didn't tell me all this from the start."

Ingham sighed and put down his empty glass. "It was an unpleasant, vague story."

"Even when the boys dragged something off your terrace?"

"Suppose Abdullah was simply knocked out? Suppose he went to another town—considering his unpopularity here?"

"I think I will have a scotch after all." When she had made it, she said, "What about the hotel people? The management. Don't they know?"

He sat down near the foot of the bed. She had leaned back against a pillow.

"I doubt it. The boys wouldn't report it, because they're supposed to keep prowlers off the grounds." He shrugged. "If the management knew, I don't think they'd tell the police. They don't want the rumor spreading that the Reine has burglars."

"Mm-m," she said on a dubious note. "Curious reasoning. But you're an American. It's customary to report things like that. I mean attempted robbery. Maybe the police wouldn't do anything to you, if he's found dead. He was invading your house. All right. But they must have a census or registration of some kind, and presumably Abdullah's missing."

Ingham smiled, amused. "I can't imagine a very accurate census here, I really can't."

"You—just didn't consider reporting it," she went on.

"I considered it, and gave the idea up." After talking with Anders, he thought, but he didn't want to mention Anders again.

It hadn't helped, his telling her. He could see that she would always disagree with him. Ingham felt adamant about not reporting it—especially at this late date it seemed silly—but he wondered if that would be the next ultimatum, the next hurdle he had to take to please her?

"In view of the atrocities going on in some parts of Africa," Ingham said, "Arabs massacring blacks south of Cairo, murders as casual as fly-swatting, I dunno why we make so much over this. I didn't murder the fellow." He took her hand. "Darling, let's not let this throw a gloom over everything."

"It's not really for me, it's for you—to worry." She said it with a shrug, looking toward the window.

The shrug hurt him. "Darling, I want to marry you. I don't like—secrets between us. You wanted me to tell you the truth, so I did."

"You compare it to a lot of Africans or whatever killing each other. But you're not an African. I just find it surprisingly callous of you, I suppose. When you see a man fall—I presume—knowing you'd hit him, wouldn't you turn on the light and see what had happened to him, at least?"

"And get hit over the head myself by his pals who might be on the terrace? Imagine yourself. You'd throw the heaviest thing you could, then shut the door!"

"Yes, a woman might."

"Then I'm not very noble. Or manly." Ingham got up. "Think about it for a bit. Till tonight. I thought you might like to be alone for a while today."

"I think I would. I've got a couple of letters to write. I'll just sit in the sun and be lazy."

A minute later, he was gone, walking down the carpeted corridor toward the wide staircase. He felt worse than ever, worse than when he had been lying to her. He stopped before he reached the bottom of the stairs, and looked up, wondering if he should go back, *now*, and talk with her. But he could not think of anything he could say that he had not already said.

He drove quickly back home, thinking only of talking with Jensen.

Jensen was home. The smell of turpentine was powerful in the warm air. Jensen was reheating a pan of boiled coffee. Ingham told him about his talk with Ina.

"I don't know why you told her," Jensen said. "You can't expect her to understand. She doesn't understand this part of the world. Anyway, women are different." He poured the coffee through a strainer into two cups. "A man may not like causing a death, but it can happen. Mountain climbing. A mistake with the rope, a slip and *fwit*—your partner, maybe a good friend, is dead. An accident. You could say what you did was an accident."

Ingham remembered his arm with the typewriter drawn back, his effort to get a perfect aim. But he knew how Jensen meant "accident." "I told you why I told her. Last night I asked her to marry me. She practically said she wouldn't or couldn't until I told her the truth about that night. She knew I wasn't telling the truth, you see."

"Um-m. Now Adams is going to hear about it. It wouldn't surprise me if he told the police. Not that you should worry."

"I asked Ina not to tell him." But Ingham couldn't remember that Ina had given him a promise that she wouldn't. "Yes—" Ingham stretched back on Jensen's sloppy bed, and pushed off his tennis shoes. "Is it social responsibility or bloody meddling?"

"Bloody meddling," said Jensen, staring with nearly closed eyes at his canvas in progress. The picture was of two enormous soles of sandals with the tips of brown toes showing. A reclining Arab's face was tiny between the sandals.

"I'm going downstairs to sleep," Ingham said, "despite your good coffee. I had a bad night last night."

"Don't let her upset you! Good God, I see she's upsetting you!" Jensen was suddenly rigid and spluttering with anger.

Ingham laughed. "I want her, you see. I love her."

"Um-m," said Jensen.

At his sink, Ingham washed his face, then put on pajama pants. It was ten to 12. He didn't care what time it was. He lay down on his bed and pulled the sheet over him, and after a minute threw it off, as usual. One last cigarette. He made himself think for a few minutes about his book. Dennison was having his semirealized crisis. His appropriations had been discovered. Dennison was stunned, though not completely puzzled, by the public's attitude. What was worse for him was that a few of his friends were shocked that he was a "crook," and had dropped him, though even these, later, were going to repay the money he had given them. Ina had had an idea the other night: have the money repaid with interest, over a long period if need be, so that Dennison's bank could not say he had cost them the money his stolen money would have earned. It was going to amount to a fantastic lot of money.

He turned on his side and shut his eyes, and suddenly he thought of Lotte. It gave him as usual a pleasant-painful jolt. He thought of getting into bed with her at night, every night, always a delicious pleasure to him, whether or not they made love. He had never tired of Lotte physically, in those two years, and he remembered thinking that he saw no reason why he should ever tire of her, despite what some people said about boredom always setting in. He had never quarreled with Lotte. It was funny. Maybe that was because they'd never talked about anything at all complex, such as what he'd just been talking to Ina about—and he'd always been quite content to let Lotte have her own way. He supposed Lotte was happier now, with the extrovert idiot she had married. Maybe she had even decided to have a child.

Ingham heard the front door being opened, a wooden squeak against the threshold. Fatma, he thought, damn her.

A knock on his door. "Howard? Anybody home?" It was OWL.

"Just a minute." Ingham pulled on his pajama jacket. He hated being seen in pajamas. He started to put on his sneakers and gave it up.

"Aha! Sleeping late. Sorry if I disturbed you."

"No, I went back to bed. I had a lousy night."

Adams wore neat Bermuda shorts, a striped shirt, and one of his little canvas caps. "How so?"

"The heat, I suppose. Gets worse and worse."

"Ah, that's August! Have you got a few minutes, Howard? It's reasonably important, I think," he said briskly.

"Of course. Sit down. Would you like a drink or a beer?"

OWL accepted a beer. Ingham got two cans from the bucket of water on the floor. The foam spewed up. They were not very cool, but Ingham didn't apologize.

"I had breakfast with your girl," OWL said with a chuckle. "If that sounds funny, I met her on the beach this morning. I invited her for scrambled eggs."

"Oh." OWL hadn't noticed his car, Ingham gathered. Ingham sat down on his bed.

OWL had taken the chair by his table. "A bright young woman. An exceptional girl. She goes to church, she told me."

"Yes, so did I tell you. I think just recently."

"Protestant. Called St. Ann's, she said. She told me about her brother, too."

What was he leading up to?

"She's a little worried about you.— She said she'd tried to talk you out of living here and get you to take a bungalow. Just for your own comfort."

"I'm not uncomfortable. I can understand that a woman wouldn't like it."

"She tells me you've got a very nice apartment in Manhattan."

Ingham resented the remark, as if it were somehow an intrusion on his privacy. And what would OWL think if he knew John Castlewood had killed himself there, and if he knew why?

"Ina'll be leaving in another week or so, she told me. You're staying on, Howard?"

"I'm not sure. If my book is finished—the first draft—I suppose I'll go back to New York."

"I thought maybe you'd be going back with her." Adams smiled pleasantly, and put his hands on his bare knees. "Anyway, I'd hang onto her, if I were you."

Ingham sipped his beer. "Is she so keen to hang onto me?"

"I would think so," OWL said with a sly wink. "Would she have come to Tunisia, if she weren't pretty sold on you? But I hope you'll be honest with her, Howard. Honest in everything."

Ingham thought suddenly, Ina hadn't told *him* much about her feelings for Castlewood, speaking of honesty. She might have given a fuller accounting. "Perhaps adults, people as old as we are always have some secrets. I don't know that I want her to tell me everything about her past. I don't know why some things can't remain private."

"Maybe. But one's heart must be open to the one we love, to the one who loves us. Open and bare."

As always, listening to OWL, Ingham saw the actual thing, the heart, cut open, full of limp valves, bloodclots, as he had seen hearts in butchers' shops. "I'm not sure I agree. I think actions in the present count more than those in the past. Especially if the other person wasn't even in that past."

"Oh, it doesn't have to be so long past. Just an honest attitude, that's all I mean."

Ingham smouldered gently. He drained the last drops of his beer and set the can down a little hard on the crate that he used for a night table. He wiped his mouth on the back of his hand. "I hope I'm honest enough to satisfy Ina."

"We'll see," said OWL, with his happy, paunchy smile. "If she leaves before you or if you both leave together, we've got to have a big send-off. I'll miss you both.— Would you like to have some lunch at Melik's, Howard?"

"Thanks, Francis. I think I'd like some sleep more than anything."

When OWL was gone, Ingham drank a big glass of water, and tried the bed again. He felt as if he seethed inside, deeper than even a sleeping pill could touch, if he had had one. It was a sensation like repressed anger, and Ingham detested it. He heard Jensen's soft tread on the outside steps, and was delighted when Jensen tapped on his door.

"Wasn't that our mutual friend OWL?" Jensen asked.

"Correct. Have a stone, my friend."

"How did you guess?" Jensen went to the kitchen. "And you?"

"I don't mind if I do."

Jensen sat down. They drank.

"OWL is urging me to confess, and he doesn't know I've already done it," Ingham said. "Imagine confessing something that you might not have done?"

"OWL should go back to New England, or wherever it is."

"And of course he's urging me to hang onto Ina." Ingham flopped back on his bed. "As if his advice would influence me in something like that!"

"He's a funny little fellow. 'What a funny little man you are,' as Bosie said to the Marquis." Jensen laughed with sudden mirth.

And Ingham smiled, too. "I'll go by the Reine around seven and see how Ina's doing."

"I have never seen such meddling people—maybe not Ina, but I can see you depend on what she thinks. Do you know what I would do to the man who stole Hasso? I won't put into words what I would do, and I would do it slowly, and I wouldn't give a damn what anybody thought of me for doing it."

Ingham drew comfort from Jensen. "It's not entirely Ina and OWL. I think I live through a same kind of crisis in my book. That happens." Ingham had told Jensen about Dennison.

"Oh, yes, that happens. You don't mind if I have another stone? Or a pebble?"

24

INGHAM WENT to find Ina at 7. He had slept a couple of hours, had gone for a swim, and had written three pages in an effort to make it seem a day like any other. But he felt odd, and had come to no conclusion as to what he should do if Ina's attitude was this or that. The church business bothered him in an amorphous way. How *much* was she involved with the church? And it was not so much the situation now that he thought about, but future ones, in which she might take an attitude with which he couldn't cope, in which she might go off on tangents that would make him feel like someone from another world—which would be in fact true.

He rang Ina's room, and she sounded in a good mood and said she would be down in ten minutes. Ingham sat down on a lobby sofa and looked at a newspaper.

Ina came down in a pale pink dress. She had a white chiffon scarf in her hand.

"You look marvelous," Ingham said.

"The scarf is in case we go for a walk. The breeze."

"You're counting on a breeze?" Her perfume, as usual, pleased him. It was so much more interesting than jasmine. "Would you like to go somewhere in particular, or should I think of something?"

"Francis rang up and asked us for a drink. Do you mind?"

"No," Ingham said. They got into Ingham's car. "What's Joey's news?"

"Nothing much. He's painting. Louise comes over nearly every day."

"She lives nearby? I forgot."

The car rolled onto the nearly silent sandy lane that curved toward Adams' bungalow. Adams' terrace light was on, and he greeted them at the door before they had time to knock.

"Welcome! I'd suggest the terrace, but it's much cooler inside. Ha-ha! Come in and see!"

Adams' terrace faced the gulf and had a glider, table and chairs. There were canapés of cheese and black olives on the mosaic table in the living room.

Ingham hoped Adams wouldn't want to join them for dinner. Then he thought it might be better if he did join them. Why was Ina so cheerful? Ingham wasn't sure how to interpret it. Had she given him up? Had she "understood" and decided to tell him so? Whatever she said tonight, Ingham thought, he would ask her just one more question about John Castlewood: had she liked him or loved him merely because he had loved her? Castlewood's declaration of passion had been a surprise to Ina, she had written. It often seemed to Ingham that women fell in love with men who were already in love with them, men whom they wouldn't otherwise have noticed.

Adams entertained Ina with bits of Arabic lore, of which he had so much. Such as that the Mohammedans expected their messiah to be born a second time, and via a man, hence the baggy pants that they wore in expectancy. And there was talk of the Arab refugees west of the Jordan River. It was astounding how much wreckage had resulted from a war lasting only six days.

"I hope you've extended your leave from your office, Ina," Adams said, refilling Ina's glass from his silver shaker. He had offered them daiquiris ("Jack Kennedy's favorite cocktail") which he had made before they arrived and stored in his refrigerator.

"Yes, I cabled today. I'm sure I can have another week."

OWL's smile took in Ingham. He beamed goodwill on both of them. "You said something about going to Paris, didn't you, Howard?"

Had he? "That was if I finished my book."

"I think I said I'd thought of it," Ina said.

"With Howard? Good. I think he's getting restless," said OWL.

Ingham wondered what had given him that idea. OWL, as the talk drifted on, glanced from one to the other of them, as if trying to perceive what they had "decided," how much in love they were, how happy or maybe not so happy. And Ingham more and more sensed a detachment in Ina. Here in OWL's living room, where he had so often sat having friendly, ordinary conversations with OWL, Ingham tried to brace himself to turn loose of Ina—in an emotional sense—because he felt that was what she was going to suggest. How much would it hurt? And would it be his ego or his heart that would be hurt? Ina looked at him, smiling with a slight amusement, and Ingham knew she was a little bored, like himself.

"I think I'm within two days of finishing," Ingham said in answer to Adams' question about his book.

"Then you should have a real holiday with a change of scene. Yes, Paris. Why not?" OWL bounced on his heels, as if he were seeing a vision of a classic honeymoon, blissful, in Paris.

They left after two drinks. OWL had showed no sign of wanting to come with them.

"He's sort of an angel, isn't he?" Ina said. "Very fond of you.— You're awfully quiet tonight."

"Sorry. I think it's the heat. I thought we might try the Hotel du Golfe tonight."

The restaurant of the Hotel du Golfe—where Ingham had looked so often for letters that never came, letters from John and Ina—was nearly full, but they were able to get a well-placed table for two.

"Well, darling," Ingham said, "did you think any more about what we were talking about today?"

"Of course I thought about it. Yes. I understand things are different here. I suppose I was making too much of it.— I really didn't mean to be telling you what to do."

And yet in a way, that was what Ingham wanted.

"If it doesn't bother you, it doesn't bother you," she added.

Did she mean it ought to? Ingham gave a laugh. "Then let's not talk about it any more."

"Do you want to go to Paris? Next week?"

Ingham knew what that meant. She had taken him back, accepted him. Go and maybe come back to Hammamet? But he knew she didn't mean it that way. "You mean, go on to New York from there?"

"Yes." She was calm, quite sure of herself. She smiled suddenly. "I don't think you're bubbling with enthusiasm."

"I was thinking I'd like to finish my book before going anywhere."

"Isn't it as good as finished?"

It was, and he was the one who had said so, but he did very much want to finish his book here, in that crazy room where he was now, with Jensen's paintings and Jensen upstairs. Not going to Paris wouldn't necessarily mean losing Ina. "If you could stay here—if you could bear it, the heat, I mean, I could be finished in less than a week."

She laughed again, but her eyes were gentle. "I don't think you'll finish in a week. But you may not want to go to Paris."

"And you want to go to Paris instead of staying here. I understand."

"Just how long do you want to stay here, darling?"

The waiter was showing them a skillet with two raw white fish in it. Without knowing a thing about the fish, Ingham nodded his approval. Ina might not have seen the thing. She was watching him.

"I'd like to stay till I finish. I really would."

"All right, then, you stay."

An awkward silence.

"I'll see you next in New York then," Ingham said. "That won't be terribly long."

"No."

Ingham knew he might have said, knew she was expecting him to say something more affectionate. He was suddenly unsure about the way he felt. And he knew this stuck out all over him. He could make it up later, he told himself. It was just a sticky moment. His uncertain feelings gave way to a sense of guilt, of a vague embarrassment. He thought of the day in the bungalow at the Reine, when he'd suddenly had a hunger for Henry James, felt that he couldn't live through the rest of the day and the evening, if he could not read some prose by him, and he had driven to Tunis and bought the only thing he could find, a Modern Library edition of *The Turn of the Screw* and *The Lesson of the Master*. He wanted to tell Ina about that, but what had it to do with tonight, with now?

They had a brandy after the meal. The evening, externally, improved. There were no more difficult moments. But Ingham continued to feel unhappy within himself. Phrases of OWL's tripe drifted through his mind maddeningly. That and the happiest recollections of being in bed with Ina. He thought of being married to Ina, living in a comfortable apartment in New York, being able to afford a maid to make life for both of them easier, entertaining interesting people (he and Ina tended to like the same people), and of maybe having a child, maybe even two. He was sure Ina would want a child. He imagined his work developing, burgeoning, in that atmosphere. So why didn't he jump at it?

He simply couldn't jump that night.

But he did go back to Ina's room with her. Ina asked him, and he accepted.

It was 3 A.M. when he got home. He had wanted to do some thinking, but he fell fast asleep almost at once. They had had, as usual, quite a nice and exhausting time in bed.

Ingham awoke in the dark, a little suddenly. He thought he had heard something at the street door, but when he listened, he heard nothing. He struck a match and looked at the time. 4:17. He lay back on his bed, tense, alert. How much did Ina love him? And wouldn't he be guilty of rather bad behavior if he pulled out now? And yet there *had* been John Castlewood, who'd entered the picture after Ingham, and presumably Ina, had taken it for granted they'd be married. Ingham had asked Ina about John tonight, in her room. He had asked her how much she had loved him. But the only thing he had got out of her was that she had felt, or she had believed, they might make a go of it. John Castlewood had loved her very much, and so forth, and maybe that was true. But Ina's answer seemed a little vague to Ingham now, or there was no definite phrase that stood out in it, anyway. His mind shied away from the problem, and he thought of the crazy situation he was in, here, and wondered how it had all come about. Castlewood's assignment, of course. Then OWL with his unbelievably corny broadcasts, and being *paid* for them! Ingham had, on one occasion in OWL's bungalow, seen an envelope with a Swiss stamp on it in the wastebasket. OWL had said he was paid via Switzerland. The return address of a bank had given no clue as to the payer, of course. Could it be possible, Ingham wondered, that OWL was having a fantasy about all of this, about having met the Russian who would pay him for such broadcasts? Was he pretending to himself that some of his own dividends, which might be coming from Switzerland, were payments for his talks? What was possible and what wasn't? Ingham's months in Tunisia had made this borderline fuzzy. The fuzziness, or inversion of things, now involved Ina. He felt it was not quite right they should marry, which was the same as saying that he didn't love her enough, and maybe she did not love him enough either, and that she was not "quite right," whatever that was, and maybe something quite right did not exist for him. But was this feeling due to some strange power of Tunisia to distort everything, like a wavy mirror or a lens that inverted the image, or was the feeling valid?

Ingham lit a cigarette.

And Jensen. Jensen had a character, a background, a history, which Ingham did not know, which he could never know any more than partially. He knew Jensen only enough to like him quite a bit. (And Ingham recalled one night when he'd gone alone to the coffeehouse called Les Arcades, and had come near to taking home a young Arab. The Arab had sat at the table with him, and Ingham had stood him a couple of beers. Ingham had been both sexually excited and lonely that evening, and the only thing that had deterred him, he thought, was that he hadn't been sure what to do in bed with a boy, and he hadn't wanted to feel silly. Hardly a moral reason for chastity.) He was surrounded by a sea of Arabs who were still mysteries to him, with the possible exceptions of Mokta, and the cheerful Melik, a kindly fellow who certainly wasn't a cheat, either.

Ingham realized he must come to a decision about Ina and tell her, preferably before she left for Paris, which she wanted to do in about five days or less. If he turned loose of Ina, would it be stupid? He could see her marrying someone else very quickly, if he did. Then he might be sorry. Or was this a bastardly way to be thinking? He had the awful feeling that in the months he had been here, his own character or principles had collapsed, or disappeared. What was he? Presumably someone with a set of attitudes on which his conduct was based. They formed a character. But Ingham now felt he couldn't think, if his life depended on it, of one principle by which he lived. Wasn't sleeping with Ina a form of deception now? And he didn't even feel uncomfortable about it. Was his whole past life then a history of phoneyness? Or was all this now the falseness? He was suddenly sweating, and lacked the initiative to get up and pour a bucket of water over himself on the terrace.

He heard a scratching noise, a whimper, down at the door on the street. Jensen must have put out his garbage. Usually it attracted cats. The scratching kept on. Anger got Ingham out of bed now. He turned on his light and took his flashlight. He went down the four steps, tense, prepared to yell at the cat who was probably trying to dislodge a sardine can from under the door.

A dog looked at him and growled low.

"Hasso?— Hasso, it *isn't*!"

It was. The dog looked awful, but it was Hasso, and Hasso remembered him—just enough not to attack him, Ingham could see.

"*Anders!*" Ingham yelled, his voice cracking wildly. "Anders, *Hasso's* here!"

The dog crawled up the steps toward Jensen's rooms, its legs limp.

"What?" Jensen leaned out his window.

Hysterical laughter started in Ingham's throat. Jensen knelt on his top step and embraced the dog. Ingham, for no reason, turned on all the lights he had, and also the terrace lights. He poured a bowl of canned milk and added a dash of water lest the milk be too rich. He took it upstairs to Jensen.

Jensen was kneeling on his floor, looking the dog over. "*Vand!*"

"What?"

"Water!"

Ingham went to Jensen's tap to get it. "I've got sardines. Also some frankfurters."

"Look at him! But he'll live. No bones broken!" That was the last thing Jensen said for several minutes that Ingham could understand. The rest was in Danish.

The dog drank water, ate ravenously of a few sardines, then abruptly abandoned the dish. He was too starving to take on much at once. An old brown collar was around his neck, trailing a length of metal chain. Ingham wondered how he had broken or chewed the chain, but the last links were worn so thin and flat, they gave no clue. The dog must have walked miles.

"He really has no wounds," Ingham said. "Isn't that a miracle?"

"Yes. Except this scar." There was a tiny bald patch in front of one of Hasso's ears. Jensen thought they had had to knock the dog out to catch him or to put the collar on him. Jensen was looking at Hasso's teeth, at his feet which were scabby and bloody. Some bad looking patches in his fur were only mud or grease.

Ingham went down to get his scotch. He brought the rest of the tinned milk. Jensen had heated some water and was washing the dog's feet.

They sat up talking a long while. The dawn came. The dog lay down on a blanket Jensen had put down for him, and fell asleep.

"He was even too tired to smile, did you notice?" Ingham said.

And so the time passed with remarks like that, remarks of no consequence, but both Ingham and Jensen were very happy. Jensen speculated as to what had happened. Someone must have taken him miles away and attempted to keep him tied up. They must have had to toss food at him, because he wouldn't have allowed anyone to come near. But how had they captured the dog in the first place? Clubbed him? Used chloroform? Not likely. And Ingham was thinking that it was all cock-eyed, except this, except Hasso's return, which was the most unlikely thing he could have imagined would ever happen. And he knew he would speak to Ina tomorrow, rather today, and tell her that he could not marry her. That was correct, the correct thing to do. And in three more days, he would finish his book, he was positive. He made this announcement to Jensen, about his book, but he doubted if Jensen took it in.

The whisky put them both, toward 7 A.M., in a relaxed, happy mood. Jensen was positively drunk. They both went to sleep in their respective beds.

25

AT 11:20 that morning, Ingham was walking along the beach, carrying his sneakers, toward the Reine de Hammamet. The sun poured down, turning the sand white. The sand, if he walked quickly, was bearable between his toes. The sky was a cloudless deep bright blue, like the shutters and doors of Tunisia. He had bought a chicken and a form of leg of beef for Hasso this morning. Jensen's hangover, if any, was totally lost in his concern for Hasso's welfare. The dog, this morning, had been well enough to smile, and he had smiled at Ingham, too.

Now Ingham was thinking, with as usual no success in preparation, of what he was going to say to Ina. The hour to him did not matter. It might as well have been 4 A.M. Ah, destiny! He was convinced that his decision to sever himself from Ina was of a little more importance to him than to her. He imagined her meeting another John Castlewood, or some substitute for himself, in a matter of weeks. He was sure she could more easily find a man she liked than he could find a woman. For this reason, he felt that he was not going to hurt her very much.

He also might not find her in. Ingham was prepared to be told that Miss Pallant had taken an all-day bus-ride somewhere.

Miss Pallant was not in but she was on the beach.

Ingham went back to the beach, and walked on in the direction from Hammamet, because he was sure he had not passed her.

He recognized her chair by her beach robe and a script bound in a blue cover. With his eyes nearly shut against the glare, he faced the sea and examined the surface of the water.

It couldn't be, but it was true: OWL's spear broke the surface with its black arrow, just a hundred yards out and a bit to the left. Ina's white-capped head emerged beside it, her face gasping and laughing, and finally OWL's ruddy visage came up behind the spear. Naturally, the spear was empty. Had OWL ever caught anything?

They saw him, and waved. Ingham stood waiting, dry and hot, the skin of his face and forearms gently toasting, while they came out of the sea.

A burst of greetings from OWL. Why hadn't he brought his swimming trunks?

"Why aren't you working?" Ina wiped her face with a towel.

"Hasso came home last night. Anders' dog," Ingham said.

"My goodness! The one who was lost?" OWL was a-goggle with surprise. "Yes, Ina! Did I tell you? Anders' dog disappeared— How long ago was it?"

"Six weeks, anyway," Ingham said.

Ina was also incredulous and glad about the good news.

Adams asked them to his bungalow for a beer, to cool off, but Ingham said:

"Thanks, Francis, can I take a raincheck?"

Adams understood. He understood, anyway, that Ingham wanted to talk to Ina.

Ingham and Ina walked toward the hotel. Ina paused to shower under the bare, outdoor tap where Ingham had seen the Americans who he had thought were Germans. In silence, they went directly to her room. Ina again removed her bathing suit in the bathroom, and came out in a terry-cloth robe like his own, but white.

"I know what you're going to say, so you don't have to say it," Ina said.

Ingham had sat down in the one big chair. Ina leaned across him, one hand braced on the arm of the chair, and she kissed his cheek, then briefly his lips.

I can't get married, Ingham thought. What should he say? Thank you?

"Would you like a scotch, darling?"

"No, thanks.— It was a strange night last night," he said, stuttering slightly. "I was awake, and I heard Anders' dog scratching at the door. Only I didn't know it was the dog. So I went down—and it was unbelievable, to see this dog after so many weeks. Skinny, of course. He looks awful, but he'll live. It's a miracle, isn't it?"

"Yes. Six weeks, did you say?" She was sitting on her bed, facing him, with a deadly air of politeness.

"Six weeks maybe, I haven't counted them."

Their eyes met briefly.

Ingham had a mad impulse to push her back on the bed and make love to her. Or if he did, would he find himself incapable? "I'm sorry I dragged you here."

"You didn't!"

He could predict the next exchanges. It was awful. They came, and at last he was saying, as he had hoped not to, "Why should I put you in a trap? I suppose I don't love anyone. I suppose I can't."

And she obliged with, "Oh, you have your work. Writers think about so many sides of things, they never choose any one thing. I'm not blaming you. I understand."

How many times had Ingham heard that in the years before Lotte? Little did the girls know. But one thing was true, they were jealous of his work. "It isn't that," Ingham said, feeling stupid.

"What do you mean, it isn't that?"

She was supposed to cut through all this underbrush with a clear rapier brain, Ingham thought. He didn't know what to say. She *did* blame him, and it might have been a lot better if she were angry. "It isn't enough to get married on," he said.

"Oh, that's obvious." Her hand moved in a limp, hopeless gesture.

Ingham looked away from her hand. "You'll meet someone else easily enough, I think. Maybe even before you leave Tunisia."

She laughed. "OWL?" Then she got up and made scotches. "How're you going to finish that book if you don't get any sleep?"

"I'll finish."

She was leaving for Paris in two days, or possibly tomorrow, and Ingham thought it would be tomorrow. She had had a cable from her office saying she could have another week. And of course the heat here was a bit much. The scotch nearly knocked Ingham out, but he didn't mind, in fact was grateful.

"Shall we all have dinner tonight? You and I and Anders? Maybe OWL?"

"I simply can't. If you don't mind." There were tears in her eyes.

Ingham knew he had said the wrong thing, that he couldn't improve things by proposing that they have dinner together alone. He stood up. The only thing he could do to please her was to leave. "Darling, I'll ring you tomorrow to find out when you're leaving."

"I didn't say I was leaving tomorrow."

She was standing barefoot in the white robe. He wanted to embrace her, but was afraid she would reject him. "I'll call you anyway." He went to the door. "Bye-bye, darling."

He pulled the door to, and thought of nothing until he was down on the beach again, where he removed his sneakers. Now the hotter sand made him run fast to the water. He splashed in, wetting his dungaree cuffs, rolled them up, and plunged on toward Hammamet, ankle-deep, splashing. He had no doubt that Ina would see OWL tonight. OWL would express regret and disapproval.

In his room, Ingham felt calmer. He made coffee, and drank it in sips as he tidied up. Jensen was quiet upstairs. Maybe both he and the dog were sleeping. With a second cup of coffee, he sat down to work. But before he could collect his thoughts about his chapter in progress, he thought of Lotte. The throb of loss, or maybe of lust or maybe love, went deeper this time. He had an impulse to write to her now (the only address he knew was their old one, but the letter might be forwarded), and to ask her how she was, ask her if she might like to see him some time in New York, for a drink or for dinner, if she ever came to New York. Was she happy or unhappy? Might she possibly like to see him? They'd had very few mutual friends. There was no one Ingham could ask in New York about her. She'd been in California for over a year. He realized he wanted her back, just as she was. She had that incredible quality—not a virtue, not an achievement—which let her do no wrong. That was to say, no wrong in his eyes. She had made mistakes, she had behaved selfishly sometimes, but Ingham had somehow never blamed her, never resented, never found fault. Was that love, he wondered, or simply madness? He decided that he must not write to her, though it was a brinkish decision.

Another five minutes walking around his room, another cigarette, then he sat down and worked. Dennison was out of prison. The period had been seven years, which Ingham had compressed into five pages of intense prose of which he was rather proud. His wife, faithful always, had remained faithful. Dennison was forty-five now. Prison had not changed him. His head was unbowed, not at all bloodied, just a trifle dazed by the ways of the world that was not his world. Dennison was going to find a job in another company, an insurance company, and start the same financial manoeuvrings all over again. Other people's hardships were intolerable to Dennison, if merely a little money could abolish them. Ingham, sweating, shirtless, in sticky white dungarees, produced five pages by 4:30, got up from his chair and dropped on his bed. The air in the room, though everything was open, was motionless and saturated with heat. He was asleep within seconds.

He awakened with the now familiar logginess of brain that always took fifteen seconds to clear. Where was he? What was up or down? What time of day was it? What day of the week? Was there anything he had to do? Hasso was back. He had talked with Ina. He had got through the awful speech to her, or she had made it for him. One more day's work, maybe a day and a half's work, would finish *Dennison's Lights.*

Ingham took off his clothes and poured a bucket of water over himself on the terrace. He put on shorts, and soaked his sweaty dungarees in the bucket which he filled at the sink. Then he went up to see Jensen.

He found Jensen painting, his blond hair dark with sweat. Jensen wore nothing but cotton underpants. The dog slept on the floor. "Can I invite you for dinner *chez moi*?" Ingham asked.

"*Avec plaisir, m'sieur! J'accepte!*" Jensen looked bleary with fatigue, but happy. He was working on his picture of the Arab with the two huge sandals in the foreground. A jar of vaseline was on the floor near Hasso.

"Did you write your family about—" Ingham pointed to Hasso.

"I cabled them. I said I'd be home in a week."

"Really?— Well, that's news." As the dog breathed, Ingham could see his ribs rise and fall under the black and buff fur.

"I don't want anything else to happen to him. The Choudis were very nice this morning. I think they were as glad as I was!"

The Choudis were the Arab family next door.

Jensen's face glowed with a simple and rather angelic happiness.

"You're going to collapse in this heat," Ingham whispered. "Shouldn't you take a nap?"

All around them, the town seemed to be sleeping. There was not a sound beyond the windows, only thick, silent sunlight.

"Maybe I will. Shall I bring some wine and some ice?"

"Don't bring anything." Ingham left.

He went out for the shopping, thinking he might be too early for the butcher's to be open, but he wanted to buy a lot, and he might have to make two trips, anyway. The ten-year-old daughter of the Choudis was sitting in her open doorway, arranging round stones on the doorstep. She grinned at him with bright eyes, and said something Ingham could not understand.

Ingham replied in French, with a smile also. He thought she had said "Hasso," but even this word was different when she said it. Her little face was warm and friendly. Ingham walked on. He felt suddenly different toward the family next door, felt they were friends of his and Jensen's, instead of just a family who lived there. He realized he had vaguely suspected them of having had something to do with Hasso's disappearance.

The dinner that night was the best Ingham could provide, given the town's resources. He had gone to the Reine's little grocery. There was salami, sliced hard-boiled eggs, lambs' tongues, cold ham and roast beef, potato salad, cheese and fresh figs. Jensen had brought boukhah, and of course there was scotch and cold white wine. Hasso was there, too, and ate bits of meat which they handed him from the table.

"I don't usually do this, but tonight's a special occasion," said Jensen.

"Is he keeping everything down?"

Hasso was, said Jensen. Jensen still looked very happy, too happy even to sleep, perhaps. "And Ina? How is she?"

"All right. I think she's with OWL tonight."

"She might stay another week, you said."

"No, I think she'll go on to Paris. Maybe day after tomorrow."

"And you, too?"

"No." Ingham said a little awkwardly, "I told her I didn't think we should marry.— It's not the end of her life, I'm sure."

Jensen looked puzzled, or maybe he had nothing to say. "Nothing to do with that dead Arab, I trust."

"No." Ingham laughed a little. He wanted to mention Lotte, to say he was still in love with her, but first he was not sure that was true. He was not at all sure Lotte had been the main reason why he had decided not to marry Ina. The Castlewood affair had shaken Ingham more than he had realized when he first heard about it. "Did you ever have someone in your life," Ingham said, "who's like the one great love? The rest just can't ever be as good."

"Ah, yes," said Jensen, leaning back in his chair, looking at the ceiling.

A boy, of course, but Ingham felt that Jensen knew exactly what he meant. "It's a funny thing—the feeling that such people can't do any wrong, no matter what they do. A feeling that you'll never have a complaint against them."

Jensen laughed. "Maybe that is easy if you don't live with them. I never lived with mine. I never even slept with him. I just loved him for two years.— Well, forever, but for two years I didn't go to bed with anybody."

But Ingham meant, even if you did live with someone, as he had with Lotte. Ingham let it go. He realized he would miss Jensen painfully when he left.

26

INGHAM SAW Ina off at the airport the next day. She left on the 2:30 P.M. flight to Paris. OWL went with them in Ingham's car. Ingham had rung her just before 11 from Melik's, and Ina had told him her arrangements.

"I was just about to send a messenger to you—or something," she said, blithely enough.

Ingham wasn't sure whether to believe her, but he knew she had his address. "I'll take you in the car. We can have some lunch at the airport."

"Francis wants to take me."

"Then ask him to come along in my car," Ingham said, a bit irked by the ever-present OWL. "I'll be there in about half an hour."

Then he went home and changed, and started out almost at once. Ina hadn't wanted to stay one more day. Ingham knew that 2:30 P.M. flight. It left every day.

Ina was settling her bill in the lobby. Then through the glass doors Ingham saw Adams' black Cadillac pull up outside the hotel. Adams had a small bouquet of flowers.

"So—you're missing a Paris holiday in delightful company," OWL said with his squirrel smile, but Ingham could see that Ina had told him they were not going to marry.

Ingham insisted, over OWL's protest, on taking his car, and they got in. There were the usual remarks on the seascape by OWL.

Ina said to Ingham, "I'll check on your apartment as soon as I get home." She was in the front seat beside Ingham.

"Don't hurry.— Anyway, I might be home in ten days myself."

She laughed a little. "How long have you been saying that?"

They lunched in the slightly mad restaurant of the airport. Service was sporadic, but they had plenty of time. Again the departure and arrival announcements were inaudible beneath the radio's claptrap. Ina made an effort (so did Ingham), but he could see a certain sadness, a disappointment in her face that pained him. He really was so fond of her! He hoped she was not going to cry on the plane, as soon as she was out of his sight.

"Is there anyone you know in Paris now?" OWL asked.

"No. But one usually runs into someone.— Oh, it doesn't matter. I like walking around the city."

2:10. It was bound to be time to start boarding. Ingham paid. A kiss at the gate, OWL got a smack on the cheek, too, a second quick, passionless kiss for Ingham, then she turned and walked away.

Ingham and Adams walked in silence back to Ingham's car. Ingham felt sad, depressed, slightly impatient, as if he had made a mistake, though he knew he had not.

"Well, I gather things didn't work out," OWL said.

Ingham set his teeth for an instant, then said, "We just decided not to marry. It doesn't mean we had a quarrel."

"Oh, no."

At least that shut Adams up for a while.

Finally Ingham said, "I know she enjoyed meeting you. You were very nice to her."

OWL nodded, staring through the windshield. "You're a funny fellow, Howard, letting a wonderful girl like that go by."

"Maybe."

"There's not someone else in your life, is there? I don't mean to be prying."

"No, there isn't."

Ingham was back home by 4. He wanted to work, but it was an hour before he could settle down. He was thinking of Ina.

He produced only two pages that day. One more day's work would certainly see the book finished, Ingham thought. As usual at the end of books, he felt tired and somehow depressed, and wondered if it was something akin to post-natal depression, or was it some doubt that the book wasn't as good as he thought it was? But he had had the same depression after books he knew were quite good, like *The Game of "If."*

The following day it took him three dragging hours to produce the four pages that ended the book. After a few minutes, he went upstairs to tell Jensen he had finished.

"Hurray!" Jensen said. "But you look gloomy!" Jensen laughed. He was cleaning brushes with a messy rag.

"I'm always like this. Pay no attention. Let's go to Melik's."

Ingham picked up with some drinks with Jensen before dinner. Jensen had gone to a hotel that afternoon and arranged his flight to Copenhagen for next Friday, just four days off. Ingham felt absurdly forlorn at the news.

"You'd—better make sure your canvases are dry, shouldn't you?"

"Yes. I won't paint any more. Just draw a little." His smiling face was in great contrast to Ingham's gloom.

Ingham replenished Jensen's scotch and water.

"Come with me, Howard!" Jensen said suddenly. "Why not? I'll tell my family I'm bringing a friend. I already told them about you. Stay a week or so. Longer! We've got a big house." Jensen was leaning toward Ingham. "Why not, Howard?"

It was exactly what Ingham wanted to do, to take off when Jensen did, to see the North, to plunge into a world completely different from this one. "You mean it?"

But there was no doubt Jensen did.

"I'll show you Copenhagen! My family's house is in Hellerup. Off the Ryvangs Alle. Hellerup's sort of a suburb, but not really. You'll meet my sister Ingrid—maybe even my Aunt Mathilde." Jensen laughed. "But we'll bum around the city mostly. Lots of good snack bars, friends to look up—and it's cool, even now."

Ingham wanted to go, desperately, but he felt that it would be a postponement of what he had to do, which was get back to New York and start his life there again. Copenhagen would be like a five-day Christmas celebration. He really did not want that.

"What's the matter?" Jensen asked.

"I'd like to very much, but I shouldn't. I can't. Not just now. Thank you, Anders."

"You're just melancholic tonight. Give me one good reason why you can't come."

"I suppose I'm a little disturbed. It would be self-indulgent. It's hard to explain. I'd better get back on my own tracks again. But can I—maybe visit you sometime, if you're there?"

Jensen looked disappointed, but Ingham thought he understood. "Sure. Make it soon. I may go away again in January."

"I'll make it soon."

27

FOUR DAYS LATER, Ingham drove Jensen to the airport. They stood in the terminus bar and drank boukhahs. Hasso had already been loaded in his box onto the plane. Ingham made a fierce effort to be cheerful, even jolly. It actually worked a little, he thought. Jensen was obviously so pleased to be going home, that Ingham felt ashamed of his own depression. They embraced at the gate like Frenchmen, and Ingham stood watching Jensen's tall, lank figure, lugging portfolios, until he reached the turning point at the end of the corridor. Jensen looked back and waved.

Ingham went straight to the ticket office of the terminus and bought a ticket for New York for Tuesday, four days off.

Jensen's empty rooms upstairs made Ingham think, perversely, of a tomb that had been robbed. He tried to put the floor above out of his mind, pretend it wasn't there, and he certainly had no intention of going up to look at the rooms, even to see if Jensen might have forgotten something. The only happy thought was that Jensen was very much alive, and that he would see him again somewhere, in a matter of months if he wished.

The other happy thought was of course his finished book. It would be pleasant to do some more polishing in the days he had left here, work that required no emotional effort. He was pleased with the book, and only hoped his publishers would not think it dull after *The Game of "If."* Dennison had a less primitive attitude than most people about money, and he hoped he had made that point. Money to him had become impersonal, essentially unimportant, like an umbrella that can be borrowed to hold over someone's head, an umbrella that could be returned like the umbrellas in the racks at some railway stations that Ingham had heard about, somewhere. Banks did the same thing, even extracting interest, and hoped that there wouldn't be a run on them.

He began slowly to prepare for leaving, though there was absurdly little he had to do. He had no bills in town. He wrote to his agent. He sent off Ina's mats, and spoke to the post office, giving them a date at which to start forwarding to his New York address, and he gave the man a tip. He called on OWL to inform him of the news, and they made a date for dinner the night before his departure. Seeing him off was unnecessary and awkward, Ingham said, because he had to return his rented car in Tunis.

"But how're you going to get to the airport then?" OWL said. "I'll come with you in my car to the rental place."

There was no dissuading OWL.

Now when there was no need of routine, because he wasn't writing, Ingham particularly stuck to one. A swim in the morning, a little work, a swim again, a short walk before lunch, work again. He was taking his last looks at the town, at the Café de la Plage, all male always, even down to the three-year-old tot seated at a table of wine-drinkers. Strange things crossed Ingham's mind, some that made him laugh, such as, how easy it would have been to hire an Arab for a few days to pose as the missing Abdullah, to satisfy Ina that Abdullah was not dead. But that would not have made any essential difference in his and Ina's relationship, Ingham knew.

The morning before he left, he had two pieces of mail, one a postcard from Jensen. It read:

> Dear Howard,
>
> Will write later, but meanwhile have this. I will torture you by saying I sleep under a blanket here. Please visit soon. Write me. Love, Anders.

The picture on the card was of a greenish-roofed building surrounded by a moat or canal.

The second item was a letter, much forwarded, and Ingham caught his breath when he saw the handwriting in the center of the envelope. It was from Lotte. The original postmark was California. Ingham opened it.

> July 20, 19—
>
> Dear Howard,
>
> I am not sure this will reach you, as I only know our old address. How are you? I hope well and happy and working well. Maybe you are married by now (I heard

something along this line via the grapevine) but if not, knowing you, I feel sure you are involved, as they say.

I am coming to New York next month and thought we might meet for a drink for old times sake. I've had a rough last year, so don't expect me to look the picture of happiness. My husband was a charmer to quite a few others too, and we at last decided to call the whole thing off. No children, thank God, though I had every intention of having some. (You won't believe that, but I have changed.) I hope to stay in New York for a while. Even sunshine can become boring, and I found California so full of weirdies I finally felt as square as the Smith Brothers in comparison. There was a rumor here that you had gone to the Near East to write a play or something. True? Write me c.o. Ditson, 121 Bleecker Street, N.Y.C. Won't be staying there, but they will forward letters to wherever I am. In New York by August 12 about.

Love,
Lotte

When he had read it, Ingham breathed again. Ah, fate! It was as if she had read his thoughts. But it was more than that. So much more had had to happen to her than to him to make the letter possible. So she was free now. Ingham began to smile in a dazed way. His first impulse was to write her that he would like very much to see her, then he realized he would be in New York tomorrow night. He could give her a ring from his own apartment—rather the Ditsons, and ask where she was. He didn't know the Ditsons.

At Melik's that night, OWL commented on his good mood. Ingham felt very merry, and talked a great deal. He realized OWL thought he was happy merely because he was leaving. Ingham could have told him about Lotte, but he did not want to. And despite his apparent good humor, he was feeling very compassionate toward Adams and a little sad about him. Adams seemed so lonely under his own cheer, and his cheer seemed as bogus as the phrases he dictated to his tape machine. How long could such pretense sustain anyone? Ingham had a terrifying feeling that one day OWL would pop like a balloon, and collapse and die, possibly of heartbreak. How many more people would turn up in the months ahead to keep OWL company? OWL had said he had met three or four people he had liked since being here, but of course they always went away after a while. OWL plainly saw himself as a lonely guardian of the American Way of Life, in a desolate outpost, keeping the lighthouse aglow.

The next morning at the airport, OWL gripped Ingham's hand hard. "Write me. I don't have to tell you my address. Ha-ha!"

"Good-bye, Francis. You know—I think you saved my life here." It may have sounded a bit gushy, but Ingham meant it.

"Nonsense, nonsense." OWL wasn't thinking about what Ingham had said. He poked a finger at Ingham. "The ways of Araby are strange as her perfumes. Yes! But you are a son of the West. May your conscience let you rest! Ha-ha! That rhymes. Unintentional. Bye-bye, Howard, and God bless you!"

Ingham walked down the corridor that Jensen had. He felt as if he were being borne slowly up into the air, higher and higher. Even the typewriter in his hand weighed nothing at all now. There is nothing, he thought, nothing so blissful in the world as falling back into the arms of a woman who is—possibly bad for you. He laughed inside himself. Who had said that? Proust? Had anyone said it?

At the end of the corridor, he turned. OWL was still standing there, and OWL waved frantically. Carrying things, Ingham couldn't wave, but he shouted a "Good-bye, Francis!" unheard in the shuffle of sandals, the din of transistors, the blare of the unintelligible flight announcements.

BIOGRAPHICAL NOTES

NOTE ON THE TEXTS

NOTES

Biographical Notes

Margaret Millar (February 5, 1915–March 26, 1994) Born Margaret Ellis Sturm in Kitchener, Ontario, to Henry William Sturm, a barber and city alderman who later served as mayor, and Lavinia Ferrier Sturm. Attended Kitchener-Waterloo Collegiate Institute, where she studied music, graduated at the top of her class, and made passing acquaintance with fellow student Kenneth Millar. Entered the University of Toronto, majoring in classics, but did not graduate. Renewed acquaintance with Kenneth Millar in 1937, and they began dating. Married Kenneth Millar in 1938, the day after his graduation from the University of Toronto; their daughter, Linda, was born a year later. Ordered to rest in bed due to cardiac problems following Linda's birth, Millar read mysteries for the next two weeks and decided to try her hand at a novel. Published first novel, *The Invisible Worm* (1941), featuring Paul Prye, a psychiatrist detective, who later appeared in *The Weak-Eyed Bat* and *The Devil Loves Me* (both 1942). Moved to Ann Arbor, Michigan, in 1943 when Kenneth quit his Toronto teaching job and accepted fellowship at the University of Michigan. Published *Wall of Eyes* (1943), featuring Toronto Police Inspector Sands, and a follow-up, *The Iron Gates* (1945), as well as a stand-alone crime novel, *Fire Will Freeze* (1944). Moved to southern California, where Kenneth served as an ensign in the Navy. Millar found work as a screenwriter, adapting *The Iron Gates* for Warner Brothers (film was never made). Sale of the screen rights enabled her to buy a bungalow in Santa Barbara and for both husband and wife to become full-time writers. (Kenneth would become celebrated for his Lew Archer novels, published under the pseudonym Ross Macdonald.) Remained in Santa Barbara while Kenneth returned to Ann Arbor to finish his doctorate at the University of Michigan. Millar published three non-mystery novels, *Experiment in Springtime* (1947), *It's All in the Family* (1948), and *The Cannibal Heart* (1949). From then on, with the exception of the novel *Wives and Lovers* (1954) and the bird-watching memoir *The Birds and the Beasts Were There* (1968), she wrote psychological suspense novels, all published by Random House and largely edited by Lee Wright. Published *Do Evil in Return* (1950), *Rose's Last Summer* (1952), *Vanish in an Instant* (1952), and *Beast in View* (1955), winner of the Edgar Allan Poe Award of the Mystery Writers of America for Best Novel. Linda was involved in a hit-and-run car accident in 1956 in which a thirteen-year-old boy was killed and another seriously injured; she was sentenced to probation after trial in juvenile court. Family lived in Menlo Park, California, 1956–57, before returning to Santa Barbara. Published *An Air That Kills* (1957), *The Listening Walls* (1959), and *A Stranger in My Grave* (1960), which was nominated for a Best Novel Edgar Award. *Rose's Last Summer* was adapted for television series *Thriller* in 1960, and *Beast in View* was adapted for *Alfred Hitchcock Presents* (1964). Published *How Like an Angel* (1962) and *The Fiend* (1964), which was also nominated for the Edgar Award. Linda died in her sleep on November 4, 1970. Published *Beyond This Point Are Monsters* (1970), dedicated to John Westwick, who had represented Linda in her hit-and-run case. After a six-year hiatus, published three mystery novels featuring Latino lawyer Tom Aragon, *Ask for Me Tomorrow* (1976), *The Murder of Miranda* (1979), and *Mermaid* (1982). Declared legally blind in 1978 due to macular degeneration but was able to keep writing with the aid of special optical equipment. Kenneth was diagnosed with Alzheimer's disease in 1981. Published *Banshee* (1983); in the same year, Millar received the Grand Master Award of the Mystery Writers of America. Kenneth died on July 11, 1983. Published *Spider Webs* (1986); *The Couple Next Door*, a short story collection, was published posthumously by Crippen & Landru in 2004. Died in her Santa Barbara home from heart failure.

Ed McBain Pseudonym of Evan Hunter (October 15, 1926–July 6, 2005). Born Salvatore Albert Lombino in East Harlem, New York, only child of Charles and Marie Coppola Lombino. Father worked for the post office and as a musician on the side. Family moved to the Bronx in 1938. Won an Art Students League scholarship and studied art at Cooper Union. Joined U.S. Navy in 1944 and served as radar operator on a destroyer. Spent time in Japan after the war; began writing short stories. Left the Navy in 1946 and attended Hunter College, where he helped found a drama society and graduated Phi Beta Kappa with degree in English in 1950. Married Anita Melnick in 1949; they had three sons, Ted, Mark, and Richard. Taught very briefly at Bronx Vocational High School. Worked as an executive editor for the Scott Meredith Literary Agency. Legally changed his name to Evan Hunter in 1952 and began publishing novels the same year. Achieved critical and commercial success with novel *The Blackboard Jungle* (1954), inspired by his teaching experience; other novels published as Evan Hunter include *Strangers When We Meet* (1958), *Mothers and Daughters* (1961), *Buddwing* (1964), *Last Summer* (1968), and *Every Little Crook and Nanny* (1972). Inaugurated pseudonym Ed McBain with *Cop Hater* (1956), first novel in the 87th Precinct series of police procedurals, which eventually encompassed fifty-four titles, including *The*

Mugger (1956), *The Pusher* (1956), *Killer's Choice* (1957), *King's Ransom* (1959), *Lady, Lady, I Did It!* (1961), *Like Love* (1962), *Ten Plus One* (1963), *He Who Hesitates* (1964), *Doll* (1965), *Shotgun* (1969), *Bread* (1974), *Blood Relatives* (1975), *Heat* (1981), *Lightning* (1984), and *Vespers* (1990). Also published crime novels as Ed McBain outside of the 87th Precinct series, as well as novels and stories under the names Richard Marsten, Hunt Collins, Curt Cannon, and John Abbott. A television series, *87th Precinct*, appeared on NBC, 1961–62. Wrote screenplay for Alfred Hitchcock's *The Birds* (1963) and worked on screenplay for Hitchcock's *Marnie* before being fired by the director; recounted experiences in memoir *Me and Hitch!* (1997). Divorced Anita in 1973 and married Mary Vann Finley. As McBain, wrote thirteen novels featuring the lawyer Matthew Hope, beginning with *Goldilocks* (1978). Named a Grand Master of the Mystery Writers of America in 1986. Divorced Mary in 1997 and married Dragica Dimitrijevic. Died of laryngeal cancer in Weston, Connecticut.

Chester Himes (July 29, 1909–November 12, 1984) Born Chester Bomar Himes in Jefferson City, Missouri, third son of Joseph Himes, a blacksmithing instructor at the Lincoln Institute, and Estelle Bomar Himes. Family moved in 1914 to Lomar, Mississippi, where father taught blacksmithing at Alcorn College; they later lived in Athens, Georgia, Pine Bluff, Arkansas, and St. Louis, Missouri, before settling in Cleveland, Ohio, in 1925. Himes graduated from high school in January 1926 and began working at a hotel, where he suffered severe injuries falling down an elevator shaft; spent four months in hospital. Entered Ohio State University in September 1926 but left in 1927. Worked as hotel bellhop. Arrested twice for armed robbery and was sentenced in December 1928 to twenty to twenty-five years in the Ohio State Penitentiary at Columbus. Survived fire on April 21, 1930, that killed 322 prisoners. Began publishing short stories in *Atlanta Daily World*, *Abbott's Monthly*, *Esquire*, and other periodicals. Paroled in April 1936; returned to Cleveland. Married Jean Johnson in July 1937. Worked at a variety of jobs, including writing assignments for the Federal Writers' Project; wrote *Yesterday Will Make You Cry*, novel based on his prison experiences. Moved to Los Angeles in 1941. Published political statement "Now Is the Time! Here Is the Place!" in *Opportunity* in September 1942, calling "for 13,000,000 Negro Americans to make their fight for freedom . . . to engage and overcome our most persistent enemies: Our native American fascists." Moved to New York City in 1944 and formed friendship with Richard Wright. Published novel, *If He Hollers Let Him Go* (1945), followed by *Lonely Crusade* (1947). Separated from Jean in 1952. Prison novel published in significantly altered form as *Cast the First Stone*

(1953); the unexpurgated manuscript was published under its original title in 1998. Moved to France in 1953. Published *The Third Generation* (1954), novel based on his family's history. Novel *The End of a Primitive* published as paperback original by New American Library in censored form as *The Primitive* (1956). Marcel Duhamel, editor of the Série Noire, a crime fiction series published by Gallimard, asked Himes in 1956 to write a detective novel for his series. The novel was published in French as *La Reine des pommes* (1958) and in English as *For Love of Imabelle* and *A Rage in Harlem*; it won an important French prize, the Grand Prix de la Littérature Policière. It was the first of a series featuring Harlem police detectives Coffin Ed Johnson and Grave Digger Jones, a number of which appeared in French before they were published in America as paperback originals: *The Real Cool Killers* (1959), *The Crazy Kill* (1960), *The Big Gold Dream* (1960), *All Shot Up* (1960), *Cotton Comes to Harlem* (1965), *The Heat's On* (1966), and *Blind Man with a Pistol* (1969). Also published the non-series novels *A Case of Rape* (1963 in French; 1984 in English), *Pinktoes* (1965), and *Run Man Run* (1959 in French, 1966 in English). Met Malcolm X in Harlem in 1962, while working on screenplay *Baby Sister* (film was never completed). Suffered stroke in 1963. Traveled to Spain with British companion Lesley Packard in 1967 and made plans to build house in Moraira. Film version of *Cotton Comes to Harlem* (1970), directed by Ossie Davis and starring Godfrey Cambridge and Raymond St. Jacques, was followed by *Come Back Charleston Blue* (1972), based on *The Heat's On*, directed by Mark Warren with the same leading actors. Suffered second stroke in 1972. *Black on Black: Baby Sister and Selected Writings* (1973) collected his screenplay and other works. Published autobiography in two volumes as *The Quality of Hurt* (1972) and *My Life of Absurdity* (1976). Divorced Jean and married Lesley Packard in 1978. Unfinished novel *Plan B* published in French in 1983 (English-language publication 1993). Died in Moraira.

Patricia Highsmith (January 19, 1921–February 4, 1995) Born Mary Patricia Plangman in Fort Worth, Texas, the only child of Jay Plangman and Mary Coates Plangman; parents divorced shortly before her birth, and mother married Stanley Highsmith, a commercial artist, in 1924. Spent childhood in New York City, Fort Worth, and Astoria, Queens. Graduated from Barnard College in 1942 with degree in English. Published short story "The Heroine" in *Harpers Bazaar* in 1945. Worked as a freelance comic book scriptwriter, 1942–48, writing romance comics for Marvel precursors Timely Comics and Atlas Comics. Stayed at Yaddo, artists' colony in Saratoga, New York, in 1948 along with Chester Himes, Truman Capote, and Katherine Anne Porter. Published first novel, *Strangers on a Train* in

1950; rights purchased for small amount by Alfred Hitchcock, whose film version was released the following year. Published *The Price of Salt* (originally titled *Carol*), a novel with a lesbian theme, under pseudonym Claire Morgan in 1952; did not publicly acknowledge authorship until 1991. Published *The Blunderer* (1954); *The Talented Mr. Ripley* (1955), in which she introduced the continuing character Tom Ripley; *Deep Water* (1957), *A Game for the Living* (1958); and, with Doris Sanders, the children's picture book *Miranda the Panda is On the Veranda* (1958). Moved to Sneden's Landing, New York, where she lived briefly with the novelist Marijane Meaker. Published *This Sweet Sickness* (1960). Moved to Europe, living in Italy, England, and France; briefly visited Tunisia in 1966. Published novels *The Cry of the Owl* (1962), *The Two Faces of January* (1964), *The Glass Cell* (1964), *The Story-teller* (1965), *Those Who Walk Away* (1967), and *The Tremor of Forgery* (1969), as well as a guide for writers, *Plotting and Writing Suspense Fiction* (1966). Moved to Moncourt, a village south of Paris, in 1970. Returned to her character Tom Ripley with *Ripley Under Ground* (1970), *Ripley's Game* (1974), *The Boy Who Followed Ripley* (1980), and *Ripley Under Water* (1991). Published short story collections *Eleven* (1970), *Little Tales of Misogyny* (1974), *The Animal Lover's Book of Beastly Murder* (1975), *Slowly, Slowly in the Wind* (1979), and *The Black House* (1981), as well as novels *A Dog's Ransom* (1972), *Edith's Diary* (1977), and *People Who Knock on the Door* (1983). Adaptations of her work by European filmmakers included René Clément's *Purple Noon* (1960), based on *The Talented Mr. Ripley*; Wim Wenders's *The American Friend* (1977), based on *Ripley's Game*; Claude Miller's *This Sweet Sickness* (1977); and Claude Chabrol's *The Cry of the Owl* (1987). Moved to Aurigeno, a small village near Locarno, Switzerland, in 1981, where she made her home for the rest of her life. Published novel *Found in the Street* (1986) and the short story collections *Mermaids on the Golf Course* (1985) and *Tales of Natural and Unnatural Catastrophes* (1987). Received Chevalier dans l'Ordre des Arts et des Lettres from the French Ministry of Culture in 1990. Died of aplastic anemia in Locarno. Her novel, *Small g: A Summer Idyll*, was published posthumously in 1995.

Note on the Texts

This volume collects four American crime novels of the 1960s: *The Fiend* by Margaret Millar (1964); *Doll* by Ed McBain (1965); *Run Man Run* by Chester Himes (1966); and *The Tremor of Forgery* by Patricia Highsmith (1969). A companion volume in the Library of America series, *Crime Novels: Five Classic Thrillers 1961–1964*, collects five earlier works: *The Murderers* by Fredric Brown (1961); *The Name of the Game Is Death* by Dan J. Marlowe (1962); *Dead Calm* by Charles Williams (1963); *The Expendable Man* by Dorothy B. Hughes (1963); and *The Score* by Richard Stark (1964).

Margaret Millar used the working title "The Remember Game" for her twenty-second novel and eighteenth work of crime fiction. *The Fiend* was published in hardcover in New York by Random House on May 13, 1964, in a printing of 10,000 copies. An English hardcover printing was published in London by Victor Gollancz in the summer of 1964. The novel was reviewed enthusiastically in *The New York Times Book Review* by Anthony Boucher: "Even by Mrs. Millar's unusually high standards, her latest, *The Fiend*, is something extraordinary. It may well be the finest example to date of the fusion of the novel of character and the puzzle of suspense." *The Fiend* was nominated for the Edgar Award for Best Novel of 1964 given by the Mystery Writers of America, losing to John le Carré's *The Spy Who Came in from the Cold*. Millar did not revise the novel after its publication. This volume prints the text of the 1964 Random House edition.

Evan Hunter achieved critical and commercial success early in his career with his novel *The Blackboard Jungle*, published in 1954. The following year he met with Herbert Alexander, the editor-in-chief of Pocket Books, who asked him if he had any ideas for a mystery series. Hunter proposed writing a police procedural series set in New York City and featuring "a *conglomerate* hero" in the form of a squad room of detectives. Alexander offered him a contract for three books, and Hunter began researching police procedures. Once he began writing he decided he would have greater creative freedom if he set the series in a "mythical city" inspired by New York, with "Isola" (Italian for "island") representing Manhattan. *Cop Hater*, the first in what soon became known as the 87th Precinct series, was published under the name Ed McBain by Permabooks (an imprint of Pocket Books) in March 1956. Beginning with *Killer's Wedge* (1959), the eighth 87th

Precinct novel, new books in the series were initially published in hardcover editions.

Doll, the nineteenth novel in the 87th Precinct series, was published in New York by Delacorte Press on October 11, 1965. An English hardcover printing was published in London by Hamish Hamilton in the summer of 1966. Hunter/McBain did not revise the novel after its publication. This volume prints the text of the 1965 Delacorte Press edition, but corrects a typesetting error that appeared in that edition: at 274.31–32, "two ounces" becomes "thirty-two ounces."

Chester Himes left the United States in April 1953 and spent the next twenty-one months in Paris, London, and Mallorca. Himes returned to New York in January 1955 to meet with editors and agents, beginning an eleven-month stay that was both personally and professionally frustrating. By the autumn he was working as a night-shift porter at the Horn & Hardart Automat at Fifth Avenue and 37th Street. Shortly before returning to France, he had a final meal with his coworkers. As Himes recounted in *My Life of Absurdity* (1976), the second volume of his autobiography: "While we were eating in the basement a drunken white detective staggered down the stairs and accused us of stealing his car and waved his pistol around. That incident was the basis for my novel *Run Man Run*. But I showed him my passport, which I had taken to have renewed, and that sobered him somewhat. He must have thought a nigger with a passport was connected with the government."

In 1956 Himes met the poet Marcel Duhamel in Paris while visiting the publishing house Éditions Gallimard. Duhamel had translated Himes's novel *If He Hollers Let Him Go* into French; he was also founder and editor of the Série Noire, a series of crime novels, established in 1945 and published by Gallimard, that presented work by French, British, and American writers. During their meeting Duhamel asked Himes to write a crime novel for the Série Noire. Himes agreed and eventually published seven books in the Série Noire from 1958 to 1961. *Run Man Run* was his third novel to appear in the series, and the only one not to feature the Harlem police detectives Coffin Ed Johnson and Grave Digger Jones. It was published in a French translation by Pierre Verrier under the title *Dare-dare* (i.e., "double quick" or "at a clip") on April 10, 1959.

Himes sent a revised typescript of the novel to William Targ, his editor at Putnam, in 1965. He made significant changes in the revised version, adding and eliminating episodes and characters and changing the ending to one in which his protagonist Jimmy Johnson dies. Himes wrote in a letter to Targ that he had altered the ending "so as to nail down the point for the U.S. public," but at his editor's request he subsequently reverted to a less tragic resolution. (The typescript he sent to Putnam is not known to be extant.) *Run Man Run* was published in hardcover in New York by G. P. Putnam's Sons on November 10, 1966. An English hardcover printing was published in London in the spring of 1967 by Frederick Muller Ltd. Himes did not revise the novel after its American publication. This volume prints the text of the 1966 Putnam edition.

Patricia Highsmith and her friend Elizabeth Lyne sailed from Marseille to Tunis in June 1966 and then traveled to the coastal town of Hammamet, where they stayed for several weeks at a bungalow hotel. While in Tunisia, Highsmith wrote in a notebook: "The element of terror—anxiety—is important. Perhaps *overconsciousness of details*—by which an individual tries to fix his place, from which he tries to gain security and confidence, but without success. It is the element of security, that is forever missing; the meaning and importance of life that is missing." She began writing a novel inspired by her Tunisian experiences in January 1967 at her home in Suffolk, England. Highsmith originally intended for her protagonist to have an affair with an Arab boy, an echo of which can be found in a passage in the published version (see 788.10–18 in this volume). In a notebook entry in March, she wrote that she wanted the novel to reflect the "general sadness and futility of much of the world." Highsmith continued to work on the manuscript after she moved to Île-de-France in June, completing a draft in December and sending a revised typescript to her American and British publishers in February 1968. Later that month she was "relieved" to learn that the book had been "well received" at Doubleday, which would publish it as "a rather straight novel." (The four books she had previously published with the firm had appeared in its Crime Club series.) *The Tremor of Forgery*, Highsmith's thirteenth novel (including the pseudonymous *The Price of Salt*), was published in hardcover in Garden City, New York, by Doubleday & Company on March 21, 1969. A hardcover English edition was published in London in January 1969 by William Heinemann Ltd. Highsmith did not revise the novel after its publication. The text printed here is taken from the 1969 Doubleday edition.

This volume presents the texts of the original printings chosen for inclusion here, but it does not attempt to reproduce nontextual features of their typographic design. The texts are presented without change, except for the correction of typographical errors (and the one other correction mentioned above). Spelling, punctuation, and capitalization are often expressive features and are not altered, even when inconsistent or irregular. The following is a list of typographical errors corrected, cited by page and line number: 20.18, sunburn."; 30.36, understand."; 89.13, pontytail; 151.1, He; 155.31, dead." [no line space]; 191.30, Arlington's; 214.6, Corocoran,; 216.18, It; 289.1, fault.'; 295.24, detective?'; 302.16, That's; 305.38, Sachs?'; 306.3, personal.; 310.21, lists,; 339.3, Willis'; 351.11, Nothing"; 366.29, lie!) They; 375.29, admissable; 378.2, you."; 387.10, Carella,; 408.29, experimently; 445.32, was," Go; 457.2, it."; 492.19–20, anyway; 495.33, for the now; 507.16, soprana; 517.21, herself."; 518.14, saying.; 519.6, third; 535.20, tequilla,; 541.15, arna bontemps; 541.19, Fisher,; 544.21, jewelery; 545.38, in buttoned-up; 548.20, left her; 561.6, hers; 562.2, doorplane; 573.39–40, Collin's; 576.25, "His; 576.26, hysterically "he's; 578.18, It'l; 578.21, straddled it; 579.33, said "that; 582.32, Malcom; 587.16 (and *passim*), cliéntèle; 590.21, better more; 626.5, consisted in one; 654.7, athiesm; 666.30, ask; 670.21, Tunisia,; 679.9, prevail . . . (Adams; 685.36–37, Wednsday; 686.28, bungalow. Ingham; 704.6, "*A bientôt*; 709.12, next the; 711.16, Maigre."; 717.30, blabble; 736.12, her—7:15; 768.8, believeing.

Notes

In the notes below, the reference numbers denote page and line of this volume (the line count includes headings). No note is made for material included in standard desk-reference books. Biblical quotations are keyed to the King James Version. Quotations from Shakespeare are keyed to *The Riverside Shakespeare*, ed. G. Blakemore Evans (Boston: Houghton Mifflin, 1974). For references to other studies and further biographical background than is contained in the Biographical Notes, see Erin E. MacDonald, *Ed McBain/Evan Hunter: A Literary Companion* (Jefferson, NC: McFarland, 2012); Lawrence P. Jackson, *Chester B. Himes: A Biography* (New York: W. W. Norton, 2017); Chester Himes, *The Quality of Hurt: The Autobiography of Chester Himes*, Volume I (Garden City, NY: Doubleday & Co., 1972); Chester Himes, *My Life of Absurdity: The Autobiography of Chester Himes*, Volume II (Garden City, NY: Doubleday & Co., 1976); Michel Fabre and Robert E. Skinner, eds., *Conversations with Chester Himes* (Jackson: University of Mississippi Press, 1995); Joan Schenkar, *The Talented Miss Highsmith: The Secret Life and Serious Art of Patricia Highsmith* (New York: St. Martin's Press, 2009); Andrew Wilson, *Beautiful Shadow: A Life of Patricia Highsmith* (London: Bloomsbury, 2003); Marijane Meaker, *Highsmith: A Romance of the 1950s* (San Francisco, CA: Cleis Press, 2003); Kathleen Sharp, "The Dangerous Housewife: Santa Barbara's Margaret Millar," *Los Angeles Review of Books*, November 28, 2013; Pete Hamill, "The Poet of Pulp: How Ed McBain made the precinct house a respectable place," *The New Yorker*, January 10, 2000; David Lehman, "Ed McBain: The Man from Isola," in David Lehman, *The Mysterious Romance of Murder: Crime, Detection, and the Spirit of Noir* (Ithaca, NY: Cornell University Press, 2022).

THE FIEND

2.1 Jewell and Russ Kriger] Jewell Kriger (1918–1998) and her husband Russell Kriger (1917–1990). Like Margaret Millar, Jewell Kriger was a member of the Santa Barbara Audubon Society and an enthusiastic bird-watcher.

3.1–4 The fiend with all . . . *Caedmon*] From *Cædmon's Metrical Paraphrase of Parts of the Holy Scriptures in Anglo-Saxon* (1832), translated by Benjamin Thorpe (1782–1870). The passage quoted is from a manuscript known as *Genesis B* that is no longer attributed to the seventh-century Anglo-Saxon poet Caedmon.

14.3 San Felice] Millar's fictional name for Santa Barbara, California.

121.4–5 "The truth about . . . ate each other up."] From "The Duel" (1894) by Eugene Field (1850–1895).

145.1 *Lancet*] *The Lancet*, weekly medical journal founded in England in 1823.

145.12–13 one of the new reserpine compounds] Blood pressure drugs first marketed in the 1950s.

189.3–4 Tom Sawyer . . . the secret hide-out] In Chapter II of Mark Twain's *Adventures of Huckleberry Finn* (1885), Tom Sawyer crosses the Mississippi in a skiff along with Huck and other boys and leads them to "a hole in the hill, right in the thickest part of the bushes. . . . We went about two hundred yards, and then the cave opened up." Inside the cave Tom announces his plan to "start this band of robbers and call it Tom Sawyer's Gang."

224.27–28 'sat on a cushion . . . sugar and cream'?] Traditional nursery rhyme.

DOLL

236.3–6 The city in these pages . . . investigatory technique.] This statement appeared in every novel in the 87th Precinct series beginning with the first book, *Cop Hater* (1956). In an introduction written in 1989 for a new edition of *Cop Hater*, Ed McBain recalled how he had met Herbert Alexander (1910–1988), the editor-in-chief of Pocket Books, in 1955. When Alexander asked him if he had any ideas for a mystery series, McBain proposed writing a police procedural series set in New York City and featuring "a *conglomerate* hero" in the form of a squad room of detectives. Alexander offered him a contract for three books, and McBain researched police procedures with the help of the New York Police Department. Once he began writing, McBain "discovered that I was calling the NYPD almost daily" to check details:

> And I realized early on that if I had to count on the NYPD to verify every detail of the procedure in the books I was writing, I would have to spend more time on the phone than I was spending at the typewriter.
>
> So, I asked myself why I had to use a *real* city. What if I premised my geography only loosely on the real city, stuck with routine that was realistic for any police department in America ("clinical verity," Herb later called it), and then winged it from there? Wouldn't this free me from the telephone and get me back to the typewriter? And wouldn't it provide me with creative freedom?
>
> Thus was the mythical city born.
>
> Out of desperation, I guess.
>
> I've never regretted the choice. If a conglomerate detective hero was something new in detective fiction, then the mythical city as a backdrop was similarly new. At least, I knew of no other writer who had used it before. Anyway, I thought it would be more fun to *create* a city than to write about an existing one. It has turned out to be a *lot* of fun. I can't

describe how much joy I experience each time I write about another section of a city that doesn't exist, inventing historical background, naming places as suits my fancy, and then fitting it all together in a jigsaw pattern that sometimes even *I* don't fully understand. It is next to impossible to overlay a map of my city on a map of New York. It's not simply a matter of north being east and south being west or Isola representing Manhattan and Calm's Point representing Brooklyn. The geography won't jibe exactly, the city remains a mystery.

The city, then, became a character.

("Isola" is Italian for island.)

238.22 Chagall] Marc Chagall (1887–1985), Russian-French artist.

239.21–22 George Washington and the unsuspecting Hessians] Washington led the Continental Army in a surprise attack against a garrison of Hessian mercenaries in Trenton, New Jersey, on the morning of December 26, 1776. In the lore of the battle, the Hessians are often depicted as unprepared and hungover from Christmas reveling the night before.

240.1 B.C.I.] Bureau of Criminal Identification.

244.5–6 I know what happened to him] The reference is to the death of Bert Kling's fiancée Claire Townsend, who was killed by a stray bullet in a shooting in a bookstore in an earlier novel in the series, *Lady, Lady, I Did It!* (1961).

248.1 Hathaway Shirt man] "The man in the Hathaway Shirt" was an advertising campaign created by David Ogilvy (1911–1999) in 1951 for a small clothing manufacturer based in Maine. It featured an elegant, mustached middle-aged man wearing an eyepatch, and proved immediately successful.

250.4 Sonny Tufts] Born Bowen Charlton Tufts III (1911–1970), who was briefly successful as a leading man in *So Proudly We Hail!* (1943) and *Here Come the Waves* (1944).

278.14 super .38-caliber Llama automatic] A Spanish semiautomatic pistol chambered to fire .38 Super ammunition.

317.20 The Hairy Ape] Name for the stoker Yank, the protagonist of *The Hairy Ape* (1922), play by Eugene O'Neill (1888–1953).

319.26 vontz] Yiddish: bedbug, pest, nuisance.

341.15 Mutt and Jeff] The taller Mutt and shorter Jeff were inseparably paired characters in the comic strip created by Harry Conway "Bud" Fisher (1885–1954) in 1907; it continued in syndication until 1983.

355.34 The Boston Strangler] Name given to the man suspected of murdering eleven women, aged nineteen to seventy-four, in the greater Boston area from June 1962 to January 1964. In March 1965 Albert DeSalvo (1931–1973), who had been committed to Bridgewater State Hospital after being arrested for sexual assault in November 1964, confessed to the murders. Because of a lack of testimony or physical evidence linking him to the killings DeSalvo was never charged with murder, but he was convicted in 1967 of armed robbery and sexual assault in several unrelated cases and sentenced to life; he was stabbed to death in prison in 1973. DNA tests performed in 2013 linked him to the murder of Mary Sullivan in January 1964, but controversy persists regarding whether he was guilty of the other murders he confessed to.

376.15 Soledad] Soledad State Prison in California.

379.8 There was no wall opposite the end door] Cf. the passage at 275.2–3 in this volume: "He braced himself against the corridor wall opposite the door . . ."

RUN MAN RUN

391.18–19 Schmidt and Schindler . . . the corner] Himes returned to New York from Europe in January 1955 and worked in the fall for several weeks as a porter at the Horn & Hardart Automat cafeteria located at Fifth Avenue and 37th Street. He returned to France in December.

412.2–3 "I looked over Jordan . . . carry me home . . ."] Opening lines of the spiritual "Swing Low, Sweet Chariot."

412.25 Joe Louis] Louis (1914–1981) was world heavyweight champion from 1937 to 1949.

414.35 the Phantom of the Opera!] A reference to the skeletal makeup worn by American actor Lon Chaney (1883–1930) in the 1925 film version of the novel by French writer Gaston Leroux (1868–1927).

435.7 Bellevue] Public hospital in New York City.

471.37 civil rights workers in Mississippi] Civil rights workers James Chaney, age twenty-one, Andrew Goodman, twenty, and Michael Schwerner, twenty-four, were abducted and murdered near Philadelphia, Mississippi, on June 21, 1964, by members of the Neshoba County sheriff's department and the Ku Klux Klan.

471.39–40 that psycho over . . . in New Jersey] Howard Unruh (1921–2009) shot and killed thirteen people with a German army pistol in Camden, New Jersey, on September 6, 1949. Unruh was ruled insane and spent the rest of his life in a psychiatric hospital.

473.26 black Topsy dolls] Dolls based on the description of an enslaved girl in the novel *Uncle Tom's Cabin* (1852) by Harriet Beecher Stowe (1811–1896); they were marketed until the 1960s.

489.14 Lindy's] Restaurant at Broadway and West 51st Street in New York City that operated from 1921 to 1969.

494.5 lain] Slang: sucker, gullible victim.

499.24–25 Commissioner Moses] Robert Moses (1888–1981), planner responsible for major highway construction and urban building projects in New York City and Long Island. Moses held numerous positions during his career, including commissioner of the New York City Department of Parks (1934–60) and chairman of the Triborough Bridge Authority (1934–68).

503.32–33 Lot's wife] See Genesis 19:15–26.

506.7 Pearl Bailey] Actress and singer (1918–1990).

507.1 Savoy Ballroom] The Savoy Ballroom at 596 Lenox Avenue in New York City opened in 1926 and closed its doors in 1958.

507.10–11 *Come to me, . . . don't you cry*] "My Melancholy Baby" (1912), popular song with music by Ernie Burnett (1884–1959) and lyrics by George A. Norton (1880–1923).

512.21–22 *I'm gonna sit right down . . . it came from you*] "I'm Gonna Sit Right Down and Write Myself a Letter" (1935), popular song by composer Fred E. Ahlert (1892–1953) and lyricist Joe Young (1889–1939), originally popularized by Thomas Wright "Fats" Waller (1904–1943).

513.22–23 *If this ain't love it'll have to do*] "Until the Real Thing Comes Along" (1936), popular song with music by Saul Chaplin (1912–1997) and saxophonist Lawrence E. Freeman and lyrics by Sammy Cahn (1913–93), based on an earlier song (1931) of the same name by composer Alberta Nichols (1898–1957) and lyricist Mann Holiner (1897–1958).

513.37 "Rocks in My Bed"] Song (1941) by Duke Ellington (1899–1974), first sung by Joe Turner (1911–1985) in the revue *Jump for Joy*, and subsequently recorded by Ivie Anderson and others.

521.12–13 *the true administration . . . good government*] Inscription on the New York State Supreme Courthouse at 60 Centre Street on Foley Square in New York City. It is derived from a letter from George Washington to Edmund Randolph, September 28, 1789, although Washington wrote "due" rather than "true."

523.3 the King Cole room at the St. Regis] The King Cole Bar opened at the St. Regis Hotel in New York City in 1948; its centerpiece, which was previously displayed at the Knickerbocker Hotel, is the painting *Old King Cole* by American painter Maxfield Parrish (1870–1966).

523.13 Lena Horne] Lena Calhoun Horn (1917–2010), American singer, actress, dancer, and political activist.

540.6–7 "*C'est fini,*" . . . *du bon travail,*"] French: "It's done," . . . "You've worked well."

540.26 Blumstein's] Blumstein's Department Store was located at 230 West 125th Street from 1923 to 1976.

540.35 Theresa Hotel] Located between West 125th Street and Seventh Avenue (now Adam Clayton Powell Jr. Boulevard), the Hotel Theresa opened in 1913 and closed in 1967, when the thirteen-story building became an office tower. It was the tallest building in Harlem until 1973.

541.14–20 *Black No More . . .* Langston Hughes.] *Black No More* (1931), satirical novel by George Schuyler (1895–1977); *Black Thunder* (1936), historical novel about the Gabriel Prosser slave revolt by Arna Bontemps (1902–1973); *The Blacker the Berry* (1929), novel by Wallace Thurman (1902–1934); *Black Metropolis* (1945), sociological study of the South Side of Chicago by St. Clair Drake (1911–1990) and Horace R. Cayton (1903–1970); *Black Boy* (1945), autobiography by Richard Wright (1908–1960); *Banana Bottom* (1933), novel by Claude McKay (1890–1948); *The Autobiography of an Ex-Colored Man* (1912), novel by James Weldon Johnson (1871–1938); *The Conjure-Man Dies* (1932), mystery novel by Rudolph Fisher (1897–1934); *Not Without Laughter* (1930), novel by Langston Hughes (1901–1967).

545.34 *Little Caesar*] Film (1930) directed by Mervyn LeRoy (1900–1987) from a novel by W. R. Burnett (1899–1982), starring Edward G. Robinson (1893–1973) in his signature role as the gangster Rico Bandello.

556.30 Kilroy was here] Graffiti inscription popular among American GIs during the 1940s.

THE TREMOR OF FORGERY

586.2 ROSALIND CONSTABLE] Constable (1907–1995) was an English-born arts journalist who worked for Time Inc. and became a close friend of Highsmith in the late 1930s.

587.25–26 Boulevard Bourguiba] Habib Bourguiba (1903–2000), a leader of the Tunisian independence movement, became the Republic of Tunisia's first president in 1957 and served until his removal from power in 1987.

589.25–26 *The Gathering Swine*] A pun on "Gadarene swine," with reference to the miracle described in Matthew 8:28–32.

590.29 "*Vingt-six, s'il vous plaît,*"] French: "Twenty-six, please."

590.40 William Golding] British novelist (1911–1993) whose works included *Lord of the Flies* (1954), *The Inheritors* (1955), *Pincher Martin* (1956), *The Spire* (1964), and *The Pyramid* (1967). He won the Nobel Prize for Literature in 1983.

594.4–5 "The Israelis have blasted a dozen airports."] Israeli air raids on Egyptian airfields on the morning of June 5, 1967, marked the beginning of the Six-Day War, which ended on June 10 with the defeat of Egypt, Jordan, and Syria and the Israeli occupation of the Sinai, the West Bank, and the Golan Heights.

607.24 Billy Graham] American evangelist (1918–2018).

612.16–17 "*Bien sûr, m'sieur! . . . pour vous!*"] French: "Of course, sir! I watch all the time—all the time for you!"

624.21 *boukhah*] Spirit made from fermented figs, first distilled in Tunisia in the nineteenth century by the Jewish Bokobsa family.

632.29–33 Oh, I come to the garden . . . my Savior's alone.] Opening lines of the American hymn "In the Garden" (1912) by C. Austin Miles (1868–1946).

635.28 Robin Goodfellow] Mischievous sprite, also known as Puck, in Shakespeare's *A Midsummer Night's Dream*.

643.4 *Rien, merci*] French: Nothing, thank you.

645.15 Raskolnikov] Rodion Raskolnikov, former law student who justifies on philosophical grounds his murder of an elderly pawnbroker and her sister in *Crime and Punishment* (1866), novel by Fyodor Dostoevsky (1821–1881).

659.6 "*Mais non, merci. Pas d'argent aujourd'hui!*"] French: "But no, thank you. No money today!"

680.20–21 Norman Douglas . . . book on Tunisia] *Fountains in the Sand: Rambles Among the Oases of Tunisia* (1912) by the British novelist and travel writer Norman Douglas (1868–1952).

688.36 *Mektoub!*] Arabic: It is written!

701.17 *tant—mieux*] Tant mieux, French: so much the better.

711.31 Porfyrivitch] Porfiry Petrovich, police detective investigating the murders committed by Raskolnikov in *Crime and Punishment* (see note 645.15).

724.10 O. Henry Awards] The O. Henry Prize for short stories was established in 1919 in honor of William Sydney Porter (1862–1910), known as O. Henry.

794.38–39 His head was unbowed, not at all bloodied,] Cf. the poem "Invictus" (1875) by William Ernest Henley (1849–1903): "Under the bludgeonings of chance / My head is bloody, but unbowed."

803.12–13 the Smith Brothers] The image of bearded faces of the Smith Brothers—William (1830–1913) and Andrew (1836–1895)—on their line of cough drops were first trademarked in 1877.

This book is set in 10 point ITC Galliard, a face designed for digital composition by Matthew Carter and based on the sixteenth-century face Granjon. The paper is acid-free lightweight opaque that will not turn yellow or brittle with age. The binding is sewn, which allows the book to open easily and lie flat. The binding board is covered in Brillianta, a woven rayon cloth made by Van Heek–Scholco Textielfabrieken, Holland.

Composition by Dianna Logan, Clearmont, MO.

Printing by Sheridan Grand Rapids, Grand Rapids, MI.

Binding by Dekker Bookbinding, Wyoming, MI.

Designed by Bruce Campbell.